Terminal Degree
An Academic Thriller
Sid Stark
Helia Press

Want to keep in touch and hear about news and special offers first? Get your free novella and sign up for my mailing list (but only if you want to!) by scanning the QR code below.

1

January

IT WAS DECEMBER 31, 2016, and most of my friends had become so woke they were intolerable to be around. I was starting to wonder who my people were, if I even had any people, what I had done to deserve this, and whether I was doomed to die friendless and alone in a grossly overpopulated world.

My questioning of friendship, belonging, and reality itself was exacerbated by social media, which was the only method I had for interacting with almost everyone in my life these days. It was great for keeping up with that friend from grad school who was now doing a poorly paid postdoc on the opposite coast, or teaching English as a Second Language in Turkey. Without it I would have been much lonelier and more isolated.

But it meant that when my so-called friends started calling out other people (people like me, for example), they were just disembodied text pumping out hateful, hurtful words from the other side of the world. Social media might be making me less lonely, but it was certainly making me more angry.

These unkind thoughts were filling my head—again—because I had made the fundamental strategic error of responding to a political post on Facebook this morning, and was now reaping the rewards of my own stupidity. Somehow an innocuous comment about pigeons had been taken as proof that I was, in fact, the Devil incarnate, or worse, a Karen. Not the actual Karen who was my department chair, who was, I freely admitted, pretty bad, but a "Karen" as an abstract concept. Apparently this was the worst thing you could be.

"All these super-woke liberals who've just discovered racism and sexism are like teenagers who've just discovered sex, only less charming," I complained to Mel.

Mel was currently the only friend whose company I could tolerate. We were hiding out from the world together by spending New Year's Eve sitting in my low-rent one-bedroom apartment and drinking non-alcoholic festive drinks.

They had to be non-alcoholic because Mel was currently on an aggressive regimen of antibiotics that did not, she had been told, mix well with alcohol. Also, she probably shouldn't drink alcohol in general if she wanted to get better. Or coffee. Or tea. The less said about sugar, gluten, and dairy, the better. And she should probably avoid lectins and salicylates as well. It was unclear what she *was* supposed to eat. Possibly just filtered water, although even that was questionable.

"Preach," she said. She took a sip of the mocktail she was holding, made a face, and set it down. "And let's not even talk about their sudden horror of homophobia that somefuckinhow is the most homophobic thing I've ever seen. Did I tell you about my first and fuckin' last meeting with Queer Crimson?"

"No," I said. "I didn't know there was such a thing."

Crimson College, named in honor of its rather tenuous association with Harvard, was a private college in Greenfields, Georgia, a small town about an hour and a half outside of Atlanta. Mel and I had the dubious honor of being Visiting Assistant Professors (VAPs) there. I taught Russian. Mel taught Arabic. Mel was an ex-Air Force veteran with a strong South Carolina accent and some bad experiences in Iraq to her credit. She was also one of the few openly gay members of the Crimson faculty.

"Yeah, someone sent out an email during finals week, saying why don't we try to put something together, you know, support each other during these trying times. So half a dozen of us who were desperate to escape our families got together a couple of days ago to talk about making something official."

"That's nice," I said.

"It started off nice, but then somehow, and I'm still not entirely sure how, I got expelled for being a trans-exclusionary radical feminist," said Mel. "Pretty much all the lesbians did. But only after getting lectured by a bunch of men about how we were bigoted and exclusionary for not liking dick."

"Well," I said. "I can't say I'm surprised, but I'm sorry you had to go through that."

Mel shrugged. "It ain't nothing I haven't been through before. It just sucked extra-bad to get it from my so-called 'allies.' Seems like no one can be friends anymore. I'm just a little worried that I might get fired over it. If I'm not fired for being sick, that is."

"I want to say that's not going to happen," I said. "But I know it's all too possible. I've got your back, though."

"Thanks," said Mel. "We can be outcasts together."

"Fabulous," I said. "Do you want anything to eat? Should we actually cook this feast we've planned?"

She made a face. "I've got to eat something, 'cause I've got to take my next dose of doxycycline, and if I don't chase it with something high-fat, I'll barf like...well, you get the picture. But I don't *want* to eat anything."

"How much longer do you have to take it?" Mel had—*finally*—been diagnosed with Lyme disease at the end of last semester, after a year of increasingly bizarre symptoms that ranged from sudden bouts of what seemed like the flu to half her face going paralyzed. She had started taking antibiotics over winter break. Since the treatment itself could be pretty debilitating, the hope was to get through the worst of it before the start of the next semester.

"I've got one more week of this round. Some people get better after one round. Some people have to take antibiotics for years, and still never get better."

"Oh," I said. "So, um...how do you feel?"

She shrugged. "My joint pain's almost gone, and I'm not twitching as much as I used to. My face looks better, too, don't you think?"

I leaned across my small table that served as both a working desk and a dining room table for entertaining, and peered at her face through my right eye, and then my left. From up close, I could see that her dark blonde hair in its boyish pixie cut was developing gray streaks around the temple, her wide, expressive mouth had fine lines all around it from too much smiling and too much sun, and there were dark blotches from permanent sun damage across her cheekbones and the bridge of her nose. Her eyes, I noticed for the first time, were blue-gray with flecks of green and gold. We were so close, our breathing had synchronized.

I jerked back. "It looks perfectly symmetrical."

"It wasn't perfectly symmetrical before the Bell's palsy, but thanks. It feels like it all works fine again, so that's great. Some things are great."

"But?"

"But I'm tired as shit, and every time I eat something, it feels like a poison bomb's going off inside of me. It was like that before, but the doxy ain't fuckin' helping, I tell you what."

"Maybe that will go away when you go off it, and you'll just feel better," I said. "Maybe a week from now, you'll be done with this and you'll be completely cured."

She gave me a smile. It said, *You think you know what I'm going through, but you don't. I'm just too nice to point that out.*

Well, at least she didn't say it out loud, I told myself.

"Let's make supper," I said. "Even if it doesn't taste good, it'll keep you from upchucking the pills that are going to cure you."

"Yeah...is that your phone?"

Two loud *pings* had filled the apartment.

"I think it's both our phones," I said. We pulled out our phones. Indeed, mine had a message notification.

Darling Inna. Happy New Year! Wishing you joy and happiness. If all goes well, in 24 hours mama and I will be with you in Atlanta!

The warmth from that message insulated me from the chill coming from the other side of the table. It was only Mel's muttered "Fuck, fuck, *fuck*" that brought me back to myself.

"What is it?"

She looked up from her phone. "Apparently I've just stolen a hundred grand."

2

MEL HAD BEEN A BUSY girl. Or rather, the person who'd been using her identity to commit fraud had been very busy indeed.

"Is it weird I feel guilty?" Mel asked. "Like, I *know* I didn't fuckin' do any of it, but other people think I did, and I feel like I owe 'em an apology or something. Like I should've been more careful about guarding my info and then they wouldn't be in this mess. Fuck! What if I get into trouble over this?"

"What, exactly, did 'you' do?" I asked.

She shrugged. "Fuck knows. I'm sure this is just the tip of the iceberg of fraud Criminal Me has committed. Maybe the black helicopters are circling over my folks' place even as we speak."

"Because that's where the packages are being sent," I stated.

The scam had been discovered because a whole slew of packages for Mel had arrived at her parents' house over the past few weeks. She had been avoiding going there for the holidays since, in her words, "We have a very fuckin' complex relationship, and it isn't improved by all the drinking my dad does during the winter."

But the volume of packages and letters had built up to the point that her parents had insisted she do something about it. She told them to open the packages and see what they were and who they were from.

The packages had been from all over the country, and had contained, bizarrely, ashes. Mel had tracked down one of the senders and demanded to know what kind of sick joke they were playing. The sender had demanded the same thing in reply. After a couple of rounds of this, it turned out that the sender had sent the ashes of her recently deceased cat, believing that Mel was going to transform them into a one-of-a-kind work of commemorative sculpture. The sender said she had already paid $1,000 for the work, plus another $500 for supplies.

"Turns out scams involving cremated remains aren't that unusual," said Mel. "They say they're going to turn them into a work of art, and then they take the money and run, or hold the ashes for ransom, or say they're caught up in customs…"

"That's scummy," I said. "But a hundred grand? That's a lot of ashes."

"It wasn't just the pet ashes thing," said Mel. "Looks like my identity's also been used for fake unemployment claims, and Evil Mel has also been catphishing people on dating sites. My parents got a notification of un-employment benefits, and several love letters from people who'd forked over a bunch of money to Evil Mel. When we started adding everything up, it turned into the better part of a hundred grand. That's what they were just texting me about. And who knows what else is out there. It makes you fuckin' wonder, doesn't it? Like, who out there is real, and how many scammers and fakers we're surrounded by every day. What do we *really* know about the people we think we have in our lives, anyway?"

"Yeah," I said. "So what are you going to do about it? Have you told the police?"

"I guess I'd better, huh? I just doubt they'll do much about it. I mean, what can they do? It's not a violent crime. The cynical part of me says they're not even going to try."

"You should still report it," I said. "At least that way they're less likely to come after *you* if something happens."

"Yeah. And maybe then I should track this motherfucker down and…I don't know. I can barely even eat dinner these days. What am I going to do if I find a master cyber criminal? 'Sides, I don't think this is a master cyber criminal. It's probably some kid in his dad's basement, or some desperately poor dude somewhere in Nigeria, trying to scrape to-gether enough cash to claw their way out of poverty. If you look at it that way, I'm the bad guy here."

"Sounds like they caused a lot of people a lot of pain with this ashes scam thing," I said. "And catphishing is scummy in general. It can really hurt people, even if you don't steal from them."

"So you're saying I should go all vigilante on their asses?"

"I'm saying you should report them," I said. "With extreme prejudice."

Mel grinned. "Report with extreme prejudice. I guess I'll start with that and see how it goes."

"Sounds like a plan," I said.

3

MEL SAID SHE DIDN'T want to think about the fraud her alter ego was committing anymore, and she needed to take her doxy, so we should go ahead and heat up supper, unappetizing as it sounded. While she was warming up the selection of Middle Eastern dishes she had brought over, I opened up the text that had been burning a hole in my brain ever since it had *pinged* onto my screen.

It still read exactly the same:

Darling Inna. Happy New Year! Wishing you joy and happiness. If all goes well, in 24 hours mama and I will be with you in Atlanta!

I checked the time. 23 1/2 hours from now, to be exact, Dima Kuznetsov, my former fiancé and current...what? I didn't know. Not my fiancé anymore. Not even my boyfriend. But more than "just a friend." Someone with whom I shared a long and painful history, and a love that just wouldn't die no matter how much we both tried to smother it.

Anyway. 23 1/2 hours from now, he and his mother would be landing in Atlanta. 23 1/2 hours from now, I would be seeing Dima in the flesh for the first time in three years. 23 1/2 hours from now, my entire life would be decided...

Stop it, stop it, stop it! That's not helpful. Just answer the damn text.

I checked the time. After midnight in Moscow. It was officially the New Year there.

Happy New Year! I wrote. *Wishing you health, happiness, and that all your dreams come true! I can't wait to see you! Hugs and kisses to Galina Ivanovna.*

Galina Ivanovna was Dima's mother. The actual reason for their visit to Atlanta was not to see me. The actual reason for their visit to the US was that Galina Ivanovna's kidney disease had progressed to the point that her only hope was either a transplant, or a new treatment being offered at a clinical trial in Atlanta. Given the average wait times for a transplant, plus the extreme disfavor in which Dima was held by many Very Important People in Moscow, the clinical trial was, realistically, her only hope. So really, they were coming to Atlanta because the alternative was death. I just happened to live nearby, and had volunteered my services as a guide and translator. They certainly weren't coming out of love for me. I should probably not send that lovey-dovey text. It was inappropriate and would only cause more hurt feelings.

I hit "Send." There had already been so many hurt feelings between me and Dima that worrying about a few more seemed pointless. Sometime in the past three weeks, since Dima had told me they'd gotten their visas and were coming to America, I'd decided to throw my hat in the ring and see if I could...what? Get him back?

"That's not a happy face," said Mel. "You had your identity stolen too?"

I looked up from my phone. My neck and shoulders had cramped up from hunching over it like Gollum over the One Ring. If I wasn't careful, I'd give myself a migraine before Dima even crossed into US airspace.

"Sorry," I said. "I should probably work on my posture. God knows what I'm doing to my neck with all this screen time."

"No fuckin' kidding," said Mel. "And with your book contract, this semester's going to be extra-brutal, too."

"Yeah." I had signed a contract at the end of the last semester with an academic publisher for a revised version of my dissertation. The contract had come with a multipage document full of confusing, contradictory, and frequently mean-spirited suggestions for improvement from my peer reviewers.

I had tried to get a jump on the revisions over winter break. So far I had made little progress. Every time I looked at the reader comments or talked to the editor, I felt more confused about what I wanted to say and how to say it, and less motivated to work on the book.

Like being on social media, the experience was making me question who my people were, what I was doing with my life, and whether I should just give it all up and go live in a box under the freeway. I was tough. Physically tough, that is. I could handle winter in a cardboard box, right? It wasn't even like it would be a Russian winter. Georgia winters hardly counted as "winter" at all.

I reminded myself—again—that living in a cardboard box, even in Georgia, would probably be a lot worse than I was thinking it was, and that I was in fact one of the lucky elect who not only had a roof over her head, but an actual book contract. Getting the book published was not supposed to be fun. It was supposed to be an excruciating rite of passage to prove my commitment to the cause and willingness to suffer in its name.

"Do you like to write?" I asked Mel.

"I fuckin' hate it. Which maybe goes to show that I'm in the wrong fuckin' profession. Maybe we should all go join a commune or something."

"Yeah. Although the commune we lived in when I was a kid fell apart after a while. They're not as idyllic as you'd like to think."

"Yeah," said Mel. "'Cause they're full of people. Come on. Let's eat this fuckin' festive dinner so we can call it a night. I gotta go lie down soon."

"Just one more week, and you'll be done with this," I said.

"If I'm lucky," said Mel.

4

MEL WENT BACK TO HER apartment by 8:00pm, saying the doxy wasn't agreeing with her—"as per fuckin' usual"—and she just wanted to go lie down.

"How you meet the New Year is how you'll spend it," I said.

"Well, maybe spending it lying down wouldn't be such a bad thing," said Mel.

"Fair enough."

"And if I feel inspired, I'll get back up and look into Evil Mel some more. Maybe this is a sign."

"A sign of what?" I asked.

"A sign that I need to give up academia and become a vigilante. Whaddya think?"

"I think being a vigilante probably pays even less than being a contingent faculty member," I said.

"What about being a private detective?"

I laughed. Then I did a double take. "Are you serious?"

She shrugged. "You know as well as I do that our contracts run out in May. We've got the chance of getting those tenure-track jobs they keep dangling in front of us, but I'm giving us even odds of getting tossed out on our asses as soon as we turn in our final grades. Well, even odds for you. In my case, I'd say they're at least two to one. I'm a pain in the ass *and* I'm sick. They probably can't wait to get rid of me."

"Yeah, but who else are they going to get to come live in Greenfields, Georgia?"

"I know at least three PhDs who'd give their right hands for this job."

"Well...okay. Same here, actually."

"Besides," said Mel, "I'm starting to think I'd give my right hand to *not* have this job. So I've started looking into alternative careers. Being a PI might be fun."

"Do you have any qualifications?" I asked.

"Besides being nosy and brash? No. But maybe I could get them. I mean, it's all research, right? What we're doing here and what we'd do if we were investigating stuff out in the 'real world,' right? Whaddya say? I can see the office door now. 'Wilson & Halley: Here to help.' Or some shit like that. We could specialize in female clientele."

"It sounds great," I said. "Except that neither of us have any relevant training and experience. I mean, yeah, it's all research in the end, but don't you have to, I don't know, know people and stuff? I mean, Dima's job is kind of similar, and it's all about contacts and knowing the right people. As well as being nosy and brash, of course. And I'm not even that nosy and brash."

"But you like to find stuff out," said Mel. "And you were thinking of joining the FBI, right?"

"Yeah, but that looks like a dead end." I had indeed applied for a job at the FBI last year as a backup in case academia failed me. I'd gone through a couple of rounds of interviews, but appeared to have stalled out at the background check phase. It seemed that Dima was still having a major effect on my life, even when he wasn't in it.

"Damn it."

"I'm kind of over that idea, anyway." Joining the FBI had been part of my California life plan with Alex and, weirdly, Frank McAvoy. Alex was now out of my life, and I hoped that Frank wasn't going to feature too much in it, either. So I had gone sour on the whole FBI thing, and it looked like they had gone sour on me, too. I just didn't have a backup plan for my backup plan.

"Yeah," said Mel. "Well, keep the PI thing in mind. And if you come up with any better ideas, let me know. I want to have something on the back burner if our interviews go badly. When's yours?"

"The tenth," I said. "Tuesday. Of course they did it during the first week of class. I guess I should be grateful they didn't decide to do it on Monday."

Mel made a face. "Fuck, yeah. Mine's on Thursday, and I thought that was harsh. Did you get the lecture about how everything had to be *scrupulously* fair, and how they wanted to move forward with this as quickly as possible?"

"I certainly did." Mel and I were both finishing out our second year as VAPs here at Crimson. To our surprise, the tenure-track jobs that had been used as bait for our current jobs had, in fact, materialized, and we had been *welcome*—in the words of our department chair—to apply. We had duly applied, and had been invited to first-round interviews. Which were, out of some peculiar sense of sadomasochism, being held during the first week of class.

And then, if that went well, we would be invited for a second, multi-day round of interviews. And if *that* went well, we would be offered the job. Which would mean we could stay here for a few more years, or—if we actually got tenure, which was by no means certain—the rest of our working lives. Both of us had very mixed feelings about that.

"Maybe Brian Michaels will hire us," I said. Brian Michaels was the chief of the campus police department. "Or at least you, since you're ex-military. That could get you started on the PI thing."

"It is crazy that I'm actually considering that?" asked Mel.

"No," I said. "Not crazy at all. You can join John there." My brother John was going to retire from the Marines soon, and was casting about for things to do. Brian Michaels had offered to help him get into law enforcement. Last I'd heard, though, John was contemplating law school at the suggestion of Camila, his girlfriend. Shocking a development as this was, maybe it meant that Mel could get that law enforcement mentorship from Brian Michaels instead.

"Maybe you'd like being a cop," I said.

"Maybe," said Mel. "But I think you have to be healthy to do that. So I'd better go rest up and try not to puke my fuckin' guts out."

"Sounds like a plan," I said. "And happy New Year."

"Happy fuckin' New Year," said Mel. "Maybe this year'll be the one where everything finally turns out right."

"Maybe," I said.

5

I WOKE UP EXTRA-EARLY on Sunday morning. Sunday, January 1. A new week, a new year, a new...*urgh*. I registered what had woken me up. It was not happy dreams of my new life. It was Fevronia, my beautiful tannish-orange longhaired rescue cat, barfing on the pillow next to mine.

A forensic examination of the barf showed no signs of anything sinister. I got up as much as I could with a paper towel, put the pillow case in the laundry, and decided we were up already anyway, so we might as well start our day.

Fevronia chowed down happily on the food I poured into her bowl. She must not be that sick, then. And she seemed to be enjoying the new, cheaper brand of cat food I'd started her on. I'd been feeding her the second-cheapest brand I could find, but in preparation for the extra expenses I knew would be coming my way with Dima and Galina Ivanovna's visit, I'd switched to the cheapest brand. I'd been afraid she would turn her nose up at it, but so far she'd been tucking into it with the same enthusiasm she'd shown for every other kind of food I'd ever given her. She didn't like much in life that I could tell, but she did like food.

I made myself a small amount of coffee and added an even smaller amount of cream. I needed to cut back on my own food expenses as well. Telling myself this was a perfectly adequate breakfast, I checked the time. Six in the morning. Dima and Galina Ivanovna wouldn't be arriving until almost six in the evening. That meant I didn't need to leave until four at the earliest. That meant I had the whole day to kill.

I texted Mel and asked if she felt up for a run. She did not. I tried going for one by myself, but my left knee, which I had injured repeatedly over the past year, let me know it was not in running shape, so I managed more of a slow and unsteady walk.

Afterwards, I remembered that I hadn't checked my mail for a couple of days, and I should see what fate had brought me. I went to the big metal cluster mailbox between my building and the next one over, and tried to open my own box. This was harder than it should have been. We'd had a bit of a freeze the week before, and ever since, the lock had tended to jam. I'd mentioned it to the complex office, and they'd sent someone out to spray it with WD-40. Now all my mail smelled like a DIY project, and the lock still jammed. This time was no exception, and as usual, once I'd finally wrestled it open, the box was empty.

When I got back, it was only 8:00am. I cleaned the apartment. Again. I'd already cleaned it twice in the past two days. Dima and his mother were going to be subletting an apartment in the same building as Mel, so it wasn't like they were going to be living here. But they would certainly be eating here, so I wanted to make it spick and span. Plus, it helped me burn off nervous energy.

After that, it was only 9:00am. I spent a little while prepping for my interview, but that left me in such a state of nerves that I could hardly sit still, so I gave up and started on my book revisions instead.

By 11:00am I was confused, demoralized, and my face and hands had gone numb from extreme nervous tension. I did some stretches and tried to crank out another couple of paragraphs, but my fingers kept striking the keys in the wrong order, creating sentences like *whlie mArnia tsVeatev'as aerly wrok wsa mrakde by*...I closed down the document and pulled out a book that one of the reviewers had recommended I include in my bibliography.

The book achieved what running, meditation, housecleaning, and yoga hadn't, and put me into a somnolent stupor that resulted in a brief but refreshing nap. When I woke up, it was already legitimately the afternoon. I gave up on scholarly endeavors for the day and called my various family members.

John was on a brisk ten-mile run with Camila, who was training for her next triathlon. I said hi to both of them, and we made vague plans to get together at some point. I'd talked to Camila over Skype, but never met her in person, and curiosity was consuming me. To the extreme astonishment of the rest of the family, Camila appeared to be a serious, intelligent woman looking for a real relationship. Since John's tastes had hitherto always run to trashy blondes looking to cheat on their husbands, we were cautiously optimistic that this new development heralded a positive change in his life.

John, meanwhile, was obviously making Herculean efforts not to say what he thought about Dima's imminent arrival. John had never met Dima, but he considered him to be a car crash who would take me out as well. The historical precedent tended to support that point of view.

"Well...let's try and do something together when...when you're free," was John's only reference to Dima's visit.

"Sounds great," I said, with all the cheeriness I could muster. "Looking forward to it!"

I tried calling my maternal grandparents, the ones who lived in Macon, and the ones I normally meant when I talked about "my grandparents," but the call went straight to voicemail. They had taken a spur-of-the-moment cruise over the holidays, and were apparently partying hard somewhere between Fort Lauderdale and the Bahamas. I wasn't sure I could summon up the strength to go on a cruise right now even if someone had offered it to me for free, so I respected their energy and their commitment to living their best lives.

My parents were taking a few days off their current project, building a tiny house on the property they'd recently purchased outside of Macon, to go spend the holidays with my father's parents. I also had a full set of paternal grandparents. We just rarely spoke to or of them. They had heartily disapproved of my father's decision to throw over regular society and live on the margins in his wild youth, and they'd never gotten over it, even decades after he'd gotten a graduate degree and a real job. In their minds, social work wasn't a real job, anyway.

And they blamed my mother for my father's alternative lifestyle, even though he'd been the one to convince her to join a commune and—and this was something we never spoke of these days at all—have a child out of wedlock. Technically as well as by temperament, John was a bastard. My parents had spurned oppressive social constructs such as marriage, and had been literally shacking it up in one of the commune's old out-buildings when John came along.

They had gotten married once they'd discovered the myriad inconveniences of having a child from an unofficial relationship. This had retroactively legitimated John and made my birth free of any stain of illegitimacy. My mother's parents had thought the whole thing a bit of a lark, but my father's parents had never forgiven or forgotten.

The first time I had ever met them was at John's graduation and commissioning ceremony. They had also come to my college graduation and my doctoral hooding ceremony. They had indicated they might be willing to attend weddings (at least first weddings) and christenings, should John or I provide them with the opportunity, but for the most part, they showed no interest in our existence.

It was therefore a shock when they had invited my parents to come spend the holidays with them in Christiansburg, Virginia. John and I had not been invited. My parents were offended on our behalf, but we were relieved to be left out of it.

All that was a long backstory to why I hit "Call" on my mother's number with a fair amount of trepidation. I needn't have bothered. That call went straight to voicemail too.

By then it was almost 3:00. I texted Mel again. She was feeling okay, she said, although not well enough to go for a run or even for a walk. She had reported Evil Mel's misdeeds to the police with as much prejudice as she was capable of, but had been left with the distinct impression that there wasn't a lot the authorities would or could do. So she'd started digging into Evil Mel in the hopes of nailing her ass herself, and did I want to help?

Sure, I texted. *Be right over.*

6

"YOU WON'T FUCKIN' BELIEVE the shit I've found." Mel jerked her head at me to come in, and then led me to the dining/living room/ breakfast nook that was the mirror image of mine, except that it was even barer of furniture. Mel didn't bother with a table and chairs. She had an extremely ratty loveseat that she'd picked up off the curb while living in LA, and a kind of coffee table she'd made out of plastic fruit crates. I'd asked her once how she managed to get any work done on that setup. She said she preferred to work lying in bed. My neck screamed in protest at the very thought, but tastes differ.

"What did you find?" I sat down gingerly on the loveseat. It creaked, shifted, and then settled into a new, slightly lower configuration. Mel moved as if to sit down next to me, thought better of it, sat down crosslegged on the floor, grimaced, muttered, "My fuckin' *knees*," and lay down on her back, her head propped against the leg of the loveseat.

"Um...are you...do you want, like, a pillow or something?" I asked. "That doesn't, uh, look very comfortable."

"Nothing's very comfortable," said Mel. "I'll just wriggle around and try to spread the pain from body part to body part. Pay no mind to it. Here. Take a look at this. Can you fuckin' *believe* this shit?"

Holding my breath in an attempt not to collapse the loveseat or knock over the teetery tower of fruit crates that was holding up Mel's laptop, I leaned forward and peered at the screen.

"What am I looking at?" I asked.

"Me! Or rather, Evil Me. This is Evil Mel's dating profile. One of 'em. I'll bet she's got half a dozen. This is just the first one I've found. I did a reverse image search, started poking around on sketchy dating sites...*et voila!* Goddamn this motherfucker!"

I peered closer at the screen. I now recognized the slightly blurry picture as being of a much younger Mel, smiling fixedly into the camera in her dress blues.

"And look!" She clicked over to the next picture. "Look what else that motherfucker has!" The next picture was equally blurry, but also showed a much younger Mel, now posing on a sand dune in her combat fatigues.

"Not only is that the worst fuckin' thing I ever fuckin' did, but now some fucker's plastering my shame all over the internet to catphish poor desperate suckers. I fuckin' *hate* this. I fuckin' *hate* her! Evil Mel needs to go the fuck *down*."

"Yeah," I said. "Have you reported it?"

"Like I said, I told the police, but I don't know there's much they can do. I thought about reporting it to the dating site. But then I thought I'd try to catch her instead."

"Catch Evil Mel?" I asked.

"Yeah. I created a profile and sent her a like and a message. Now I'm just waiting to hear back from her."

"Do you think that'll work?" I asked. "'She' is probably a 'he' somewhere on the other side of the world. And even if she's somewhere nearby, catphishers don't normally let you interact with them in the real world. They won't even talk to you on the phone."

"I can be real persuasive," said Mel.

"Yeah, but..."

"Look, I gotta try, okay?" Mel was often angry with the world, but this was the first time I'd ever heard that tone directed at me.

It must have shown on my face, because she stopped, took a deep breath, and then said, speaking with forced calm, "I hate what I did in Iraq. It wasn't that bad compared with what a lot of other people did, but I hate that I was there at all. Every day I wake up with that guilt, and every night it goes to bed with me."

One side of her wide, mobile mouth twisted. "A toxic lover I can't fuckin' get rid of, I guess. Anyway. It's inside of me like poison, like this *fuckin'* disease I can't beat. And now some shithead is using pictures of it she's stolen somewhere to lure poor shlubs into giving her their love, and maybe their money too. She's *hurting* people. She's using the worst thing I ever did to make this fucked-up world an even worse place than it already is, and the poor fuckers she's doing this to think it's *me* doing it to them. I can't...Ro...I don't know how to make you understand...you don't have anything this fucked up to atone for...but the world's a worse place because of what I did. Now...it feels like this is my big chance to make it right. I can't go back and change what's already been done. But maybe I can stop this."

"I understand," I said. "I just...well, be careful, okay? Evil Mel is probably some low-down, lowlife loser, but lowlife losers can be dangerous. And so can an obsessive chase after something you can't catch."

My hand had instinctively slipped down onto Mel's shoulder. She reached up and caught it. For a moment we sat like that, unmoving, not even breathing. Then she let go and, shaking her neck like it had gone stiff, pulled herself up to sitting.

"Thanks." Her voice was rough. Her shoulder was touching my leg.

"You know I've got your back," I said. "As much as I can. But right now"—I pulled out my phone—"I should probably get to the airport." It was only 3:30, but I was starting to have anxious visions of New Year's Day traffic jams. And there was something in the air between us that I didn't want to encourage.

"Yeah." Mel cleared her throat. "Yeah, you're right. And you're right about the not finding her thing, too. Evil Mel is probably some dude in Bangladesh or something. I just...I might as well try, right?"

"Right," I said. "No harm in trying."

7

I LEFT MEL'S APARTMENT feeling disturbed on multiple levels. I was worried about this plan of hers to go after her imposter. I was afraid that she would get caught up in a wild goose chase that would destroy her emotionally at a time when she was already at the end of her tether physically, mentally, and financially. I was also afraid she might actually catch Evil Mel, and either get hurt, or do something stupid.

And I was afraid of this...thing that was growing between us. That way led to madness and heartbreak. Every now and then I asked myself if maybe all this mooning over men had been a mistake, and Mel was actually the woman for me, and I just needed to take that leap and find out. Thus far I'd always rejected the thought. Both my reasoning and my feelings for doing so seemed sound. But right now, with the sensation of her shoulder still alive on my leg, and facing the prospect of another round of rejection and misery with Dima, I found myself asking if maybe I was making a giant, giant mistake.

You're not. And you need to get to the airport. With that bracing thought, I checked on Fevronia—napping on my pillow—got my keys, purse, jacket, and everything else someone might need for a expedition to Hartsfield-Jackson airport, and set off.

8

MY FEARS OF MASSIVE New Year's Day wrecks outside of the airport failed to materialize. That meant I had to hang around the arrivals lobby for the better part of an hour, wondering if I shouldn't have just parked in the cell phone lot and told Dima to call me when they landed. But that had seemed like an extra layer of stress on top of an already stressful and difficult situation. Galina Ivanovna would be exhausted, and probably terrified as well. Anything we could do to make things more comfortable for her should be done. And it had also somehow seemed just plain wrong to wait in the cell phone lot. After a broken engagement and three-year separation, our first meeting shouldn't be at the curbside pickup zone, getting honked at by everyone waiting to take our spot.

As I hung around at the waiting area at the top of the escalators, though, trying harder and harder not to chew my nails or my hair from nerves, I doubted the wisdom of this. The short-term parking fees were pretty steep for someone as strapped for cash as me. If Galina Ivanovna was too tired to walk far, I was still going to have to go get the car and bring it around to the curbside pickup zone, and that would take longer than just driving over from the cell phone lot.

And...my first meeting with Dima after a broken engagement and three-year separation was going to be in front of hundreds of random strangers. In my fondest fantasies, it could take the form of a romantic sweeping-off-my-feet and ecstatic embrace. In my more realistic moments, I knew that it was probably going to be a cold nod, followed quite possibly by an argument. And/or me bursting into tears.

There...over there...was that...goodness, I'd forgotten how *tall* he was. 190cm, or 6'3", which was only an inch taller than John, but somehow it seemed like a lot more. Or maybe Dima just loomed large in my eyes and my mind and my life.

He was looking down and saying something to Galina Ivanovna, who was leaning on his arm, appearing on the verge of collapse. I'd always thought of her as a vigorous woman, still young despite being over 60, but now her face was ashen, with dark gray lines of pain and exhaustion cutting through it. Her hair had gone from the dark brown shot with steel I remembered, to almost white. It had come loose from the severe braid she normally kept it in and was floating around her face. She must have lost thirty pounds since I'd last seen her. I'd heard old women called "God's dandelions" in Russia, and right now, she looked like a dandelion that was about to be blown away in the first puff of wind.

She looked up. Saw me. Stopped dead, clutching at Dima's arm and dragging him to a stop too. He looked up. His eyes met mine.

*This is **it**. There's no walking away from this.*

A kid bumped into me from behind, so hard I staggered and almost went down.

"Oh, I'm *so* sorry! Noah, tell the lady you're sorry!"

Noah's parents crowded around me, offering apologies and trying to get Noah to apologize, too. Noah, who looked to be about eight, fidgeted and squirmed and refused to speak to me or look me in the eye, mumbling and then shrieking to himself instead. Eventually his father picked him up and carried him off, while his mother said something about how he was "on the spectrum" and "struggled with appropriate social behavior" and "wasn't entirely verbal."

"No worries," I said.

"Anyway, I'm *so* sorry...are you sure you're okay? If you're sure...I'd better go meet my mother-in-law..." She made an involuntary face of distaste.

"Go," I said. "I'm fine. It's no problem, really. And I'd better go meet my..."

"Oh, are you picking up your mother-in-law too?" Now the woman made a face of sisterly solidarity.

"Something like that," I said.

She patted my arm. "Good luck, hun. And sorry again...they say he'll probably get better as he gets older, but not to...anyway, not your problem...good luck, hun. Oh! Is this...is *this* your husband?"

"Something like that. Good luck."

The woman rushed off. I looked up. Dima was standing right next to me, so close I could feel the heat coming off his body.

"Inna," he said.

I hadn't known what I was going to say when I saw him. Nothing, it turned out. I couldn't think of anything to say, especially in Russian. Almost twenty years of intensive language training were blanked out by his presence. Oh my God! This was mortifying! I had to say something, both for my own self-respect as a language instructor, and to keep from bursting into tears just like I'd feared I would.

"Welcome to America," I said. "Finally."

Dammmmmmmmmnnnnnn. I'd meant that to sound jaunty and cheerful. It came out more waspish and passive-aggressive. Also, I'd failed to differentiate my hard and soft consonants adequately. That was going to eat at me all evening.

"Finally." Dima smiled. Maybe it hadn't been as waspish and passive-aggressive as I'd feared. "You look good, Inna."

"You too." Had I used the correct case? Was I even speaking Russian? I wasn't sure.

Dima did look good, though. Tired and like he'd been through a particularly rough mill a few times since I'd last seen him, but still good. He had one of those Russian faces that was pale but had sharply defined cheekbones, and gray eyes whose shape hinted at Central Asia. His brown hair had grown out and was falling in his eyes in a way I knew drove him crazy. He brushed it back, and the airport lights caught a glint of gray that hadn't been there three years ago. He had shaved off the stubble he'd been sporting for a while. If he'd smiled, it would have shown off the dimple on his left cheek that only came out when he was really happy. Since right now he had on his "don't fuck with me" face, it just showed off the new scar on his jaw from the altercation that had ultimately led to our breakup. It went well with his other scars, some from war, some from torture, and some from pickup hockey games.

"Innochka! Darling! At last!" Galina Ivanovna pushed forward and threw her arms around me. She stepped back and examined me. "You look...wonderful! So healthy!"

I knew this was her way of saying that I'd gained weight. With my knee problems stopping me from running, I'd put on weight the previous year, to the point that all my clothes had become uncomfortably tight. She, as a Russian, was no doubt absolutely sincere when she said it made me look healthy, but as an American, I couldn't help but feel self-conscious about it.

"It's been so long," I said.

"It has been so long...and I'm absolutely spent...take us home, Innochka."

"Sure," I said. "This way."

9

GALINA IVANOVNA'S CLINICAL trial was being run out of Grady Memorial in downtown Atlanta. It would start on Tuesday, with a three-day inpatient stay followed by weekly visits, and was expected to go for at least a month, or possibly three or four months. Dima and Galina Ivanovna had gotten return tickets to Moscow for the end of May. Originally they had planned to spend the entire time staying near the hospital. Then they had looked at hotel and short-term rental prices there, and realized they couldn't afford them without selling a kidney, possibly several kidneys.

Since Galina Ivanovna was here precisely because her kidneys were failing, that seemed like a bad plan. I had offered to let them stay with me for free. That offer had been met with a long pause, followed by the argument that it wouldn't be comfortable enough for Galina Ivanovna, who would certainly need her rest.

We had finally compromised on a cheap sublet in my apartment complex. I had offered to drive them around, including taking Galina Ivanovna back and forth to her hospital appointments. If they didn't have to rent a car, they could—just barely—make the rent on the sublet.

"Are you hungry?" I asked them. "It's an hour and a half back to Greenfields. We could have supper in the airport."

They both made a face. "Expensive," said Galina Ivanovna. "Can't we pick up some groceries on the way, and I'll make you supper when we get home?" Her voice, always so strong before, sounded weak, almost plaintive.

"I told you, mama: no more cooking! I'll be doing all the cooking," Dima told her.

She made a face. "Then I'll die of hunger for sure."

Dima opened his mouth to make some sharp retort.

"Let me treat you to dinner at a restaurant here, if you're hungry now," I said. "Or if you prefer, let me make supper for you when we get to Greenfields. I've got plenty of groceries for supper and breakfast, and I'll take you shopping tomorrow morning." My Russian, I noted with relief, was returning. I could even pronounce soft consonants correctly again.

Dima opened his mouth to argue some more. Galina Ivanovna elbowed him in the side and patted my arm.

"Thank you, Innochka," she said. "Supper in Greenfields sounds lovely. But we should get Dima something right now. He refused to get a wink of sleep or to eat or drink anything the cabin crew brought him. He's...well, he thinks he can't be too careful. But we should be safe now. And I can't wait to try your American food! You used to cook the most delicious dishes for us. Do you remember the pasta and tomato sauce she used to make, Dima?"

"Pasta and tomato sauce is Italian." Dima's face had taken on an argumentative cast. He tended to pick fights when he was tired or stressed out. He looked more tired and stressed out than I'd ever seen him before. He must be about to explode from the strain of not shouting at someone.

"I've got plenty of pasta and tomato sauce at home," I said. "And salad. Everything we need for a light, healthful supper. And I've some crackers and a bottle of water in the car. Let's go."

Dima opened his mouth a third time, and I *knew*, as if the thoughts were my own, that he was about to start a fight about my vegetarianism. Where, I asked myself, was the certainty I'd had just a few minutes ago that this was the man for me, the one and only? How had I forgotten what a pain in the ass he could be, and so often was?

Dima closed his mouth. Whoa. This was a level of self-restraint I'd never seen in him before. He'd told me in one of our conversations over the past few weeks that he'd changed, that things had happened to make him reconsider his past actions and future behavior, that he'd gained in humility and wisdom, that he was ready to be the man his mother needed him to be.

Since Dima always spoke with white-hot conviction, I'd believed him at the time, or at least believed that he believed it. But Dima said all kinds of things with white-hot conviction that didn't always turn out to be for the long haul.

It wasn't that he was fickle. About the things that really mattered to him, he was steady as a rock. But he was passionate and intense about everything he did, ranging from taking on warlords and oligarchs, to deciding what to eat for lunch. The passion and intensity for warlords and oligarchs had yet to fade. The passion and intensity for, for example, sushi, which had taken Moscow by storm a few years back, had faded within a couple of days. So it was hard to know where this new passion for self-restraint, wisdom, and humility lay in the general scheme of things. It was more than a passing fad, though. A reason for hope? And if so, hope for what?

"Let's go," I repeated. "Or you can sit here and wait and I'll come pick you up."

"I've been sitting so long my ass has gone numb," Galina Ivanovna said. "I need to walk. If you don't mind an old lady's slow shuffle, let's all go together. That way we can have a good chat, catch up. We have so much to talk about, Innochka. You'll have to tell me all about your life here in America."

"Sure," I said. "I can't wait."

10

GALINA IVANOVNA DID in fact perk up by the time we got to the car. She looked around with fascination at everyone and everything we met, as if even an airport parking garage might offer her fabulous sights of America, the country she'd heard about her entire life but had never been to.

Dima offered her the front passenger seat so she could get a good view of Atlanta, but she said she'd take the back, since she was the shortest. How such a small woman had produced such a large son was a source of frequent amazement, but Galina Ivanovna always said Dima took after her father as well as his, and there were a lot of fine, strapping boys on both sides of the family. She, she claimed, was the shrimpy anomaly.

When we got to the car, she asked me if I wanted Dima to drive. It was dark in the far corner of the garage where I'd tucked my little Honda Civic into a compact car spot, but I thought I caught a glimpse of a tightened jaw muscle, as if, just for an instant, he was nervous about driving a strange car through a strange city in a strange country with a strange alphabet he could barely read, and all after a transatlantic flight that he'd spent without food, water, or sleep. Then he held out his hand for the keys.

"Why don't I drive," I said. "I know the way, and I know the car. It's a bit...finicky. I'll show Dima how to drive it tomorrow."

Galina Ivanovna chewed her lip a little, but agreed that made sense, and that I should drive.

"Let me just check it," said Dima. He had me and Galina Ivanovna stand back while he opened the hood so he could check the engine, and then got down on his back and peered at the undercarriage with his phone flashlight.

"I think it's clear," he said, getting up and dusting himself off. "I know it's unlikely anyone will be targeting me here, but..."

"Is there anyone in particular I should be worrying about?" I asked.

"I'll fill you in later. Let's go."

We all got in and set off. I had a moment of terror when I turned the key, but the car started up with no hint of a fireball.

The price of the ticket to get out of the lot filled the car with a horrified chill, especially when I translated it, at Galina Ivanovna's strangled request, into rubles. Galina Ivanovna told Dima to pay me back, but I told them they were my guests and under no circumstances would I accept money from them. Instead, I tried to get Dima to take the water and crackers. We argued about this until we got on the freeway, and then Galina Ivanovna stared out the window with rapt fascination.

Dima, who had finally broken down and accepted the water and crackers, was also gazing out the window between bites with a curiosity he couldn't quite conceal. He had an inward look, as if he were already composing an article, finding just the right words to convey his first impression of America to his Russian readers.

Once we were out of the city limits, both of them turned away from the windows. "How much longer, Innochka?" Galina Ivanovna asked.

"About an hour."

"So, it will be three hours of driving each week to take me back and forth to the clinic," she said.

"More or less."

"And you'll be busy with work. When do classes start?"

"January 10th."

"Only a week and a half from now, then. What will you be teaching?"

"Introductory and intermediate Russian language, and Russian literature," I told her.

"Literature! That's good. At least they've got you teaching something important, something in your specialization. And you have your book. That's good. How's that going?"

I gave her an upbeat assessment of the book and my progress on it. Then we discussed my upcoming interview. Galina Ivanovna did all the questioning. Dima alternated between staring out the window, and looking at me as if he desperately wanted to say something, but couldn't get the words past some obstruction in his throat.

"It sounds like you've been having a hard time, Innochka, but things are looking up for you," Galina Ivanovna concluded. "And it sounds like you've got friends who've been helping you out, which is always good."

At the word "friends," Dima snorted and muttered something about "One friend in particular."

"Well...yes..." I said.

Dima made a pained kind of gagging sound and muttered something about "*Special* friends."

"Be quiet, Dima," Galina Ivanovna ordered. "Tell me about this friend of yours, Innochka. We haven't had a chance to talk in, well, years. I want to hear everything about your life. I consider you to be a daughter to me. I know you had an American man. Tell me about him."

"Um, well...he helped me move. And, he, well, he helped me. But, uh...as you know, we broke up."

"It's good you had someone to help you, Innochka," said Galina Ivanovna.

"Um...yes..."

"And we know how he helped you," Dima said.

Galina Ivanovna made an exasperated *tsking* sound from the back of the car. A prudent man would have stopped. Dima, as usual, was not prudent.

"I know you like...love, Innochka, but did you have to go chasing after an American? An American! How could you be that desperate?!?"

Surprisingly, I couldn't hear the steering wheel cracking under the grip of my fingers. Maybe because the sound was drowned out by Galina Ivanovna's inhale as she prepared to ream Dima out.

"You told me to go get fucked," I said. "So I did."

Dima growled. Galina Ivanovna smacked him on the back of the head.

"Dimulya, aren't you ashamed of yourself?" A torrent of words that sounded as if it had been building up inside her for days, perhaps weeks, maybe months or years, came bursting out. "You go asking stupid questions, begging to be told things you don't want to hear, and what happens? You get told things you don't want to hear. And you heard our Innochka: you have no one to blame but yourself. You sent a pretty girl like her away, and what happened? Some other man came along. He sounds very nice, Innochka. You say you broke up, but these things happen on the way to true love. Do you think you'll marry him?"

"No," I said. "I don't think he's going to marry anyone."

Galina Ivanovna *tsked* again. "Moron! You hear that, Dimochka? Still a chance for you, not that you deserve it. Lucky for you that other men are even stupider when it comes to women than you are! Maybe you can get in around this American who's been courting your girl while you've been running off playing at soldiers after all."

Dima inhaled sharply, just like his mother, and turned to look out the window, a muscle in his jaw jumping. We passed the rest of the ride in silence.

11

WE ONLY BROKE THE SILENCE when we pulled into the apartment complex. By then it was almost 8:00pm. I was tired. Dima was surreptitiously rubbing his eyes and stifling yawns. Galina Ivanovna must have been on the verge of passing out. But she made complimentary remarks, and reached forward and patted my shoulder approvingly when I told her I'd already gotten the key for their apartment and they could move into it whenever they wished.

"Is it in your building, Innochka?" Galina Ivanovna asked.

"Unfortunately not, but it's in the same building that Mel lives in."

"Mel...he isn't..."—Galina Ivanovna gave Dima a squinty-eyed glare—"your American friend who helped you?"

"Mel is a woman. She also teaches at Crimson. And we help each other."

Dima snorted, but more quietly than before.

"That's lovely that you help each other," said Galina Ivanovna, giving Dima another squinty-eyed glare. "I've heard so many bad things about America. I was afraid people didn't help each other here like they do back home. But of course you do. After all, you're an American, Innochka, and you help people all the time. And now, if you won't mind helping me, Innochka, I'm afraid I'm rather hungry and tired. Can you take me into your apartment and this supper you've promised? Dima: unload the car. Put the suitcases where Innochka tells you."

Galina Ivanovna was openly appreciative of my cheap one-bedroom apartment. Dima was also impressed, although he tried not to show it. American apartments were much bigger than the equivalent in Europe

or Russia. Which might be one reason we were having both an environmental and a housing crisis.

But right now, I obviously rose in Dima and Galina Ivanovna's estimation as a person of means. I didn't try to get into a discussion with
them about purchasing power and how, since everything was so expensive in America, and the requirements for being a respectable member of
society and not an indigent street person were so high, I was no richer
than they were, or maybe poorer.

Galina Ivanovna was lavishly complimentary of the quick and simple
supper I prepared for them, and Dima, after a sharp glance from her, said
nothing about the lack of meat in it. He had for the most part admired
my vegetarianism when we'd been together, as a sign of my commitment
to living according to my convictions, as well as my general exoticness.

However, he'd never been entirely comfortable with it, and whenever
he wanted to pick a fight, it had provided a handy pretext. Galina Ivanovna, as a Soviet-trained medical doctor, had initially been deeply skeptical,
but once she'd looked into the latest research on the potential health
benefits of plant-based eating, she'd come around. Now she told me how
fortunate it was that I didn't eat meat, because she was supposed to avoid
it herself these days.

"In fact, I have been eating nothing but tasteless, low-protein cosmonaut meals, and I'll be eating more of them as part of the treatment here.
But I'll start eating them at the hospital. I just want to enjoy your good
cooking tonight, Innochka."

My cooking was passable at best, but I supposed that after months of
low-protein, low-sodium pre-prepared meals, as well as airplane food, it
was probably downright delicious.

After we were done, Galina Ivanovna's eyes started to close. She
forced them open once, twice, but on the third time, she almost fell
asleep with her head on the table.

"Why don't you rest here for a bit while I show Dima your apartment," I said. "You can lie down on my bed if you'd like."

"No...I'll just doze here for a bit at the table...Dima, go with Inna."

A minute later, Dima and I were walking side by side across the dark parking lot, carrying their luggage. Dima walked slightly behind me, as if acting as my bodyguard or trying to avoid having to say anything to me.

"Here's the entrance," I said, stopping in front of their stairwell. "You're on the second floor. I hope it isn't too much for Galina Ivanovna."

"She'll be fine. The second floor is good. Less crime. More secure."

"Good. Well, it's up here."

Dima looked up into the dark stairwell. "Don't they have a light?"

"I guess it's gone out."

"Wait here. Guard the suitcases."

He went cautiously up the stairs, pressed against the wall to make a smaller target. After a moment of looking around, he came back down, got the suitcases, and nodded at me to follow him up into the darkness.

We stopped in front of the apartment door. I fished the key out of my pocket. My fingers were clumsy and slippery, and I dropped the key on the dirty concrete with a dull tinkle.

"Inna," said Dima. He went down on one knee and felt around for the key, his eyes fixed on the ground.

"Yes?" I found my own eyes scanning the darkness, as if searching for the enemies that Dima was convinced were out there.

"Thank you. For everything."

"Of course."

"I didn't mean to be such a shit to you. I just...this whole thing with mama...and your American man...it really fucked me up to hear you and mama talk about him...it made me realize...do you remember that Tsvetaeva line I told you, the first time..." He stopped and swallowed, as if he couldn't get the words *we kissed* out past a lump in his throat.

"Of course," I said. "'You are foreign blood to me / Foreign blood / Is more alien and desirable than all others.' It was the first time I'd ever heard any Tsvetaeva. And I ended up writing my dissertation on her. I have you to thank for that."

"I said it then. But I only truly felt it now, seeing you in America, hearing about your American friends. You *are* foreign blood to me, Inna, with all that entails."

"And what does that entail?"

He stood up. We were no more than a handspan apart. One simple movement, and we would be in each other's arms, where we'd spent so much time, been so happy...

A door on the landing above opened, spilling light onto us. We stepped back from each other. A couple of teenagers clattered past us down the stairs, chattering excitedly about the movie they were going to go see.

"I don't know what it entails," Dima said. "Maybe that's what I'm here to find out. Step back, Inna. I'm going to open the door."

I stepped back against the wall. Despite the darkness, he slid the key into the keyhole on the first try, turned it smoothly in the lock, and swung open the door.

12

I GOT DIMA AND GALINA Ivanovna settled into their new place by 10:00pm. It took a while because Dima insisted on sweeping the entire apartment before letting me and Galina Ivanovna in.

"Who *are* you expecting to come after you?" I asked. "The FSB? Is that why you wouldn't eat or drink anything on the plane?" There had been cases of Russian journalists getting poisoned on planes, possibly by the FSB.

He shrugged. "Probably not the FSB. I just wanted to be careful, just in case. I'm more worried about private hits. I've pissed off a number of private enterprises, especially Kavboyets and their friends." Kavboyets was a private military company out of the North Caucasus that was displeased with Dima's investigations into their ties with oil and gas, Russian state security structures, and US companies. They were scary. Very scary. I just hoped that they couldn't get US visas.

"Or maybe the Ukrainians," Dima went on. "They're still pretty sore over what I wrote about their dirty gas deals, and the fact that I embedded with a DNR battalion. There could be a car bomb with my name on it out there."

"Could any of them actually send someone all the way to America to get you?"

He shrugged again. "I don't know. But my good friends at Kavboyets might not have to send someone. They've got Security Solutions, right here in Georgia."

"True." Security Solutions was the private prison and security company that was also, as it happened, a major donor to Crimson College. I had—I assumed—displeased them mightily by getting the son of the

37

owner arrested on drug and sexual assault charges. So far they hadn't shown any signs of retaliation, but realistically, all they had to do was make sure I didn't get the tenure-track job I would be interviewing for next week. I could be invited for a first-round interview to show that everything was fair and above-board, but when it came time to actually make an offer, it would go to someone who was a "better fit" for the job description or campus community. All perfectly legal and correct, and it would get me out of their hair and maybe end my career.

However, they might prefer something a little more violent for Dima. They had been expanding into the private army business in Russia, including a deal with Kavboyets, and they had raised Dima's wrath in the process. He had gone after them, in his typically no-holds-barred style.

I didn't know the details and wasn't sure I wanted to know them, but I was under the impression that he had caused them a certain amount of inconvenience. And now both of us were right here, in the same cheap apartment complex in Greenfields, Georgia, just down the road from their headquarters.

I was starting to think this whole trip to America was a terrible mistake. On the other hand, what was Galina Ivanovna supposed to do? Doctors back in Moscow were refusing to treat her because of who her son was. And she wasn't responding to treatment anyway. This clinical trial was her only hope.

And Dima was probably in no more danger here than anywhere else, since he normally spent most of his time rushing into war zones and picking fights with the rich, highly connected, and amoral. They might be endangering me a little, but again, what was the alternative? Condemn Galina Ivanovna to certain death because I was scared? Not an option. We'd just have to take precautions.

Maybe I could convince Dima to keep a low profile and not publish anything too sensational while his mother was receiving treatment. He'd never been amenable to that kind of argument before, but he did seem semi-sincere about turning over a new leaf. Maybe that meant not recklessly endangering his mother. And maybe we were blowing this whole thing way out of proportion and he was not being stalked by Chechen jihadists, FSB poisoners, Ukrainian car bombers, and American hitmen, all determined to rid themselves once and for all of this unbelievably troublesome, meddlesome, and turbulent modern-day priest.

I was just convincing myself of this and settling myself into a state conducive to sleep when a text *pinged* on my phone. Not from Dima. From Frank.

Hey Ro. Is it true your Russian boyfriend is here in the States?

"Argh!" My involuntary groan was so loud it sent Fevronia scampering off the bed. I thought for a nanosecond about ignoring the text. But I'd already seen it, and it would torment me all night if I didn't deal with it now. Besides, while Frank was annoying, he sometimes had good intel and, weirdly, good advice. He was an FBI agent and was competent at his job, whatever else he was.

My acquaintance with Frank had arisen under complicated and fraught circumstances during my visits to California last year. Somewhat against my will, we had ended up staying in touch after things had ended with Alex. Frank had even come all the way to Georgia to save me from—oh God, the irony—danger that people I actually liked had brought into my life.

So, weirdly, horribly, from a certain light, Frank was now one of the most reliable people in my life. This despite his domineering behavior and unfortunate tendency to engage in low-level sexual harassment at every opportunity. You'd think the FBI would have trained that out of him by now, but I guess some people are incorrigible.

I told myself I was up for dealing with Frank, and that I might need to hear what he wanted to tell me. *It's true*, I texted back.

Is he with you?

He's here in Georgia, I texted. *He's not with me in the room at this instant, if that's what you're asking.*

Okay. Be careful. I don't know what he's told you about what he's been up to, but you need to watch your back, Ro.

He's made that clear, I wrote. *I think he thinks multiple people could be after him. Do you know something?*

I don't know anything about a hit on him, Frank wrote back. *What I do know is that word on the street is that he's turned. He's working for the Russian government now, Ro. A really unsavory branch of it.*

That seems unlikely, I wrote back.

My intel is solid.

Okay. I'll ask him, I wrote.

You sure that's safe?

I don't think he'll *hurt* me, if that's what you're asking, I texted.

You sure about that?

Yes.

Okay. Maybe you're right. But he's working for people who will hurt you bad, Ro.

I thought about texting *So what else is new?* I didn't. *I'll watch out,* I wrote instead.

Good. Let me know if you need anything.

Will do, I wrote. And then I tried, and failed, to go to sleep.

13

I HAD PLANNED TO LET Dima and Galina Ivanovna sleep in. I assumed they were exhausted. I was a little exhausted myself, to be honest. But Fevronia woke me up with some 5:00am barfing, and shortly after I finished cleaning that up, my phone *pinged* with a text from Dima.

Are you awake?

Apparently, I texted back, pouring out some more cat crunchies for Fevronia. She tucked into them happily.

We woke up hours ago. I've been trying to get mama to go back to sleep, but she says she can't. She doesn't want me to bother you, but I figured you might be up by now too. Do you have any tea? Coffee?

Both, I wrote. *Do you want me to bring some over?*

What if we come over to you?

Come on over, I texted. Then I went and looked at myself in the bathroom mirror. My hair, which normally hung down in more or less controlled waves to my shoulders, was sticking up in a wild variety of funhouse crazy angles. My eyes were red and not quite focused, and I had a crease on my right cheek. I was in my oldest, rattiest t-shirt and running shorts, which was my version of pajamas.

Oh, whatever, I told myself. It wasn't like Dima hadn't seen me just out of bed hundreds of times before. He'd probably recognize the shirt and shorts. I rinsed out my mouth, splashed some water on my face, made a vain stab at smoothing out my hair, and went into the kitchen to start water for tea and coffee.

Two minutes later, Dima knocked at the door. I told myself that I recognized his knock because I knew it was him doing it, but it was also a comforting, familiar sound that I was convinced I would know anytime, anywhere.

He, unlike me, had showered, shaved, and put on clean clothes. Galina Ivanovna had also put on clean clothes, done up her hair, and even applied a little rouge and lipstick. She had always said she approved of my no-makeup aesthetic, but she also confessed that she enjoyed dressing up when she could. This time, I sensed that she was putting on a brave face for the world, perhaps for the last time before an ordeal that might strip away all her love of culture, elegance, and beauty.

My heart clenched painfully. Galina Ivanovna had been the one to inculcate a love of culture, elegance, and beauty in me. My parents valued education, but they'd always been more interested in social action than in art. Galina Ivanovna had been the one who'd taken me to the ballet, to the opera, to art museums, to a whole world of high culture that I hadn't even known existed before she'd introduced me to it. And of course, Dima had recited that Tsvetaeva poem to me, and Galina Ivanovna had pressed precious little poetry collections into my hands and insisted I read them, and...well, here we were. She had been one of the most influential people in my life, the person who had turned me from a gauche American into a cultured intellectual, and I might be about to lose...

"You look good," I said, cutting off that thought before I could finish it. "Is that a new dress?"

"Oh, thank you, Innochka. Yes, it's a new dress. I got it for this trip. Silly, I know, but I wanted something to cheer me up...and Dima was talking about going to Pesaro in September, for the world championships...he says he has connections that might enable us to go there for cheap...and I thought, if I can make it that far, this dress will serve for that, too. I might not have a lot of world championships left, and for once in my life, I'd like to cheer our girls on in person, you know?"

"I know," I said. Galina Ivanovna was a passionate fan of rhythmic gymnastics, and had converted me to it as well. We had watched all the major events together when I'd been living with them, and I'd gained an impressive array of esoteric phrases in Russian like "all-around champion," "penché turn," and "group exercise with three balls and two ropes."

Since the latter involved putting numbers in the instrumental case, it was particularly gratifying to be able to whip out at odd moments.

"A colleague has offered us a place to stay, and we might be able to get discount flights," Dima put in. "Mama has her heart set on it, and I won't lie, it would be nice to see something where I can be unashamedly proud of my country. My foreign friends are always reminding me that Russia is a place where the police can hit you over the head and drag you off to jail because they don't like the way you look. As if I could forget. I'd like to have a chance to point out to the world that Russia is also a place that produces beautiful women who perform great feats of athleticism and incomparable works of art."

In my experience, Westerners responded to the sight of beautiful Russian women performing great feats of athleticism and incomparable works of art by talking loudly and anxiously about how they were cheating, they were old-fashioned, they were unhappy, they were...pick whatever excuse you like. I didn't say that. I didn't want to do anything to spoil Galina Ivanovna's anticipation. The more I looked at her, the more I thought she was right and she might not have a lot of world championships left. In fact, I thought she might need this world championship as something to look forward to in order to make it to September.

"How about some tea," I said. "And we should make a grocery list. I can take you shopping whenever. I'm at your disposal all day. I thought, if you felt up to it, we could take a little excursion around town and campus, as well. It's small, but you might find it interesting."

"Thank you, Innochka. That would be lovely, and I'd like to do it today. I'm tired, but I'll be spending the rest of the week in the hospital, and then God knows how I'll feel. They say if the treatment works, I could start feeling better within a couple of weeks, but for some people it takes longer, and it can be very tiring, especially at first. So I'd like to see your college while I'm still able to enjoy it. It does my heart good to know that you're here, in this out-of-the-way place, teaching students about the classics. Will you be reading Pushkin?"

"We will," I said.

"That's good. It's good to know that at least a few Americans will read him. It's good to know that *anyone* will read him. Sometimes, when

I think about the future, I..." She blew out a deep breath, sat there for a moment with her eyes closed, clutching at her mug of tea as if it were keeping her from falling right off her chair, and then said, with forced cheeriness, "But enough about that. You said we could go grocery shopping. What time do the stores open?"

"I think they're open around the clock," I said. "We can go whenever you like. Would you like some breakfast first? I have...well, I have yogurt and toast."

"Yogurt and toast sound lovely, Innochka. A real treat, actually. I'll go back on my cosmonaut meals for lunch. Dim! Dimulya, help Inna with breakfast."

Dima looked up from his phone. His expression was grim and focused inwards, and I knew he'd just gotten news about a story.

"Sure," he said. "Breakfast, and then an excursion. And then...Inna, how far away is the headquarters for Security Solutions from here?"

"About an hour, I think," I said. "Um...why?"

"I was thinking of checking it out."

"Um..." I said again. "Why?"

"Because," he said, "I think they might have a testing facility there. I was thinking of trying to get a look at it."

"What kind of testing?" I asked, at the same time as Galina Ivanovna said, "*NO*, Dimochka. Not now. Not when we're Inna's guests. Not when I'm about to go into the hospital. Not when you don't know the territory or even the language. Let it lie, at least for now."

A muscle bunched on Dima's jaw. Then he visibly, intentionally, relaxed it, and said, in the most conciliatory voice I'd ever heard him use, "You're right, mama. Now is not the time. I need to focus on taking care of you, and I don't want to put Inna in danger. And I should do a lot more background checking first, anyway. I won't go anywhere near Security Solutions."

"You promise?" she said.

"My word of honor. Inna, how can I help?"

We went into the little kitchenette together. As I was getting out the toaster, he leaned close and said, very low, into my ear, "I'll tell you more later. I can see you're curious. And you need to know. It's for your safety too."

"Okay," I said. "I can't wait."

14

BY 8:00AM, WE WERE ready to set off. There was a brief delay as we put on our coats and Galina Ivanovna expressed dismay over the thinness of my winter jacket. She and Dima were both dressed for January in Moscow, her in a below-the-knee quilted coat, and him in a fur-trimmed parka. My jacket, she said in horror, would hardly be appropriate for October.

"It's actually above freezing right now," I pointed out. "We don't need winter coats here."

She initially refused to believe it, although she had commented on the warm air on the walk from their apartment to mine, but when Dima showed her the weather app on his phone, she agreed that it did, indeed, show the temperature as above freezing. Even so, she stepped out the door with distrust, as if expecting to be hit by a wall of snow and ice.

"It's so bright!" she exclaimed. "The sun's already up! And it really is above freezing. We're in the south for sure, Dimochka. I'd read about this kind of weather, but I'd never experienced it. Is this what Moscow will be like with global warming, do you think?"

"Unfortunately, no," said Dima. "I think it will be like the summer with all those fires."

All three of us made a face. Moscow had been surrounded by wildfires in the summer of 2010, choking the city in a dense cloud of smoke that spread out over several neighboring countries, and it had taken months for them to go out. It was then, Galina Ivanovna had said, that she began to believe that global warming was a real threat, not something that hysterical Westerners kept yammering on about because they didn't have anything better to worry about.

"Well, no fires here right now," said Galina Ivanovna. "Show us your campus, Inna. And show Dima how to drive your car. That way he can drive us both around."

After a brief orientation of the car, which taxed my Russian to the utmost—car and driving vocab was a highly specialized subject—we set off, with Dima behind the wheel and me in the passenger seat giving directions. This was rather more stressful for me than driving myself would have been, but now was a good time for Dima to familiarize himself with American traffic conventions and my car's tricky clutch and tendency to rebel when asked to shift into second gear.

There was some unpleasant lurching and grinding on the way out the parking lot, but by the time we made it onto the main road, Dima and the car appeared to have come to an agreement of mutual cooperation and harmony. Dima had always been more interested in cars than I had, and had nursed his elderly Niva jeep through many years of bad roads and worse weather with skill and flair. Maybe Galina Ivanovna was onto something with this idea of him driving me around...

My phone *pinged* as we were pulling through the gates of campus. I stopped my tour guide spiel to check my notifications. A text from Mel popped up onto the screen.

Got her! I think I made contact with Evil Mel. About to try my wiles on her. Wish me luck!

15

I MUST HAVE GROANED out loud, because Dima looked over at me, an equal mixture of curiosity and alarm on his face.

Good luck, and *be careful*! I texted back.

"What is it, Inna?" Dima asked. I must have looked even more worried than I thought, because something in my face made him pull over into a loading zone in front of the library and park the car.

I sketched out the situation with Evil Mel.

"The internet is such a dangerous place!" said Galina Ivanovna. "A colleague of mine, an intelligent, educated woman with two degrees and four decades of experience practicing medicine, was swindled out of her life savings recently. Her husband had died the year before, her son had emigrated to Australia, she was feeling lonely, she went online looking for friends, but the friends she found were lowlife thieves who lied to her and took every kopeck she had. She's had to come out of retirement. She's almost seventy and she works fifty hours a week just to put food on the table.

"Her son is rich, but when he found out about it, he not only refused to help her, he told her if she was that stupid, she deserved it, and he didn't want to have anything to do with her. This isn't...you know, there were a lot of problems in Soviet times, but when something like that happens, I understand why a lot of my friends get out their red banners and vote for the Communists. If this is modernism, capitalism, democracy...I don't know that we need it. A lot of us certainly don't want it. Maybe it works for some people. For us, it's turned into a heartless law of the jungle where sons turn on their own mothers for not being sufficiently profitable."

"Yeah," I said. "You're not alone in thinking that. And the internet can definitely be a very dangerous place. Mel's smart and tough, but I'm worried about her getting into something really dangerous with this crusade."

"Crusades can be dangerous," said Dima, while Galina Ivanovna said, "Can you help her? Watch her back?"

"I can try," I said. "I just don't know how."

"I've been telling Dima he should look into this," Galina Ivanovna said. "The oligarchs and warlords he goes after are dangerous and bad, yes, but for most of us, it's these petty thieves and scammers who are the real danger. He should make this his next story. In fact, he should do it now. He should help your friend and work on his next story simultaneously."

Now it was Dima's turn to groan. "Mama..."

"Are you saying it's a bad idea?" demanded Galina Ivanovna.

"I'll be busy taking care of you."

"Not so busy you weren't planning to go stake out the headquarters of Security Solutions. If you can find the time to do that, you can find the time to help out Inna's friend. She's literally right next door to us, you'd be doing Inna a favor, and getting good background for your next story. One that might be more likely to get published in a big Western publication.

"How many times have you complained that they love stories about Russian corruption, but they don't want to hear a word about Western corruption? If you do manage to find something out about Security Solutions, who do you think is going to publish it? Chances are it will just leave you broke and heartbroken, and maybe with your face smashed in, just like so many stories you've chased after in the past. While here's a story that's fallen straight into your lap that could actually do some good *and* earn you some money, and probably with a lot less danger than what you normally do."

"It's not really my type of thing..." said Dima.

"Well, maybe you need to find a new type of thing," Galina Ivanovna told him. "You keep talking about it, but never doing it. Maybe now is the time to actually do it."

"She probably doesn't speak any Russian, and I don't speak much English," said Dima.

"So Inna can translate for you."

"I'd be happy to," I put in at this point. I was not, in fact, sure that I would be happy to. I shared all of Galina Ivanovna's reasons for thinking this was a good idea. I also shared all of Dima's reasons for thinking this was a bad idea. As much as he had excellent reasons for finding a safer, more remunerative line of work, he hadn't managed to make himself do so yet, and I had doubts that if he did so, it would turn out well. He was addicted to danger, and if he found a safer job, he'd probably just turn to drugs or BASE jumping or skydiving to get his adrenaline levels up.

So I wasn't sure that this was a great pivot for Dima, professionally speaking, and I also wasn't sure that I wanted to spend a lot of time translating for him and Mel. I mean, in theory of course I wanted to help them both out. In practice, this sounded like a massive headache that could easily spiral into relationship-ending arguments.

On the other hand, what was I going to say, no? Mel did need help, and Dima did need to try something different, and they both needed me in order to make it happen. Refusing was unlikely to make things any better for the three of us, and would probably make them worse.

"Would you like to meet her this afternoon?" I asked.

Galina Ivanovna beamed. For that instant, her face lost its exhausted, sick look, and she was once again the vigorous woman I remembered. "That would be lovely, Innochka," she said. "I'll probably need to rest, but I'm sure Dima would love to meet a friend of yours, and maybe we can all help each other out, too."

"I'll set it up," I said.

16

GALINA IVANOVNA WAS in raptures over campus, which she said looked just like something from an American movie.

"Like...what was it called...*The Club of Dead Poets?* Something like that," she said as we were driving away from it.

"Yeah," I said. "Something like that. Although our buildings aren't so nice inside. In fact, they might be really bad." I gave a short overview of Chloe, her health problems, my own possible problems with the buildings, and the possibility that they might be moldy or otherwise toxic.

"Akh!" said Galina Ivanovna. "That's really bad. Dirty air is very dangerous. There is talk at my polyclinic that maybe we have a bad building too. It turns out that three more of my colleagues have developed kidney disease this year, and there is an unexpectedly high rate of cancer amongst us, as well. Plus asthma. Asthma is very dangerous, Inna. Have you told a doctor about your problems breathing?"

"No..." I began.

"She's telling you, mama," Dima interrupted. "She's telling a doctor right now."

"Good point. When we get back, I'll dig out my stethoscope and listen to your lungs, Inna. I don't like what you're telling me about chest tightness. Of course, it could be 'just' stress. But stress is very dangerous, too. And if there really is mold in the buildings...I was reading an article recently about ghosts. The author was arguing that haunted buildings are really full of mold or toxins. That's why you feel so anxious, shivery and lightheaded, start hallucinating when you're in them...it was a very interesting article, but I wasn't expecting to implement it in my practice.

However, science never stops. I'll listen to your lungs as soon as we get home, Innochka."

"Great," I said. "Thanks." I was haunted, pun intended, by the fear that now Galina Ivanovna would be hounding me about my health her entire time here, but I couldn't see a way around it. Plus, she *was* a medical doctor. Maybe she'd find out something useful.

"And call your friend Mel when you get back home. I need to rest after this, but Dima will be bored. If your friend is free, you can take him to her and they can start working on her problem."

"Sure," I said. "That sounds great."

17

WHEN WE GOT BACK FROM our expedition, we unloaded a week's worth of groceries from the car, and Galina Ivanovna got out her stethoscope and listened to my lungs. She spent a while at it, frowning and moving the stethoscope around, before finally saying they didn't sound terrible but they were a little congested and tight, and I should monitor them carefully, especially in bad buildings. Then she suddenly drooped and said she needed to go home and rest, and I should call Mel.

A few minutes later, I was alone in my apartment with Dima. It felt incredibly natural, and the weirdest, most awkward thing I'd ever done, all at once.

Maybe Dima felt the same way, because he stood for a while looking out the window of the kitchenette, his back turned towards me as if he couldn't bear to meet my eyes. I reflected, and not for the first time, how awful it was that the people I cared about most in the world often seemed to find my presence actively painful. Of course, if we hadn't cared about each other so much, there wouldn't be so much pain between us.

"Inna." Dima still had his back to me. "Thank you again. You're being so patient with mama. I know she can be pushy..."

"She's just trying to help," I said.

"Yeah, but she's helping in a pushy, annoying way. You've always said the most important thing for you in a relationship is autonomy and respect, but she can't give that. It's how she is."

"I know," I said. "And I don't mind. She's like a second mother to me..." Oh God, my voice was starting to break. Another second and I was going to burst into tears. But dammit, the situation was genuinely tragic. It deserved a few tears.

"She feels the same. You know, she was so angry with me when I told her I'd sent you away. She told me you were the daughter she'd never had, and it was cruel and unfair to deprive her of you just because I was afraid."

"It was a bad situation," I said. "You were doing what you thought was right." Those were both true statements. And maybe, by sending me away, Dima had in fact kept me safe. But we'd never know, and he'd also hurt me badly and maybe kept me and Galina Ivanovna apart during what could be the last years of her life. For the first time it occurred to me that perhaps we could have gone against Dima's wishes and kept in touch anyway. Why hadn't we?

"I thought was acting in your best interest," he said. He turned to look at me. One corner of his mouth was turned up in a wry smile. "It has been pointed out to me that our president, whom I've hated with every fiber of my being for years, thinks he is acting in Russia's best interests. A humbling thought."

"Humbling indeed," I said. "And this doesn't sound like the kind of conversation your friends normally have with you."

"I've acquired some new friends. Or gotten back together with some old friends. In any case, it's made me rethink things I've taken for granted for years. And one of those things is whether or not I was acting in anyone's best interests. Maybe my own. I was scared. But I didn't give you the autonomy and respect you need more than anything from me, and I think I mainly hurt myself as well."

He was looking down at the floor as he said this. I'd heard many times that most men couldn't bear to look people in the eyes when they're saying something revealing. I reminded myself of this, and that I shouldn't take it personally.

"And I want to make things right," he said, still looking at the floor. "I don't know what that means, exactly, but I need to atone for what I've done to you and to mama. I want you to be able to turn to me for help, instead of being a burden and a source of pain to you. Mama..." He swallowed. "Mama's going to need a lot of help, whatever happens. And I'm...I'm afraid...I'm afraid I won't be brave enough." The last words came out as a strangled whisper.

"You'll be brave enough."

"I never have before. Sure, I'm brave when it's just bombs and bullets, but when it's something really scary, like hurt feelings, I've always turned tail and run."

I opened my mouth to tell him that wasn't true. The fact that it *was* true blocked my words from coming out, leaving me gaping and gasping like a fish out of water.

"I want to trust you," I finally managed. "I believe that this time, you'll find the courage not to run away when things get hard."

"Meaning that I couldn't find the courage before?" He didn't sound angry. He was now examining my cabinets as if they were the most fascinating objects in the world. "Don't deny it, Inna: that's what I did. I ran away when things got hard. You're right not to trust me. I don't trust myself."

"Sometimes," I said, "when you can't trust yourself, you need someone else to trust you instead. Their faith can give you the strength you need to deserve their belief."

"That," said Dima, "is the kind of speech I would expect from you, Inna. Maybe that's even what I was secretly hoping you'd tell me. I certainly don't deserve it. But I'll take it anyway, because I'm weak and selfish and I need all the support I can get to be brave for mama."

He swallowed again, then shook his shoulders as if shaking off unbearable thoughts. "But right now she's charged us with a mission, and we should fulfill it. Call your friend and let's find out if there's anything we can do to help her."

18

MEL WAS SURPRISED BY the offer/demand to help her, but after a few rounds of texting, said that we probably couldn't make things any worse, and maybe we could make them better, so we might as well come over.

She greeted us at the door in ratty sweats and oversized sunglasses. "Sorry for the weird getup," she said. "Not feeling great at the moment."

"We can come back another time..." I began.

"Nah. Stay. What else am I gonna do? At least this'll give me something to think about." She took off her sunglasses and gave Dima an up-and-down. "So. You're him."

"Yes." Dima didn't wait for me to translate. He stepped out from where he'd been standing behind my shoulder, and held out his hand. "Kuznetsov. A pleasure."

There was a handshake that was a little longer and firmer than it needed to be. I could see they were both holding themselves back from a full-on dominance struggle. Mel was doing a better job of it than Dima.

"So," I said, taking a step to the side so that they both turned to look at me, breaking off the handshake/staring contest that seemed in danger of devolving into a standoff. "What's the latest on Evil Mel?"

"Brace yourself, *habeeba*," said Mel. At my side, I felt Dima stiffen. He must know that *habeeba* meant "darling." He knew almost as much Arabic as he did English. Which is to say, not very much at all, but enough to throw around a few key phrases. He turned to look at me, about to utter some outburst. Then he visibly forced himself to take a deep breath, relax, and give Mel a pleasant smile.

"So," Mel was saying, "you know how I was cyber-stalking her on dating sites?" She was looking at me as she said it, but also watching Dima out of the corner of her eye. Oh God, this was going to be exhausting.

"Uh-huh," I said. "Do you mind if we go sit down? My knee's bothering me." It wasn't actually bothering me that much, and sitting might make it worse, not better, but maybe changing location and configuration would break things up between Dima and Mel. At least I could try to arrange them so they weren't giving each other squinty side-eye.

"Sure thing. You two take the loveseat. I *think* it'll hold you both. I'll take the floor."

The loveseat creaked threateningly when we sat down on it, but didn't actually collapse. Mel sat down stiffly on the floor, grimacing in pain.

Dima jumped up, making the loveseat creak threateningly again. "She should sit here," he told me. "I'll sit on the floor."

I conveyed this to Mel. She argued. Dima argued back, and then sat down on the floor. After a moment, Mel grudgingly got up, grimacing in pain again, and took his place next to me on the loveseat.

"Okay," I said. "You were cyber-stalking Evil Mel on dating sites. You created a profile and got in touch with her. Didn't she notice that you and she were using the same photos?"

"First of all, I wouldn't have used the exact same photos, since the ones she had were about a decade and a half out of date. But second of all, I didn't use my own photos. I used my cousin's. And her name as well, since Evil Mel is already using my name."

I resisted the urge to groan, roll my eyes, slap my forehead, and otherwise express dismay. "I thought you were hoping to actually talk to her. How can you do that if you're catphishing her?"

"My cousin and I look a lot alike," said Mel.

"But..." I began. "Won't that make her suspicious, too? I mean, you're still posing as someone who looks a lot like her. Or like you...you get what I mean."

"Yeah, I get what you mean. But my cousin's all girly-girl, so at first glance we look real different. Plus, I kinda think that Evil Mel isn't that bright."

I was willing to suppose that Evil Mel wasn't that bright, since someone really bright probably wouldn't be doing these kinds of low-level
scams. I also thought that was a dangerous assumption to make, and
also that, even if she wasn't that bright, she probably possessed a certain
amount of low animal cunning. But I figured saying that wouldn't help
things. Mel probably already knew all that, and wouldn't appreciate me
nagging her about it further.

"Okay," I said. "And then, what? You actually connected with her?"

"Yeah. We chatted a little bit on the app, and then she told me she
didn't spend a lot of time on it and asked me to move off it—of course."

"Uh-huh." A common sign of catphishing was when someone said
shortly after the initial match that they didn't spend a lot of time on the
original app or site, and suggested moving off it to a private communication channel like email or text. Of course, non-catphishers would often
suggest moving off the app eventually too, but catphishers normally did
it within the first few hours of matching.

"So I said *sure,* I'd *love* to connect with her on a private chat, and I
gave her the WhatsApp account I'd made just for this, and we've been
chatting away like little lovebirds. She's told me that she had a tough
childhood, her family wouldn't accept her for who she is, they kicked her
out when she came out to them, and she was living on the streets for a
while after that, but then she met this *wonderful* woman who rescued
her, only the woman *died*"—Mel stopped her roll her eyes—"leaving her
heartbroken and alone, but now she's ready to move on and find someone who will heal her wounded heart and make her believe in love again."

I conveyed the gist of this to Dima. He nodded cynically. I tried to
be less cynical, but with poor success. Lots of people, including people
on dating sites and other internet watering holes, had real tragedies that
they were genuinely trying to recover from. However, catphishers loved
to pile on the sob stories. The sad reality was that anyone who claimed to
be widowed, or to have a serious medical condition, or otherwise be in a
bad way and need help, needed to be treated with extreme caution.

Unfortunately, this meant that people like Mel who really did have
tragic backstories and serious medical conditions were targets of con-

stant suspicion *and* of constant catphishing attacks, since the catphishers saw them as vulnerable.

"Any information from her WhatsApp number?" Dima asked. "Anything meaningful about its area code?"

I translated. Mel shrugged. "I checked. It's an Augusta number. But since I'm using a burner number, I can't exactly expect her to be using her own number either. Although maybe she really is that dumb. Since she targeted me and sent stuff to my house, I wonder if she actually is from around here. That's what I'm hoping, anyway. That way I could track her down and nail her to the wall pretty easily."

"Uh-huh," I said. "So have you found out anything else? It sounds like you think you've made some progress in finding out who she actually is."

"Yeah," said Mel. "I went along with her sob story, shared my own, and hinted that I was low on cash and could use an easy way to get some more. And she hinted she might have some ideas. I said I was all ears. And she said maybe we could go into business together. I said I was all for it. And she kind of hinted at her ashes scheme to me, asked me if I wanted to go halvesies on it. I said heck yeah, tell me more. So I might be in like Flynn on the scam to blackmail people with their pet's cremated remains."

19

"WOW," I SAID. "DO YOU really think she's that dumb? Or is she playing *you* somehow?"

Mel shrugged. "Like I said, I got the impression that she wasn't real bright. I mean, obviously she's clever enough to put together a scheme like this. But she doesn't seem like the sharpest tool in the shed, even so. And not real well-read, either. She writes like English is her native language, but she grew up in a trailer park. I mean, I grew up in a trailer too, so that doesn't necessarily mean you're an idiot, but I also learned how to put together a sentence."

"Or she's playing you," I repeated. "I've heard that sometimes they make really obvious errors because they're trying to weed out the smart people. They want someone who's stupid, gullible, or desperate enough to overlook major red flags."

"Yeah," said Mel. "Could be. Or could be that she really is exactly what she says she is. Other than being me, of course."

Dima was looking at us intently, trying to catch all the words that he could. I stopped and translated for him.

"Ah," he said when I was done. "Yes. Hard to know. More investigation is required. Talking to her is good. And do you still have the documents and boxes sent to your house?"

Mel made a face. "I was hoping to avoid that," she said. "Since it would involve going home and talking to my parents."

I translated. Dima nodded.

"Yes. Very understandable. But if this were my story, that's what I would do next. Actual physical evidence can be very useful."

Mel made another face, but agreed that Dima spoke sense. "Why don't you come with me?" she added. "If you really are thinking of doing a story on this."

Dima's eyes lit up. I could see the old thrill of the chase kindling in him. It was good to see him excited about something. I wasn't sure that this was a great thing for him to be excited about. On the other hand, it was probably better than staking out Security Solutions.

"Why don't we all go," I proposed. "Maybe this weekend? We could make a day trip of it, show Dima some more of America, and check out the evidence."

"Yeah!" Mel was perking up as well. "And with you two there, my parents might act decent for once. My dad might even stay sober. Worth trying."

"Sounds like we have a plan, then," I said.

"Yeah. And meanwhile, I'll keep seeing if I can get anything out of Evil Mel. Maybe we can get this whole thing done and dusted by the time the semester starts."

"Maybe," I said.

20

GALINA IVANOVNA WAS supposed to check in at the hospital at 8:00am Tuesday morning. This meant leaving Greenfields shortly after 6:00am. Luckily for them, she and Dima were still more or less on Moscow time, so 6:00am felt like early afternoon to them. To me, it felt like 6:00am.

Maybe 6:00am wouldn't have felt so unpleasantly early if it hadn't been the beginning of January and so dark and dank, or if I'd actually gotten some decent sleep the night before.

After the meeting with Mel, we'd taken Galina Ivanovna to stroll very slowly around Greenfields's tiny town square. Galina Ivanovna had been more impressed with the town square than it had deserved, again, as far as I could tell, because it looked like what she'd seen so many times in American movies. I supposed it wasn't that different from American visitors gawking at Red Square, unable to grasp that they were finally standing in front of something they'd seen so many times but had never believed to be real. It was just funny to think of someone feeling the same way about the town square of Greenfields, Georgia as I'd felt about Red Square, Moscow.

After that we'd headed back home, and I'd made them supper again, insisting that they were my guests and I would cook for them rather than having them cook for me, as Galina Ivanovna kept offering to do. I was half tempted to take her up on the offer, since I knew it would make her feel better to do something for me, but she looked so exhausted from her walk that I insisted that she rest and let me do all the work. She'd agreed, which alarmed me even more than the ashen pallor of her face and the deep gray grooves etched into it.

She'd almost nodded off twice over her plate. She woke up enough when we were through to suggest listening to my lungs again. Instead, Dima had insisted on shepherding her to their apartment right after supper, and we'd all agreed we'd have an early night.

Going to bed early had only given me more time to lie there, thinking anxious and unwelcome thoughts about Galina Ivanovna, Mel, Dima, my job, whatever my father's parents were up to...just as I'd finally been on the verge of dropping off, Fevronia had barfed all over my pillow. Quite a lot of the barf got in my hair. This had necessitated a midnight shower and bedding change, which woke me up all over again and gave me another thing to worry about: namely, was Fevronia sick too? Should I be hustling her off to the vet? Was I about to lose the only faithful companion I'd had for the last three years?

If Fevronia was dying, it was a slow illness, I finally decided, since she had settled herself on the new pillow and started a stentorian purr right in my ear. This was sweet, but not conducive to sleep. It did suggest that whatever health problems she might have, they weren't an emergency. I should focus on getting Galina Ivanovna to the hospital, I'd decided, and worry about Fevronia later.

Fevronia continued to appear hale and hearty the next morning, which came just about the time I'd finally fallen into a deep sleep. She was thrilled by this unexpectedly early breakfast. Me, not so much.

Dima also looked annoyingly hale and hearty when I met them in the dark parking lot at 6:10am. Even Galina Ivanovna appeared to have revived overnight. Apparently, I was the only one who wanted to crawl back into bed and sleep for another couple of hours. But I couldn't, because I needed to drive Galina Ivanovna to what might be the most important medical appointment of her entire life...now I was freaking myself out. I needed to get a grip.

"Are we all ready? Got everything? Let's go!" I said, with so much false chipperness I was afraid Galina Ivanovna would ask if I was experiencing a sudden manic attack. But she only patted my hand and got into the backseat.

I tried to carry on a perky conversation as we headed off to Atlanta. Speaking Russian while driving had always made me lose control of my case endings, and this time was worse than usual. I initially blamed the early start, but as we got onto the highway and Dima stared out the window, making monosyllabic answers only when pressed for a response, I had to admit that my speaking problems were also from nerves. I was terrified of this medical appointment.

Dima appeared to be in an even worse state. Galina Ivanovna was the calmest of us, even though it was her life-or-death event. I considered asking her how she managed to keep such an even keel, and whether this was something I could look forward to with age, but I couldn't think of a way to phrase it that didn't sound insensitive and whiny, and I was having more and more trouble with my grammar as traffic picked up around me, so eventually we all lapsed into silence.

We maintained a grim silence as I navigated through the city and dropped them off in the front of the hospital. It was a relief to be by myself while parking and walking over from the parking deck. When I found them, still waiting for me by the hospital entrance, they looked visibly relieved, too, as if being alone together had been almost more than they could bear.

Galina Ivanovna broke our vows of silence to comment admiringly on the size and cleanliness of the hospital. Dima said, "Huh," and I made what I hoped was a suitable response. Then we got lost, and I had to ask directions—twice—and then we were at the check-in desk and I had to explain who we were and why we were here. My mouth felt weirdly stiff and far away as I explained it to the receptionist, and I found myself struggling to switch back and forth between English and Russian, including blanking out on the English phrase "clinical trial" and saying it in Russian before realizing my mistake.

To my mixed trepidation and relief, we were not left to sit for hours in the waiting room, but whisked away to an examining room immediately. We weren't left to sit for hours there, either, but had a nurse come in to take vitals before we'd hardly had time to take our seats.

The nurse's questions provided some unexpected comic relief, as she started off by asking Galina Ivanovna about her preferred pronouns and gender identity. After several rounds of back-and-forthing, I was able to convey to Galina Ivanovna what this meant.

"Is she serious, Innochka?" she asked once she'd finally grasped the concept. "This isn't a joke they're playing on a poor foreigner?"

I assured her they were serious.

"In that case..." Galina Ivanovna drew herself up to her full height of 162 cm and informed the nurse that she'd been born a woman, she'd lived all her 67 years as a woman, and God willing, she'd die a woman. If the staff wanted to use the polite form of address for her, they would refer to her as "Galina Ivanovna," which, in case they'd flunked out of grade school, took feminine grammatical forms. Furthermore, as medical professionals, shouldn't they be ashamed of themselves for peddling bizarre pseudoscience?

Dima almost smiled. The nurse looked at me questioningly.

"That was probably rude, wasn't it, Innochka," said Galina Ivanovna. "I apologize. I'm not quite myself—jet lag. Make it more polite when you translate it."

I told the nurse that Galina Ivanovna identified as a woman and used she/her pronouns. The nurse, sensing that there had almost been an outburst, looked relieved and hurried through the rest of the exam, before telling us the doctor would be with us shortly, and fleeing the room.

We spent the next few minutes discussing the strangeness and obsession with superficialities of Western culture. This was interrupted by the actual doctor showing up at 8:45am. She introduced herself as Dr. Azarian, which prompted a conversation about her Armenian background and fulsome compliments from Galina Ivanovna on the beauty of Armenian culture. This was followed by a lengthy discussion of Galina Ivanovna's symptoms and chart, which taxed my Russian abilities to the fullest. Also, Galina Ivanovna introduced me as "my daughter-in-law," causing Dima to twitch violently and me to stumble and flail and finally call myself "a friend of the family." Dr. Azarian gave us all an appraising once-over at that, but, to my relief, said nothing.

"Well," she said, once she was done examining Galina Ivanovna, "I think you are a promising candidate, although I think it would have been preferable to have started six months or a year ago. However, I do think it's still worth trying, if your initial labs come back with the kind of values we're looking for—and I think there's a good chance they will. If you still want to continue with this, you'll need to sign these consent forms—here, here, and here—and get checked in for the initial in-hospital stay, which will include those labs I mentioned, and, if they come back with favorable results, the first course of treatment. I can leave you to read over the consent forms together if you'd like."

"I don't need to read them again," said Galina Ivanovna firmly. "I want to do it. Even if it doesn't help me, it might help science. Let my illness be worth something."

Dr. Azarian looked inquiringly at me. I translated. She smiled in a way that might have been impressed or might have been condescending. Galina Ivanovna picked up the pen and signed the forms before we could discuss it any further.

"Now," she said. "Where do I go for those labs?"

21

THE INITIAL BRISK EFFICIENCY of the check-in and exam process soon, of course, slowed down. We spent the rest of the morning getting Galina Ivanovna set up in her room, and the rest of the afternoon getting the various labs taken care of, which included so much blood being drawn I was half afraid she would collapse from blood loss on the spot. However, she remained cheerful and energetic throughout.

It was Dima who became more and more drawn and drained-looking as the day wore on. I tried not to think about how I probably looked. I gave myself various bracing pep talks about how this wasn't about me and it didn't matter that I no doubt looked like death warmed over, and also that it was okay that several high-stress hours of translating complex medical terms were rapidly turning my brain to mush and I was having more and more trouble putting together a coherent sentence in any language.

By early evening Galina Ivanovna was also starting to flag. When her supper arrived—part of the trial involved being on a special diet—she told me and Dima that we should go get dinner and then go home.

"I was going to spend the night here with you," Dima protested.

"Where? On that chair?" She nodded towards the chair by her bed. "You won't sleep a wink, and you'll keep me up all night too. We'll all be better off if you go home and get something decent to eat"—she gave the special meal a dubious look—"and a good night's sleep."

"I can't leave you! Besides, you don't speak English."

"You don't speak English, either," Galina Ivanovna pointed out.

"I speak more than you do! And Inna can stay with us, too..."

"Absolutely not," said Galina Ivanovna. "The poor girl's falling asleep on her feet. Take her home, Dima, and make sure she eats something. And if you're still really tired tomorrow, you should just stay home and rest instead of coming back here to see me."

That set off such a furious rebuttal from Dima that eventually Galina Ivanovna agreed that we could and should come spend the day with her tomorrow, but only if we solemnly promised to go home, eat a nourishing supper, and go straight to bed.

"My word of honor," Dima said. "And we'll be back here by eight tomorrow morning at the latest."

Galina Ivanovna must have seen something in my face at that, because she said she didn't want to see us here any earlier than nine.

"Fine," said Dima. "Nine on the dot. Come on, Inna. We have a mission to complete. Let's go home."

22

WE MADE THE ENTIRE 90-minute drive back to Greenfields in silence. Occasionally I attempted to start a conversation about what to have for supper, or about what we would do tomorrow, or Mel's situation, but Dima only answered with brusque "hmmm" sounds.

When we got back into the apartment, Fevronia came running out to greet us. Dima smiled for the first time that day and scratched her behind the ears. She responded by purring and twining her tail around his hand. He scratched more. She purred more. This love feast went on until she suddenly grew tired of the attention and hissed and swiped at him. He laughed.

"I like your cat, Inna," he said. "She reminds me of myself."

"Well..." I said. "Yes. Pasta for supper? It's all I feel like making."

"Sure, sounds great."

The Fevronia-induced good cheer continued while we were making and eating supper. Dima offered to wash up afterwards while I checked my email, which I had sadly neglected all day.

There was nothing urgent in my inboxes, but the amount of junk mail and trivial announcements required a while to clean out. When I looked up from it, Dima had finished washing the dishes and was standing with his back to me, looking out the window.

"I'm done here," I said. I thought about going over to Dima, but his back didn't look very inviting.

"You must be exhausted," I said. "Why don't we just go to bed. We've got another early morning tomorrow, and I know *I'm* exhausted."

"I'm sorry you're having to wear yourself out for me, Inna," he said to the window.

"I'm happy to do it. Your mother is very important to me, too. And I think we're doing the right thing. I have a lot of hope for this treatment."

"My mother is dying, Inna," he said, still speaking to the window.

"There's a very good chance that the treatment will help her."

"She's sixty-seven years old, Inna," he said.

"She could have another thirty years or more. Half her life again."

"My mother is dying, Inna. Sooner or later, I'll lose her. Or she'll lose me. Probably sooner."

"You can't know that."

"No? Should I say, how is it in English, 'Ewerysing vill be all rait'? Make one of your American optimistic smiles?"

I rubbed my face. It had been a long day, and Dima was making it longer. "Would it help?"

"No!"

"You're probably right," I agreed. "It never helps me much."

"You heard what the doctor said, Inna. You translated it. She should have started treatment much earlier."

"You shouldn't..."

"I should! Because you know why she didn't start treatment earlier? Because *Dima Kuznetsov's* mother can't get treated! There's no doctor in Moscow who will treat *Dima Kuznetsov's* mother! *Dima Kuznetsov's* mother had to spend six months going from clinic to clinic, begging for help, only to be turned away every time as soon as they found out who her son was! Galina Ivanovna Kuznetsova is a respected medical doctor and the widow of a Hero of the Soviet Union, but it didn't matter because she's also *Dima Kuznetsov's* mother! The pro-Kremlin ass-lickers wouldn't help her because they think I'm a traitor, an enemy of the people, and the liberals wouldn't help her because I was an OMON head-breaker, with a thousand human rights violations at my back! The sins of the son were visited upon the mother! Just like Dima Kuznetsov's fiancée couldn't even walk down the street in safety! And even after I...I...we *still* had to leave the country to find any chance of a cure for her! Now both Dima Kuznetsov's mother and Dima Kuznetsov's fiancée had to go throwing themselves at the feet of foreigners! Now we're in a foreign country, surrounded by foreigners, dependent on foreigners, because our own people won't help us!"

I opened my mouth to say that they weren't foreigners to me, but thought better of it and said, "It's not your fault," instead.

"So whose fault is it, then?"

He was clenching and unclenching his fists, looking like he might put them through the window, or burst into tears, or both.

"Your struggle is righteous," I said.

He mumbled something that sounded like, "Don't be an idiot, Inna."

"Someone has to tell the truth," I told him. "Who better than you?"

"Anyone," he said, still not turning to look me in the face. "Anyone would do a better job than me."

"But no one else is doing it. So it has to be you."

"And if you and my mother have to suffer because of it?"

"Then that's what will happen. We won't complain, and we won't blame you, because your struggle is righteous."

He buried his face in his hands. His shoulders were shaking.

"Your mother loves you, you know that," I told him. "She takes pride in your struggle. In you."

"And you?" he said, his voice muffled by his hands.

"I take pride in you too."

"Even now? Even though I'm a complete dickhead who sent you off to go get fucked by some foreigner when you offered to stand by me like a Decembrist's wife?"

"I didn't say I wasn't annoyed with you. But I still take pride in you."

He laughed, pulling his face away from his hands, and then inhaled deeply. "It smells nice here. Like you. Like foreign blood."

"'Foreign blood is the most desirable, and alien, of all,'" I said.

"I don't want to be alien to you, Inna. Just desirable."

"You are."

"Really?" He still had his back to me. "And how does it end? What does Jesus say to Magdalene at the end?"

"That he was stiff, and she taught him tenderness by falling?"

"Yes, that. And then she washed over him like a wave." He took a deep breath, but still didn't turn around. "Maybe that's what I need.

Maybe I need you to teach me tenderness, Inna. To wash over me like a wave."

I opened my mouth to say...what? Both our phones *pinged* simultaneously. We froze.

"It might be mama," Dima whispered. "I have to answer it." He pulled his phone out of his pocket and checked the screen.

"Fuck!" he said.

"What is it?!?"

He shook his head instead of answering. I picked up my own phone, afraid to find it was a message from the hospital telling me something dreadful had happened to Galina Ivanovna. But instead, it was a text from Frank McAvoy.

Ro! Call me as soon as you get this. We *need* to talk ASAP. It's about your boyfriend.

"Dima!" I said. "What's going on?"

But he was already out the door.

23

I RAN OUT THE DOOR after him. He was already on the phone, hissing into it in a strangled, rage-filled whisper as he went down the stairs and set off across the parking lot, not looking back.

I went back into my apartment. I wanted to laugh, cry, and hit something all at once. Instead, much against my inclination, I called Frank.

He picked up on the first ring. "Ro! You got my message. Good."

"What's going on?" I demanded.

"Whoa, you sound stressed out. What's going on with *you*?"

"It's been a long day." I exhaled and made a conscious effort to sound less stressed. "What's so important that I needed to call you right away?"

"Is he there with you? Can he hear you?"

"Dima?"

"Is that what you call him? Kuznetsov?"

"Yes," I said, making another supreme effort not to sound stressed out or aggravated past all bearing. "It's his name."

"Cool. So can he hear you?"

"No," I said. "He just left. He got some kind of really important message too. So what's going on?"

"So, you remember when I said he was working for the government? And that he walked on the dark side?"

"Ye-es," I said. "But..."

"But it turns out it's even worse than we first thought."

"Um," I said. "Okaaaay. But you can't convince me that he's here to, I don't know, assassinate someone or something like that."

"The thought has crossed our minds," said Frank. "See, it turns out he owes some very unpleasant, very high-up people some very big favors.

And these very unpleasant, very high-up people might want some folks in your neck of the woods removed. Permanently, if you get my drift."

"How do you know this?" I asked. "Isn't this a little out of the purview of the FBI?"

"I have my sources." The words sounded more like a threat than a joke. And I could believe them. Frank had spent his entire career in the military and law enforcement. He was probably very well connected with lots of people in lots of sensitive positions. He probably had an old basic training buddy who was now in the CIA, who had a source inside the FSB, who was passing on interesting tidbits about Dima...No doubt any attempts on my part to gain more clarity would be fruitless, but I had to believe that Frank believed that his information was credible.

"Okaaay," I said again. "I guess I can believe that there's some kind of...connection between Dima and, uh, people in the security structures there. But it's not like he's an assassin or anything. He never was. That kind of thing was completely out of his line of work."

"But I'll bet he'd be a quick study," said Frank.

"Well...maybe, but..."

"Listen. Has he shown any interest in anyone at Security Solutions?"

"Well, of course, but..."

"We have reason to believe," said Frank, speaking slowly and distinctly, "that he's been sent over here to assassinate the head of Security Solutions."

24

I LAUGHED.

"It's no fuckin' joke, Ro. You could be sleeping with a killer."

I laughed again. I thought about telling Frank that Dima and I weren't sleeping together. Then I decided that was A) none of his business, and B) not entirely true. Because while, okay, we weren't sleeping together, that little interlude before our phones pulled us apart had been...*something*. We may have been on opposite sides of the room, but that might have been the most intimate Dima had ever been with me.

"Seriously," I said. "That's not what Dima does. Frankly, I suspect he'd make a terrible hitman. Aren't they supposed to be low-profile, innocuous, unnoticeable kind of people? That's not Dima at *all*. I don't think he could do low-profile if he tried. And he can't do a frontal assault on his own. I just don't see how he could do it, even if he's supposed to, which I sincerely doubt he is. No one in the government would trust him with anything like this. They'd be sure he'd run off and publish every detail of the assignment, and they'd probably be right."

"That's not what my sources say." Frank's voice was tight.

"Okay, but still..."

"I think you should stay away from him."

I laughed a third time. "How? His mother is in the hospital here right now. They're relying on me to get her through this. And what am I going to do: tell him sorry, I know you flew all the way to America for the specific purpose of getting my help, and you don't know a soul other than me here, but get out of my sight?"

"I think you need to be thinking about your own safety right now, Ro," said Frank.

"Okay, but even if what you're saying is true, and that's a big if, telling him to get away from me would probably just set him off, right?"

"I guess." Frank's voice was slow and grudging. "Maybe. You know him better than I do."

"I do, and all my knowledge of him says that he'd never do anything like this."

"You should still be careful, Ro."

"Well...okay," I conceded. "He does tend to bring trouble with him, wherever he goes."

"Does he act like he thinks trouble's after him here?" Frank asked.

"Well...yes, he does."

"Has he said what kind of trouble?"

"Not exactly," I said. "Just the usual trouble, I guess."

Frank was silent at the other end of the line for a while. When he spoke, his voice was even more slow and grudging than before.

"I'm trying to decide what to tell you to do," he said. "I don't want to put you in any more danger than you're already in. I don't want you prying into his affairs. But if you could find out what he's up to, that might give you the information you need to keep yourself safe."

"How about this," I said. "I'll keep my eyes and ears open, and if I come across anything that worries me, or that I think you might want to know, I'll tell you."

"Don't go snooping around, Ro," Frank said sharply. "Don't go doing anything like that. Leave this to the professionals."

"I'm not going to snoop," I promised. Truthfully. I had no interest in snooping around in Dima's private affairs. That way spelled disaster on multiple levels. "I'm just going to pay attention, and if anything worries me, I'll let you know. Deal?"

"Deal," said Frank. "I guess. But be very careful, Ro. And I'm going to be checking in on you regularly."

"Great," I said. "Really appreciate that. Really."

25

AFTER FRANK HUNG UP, I waited. And waited. And waited. An hour later, Dima still hadn't come back.

Where are you? I texted.

I waited some more. Still nothing. It was now after 9:00pm. We really should be getting to bed.

I'll just go check on him. He'd probably gone back to his apartment to take the call, and...what? Fallen asleep? Or maybe he was still on the phone, and I shouldn't disturb him. Or maybe something terrible had happened to him...maybe whoever he was so concerned about had found him, and jumped him in the stairwell, and...and did I really want to go out into the darkness? What if the people after him were still there, waiting in the stairwell for *me*? What if going out there was the last thing I ever did? What if...

I shoved my feet into my shoes, my arms through the sleeves of my jacket, and my body out the door before I could come up with any more *what ifs*. Enough with the doom-mongering. Dima had probably fallen fast asleep on the couch after a very long and tiring day. I'd wake him up, we'd apologize to each other, and then we'd both head off to our respective beds, in preparation for another long and tiring day.

It was dark in the parking lot. Most of the parking spaces were filled, with deep pools of shadow beneath and between the cars. The thin ring of longleaf pines that surrounded the complex seemed extra-tall and extra-deep, as if they had morphed into a hundred acres of trackless wilderness with the setting of the sun. A gust of wind blew through them, raising a sound from the needles like the whispering of secrets or the hissing of snakes. Clouds scudded across the sky, covering the slender crescent of the waxing moon and blotting out its faint light.

Walk! Just walk! My legs started carrying me past the dark cars and the darker wells of shadow underneath them. Nothing jumped out at me. My ankles tried to shrink in on themselves even so, away from the icy-hot grasp of ghostly hands they were sure were groping for them. Sweat trickled down my sides, and there was a strange, electric-shock-like crawling sensation up the back of my neck as the tiny, feeble hairs there tried to stand on end in a useless gesture of defense and protection.

I wonder if this is how Mel feels all the time? Part of her illness was a whole host of strange sensations, including the feeling of having a taser attached to the back of her neck and slowly being turned up.

I glanced behind me involuntarily. What had that sound been? Was someone coming up on me? Was there someone here in the parking lot with me, just out of sight?

It's a dog, I told myself. *Someone's taking their dog out before bed. It's probably that woman with the toy poodle who lives in the next building over.* I squinted at the dark figure that was now resolving on the edge of my vision. No matter how much I strained my eyes, I couldn't turn it into a woman and a toy poodle.

Are they coming this way? They're coming this way! They're coming right toward me! What should I do? Run? Back to my apartment? Or try to hide in the unlit stairwell ahead?

The dark figure was picking up speed. I broke into a half-jog. What was that sound? Like a goblin shriek...

"AAAAAGH!" Another figure, even bigger and darker than the one pursuing me, loomed out of the stairwell in front of me. Before I could turn and run, it grabbed my upper arms.

"AAA—" I started to scream.

"Innochka! What's the matter?"

"Dima! It's you!"

"Yeah, it's me. I came out looking for you, and you practically ran straight into my arms. Are you okay?" His grip tightened. "Is someone after you?"

I looked back. The goblin shrieks had resolved into the yapping of the toy poodle, who had dragged her owner over to greet her best friend, the mini-pinscher from the row of cottages along the edge of the complex. I could now make out the clear and unambiguous outlines of two rather small and unathletic women, who were standing and chatting in the middle of the parking lot while their dogs sniffed and circled each other.

"Only my own unbridled imagination." I tried to say it lightly, but my voice cracked at the end of the sentence.

Dima looked around. "Even so, let's get inside. You're right to be worried about being outside alone after dark. Come on." He turned and led me up the stairs to his apartment.

26

DIMA HELD ONTO MY ARM as we went up the stairs to his apartment. When he opened the door and made to step inside, though, I found myself freezing.

"What is it?" His voice grew sharp. "Do you see something?"

"Nothing," I said. "It's nothing." I let him pull me through the door. He closed it softly but firmly, and threw the bolt and set the security chain as well. Still holding onto my arm, he peered out the peephole.

"Nothing," he agreed. "Come on. You need to sit."

He flipped on the light in the living/dining room area. It was a floor lamp with a dusty red shade and a single bulb that came on reluctantly and shed shadows as much as light throughout the room. Dima led me through the gloom over to the ratty couch and sat me down on it. He turned one of the rickety chairs at the rickety dining table around and sat on it backwards, his arms folded over the back. It was his favorite way to sit, especially when he needed to think.

"So," he said. "What happened? You're white as a sheet, Inna."

"That's a lazy figure of speech," I told him. "You hate that kind of sloppy language."

He almost grinned. "True. It lacks impact and isn't accurate. You look like you're about to pass out, then. Also a lazy cliché, but more correct."

"I *feel* like I'm about to pass out."

"Do you want something? Water? That's all I can offer. I don't even have any vodka." He almost grinned again. "Don't tell anyone, or they'll revoke my citizenship."

"I'm fine. I just got scared. It was silly."

"You don't get scared for silly reasons, Inna." His eyes were turning serious again. The red half-light of the reluctant lamp only lit one side of him, leaving the other in deep shadow. It made him look foreign, otherworldly, with sharply etched lines and grooves on one side of his face, and nothing at all on the other.

Like Hel, goddess of the underworld, only male.

"What is it, Inna? You've had some kind of a funny thought, I can tell."

"I was just thinking you looked like Hel."

"The Norse goddess? Thanks. I guess. No one's ever compared me to a deity before. So what's got you so scared? Other than Hel, of course."

"I got a call."

I stopped. What to tell him? Part of me wanted to tell him everything Frank had said, so that he could reassure me it was all nonsense and we could laugh about it together. Another, smaller and more scared, part of me couldn't help but wonder if everything Frank had said wasn't true. Most of me still stood by my initial disbelief in his story, and my belief that Dima would never do anything to hurt me. But there was still a tiny voice in the back of my mind telling me that you never really knew another person, not really, and Dima *had* hurt me. I couldn't trust him, not really, and he'd said he couldn't even really trust himself. Maybe I should be afraid of him. Maybe I should get up and run out of this room right now.

Don't be ridiculous! The rational part of my brain told me that 1) I would never be able to get away from Dima if he really wanted to stop me, and 2) when it came right down to it, he'd always been the one to run away from me. I should trust my knowledge of him and myself and our past, which told me that the main risk of me telling him what Frank had said was that he'd cut me off from him again. Admittedly, that was a pretty big risk, but it wasn't like I'd be in physical danger.

"I got a call from someone who's concerned about you," I said.

"Concerned about me? How kind of them."

"More concerned that you might be dangerous," I said.

"Dangerous to whom?"

"Well...maybe to me...but mainly they're concerned you've been sent here as a hitman. They're worried that you've been asked to take out the head of Security Solutions."

"Oh. Well, as it happens...they're right."

27

I BURST OUT LAUGHING. Dima stared at me. Then he laughed, too.

"Well," he said. "It's good to know you still have faith in me, Inna. Or maybe you have so little faith in me that you're mocking my ability to take someone out. I guess that's good too. I mean, you're still laughing...or is this a fit of hysterics? Should I get a glass of water? Valerian? Validol? Inna! Pull yourself together. You'll make yourself sick if you keep on like this, and then who will take me to see mama tomorrow? I haven't sufficiently subdued your car yet to drive all the way to Atlanta. It needs another day or two for me to demonstrate my complete and total mastery of its transmission."

I tried to stop laughing. Hysterical half-laughs, half-sobs kept building up painfully in the top of my chest and bursting through, despite my best efforts to restrain them. Tears were forming in the corners of my eyes, and I was shivering.

"I'm sorry," I said between gasps. My teeth were chattering now, too. "I don't know what's wrong with me..."

"It's stress," said Dima. "Completely understandable, if inconvenient." He rummaged through his jacket pockets. "I could have sworn I had a bottle of valerian on me somewhere...mama insisted, just in case...but I must have left it with her..."

"It's okay." The laughter had stopped and my jaw was unclenching, although my body was still shuddering slightly. "It's okay. I'm fine. I don't need anything. Other than the truth."

"The truth." Dima looked down at the floor, then back up at me. "The truth. You deserve to know the truth, Inna. If only I knew what it was."

"I don't mean in some kind of general or metaphysical sense," I said. "I mean the truth about what you're doing here."

"Yeah," said Dima." I wish I knew that, too."

I laughed again, choked, and brought myself sharply under control. Anger was replacing the nerves and hysteria, filling me with welcome strength and warmth, but pushing me into dangerous territory, towards a place where I might do or say something I'd regret for the rest of my life.

"Well," I said, swallowing down the anger before it erupted all over both of us. "Tell me what you *do* know, then."

"What I know..." Dima propped his elbows on the chair back and rested his chin in his hands. Then he made a face and went back to sitting with his arms folded. I'd seen him do that dozens, maybe hundreds of times. He'd told me once that he always thought he'd feel more support-ed with his chin in his hands, but every time he tried it, he discovered that it strained his neck, and the back of the chair dug painfully into his elbows. And yet the next time he started feeling anxious or insecure, he'd do it again, as if a lifetime of experience meant nothing. Probably there was some kind of moral in that somewhere.

"What I know," he repeated, "is that Security Solutions is bad news. And there are some high-up people back home who would love to see them get taken out. I owe some of these high-up people favors." He was still smiling, but his eyes were bleak now. "They have intimated that, since I'm right here already, maybe I should do something about Security Solutions, or at least its owner, Anthony Wainwright."

"So, what?" I asked. "They expect you to, what, stroll into his office and shoot him down in front of everyone?"

"I think"—he spoke slowly, as if he was thinking through everything he was saying, as he was saying it—"they would be just fine with that, if I could actually do it. As long as I got shot and killed by his bodyguards in the process. They would be displeased if I were captured by American security forces and subjected to interrogation. Who knows what I might say?" He grimaced. "I'd like to think I'd hold out pretty well, but to be honest, I don't know how I'd do against waterboarding. And who knows what kind of drugs your intelligence forces have?"

I wanted to protest that A) I was sure Dima would hold out just fine against waterboarding, and B) the US didn't do things like that anyway, but I knew for a fact that B wasn't true, and I wasn't sure about A either. Anyone can be broken.

"And besides"—Dima's grimace turned to a lopsided grin—"I think their main fear is that I'd blab everything to my captors in hopes it would get into the press. And that could very well be true. And now I'm going to blab to you, Inna, so that if I *am* shot down in a hail of bullets or whisked off in an unmarked car to some undocumented black site, *you* can go give exclusive tell-alls to every news source in the country."

"Deal," I said.

"Okay. So, you know about Security Solutions and their connection with Kavneft and Kavboyets back home?"

I nodded. Kavneft was an oil company based in the Caucasus, and Kavboyets was a mercenary company, also based in the Caucasus. They had close, if somewhat questionable, ties with each other, with other oil and gas companies, and with the Kremlin. And it turned out that Security Solutions had been working on some kind of a partnership with Kavboyets to develop an international soldier-for-hire business. What could possibly go wrong?

"So." Dima took a deep breath. "It seems that Kavboyets has been working with a drug development company called PitLek to create drugs to use on the battlefield. Some people believe this line of research has great promise, but others are concerned it would lead to mass instability, both at home and abroad. And the powers that be are concerned about that instability." He shrugged. "You know how it is, Inna. 80% of the country is firmly behind the current regime. The other 20% is a motley crew composed of pro-western liberals, troublemakers like me, old-school communists, neo-Nazis...and opportunists who'd love to come to power themselves, and don't care how. There is concern that, despite their current professions of loyalty, Kavneft, Kavboyets, and PitLek fall into this last group—as does Security Solutions."

Dima made a wry face. "Ten years ago, I would have been offering my services to them. The enemy of my enemy is my friend, and all that. But now...you know, when I thought of doing it, I thought of how you used to try to warn me of the kind of chaos I was courting when I did that kind of thing. And how I was too arrogant to listen."

"You were idealistic," I said.

"Idealism without common sense is the most dangerous force in the world."

"Even worse than stupidity?" I asked.

Dima laughed, and then looked surprised. "Well...maybe idealism without common sense *is* stupidity. One of its worst forms. Anyway. You and I both know, with the wisdom of advanced age, what could happen if there were a major shakeup in the Kremlin. Widespread civil war. It would be like Yugoslavia in the nineties all over again, only stretching from the Baltic to the Pacific, and with nuclear weapons."

"Not a very attractive prospect," I said.

"No. No, even I could see that. So, when it was proposed to me...somehow I found myself on the other side again, back with my old comrades in the forces of law and order. Sort of. We're currently fellow travelers, you could say. They helped me out with mama, and in return I...well, I agreed to help them. Including with their little problem with Security Solutions and Mr. Anthony Wainwright."

"By killing him?" I asked.

"Like I said, I think they'd be perfectly happy for me to blow him to kingdom come. But no. They said I didn't have to compromise my principles like that. Instead"—another grimace—"they asked me to compromise my principles in a way that might be even worse. They don't want a physical assassination from me. They want a character assassination."

28

"HOW?" I ASKED. "HOW are you supposed to assassinate the character of someone like Anthony Wainwright? I don't mean to insult your ability to tear someone's character to shreds. But who's going to care?"

Dima sighed. "That's what I said. And then *they* said..."

"Who's they?" I interrupted. "Or do I not want to know?"

"Former comrades," said Dima. "Broadly speaking. People who took the legal route after getting out of the military—if you consider government service the legal route. And their bosses." His lips twisted into what couldn't even be called a wry smile. More a death spasm. "It turns out that I'm able to win friends and influence people, even in very high places. Providing I behave myself."

"That must be difficult." The words slipped out before I could stop them. But Dima laughed, his face relaxing from its death spasm into something like the boyish humor that had always been his most charming aspect.

"Very difficult. But I'm trying to behave myself. I'm trying all around. Have you noticed?"

"I have. I've been very impressed by how hard you're trying."

"Thanks. And I mean that, Inna. It's a hard-fought battle that I'm still in the middle of, and no one's said so much as an 'attaboy' once. It's nice to have it acknowledged. And coming from you...it means a lot, Innochka."

His voice had dropped into a register that made the hair on my arms stand up. Another sentence or two, and who knew what might happen...

Dima's phone *pinged.* He cursed. I silently echoed him. What was it with these goddamn phones?

He looked down at the screen. His face tightened into its death spasm again. When he looked back up at me, his eyes were bleak.

"Inna..."

"You have to take this call," I guessed.

"I hate to impose upon your angelic patience, but..."

I stood up. "Take the call," I said. "There've probably been enough revelations for today, anyway. And morning is wiser than evening. Take the call, go to bed, and we'll talk again tomorrow." I paused. "Is it safe for me to walk back to my apartment?"

He stood up too. "Probably, but I don't want to take any chances, and I should do at least one gallant thing for you today. I'll walk you to your door and answer the call afterwards."

"Fine. Thank you."

"It's the least I can do." We went in silence out the door. When we came to the top of the stairs in the dark stairway, he automatically put his hand on my arm. He kept it there all the way down, not even holding me, but just resting his hand on my arm, ready to catch me if I should trip and fall. He kept it there until we were all the way out of the darkness and under the single working streetlight in the parking lot. When he removed his hand, he flexed it twice before putting it in his pocket, as if my jacket had left some imprint on his skin, half of pleasure, half of pain.

"I'll tell you," he said suddenly, when we reached my door. "I'll tell you everything, Inna. Tomorrow. I'll make a full and openhearted confession."

"Only tell me what you want to," I told him. "Only tell me what you think I should know. Don't tell me anything that would hurt either of us."

He was standing so close to me that when he spoke, it was to my hair, not my face. Maybe that made it easier for him to talk. "I'm afraid all of it will hurt both of us," he said. "But I'm afraid staying silent will hurt us more. And I was serious when I said I wanted you to know so you could take the story to your vaunted free press if something happens to me. I don't quite know everything yet myself, but everything I do know, I'll tell you, and you can decide what to do with it—with me. Wait a second."

He reached out and brushed back a strand of hair that had fallen across my cheek.

"Thanks," I said.

"Good night, Inna. Sweet dreams. And now I'd better go take that call."

I opened my door and stepped in. When I turned around and looked back, Dima was still standing there, watching to make sure I got inside safely. I waved. He waved back, with the same hand he'd used to brush back the strand of hair. When he walked away, he held that hand to his own cheek, as if keeping his face warm against the cold of the January night.

29

MORNING MIGHT BE WISER than evening, but it arrived much too soon, and didn't bring a lot of obvious wisdom with it. I dragged myself out of bed after half a night of tossing and turning, and half a night of the drugged, heavy sleep of physical and emotional exhaustion.

The drugged, heavy feeling stayed with me as I hauled myself out of bed, and as I made coffee, and as I got into the car. Dima, who'd elected to meet me in the parking lot, took one look at me and said, "You look terrible, Inna. Should I drive?"

"Thanks," I said. "And I thought you said you weren't ready to drive yet. And you look terrible, too."

He rubbed his eyes. "Long night. And it wasn't just insomnia, although there was a lot of that, too."

"I'll drive," I said. "And you can tell me everything you think I should know."

He blew out a breath, but agreed, and folded himself into the front passenger seat. It wasn't quite big enough for him. Most things weren't. Even when he fit into them physically, which wasn't often, he couldn't fit into them psychologically. He was one of those people who always filled any space they were in to overflowing. It was attractive. It was also stressful and exhausting. I wondered if it was even more stressful and exhausting for him. I guessed that it was. Dima had spent his entire life burning the candle at both ends. And like Edna St. Vincent Millay, he gave a lovely light. From a distance. And I sensed that his candle was just about burnt out.

"What's wrong?" he asked.

"Nothing."

"You shivered. Are you cold?"

"I'm fine." In fact, I was a little chilly. The car's heater took a while to get going and was anemic at the best of times. We wouldn't be warm until we got onto the highway, and even then we would only be warmish at best. But I had shivered from the chill of my thoughts, not the January air currently filling the cabin.

"So," I said. "Tell me what you think I need to know."

He ran his hand through his hair. Blew out another breath. "So," he said. "I can't tell you everything. I thought I could. I wanted to. But the more I thought about it...and it was impressed upon me last night..."

"That's okay. I know. Just tell me what you can."

"Okay. So. You know the background about Kavboyets and Security Solutions."

"Uh-huh."

"Well. And I mentioned something about the drugs."

"A little," I said.

"Right. So, they were researching drugs to use on people they want to...mmm, let's say they want to modify their behavior. Truth drugs, and sedatives—that's where Security Solutions initially came in, looking for better sedatives for the inmates in their private prisons—and things they can use on the battlefield."

He stopped and wrinkled his nose. "I had a firsthand encounter with those. Not nice. They were originally working on a drug to make people more malleable, biddable, so you can send an aerosol of it over into enemy positions and then tell them to surrender. But sometimes they make people vicious instead."

He curled up his top lip in distaste. "So then they decided to work on a separate drug, one to use on their own people, that amps up the aggression side effect. From what I understand, it uses the body's own hormones to increase in-group bonding while triggering extremely violent reactions to anyone outside of the group, as well as giving people superhuman strength and speed. It sounds sci-fi, but it's all science. They've been working on it very hard back home and testing it out on the various mercenary groups and battlefields in the former USSR. Now they're saying it's ready for wider distribution. What could possibly go wrong?"

Now we both shivered. The mind boggled at all the things that could go wrong.

"Meanwhile," Dima continued, after we'd both given a moment's silence to the current and future victims of these drugs, "Mr. Anthony Wainwright, the head of Security Solutions and, I note, a major donor to your college, Inna, has connections high up in the US government and also the Russian government, as well as ties with major corporations in both countries. He's a well-connected guy."

"I wouldn't expect anything less from him," I said.

Dima gave me a sideways glance. "Have you met him?"

"The father? No. Just the son. He was in my class. And then, of course, he attacked me. So I guess you could say we're close."

"There's nothing like breaking someone's leg to foster closeness," said Dima, nodding.

"I don't think I actually broke his leg..."

"Too bad. I wish you'd crippled him for life."

"Yeah...I'm sure lots of other terrible things are happening to him. Prison's gotta be tough for him."

"For sure." Dima brightened, smiling widely enough that the dimple on his left cheek appeared for a moment. "Justice is sweet, sometimes. Anyway, like father, like son, although I think the father might be even worse. The son just drugged and violated vulnerable young women. The father wants to drug and violate his own motherland, and mine too."

"Does he want to make these drugs widely used?" I asked.

"That's the suspicion. He wants to distribute them to his mercenaries, and—and this is where the real money is—get a contract with the US Department of Defense to use them on US military personnel."

There was another moment of silence in the cabin.

"Really," I finally said.

Dima shrugged. "That's what certain people high up in the security apparatus back home believe. They believe that Security Solutions is working with PitLek to develop and patent this drug, which they will then sell at astronomical prices to both the Russian and US governments. If they can. The Russian government has been involved in the research from the beginning, so they believe the drug should be theirs and theirs alone."

"I can see that," I said.

"Yeah. They wanted to have their cake and eat it too: let private companies take on the work and the risk, and then take over when the product was ready to be deployed. But then Security Solutions got involved, and now it looks like the Americans want it too—and are likely to get it."

"If it works," I said.

"If it works. From what I've seen…" He shook his head, a brief spasmodic movement of distaste. "From what I've seen, it doesn't work very well. But it might work well enough for both governments to be willing to sacrifice a few soldiers to it."

"And, what, you're supposed to stop it?" I asked.

He shrugged again. "I don't think I'm their only weapon in this fight. But they want me to dig up everything I can about Anthony Wainwright and publish it. The hope is that if I do that, there'll be such a stink around him that his government pals will cut off all ties and cancel any contracts."

"And what do you think?" I asked. "Will it work?"

Another shrug. "I don't know. I don't know how sensitive Americans are to scandal and corruption. But"—he looked over at me, a dry smile turning up one corner of his mouth—"I needed a crusade, and I hate Anthony Wainwright, so I agreed. I've doubted myself every day since, wondering if I'm selling out and serving evil, but…here I am."

"You're just supposed to tell the truth, right?" I said.

"Yes. Just the truth."

"Well, then," I said. "Just tell the truth, the whole truth, and nothing the truth, and you'll be fine."

"I'd like to think so, Inna. But these people are so dirty, they can spoil even the purest truth in the world. By the time I'm done, I'm afraid my beautiful truth is going to be all stained and grimy. I'm afraid it won't even look like the truth anymore."

"I hope not," I said. "I guess we'll find out."

30

WE BOTH PUT ON OUR game faces when we showed up at the hospital and made our way to Galina Ivanovna's room. She greeted us with her game face too, insisting that she had slept well and was perfectly comfortable.

"You look worn out," Dima protested.

She waved a hand dismissively. "That's just how I look now. Really, this is the most comfortable place I've been in years. Like a spa, to be honest."

Dima and I looked around skeptically. It was a typical American single-patient hospital unit. So it probably was much nicer than your average Russian hospital, but it still wasn't what you would call "nice." You could hear everything going on in the ward, and Galina Ivanovna let slip that she had been awakened at two o'clock in the morning for a vitals check, and again at four when something had happened in the unit next door.

"But really," she said, as she stirred a small bowl of something that looked kind of like chocolate pudding, but less appetizing, "it was fine. I sleep so poorly now that it really was like a vacation."

"It's only for one more night, anyway," said Dima. "But I think I should spend the night with you tonight, just in case..."

"Then I really won't sleep," she told him sternly. "And neither will you. What a waste! You should rest when you can. And have you made any progress on Inna's friend's problem? You need to get started soon, especially since you might not be here for long."

I started. "What? I thought you both were supposed to spend all spring here, for the length of the trial. Or..." I couldn't make my mouth form the words *Have the results come back unfavorable? Are you being kicked out of the trial?*

"I am," Galina Ivanovna said. She gave Dima a sharp look. "But Dimochka here might have work to do. He might have to leave Georgia, or even leave the country entirely." She gave him another sharp look. "Unless you've rethought your decision?"

"I haven't rethought it." He was looking down at the coverlet on Galina Ivanovna's bed, carefully not meeting my gaze. "I just don't know yet what I'll have to do, so I haven't said anything about it yet." He gave me a swift apologetic glance, then went back to staring at the coverlet.

I bit back the words *So when were you going to tell me?!?!* "When do you think you'll know?" I asked, as calmly as possible.

He shrugged. "Management knows best," he said, which I took to mean that this depended on the pleasure of the people he was—what? Serving? No, that wasn't right. Temporarily allied with? That was more like it. But it seemed they still called the shots.

"Wait," I said, suddenly struck by another worry. "Don't you have a B2 visa? Doesn't that mean you can't engage in journalistic activities for a foreign press? Don't you need an I visa for that?"

Dima grinned, then held his finger to his lips. "First of all, this won't necessarily be journalistic activities. Second of all, we're not going to tell anyone. As far as the US government is concerned, I'm just here to help out my ailing mother"—he nodded at Galina Ivanovna—"and visit an old friend"—he nodded at me.

"The US government thinks you're up to something," I said. "At least, certain members of the forces of law and order do."

He grinned again. "But are they planning to deport me?"

"Not right this moment, at least as far as I know."

"Then we're safe. Besides, if anyone accuses me of being a foreign media representative, I'll tell them I'm freelancing in the hopes of selling a story to an American press."

"Okaaaaay," I said. It was as good as I was going to get. And in theory I approved of Dima's devil-may-care attitude in the face of the Byzantine and heartless American bureaucracy around visas and immigration. In practice, it made me nervous. What if he got deported *forever*? What if we were separated *forever* because he had the typically Russian relaxed approach to obeying the law? What if...

There was a bustle outside the door. Then Dr. Azarian, with a whole crew of nurses, interns, and other hangers-on in her train, came striding into the room.

"How are we doing today?" she asked.

Galina Ivanovna looked over at me. "She wants to know how you're doing," I translated.

"Excellent," said Galina Ivanovna, giving Dr. Azarian a look that was both cheerful and measuring at the same time. She raised her spoon. "The food is delicious."

I translated. Dr. Azarian laughed. "Most of our subjects aren't quite that enthusiastic," she said. "You must be either very polite, or very hungry."

I translated. "Both," said Galina Ivanovna. She fixed Dr. Azarian with another gaze, this one more measuring than cheerful. "What do my results say?"

"Ah, yes. Well..." Dr. Azarian pulled a folder out of the sheaf of folders she was carrying, opened it, and consulted a piece of paper inside. "Well, overall, the news is pretty good," she said.

I translated. Dima visibly relaxed. Galina Ivanovna fixed her with an even sterner stare. "Inna, tell her I know what that means. It means the news isn't actually very good at all."

I translated. Dr. Azarian laughed again, but her laughter sounded forced. "Well...it's true that the results aren't as good as we'd like. Those creatinine levels...and the BUN levels aren't great either..."

"I know that," said Galina Ivanovna, once I'd translated it for her. "I have kidney failure. My creatinine and BUN levels are terrible. What I'm asking is: is it worth starting the trial? Or have I been eating this tasteless cosmonaut food"—she lifted up her spoon again—"for nothing?"

Dr. Azarian consulted her piece of paper again. "Overall, the results aren't great. I'd prefer them to be better. If you'd started six months ago...but I think it's still worth beginning the trial. We've had patients almost as bad off as you who've seen real improvement from it. So if you're game, we'll go ahead and start the first infusion today."

I translated. Galina Ivanovna nodded firmly. "Start the infusions," she said. "What have I got to lose? At the very least, it will contribute to science."

I translated. Dr. Azarian looked taken aback, but then said, "I like your attitude! I'll tell them to prep you for the first infusion. It will take all afternoon. The good news is you won't have to do anything. It's just a simple IV, and most patients don't feel a thing. You can just lie back, watch TV, and enjoy yourself while you get better."

I translated. Galina Ivanovna pulled a dark green hardback with gold lettering on the cover out from under her sheets. I immediately recognized the distinctive design of the "Poet's New Library" series. This one said *Complete Collected Poems of E.A. Baratynsky* on the front.

"I'm not going to watch TV," she said. "If these are my last days, I'm not going to waste them on TV, and if they're not my last days, I'm going to take this time to improve my mind. I've been meaning to delve into metaphysical poetry for years now, but I've always been too lazy. Now is the perfect time."

"She's going to spend the time improving her mind by reading metaphysical poetry," I translated.

Dr. Azarian's laugh sounded distinctly uncertain. "Well, good for her!" she said. "I'll go tell them to start the prep. We'll come get you in a couple of hours."

31

"ISN'T THAT NICE," SAID Galina Ivanovna once Dr. Azarian had left. "Not long to wait. Just enough time for me to finish *this*"—she held up her spoon again—"and have a nice chat. What's up with you, Dimulya?"

Dima was surreptitiously checking his phone. He put it away, a guilty look on his face. "Just wanted to get a jump on Inna's friend's problem," he said.

Galina Ivanovna gave him a sharp look. "Really?"

"Really, mama."

"I can see you're hiding something from me. You never were much of a liar, Dimulya, and you still aren't. Just watch out you're not hiding something from me that I need to know."

"I'm not..." Dima protested, but with so little conviction that he couldn't even finish the sentence. "I'll stop," he added. "I should be paying attention to you right now, anyway."

But he kept fidgeting and glancing at his phone as Galina Ivanovna finished her non-pudding, and as she asked me about my research, and as she opened the book and read "Two Lots" out loud.

"That was depressing," she said when she'd finished. "'You will awaken only for suffering, / For new pain in old wounds.'" She checked the date of the poem. "And he was only twenty-three when he wrote it, too. What does a twenty-three-year-old know about suffering, anyway?"

"I'd already suffered plenty by the time I was twenty-three," said Dima.

Galina Ivanovna fixed him with another stern look, which softened. By the age of twenty-three, Dima had already lost his father, watched his country collapse, and fought in a war. "True," she said. "Although you were still full of the blind optimism of youth, even so. Maybe you'll find his"—she held up the book—"early work more to your taste than me. Maybe you have to be a man and a soldier to understand it." She flipped towards the back of the book. "Let's take a look at his later work..."

A nurse came in. "Time to get you prepped!" she announced cheerily.

I translated. Galina Ivanovna smiled. Dima's face tightened.

It tightened even more as the nurse transferred Galina Ivanovna into a wheelchair—"Just to make things easier!" she announced brightly—and wheeled her down a long corridor and into a large room with three other people already hooked up to IVs. When the nurse swabbed the crook of Galina Ivanovna's arm with alcohol, Dima covered his mouth with his hand, as if holding back vomit. And when she inserted the needle into Galina Ivanovna's vein, he staggered slightly and clutched at the back of her chair.

"Forgive my son," Galina Ivanovna told the nurse. "He faints at the sight of needles."

I translated. The nurse looked concerned. "Sir, why don't you take a seat," she said. "Or maybe you should go outside, get some fresh air. Do you want me to call for a wheelchair for you?"

I translated. Then I had to fight back the intense desire to burst out laughing at the conflict between horror, outrage, and relief on Dima's face.

"Thanks," he muttered. "I'll manage. Mama, I'll, uh..."

"Go," she told him. "I don't want you messing up my treatment. Inna will stay with me. We'll call for you when I'm done. Go!" She made shooing motions at him.

"Okay. I'll, uh...I'll just..." He nodded at both of us, let go of the chair back, and made his way, wobbling slightly, out of the ward.

"It's always the tough guys who can't deal with blood and needles," said Galina Ivanovna. "They can cause harm, but they can't handle healing."

The nurse looked at me inquiringly. I translated.

"Oh, for sure," she said. "My husband's ex-army, a real tough guy, loves hunting and fishing, doesn't have any problem with gutting a fish or dressing a deer, but one look at a needle and he's on the floor. I have to take our dog to the vet because he can't bear to watch her get her shots. And when our niece with diabetes was visiting and she had to do the finger sticks and insulin injections, well, I thought he wasn't going to make it. He basically lived in the garage the entire time she was there so that he wouldn't have to look at her."

I translated. Galina Ivanovna nodded. "It was the same with my husband," she said. "I think he only saw me give myself insulin once in our entire marriage. Of course, we weren't married very long. But still. He almost vomited every time he so much as glanced at the needles. One time he *did* vomit."

I translated. The nurse laughed. They swapped a few more stories of tough men they knew who fainted at the sight of blood and needles while the nurse hooked up the drip. I was starting to feel a little faint myself. Normally I had a high tolerance for medical things, but all this talk of vomiting and passing out was getting to me.

Fortunately, Dr. Azarian arrived, cutting off the flow of reminiscences. She checked the needle, the drip, and the bags of fluid that were hanging from the IV stand.

"Everything looks good," she told Galina Ivanovna. "Of course, with Kathy here"—she nodded at the nurse—"I always know it will be. I just like to be here when we first start the infusions. It's such an exciting moment!"

Kathy smiled, pleased. And she had seemed competent, despite her extreme cheeriness.

"So," said Dr. Azarian, "are you ready to start getting better?"

"As Yury Gagarin said, 'let's go!'" said Galina Ivanovna.

Dr. Azarian pressed some buttons. Fluid starting dripping down from the bags into the IV tube.

"You might feel a little coolness, a little tingling, at first," said Dr. Azarian. "But that should be it. And you might feel pretty tired towards the end, or afterwards. A lot of patients experience some temporary fatigue after the first few sessions."

"I feel the tingling!" said Galina Ivanovna, laughing. "I feel like it's working already!"

Dr. Azarian smiled. Kathy smiled. I tried to smile, but I could feel the smile wanting to turn into hysterical laughter.

"Well, I'll leave you to it," said Dr. Azarian. "There's a call button there"—she pointed at the IV stand—"in case you need anything. Kathy will be here in the ward with everyone, and we'll come get you and take you back to your room in a couple of hours."

Galina Ivanovna gave a double thumbs-up. Dr. Azarian gave her an encouraging smile that was only a little bit false, and left. Kathy said she was going to go check on another patient, but to call her if we needed anything.

"Everyone is so kind here," said Galina Ivanovna. "And the tingling feels so funny! Not painful, but funny. I think it's a good sign. Now, where's the book, Inna? We have poetry to read."

32

THERE WAS NO SIGN OF Dima as Galina Ivanovna and I sat in the ward and read poetry. After an hour, when two of the other three people were unhooked from their IVs and wheeled away, he sent me a brief text.

How's mama?

Fine, I texted back. *Maybe a little tired now.* Her eyes kept drifting closed as I read to her.

Should you summon the doctor?

Kathy returned from wheeling away one of the other patients, and came over to us. "How are we doing?" she asked. "A little sleepy?"

Galina Ivanovna yawned and nodded.

"It's to be expected," Kathy told her. "For the first couple of treatments, until your body gets used to it. But you just saw me with Mrs. Trevelyan. She's been with us a month now. The first couple of times, she got so tired she fell asleep in the middle of the treatment! But you saw her now, as lively as a spring lamb. That'll be you in a few weeks!"

I translated. Galina Ivanovna nodded again and tried to smile. "How much longer?" she asked. Her words were slightly slurred.

Kathy checked the bags hanging from the IV pole, which were more than half empty. "About another 45 minutes. If you need to, just lay your head back and take a little nap. We'll be watching out for you."

Galina Ivanovna shook her head. "I'll nap afterwards. I want to monitor my condition now. Out of scientific curiosity, you understand."

I translated. Kathy looked puzzled. "She's a doctor herself," I explained.

"Oh, is that *so?* So I guess we should be calling you"—Kathy checked her chart—"Doctor, uh, Ku—Kuzne—uh..."

"Kuznetsova," I supplied.

"Well, I'm sure this must all be *very* interesting to you, Doctor, uh..." said Kathy, while her eyes said *Doctors make the worst patients.*

"Inna, if she can't say my name, tell her she can call me—let's see, Galina is probably too hard for her too...do you think she can manage Galya?"

"She says you should call her Galya, if it's easier for you," I said.

Kathy tried it, and winced.

"What about Doctor K?" she asked.

"Doctor K," Galina Ivanovna repeated thoughtfully. "I like it. Yes. That will be my new title from now on."

Kathy said that sounded great, and bustled off to see the other patient.

The nurse thinks everything's fine, I texted Dima.

Good. I'm in the middle of something here. Can I come get you in an hour?

Sure, I texted back. *The treatment will be over in 45 minutes.*

I'll meet you back at mama's room in an hour, he wrote.

"Is that Dima?" Galina Ivanovna asked. "Is he sending his excuses?" She had gotten a fresh surge of energy from the conversation with Kathy, and was speaking clearly now.

"He's in the middle of something," I said.

"Of course he is," said Galina Ivanovna. Her tone was fond, but also acerbic. "He's always in the middle of something. One day he's going to look up and see that he's missed the most important things in life because he was in the middle of something whenever they were happening."

"He, uh, he might be working on something pretty important," I said.

Galina Ivanovna patted my hand. "I appreciate that you always defend him, Innochka," she said. "That's a good quality in a fiancée, any mother will agree. But any mother of sense would tell you that sometimes your fiancé doesn't need defending. Sometimes he needs a good sharp kick up the ass. Or at least some very plain truth, spoken straight to his face."

"Well..." I said.

She yawned. The burst of energy from Kathy's visit was fading, leaving her even more drained than before. "But we can talk about that later," she said. "Once he's ready to face the fact that he mustn't throw you away again, no matter how many important things he's in the middle of. Now, let's read that last poem again. There were some good lines in it. What was it? 'Many lands have I left behind me, / My agitated soul has borne / Many false joys, true evils; / Many mutinous questions have I resolved.'"

She sighed. "False joys, true evils. It's true. There are so many of them." Her eyes were drooping closed, despite her efforts to keep them open. The book slid out of her hand and slithered along the blanket, slipping right off her lap and onto the ground. She didn't notice. "False joys, true evils," she repeated, her voice thick and sleepy. "Wake me up when it's over, Inna. I think I'm going to have to take a little nap after all. You can keep watch over me. Make observations for science."

"Of course," I promised.

Her head drooped to the side, and she fell asleep.

33

I PICKED UP THE BOOK. It fell open to the poem we'd just been reading.

It matters not whether the shore is near or far!
Desire for it has been readied in my heart.
I see Thetis: From her azure urn
She is drawing a kind fate for me.
Tomorrow I will see the towers of Livorno!
Tomorrow I will see that earthly Elysium!

I decided I'd stop at that high point and go check Facebook to see what my friends and family were up to.

Ten minutes later, I was completely enraged by what my nearest and dearest were posting. I turned off my phone and went back to the book. I was so busy contemplating the tension between personal desires and the blind forces of the universe that I didn't even notice that the time was up and Galina Ivanovna's treatment was over until Kathy came in to unhook her and take her away.

"Fell asleep, did she?" she whispered to me. "It happens a lot, especially the first time. We'll just take her back to her room. She'll probably want to sleep all afternoon. She might not even wake up until suppertime."

"Oh," I said. Kathy seemed very calm about it, so I had to hope this wasn't sinister. I texted Dima that the treatment was over.

He still hadn't replied by the time we got back to the room. Galina Ivanovna woke up briefly, only to say that she just wanted to rest and I should go home, and fell promptly back asleep. I texted Dima again. Still nothing. Galina Ivanovna appeared to be sleeping deeply. Kathy said I didn't need to stay there if I didn't want to, that she would keep an eye on her if I wanted to go out and stretch my legs.

I went along various corridors and down various elevators and through various automatic doors until I came out into the January afternoon sunshine. There was an urn for smokers placed off to the side, under a small overhang. Dima was standing there, smoking furiously.

"Galina Ivanovna is resting," I told him. I carefully did not say anything about the smoking. I was pretty sure he'd stopped—again—and hadn't smoked once since he'd arrived in America. I certainly hadn't smelled it on him. But apparently the ordeal was getting to him. Picking a fight with him over it was likely to be counterproductive, though. "She just wants to rest now," I said. "She told me to go ahead and go home."

He nodded without looking at me.

"I'll go get the car, then," I said.

"I'll come with you," he said, still not looking at me.

"No need. You finish your cigarette."

"Why..."

"Why what?" I asked.

"Why do you always have to be so *fucking* independent, Innochka?"

"I don't know. Why do you always have to be so stubborn?"

"I'm not stubborn." He turned so that I could see his face in profile. One side of his mouth was almost smiling. "I'm a man of principle."

"And the difference is..?"

"Not a damn thing." He stubbed out his cigarette, grinding it into the sand until it came apart in his fingers. "Innochka..."

"Yes?"

"Innochka, what you said, back there in the car. I never told you to go get fucked. I never wanted you to fuck anybody. I only ever wanted you to make love. With me."

I repressed a sigh. Were we really having this conversation? Now? Out on the sidewalk, next to the hospital parking lot? Apparently, we were.

"Yes, well," I said, "you still sent me away."

"You know why!"

"And I told you I would stay anyway. So when you sent me away, it was like you told me to go fuck off and never come back."

The other side of his mouth smiled. "You always sound so funny when you say 'fuck,' Innochka. It's the only time you can't hide your American accent. Except when you're doing it, of course. Then it's even stronger."

I repressed another sigh. "A gallant observation."

"I'm a real knight in shining armor. Valor, deeds, and glory, just like Blok. But I meant what I just said, Innochka."

"Yes, well..."

"Excuse me? Are you speaking Russian?"

We both turned. An undergraduate-looking girl was standing there beaming at us, flanked by her parents.

"Yes," I said. "Do you, um, speak Russian?"

"I'm in my second year! And I was so excited! I actually understood a few words!"

"That's, um, that's great," I said. "Like, uh, what?"

"Like 'yes.' And 'said.' And 'American.'"

"Good for you," I said.

"So are you Russian?"

"He is." I nodded at Dima. "I'm an American. But I teach Russian."

"Wow, that must be why your Russian is *soooo* good! Whoa! I've never met an actual Russian before!" She goggled at Dima with a mixture of fascination and trepidation.

"Nice to meet you," Dima said in Russian.

"Whoa, I, like, totally understood that! Uh, nice to meet you too!" She giggled in triumph at getting the words out.

"Your Russian is excellent," said Dima.

"Yes?"

"Yes, and I'm speaking the purest truth, because most Americans can't even say 'yes.'"

"Yes?" said the girl, with the fixed smile of someone who's only understood two words out of ten.

"It's wonderful that you're getting to practice your Russian, Caitlyn, but we should leave these folks to get on with their business," her mother interjected. "Thanks so much for talking to her, uh, Professor?"

"Um, yeah. I'm a Russian professor at Crimson College."

"Oh, how *lovely*! I went there, you know! Caitlyn considered it, but ended up going to UGA, didn't you, darling?"

"I did my undergrad at UGA," I told her. "You've probably had some of the same professors I did."

Caitlyn beamed even broader. "Oh, wow! What's your name?"

"Rowena Halley."

"Awesome! I'll be sure to tell them I saw you!"

"You do that, honey, and thank you, Professor Halley." Her mother gave me a big smile. "We were just visiting her grandmother, who doesn't have a lot of time left, so it's been a hard day, but meeting you has sure cheered us all up."

"I'm sorry about your grandmother," I said. "And glad I could cheer you up. Say hi to everyone at UGA for me."

"Thanks, professor, I sure will!" Caitlyn skipped off, followed more sedately by her parents.

"Wow," said Dima, with his strongest parody of an American accent. "You talk Russian so good, Professor Halley."

"She was trying very hard."

"I know. That's what's so sad. Because even so, I was still just a bear in a zoo to her. Go get the car, Innochka, while I go say goodbye to mama. And then we should talk. I have more information. Which was what I'd meant to tell you instead of...what I said." He looked slightly ashamed. "All that just came out by accident."

"I'm very familiar with those kinds of accidents." I hoped I sounded more patient than I felt. I was trying to be compassionate and forgiving about the fact that I had spent most of the day sitting with Galina Ivanovna, who, when you came right down to it, had no official relationship with me, while Dima, her own and only son, had been off doing...what? I didn't mind helping out Galina Ivanovna—in fact, I was happy to do so. But it also felt a little like I was being taken advantage of.

I wasn't sure how much was sexism and how much was selfishness, but Dima had run out of that room because of his own fear, and hadn't expressed any concern about how I might feel. Apparently, I was supposed to tolerate blood and needles and sickness and fear and hospitals and the tedium of hours by a sickbed just fine, and with no expectation of reciprocity from him or anyone else...I made myself stop thinking those thoughts before they caused me to experience a little accidental blurting of awkward truths myself.

"Yes, well..." He made an indeterminate movement with his shoulders. "I'll...I'll go see mama, and then...then we'll discuss things." He disappeared through the sliding doors before I could ask him what, exactly, we were going to discuss.

34

DIMA WAS ALREADY WAITING for me on the sidewalk when I pulled the car through the parking lot exit. His face was tight, making the scars on his cheekbones and jawline stand out sharply.

"How's Galina Ivanovna?" I asked.

He shrugged. After a moment, he said, "Sleeping."

"Good," I said.

"They said she wouldn't feel anything! They said she'd start to feel better right away!"

"Well..." I said. "They did say she might feel a little tired at first. Which is doctor-speak for 'She'll probably be in a coma for a while.'"

"What if something's wrong?" Dima demanded. "What if...Inna, should we be leaving her? Maybe we should go back. Maybe we should stand guard over her bed the whole time. Maybe..."

"She told us to leave her," I said.

"Yes, but..."

"Maybe this is finally her chance to get some rest on her own, without worrying about us, or us fussing over her," I said.

"Yes, but..."

"She's got her cell phone," I pointed out. "She can call us if she needs anything. No one seems to think she's in any danger right now, including her. And we'll come back tomorrow morning, and take her home tomorrow afternoon."

"Yes, but...I feel like I should do something. To make up for, well...for running off and leaving both of you like a coward."

So at least you recognize it. I thought the words but very carefully did not say them. "If you want to help Galina Ivanovna," I said gently, "you could start by listening to her when she tells you what she wants."

He made a face. "Yeah, that's what she says, too. Maybe I should start listening, huh?"

"Maybe," I said. "So what's this news you wanted to share with me?"

"Oh, that...I might have to leave even sooner than I thought."

"Oh." I very carefully did not grind my teeth. "To do what?"

"To go back to the front."

He didn't look at me as he said the words. That was good. It meant I didn't have to work quite so hard at controlling my face. "To do what, exactly?" I asked. I meant it to sound gentle, but judging by Dima's wince, some of the icy rage I was feeling came through.

"To, well...there's always something, some story, that needs to be covered..."

"No doubt," I said. "But is there some specific story that needs to be covered right now, while Galina Ivanovna is in the hospital?"

He winced again. "Well...I've been getting calls...they need me over there." Now he did look at me. His face was as close to beseeching as I'd ever seen it. "Have you ever felt, Inna, like a bird of passage trapped in a cage? Like there's something in you, something in every nerve, every sinew, every cell, that's calling and calling, telling you that you *have* to do something, do it right now, or catastrophe will strike, you'll lose everything, disaster will overtake you? Apparently it's biological. It's called *Zugunruhe*. I looked it up."

"Ye—" I choked, coughed, and tried again. "Yes," I said.

He did a doubletake. "Really? About what?"

"About..." I choked, coughed, and tried again. "About...family."

He looked confused.

"About getting married and having children," I said bluntly.

He looked shocked. "Really? Why would anyone feel that way about *that*?"

We were approaching the on-ramp for the interstate. That was lucky. It made me concentrate on my driving instead of screaming at him, or possibly throttling him.

"Lots of people," I said, once we were safely merged into traffic and I could speak normally again. "Although I think it might mainly be women."

"Yeah...I guess..." Dima's gaze was turned inwards. "It never occurred to me that anyone would feel that way about *that,* especially you, Inna. It's so...silly. So *selfish.* Just wanting to love and reproduce instead of something more important. Just wanting to have children for your own gratification. Have you ever thought about what you'd be putting *them* through?"

"I have." That sharp, shrewish tone that came through despite all my best efforts to suppress it was probably not conducive to a productive discussion. "And by that measure, merely existing is selfish. By that measure, we should all just lie down and die right now. But I refuse. I insist that my existence have value, that my life have meaning. And for me, a big part of that meaning is family. I *feel* it, like a calling from a higher power."

"Yeah." Dima was still looking inwards. Maybe he needed to hear that sharp, shrewish tone. Maybe that was the thing that would finally break through that shell of delusion and cluelessness he had spent the past—was it *ten* years already?—encased in.

"I guess I've been like Chekhov's 'Man in a Case,'" he said. "Or maybe I need someone to always be tap-tap-tapping at my window, reminding me of others' suffering, or otherwise I'll forget. Isn't that also Chekhov?"

I shivered. Just when I was so angry at him I was afraid I might do something really terrible, he did that thing that he'd always done, that no other man—or woman—I'd ever known, did. He'd always had a tendency to echo my thoughts with uncanny accuracy. We'd noticed from our very first meeting how we were strangely in synch, how we often did the same things at the same time, said the same things at the same time, thought the same thoughts at the same time. Even when we were furious with each other, that strange, almost uncanny synchronization remained, as if we were always operating on the same wavelength.

"Yes," I said. "That's also Chekhov. From the same Little Trilogy."

He nodded. "Mama used to talk about it a lot. I never paid much attention...but I probably should have." He sighed, and fell silent.

We drove several more miles down the road in a silence that wasn't quite companionable, but at least wasn't seething with suppressed rage.

"See, it's like this, Inna," he said suddenly. "That way you say you feel about...that feeling that you *have* to do something, you're being called to it by a power stronger than you...that's how I feel about the front, about battle. Especially if my comrades are there. And several of them are going back there now. They're inviting me to come with them...there really are stories that need to be covered...and they need me...most of them are foreigners, they need my help, they need me to be their fixer, basically...I just got a call from Dave Wilkinson, my friend I told you about...he's going back to the front...and what do I tell him? Do I tell him 'no'? I can't imagine telling him no! I can't imagine abandoning him, not when he needs me..."

"Galina Ivanovna needs you, too," I interrupted him. "And there are other local journalists, other fixers, that Dave Wilkinson can find. But your mother only has one son."

He looked over at me. "Something tells me, Inna, that you are thinking that I should be feeling that call to stay with her, not to run off and leave her."

"I can't say what you should or should not be feeling." In fact, I was judging him pretty harshly right now for it, but once again, I decided that would not be a productive thing to mention. "I can only say what you should or should not do. And right now, I am very firmly of the opinion that you should stay with your mother. At least until she's through the first couple of weeks. There will still be war and calamity and corruption next month. But your mother's treatment is happening right now, and you're the only son she has to sit by her side while she's undergoing it."

Dima looked over at me again. "Thank you, Inna," he said.

"For what?"

"For insisting that I shape up and act right. No one else will do it, not even mama."

"I haven't been very successful so far," I said.

"Maybe the fruits of your labor are only just coming to bear," he said. "And in any case, thank you for believing that I *can* shape up and act right. I'll try to live up to your belief, *Zugunruhe* or no *Zugunruhe*."

"Great," I said. "That's great."

35

AFTER OUR LITTLE CONVERSATION in the car, Dima remained pensive and withdrawn for the rest of the afternoon. He only brightened up when I told him halfway through supper that I'd gotten a text from Mel.

"Any news with her?" he asked. "Has she found anything more out about her doppelganger? I should have been looking into that more, I know, but..."

"She said she has a phone date scheduled with her this evening," I told him.

He raised his eyebrows. "A phone date? Scammers won't normally do phone dates."

"I know. But that's what she says. She's asking if we want to come over and listen in."

He pushed his half-eaten plate away from him. "What time? Should we go over now?"

"In half an hour. If it happens at all. She's as skeptical as you are. But she thought it was worth trying."

"Of course it's worth trying." Dima was growing more animated. He pulled his plate back towards him and ate a mouthful with more enthusiasm than he'd shown all day. "It's always worth trying to talk to a source. But normally they let you down."

"I know. Frankly, I'm expecting nothing to come of this."

"Me too." Dima took another couple of enthusiastic mouthfuls. "But it's still something to try. Try enough times and something will come through." He scraped up the last of the food from his plate, then looked down at it in surprise.

"Do you want more?" I asked.

"No...although it was much better than I'd expected."

"Thanks," I said dryly.

"You're converting me, Inna. Next thing you know, I'll be a full-time vegetarian, too."

"It's a good way to demonstrate the courage of your convictions," I said.

"Yeah...should we go over now? We should probably get there early."

A few minutes later, we were knocking at Mel's front door. She threw it open with more verve and pizzazz than I'd seen from her in months.

"You look good," I said.

"I *feel* good! I think the antibiotics are finally working. My thumbs don't hurt, I haven't had a single seizure all day, and I actually feel like *doing* stuff! Funny how you take that for granted until it gets taken away from you. Anyway. Come on in. We're T minus ten minutes till the great phone date."

"Do you think she'll actually call?" I asked.

She held up her hands in a who-knows gesture. "I'm giving it less than even odds, to be honest. She suggested it, and then when I said yes, she said that she'd call me, I shouldn't call her, or words to that effect."

"But you have her WhatsApp number, right?" I asked. "You could just go ahead and call her, I suppose."

"Yeah, but there's no reason she'd pick up. I figured I'd go ahead and let her call, just like she said she would. Well, unless she doesn't actually call. Then I might go ahead and call her." Mel grinned. "It'll be interesting to hear her voice, see if she's really from South Carolina like she says she is. It's going to be voice only, by the way. She told me she's shy, gets nervous on video calls, at least until we get to know each other better, so can we just do audio."

"Uh-huh," I said. "Probably best that way anyway. The moment when she actually sees you and sees that you're you is bound to be an awkward conversation-stopper. You're probably best off trying to get as much information out of her as you can before you move to video. If it ever happens."

"Yeah. Come on, have a seat. Can I get you anything? Are you comfortable?"

"We're great," I told her. In fact, Dima and I were arranged fairly precariously on the loveseat, which I was convinced was swaying under us, but there weren't many other options available. Mel plopped down on the floor beside us and got into a crosslegged position with no sign of pain.

"All right," she said, pulling out her phone. "What's the game plan? Do we try to record the conversation? Should I be asking her specific questions?"

"Recording conversations is always good," Dima said once I'd translated. "We can use my phone. And what do you want to know most of all? What is the goal of this conversation?"

"I guess...I'm not actually expecting to learn much, to be honest, although you never know. We might get lucky. I really just want to build up some trust with her, try to get her talking to me regularly, so that I can find out more about her and *shut her the fuck down*." Mel said the last words with bitter conviction.

"In that case," said Dima, "you want to be as friendly and relaxed as possible. Don't even think about your anger, about how she's done you wrong. Hold only good thoughts and feelings about her in your heart, in your mind. Otherwise, she'll know." He spoke seriously, confidently, with the casual competence of an expert. He was entering into his professional persona, and I could see him shedding the anguish, the doubt, the self-loathing that normally hung over his personal life like a cloud. No wonder he preferred working to anything else.

Maybe he can learn to have that confidence and competence in his personal life, I thought. *Maybe that's the best way to get him to* **have** *a personal life at all.*

"Oh shit!" said Mel. Her phone lit up and started buzzing. "Incoming! Here we go."

36

"HEY," SAID MEL INTO the phone. "Mel? Is that you?"

I started. Then I remembered that, of course, Evil Mel wasn't just using a couple of pictures of Mel on dating sites. She was also using Mel's name and her parents' address to carry out a variety of scams. Ugh.

"It sure is, baby," said the phone. The voice sounded remarkably like Mel's, only higher, softer...was it because I already knew she was a scammer, or was there something inherently dishonest about it? She was definitely trying to pile on the charm. "Is this Nicole? But you go by Nickie, don't you, baby?"

I made an involuntary face, as if I'd just glugged down a gulp of iced tea that turned out to have about twelve packets of saccharine in it. Dima was concentrating on his phone, which he was using to record the conversation, but I thought he might be making a face too.

"I sure do, baby," Mel cooed. "That's so sweet of you to remember." She gave a little giggle, a breathy, girlish sound I'd had no idea she could produce. I had to give her credit for her hitherto-unsuspected acting skills.

"Well, I'm pretty sweet on you already, baby," Evil Mel cooed back.

"Same here, sugar, same here. I think we've really got something going already, don't you?" For an instant, Mel broke character and grimaced, but quickly regained the look of stupidity, infatuation, and artificial sweetener she'd been wearing since the start of the call.

"We sure do, sweetie! We sure do. It's amazing, isn't it?"

"It's like we've got so much in common," said Mel. "It's like we're practically twins, ain't it?" A look of malicious humor crossed her face, then disappeared.

"I know!" said Evil Mel. "It's like it's meant to be!"

"I think it is," said Mel. "Do you believe in fate? 'Cause I think we were destined to meet each other."

"I believe it too, sugar, I believe it too!"

"Well, let's do something about it," said Mel. "Let's actually meet up."

"In person, sugar?"

"Sure thing, sugar," said Mel. "I want to actually see you, baby, see if you're as pretty in person as you are in your pictures..."

"Oh, sweetie..." I could practically hear the wheels churning in Evil Mel's head. "I want to meet you *so bad*, hun, but...I don't know...I don't want to ruin what we've got, you know what I'm saying? I don't want to rush into anything when we've got such a *special* thing going on, you know?"

"Sure," said Mel. "I sure do. And you're right. I was just so impatient to see you, babe, that I jumped the gun. But you're right. We should take it slow, not ruin this good thing that we've got. We can just keep talking on the phone for as long as you need to feel comfortable, sweetie."

"You're so *considerate*, Nickie," said Evil Mel with a breathy giggle. "I knew I could trust you from the moment I got your first message. Sometimes you just *know*, you know? It's like we're soulmates!"

"I sure do," said Mel. "And I think we've got even more in common than you know. I can't wait for us to find out all the things we've got in common." Another look of spiteful humor flashed across her face, and was quickly suppressed.

"I know, sweetie...and you know, babe, I've been thinking..."

"Yes?" said Mel.

"You said you were having a hard time, you needed some cash..."

"I could sure use some cash, that's true," said Mel. "It's been a pretty tough year. You know how it goes."

"I sure do, baby, I sure do. I was having one of those years myself, but then..." She trailed off suggestively.

"Yeah," said Mel. "You told me you found a side hustle that was bringing in some good cash, enough to keep you going when you lost your job."

"I sure did, babe. At this point, it's bringing in more than my day job did." She laughed. Spitefully. "With any luck, I'll never have to go back to work for that asshole at the grocery store again. I told you what he did to me, right?" Her voice had deepened, roughened, sincerity coming through for the first time. Whatever had happened at her old job, I guessed it had been real, and it had been bad. I repressed a twinge of sympathy. So she'd had a hard time. Lots of people had hard times. Not all of them dragged my friends into deception and crime.

"You sure did, hun, and I'm real sorry you had to go through that," said Mel. "Men are assholes like that. And if there's anything I can do to help you so you never have to go back to work for him, I'll do it. Just let me know."

"That's so sweet, honey." Evil Mel paused. "Actually," she said slowly, as if testing the waters, "there might be...you said you were good at art, right?"

"Right," said Mel.

"How do you feel about actually making some money from it?"

"I've never had much luck with that before," said Mel.

"Well, this might be your lucky break, sweetie," said Evil Mel. "Can you send me some pictures of your stuff? I'd like to look at it, see if it works with what I'm doing. And, of course, I'd like to see anything *you* do, sweetie."

"Yeah," said Mel. "Yeah, of course! There's no one I'd rather share my pictures with than you."

"I knew we were meant to be together," said Evil Mel. She giggled some more. "I have a really good feeling about this, don't you? I think this could be the start of something beautiful."

"You betcha," said Mel.

37

"FUCK YEAH!" MEL DID a double fist-pump. She turned to Dima. "You get that? Is it all on tape?"

I translated. Dima nodded. "Listen," he said, and played the beginning of the call for us on his phone.

"Hot damn!" said Mel. "Can you send it to me?"

"It's done," Dima told her. "Just give me your number."

A minute later, and the recording was on Mel's phone.

"'Course, I don't know how much good it will do," she said. "She didn't say anything outright incriminating, dammit. But it's a start. Now I just gotta get her to let me in on this 'side hustle' of hers."

"Yeah," I said. "Does the real Nickie know that you're using her identity to engage in activities of dubious legality?"

"Not yet, but she won't mind."

"Really?" I said.

Mel gave another careless shrug. "To be honest, I'm hoping she never finds out, but if she does, I'll smooth things over somehow. I always have before. Nickie and I have a...complicated relationship. She disapproves of me and everything I do, but we're also the only two girls in our generation, so we've been forced to be friends our whole lives. I don't think she'll leave me in the lurch."

"Okay," I said. "That's, uh, great. And do you have a plan for avoiding criminal charges if you get caught with a bunch of cremated remains acquired under false pretenses?"

"I doubt I'll get caught," said Mel breezily. "The victims aren't going to go to the police, and if they do, the police won't care."

"It's an evil world," I said.

"Damn straight it is. But we've just taken a step to clean it up a tiny bit. I can't wait to catch Evil Mel in the act and nail her ass to the fucking wall." Mel grinned, but the spite on her face far outweighed the humor. "I'll let you know what happens with the side hustle, and if she agrees to meet with me."

"Please do. And maybe we should come with you as backup."

"Yeah…That might not be a bad idea…" Mel was looking a little more sober now, as the idea of meeting a criminal, and one who'd specifically targeted her, started to sink in. "I mean, I don't think she's *dangerous*," she added quickly. "I think she's basically pathetic. I think the story she told me about losing her job after being sexually harassed by the manager at the grocery store where she used to work is probably true. I think she probably turned to a life of crime out of desperation."

"I think you might be right," I said. "That doesn't make her any less dangerous. Maybe she won't come kill you in your sleep, it's true, but she preys on sad and desperate people. And she might turn violent if she's pressured, or she might have violent confederates."

"Maybe." Mel shrugged again. "I'm still looking forward to nailing her ass to the wall. And I think I'm showing a flair for this detecting work, don't you?"

"Yes," I said. "Just don't get carried away by it. Let the professionals take over as soon as you can."

Mel snorted. "I think we're on our own with this one, Ro. I think they wouldn't care even if there was anything they could do, which there isn't. They're too busy with murders and shit to care about a little scamming."

"Fair enough," I said.

38

DIMA WALKED ME OVER to my place after our meeting with Mel, and then left to go back to his apartment. This time the nighttime parking lot just seemed like an ordinary parking lot in a small, rather boring, apartment complex in smalltown Georgia. The only special thing about it was having Dima by my side.

After he left and I went to bed, I spent a while wondering if I really wanted him by my side. He'd displayed many of his most annoying traits today, one after the other in quick succession. Would my life really be better with him in it? In many ways, it would probably be worse. But. But, but, but...

When I woke up the next morning, I still didn't have an answer to that question. It continued to elude me as we drove into Atlanta. Dima mostly worked on his phone for the whole trip, which I had to admit, was maybe an argument against having him in my life on a more permanent, full-time basis.

But when we got to the hospital, he went inside with me. When we went into Galina Ivanovna's room, he was calm and cheerful, telling her that she looked great (she didn't, although she didn't look much worse than she had the day before), and that he was going to spend the whole day with her, including sitting with her for her entire treatment session.

"Don't deceive yourself, Dimulya," she told him. "You've never been able to handle blood and needles. You almost passed out just from watching them insert an IV yesterday."

"But they won't have to do that again, will they?" he countered with a grin.

"Well, no. They left it in overnight."

"So no worries. The actual level of blood and needles will be very low, right? And even if it's high, I need to be with you. It was wrong of me to abandon the field of battle and leave my comrades in the lurch yesterday. Cowardly. I need to redeem myself and prove my courage. So I'm going to do it by sitting with you the whole time."

He was smiling, half-joking, as he said it, but we could tell he was serious underneath.

"Well...as you will, then," said Galina Ivanovna. "If you manage, it'll be a first, that's all I'm saying."

Dima hardly checked his phone at all as we sat in Galina Ivanovna's room and waited for the procedure to start. He swallowed hard when Kathy showed up with the wheelchair and asked if we were all ready to go, but walked bravely with us along the corridors to the treatment room. He swallowed even harder when we stepped into the room, and looked like he might actually vomit when Kathy hooked the IV up to Galina Ivanovna and started the drip, but after a couple of deep breaths, he sat down in one of the guest chairs and said, his voice hardly shaking at all, "Would you like me to read to you, mama?"

She handed him the same book we'd been reading yesterday. "Pick something," she ordered. "At random. I've decided I'm not going to try to go through all the poems in chronological order until I'm feeling better and can stay awake for them."

Dima, looking heartened by the words "until I'm feeling better," opened up the book around the middle and started reading.

"Of what use are dreams of freedom to a slave? /Look..."

His phone *pinged*. He grimaced, silenced it, and went back to reading.

"We too shall be submissive to our fate..."

His phone *pinged* again a few lines later. He made a face, put it in his jacket pocket, and continued reading.

"Madman! Is it not the higher will / Who gives us our passions? Is it not / Its voice in their voice we hear? O, burdensome for us / Is life..."

His phone started ring. He raised his voice, talking over the sound.

"...beating in our hearts like a mighty wave / And squeezed into narrow boundaries by fate. For fuck's sake! What the fuck do they want now!"

"I don't think that last bit was part of the original version," said Galina Ivanovna dryly. "Even if Baratynsky wrote that—and I'm sure he said it to himself many times—I doubt he could have gotten it past the censor."

"I'm sorry, mama. I'll turn my phone off completely."

"And if it's something important?"

"Nothing is more important than sitting here with you, mama." His gaze flicked over at me as he said it, then flicked away, as if embarrassed.

"Check it," said Galina Ivanovna. "Otherwise it'll eat at all of us all day, wondering if you've won the lottery or something."

"I don't play the lottery, mama."

"Yes, you do." Her voice was gentle. "You play the lottery harder than anyone I've ever known. You're just not looking to get money out of it. But you cast your lot at the gods and go toe-to-toe with fate every single day of the week. Now go. Answer your thrice-cursed phone before I smash it. If it's ringing and ringing after you've put it on silent, that means someone's calling you over and over again. They must have something they really need to tell you."

Dima looked over at me. "Go," I told him. "We'll be fine here. You can come back after you take your call."

"Well...okay. One call, and then I'll be right back." He stood up and pulled on his jacket with the air of a man who can't wait to get out into fresh air. "And then we can read more depressing poetry about fate and lots and all that. If I were you, mama, I would have picked something more cheerful. About love, maybe."

"After a while," said Galina Ivanovna, "love starts to seem pretty depressing. But this stuff is just what the doctor ordered. Now go, before I push you out myself."

"Okay. I'm off. But I'll be right back." He had already broken into a half-jog by the time he reached the swinging doors leading to the corridor and fresh air and freedom.

39

AFTER DIMA LEFT, GALINA Ivanovna's eyes started to close. She was already being hit by the drowsiness the treatment caused, and she wasn't even halfway through today's session yet. I hoped that all the promises we'd been given about the side effects going away and people feeling much better after the third or fourth infusion were true.

"Read me something cheerful, Inna," she said, her voice thick with sleepiness.

I flipped through the book without much hope, but then found something surprisingly appropriate, and started reading.

"'Spring, spring! How pure the air! / How clear the horizon!...'"

Galina Ivanovna started to nod off. I read, my voice growing softer and softer, as she slipped into sleep.

"'What's happening to my soul? / It's a brook with a brook / And a bird with a bird...'"

My phone *pinged*. I winced, afraid it would jolt Galina Ivanovna awake, but she kept sleeping soundly. I pulled out the phone, expecting it to be a message from Dima. But it wasn't.

Ro! Didn't want to call you in case you were in the middle of something, but *call me as soon as you get this message*!!! Something's going on with Mom and Dad. We need to have a family powwow. I've already put in for leave in case I need to go up to VA and extract them from enemy territory. Just kidding. Not really. Call me ASAP!

I turned back to Galina Ivanovna. She was still sleeping soundly. I hit "Reply" to the message, and chose a voice call.

"John?" I said, trying to keep my voice as low as possible. "What's going on?"

40

"RO? WHY'RE YOU WHISPERING?"

"I'm in the hospital," I whispered.

"What the fuck?!?! Why?!?!"

"I'm with Galina Ivanovna. For her treatment," I clarified.

A pause. "That's *his* mother, right?" John said eventually.

John loathed Dima with a fiery passion, despite never having met him. I suspected a lot of that loathing was because John saw way more of himself in Dima than he was comfortable with. Mostly, it was expressed as an absolute refusal to ever utter his name, and strong encouragement for me to find someone better.

Alas, my attempts in that realm had not been crowned with success. The man John had approved of had left me for another woman, which had been rather a blow to both our egos. Apparently it hadn't raised John's opinion of Dima any, though.

"Yes," I said. "I'm sitting with her right now, but she's fallen asleep, and I don't want to wake her."

"Is *he* there?"

"Not right now," I said.

"So he's fuckin' left you to sit with *his* mother while he fucks around doing fuck knows what?"

"A work thing came up," I said. "We both told him to take care of it. Anyway. What's this about Mom and Dad?"

Another pause. I could feel John shifting mental gears, deliberately squashing down his Dima-loathing and pulling out his concern for our parents.

"So," he said. "You know how Dad's parents never wanted to have anything to do with us?"

"Uh-huh," I said.

"And they always thought Mom was a painted Jezebel who, like, fuckin' seduced Dad and, like, fucked with his mind and shit, turned him away from the path of righteousness and all that?"

Laughter was coming through John's voice despite the seriousness of the situation. The thought of our mother, who had never to my knowledge worn makeup, jewelry, or even nice clothing, being considered a painted Jezebel was risible in the extreme. And, while I was hardly the best judge in this case, she had always seemed to me to be lacking that sexual fire that came off some people in waves. My grandmother—her mother—had certainly always considered her a boring stick-in-the-mud that way. So it was hard to picture her in the role of irresistible seductress.

I mean, yes, she and my father had gotten together and produced two children, so there had to be *something* going on between them, but their relationship had always on the surface been the kind of mellow, easygoing thing that was held up by counselors and relationship coaches as the ideal we should all aspire to. Where John and I had gotten our tumultuous natures was anyone's guess. Maybe these relatives who wouldn't have anything to do with us. *That* smacked of repressed passion for sure.

"I've heard hints," I said. "But it seemed like they wanted to extend the olive branch. Isn't that what this holiday visit is all about?"

"Kinda sorta. So, it turns out our grandpa—Dad's dad—has cancer or some shit like that."

"Oh," I said. "I'm sorry to hear that." My sorrow was more pro forma than sincere, since I'd met him precisely three times in my life, and he'd been so cold to me I'd felt the beginnings of an ice cream headache just from standing next to him. Still, I didn't wish him to suffer. Much.

"Yeah, whatevs. He's always been a shit to us, so I'm not about to cry a bunch of crocodile tears over it now. Anyway, he's starting chemo next week, but they're not sure how it's going to go. So *that's* why he wanted Mom and Dad to come. He's all concerned about his legacy and shit. Actually, he just wanted Dad to come. Dad and me."

"Really? I thought…" I stopped myself before I said anything about John's birth and how I'd always thought our father's parents felt about it.

"Yeah, I guess he got over the fact I'm a bastard when death was staring him in the face." Apparently John didn't feel the same need for delicacy that I did.

"Technically, you're no longer a bastard," I pointed out. "Once our parents got married, you were automatically legitimated."

"Yeah, but those motherfuckers never cared, did they? Until now. Until the grandpa who never gave a fuck about me decided he needed an heir. A *male* heir. Fuck! I thought feminism was supposed to save me from this kind of fuckery."

John's voice was growing more and more heated. He'd always put on a show of nonchalance over our paternal grandparents' rejection, but it seemed that 40 years later, it still rankled. Well, it would.

"Feminism can only save you from this kind of fuckery if the people involved buy into it," I said.

"Well, I'm gonna start a big annual donation to NOW or some shit," said John. "I guess I'm a believer now, 'cause you will not fuckin' *believe* this shit…"

"What, exactly, is the problem?" I cut him off before he could descend into a full-on tirade. Galina Ivanovna was stirring in her chair. I didn't want to wake her up, and I wanted to finish this call before she had to go back to her room.

"So, you know how Dad's parents were all in a state because they were convinced he was in a cult and all?"

"That's what I heard," I said. "And to be fair, we *did* live in a commune."

"A commune isn't a cult," John said sharply. "There's a big fuckin' difference between the two."

"Well…true." I didn't think I'd ever heard John defend our early lifestyle before.

"But now—you'll fuckin' bust a gut laughing—it turns out *they're* the ones in a cult. And they're trying to get Mom and Dad to sign up. And I think they might succeed."

41

"UM," I SAID. "WHAT makes you think that?"

"'Cause I got a call from Dad this morning, asking me to come up and visit them. At first it seemed like it was just what you said about extending the olive branch and shit, and I was all like, 'Sure, Dad, let me see if I can swing it,' but then the more he talked, the more I started getting creepy cult vibes. Especially once he told me the fucking name of it."

"What's the name of it?" I asked.

"Church of the Holy Light. Total cult name, right? Anyway, they're saying something about how Dad's dad's money and house belong to the male line or some shit like that, and they want to sign it over to me so I can, I guess, sign it over to the church or some shit like that. It's like some fuckin' Jane Austen story, but way creepier."

"Yeah," I said, carefully not expressing my surprise that John was A) familiar with Jane Austen novels, and B) willing to mention it in public. Camila must be having an even more profound effect than I'd thought. "Is that even legal?"

"It seems to be working for them. And Dad wants me to do it. That's the scariest thing."

"Yeah," I said. "That is scary. What are you going to do?"

Another pause, this one even longer than the others. "I guess I'm going to go up there," John finally said. "See how doolally these other grandparents really are, and how batshit crazy this church is, and how much Mom and Dad have been sucked into it, and if I can get them out of there."

"Do you think it's dangerous?" I asked.

"I don't want to think so, but cults are fuckin' nuts by nature," John said.

"Oh," I said. "Do you want me to try to talk to Mom and Dad?"

He sighed. "No. Not yet. Mainly I wanted to let you know, in case something goes wrong with the extraction and I need to be extracted myself."

"Oh," I said. "Okay. When are you going up there?"

"Tomorrow. Hoping to be back by Monday. But let's stay in contact, okay? Regular check-ins, and all that."

"Yeah," I said. "For sure. I'll expect to hear from you every day till you get back."

"Sounds good." John's voice was becoming calmer. "Hopefully it'll all be nothing, but you never know with this shit. And hey." His voice filled with forced cheer. "If *he's* still around, maybe he can come in and rescue me. Isn't that the kind of thing he does?"

"Not really," I said. "Not anymore. But I'm sure he'd try if it seems necessary."

"Great," said John. "Nice to know I've got a crazy Russian vigilante as backup in case things start going down the crapper."

"Yeah," I said. "Good luck."

"Thanks. And, uh, good luck to his mom, too. That sounds rough. I hope the treatment works. I want to hate 'em both, but she's just a little old lady who's gotten sick, so I can't really hate her, can I?"

"She's more than just a little old lady who's gotten sick," I said. "But you shouldn't hate her anyway. I think you'd like her."

"I'll take your word for it, Ro. Okay. I'd better get ready. Over and out."

"Good luck," I said again. But John had already hung up.

42

DIMA CAME BACK INTO the ward just as my conversation with John was over. He looked grim, his scars standing out sharply the way they did when he tensed his face.

"What's the matter?" I asked.

"What's the matter with *you*?" he countered. "You look terrible."

I gave him a short précis of my conversation with John.

"Do you need to go up there?" Dima asked immediately. "Do you...where *is* Virginia? Can you drive there from here? Or is there a train..."

"I don't need to go quite yet," I told him. "John said he'll take care of it."

"Yes, but, Inna, if you'll forgive me for saying it, and with all the respect in the world for your brother, he strikes me as a real hothead. This sounds like something more in your line."

"Normally, I'd agree. But they're specifically expecting him. Besides, you and Galina Ivanovna need me."

"We can take care of ourselves."

The IV stand *pinged*. A moment later, Kathy reappeared and began unhooking Galina Ivanovna from it. Dima shuddered and turned away, but then resolutely turned back and watched the procedure to the end.

Galina Ivanovna woke up just as Kathy was finishing. "What?" she asked sleepily. "That's it?"

I translated. Kathy laughed. "You'll need to wait in your room for a bit, so the doctor can see you about next steps," she said. "Then we'll get you all checked out, and you can go home and rest up for next week."

"I've been getting lots of rest here," Galina Ivanovna said when I translated that. "I'm hoping to get out and about and do stuff once I'm home. Should I expect to fall asleep like this every time I do an infusion?"

"The normal pattern is to have a lot of drowsiness for the first three, and then for it to fade after that," Kathy told her.

I translated. Galina Ivanovna nodded. "And should I expect to experience a lot of drowsiness between now and the next infusion?"

"You'll have to talk to the doctor about that—she can tell you everything you need to know about side effects, care, all that," said Kathy, in a tone that told us yes, Galina Ivanovna could expect to feel very drowsy and tired for the next week.

She nodded off on the wheelchair ride back to her room, and then again as we were waiting for the doctor.

"I don't know if this will make things easier or harder for me if you have to go away," said Dima, looking down at her sleeping form.

"I'm not going to go away."

"And if your parents need you?"

"John will take care of it," I said, with more conviction than I felt.

Dr. Azarian came in before we could argue about it any more. We woke Galina Ivanovna up, and Dr. Azarian checked her over, asked her how she felt, discussed her latest chart readings with her, and went over what she should do between now and the next infusion, which would be next Thursday.

Mainly she was supposed to stick rigorously to the special diet. As part of that, we were given a large box of pre-prepared meals. It was so big that Dima had to lug it, struggling slightly to keep it from slipping out of his grasp, behind us while Kathy wheeled Galina Ivanovna out of the room, down the various corridors and elevators, and out onto the sidewalk.

"Here you are!" she said cheerfully. "See you next week!"

Dima set down the box gratefully. "Do you want me to go get the car, Inna?"

"You wait here. Guard the food. I'll be back in a second."

"True," Dima said solemnly. "This food is so expensive, and has been transported here with so much heroic effort, that someone needs to be prepared to lay down his life to protect it. I guess that person is me. Mama, do you have any weapons handy? I might need backup. That purse of yours looks like it could take down a would-be thief prettily handily."

Galina Ivanovna laughed. Weakly, but she laughed. "Why do you think I carry it? It's reinforced with steel at the bottom. I'll help you stand guard if you promise to let me sleep all the way back home."

"Deal," said Dima.

43

GALINA IVANOVNA SLEPT most of the drive back to Greenfields. Dima mostly sat in silence too, although he seemed too tense to fall asleep. Occasionally he looked over at me and opened his mouth as if to tell me something important, but every time he closed his mouth again without ever saying a word. Once he got into a furious texting exchange that lasted for the better part of half an hour, after which he put his phone on silent with an air of finality and went back to staring out the window.

By the time we got back to Greenfields, it was almost suppertime. Galina Ivanovna woke up enough to eat with us. We were all pleasantly surprised to discover that the special meals in the giant box included not just "breakfast pudding" (whatever that meant—we judged it best not to inquire too deeply) but things that looked like actual food. American food, but it was still a step up from the "cosmonaut meals" Galina Ivanovna had been living off of for the past few months.

She tucked into something that was supposed to be Spaghetti Bolognese, and did appear to be noodles with red sauce with chunky bits in it, and said it was the best thing, barring the food I'd cooked for her from scratch, that she'd had for half a year. She ate with an appetite that surprised all of us, and then started to nod off again.

"I'll walk you back to the apartment, mama," Dima told her.

"It's too early for you to go to bed," she objected, yawning hugely.

"I'll just tuck you into bed like you used to do for me when I was little, and then I'll come help Inna clean up."

"Fair enough," said Galina Ivanovna with another yawn.

He wrapped her up in her coat, hat, and scarf, which she insisted on wearing despite the practically tropical—by Russian standards—temperature of 50 degrees Fahrenheit, and led her towards the door. As he walked her through it, he turned back and mouthed *We have to talk* at me. Then he ushered her down the stairs and disappeared into the dark parking lot.

44

WHILE I WAS WAITING for Dima to come back, John texted to confirm that he'd be setting off for Christiansburg first thing the next morning.

And look into the Church of the Holy Light, he wrote. *I tried searching around a little, but didn't get far. Maybe you can dig something up.*

When Dima came back, I was staring at a screenful of useless hits on the phrase "Church of the Holy Light." All of them were about World of Warcraft, not about a tiny cult in Virginia.

"What's this?" Dima asked when he saw my screen. "Researching video games?"

I explained.

"Right. Cults can be hard. Do you want me to help?"

"First tell me what it is you have to tell me," I said.

He sighed, ran his fingers through his hair, and stared at the screen for several beats before finally turning to face me.

"I have to go," he said.

"Right now? Go where?"

He chewed on his lip. I could sense that he was weighing how much to tell me. I reminded myself to remain calm and not give into angry outbursts. The fact that we were discussing this at all was progress. And maybe he really did have to go.

"You know how Security Solutions was bringing in trainers for their mercenaries from Ukraine?" he said.

"I hate this already," I said. "They've got a group of Ukrainian trainers here right now, and you're supposed to go interview them, aren't you?"

Dima grinned. "You're a genius, Inna."

"No, I'm not. I just know you."

"That you do." He turned serious. "I don't know if we're two hearts that beat as one, but sometimes we're definitely two minds that think as one. And yes. I'm supposed to go up on Monday and interview the new Ukrainians. It's already set up. I should be gone for a couple of days, and then back here in time for mama's next treatment."

"What if some of these guys recognize you? You've made a lot of enemies there."

"That," said Dima, "is a chance I'll have to take. I'm hoping that if they do recognize me, they'll protect an old comrade for the sake of our bonds of brotherhood."

"You're not an old comrade! If these people are anything like the last group, they're a bunch of swastika-tattooed extremists who signed up to fight specifically in order to fulfill their lifelong fantasies of killing Russians!"

"I'll think of something," said Dima. He tried to say it soothingly. But his eyes were alight with excitement at the thought of infiltrating a hostile encampment under false pretenses.

"I'm sure you will." And I was. Dima had an excellent track record of getting out of these kinds of situations alive. But the problem was that he had to be both brilliant and lucky every single time, whereas his enemies only had to be brilliant and lucky once.

"Are you angry with me, Inna?" He was trying to sound concerned. But that excited gleam in his eyes, and that grin, kept breaking through.

"No." It came out as more of a groan than a word, but I meant it. "I know you're doing this because it's necessary. I assume it's your, uh, new friends up above who are asking you to do this?"

He nodded.

"So you can't exactly say no."

He shrugged. "Of course I could say no. But there might be unpleasant consequences. Including our dear friend Mister Anthony Wainwright doing something terrible right here in your native land."

"Well...true. This sounds more like something for the FBI to take care of than you, though."

He shrugged again. "Maybe the FBI doesn't have the information we do. Maybe they don't care."

"Um...do you want me to pass this on to someone in the FBI?"

He started to shake his head, then stopped. I could see serious thought going on inside.

"I'm leaving on Monday morning," he said. "I should be back by Wednesday afternoon. If I'm not, or you're suspicious of something, then yes, tell your friend in the FBI." His grin came back. "It'll be nice to see the vaunted American intelligence community in action. I've seen so many movies about them, but I've never seen them in the flesh. Maybe this will be my chance!"

"I hope not," I said. "But I'll call them if I need to."

45

FRIDAY WE SPENT AT home, watching over Galina Ivanovna. Other than drowsiness, which wore off by the end of the day, she showed no ill effects from her first round of treatment. She also, to Dima's disappointment, showed no signs of miraculous healing, but she told him tartly that it was to be expected.

We had agreed to go with Mel to her family's place in South Carolina on Saturday morning. Dima initially wanted to cancel, not wanting to leave Galina Ivanovna on her own, but she insisted that he go.

"I'll never get any rest with you hovering over me," she told him. She waved *The Complete Collected Poems of E. A. Baratynsky* at him. "Go! Evgeny Abramovich will keep me company."

"Evgeny Abramovich can't call an ambulance if you start feeling poorly," Dima said.

"I'm only going to start feeling poorly if you keep pestering me like this! Go!"

Dima eventually acquiesced. And so at 8:00am the next morning, we set off for South Carolina.

We were taking my car, since it got better gas mileage than Mel's elderly Jeep Grand Cherokee. Mel's parents lived just north of Augusta, on the South Carolina side of the Savannah River. It was a little over two hours each way, barring traffic. So another four or five hours in the car, on top of all the three-hour days I'd been pulling this week. I wished I liked driving more. At least, I consoled myself, this would involve farmland, not downtown Atlanta.

Dima watched with fascination as we drove past farms and small towns, and around greater Augusta, and finally up the long gravel driveway to the rusting doublewide trailer that was Mel's family home.

"This is another side of America," he said. "One we don't see on TV so much."

"Welcome to the real America," Mel told him when I translated. "At least, that's what all my folks would like you to believe. For them, New York and LA, and even Atlanta, are all just fantasyland."

"It's the same back home," Dima told her. "The people out in the deep country live completely differently from those in the center, and they can't understand or even believe in each other's reality. Is that your mother?"

A tall, rawboned woman with a face covered in freckles and long gray hair falling out of a sloppy braid had come out the front door of the house and was staring at us with suspicion. She was wearing a worn man's flannel jacket over even more worn overalls, and cracked rubber boots with holes in the big toes. If you cut off her hair and removed the permanent grooves of angry suspicion on her face, you could see, sort of, that she and Mel were close kin. They both had the same strong features, the same wide, mobile mouth, the same large hazel eyes. But this woman, I was sure, had never possessed Mel's air of restless intelligence and her quick sense of humor.

"So you brought 'em," she said, when Mel got out of the car. "Didn't think you were gonna actually come, but you did and you brought 'em." Her country accent was even stronger than Mel's, and she had the throaty voice of longtime smoker.

"Yeah, Mom, here we are." Mel's voice was falsely bright. "This is my friend Rowena, from school, and her friend Dima. He's an investigative journalist. They're here to help me look into...all the stuff you've been getting. Ro, Dima, this is my mother, Jolene."

Jolene gave both of us a narrow look. I smiled. She narrowed her eyes even more. Dima turned on what he called his "little-old-lady smile," which was about a thousand times warmer and more charming than his usual expression, and worked his dimple to its best effect. Jolene tried to glare back, but involuntarily broke into a smile herself.

"Well," said Jolene, "guess y'all might as well come on in. Your dad's out in the back fields, checking the winter wheat. Dunno when he'll be back." She turned and went into the house, letting the flimsy screen door bang closed behind her. After a moment, Mel went up the steps and led us in.

Inside, it was stiflingly hot and reeked of cigarette smoke, fried food, and artificial "air fresheners." The living room was crammed with un-matched, very elderly overstuffed furniture, and a brand-new, widescreen TV. We went up the half step to the kitchen area, which appeared to have been decorated sometime around 1985.

"Watch that tear in the linoleum," Jolene told me, just as I caught my toe on a foot-long section of linoleum that was curling up off the under-flooring. "You okay, hun?" She spoke without looking at me, her voice indifferent.

"Fine," I said, and broke into a coughing fit. My upper chest felt un-pleasantly hot and tight inside, as if I were coming down with bronchitis.

"It's all still in my bedroom, right?" Mel asked. "All the stuff that's been coming in?"

"Dunno why we keep calling it your bedroom," said her mother. "Seeing as how you ain't lived here for more'n a decade. We've been using it as a storage room for years now. We've been piling it all up on your bed. You can go have a look if you want."

She broke into a harsh coughing fit that went on for several seconds. When she was done, she pulled a pack of cigarettes and a lighter out of her shirt pocket, stuck a cigarette in her mouth, and lit up. Her hands were shaking slightly. From the coughing fit, or Mel's visit? She inhaled deeply, held it for longer than I would have thought possible, and then blew it out in a long exhale that filled the whole kitchen with smoke.

"Wish you'd go ahead an' take it with you," she said. Her previous indifference had returned, stronger than before. "Lord knows we don't need none of that stuff junking up the place. We've got enough junk here as it is."

She looked around the house with a critical eye while taking another deep drag. I found myself looking around with her. The doublewide was in fact crammed to the gills with what certainly looked like junk to me.

The mere sight of all that ratty old furniture, piles of old newspapers and magazines, and dust-covered knickknacks that had been cheap crap thirty years ago, and were now even crappier, gave me a strong desire to set a match to all of it. Judging by the way her eyes narrowed again as she surveyed it, Jolene was experiencing a similar desire.

"That's a nasty cough you got there, hun," she said to me. "You coming down with something?"

"Not that I'm aware of," I said, as another wave of coughing went through me. "Maybe it's just the dry air."

"Maybe you need to get out of here," Mel said. "Come on. I'll show you around the place. Maybe we'll run into my dad."

"Sounds good," I tried to say, but I was coughing so hard I could barely get the words out.

46

THE COUGHING EASED as soon as we stepped outside into the chill January air. After a couple of minutes, I was back to normal.

"You sure you okay?" Mel asked.

"I think I might be allergic to cigarette smoke," I said. "Although it's never been a problem before."

Mel made a face. "Cigarette smoke is the least of your worries in that house. There's so much nasty mold and shit it's a wonder they're alive at all. And they cover it up with even nastier 'air fresheners.' I always end up with a sore throat and big dark circles under my eyes after I spend the night there. But I'm afraid you'll have an asthma attack if you go back in."

"Maybe your room is better," I said. I was also a little afraid I might have an asthma attack if I went back inside, but the thought of spending a dank, chilly January afternoon sitting in the car, prior to spending another two hours driving back home, did not appeal.

"Tell you what," Mel said. "Let's try going in the back. Maybe that'll be better."

We went around to the back of the doublewide and through another rusty screen door. This one opened up to a cramped utility room full of muddy boots and other farm detritus. It smelled of dirt, but that was an improvement over the front of the house. We went through that and into a tiny bedroom, stacked floor to ceiling with boxes. A stack of mail and packages was piled on top of what looked like old sewing projects that had been thrown onto the bed.

"How you feeling?" Mel asked me.

"Better." If I concentrated on breathing shallowly, I could keep from coughing.

"Wrap your scarf over your face," Dima advised.

I did. Mel said I looked like I was about to rob a bank, but it was a hot look for me. I said I was okay with that if it meant I could breathe.

"Okay," said Mel, interlacing her fingers and stretching them, as if in preparation for an arduous physical task. "What've we got here?"

What we had was ten packages that, when we opened them, did appear to have ashes in them.

"Well," said Mel, screwing up her face in disgust as she closed the last of the packages back up, "at least we have their return addresses. So we can send the ashes back. What kind of a sick person extorts money from grieving people?"

"Scumbags and the very desperate," said Dima when I translated.

"Fair enough," said Mel. "I'll take all these home—hopefully I won't get in trouble for having a bunch of pet ashes in the apartment—and see if I can find out who all these people are. Maybe they can give me some good intel, and I can send their ashes back. And then there's this." She held up a sheaf of envelopes. "Stuff from unemployment, it all looks like. I'll go through that too, see if it gets me anywhere. Is there anything else?"

We looked around the pile of junk filling up the room. There could be a vital clue in here swallowed up by all the other stuff that Mel's parents had tossed into here and forgotten.

"That's all that I can see," I said.

Dima, his role as a guest overtaken by his role as a nosy reporter, was poking through the piles of stuff. He moved a stack of old *Seventeen* magazines, raising a cloud of dust and setting us all to sneezing.

"Jesus," said Mel once she could speak again. "Those must be twenty-five years old. Mom got me a subscription as part of her plan to make me more girly and less, well, what I am. She never would let me throw them away. 'Course, she never would let me throw *anything* away, but she was particularly attached to those. I guess they were like a talisman or magic spell or something for her. Something that would transform me into the daughter she wanted instead of the daughter she had. I think she would have forgiven me the lesbian thing if I'd only I'd been small and cute and girly."

There was a moment of silence for Mel's family tragedy, and also for the pointlessness of big, mannish Jolene trying to turn her daughter into someone small and cute and girly.

"I'm sorry," said Dima when the moment of silence started to stretch on too long. "Families are difficult." Was he giving me side eye as he said it? Trying to show me just what I was saving myself from by not having a family? Did he *really* think I'd be the same kind of mother as Jolene?!?!...

Stop, stop, stop! I told myself. *Not helpful!* "Let's take this stuff out to the car," I said out loud. "Is there anything else you need to do here?"

"I'd like to say hi to my dad," said Mel. "If he's in the mood to see me. Hard to know with him."

"Dima and I can load up the car while you look for him," I said.

"Sounds good. I'll ask Mom if she knows where he is." Mel squared her shoulders and went out to talk to her mother.

47

WHEN DIMA AND I STEPPED out the back door, our arms full of packages, we saw a tall, thin man in ragged overalls, a worn work coat, and rubber boots coming towards us. He had lots of flyaway salt-and-pepper hair, and a wild tangle of a salt-and-pepper beard that was blowing around his face in the wind. He stopped at the sight of us, taken aback, but then, nodding to himself as if suddenly realizing something, came over to us.

"You must be Mel's friends," he said. "She said y'all might be coming with her today." His country twang was at least as strong as his wife's.

"Yes, that's right. I'm Rowena. This is Dima. He doesn't speak much English."

Dima nodded politely. Mel's father stared at him with unabashed curiosity. His eyes were a faded blue instead of bright hazel, but they had the same lively humor and interest in the world around him that was so prominent in Mel's gaze, and so absent in Jolene's.

"Mel around?" he asked abruptly.

"I think she's inside, with her mother. She was hoping to see you before we left."

He nodded with a sharp, jerky motion that set his hair and beard to waving wildly around his head. "I'd offer to shake your hands," he said, "but you can see mine ain't too clean at the moment." He held up his hands, thickened and roughened by years of hard labor, with dirt and what looked like engine grease in all the lines and grooves. The index and middle fingers on his left hand ended in stubby scars at the last knuckle, and his right pinky was crooked, as if it had been broken and never healed right.

147

"No worries," I said. "Consider our hands shaken."

He grinned. It was hard to tell through the wild tangle of beard, but he also appeared to have a wide, mobile mouth. I wondered how closely he and Jolene were related. Everyone was everyone's third cousin in these rural farming regions. Even though we were only a few miles down the road from Augusta, it felt like it was some other, exotic and impossible, world. I doubted there was much intermarriage between the two communities.

"You loading up all that stuff she got?" he asked, nodding at the packages.

"Yep. She's hoping it will give her some clues...or at least let her return the, uh, the ashes to their, uh...the people who sent them."

"Yeah. Maybe something'll come of it. What kinda person'd be so low as to steal the ashes of someone's dog?"

As if on cue, a motley-looking dog with a fair amount of bluetick hound in her parentage came trotting up. She fixed me with an intelligent gaze, cocking her head and looking first me, then Dima, up and down, then went over to Mel's father. He scratched behind her ears with obvious affection.

"This is Bluey," he told us. "Best dog this side of the Savannah."

"I'm sure," I said.

"Best hunter I've ever had," he told me proudly. "I take it you folk aren't hunters?"

"Not really," I said. "But she looks like a very good dog."

"Never lost a scent once...seeing all those ashes, it made me think..." His voice broke off, and he had to pause for a moment before going on, "well, that's a dang scummy thing to do. I sure hope Mel gets whoever did it. They deserve...well, I'd set Bluey on 'em, only she's too sweet to go after 'em like they deserve..."

"Uh-huh," I said. The screen door banged behind us, making me jump.

"Dad!" said Mel. "There you are! I've been looking for you. I wanted to make sure to say hi before we left."

"Just showing Bluey to these folks," her father told her proudly.

Bluey ran up to Mel, her ears flapping. Mel gave her a scratch on the back of her head and then at the base of her tail, causing her to wriggle all over.

"Couldn't leave without seeing you, old girl, now could I?" Mel told her.

Bluey scratched her side with joyous agreement and rubbed against Mel.

"You folks have to leave right away?" asked Mel's father. "Or can you stay and have a drink?"

An expression of pain flitted across Mel's face and was quickly replaced with false cheer. "I'm afraid we'd better get going," she said. "Dima's mother isn't doing well, and we don't want to leave her for too long. But I wanted to be sure to say hi before we left. And thanks for saving all this stuff." She held up the sheaf of envelopes. "I'm hoping it'll help."

"You know your mother," her father said. "Never throws anything away. Sometimes it comes in handy."

"It sure does," said Mel. "And now we'd better get going." She gave Bluey one more scratch, then turned and headed towards the car. Dima and I went after her, with Bluey following at our heels, her ears cocked with interest.

Mel's father disappeared into the house. By the time we'd gotten all the packages and letters loaded into the back of my car, he'd come back out. He had a chipped tumbler of what looked and smelled like cheap scotch in one hand.

"Sure you don't want one for the road?" he asked, proffering the tumbler at Mel.

"Thanks, Dad, but I'd better not," she said.

"Aw, come on..."

"She said she don't want it, Gary!" Jolene had come out to stand beside him.

"Don't be such a sourpuss, Jolene! I was just being friendly..."

"Well, don't! She don't want it, and that's final!"

Gary and Jolene glared at each other. This was clearly a long-running argument. I guessed that it was one of the few things holding them together at this point. Whatever affection they might have once had for each other was long-gone, and the only thing they had left was mutual antagonism and an unwillingness to change things, no matter how unhappy they were.

I suppressed a shudder. How many relationships ended up like this? Was this what awaited me and Dima if we decided to try things again? Would I one day be like Jolene, bitter and angry at my husband, my children, and my miserable life?

"Take care, you two," Mel said, interrupting the argument before it could progress to open shouting. "And thanks for all this." She held up the envelopes again. "Let me know if you get anything more."

"It'll be the only way we see you, won't it?" Jolene demanded. "You only come if you want something from us."

"No, Mom, I'm just real busy..."

"No one's too busy for family!"

"Now, Jolene, don't you go starting a fight with her about it, or we'll never see her again!" Gary grinned, but there was an edge of anger and meanness behind the grin. Bluey surreptitiously edged away from him, half-standing behind Dima.

"I'll give y'all a call soon, let you know how I get on with this," said Mel, smiling even more falsely than before. "Come on, Ro, we'd better get going. Don't wanna leave Dima's mom by herself any longer."

She gave Bluey another scratch and opened the car door. Dima and I said goodbye to her parents and followed suit. As we drove away down the long driveway, I could see both Jolene and Gary in the rearview mirror, watching us go and arguing, their figures full of misery and despair until they were swallowed up by the horizon and disappeared from sight.

48

THERE WAS A LOT OF silence in the car ride back to Greenfields. And it wasn't the comfortable silence of good friends hanging out together wordlessly, either. It was the uncomfortable silence of people who've witnessed someone else's pain and don't know what to say about it.

"So," Mel said after a while. "Now you know where I come from."

"The Air Force must have seemed like a welcome escape," I said.

"It did. At first. And academia seemed like a godsend. At first. But the more time I spent in all those places, the more I realized that people are people, no matter where you go."

"Yeah," I said.

"Although, that being said, my folks are some pretty people-y people. They're not bad, exactly, but they don't really like their lives, and they don't really like who I turned out to be. My dad always wanted to be something more than a hardscrabble South Carolina farmer, but he was never willing to give up the farm. My mom wanted to be something more too, but she never knew what that was. And frankly, I'm not sure there was much else that she coulda been. They wanted to live out their lives through me, but I kept following my own dreams instead." She smiled wryly. "And look how well that's working out for me. By the way, Ro, how's the prep for the interview next week going?"

"I've mainly been trying to repress any thought of it," I said. "You?"

"Same."

"You have interviews?" Dima, who had been sort of following along, asked.

I explained about our upcoming first-round interviews for the tenure-track jobs at Crimson. This was challenging, since the American academic interview process was complex and arcane and didn't translate well into other cultural contexts.

"So, this is to keep your current jobs," he finally said, after several rounds of questioning.

"Sort of. Our contracts end in May. This is to get new, longer contracts."

"For how long?"

"Six years, basically, unless they decide to terminate us at the halfway point for lack of research productivity."

"What does lack of research productivity mean? Is there some number of articles you have to write?"

Mel and I shrugged. "It means whatever they want it to mean," I explained. "As far as I can tell, it's a fairly arbitrary process, no matter what they say about transparency and fairness."

"Well, of course. And then after six years?"

"We'll be required to go up for a review process. Then we either get a permanent contract, or we get terminated."

"And then what?"

Mel and I shrugged again. "You can try again at another university, but it's likely you'll never get a permanent contract," I said.

"And these temporary contracts—are they really so bad?"

"Some are okay," I said. "But most have lower salaries—sometimes less than half of what a permanent contract would have. And of course, you can be terminated at any point. At Crimson they have a rule that you can only work for a maximum of three years on a temporary contract, and lots of other places have similar rules. So it can involve a lot of moving around, starting new jobs over and over again. It's not a good life."

Dima nodded. "I can see that. Do you want to stay here in Georgia?"

He said it casually. Only after he said it did both of us realize the significance of it. He gave me one swift, burning glance, then turned and looked out the passenger side window.

"I don't know," I said. After a moment, I added, "It's not my life's dream. I just don't have any better offers at the moment."

"Got it," Dima said into the window. "Got it."

49

MEL HAD CHEERED UP by the time we got back, and was already making plans to start sending the ashes back. We unloaded all the packages and mail and helped her carry it up to her apartment. Then Dima and I went over to Galina Ivanovna.

Galina Ivanovna was awake and glad to see us. She said she'd spent the day very happily reading and walking around the neighborhood.

"Walking? By yourself?" demanded Dima, breaking out of the silent funk he'd been in ever since that last conversation in the car. "I told you not to go walking by yourself!"

"Relax," Galina Ivanovna told him. "What's going to happen to me here?"

"You could have a dizzy spell...fall...get mugged..."

"Get mugged? Here?"

Both she and Dima turned and looked at me questioningly.

"We don't have a lot of muggings," I said. "Although I wouldn't walk around with a lot of cash and jewelry, just in case..."

"You see," Galina Ivanovna said triumphantly. "I was perfectly safe!"

"And the dizzy spells? The falling?"

"What dizzy spells? What falling? I feel fine."

Dima gave her a look.

"Well, as fine as I've felt for months. I was perfectly safe, Dimulya. How was your trip? Tell me about it. Oh, and I need to listen to Innochka's lungs again. She's coughed twice already."

I told her about the dusty doublewide. She whipped out her stethoscope and listened to different parts of my chest, her face serious.

"Not an emergency, but I don't like it," she declared. "You need more fresh air, Innochka. So let's walk over to your apartment, and Dima can give me his impressions of South Carolina and rural America."

Dima filled her in on his impressions of South Carolina and rural America, which probably would have surprised many South Carolinians and rural Americans greatly, while I made supper. Galina Ivanovna appeared extremely interested in everything Dima told her, and said that she wished she could have seen it too.

I thought of the cheerless farmland, currently in its dead season, and the poverty, misery, and general air of dirt and depression that permeated every inch of Mel's family's house. No doubt Galina Ivanovna would have found it fascinating, and it would have dispelled a lot of her romantic notions about America, but I was glad she hadn't seen it. This was the side of America that most Russians knew nothing about, and even though I kept trying to explain it to them, so they could understand what America really was, I wasn't actually sure I wanted them to see it with their own eyes. Some things are too sad and shameful to share with strangers, even strangers you've known for years.

Of course, I'd seen lots of sad and shameful things about Russia, so it was only fair that Dima and Galina Ivanovna saw this side of America. But...but now that it was *my* country that was the one evoking pity and shame, it was a very different matter. I understood for the first time, truly understood, a tiny part of how Dima must have felt every time we discussed something that was going wrong in Russia.

I remembered my early years there, as a naive and bright-eyed NGO worker, gathering stories of election fraud and human rights abuses. Now, looking back on it, I winced. I and all my colleagues had had nothing but the absolutely best of intentions. But what kind of impression had we made?

I imagined how I would feel, faced with a bunch of idealistic recent college grads from Russia, here in America to investigate opioid addiction, gerrymandering, voter suppression, police brutality, and all the other ills of American society, and to show us how to make things better by doing them the Russian, rather than American, way. I would be bemused, then offended, then outraged—and I had to assume that I would be more tolerant and understanding of that kind of thing that 99% of my fellow Americans.

Yes, I and my fellow idealists had indeed uncovered misdeeds and abuses while we were in Russia—but we hadn't stopped further misdeeds and abuses from happening. More than that, I now wondered if we hadn't ultimately made things worse. By stoking, even if unintentionally, dislike and mistrust between the US and Russia, had we contributed in our own small way to this new cold war that was growing between our two peoples? Had we, in fact, done the exact opposite of what we'd set out to do, fostering violence and hatred rather than peace and love?

"You look grim," Dima said. He came over to where I was gathering up the plates from the table, took them from me, and carried them over to the sink. "Contemplating the state of the world?"

"Something like that." I peeked over at Galina Ivanovna. She was absorbed in her reading. She had moved from Baratynsky to Tyutchev, I saw.

"Any conclusions?" Dima asked. Automatically, he started washing the dishes by hand. He still couldn't get used to having a dishwasher, and trying to retrain him seemed like a waste of effort.

"Just wondering if I've made the world a worse place," I said. "If I've accidentally fostered hate rather than love between the American and Russian peoples."

Dima looked over at me. It was supposed to be a quick glance, I could tell, but his eyes met mine, and held.

"I think," he said, his voice dropping, thickening, filling with that special *something* that had only ever been between us, "you've managed to foster some pretty warm and close relations between the American and Russian peoples. At least between a few select representatives of them."

I opened my mouth to speak. No words came. I couldn't think of anything I could say that wouldn't somehow ruin this moment, that wouldn't somehow destroy this fragile seedling I was hoping so desperately would grow into a strong flower and bloom...

My phone *pinged*.

"Dammit!" I said.

Dima laughed, although his laughter was still lower than normal, warmer, the laughter of a man who wants to make love with you. He cut it off abruptly and cleared his throat.

"Check your phone, Inna," he said, going back to washing the dishes, his body half-turned away from me. "Maybe it's your brother with important information. You wouldn't want to miss that."

"Right," I said. "You're right. God alone knows what kind of trouble John has gotten into by now."

50

THE TEXT WAS INDEED from John. *Am now embedded in enemy territory*, he wrote. *Will send for reinforcements if necessary.*

I texted back asking for more details, but got no reply. I hoped that was because he was charming our estranged grandparents with his gift for the gab—and John could be charming when he wanted to—and not because he was chained up in a basement somewhere.

Galina Ivanovna, who had chatted perkily all throughout supper—hers had been something resembling meatloaf, another American dish she declared to be "better than I expected"—started to yawn more and more after we'd finished cleaning up.

"Let's get you to bed, mama," Dima told her. "Let's go back to our place."

"It's barely eight in the evening," she protested. "You can't possibly be ready for bed yet, even if I am!"

Dima gave me one swift glance, and I *knew* he was thinking about coming back over here after his mother fell asleep. Then he looked away just as quickly.

"It's been a long day, and I'm still half on Moscow time," he said, his eyes not meeting mine. "If you don't mind, Inna, we'll say goodnight now."

"I don't mind," I said. That was only sort of true. I was disappointed he was leaving, and also relieved. Every day we spent together, I could sense the ties between us regrowing, winding themselves tighter and tighter around us, drawing us closer and closer together. I could sense that they were telling me that *this was it, this was the **one***. But I couldn't quite sense yet whether it was *time*, whether *now* was the moment we'd been waiting and waiting for. I didn't want to jump the gun on this, mess it up once again.

I could sense Galina Ivanovna looking back and forth between us, even though she was trying to be surreptitious about it. "If you're sure," she said. She didn't sound too sure herself now, but another yawn overwhelmed her before she could say anything else.

"Bed," Dima said firmly. "Goodnight, Inna. Sleep well. We'll talk more in the morning."

"Until the morning," I said, and watched them go out the door.

51

JOHN DIDN'T GET BACK to me until the next morning. There was a string of texts waiting for me when I woke up.

Okay, get your research hat on, Ro, he'd written. *Or your lab coat, or whatever it is you wear when you're doing this shit. The Church of the Holy Light is way more fucked up than I thought, and that's saying something.*

The next text read: *The Halleys—don't want to call them Grandma and Grandpa, it's too weird—don't believe in internet or cell phones, so I'm texting this in secret from under the covers. At least I've still got cell service here, although I'm sure they'd block it if they could. They tried to get Mom and Dad to give up their phones when they got here. Dad refused, but they're not allowed to use them in the house. They gave me a long lecture about it*

The message cut off and started up in a new text bubble.

and how I was rotting my soul by using the internet when I first got here and how I was doomed to Perdition or some shit like that, but they were going to save me, and how if I listened to them, I could overcome the shame of my birth, but I had to do exactly as they said. I said sure, sure, whatever you want. Not sure how to play this yet.

Another message had been sent five minutes later.

I mean it, Ro: these guys are totally batshit crazy. Can't believe they're our flesh and blood :) Or maybe I can, but they're still scary. They're scaring ME, and that's saying something.

Two minutes later, he'd sent another one.

So if you could do some digging, see what you can find out about our grandparents and about the Church of the Holy Light, that'd be great. I'll try to stay in contact, but I'm a little afraid they're going to take my phone away when I'm not looking or some shit like that. I'm sleeping with it under my pillow, which will probably give me brain cancer, but I don't want to risk losing my only weapon :) Wish I'd brought a sidearm at least

The text cut off and continued in another bubble.

but I thought it would be overkill for my grandparents' house, and I didn't want to deliver a weapon into enemy hands :):) I haven't seen any signs of weapons here yet, and they haven't talked about their stashes or anything. I don't think they're preppers, but there's something NOT RIGHT about them. Wouldn't surprise me to discover they've got some weird dungeon or cache of bizarro weapons or some shit like that somewhere.

The next text had been sent fifteen minutes later.

Shit, almost got caught there with the phone. Alexandra—Mrs. Halley, Grandma, whatever you want to call her—came to the door and asked me if everything was okay, and then just barged the fuck right in. Almost told her she was lucky I didn't have porn with me :):):) but decided it would be a bad move. Barely had time to hide the phone under my pillow and pull out a book before she came in. And it's a good thing I did, because

Another text bubble started.

she took away my book and gave me one of their church pamphlets to read instead. Told me I needed to stop rotting my soul with Tom Clancy (I don't think she knew Tom Clancy from Tom Cruise, but she didn't approve of the picture on the cover) and start thinking about the purity of my heart and what kind of eternal life I was earning for myself. I didn't tell her it was a little late for that.

Another five minute pause, like maybe John had stopped texting in order to wrestle with his own despair and self-recrimination before carrying on.

Anyway, anything you can find out about them would be great. Pass along anything you think is relevant. Maybe send it via email unless you think it's time-critical. I don't want my phone notifications to give me away if I can help it, but I don't get screen notifications from my personal email account. So send stuff there unless you think I absolutely have to know AS-AP. I guess if you find out something really dangerous, go ahead and call me. I don't know how much you're going to find

A new text bubble started.

given their anti-internet stance. I doubt they have a website or anything useful like that. But maybe there's some subreddit somewhere with info on them. Take a look, will you, and let me know if it looks like I'm about to be a victim of human sacrifice. JK—sort of. These guys are creepy as fuck, Ro. And they're turning Mom and Dad. You know how they love anything counterculture. And there's all this weird stuff that they actually agree on. Hell, there's all this weird stuff that *I* actually agree with them on. But they're still creepy as fuck and I can't

Another text bubble started.

let myself get distracted from the mission. So look into it, okay? I've already discovered their pastor is named Jeremiah Jones. I'm supposed to meet him tomorrow. I'd like to know something about what I'll be up against before I do.

I texted back *I'll look into it right away.* Then I got up, made coffee, and opened up my laptop.

52

WHEN DIMA AND GALINA Ivanovna came over a couple of hours later, I was still staring at my laptop, feeling increasingly frustrated.

As John had predicted, there was no website for the church. There were also no press releases, no blogs, no social media posts, or even articles in the local press. All I got was page after page about World of Warcraft.

Jeremiah Jones was also a dead end. They were both such common names that I turned up millions of hits, but of the first few dozen that I looked through, none of them suggested they had anything to do with a cult in Virginia. I tried the two search terms together, and got nothing. I tried adding "cult" and "Virginia" and "Christiansburg" and still got nothing. If I hadn't known that this was not the kind of thing John was likely to be mistaken about, I would have started to think that maybe he'd made the whole thing up. But while John could be a kidder about some things, I knew he'd never say anything other than the purest, most concrete truth as he knew it about something like this. So I had to believe that there was indeed such a cult, and our grandparents were indeed up to their necks in it, and there just wasn't anything immediately available on the internet about it.

"What's the matter?" Dima asked as soon as he came in. "You look like your eyes hurt. Have you been up working already?" It was eight o'clock in the morning on a Sunday. Not that I didn't work on Sunday mornings all the time. But a reasonable person could be expected to be resting then.

I explained about John's texts and my so-far fruitless search for information.

"Try searching for something related to your grandparents," Dima suggested. "What about aunts, uncles, cousins? Are there other Halleys you could reach out to?"

"Wow," I said. "Why didn't I think of that?"

Dima grinned. "Years of professional experience are speaking here," he told me. "Years of hunting down people who don't want to be found."

A search of my grandparents' names turned up the information that Alexandra Halley had, back in 2012, had been leading the women's Bible study group and also directing the children's choir at her local Presbyterian church. The choir had performed at several local events and been written up in the local paper. Alexandra had been mentioned as a dedicated and energetic member of the church and the community, involved in multiple social and charitable organizations, along with her sister-in-law, Roseanna Arlene Halley.

I stared at the name. My scalp and the nape of my neck prickled. I *had* to have been named after her. Oh, not exactly, of course, but my parents *had* to have intended the similarities between our names. She was Roseanna Arlene Halley, and I was the much hippier but basically the same Rowena Arwen Halley. There *had* to be a story here, one that was so important they decided to name me after her, but not tell me about her. I'd never even known she'd existed.

"Are you okay, Inna?" Dima asked.

"I'm fine." It came out as a quavery croak. Sweat was trickling down my sides, despite the early-morning January chill in the apartment that I was too frugal to heat for more than an hour or two a day.

With trembling fingers, I performed a search for Roseanna Arlene Halley. A whole series of hits popped up on my screen, starting with a Facebook page. I clicked on it.

"Is that your grandmother, Inna?" asked Galina Ivanovna. She had made herself some tea and come to join me at the table. She eyed the pictures filling Roseanna's feed approvingly. "She looks just like you. Very pretty. I always knew you'd age well. You've only grown better-looking in the past ten years, and if you look at her, you can see what you'll be like forty years from now. Something to look forward to in your old age. Do you know if she has any special beauty regime?"

"My great-aunt," I told her. "I don't know anything about her beauty regime. I don't know anything about her at all. But I think I need to find out."

53

I STARTED BY SCROLLING through her Facebook feed. Despite being over 80 years old, Roseanna kept up a surprisingly active presence on social media, sharing and posting several times a week. From that I gathered that she was still active in the local Presbyterian church, and also ran a community volunteering club for local seniors.

I drummed my fingers on the table. I was hesitant to contact Roseanna straight away. We must be estranged for a reason, and I didn't know what that reason was. Barging in unannounced and uninvited could potentially make things worse. I couldn't guess how they might get worse than total estrangement, but I could trigger something that might somehow cause John problems, and I didn't want to do that if I could help it.

I chewed on my thumbnail until I caught myself at it and stopped. Try to reach out to other members of the church or the club? But they didn't know me from Eve, and they might go blabbing straight away to Roseanna, thereby triggering the unforeseeable problems for John that I was determined to avoid. I decided to start a little closer to home.

My mother's parents should have gotten home from their cruise yesterday. They were probably exhausted, but on the other hand, my grandmother—my maternal grandmother—never met a piece of gossip she didn't like. If she knew anything about my father's parents or aunt, she'd wake up from a coma in order to tell it to me. If she had actually been sitting on a juicy family secret for the past several decades, it must have been killing her. If I told her John's safety was on the line, she'd spill everything, no matter what kind of solemn oaths of silence she'd taken. I dialed her up.

"Weena! How good to hear from you!"

As I'd guessed, she answered on the first ring, sounding hale and hearty and full of energy for socializing. Excellent.

I asked her about the cruise, and made appropriate comments as she gave me an enthusiastic rundown of the highlights.

"But what about you, darling?" she concluded. "How have your holidays been? Have you seen Vannie"—Vannie was what she called John, whose original given name had been Ivanhoe—"or your parents? When do you think we'll see you, honey?"

"Well," I said. "I'm actually calling about them. About John and Mom and Dad. Do you know what's going on with them?"

"I heard Bev and Bobby"—my parents—"were going to spend some time with Bobby's parents." Her voice rang with doubt. "I have to say I was surprised, but if they're looking to smooth things over, it's past high time, so good for them."

"Yeah," I said. "Mom and Dad and John are all there right now, but...there's some weird stuff going on."

"There always is, with Alexandra and Dennis," my grandmother said tartly.

"Yeah...did you know that they'd joined, well, a, um, cult? The Church of the Holy Light?"

"I haven't seen or heard from them since your hooding ceremony, sweetie, and we barely spoke two words to each other then. They..." Her voice slowed as she recalled the events of almost three years ago. "They mentioned something about joining a new church, I think. But I don't remember them saying anything else about it. Like I said, we barely spoke two words to each other. And it's not like they'd go around announcing that it's a cult. Most people who end up in cults don't recognize them for what they are, anyway."

"True," I said. "Well, um...I'm looking into it, trying to find out more about the church and, well, them, since I know hardly anything about them. I found some old newspaper articles about, um, Alexandra"—it was hard to know what to call her—"and they mentioned her doing a lot of events and stuff with her sister-in-law."

I could feel a sharp change in the atmosphere on the other end of the line. My grandmother's silence suddenly became much more profound, but also pressurized. The right stimulus, and she'd pour out everything I needed to know.

"Roseanna Arlene Halley," I said. "Do you know her? Or know anything about her? I'm hoping she might be able to help me. But I didn't want to get in touch with her out of the blue, in case...well, obviously there's *something* going on between her and my parents, and I didn't know..."

I trailed off. I could feel the pressurized silence on the other end of the line building and building.

"You did right, hun," my grandmother said. "Roseanna is the most likely person to know what's going on with Alexandra and Dennis, but...your parents never told you about her?"

"Not a word," I said.

"Well...well..." She took a deep breath. "It's high time *someone* told you, then. I don't care what your mother thinks. Let me fill you in."

54

"IT WASN'T TALKED ABOUT much back then," my grandmother said. "Sometimes people'd make remarks about the 'baby blues.' Then they'd laugh and roll their eyes. Just one of those silly women's problems that didn't matter."

"Uh-huh," I said. Of course. Women were destined to be sad and pathetic and in pain, everyone knew that, even if they didn't know it consciously, even if they'd argue with you fiercely if you said it to them straight out. But if you looked at how people and societies actually acted, then it was clear that the underlying assumption by pretty much everyone was that women were inherently sad and pathetic and in pain (also weak, stupid, and evil, of course), and there was no point in doing anything about it.

"Alexandra...I'm just going by what I heard, you understand. But what I heard is that Alexandra had it bad. Real bad. You know, sometimes it's so bad women kill their newborn babies, do all kinds of terrible things...I can't imagine how awful they must feel." My grandmother's voice went soft as she tried, and failed, to imagine it.

"I guess I was lucky," she continued, still in that soft voice. "I was so happy when your mother was born. I loved being a mommy to a little newborn girl." Her voice gained strength. "She'd reach out her little hands to me, and my heart would just melt...but sometimes something goes wrong. Hormones, I guess. It's all hormones. Strange to think about it, isn't it? That we're not in control of our feelings, and it's all hormones. All that love I felt for that baby girl was all just hormones."

"I wouldn't say it was 'just' hormones," I said. "We've always known that there's a powerful force that makes us love babies. Now we know enough to call it hormones. That doesn't make it any less real. You could say it makes it more real."

"True. I guess that's one way of looking at it. Anyway, for Alexandra, something went wrong. What I heard..." She stopped, swallowed, and started again. "What I heard—from your father, and from Roseanna—is that she'd already had one baby. A little girl. But there was"—her voice caught—"there was something terribly wrong with her, and she didn't survive more than a few hours."

"Oh," I said. Something seemed to be splitting up inside of me. One part of me was listening to this story with cool indifference, as if it were about complete strangers—which it was. Another part of me was crying out, *That was your aunt! That was your close kin!* I'd felt the call of blood vengeance before. This was different, but somehow similar. It was still a call of something primal, something tragic and terrible that threatened to take over me.

"Then she had your father," my grandmother continued. "And he was perfectly healthy. But...she wasn't. This time, there was something terribly wrong with her. She...she..." Her voice caught once more, trembled, and then started again. "She tried to set him on fire. Well, both of them. She tried to set the both of them on fire. Roseanna stopped her."

"Oh," I said.

"And then Roseanna took Bobby and raised him like her own. Raised him till he was five years old, while Alexandra was in and out of clinics."

"Oh," I said. *Why didn't I know ANY OF THIS?* I thought. I was ashamed for immediately thinking of myself in the face of a story like this, but my first feeling was one of hurt at not being told this important piece of family history.

"Then Alexandra got him back," my grandmother continued. "She tried to raise him as her own son—which he was, of course—but they never really got on as mother and son. He'd already bonded with Roseanna, and there was...there was always something wrong with Alexandra. She never recovered."

I could hear my grandmother shudder over the phone. "I don't want to think about what happened to her in those clinics. I know she had a hysterectomy—against her will, I believe—and electroshock therapy, and whatever drugs they were giving people back then. She's lucky she didn't end up with a lobotomy. The end result was, well...she just never seemed to have normal feelings like a normal person after that. She couldn't relate to anyone, especially the son she'd wanted so much and suffered so much from and almost killed."

"That's terrible," I said.

"It is, sweetie, isn't it? You can see why we didn't want to tell you, can't you?" My grandmother's voice rose anxiously. "We didn't want you thinking that there was something...*wrong* with you, with a grandmother like that. We were especially worried about you, sweetie. What if you were too scared to have children, after hearing about it? Of course, I'm *sure* you have nothing to worry about, hun. Like I said, I loved your mother so much from the moment she was born...and your mother never had a hint of postpartum depression, either, so I'm sure you're safe, hun, I'm sure you're safe..."

"I'm sure," I said reassuringly, although at the moment I was far from sure. "So, um...was I named after her? Roseanna? I couldn't help but notice the similarity between our names."

"You were, sweetie, you were...by the time you came along, the big break had already happened, they didn't dare name you after her directly, but your father had his heart set on honoring her somehow or another, so they came up with a name that sounded a lot like hers, but that no one but them would know what it really meant...you don't mind, do you, sweetheart? Your name...well, it's a bit funny, I admit, but it's a nice name, isn't it?"

"It's a great name," I said. "So, um...how come I never met her? Roseanna?"

"Well..." My grandmother blew out a breath. "You sure you want to hear all this right away, hun? It's a lot to take in...maybe we'd better take a break..."

"John really needs to know," I said. "It's kind of crucial. And time-sensitive. I'm fine. You can tell me anything." I'd said those words so many times. So often it had been a prelude to someone else's tragedy and pain. But this time, it would be my own tragedy and pain, or at least my family's. That was probably why the words felt particularly false as they left my mouth. And I wasn't sure I actually wanted to hear any more of the story. But I'd already said them, and John really was counting on me. Whatever I heard, I told myself, I could stand it.

"Well..." said my grandmother. "I guess..." She sounded reluctant, something I'd never expected to hear from her when it came to dishing out gossip. What, I wondered, could possibly be worse than what she'd already told me?

"I guess it's time it all came out," she said. Her voice grew stronger. "No, it's definitely time. You and John need to know. And it's been eating at me for the better part of forty years. I'll just tell you the whole sorry story all at once."

55

"THE THING IS, SWEETIE," my grandmother said, "that Alexandra was always jealous of Roseanna and her relationship with Bobby. Well, that's not surprising. I'd probably feel the same way. Especially since Roseanna was her sister-in-law, not even her sister. That'd be pretty terrible. You have to understand where she was coming from, hun."

"I understand," I said. "I'd probably be pretty jealous in that situation too. And she might not have been...in her right mind after whatever treatments she was subjected to."

"Exactly." Relief filled my grandmother's voice. "She was never normal after that. Of course, I didn't know her before, I only met with her a few times years and years afterwards, but it was obvious that something wasn't right with her. And, well, when your parents got together, I guess it all...I guess it all came out again."

"Uh-huh?" I said.

"From what I gathered, both she and Dennis were in despair when Bobby ran off and joined that commune. Well, your grandfather and I weren't too thrilled about it either, but we knew better than to try to do anything about it. Bobby and Bev had met just a few months before, you know, and, well, I guess it was love at first sight."

My grandmother cheered up, remembering that. "Your mother had always seemed much too, I don't know what, too cool and self-contained for that kind of thing, too interested in other things, but I guess she'd just been waiting for the right man to come along, and, well, that's what you want, isn't it? Providing he *does* come along."

"Uh-huh," I said.

"So Bobby and Bev were mad for each other from the moment they laid eyes on each other, and within a couple of months they were living together—this was back when it wasn't done as a matter of course, the way it is now, you know—and a couple of months after that, they'd left everything and were living in this commune. We weren't too happy about it, but we figured it was just a phase and the less we said about it, the less Bev would insist on staying there just to prove us wrong. So we gave 'em our blessing and invited 'em over for holidays and even went to visit a few times. It wasn't too bad, you know. I don't know how much you remember of it, sweetie..."

"I remember it well," I said. "It was *awesome*. Everyone should be so lucky."

"I'm glad to hear you say that, hun. Your grandfather and I worried about you and Vannie so much, but it seems Bobby and Bev knew what they were doing after all. When I see how so many of my friends' grandkids have turned out...no, the commune was probably the best thing they could have done for you. I should tell Bev that, someday."

"I'm sure she'd welcome hearing that," I said.

"I'm sure she would, darling. Well, anyway, as I was saying, we tried to be as supportive as possible, but not Dennis and Alexandra. They were devastated. They were convinced that there was something terribly wrong with Bobby, that whatever...I guess you could say *curse*, or however you want to put it...bad genes, I guess we'd say nowadays...anyway, you get the picture. Whatever had caused Alexandra's first baby to die, and whatever had caused her to go crazy after Bobby was born, had been hiding in Bobby all along, and it was finally coming out."

"Oh," I said.

"Of course, they—well, Alexandra—couldn't bear to think of it like that. From what I heard, Dennis blamed Alexandra for it, told her it was her fault. And she blamed Roseanna. Said if Roseanna had raised him right, instead of giving him all these crazy liberal notions she kept trying to instill in him, none of this would have happened."

"Oh," I said. "But...I thought they were still friends, or at least still doing stuff together in the church, just a few years ago."

"I'm getting to that, hun. So, things were pretty bad between Bobby and his parents, and between Dennis and Alexandra, and between Alexandra and Roseanna, for a while. Then Vannie came along, and they got much worse."

"Oh," I said. "Oh dear."

"Yes. You'd think a baby would get them to get their heads on straight, wouldn't it? But they were *beside* themselves that, well, that Bev and Bobby weren't married. They showed up at the commune, came thrusting their way into the yurt—do you remember the yurt, hun?"

"I remember the yurt," I said. "It was *awesome.*"

"It was, wasn't it, sweetie? Your mother built it with her own two hands. While she was pregnant. I was so proud of that...I mean, I thought she was crazy as a bedbug, but I also started to think that maybe, just maybe, she could pull this off.

"So anyway, Alexandra and Dennis came bursting in, shouting and screaming, saying they were going to take the baby away...and then Roseanna came in after them. She grabbed Alexandra by the arm and told her she'd *never* let her have another baby in her house, never, never, never, and if anyone was going to take care of this baby, it was going to be her and no one else."

"Oh," I said.

"Your mother didn't take too kindly to that, as you might imagine," my grandmother said. "Stood up and told them all to go straight to hell and never come back. And then Alexandra *grabbed* at the baby, tried to pull him right out of your mother's arms...your father tried to get to her, but Dennis grabbed him and wouldn't let him...your mother didn't know what to do, she was afraid that if she kept fighting, she'd hurt the baby, but she didn't want to let him go to this madwoman...and then Roseanna stepped in. She was the one who pulled Alexandra away. She might have saved little Vannie's life that day."

"Oh," I said.

"She told Alexandra that if she ever tried anything like that again, she'd have her committed. And then she said that if your parents didn't get married and smooth things over with Dennis and Alexandra, she would petition the court to have custody of Vannie given over to her."

"Oh," I said.

"Indeed. Roseanna...I only met her a couple of times, you know. But she always had a backbone of steel. Anyway...when your parents still hadn't gotten married after a couple of months, she did in fact start proceedings to get custody of Vannie."

"Oh my God," I said.

"Your mother was furious...Roseanna told her it was the only way to save Alexandra's sanity, she was going crazy thinking about her only grandson being illegitimate, if they didn't do something she was going to end up back in an institution, and this time she'd never get out...that is, if she didn't do something desperate first, hurt herself...your parents...Vannie...your parents finally gave in and got married. Roseanna came and watched...they didn't want to invite her, but I insisted, and I think she would have come anyway...you never noticed her in the pictures of the wedding?"

"I don't know that I've ever seen any pictures of the wedding." I racked my brains, trying to remember. There had certainly never been any wedding pictures displayed around the house. There had never been any wedding album. I'd never seen my mother's wedding dress. The one time I'd asked about it, she'd said that she didn't hold with that kind of thing, and she'd just worn an everyday work dress, and kept on wearing it afterwards until it had worn out.

"Do you remember...I've got one picture of it—just one!—in my bedroom. On the side table. It shows all of us together—your parents, me and your grandfather, Dennis and Alexandra...and Roseanna. Do you remember? You asked about her once, when you were little. You wanted to know who the extra person in the picture was. Everyone else was in pairs, except for this one lady who didn't have a man with her. You wanted to know who she was and why she didn't have a man like all the other ladies in the picture. I told she was there to take care of Vannie, that he was her man, but he'd messed up his clothes and couldn't be in the picture."

She laughed, the sound half-mirth, half-pain. "That was half-true. Roseanna had held him throughout the ceremony, spent the whole time watching over him. But then he got excited and spit up all over his clothes—he used to do that until he was more than a year old. She cleaned him off, and your mother wanted him in the picture, but Alexandra had a fit, said she wasn't going to have the wedding pictures ruined by a bastard being in them...there was a lot of shouting after that...Roseanna was the one who calmed everyone down, got your parents to agree to take that picture with Alexandra and Dennis and without Vannie...but your mother couldn't countenance any of those pictures after that. I kept that one where she wasn't likely to see it, just because I couldn't not have a picture of my daughter's wedding somewhere around the house."

"Oh," I said. I had only the vaguest memories of that picture and asking who the people in it were. I couldn't bring up an image of Roseanna at all. She was just a shadowy figure off to the side, eclipsed in my mind by the people I actually knew. But without her, I might not be here. Without her, my father might not have survived, something terrible might have happened to John, my parents might never have gotten married...I might not have been born. That shadowy figure to the side might be the reason that we were all here today.

"Anyway, your mother never could forgive her...she cut off all contact with her...especially since Roseanna stayed, well, *friends* is the wrong word, but she stood by Alexandra and Dennis through thick and thin...but when Vannie got terribly sick when he was two and your parents didn't have any insurance, it was Roseanna who paid for his treatment. When your parents decided to leave the commune and go back to school, it was Roseanna who gave them enough money to get themselves on their feet in the 'real world,' as you might call it. So...your mother never could forgive her, like I said, your parents always acted like she didn't exist...but they named you after her all the same."

"Does..." I had to stop and clear my throat before I could continue. "Does she know? Does she know about me?"

"She must, hun, since you'd already come along when she gave your parents that money for school. But somehow things never thawed out between them. Your mother was always afraid that she'd try to take you kids, I think. She tried to have as little to do with her as possible."

"So..." I said. "Do you think she'd talk to me if I contacted her?"

"I think you have to try, hun," said my grandmother. "I think it's a crying shame that you don't know the woman you were named after. I think it's your duty to reach out to her. I think she'd probably move heaven and earth to help you if there's anything she can do. And if your mother doesn't like it, well"—my grandmother's voice grew strong—"she can just lump it!"

56

"WHAT'S THE MATTER?" Dima's voice seemed to be coming from very far away. "You look terrible. Did you find out what you needed to know?"

"I..." I fought the impulse to run off into the bedroom and cry. I still felt strangely split, with part of me reacting to the revelations about my family as if they were about complete strangers (which was partly true) and part of me shaken to the core by this new view of my blood kin (which was also true).

"I found out a lot, yes," I said. "Hopefully enough." I drummed my fingers on the tabletop some more. "What do you think?" I asked. "I need to get in touch with an aunt I've just found out about. Should I message her on Facebook, or try to call her on the phone?"

"Do you have a good phone number for her?" Dima asked practically.

"No."

"I'd start with Facebook, then," he said.

That seemed like the easiest approach, so after flexing my fingers, taking several deep breaths, and generally psyching myself up, I wrote:

Dear Roseanna,

This is probably coming out of the blue, but this is your great-niece, Rowena Halley. I'm writing because I am trying to find out more about my father's family. My father's parents have recently initiated contact with my parents and my brother. My brother and I know almost nothing about them. We would like to know more about this side of our family. We are also concerned that some of our grandparents' new acquaintances may be tak-ing advantage of them [I rewrote that passage at least half a dozen times, struggling to find exactly the right balance of expressing concern and whetting Roseanna's curiosity but not alarming her or sounding like a conspiracy nut]. *We would also like to get to know you better. I only recently discovered that you existed, and everything I've heard about you makes me want to know you better and, I hope, stay in contact with you.*

With best wishes,

Rowena

I stared at the message, erased sections, rewrote them, erased more sections, rewrote them, almost sent the message by accident several times before it was finished, and generally worked myself into a fine state over it. But after at least twenty minutes of hard labor, I decided it was as good as I was going to make it. I hit "Enter" and watched it send.

"Well?" asked Dima.

"It's sent," I told him. "Now we're all just walking under God."

I checked my Facebook messages at least twenty times that evening. But Roseanna didn't got back to me.

57

DIMA WAS SCHEDULED to leave for the Security Solutions head-quarters Monday morning. After a lengthy hashing-out of our options, we decided that he had to rent a car. He wouldn't be back until Wednes-day evening. My classes started Monday morning. I had said that maybe Mel and I could carpool together to campus and Dima could borrow my car, but despite his extreme lack of desire to shell out for a rental, he even-tually decided that he couldn't stand the idea of me relying on rides from Mel to get back and forth to campus on such an important week, and his mother relying on her if there was an emergency. We needed my car, and he'd just suck it up and rent one.

"I still can't believe there's no public transport to campus," he said for the tenth time.

"Welcome to America," I told him.

"Do they expect all the students to have their own cars?"

"They sure do," I said.

He shook his head and went onto the website of the one rental place in town. To Dima's chagrin, we discovered that picking up the car Mon-day morning before class would be cutting it rather fine for both of us to show up at our respective responsibilities on time, so he needed to get it now and to pay for an extra night.

"Maybe you can get reimbursed," I said. "You're doing this for, well, someone, right? They should pay your expenses."

He laughed and made a face at the same time. "I'm trying to imagine how I would submit that expense report."

"They should give you cash," I said. "They have to know that this kind of thing will come up. They should give you cash up front for expenses."

"You have a very high opinion of their generosity, Inna."

"I have a middling opinion of their desire for you to fulfill your mission successfully," I said. "I'm assuming they're willing to pay a few hundred bucks to make it happen."

"I'll be sure to mention that to them, the next time I talk to them. In the meanwhile, we'd better hope that my credit card doesn't have a stroke from the sudden inrush of hard currency purchases."

"We can put it on mine," I offered automatically.

Dima laughed and put his arm around me, pulling me firmly to him and kissing the top of my head. The action had been as automatic as my offer. A breath later he froze, his lips still pressed into the part in my hair.

"Sorry." He let go of me and pulled away, moving slowly and stiffly, as if all his joints had suddenly turned to rust. "I forgot...I forgot myself."

"No worries." My voice was high and cracked. "I'll just...I'd better...just let me know if you need help with anything." I hurried over to the kitchenette and handwashed a couple of dishes that didn't need washing.

A few minutes later, Dima came over. He stayed on the other side of the counter separating the dining/living room from the kitchenette, and spoke without looking at me directly. "It's done. Only...if you don't mind...we need to go get the car right away."

"Fine." I got my keys. "Let's go."

We made the drive over to the rental place in silence. I could still feel his arm around me, his lips on the part in my hair. Somehow I could sense by the charge in the twilight air between us that he could feel those same things. A couple of times we both tried to speak, but we couldn't break through that force field that was humming between us.

I was afraid that something would go wrong with the rental, that Dima's Russian passport and driver's license would cause them to refuse him, but we made it in five minutes before closing, and they were in such a hurry to get out of there that they barely glanced at his documents. A few minutes later, and we were back home. We spent the evening in strained politeness to each other. Galina Ivanovna looked back and forth between us a few times, which was embarrassing, but couldn't seem to draw any conclusions from our behavior.

"I'll be setting off first thing in the morning," Dima said as he prepared to walk Galina Ivanovna over to their apartment. "So I'll say goodbye now. I'll be in touch with both of you if I can, but if you don't hear from me that often, don't worry."

I raised my eyebrows at him. "How long should I wait before I call in the cavalry?"

His face lit up in involuntary humor, and for an instant I could feel the connection between us, stronger than ever. Our eyes held, held...and broke. The connection between us snapped.

"There's no cavalry that will come save me," he said. "Come, mama, let's leave Inna in peace. She's got a big day tomorrow." He ushered Galina Ivanovna out the door and down the stairs. I stood in the doorway and watched. Just as he was about to disappear down the staircase, he stopped and looked back.

Pray for me, he mouthed.

Go with God, I mouthed back. Then he was gone.

58

I WOKE UP TO A TEXT from Dima.

Leaving now. Want to get an early start)))) Good luck with classes!

I texted back, but the empty little check marks told me that Dima wasn't connected to the internet and wouldn't get the message until he was back in range.

I got up and started coffee. Half of my heart felt blank, empty, and torn—contradictory as that was—without Dima around. The other half felt like I'd just gotten out of a pressure cooker. His presence was so intense that it overwhelmed everything else. The first week of classes, plus an interview, seemed trivial and relaxing in comparison.

Is this what it would be like to be married to him? I wondered. *Would I be overwhelmed, almost oppressed, by our love, all day, every day, so that I couldn't concentrate on anything else? Would I crumple under the pressure? Or would it ease off, become normal, just an ordinary aspect of my ordinary days? And if that happened, would I be disappointed? Would I be unhappy either way?*

I cast my mind back to our time living together. It had been intense, but we'd managed to do other things—mainly, I admitted to myself, because Dima had always been off chasing a story. He would keep pushing and pushing—oh God, why was I only recognizing this pattern now?—for more open declarations of love from me, more explicit commitments and promises that I loved him above all else and would never leave him.

And then when I'd respond and say yes, of course I loved him above everyone and everything else, he was the one and only man for me and I was determined to stay with him until the very end, he'd rush off. It was as if he couldn't bear to receive the love he was so desperate to get, and had to pick a fight or run away every time he got what he wanted and needed so badly.

Only his frequent absences meant that when we were together again, things were even more pressurized, as all the heat we'd been building up when we were apart raised the pressure cooker that was our relationship to dangerous temperatures. It had been glorious, and terrible, and unsustainable. Both of us had known it, but we'd told ourselves that it was from our temporary situation. Once we were married and could relax in the knowledge that we were together forever, we'd naturally settle into a more sustainable long-term pattern. Except that we hadn't. Instead, he'd been unable to sustain it, and broken things off.

I can't let that happen again. The thought rose up from somewhere deep in my chest, and filled my whole being, telling me that this was the most important thing in my life, the thing I needed to dedicate myself to above all else. Unfortunately, I didn't know how to realize that goal—no, that vow.

Stop worrying about that and worry about your job for a bit. I finished my coffee and started checking through everything I'd packed in my bookbag the day before, determinedly not thinking about Dima.

59

I STOPPED BY GALINA Ivanovna's and was reassured that she was fine, she'd had her tea and her special new astronaut food ("I'm calling it astronaut food in honor of your American space program, Innochka"), and then knocked on Mel's door.

"Are you ready?" I asked when she answered. We'd agreed that I'd drive both of us to campus today. We tried to carpool when we could, both for abstract environmental reasons and to cut costs, since neither of us were exactly rolling in riches.

"Am I fuck," she said. She had big dark circles under her eyes, which she promptly hid with her oversized aviator sunglasses, despite the January clouds covering the sky. "'Course today is a day I feel like shit. Although I got no one to blame but myself."

"Uh-huh?" I said as we headed down the stairs to my car.

"Yeah, I was up late talking to Evil Mel on the phone. Like a proper phone date kind of thing." She made a face. "Is it pathetic and awful and a sign that the world is going to hell in a handbasket that it was the best—and fuckin' only—date I've had in at least two years?"

"It's sad, yes," I said. "I'm not sure it's a sign that the world is going to hell in a handbasket. Maybe more a sign that you need to get out and try to meet someone. Someone who isn't a scammer and a criminal."

"Damn hard to do." She grimaced as she got into the car. "Damn knees are acting up again. I thought I'd cured 'em, but nope, they're fuckin' acting like they're 90 years old again today."

"Ugh," I said. "Do you know why?"

"It just happens sometimes. Especially when I'm tense. Like it *is* all in my head, just like all those fuckin' waste-of-space doctors kept trying to convince me."

"Emotional stress causes muscle tension, which can cause joint pain," I said. "That doesn't mean you don't also have damage to the joints themselves."

"Yeah. That sounds like you know what you're talking about."

"My mother is a doctor," I pointed out. "I'd like to think that she's a good one. It's the kind of thing she says, anyway."

"Maybe she woulda helped me if I'da gone to her," Mel said.

"I'd like to think so," I said. "Although she mainly works with addicts. Well, worked. She's switching to a local family practice. But anyway. You've got a doctor now. You're doing treatment. And it's working, even if there are bad days sometimes."

"Yeah," said Mel, not sounding convinced.

"So did you find out anything interesting about Evil Mel?" I asked.

Mel shrugged. "Lots. She filled me in on her rough childhood, and her series of shitty jobs, and her boss who attacked her in the storeroom and then got her fired when she complained."

"Do you think all that's true?" I asked.

"Yeah." Mel was looking out the window at the uninspiring January morning rolling by. "I do. More or less. I think she really did have a shitty childhood, whether or not the details she gave me were all 100% accurate. I think she really did hold a series of shitty jobs, whether or not they were actually the ones she told me about. And I think she really was propositioned and assaulted by her boss, who got her fired when she complained, and she really was broke and desperate and had to figure out what to do in order not to end up on the streets—again."

"So she decided to steal your identity to commit fraud and break people's hearts," I said. Firmly. I was a little worried that Mel was forgetting just what Evil Mel had done and how lots of people, including Real Mel, had suffered and would continue to suffer for it.

"Yeah." Mel didn't sound as certain as I would have liked. "I know all that. And I'm still pissed as fuck at her. But I also feel sorry for her.

I mean, she's been through a lot of shit, and most of it wasn't her fault. And it really was the best date I've been on in years."

"It's the *only* date you've been on in years," I pointed out. "Your bar may be low. Are you any closer to finding out Evil Mel's actual identity, or figuring out how to stop her?"

Mel started to shrug again, and ended with her shoulders in a defeated slump. "No. I tracked down a couple of the people who sent those ashes yesterday, but they all think she's me. Turns out there's a Facebook page with her business and my name and address, and that's how they found her. They were pretty upset when they found out the truth. Made me mad at her all over again. But then I talked to her last night, and I started thinking about how if I do everything I set out to do, she'll probably end up with a criminal conviction, maybe jail time. What good's that going to do for anyone?"

"She won't break any more hearts and wreck any more lives," I said. Even more firmly.

"Yeah...I guess...you know what our criminal justice system is like. She'll just end up in and out of prison the rest of her life, committing petty crimes because it'll be the only way she can stay afloat. Not sure that's an improvement over letting her run free."

Mel's shoulders slumped even more. "I guess if I do that PI thing I was talking about, this'd be what it'd be like all the time, huh? Catching people committing petty fraud and stupid little crimes and then ruining their lives because of it? It's probably all insurance fraud and cheating spouses. What do I care about any of that? The world won't be a better place for me catching any of those folks."

"What would the world be a better place from you doing?" I asked.

"Fucked if I know," Mel said into the window.

"I think this is the doxy talking," I said. "This isn't you, it's the drugs. Once you're done with them, all this will be over and you'll feel completely different."

"Maybe," Mel said, still speaking to the window. She turned back towards me, a forced smile on her face. "It's sure fuckin' true that antibiotics do crazy things to your mood. I'd heard about it but I didn't believe it till I started taking them. I never thought of myself as a moody person before, but now I'm yoyoing all over the place. It's fuckin' humbling, really."

A little genuine humor filled out the forced smile. "Don't know if the students know what's about to hit them. I might have a breakdown or a vomiting spree right in the middle of class. That'd give 'em something to think about, wouldn't it?"

"Do you really think you might?" I asked.

"Nah. If I really thought that, I'd've canceled today. But I can feel that the possibility's always there. Not only do I have this monster inside me, trying to take me over, I've got a bunch of monster slayers inside of me now too, and my body's the battleground. Being a battleground isn't very fun, it turns out."

"Yeah," I said. "I'm sure."

"But look on the bright side," said Mel. "At least we've got those interviews to look forward to."

"Gee, thanks," I said. "I think I just started to hyperventilate at the very thought."

"Anytime," said Mel. "Just trying to spread the pain around as best I can. And here we are. Who knows what delights await us this semester?"

"Who knows," I said.

60

WE PARKED IN THE FACULTY lot behind the football stadium—the old football stadium; a new one was being built on the other side of campus with Security Solutions money—and headed towards Bedford Hall.

"At least we can both make the walk," Mel said. I'd spent a good deal of last semester on crutches, while Mel's knee problems had gotten worse and worse, making the hike around the football stadium difficult, if not impossible.

"Yeah!" I said. "This is good, right? We're both walking pretty normally. A couple of months ago we couldn't have done this."

"Yeah," said Mel, less cheerfully than I would have liked. "Oh, look, there's Chloe. Chloe! What's up?"

"Oh, hi." Chloe came over to join us. "Do you both have 9:00am classes too?"

We nodded. "Nine, ten, and twelve," I said.

"Nine, eleven, and twelve," said Mel.

"I've got nine and eleven," Chloe told us. "I guess the senior faculty never want to teach at nine, do they? But this way we can get all our teaching done in the morning and do research and writing in the afternoon."

"Uh-huh," I said. I didn't say anything about how I rarely got much research or writing done in the afternoon. I was kind of a slouch on the research and writing front. Unlike Chloe. She was Crimson College's only tenure-track African American faculty member, hired on a special diversity appointment straight out of Columbia, where she'd already been marked as a rising star in Chinese studies. It was a testament to how bad the job market was that she was even at a place like Crimson, let alone that she considered herself lucky to be there. Well, sort of lucky. She hadn't enjoyed her time here very much so far, and she was also experiencing weird and mysterious health problems that we were all starting to suspect were coming from the old, moldy, nasty buildings we taught in. Or maybe it was the emotionally toxic environment. Hard to say, really.

"How's the book going?" I asked.

She smiled. "They say it should come out this summer!"

"That's amazing!" I said. "And quick."

"I know! It doesn't feel quick, but I know it is. And they're already interested in my next project. I haven't signed a contract yet, though. I'm still thinking about what to do. I mean, it would be great to have another book under contract already. On the other hand, it would be even better to have a contract with a more prestigious publisher. My current publisher is fine, but...I don't know. I think my next project might be really...it's probably overwhelming hubris to say *groundbreaking*, right? But I think it might be big, and I have all these dreams of being published by Oxford. Is that crazy? Is that *terrible*? Should I even be thinking about submitting to a more prestigious press when my current publisher has been so decent to me?"

"I think there's nothing wrong with aiming for the stars," I said. "Especially when it comes to getting tenure. If you think you could get published by Oxford, I say go for it. Everyone would understand."

"Maybe...of course, there's no guarantee at all that they'd accept me...they'd probably just laugh in my face...oh, look, there's Diane and Julie! Hi! How are you?"

Julie and Diane came over. We were now forming a little knot by the entrance to the faculty parking lot. Was this the "faculty togetherness" and "campus community" that people kept talking about, but had always seemed like an elusive phantom to me? I'd felt a certain amount of community with the other grad students in my cohort, but since graduating, I'd bounced from temporary position to temporary position, as had all my grad school friends. Now we were scattered all over the world, and the people we currently worked with were either in the same here-today-gone-tomorrow situation as we were, or were the people responsible for enforcing our precarity and desperation, and were therefore our de facto enemies.

Chloe, Julie, and Diane were discussing Chloe's upcoming book release with animation. Maybe there was hope, at least for Chloe.

"And Rowena has a book coming out soon, too, don't you?" she said, turning to me.

"I'm still doing the revisions," I said. "It's going very slowly."

Everyone nodded with understanding. I thought about telling them how I could barely stand to open the computer document, and that every time I looked at the reader comments, it took so much strength to keep from bursting into screams or dissolving into tears that I didn't have much left for any actual writing. I thought about telling them that the more I tried to work on it, the more I was overwhelmed by crippling doubt and near-suicidal despair. I thought about telling them that every time I so much as thought about it, I questioned its worth as a project, my own worth as a scholar, and my very right to exist as a sentient being. If I was wasting my time on this "poorly researched," "fundamentally flawed at the theoretical level," and "completely out of touch with the last thirty years of scholarship" project that "would be shameful to publish," to quote various reviewers, did I even deserve to exist at all? Shouldn't I be chucking it all in and devoting myself to pulling orphans out of burning buildings, which was the only thing that could possibly justify my continued existence after wasting the past half-decade of my life on something so stupid, pointless, and actively evil?

"I'm planning to be done by the end of the semester," I said. "They're saying that if I stick to that timeline, it should be ready to come out early next year."

"I'm so glad I never had to do a book," said Diane. She and Julie were both in the Biology department. The sciences rarely expected books. Just lots of articles and, preferably, major grants for big projects. "Although it sure feels like I've written at least a book's worth of grant proposals."

"No doubt," I said. I guess there was no way forward without extensive pain and punishment.

"Speaking of publishing..." Diane looked around conspiratorially. "I submitted an article about our buildings over break."

"Oh?" Diane had started an off-the-books project last semester taking samples for mold and other unpleasant substances in our buildings.

"Yeah. About what I found about elevated levels of *Stachybotrys, Aspergillus*, and other nasties." She made a face. "I'm keeping my expectations low, but I thought I might as well start getting it out there. I really need to partner with someone in health sciences, though. We need to correlate what's going on in the buildings with what's going on in us. Like, for example, all this *Aspergillus fumigatus* I've been finding in our classrooms. It's a well-known fact that *A. fumigatus* can colonize the human body, but it's normally only considered a danger to severely immunocompromised people, like folks who're undergoing chemo. But is it actually colonizing less sick people in lower doses, too, and causing low-level—or not so low-level—chronic health problems? We don't know enough to know. What we do know is that many people with 'sick building syndrome' improve after taking antifungal medications."

"Gosh," I said, while Mel said, "Fuck!"

"I don't want to alarm you," said Diane. "But you might consider adding more probiotics to your diet to try to out-compete the bad guys, just in case." She shrugged. "It's worth trying, anyway. I'm doing it." She glanced at her phone. "Is that the time?! Jules, we'd better hustle if we're going to make it to the Bio building by class time."

Mel, Chloe, and I all glanced at our phones too. 8:49.

"Shit!" said Mel. "Better double-time it. Come on, girls, let's get going."

61

BY MOVING AT A SEMI-jog that left us all breathless, Chloe, Mel, and I burst through the front doors of Bedford Hall at 8:57am. I told myself it was my own unfitness combined with the heavy bookbag and the sudden change from cold, damp air to warm, dry air that caused me to break out coughing as soon as I entered the building.

That was probably also the reason a stabbing pain struck above my left eye as soon as I stepped into the classroom, and I had a weird moment of disassociation and dizziness as I pulled out my materials and started arranging them on the lectern. It was unfitness and maybe acute nerves that I couldn't consciously acknowledge. That was it. It definitely wasn't because there was something wrong with the air. Other than the choking cloud of scent from personal products, dryer sheets, mildewed carpeting, and what I started thinking was mold from the big water stain in the ceiling above my head.

You're safe! I told myself. *You're safe, you're safe, you're safe!* If I said it enough times, it would be true. Of course, it hadn't been true when a student had come strolling into Bedford Hall armed to the teeth with automatic weapons and looking for one of my students. But actually, *I'd* been fine, right? Nothing—mainly due to luck—had happened to me. And the tightness in my chest and the stabbing pain in my left eye and the feeling that I wasn't in my body, but was instead floating somewhere above my left shoulder, was all probably just PTSD and maybe a little hypoxia from my aforementioned lack of fitness. I was totally fine and safe and everything would be okay.

Fixing on my best, brightest smile, and deliberately speaking as calmly and non-breathlessly as I could, I welcomed the 102 students back to Russian class, and started review.

Fortunately, their memory of the content of 101 was pretty much non-existent, so review took up most of my concentration, distracting me from my fears (that were completely groundless, right?). By the end of class, I felt more or less like I was back in my own body, although strangely jetlagged, as if I'd just gotten off the plane in Moscow and was standing in the line at passport control at what the local clocks were telling me was six in the morning, but my body was telling me was the previous evening. That was perfectly understandable, though. I'd been through a physical and emotional wringer over the past week, and I probably had a lot more physical and emotional wringing ahead of me.

There was a crush at the door as the 102 students tried to rush out and the 202 students tried to file in. Over everyone's milling heads, I caught sight of Miranda Arenson, the student I was closest to. Of course you weren't supposed to have favorites, or get close to any of your students, but...I saw so much of my younger self in Miranda it was impossible not to like her.

"Mira—" I started to call. Then I saw her turn around, rise up on her toes, and give a swift kiss to the boy behind her. I turned away, although everyone else was staring. Jamal, the boy, was Crimson's star football player. Everything he did was news, and kissing a girl in the hallway was particularly noteworthy.

Glad they're still together. Miranda and Jamal's relationship was definitely a case of opposites attract, and they'd both had more than their share of problems here at Crimson, which could have been another wedge between them. But here they were, apparently even more in love than before. It was heartening, as much as constancy in affection could be heartening in a couple who weren't even old enough to buy beer yet.

I watched out of the corner of my eye as Miranda and Jamal pulled apart, seemingly by force, and backed slowly away from each other, keeping eye contact until Miranda backed all the way into the classroom and the door frame cut them off from view of each other.

"Oh hey, Professor!" Miranda turned to face me, her pale cheeks flushed. Not, I guessed, from the excitement of an upcoming semester of learning about the imperative mood and verbs of motion (both prefixed and unprefixed). "Did you have a good break?"

"Pretty good," I said. "And you?"

"Okay. Actually, there's some stuff I wanted to talk to you about..." She looked around at the students filling up the cramped classroom. "Can we talk later? After class, maybe? I've got a request, actually."

"Sure," I said. "I have office hours right after this class. Or we can set up a time later, although I have to warn you that I'm, um, kind of busy with, um, other stuff right now."

"Yeah, me too. After class would be great. I've got...well, like, good news and bad news, I guess, and I wanted to talk to you about both."

"Great," I said. "Happy to help."

62

MIRANDA AND I REPAIRED to my broom-closet-like office after class. She filled me in on the doings at the *Crimson Champion*, the college paper, as we walked over. Once we got into my office, though, she fell silent, as if she didn't know where to start with her good news/bad news. Or maybe it was the dark, windowless, airless atmosphere of the tiny office.

"You said you had a request?" I prompted.

"Oh, yeah." Her face cleared at this apparently easy and straightforward question. "So, I'm already applying for internships for the summer..."

"That's great!" I said encouragingly.

"Yeah. Actually, I'm pretty excited about some of them...especially one that's at a community paper in Brighton Beach. You know Brighton Beach?"

"I've heard of it," I said.

"Apparently it's, like, all Russian. Like, all the stores and restaurants and stuff are Russian, and even some of the street signs."

"This is what I hear," I said.

"Yeah. Sounds awesome, right? At least, I think so. So I'm applying to an internship there, and they're asking for a letter of recommendation from my Russian teacher..."

Miranda trailed off, not meeting my eyes. Asking for letters of recommendation was one of those hazing rituals/rites of passage that college students got to experience a lot. I was guessing this was the first time she'd done it. By the time she was a senior, she'd be hardened to the embarrassment, but at the moment, it was almost unbearable.

"I'd be happy to write a letter of recommendation for you," I said. "Just let me know what kind of information they need and where to send it. If you have a statement of purpose or something like that, it would be very helpful."

"Really? That's great!"

"No problem," I said. "Happy to help."

"Great! I can't wait to tell Jamal..." Her animation suddenly drained away. "That's...that's the other thing I wanted to talk to you about." She was speaking in a half-whisper now, leaning towards me across the desk, as if afraid of being overheard by hostile forces. "I'm afraid...Jamal's coming under a lot of pressure over...well, his advocacy for, you know..."

Her voice dropped to a complete whisper. "*Changing sports culture*," she hissed. "He's been pretty outspoken about it. And the team and the college are supporting him publicly. But he thinks they're not happy about it. And he's afraid...he's afraid he's going to be cut from the team. And if he gets cut from the team, he'll lose his scholarship, and if he loses his scholarship, he'll have to drop out. And then what'll he do? He won't have football *or* a degree. He doesn't know what he'll do then."

"That does sound bad," I said.

"Yeah. I know there's nothing you can do about it directly. I mean, it's not like you can make the team keep him on or anything. I guess I just wanted to tell someone about it."

"Has he talked to Irene about it?" I asked. Irene was a retired lawyer who had taken on Jamal's case pro bono last year when it looked like he was going to be expelled, if not worse, over his involvement in some very ill-advised fraternity activities.

She shook her head. "Not yet. I think he's afraid to go to her...she was just helping him out for free last year...and he's embarrassed to tell her he's having problems again..."

"Let me talk to her," I said. "Maybe she'll have some good advice."

"You'd do that? Wow, thanks!" Miranda straightened up, her pale cheeks flushing again, this time with happiness and hope.

"No problem," I said. "Happy to help however I can."

63

NO ONE ELSE CAME DURING office hours. I spent the time clearing out a couple dozen inconsequential emails, and then headed for my lit class. I was on a 2/3 schedule, meaning I taught two classes in the fall and three in the spring: the first- and second-year language sequences both semesters, and then an extra literature and culture survey class in the spring. That class fulfilled the World Cultures requirement, and was vastly more popular than the language courses.

I entered the classroom—not the cramped windowless corner we used for the language classes, but a bigger windowless corner that still managed to be filled to overflowing once all the students crammed in—with a certain amount of apprehension. The last time I'd taught this class, it had involved a fair amount of drama. But other than the battery-farm-style overcrowding, there was no drama today. Maybe it was waiting for the middle of the semester to reveal itself.

I was half-hoping, half-fearing that Karen would corner me in the hallway after class with vaguely muttered threats about tomorrow's interview, but I saw no sign of her. Karen was our much-hated department chair, who combined boundless ill will with stunning incompetence. I liked to believe that she was the exception rather than the rule, but I was coming to the bleak conclusion that people like her were the norm in higher ed. That's what a couple decades of the system did to you. In my lower moments—which happened about three times a day, at least—I saw my future as becoming Karen. If I didn't manage to save myself somehow, it could and almost certainly would happen. I reminded myself that I was aware of the problem and could make the conscious choice to avoid it. That was less comforting than I would have liked.

"No sign of Karen?" I asked Mel when we met up after our last classes.

Mel shook her head. "Nope. Haven't seen hide nor hair of her all day. And I heard people talking about her in the ladies' room. Apparently she's out sick."

"Oh. Wonder what that means for our interviews?"

"I've been wondering the exact same damn thing," said Mel. "But so far I haven't heard a word about it."

I pulled out my phone. "Nothing in my inbox...Oh. Wow. Golly."

"What is it?" asked Mel. She gave me a second, sharper look. "Bad news?"

"I don't...I don't think so. It's just...it's a long story, but I've been trying to get in touch with a...with a family member. I had kind of given up on her getting back to me. But she just responded."

In the middle of my phone screen was a notification from Facebook Messenger. From Roseanna.

Dear Rowena, it said. *Please give me a call. Here's my number.*

64

I SAID WE SHOULD GO ahead and go home. I'd call Roseanna there, without any rush or interruptions. Mel agreed that was the best plan.

"You got a history with this family member?" she asked as we pulled out of the faculty parking lot. "You have that look. I know it well. And you don't have to tell me about it, but if you ever want to unload about difficult family stuff, I'm always here to listen. Like I said, I'm a world champion at difficult family stuff. Well, not at solving it. At surviving it."

"Thanks," I said. "It's...complicated. And I don't know the whole story. But it turns out there's this whole other side of my family I didn't know about, and they have...history. Also, some of them might be in a cult."

"Got some of those people in my family, too," said Mel.

"Really? Any success at getting them out?"

"No, but my mom totally wrecked her relationship with her sister by trying. So I guess I'd say be careful how you go about it."

"Good to know," I said. "How was class?"

We spent the rest of the ride home comparing notes on the first day of classes. Neither of us had any major incidents to report, which was always a plus. Mel was also cautiously optimistic about her health after getting through all three classes with minimal difficulty.

"That's great!" I said. I didn't say anything about my weird headache and disassociation at the start of the first class. Thinking about it was too scary. Besides, it was probably all from stress, right?

I dropped Mel off at her apartment and checked in with Galina Ivanovna. She was up and about when I knocked at her door. I offered to make her lunch, but she waved me away.

"You look tired, Innochka, and no wonder. I'll just have one of my astronaut meals by myself and then take a little nap. You go rest and catch up on work, and we'll have supper together. Dima texted, by the way. He said he made it to Security Solutions headquarters just fine."

"That's great." I repressed a twinge of hurt that Dima hadn't texted me as well. He probably hadn't wanted to disturb me during class. He'd probably get in touch with me this evening. He'd want to share his impressions of his first day at Security Solutions, and we'd have a good long talk about it...I jerked myself out of that fantasy. Maybe it would happen, or maybe he'd go incommunicado and not even think of contacting me until he was back. I couldn't hang all my hopes on him being in a sharing mood.

"I'll let you rest, then," I said to Galina Ivanovna. "I have some things to do, but it shouldn't take too long. Let me know if you need something, or you want to go somewhere, or you just want to come over and visit."

She patted my hand. "Of course, dear, of course. You go take care of everything you need to take care of, and we'll have supper together later. Don't worry about me. I have reading to do." She held up a dark green hardback with gold lettering.

"Sounds great," I said. And I went to make my phone calls.

65

I DECIDED TO START off with Irene Collins. I always found that promises hung over me balefully until I fulfilled them. Talking to Irene about Jamal would get that out of the way, and give me a little more time to prepare myself to talk to Roseanna.

Irene picked up on the first ring. "Rowena, darling!" she cried. "So good to hear from you!"

"Good to hear from you, too," I said.

"Please tell me you're calling to ask for a favor!" she said. "I'm so bored in retirement I could just *die*. Helping out that Jamal kid was the only thing that brought *any* spice into my life last year. Alan"—Alan was Irene's husband—"didn't like it; he keeps telling me I need to take it easy, work on my golf game, but I swear, it's like my whole soul just *dies* every time I find myself standing around and chit-chatting with the little old ladies there—and I can't *believe*, darling, that I'm a little old lady too—I'm not, am I? I'm *not* a little old lady, no matter what my birthdate is and what everyone keeps trying to tell me."

"Well," I said, "in that case, I have good news. I'm actually calling you about Jamal."

"Oh good!" Irene cleared her throat. "I suppose I shouldn't have expressed my joy *quite* so openly, should I? I suppose you're calling me about him because he's in trouble again?"

I outlined Jamal's current situation as Miranda had described it.

"Grrrr!" Irene tried to make a growl of rage, but it came out as more of a purr of satisfaction. "Of *course* they're doing this to him, hun. That's how they are—terrified of bad press, and doing everything they can to bring it crashing down on their heads. Bless their little hearts. Well, it keeps folks like me busy. I'll call up a couple of other board members...no, wait, I should talk to Jamal first...I'll give him a call right away...you don't mind if I hang up right now so I can call him, do you, sweetheart?"

"Not at all," I said. "Thanks for helping."

"Thank *you*, darling...I can't *wait* to take on a project like this again..." And, practically chortling with glee, Irene hung up.

66

WELL, THAT WAS EASY. I sent up a quick prayer that Jamal's problems would be just tricky enough to keep Irene entertained for a few weeks, but not so serious that they actually caused him any real trouble. Now for the more difficult call.

I had lunch, played with Fevronia, checked my inbox, answered a few of the more time-critical emails, started a load of laundry, wrote out a grocery list, and did a quick lesson-planning session. Only when I'd finished all the easy tasks and was trying to psych myself up for the final round of prep for my interview tomorrow did the pain of procrastinating become worse than the pain of picking up the phone.

When I did pick up the phone, my fingers were clumsy and cold, and I misdialed Roseanna's number twice before I finally got it right and got through.

It rang. Once. Twice. Three times. Four times. Five...Just when I was thinking that Roseanna wasn't there, and trying to decide whether I was more disappointed or relieved, she answered.

"Hello?" The voice on the other end of the call was firm, and much younger than I would have expected from a woman in her eighties. Also slightly suspicious, as if she expected the worst from unexpected callers, but was determined to give them the benefit of a tiny sliver of doubt nonetheless.

"Uh, hi," I said. "Is this Roseanna Halley?"

"Yes. Who's calling?" The suspicion had sharpened, as had the suffer-no-fools attitude. A faint steel magnolia Southern accent.

"It's, ah, Rowena. Rowena Halley."

"Oh." There was a pause on the other end of the line.

"Little Rowena," she said eventually. "I don't supposed you're so little anymore."

"Not really," I said. I thought about adding that I was 5'10" and almost 37 years old, but decided that would be childish.

"You probably don't remember me," she said after another pause.

"Well...no. To be honest, I, um, didn't even know you existed until this weekend."

There was a long exhale on the other end of the line. "I guess I shouldn't be surprised," she said. "And I guess that means I shouldn't feel hurt anymore that you never contacted me."

"Well," I said. "Um, no? I got in touch with you as soon as I found out about you."

"So who told you about me?" She sounded genuinely curious. I could hear the native intellect coming through the suspicion and hurt.

"I, um, did some digging on my own and, uh, came across your name, and then I asked my grandmother...um, my other grandmother, I guess, and she told me...all kinds of things," I finished lamely.

Another long exhale, this time with a hint of a chuckle to it. "Edith must have been bursting to tell that tale for decades," she said. "I'm astonished she managed to hold it in for as long as she did."

"She said it was difficult," I admitted.

A short laugh. "I'll bet she did. But I'm glad she told you. Someone needed to. I kept waiting to hear from you...I never could understand why Dennis and Alexandra didn't try harder to keep in contact with you...well, I did, but I thought they were being foolish...and your parents should have forgiven and forgotten long ago...have you talked to them recently?"

"Um, Dennis and Alexandra?" It felt weird to call them by their names, but calling them "my grandparents" felt even weirder, so I didn't.

"Yes. Have you been in contact with them?"

"Not me personally, no, but my parents and my brother are with them right now."

"Little Vannie," Roseanna said, her voice full of a new warmth. "But he doesn't go by that name anymore, does he?"

"He goes by John now," I told her.

"And he's in the Marines? An officer?"

"That's right."

"I always knew he'd do something good with his life." Her voice was warmer and warmer. "I always knew he'd do something worthwhile."

"Yeah," I said.

"And what about you? Are you doing something worthwhile with your life?"

"Um," I said. "I guess. I'm, uh, a teacher."

"A teacher!" I couldn't tell whether the surprise in her voice was approval or disapproval. "Where do you teach? What subject?"

"Russian," I said. "At Crimson College, at the moment."

"Oh! You mean you're a professor."

"Um," I said. "Sort of."

"Dennis did tell me a few years ago that you'd gotten into graduate school...he actually sounded proud for once...but I never heard whether you'd finished or not...we haven't..." She trailed off.

"I finished," I said.

"So you got a Master's?"

"Um, no, I got a PhD."

"A PhD! You earned a doctorate! In Russian?"

"Um," I said. "Yeah."

"Well! Isn't that something. And I'd say you're doing something worthwhile with your life for sure. I don't know very many others in my church whose granddaughters...I mean..." She trailed off again, awkwardly.

"Um, yeah," I said, to fill the silence. "My grandmother...Edith...said you sort of...raised my father?"

Another long exhale. "I suppose she told you the whole sorry story? About Alexandra's...problems?"

"She said she had post-partum depression," I said. "And what sounds like some pretty, um, invasive treatments. It's no wonder..."

"It's no wonder," Roseanna interrupted me. "Yes, I know. No one feels sorrier for her than I do. No one knows better what she went through than I do. She was an only child, you know, with no sisters to help her out. Her mother passed away when she was a teenager, and she had no aunts. So I was the only female relative she had, even if I was just a sister-in-law. Dennis..." She made an exasperated sound, stopped, brought herself under control, and continued. "Dennis was worse than useless. Forgive me for speaking ill of your grandfather. I know you and he aren't close, and while I love him like a brother, I also know all his faults like only a sister can. So you might as well know the truth."

"Thanks," I said. "My feelings won't be hurt by the truth, I promise."

Actually, hearing her say bad things about my grandparents *was* causing me pain, even though the very little I knew about them was pretty much all bad. Hearing John, or even my other grandmother, say bad things about them hadn't bothered me at all; in fact, I had enjoyed hearing the truth and getting this proof of the close relationship between me and the truth-teller. But Roseanna felt like more of a stranger, and I instinctively bristled at what felt like an attack from a stranger on people who were...I didn't know what to call them...Russian had better words for this; in Russian I could simply call them *svoi* and *chuzhiye* and everyone would know what I meant. But "my own" and "alien" didn't have the same connotations in English.

In any case, I noted that my subconscious considered Alexandra and Dennis to be "my own" and Roseanna to be "alien," even though by some measures it should be the other way around. Because I'd just learned of her existence? Because for me she was still just an ephemeral concept, nothing more than a voice on the phone, while Dennis and Alexandra had actually made a flesh-and-blood appearance in my life on a couple of (supremely uncomfortable) occasions? Or the closer genetic connection of grandparent rather than great-aunt exerting an unconscious pull?

"You can tell me anything," I said firmly. "I want to know the truth, and...I'm used to hearing shocking things."

"Really? Like what?" Roseanna sounded genuinely curious once again, and also a little skeptical.

"Um...like the confession of a boy who murdered his sister in an honor killing and then ran off to join a terrorist training camp? Like, the story of someone who had his fingernails ripped out during interrogation? Or, um, the story of the person who did the ripping? Or, um..."

"I get it. Where on *earth* did you hear stories like that?"

"I worked for a human rights NGO for a while. We got around."

"I see. Well, maybe you *are* ready to hear what I have to say, although in my experience, it's different when it's your own family instead of someone else's."

"I'm sure," I said.

"Well. Anyway. Dennis." She *tsked*. "My little brother. Does it surprise you to know that your little brother is always your little brother, even when you're our age?"

"No," I said.

"He never was very brave about things like this," she said. "Ever since he was a child. When we were little...but I'd better save early childhood stories for later. But suffice to say that Dennis completely fell apart when their first child...did Edith tell you about that?"

"She did," I said. "It sounds terrible."

"It was even more terrible than it sounded," Roseanna said. "Those things always are. So Dennis completely fell apart, which he showed by ignoring the situation as much as possible. Tried to pretend it hadn't happened, and that Alexandra wasn't going out of her mind from grief. Told her it was God's will, and she was ungrateful not to accept that. Are you religious?" The last question was fired out abruptly.

"Um," I said. "Not really, no."

She made a *hmphing* noise. "I shouldn't be surprised, knowing how I'm sure you were raised. How long were you at that commune?"

"Till I was eight," I said. "It was *awesome*."

"No doubt it was." Her voice softened. "No doubt it was all kinds of fun for a little child. But it might not have been what you needed to get you set up for life."

I held my tongue. I thought it had been better than almost anything else I could have had, realistically, to set me up for life, but getting into an argument over that would do nothing to help John. Gotta keep my eye on the mission.

"Anyway," said Roseanna after a moment. "That's neither here nor there. You'll find as you get older that you need something to help you through life's hard times, and for most of us, that's religion. But you have to know how to use it. How to let it help you. Dennis always tried to use it as a shield to save him from real life. And poor Alexandra...that was probably the worst thing he could have done."

"Mmm," I said.

"And then when little Bobby was born...your father...Alexandra had been in such a state throughout the entire pregnancy, she was so afraid that...well, you understand. And Dennis just kept talking about God's will and telling her she needed to calm down. And then, after the birth, Alexandra was so happy...so happy...for a couple of days. And then..."

There was a sound like she was shaking her head. "I don't know what happened," she said. "But *something* happened the day she brought that baby home from the hospital. Some switch was flipped inside her. And she became...well, you heard about it. Maybe Edith embellished the tale with her own prejudices—Edith and Alexandra never could stand each other, of course—but I don't know that someone like Edith could imagine the darkness that Alexandra found herself drowning in."

Another rustling shake of the head. Another long inhale and exhale. "And Dennis didn't want to have anything to do with the baby, of course," she said. "Or with his own wife. Just kept going on about God's will. And then...well, you know the main thing. Alexandra went away to be treated in a clinic, and I took in Bobby. There was no question of Dennis being his caregiver, you understand."

"Mmm-hmmm," I said.

"Bobby was the sweetest little boy." Roseanna's voice warmed again, remembering. "A perfect little boy. I couldn't have asked for a better son...I don't know where he came from...and then he went back to Alexandra, back to Dennis...and then he grew up and ran off with that woman...your mother, I mean...but they had another perfect little boy...the moment I laid eyes on him, I knew he was the most perfect little boy who'd ever been born, even more perfect than Bobby...I could already tell he'd look like me, just like me...and then there was that scene...the wedding...and your mother never got over it...I understand why, even though I can't forgive her for it...but Alexandra had no one else other than me; Dennis didn't count, of course, so I had to stand up for her, stick with her...and then...and then...I spent my whole life standing up for them, sticking with them, and they left me, they left me for that *liar*, that *fraud*...it makes me want to spit just thinking about him..."

"Are you talking about Jeremiah Jones?" I asked.

67

THERE WAS A LONG SILENCE at the other end of the line.

"Are you connected with the church?" Roseanna eventually asked. "The Church of the Holy Light?"

"No," I said. "I only just heard of them. You see, um, Dennis and Alexandra reached out to my parents recently, and then to John. They're all over with them right now. John's concerned about their involvement in this, ah, church, and he asked me to look into it. I haven't had much luck so far, but while I was reading old newspaper articles I came across your name, and I thought you might know something...I had no idea what I was going to stumble into..."

Another long silence from Roseanna. Then she laughed. A short, harsh laugh, but definitely an expression of mirth.

"Isn't life funny," she said. "I was so angry with Dennis and Alexandra for leaving me and our church to take up with that...that *charlatan*. After everything I'd done for them! After I'd chosen to stand by them, even though it meant giving up..." She stopped, swallowed, and carried on, her voice thick. "...Giving up Bobby...his beautiful little boy...his beautiful little girl...I should have been there for you! I should have been there for you. Every day...anyway."

Her voice grew firm again, all the steel in her steel magnolia showing its strength. "I was *furious* with them. And I thought...a dozen, no, a hundred, times I thought about reaching out to you...actually, I *did* reach out to Bobby and Bev. But they never got back to me, and I thought, 'Well, I guess that's that.' I've just been sitting here feeling sorry for myself instead of doing anything." Humor tinged the despair in her voice. "But then here you come, tracking me down because of Dennis and Alexandra's foolishness and ingratitude."

"Fate works in mysterious ways," I said.

"It does. And so do prayers, it seems. Anyway, you wanted to know about Jeremiah Jones? That's the real reason you called?"

"Well, once I found out about you, I wanted to get to know you, too," I said. "But my original motivation was to find out more about the church and whether, ah, there might be...issues. John is, um, concerned."

"How concerned?" she asked briskly. I wondered what she'd done with her life other than taking care of her sister-in-law and volunteering at church. Here was a born manager if there ever was one.

"Concerned enough to ask me to dig around and see what I can find," I said. "Concerned enough to set up daily check-ins, with instructions to contact the authorities if I don't hear from him."

"Goodness!" She paused. "I knew that church was trouble, but I never thought they might be in *danger*. Does Vannie...does *John* have concrete reasons for his suspicions?"

"I think it's mainly just vibes," I said. "But he doesn't like that they're pressuring him and our parents to convert and sign over money, or that they're trying to monitor and control his internet usage."

"Yes." It came out as an exasperated sigh. "Alexandra always was afraid of the internet. Not that she's entirely wrong...it certainly causes so much trouble...but one can take things too far. I know it was one of the things that attracted her to them in the first place. She didn't like that our church was trying to move with the times, get a fancy new website, set up social media accounts, even experiment with joint live-streamed meetings and events. As the co-director of the choir, she was getting asked to post about it on social media, or at least provide material so others could post about it—you know, stay relevant for the youth, that kind of thing.

"I could understand why they wanted to do that, even though I'm old enough to be suspicious of all these new-fangled gadgets and the fads that go with them. But Alexandra practically had a nervous breakdown when they brought it up. She's one of those people who's had a hard life and been mistreated, and so she tries to bully others and get her way over minor things. She's been forced to give up so much that mattered that she can never give way graciously over things that don't matter.

"She made this her crusade...and in general she and Dennis were having a hard time...you know, in every relationship, there come moments when you question what you're doing, you start to doubt and dislike the other person...and I think things were weighing on them both. They were both realizing that the bulk of their life was behind them and they needed to take stock of how they'd lived and prepare to answer for their actions...anyway. What I'm saying is that they were ripe for the picking. Then Jeremiah Jones came along. He probably seemed safe. He was in our church, you know, back in the day. Then his wife died, and he started a grief group. What he *should* have been doing was taking care of his poor motherless little boy, but he ignored his son and threw himself into what he called 'God's work' instead. The next thing we knew, he was off starting his own church—and taking a lot of our members with him. They went with him because he was telling them exactly what they wanted to hear. Telling them that they could fix everything, make up for everything they'd done, if only they joined his church. 'Church.'

She snorted. "Typical cult behavior. Promising to fix problems that can't be fixed, in exchange for total obedience and, oh, by the way, half your money. Or all of it."

"Uh-huh," I said.

"I tried to talk them out of it," she continued. "I did look into it, asked around, even went to a couple of services. I never found anything that you could call *illegal*, but I did get a 'bad vibe,' as you said. I told them that, and they told me they didn't want to have anything to do with me, I was a bad influence and they didn't want to taint their chances of salvation by associating with me. And I—I admit—I lost my temper. I decided I'd had enough, threw up my hands, and walked away. And I haven't tried again."

"Very understandable," I said. "But I'm probably going to have to try, so anything you can suggest that might help would be welcome."

Roseanna laughed another short, sharp laugh. "Goodness, you are a little bloodhound, aren't you?"

"It sounds like I come by it honestly," I said.

"That's nice of you to think so, but frankly speaking, I never saw much sign of curiosity or tenacity in either Dennis or Alexandra."

"I wasn't talking about them," I said. "I was talking about you."

Another long silence at the other end of the line. When Roseanna broke it, her voice was thick again. "Thank you, darling," she said. "I think you might be right. And...if I were you, I'd try to talk to Isaiah Jones, Jeremiah's son. He's his father's righthand man now, but he ran off in the past and I wouldn't be surprised if he still bears a grudge for the way his father treated him. He might be the lever you need to pry out some dirt on Jeremiah and the church. And either way, I think you and I should meet."

"I think so too," I said.

68

WE AGREED THAT I WOULD at some point go up to Virginia to meet with Roseanna in person, although it might not be right away. I told her that the semester was just starting, I had an interview tomorrow, and I was also taking care of a friend who was in a clinical trial.

"Goodness," she said. "For cancer?"

"Kidney failure," I told her.

"My word. Poor thing. You don't see a lot of people your age with kidney failure."

"She's older. She's, um...it's complicated, but she's the mother of, um, a friend of mine from Russia. They came over here specifically for the treatment."

"Well. That does sound like there's quite a story there. And how kind of you to help them out."

"They would do the same for me, and more," I said. "But I'm not sure when I'll be able to leave them."

"I understand. But we'll keep in touch, won't we, and we'll set up a meeting as soon as you're available."

"For sure," I promised. "And let me know if you hear anything, or think of anything...to be honest, I'm pretty worried. John is spooked, and John doesn't get spooked. I won't feel better until he and our parents are back home, and I won't really feel better until I know for sure what's going on with, um, Dennis and Alexandra."

"I will. And I suppose we might as well 'friend' each other on Facebook. Do you go on there often? I'm on there a few times a week. Somehow it seems like that's where most of my friends are, these days. So many of them have moved away to be with their families, or they're in nursing homes or care facilities. So we all share news about our lives on Facebook, and pretend it's the same as actually being friends.

"We don't even pick up the phone anymore...although, truth be told, we probably wouldn't have anyway. Most of us were only ever friends because we saw each other Sunday mornings and Wednesday evenings. I guess this is the same, except we're casual friends on the internet instead of in church. Although this way it certainly seems like people are a lot meaner to each other. Do you notice that?"

"I do," I said.

"Well, promise you won't be mean to me on Facebook, and I'll 'friend' you there. That way I can at least learn a little about your life."

"I don't post there a lot anymore," I said. "But please do friend me. Maybe I'll start posting more again someday." I almost said *when I have some news worth sharing*, but stopped myself. Then she'd want to know what kind of news I might have, and I didn't want to talk about it, especially since I wasn't sure what kind of news worth sharing I wanted to have. Instead, we said our goodbyes, and hung up.

I wanted to call John right away, but decided I should wait for his evening check-in before trying to contact him. Didn't want to put him in danger through a thoughtless phone call. My conversation with Roseanna had reassured me slightly about their physical safety, but worried me more about their spiritual and financial safety. But there wasn't a lot I could do about it right now.

There was no help for it. I had to prep for tomorrow's interview.

69

I REVIEWED THE COVER letter, CV, teaching and research statements, sample syllabi, and representative article I'd submitted, as well as the college and department websites. There was no new information there, but it was a soothing ritual. I tried to come up with some kind of super-excellent argument of why they should hire me for the tenure-track position. The best one I could think of was that I was already here. And I really needed the job, but that was better not to share. I should frame it as "I really *wanted* the job." Unfortunately, that wasn't true. I didn't particularly want the job, but I did really need it. So I should get myself together and prepare to put my best foot forward.

Galina Ivanovna came over just when I thought I couldn't bear another minute of looking at my application materials and preparing to answer questions that would be both completely rote and frighteningly out of left field. We had a cheery supper and discussed her readings from the day, which pulled me out of my weepy mood.

If I had this every evening, would my job seem less awful? I wondered. *If I was working to support someone else, would I find it more meaningful?* Somehow working to support myself had always felt hollow and selfish. Of course, my current job was supposedly benefiting others as well, but mostly it felt like I was being used to make money for people who didn't know I existed and whose core values were diametrically opposed to my own. But if I were doing it for someone else, someone who needed me, would the job itself take on a more meaningful glow, or at least seem like less of a giant waste of time? Something to contemplate.

Galina Ivanovna started to yawn shortly after we finished supper. I suggested she head off to bed.

"I'm waiting for a call from Dima—has he contacted you today?"

I shook my head. "No news is good news," I said, as lightly as I could.

Galina Ivanovna shook her head too, but with disapproval. "He never seems to understand that we're waiting to hear from him," she said. "For all that he's a writer—and my mother's heart leaps with pride very time I say those words!—he has a hard time putting himself in others' shoes, others' hearts. I guess this is why he's a journalist, not a novelist. Maybe someday he'll grow into being a novelist, but not yet, not yet."

I smiled and shrugged and didn't say anything. After a moment, Galina Ivanovna patted my shoulder, said she'd let me know if she got a message from Dima, and left.

The apartment seemed especially lonely after that. I spent a while carefully handwashing the dishes, just for the sound of the running water. Fevronia came out and watched me for a while, but when I bent down to pet her, she swiped at me and dashed back to the bedroom.

I followed her, unable to think of anything better to do. She was standing on her hind legs, batting at the edge of the comforter, playing like a kitten.

"Do you want to play?" I asked her.

She stopped and looked at me suspiciously. I tried twitching the corner of the comforter. She continued to stare suspiciously, then retreated under the bed. Oh well. At least I'd tried.

I was considering working on my book just for something to do, when my phone *pinged.*

I snatched it up, hoping it would be Dima. Instead, it was a message from John.

You able to take a call right now?

70

I HIT "CALL." JOHN picked up on the first ring.

"Ro! Thank fuck you called. I'm going crazy here."

"Are you okay?" I asked. "Is everyone okay?"

"We haven't been chained to a rock and used for human sacrifice yet, if that's what you mean."

"Well, that's something," I said.

"Yeah, it's mainly the boredom that's killing me. That, and the psy ops tactics they're using on me. Have you ever been told something you know is wrong so many times that you start to doubt your own fuckin' mind?"

"Many times," I said.

"Yeah...the more I get told about the Church of the Holy Light and why I should join it, the more freaked out I get—and the more I wonder if they're not right."

"That is often the way," I said. "But you probably should go with your initial instinct and not join. I've had a break in the case. I've got some intel for you, and I might have more soon."

"Hit me," said John.

"Have you ever heard of our aunt, Roseanna Arlene Halley?" I asked.

"No...wait. Alexandra—she likes to be called 'Grandmother,' by the fuckin' way, but I can hardly make my mouth say the fuckin' words—said something about 'Roseanna' the other day, and everyone looked at her like she'd grown a giant weird-ass second head or some shit, and she shut the fuck up. Even Mom and Dad gave her some serious fuckin' death glare hate shit. Sorry about all the fucks, by the way. I'm trying to keep them inside, 'cause I know they'd kill 'Grandmother' and 'Grandfather' if they heard 'em, and now I'm so full of fucks I think I'm gonna explode."

"Very understandable," I said. "Feel free to spew them out now so you don't burst."

"Thanks, Ro. You're the best fuckin' kid sister I've ever the fuck had."

"It's nice to know I beat out such a large field," I said.

"Fuckin' wiseass," said John, but he was already sounding less frantic.

"Anyway," I said. "I talked to our aunt, Dennis's sister, Roseanna Arlene today. I was named after her, by the way."

"Fuuuuuuuuuck," said John. "And you and I never even heard about her? What the fuck is going on there?"

"That's probably something we should talk to Mom and Dad about, but maybe not right now," I said. "Suffice to say that there's a lot of family drama in that backstory, but you should wait until you're all back home and safe to get into it."

"Just when I thought things couldn't get any more fucked up," said John. "You know, I always thought we were pretty good in the family department. Yeah, Mom and Dad are fruitcakes, but they're good fruitcakes, you know what I mean? I was all pissed off at them when I was a teenager, but when I saw the scars on the backs of a lot of the other kids at basic...or heard about all their half-brothers and sisters scattered around the country...or their crackwhore moms or sex predator deadbeat dads...well, even my thick head could grasp that maybe I hadn't had it so tough after all."

"Yeah," I said.

"But now you're saying we've got an aunt, an aunt you're named after, that they've been keeping secret from us all this time? That's some seriously fucked-up shit."

"Yeah," I said again. "She actually still lives up there in Virginia, right in Christiansburg. But seriously, don't bring her up. Not unless you want a huge scene."

"Got it. Is she completely batshit crazy?"

"Not as far as I can tell," I said.

"So...it's the folks here who are batshit crazy?"

"There was a lot going on in the family, it seems," I said.

"No fuckin' kidding. You'll have to fill me in when I get home. Anyway, I wanted to talk to you about two things. Number one: The whole situation with the will here. Turns out that our grandparents have a lot more money than any of us thought."

"Oh," I said.

"Yeah. Like, if they split it between us, we'd both be...well, I won't say rich, exactly, but we'd never have to worry about living in poverty or working some shitty job just to pay rent ever again."

"Oh." I physically bit down on my tongue to stop myself from asking if they were, in fact, planning to split the money between us. I was afraid I would sound desperately eager.

"Yeah. Only they're not planning on doing that."

"Oh." *Good thing I didn't ask.* I tried to pretend a bolt of extreme disappointment hadn't just lanced through my insides.

"Instead, they're sticking with their original plan, which is to give their house and a lot of their money to me—*if* I join their fuckin' church and give most of the money back to it."

"Oh." I told myself that the weird feeling writhing inside my chest was relief at not having to deal with that, not crippling envy and resentment that John, who needed it a lot less than I did, was being offered a life-altering amount of money, while I was being ignored entirely.

"So I was like, fuck, no, first of all, I don't know about this fuckin' church of yours, and second and most fuckin' importantly of all, what the fuck about Ro? You just gonna leave her out in the fuckin' cold?"

"Thanks," I said. "I appreciate that."

"If you'd seen how they looked at me when I said your name, you'd be a lot less fuckin' appreciative," said John. "First they said it needed to go from first-born son to first-born son. I was all like what the fuck is this, the fuckin' House of Windsor or some shit like that. Also, who the fuck do you think I am, taking money that should be my sister's." John's voice was rising from a semi-whisper to a semi-shout.

"Sorry," he said, going back to the semi-whisper. "Don't wanna get caught. But I was so fuckin' pissed—I mean, who *do* they think I fuckin' am? What kinda brother steals his sister's money?"

"Apparently the kind who goes to their church," I said. "Although I suppose technically you wouldn't be stealing it. It's their money. They can give it to whomever they want."

"Yeah, what the fuck ever. That's a shitty thing to do and a shitty thing to try to pin on me, so don't you try to fuckin' justify it, Ro."

"I'm not," I said. "But it is their money, and they can do whatever they want with it, and I'm not going to try to force or wheedle them into giving me any if they don't want to."

John laughed. "Good on you, Ro. Anyway, when I told them I wasn't taking a cent of their fuckin' money unless they gave you half, first they said it had to go from firstborn son to firstborn son, and then they said, no, wait a minute, sure, we'll give some to Rowena—if she marries someone from the church."

"Um..." I said.

"I already said I doubted you'd fuckin' go for it," said John.

"Thanks," I said.

"Anytime. But I wanted to let you know, just in case...well, Mom and Dad are kinda for it. It's fuckin' freaky. Like I said, I always knew they were fruitcakes, I just thought they were good fruitcakes—but now their fundamental fruitcakeness is starting to show. We all went to a service at their crazy church. I thought I was gonna fuckin' bust a gut trying not to scream in agony from all the shit that the preacher was spouting. But afterwards Mom and Dad started talking about how great it was to feel like part of a community again, and all kindsa shit about the decline of communal life and communal values and relationships and shit, and how we needed more of what the church was offering."

"Well..." I said.

"Oh, don't the fuck try and fuckin' justify this shit, Ro! I'm all about brotherhood and shit, you *know* that, but this shit is just too fucked up!"

"Yeah," I agreed.

"Anyway, I was afraid Mom and Dad would get a wild hair up their asses and call you and try to get you to come up and marry one of these degenerates for money, so I wanted to head them off at the pass."

"I appreciate it," I said.

"Plus I got a favor to ask you."

"Go ahead," I said.

"It's..." He paused. I could hear him shifting around on whatever he was sitting on. "Well...I didn't know who else to ask...I figured I needed a female perspective..."

"Uh-huh?" I said.

"It's about Camila."

"Uh-huh?" I said again.

"So...and of course it fuckin' happened now, when I'm up to my ass in this shit...I've been getting, well...I don't wanna say stalked, but it is kinda...*stalked* by her ex-boyfriend."

"Oh," I said.

"Yeah. Turns out they were still technically a couple, at least in his mind, when she and I first met. I asked her about it and she said he'd told her he needed his space, then basically fuckin' ghosted her, so she figured it was over and she could go do whoever the fuck she liked, but now he's back in the picture and saying she's a cheater and I stole her away and he's gonna take her back from me and all kindsa shit like that. He's been blowing up my phone all weekend about it."

"Has he been doing the same to Camila?" I asked.

"She says no, but..." He groaned. "I don't know what to do. I'm pretty sure she's fuckin' hiding something from me, like maybe he's stalking her too and she's scared to tell me. I've tried to have it out with her, but she basically handed me my ass back on a fuckin' platter. Guess that's what I get for dating a fuckin' lawyer."

"Uh-huh," I said.

"And I'm in the middle of all this shit here, and I...I thought maybe you'd have some good advice for me. I don't fuckin' know what to do, Ro. What if she's in real trouble? What if he's a psycho and he decides to attack her? Even if he doesn't hurt her, what if he's making her life a living hell, and I'm up here in fuckin' Virginia, and she won't tell me what the fuck's going on? How do I get her to tell me what's happening?"

"Do you think she was stalked before?" I asked. "Or otherwise in an abusive relationship?"

He groaned again. "I hate to even fuckin' think about it...but the more I think about stuff, all kindsa little stuff that flew over my head when we first got together, the more I think that yeah, maybe she was just getting out of a, whaddya call 'em, a toxic relationship with a creepy stalker guy. I'm now thinking she picked me 'cause she was on the rebound from that and she figured I wasn't anything serious, so she could just fuck me and leave me as her first step to freedom, 'cause I wasn't worth anything more. 'Course, she's right, but...it's going round and round in my head, so that I'm so fucked up inside...was she using me? Is she cheating on me with him now? Is she right and this is all I'm worth..."

"When was the last time you went for a run?" I interrupted.

"What?"

"When was the last time you went for a run?" I repeated. "This is the kind of emotional death spiral you get into when you don't exercise."

"Oh. Yeah. You're fuckin' right. I didn't even think about that. I haven't worked out since I got here. Not even a single pushup. I don't know what the fuck's wrong with me."

"Go for a run," I told him. "Then, when you're feeling calmer, tell her that you're worried about her ex-boyfriend, ask her if there's anything you can do, and tell her you'll be guided by whatever she says. If she's been in an abusive relationship or had a stalker, she'll probably be spooked by any kind of pressure, even if it's well meant. Make it clear that she calls all the shots here, and you'll back her up."

I tried to think how to tell John that he, like 98% of the men I'd ever known, came across as threatening and predatory when he got upset. Saying that normally caused, not self-reflection and self-control, but frightening outbursts of rage directed at the people he was already hurting. And John, as I'd told him before, was one of the good guys. At least he'd had the self-awareness to stop attacking Camila and come to me for advice. Progress.

"Try to keep the adrenaline levels down and don't do anything to trip anyone's fight-or-flight response," I said, trying to find just the right balance of gentleness, firmness, and that tinge of humor I hoped would defuse any angry explosions. "Do not, and I cannot stress this enough, get into the whole issue of whether or not she was using you when you first got together. And, just so you know, even if she was, she obviously found something in you worth sticking around for. So you *are* worth more than, um...being used for short-term consolation. I know it, and she obviously thinks so too."

John was silent for several long breaths. Then he said, "Thanks, Ro. Knew I could count on you. Didn't even think about how she might be triggered by me pushing her like that. Shows what a dumb fuck I am, huh? I'm gonna go for that run, clear my head, see if everything looks better then. It normally does."

"Yeah," I said. "It does."

"'Night, Ro," he said. "I'll check in tomorrow, okay? Let you know what the fuck is going on in this madhouse. Meanwhile, take care, okay?"

"You too," I said.

71

MY INTERVIEW WAS SCHEDULED for noon on Tuesday. I went in and taught my two language classes at nine and ten, telling myself that the tightness in my chest and stabbing pains in my temples were from stress—which was probably true. Then I went and sat in my broom closet of an office and observed my growing nausea and the sweat trickling down my sides while I pretended to look over my notes.

There's no need to be so nervous, I told myself. *It's not like you're in any physical danger. They probably won't even be rude to you. And you don't even want this job that badly. Not getting it might be a blessing.*

These pep talks had absolutely no effect on my body, which continued to ratchet up the anxiety until, when I headed over to Karen's office at 11:55, the ground felt unstable under my feet, and my knees kept buckling. I noted this as something of interest—I had read so many descriptions of people going weak at the knees when under extreme stress, but I'd always assumed it was a set expression with little physical reality, like blanching in response to bad news. But no. I guess I'd just never been scared enough before. It was humiliating that it was this stupid interview bringing me to this state, but I had to assume it wasn't just this particular interview, it was the accumulated PTSD from all the interviews I'd already been through.

It felt like everyone I passed in the hallway did a doubletake and then looked away, as if encountering someone on their way to the gallows. That was probably just my imagination. I checked my facial expression. Was I smiling? No, my face seemed frozen in a weird expression that was hurting my lips. Using way more effort than it should have taken, I molded my stiff muscles into something approximating a smile, and went up to the chair's corner office.

I knocked at the door, which was, unusually, closed. I was half-expecting to be told to wait—were they holding other interviews I didn't know about right now?—but Karen's Debbie Downer voice called out, "Rowena, is that you? Come in!"

I pulled open the door with stiff fingers and walked through on unbending knees. My chest, I noticed with detached interest, felt unable to rise and fall.

Karen was sitting in her usual chair. Jessica and Klaus, both Germanists, were perched awkwardly on rolling chairs they'd pushed into the back corner, which was the only available space on the "interviewer" side of the desk that filled most of the office. At a nod from Karen, I sat down on the one remaining chair. It was my old nemesis with the sticky seat that tended to make rude noises if you shifted in it. I told myself it would keep me from fidgeting.

"So, Rowena." Karen picked up a folder from her desk. A cascade of folders, blue books, receipts, cough drop wrappers, and random bits of paper poured off the desk and onto the floor at her feet.

"Goodness!" She stared at the mess, befuddled. She bent down to try to pick it up, but started coughing until tears came to her eyes.

"I'm"—cough—"sorry," she said breathlessly. "I've got this cold...I really *should* have stayed home...but I was *determined* to hold this interview..." She broke out into another racking cough. I felt myself instinctively edging back from her, and saw out of the corner of my eye that Jessica and Klaus were doing the same thing.

Karen finally brought her cough under control with a swig of water from a dented water bottle, and two extra-strength cough drops at once.

"So, Rowena," she said, once she could talk again. "You've decided to apply for our tenure-track job here. Can you tell us why you did that?"

"Um..." I said. It wasn't unusual to ask something about why a candidate was interested in a job. But she'd framed it like an accusation.

I came up with something about enjoying my time here at Crimson, bonding with the students, and wanting to nurture and grow the fledgling Russian program that, damn it (I left that bit out), had been my charge since its inception.

Karen burst out coughing again as I finished. I hoped that was just throat irritation and not her way of showing she thought it was all BS. Jessica and Klaus were at least nodding sympathetically, suggesting that I'd said something more or less appropriate.

"Normally at this point we'd switch into the target language," Jessica said. "But since none of us speak Russian, we'll just have to stay in English. Could you tell us a little about your research and future plans?"

I said something, my lips still feeling weird and stiff, about my current book—everyone livened up considerably when I said I had a book contract and was actively revising my manuscript—and something about where I saw my research going after that. My hearing kept cutting in and out as I spoke. I'd say something without knowing what it was, and then suddenly my words would seem almost unbearably loud and yet also coming from very far away, as if some alien entity were speaking them. But Klaus and Jessica kept nodding sympathetically, as if what I said made sense.

Karen continued to cough and root around on her desk, looking for the cough drop packet she'd somehow lost in the last five minutes. Finally, as I was wrapping up my answer, Jessica slid off her chair onto her knees, crawled across the floor to where she'd spotted the packet under the desk, picked it up and handed it to Karen, and crawled back wordlessly into her chair. Karen made no acknowledgement other than to take out two more cough drops, pop them into her mouth, and drop the wrappers onto the pile of detritus on the floor as she attempted to put them into the trash.

"So, Rowena," Karen said around her two cough drops. "Tell us where you see the Russian program in five years."

I said something about expanding it into a minor. Karen pursed her lips at that, puckering up her saggy mouth into her familiar expression of someone who'd just bitten into an unripe persimmon.

"Do you really think you'll be able to manage an entire minor on your own?" she asked.

"Well," I said, "ideally, we would grow to the point where we could hire a second person..."

She pursed up her mouth even more. "So you don't think you're capable of managing the program on your own?"

"Well..." I said, "of course I am running it solo now, but I would like to expand our course offerings to include more high-enrollment survey courses in literature and culture, and that would eventually require a second instructor..."

"Really, Rowena," she said. "You should understand by now that the department doesn't have the money to hire a second person. I'd expect whoever ends up in this position to be able to grow the program on their own, *even if* that means putting in a little extra work from time to time."

"Well," I said, "of course I'd be happy to take on the occasional overload class, especially in the early years of the program as we're working to expand it..."

"You'd need to do more than 'take on the occasional overload course,'" she said severely. "I don't think you understand the magnitude of what you'd be required to undertake here."

"Um," I said. The words *Yet another lazy-ass quitter who thinks they can fix their problems by giving me tough love!* flashed through my head. My hearing suddenly returned, and everything seemed to snap into focus around me.

"Of course I'd love to hear your ideas as well," I said, looking at each member of the committee in turn. "One of the best things about Crimson, and the thing that attracts me the most to this position, is the close and collegial relationships between the different programs. I'd love to be able to collaborate with other departments—perhaps by creating high-enrollment, team-taught interdisciplinary survey courses designed to introduce a wide variety of students to our offerings?—and, of course, hear from my colleagues about what has and hasn't worked for them, and how we can best work together to grow all our programs."

Klaus and Jessica were smiling and nodding. *Bullseye.* Karen's mouth was so tightly pursed her lips had almost completely disappeared. She seemed unable to unpurse it, so Klaus took the lead by asking me if I had any questions, answering my softball lob about funding sources for professional and course development, and then, with what seemed like genuine collegial good will, thanking me for my time and ushering me out the door.

72

I WALKED BACK TO MY car on legs that were now working perfectly, but with a badly bruised soul. Looking back on the interview, I knew I'd done the absolute best I could, and that I'd probably, by objective measures, nailed it. Klaus and Jessica had certainly seemed to think so by the end. But I couldn't help but feel that by nailing it, I'd driven the final nail into my own coffin as far as Karen was concerned, and she was chair of the interview committee and the entire department.

You don't really even want this job, remember? I told myself as I started up the car and headed away from campus. Thinking of spending the next thirty years surrounded by these same views, these same people, this same sameness, made something heavy settle in my chest. But thinking of being rejected at the one thing I'd trained so hard to do, and for the job I'd already put so much work into, made something even heavier settle in my stomach. And the thought of being broke and unemployed turned those heavy things into sacks of snakes.

I checked in with Galina Ivanovna when I got back. She told me she was fine and asked about the interview.

"It was fine," I said.

She gave me a sharp look. "You don't look like it was fine, Innochka."

"Stress," I said shortly, and then, unable to keep it to myself any longer, burst out with a lengthy speech about my mixed feelings about the interview itself and the entire job situation.

She listened with quiet attention until I was done. Then she said, "Innochka, what do you think about finding work somewhere else? Outside of America, I mean."

"Like in Russia?" I asked.

She turned down the corners of her mouth. "I wish I could say yes, in Russia, but in fact the situation at most institutions of higher education is...strained. More and more problems with academic freedom. Of course, you have many problems with that now in America, no?"

I nodded. She nodded back at me. "And I think your connection with Dima would disqualify you for most jobs in Russia in any case. So, not America and not Russia. What about somewhere else?"

"Like where?" The words came out much angrier than I had intended. "I'm sorry," I added quickly. "You're right, of course, I just don't know where..."

"Just keep your eyes open, Innochka," she said. "Maybe an opportunity will present itself."

"I will," I promised. I kept my doubts to myself

"Oh, and Dima texted. He's on his way back."

"Great." I told myself very sternly that I shouldn't feel rejected because he'd texted his mother and not me. He'd known I had an interview today. He probably hadn't wanted to disturb me.

If he hadn't had a long history of disappearing and cutting me off, I would have believed it.

73

I WENT BACK TO MY APARTMENT and spent a while prepping for Wednesday's classes. When I finished, it was late afternoon. Really, it was too early to quit for the day, but when I looked at my manuscript file, a wave of such intense lethargy washed over me that I shut down my computer and went for a run instead.

"Run" was a bit of an exaggeration. After the daily wrestle with the mailbox, which as usual yielded nothing (fate was not a very munificent benefactor, in my experience), I jogged slowly for about half a mile up and down the road outside the complex. The good news was that the knee I'd injured last year didn't so much as twinge. The bad news was that everything else twinged pretty badly.

Twilight was already closing in around me when I arrived back at the apartment complex gates. A cold January wind was picking up, rustling the thin stand of pines around the complex, whispering of far-off places and eerie things beyond the edge of vision. The juxtaposition of the lowering dark and rising wind made me feel both hemmed in and desperate to break free, run off and make my way through the wide world, far, far away from my petty problems here.

"Inna! Innochka!"

I started and whirled around. While I'd been staring at the pine tops whipping in the wind, Dima had driven up behind me and was now leaning out his open window, calling my name.

"You're back," I said.

"Yes, earlier than expected. It was a very, mmm, *fruitful* visit, but I decided it would be best to exit before things got any more interesting. You look cold. Get in the car."

He leaned over and opened the passenger side door. I went around and slid in. The car was almost oppressively warm after the bracing chill of the wild wind outside.

"How'd the interview go?" he asked.

"Fine," I said.

"You don't look fine," he said.

"Well..."

A loud *honk* cut off the rest of my words. Three other people had pulled in behind us and were waiting to go through the complex gates.

Dima pulled through the gate. Instead of turning left and driving over to the building where he and his mother were staying, though, he turned right, heading for the other side of the complex.

"I thought we should talk," he said. "Before I talk to mama. And in order not to worry her, let's go park over there, where she can't see us." His face suddenly lit up. "Do you remember..." His face closed just as quickly as it had opened, and he cut off his words. But I was 100% sure he had been about to say something about how we used to drive around Moscow in his elderly Niva jeep for the express purpose of finding a quiet place to park and make out.

"I remember," I said.

"Back then, when we first met, I wasn't thinking about whether or not you'd be any good in a situation like this," he said. "I won't conceal it: I was mainly thinking about your beauty. Your outer beauty. But now..." He exhaled deeply, as if ridding himself of the weight of the world. "Now I'm thinking about your strength. About whether you're strong enough to hear what I have to tell you."

A giant sack of snakes, heavier and more venomous than anything I'd felt after the interview, filled my chest. *Don't tell me!* I wanted to cry out. *Let's just talk about happy memories! Let's try and relive some of those happy memories, instead of creating new, sad memories!*

"You can tell me anything," I said. "I'll be strong enough to hear it. I swear."

74

"SO, SECURITY SOLUTIONS was interesting," Dima said after a moment. "Pretty much what I'd expected. A devilish mixture of big business and the military. But they were nice to me when I first arrived."

"When you first arrived," I repeated.

"Well, you know me, Inna."

"I do. Carry on."

"I told them my story again about writing for a pro-military publication that was featuring private military companies from around the world this year. The face of modern military activities, blahblahblah."

"Mmm-hmm," I said.

"And I talked about how we were particularly interested in international cooperation and I'd been sent out here because we needed a Russian-speaker to interview the Ukrainian trainers.

"The trainees were from all around the world. Plenty from here in the US, but plenty from South and Central America as well, along with a smattering from Eastern Europe, and even a couple from the Middle East and sub-Saharan Africa. The trainers were the Wolf Battalion that's been fighting in the Donbass since 2014. They're not exactly part of the regular Ukrainian military, but they're not exactly not part of the regular Ukrainian military. They've been sent over to the US to give and receive training, but all off to the side of official channels. Officially, right now, they're a private company doing joint training exercises with another private company."

"But unofficially?" I asked.

"Unofficially, there were a lot of governmental-looking people around there. Unofficially, this looks like a way for training and recruitment exercises to happen that aren't under the official aegis of their re-spective governments, but are what their respective governments want to happen."

"No surprises," I said.

"No, no surprises. And I guess I shouldn't have been surprised at the kind of people I found there. Of course, a lot of them were like me. If things had been different, one of them probably would have been me."

"That would have required you to be a different person from who you are," I said. "So things would have had to be very different."

"I guess." He didn't sound convinced. Because he knew things about himself that I didn't, or because he didn't know himself as well as I did?

"And then there were the lunatics," he continued. "Lunatics of vari-ous stripes, but all lunatics. Honestly, Inna, I always thought we were spe-cial back in the motherland for the quantity and quality of lunatics we produced. But now I see that America produces an impressive array of lunatics as well."

"We do," I agreed.

"But I will give credit to the former USSR and say that the Wolf Bat-talion had the best lunatics of all. Their leader goes by the call sign 'Dah-mer' and their second-in-command goes by 'Bundy.' Those are American serial killers, right? I looked them up."

"Right," I said.

"Weird that they didn't at least use home-grown serial killers for their call signs, but I guess it's kind of totemic or something? Like Ameri-can serial killers are just another exotic fiction coming out of Hollywood, so it's like taking a movie character's name as your call sign."

"I guess," I said. "It's still gross, in my opinion."

He made a face. "Mine too. None of us"—I knew he was referring to when he had been in the military—"ever even considered taking a se-rial killer as a call sign. And we were not nice guys. But we weren't con-sciously setting out to emulate child-killers and cannibals. But these guys seemed to want to look as vicious as possible." He paused. "Do you think it's something Freudian? Like, well, maybe they don't feel very vicious in-side, so they have to pretend to be as vicious as possible on the outside?"

"Do you think they're pretending?" I asked.

He shrugged. "If they are, they're really entering into the role. Total method acting. Stanislavsky would be proud. Because they scared me, and I don't scare easily."

"No." My scalp prickled at the very thought of someone so bad that he scared Dima. I had to assume that anyone who could do that was, in fact, a serial killer or something even worse.

"So then what?" I asked. "Why did you have to leave early?"

"I started talking to each of the guys in the Wolf Battalion. You know, getting their backstory, asking about their motivations—in a subtle way—and generally getting to know them. It was all going well...until one of them recognized me."

"No surprise," I said.

"No, of course we knew that was a risk, but I thought I was going to get away with it—until this guy remembered seeing me around Avdeyevka, remembered who I was."

"Oh," I said. Avdeyevka/Avdiivka was a hamlet in eastern Ukraine that had seen so many battles in the past few years, it was a wonder there was anything there worth fighting over.

"Yeah. And he blurted it out before I could stop him. He looked sorry as soon as he'd done in. He seemed like a pretty stand-up guy. Don't know what he was doing there, but war makes strange bedfellows. He tried to fix it, say that I was one of the good guys and they should all talk to me, but once Dahmer and Bundy found out, I had to get out of there. They didn't want any good guys around, I guess. I won't hide that there were a tense few minutes before I managed to talk my way out of the circle they were forming around me, and then make a break for it."

I repressed a shudder. "You think they wanted to hurt you?"

"Dahmer and Bundy had a gleeful, predatory look in their eyes that would have done their namesakes proud. They got right in my face and started telling me about the captive wolf they kept back home whom they fed exclusively on the flesh and bones of Russian-speaking children. I think they were lying, or at least exaggerating, but they definitely wanted to provoke me into doing something. So I smiled and said that was quite a story and I'd love to do a feature on them, and then someone I think was their political handler came and took them aside, and I got out of there. Went out into parking lot, got in my car, and just started driving. Haven't had to run away from an interview like that for a long time."

"Running away was the right thing to do," I said.

"Undoubtedly. And now we're getting to the hard part."

"Mmmm?" I said, when he stared silently at the dark windshield for longer than I could stand. The January chill was seeping in through the closed windows, and I was dressed for jogging, not sitting out in the cold.

"After I got far enough away I thought it was safe, I stopped and put in a call to...well, let's call them *my* political handlers." He turned and gave me the faint ghost of a grin. "You're probably thinking that would be a thankless task, and you'd be right."

"Uh-huh?" I said.

He blew out a long breath. "They were *very* interested in what I had to say. *Very*, very interested. So interested that they told me to try to embed with the Wolf Battalion."

75

"EMBED WITH THE WOLF Battalion," I repeated. I was hoping that my Russian had failed me. "Like, go undercover with them?"

He shook his head. "Not undercover. They already know who I am, like I said. No, I'd be doing it as myself. But embed with them, spend all my time with them, do everything with them. Journalists do it all the time. I've done it before myself."

"Uh-huh," I said. "They—your political handlers—don't think it will be dangerous?"

"I think they think it will be very dangerous," he said. "But I'm disposable in their eyes, so why not try?"

"You're not disposable in my eyes!" I had meant that to come out as a calm statement. It came out more as a furious shout.

Dima was silent for another uncomfortably long period. Finally he said, "You know, I actually believe you."

"And what, you never believed me before? You, what, thought I was lying?" That came out much too angrily too. If I didn't get myself under control, I was going to start screaming with rage.

"No. I know you don't lie, Inna. I just thought you...didn't understand. You didn't understand how disposable I was. You were too kind to see the truth."

"And what's the truth?" The words came out as a hoarse whisper from the strain of not bursting into shrieks of anguish.

"The truth...the truth, Innochka, as far as I can see now, is that you always loved me more than I deserved, but that love was real."

I said nothing. Too many emotions, the dominant one being fury, were trying to claw their way out of my throat, choking off all the words that might have released them. No doubt that was a good thing.

"I don't know how you feel right now," he said. "But I know what you've done for mama. For me. I have to accept that for you, neither of us is disposable. Hard as I find it to believe, I have to accept that if something happened to us, you would suffer. You know"—he turned to me, his face bright and open with sudden realization—"all my life, I've had a hard time accepting love, or anything else anyone did for me. I've never been able to receive what others wanted to give me. Especially when it was love."

"And now?" My voice was still thick and hoarse, but at least I wasn't screaming in uncontrollable rage.

"Now...I don't know...I feel like I'm standing on the edge of a vast precipice, an abyss opening beneath my feet. That precipice is my choice whether or not to accept love of my own free will. I'd always believed—always depended on the fact that others would force it on me, that I wouldn't have to make any decisions, any choices, on my own. That I wouldn't have to speak up and say, 'This is what I want, this is what I need, this is what I'm asking for.' That was...that was *unbearably* terrifying. I couldn't do it. Every time that abyss opened up before me, I'd turn and run."

"Oh," I said.

"But you know what Bulgakov says," he went on. "Cowardice is the worst of all vices."

"Yes," I said.

"So I'm finally trying to face up to my cowardice, but...but this is a battle I'm not sure I can win. I'm not afraid of external enemies, but this internal cowardice, sitting square in the middle of me and controlling my every word, my every move...my every thought...this is a fight that might be beyond my strength."

"You're very strong," I said. "Even stronger than you think."

He reached over and patted my knee. "Thanks, Innochka. I think you meant that sincerely, too."

"I did."

He blew out another breath. "That was the kind of thing that always used to terrify me. It *still* terrifies me. Because if you really believe that, then I have to justify that faith. The very thought makes me want to turn and run and abandon the field of battle. And I can come up with scores of sensible, logical reasons why I should. But you don't win battles through logic. Or not entirely. There has to be faith as well. And that's what I need to find for myself."

"Oh," I said.

"And I'll tell you one more thing." He was turned towards me again, his face once more bright and open. "You should have gone ahead and taken what you wanted—what you *needed*—from me, Inna. If having a family is so important to you, you should have gone and gotten pregnant even though I told you not to."

"I've been thinking that recently," I admitted. "But the more I think about it, the more I think I was right not to do it. Betraying you like that would have made me miserable, and what kind of future would the child have had?"

He made a dismissive gesture. "Mama would have moved heaven and earth to make sure that child had the brightest future any child has ever had. She would have abandoned me in a heartbeat to take care of it full-time."

"I know," I said. "But...but maybe..."

"But maybe I'm fantasizing about someone else forcing what I want and need onto me against my will," he finished for me.

"Well...yes."

"So you're saying, if I want this to happen, I have to learn how to choose it of my own free will too?"

"Yes," I said firmly.

He blew out the longest breath yet. "You're a stern taskmistress, Inna. But I'm afraid you're right. I just...I don't know that I'm able to justify your faith in me quite yet. I think the toad of cowardice is still squatting in my chest, controlling my every move, especially when I'm least aware of it."

"Maybe now that you know it's there, you can transform it from the toad of cowardice to..."—I racked my brains to come up with an elegant and appropriate metaphor using words I knew in Russian—"the, um, unicorn of courage."

He burst out laughing. "The unicorn of courage?! Is that even a thing?"

"It was the only word I could think of under pressure," I said.

"Fair enough." He was still laughing. "At least you cheered me up before the next bit. Now I have to go tell mama that I'm about to leave you both to go on a dangerous mission. I'm going to need a whole herd of unicorns to survive that conversation."

76

GALINA IVANOVNA WAS, predictably, not pleased about Dima's intention to go embed with the Wolf Battalion. She also, predictably, didn't resist too much. Critical as she was of him, she rarely tried to stop him when he wanted to do something questionable. Wisdom, cowardice, or coddling? Hard to know. For the first time, it occurred to me with full clarity that having true love for Dima might not mean going along with what he thought was best. It might mean standing up to his worst impulses, even if he didn't like it. Unfortunately, my feeble attempts to do that had always ended in failure thus far.

And in this particular case, I understood that Dima's reasons for doing this were sound. He couldn't really say no to his sponsors back home, and whatever was going on over there with Security Solutions and the Wolf Battalion, it sounded bad. Someone should do something about it, and the person who was currently in the best position to do that was Dima.

But somehow it seemed so often that he was the best and only man for the job, which meant he was constantly running away from the most important people in his life and his own inner demons. Someday he was going to have to come up with the courage to say no to things that he had very strong reasons to say yes to, so that he could say yes to things that were even more important. I just didn't know if that day was going to come soon enough—or ever.

In this case, though, he wasn't going to say no, but he wouldn't have to leave right away. Setting up the embed could take a little time. He expected to be able to come to Galina Ivanovna's next treatment, at least.

By the time we had discussed all this, it was almost bedtime. I left him and Galina Ivanovna in their apartment, and went back to my own. I felt my phone buzz in my pocket as I made the walk. When I pulled it out and checked it, I found a text message from John.

Great news! Mom and Dad have broken free of the brainwashing enough to agree to go home. We're all set to head out at first light tomorrow.

That's great! I texted back. *Are Dennis and Alexandra very upset about it?*

The reply came immediately.

Less good news is that they think Mom and Dad are about to join them in the church, so they're okay with us all leaving because they think they've already convinced us.

Have they already convinced Mom and Dad? I wrote back.

The next reply took a little longer, as if John were thinking over his answer carefully.

I don't know. They're acting pretty convinced. I'm worried, Ro. But maybe they're putting on an act in order to get out of here quicker. I know *I've* been putting on an act, so why can't they? Or maybe they're not putting on an act but they'll snap out of it as soon as they get back to freedom and sanity. I can't say for certain either way now.

Okay, I texted. *Getting out of there is still good.*

Yeah. Okay, night, Ro. I'll check in tomorrow once we're all safely away.

Good luck! I wrote.

77

AFTER THE INTENSE START to the week, the rest of it went fairly smoothly. John texted at eight the next morning to say that Mom and Dad had just pulled out of Dennis and Alexandra's driveway, and he was about to follow them. He texted again that evening to tell me that he'd made it home with no trouble.

But seriously, Ro, we need to keep an eye on Mom and Dad, he wrote. *Who knows what kind of wild hair they'll get up their butts next. They seemed pretty convinced about that church thing.*

I'll keep an eye on them, I promised. *Hopefully, like you said, once they're out in freedom again, they'll go back to their old selves.*

Their old fruitcake selves, LOL, John texted back. *But better than cultists.*

On Thursday I drove Dima and Galina Ivanovna into Atlanta for Galina Ivanovna's next treatment. She was weighed, measured, poked, and prodded ahead of time, and significant quantities of blood were taken. Both Kathy and Dr. Azarian appeared to think that everything was in order, and she spent the afternoon hooked up to the drip again. This time she fell asleep even faster and slept through most of the infusion, waking up only when the IV was disconnected and she was wheeled out to the car. Kathy assured us this was normal and we could expect her to start perking up after another couple of treatments.

Dima sat there with me for the whole thing, although he did flinch and turn away whenever actual needles were being inserted into or pulled out of his mother's flesh. Much of the time he worked on his phone or sat there in silence. I wasn't sure if he didn't want to talk about sensitive things with his mother right there between us, or if he didn't want to talk about sensitive things, period. Still, a lot of the silence between us was the comfortable quiet of people who'd known each other for a long time and could sit in each other's presence without chattering constantly.

When we got back from Atlanta on Thursday evening, I was met with a lengthy series of texts from Mel about her interview that day.

I think it went okay, she wrote. *Although Karen was her usual self. She went on and on about how I hadn't done enough service work or organized enough extracurricular activities. She was pissed I'd "wasted my time"—her words—doing translations instead of organizing events. I mean, I *did* organize film screenings and conversation tables, but no one ever came to them. The students are too fucking busy already.*

Yeah, I wrote back. We'd both been dispirited by our attempts to organize conversation tables and language clubs. Student interest had been thin, which was not surprising. The programs were still tiny, students didn't get useful résumé credit from our activities, and they were already overscheduled with things that they thought would actually help get them into the internship or grad program that would, they were certain, set them on the path to fame, fortune, and worldly prosperity. Taking the afternoon off to come to Arabic club or Russian conversation hour, on the other hand, might doom their chances, thus plunging them into a lifetime of poverty and despair. I wasn't sure how true that was, but they definitely felt it to be true.

Maybe, if we're still here next semester, we should try again with extracurricular activities and make them mandatory for our classes, I suggested.

Maybe, Mel wrote back. *Although right now I don't really feel like being here next semester. The interview kind of left a bad taste in my mouth.*

I know how you feel, I texted. *I guess we'll just have to see what happens. Did they give you a timeline of when they expected to send out invitations for second-round interviews?* I'd just been told "sometime in the next few weeks," and hadn't had the nerve to demand a more precise answer.

Sometime in the next few weeks, Mel texted back.

Great, I wrote. *Something to look forward to.*

Friday afternoon, when I got back from class, Dima was waiting for me by my door.

"I wanted to talk to you, Inna," he said. "Alone."

He was too calm for it to be something wrong with Galina Ivanovna. "Okay," I said, and unlocked the door and let us both in.

"I got an answer back from the Wolf Battalion," he said. "Quicker than I expected. I guess they couldn't resist the opportunity to be shits to me."

"So they're letting you in?"

"Yep. Just like I suspected, the lure of publicity and of harassing me was too strong. I just got the email. Six to eight weeks embedded with them."

"Oh," I said.

"Are you angry?" he asked. "Very angry?"

"No," I said. Truthfully. Sort of. "I know why you're doing this. I even think you're right to do it. I just wish you didn't have to do it."

"So do I, Innochka. I think." He frowned. "I don't even trust my own motivations these days. But tell me the truth: am I making a huge mistake?"

"What are the likely outcomes of you not doing this?" I asked.

"At best, major trouble for me at home. Maybe started by extradition back to Russia. I assume the American government would agree, but if they didn't, then I'd be an exile forever." He wrinkled up his nose. "I can't quite face that yet. And that's just the best-case scenario. The worst-case scenario could be a lot more permanent than that."

"You think they'd kill you?" I asked.

"I think one of the many 'theys' I've pissed off over the years would be encouraged to find a way. Or maybe the Wolf Battalion would do something. I'm under the impression that if I don't go along with their proposal, then I'll be declared an enemy, and their enemies tend to meet explosively violent ends."

"But you think you'll be safe if you're actually embedded with them?" I asked.

He shrugged. "I think I'll be in slightly less danger. And maybe if I succeed, we'll all be in a lot less danger. So what do you think?"

"I think," I said, forcing the words out with extreme reluctance, "that you should do it. But I also think," I added quickly, "that maybe you should think about ways you could avoid doing something like this in the future."

He nodded. "Got it. My last mission, that's what you're saying?"

"Something like that."

He grinned. "Well, if it's going to be my last mission, I guess I'd better make sure it's a good one. And now, can you come with me and provide backup while I tell mama about it? She's not going to be happy to find out I'll be leaving you both first thing tomorrow morning."

Something leaden and cold gripped my chest. "Sure," I said. "I'd be happy to."

78

GALINA IVANOVNA WAS not, as predicted, pleased. But she also didn't fight it. The same arguments that had convinced me were even more convincing to her. Plus, she was still zonked by the treatment. She grumbled a bit for form's sake over supper and then fell asleep for the rest of the evening.

Dima came back from dropping her off at their apartment and immediately started washing the dishes without being asked. I was sitting at the table, reading my email, but as he washed away, with more enthusiasm but also more splashing than I would have done myself, I found myself looking at him more and more, and then I was no longer reading my email at all, but just watching him.

"What?" he asked, looking up and catching my gaze.

"Did you always wash the dishes without being asked, and I just forgot?" I asked.

He laughed, but with an edge of embarrassment. "No. Well, I did when I was in all-male company and we were responsible for taking care of ourselves. But whenever there were women around, I always left it for them to do. To be fair to myself, most of them wouldn't have let me do it. I think. Maybe I was wrong about that, too. Anyway, as mama got...worse and worse, she started having trouble doing it on her own. And then before we left for here, we were watching *The Irony of Fate*, and we came to the scene where Zhenya washes the dishes without being asked—you know the scene?"

"I know it well." *The Irony of Fate* was a 1970s Soviet musical comedy that most people in the post-Soviet world knew by heart and watched in the runup to New Year's Eve every year. One of the ways the hero demonstrates his desirability and enlightenment to the heroine was by washing the dishes without being asked.

"Yes, of course. Well, mama and I were watching it, and we got to that scene, and she said something about how that was the moment that Zhenya conquered her heart, and she'd never found a man who could realize that particular ideal for her...I don't think she even meant anything by it; it wasn't supposed to be a hint to me or a reproach to my father...but the next day I started washing the dishes. Let her have all the things she ever wished for. Especially something that's so easy for me to give her. And you know what? I don't even mind. It makes me feel...I don't know what. Like I'm useful. Like I'm part of something. Like I'm giving something back to those who've given so much to me. I guess all those Soviet slogans about *bruderschaft* and working together were really true."

"They were about that," I said.

He finished washing the dishes and came over to sit at the other side of the table. "Are you busy?" he asked.

"Email." I shut the laptop. "It can wait. It's Friday evening, for God's sake. They can wait until Saturday to get their answers."

"Yeah..." He was looking down at the table. "Is there...is there anything you need from me before I go, Inna? Anything I can do to make things better for you and mama before I leave? I am very well aware that I'll be leaving you yet again. I am very well aware that I'll be leaving you to do the job that should be mine. The job that only I can do."

"No," I said. "I can take Galina Ivanovna to the hospital and sit with her, maybe better than you can. This thing with the Wolf Battalion, though—only you can do that."

He grimaced. "You sure as hell shouldn't. I wouldn't let any woman within half a kilometer of them."

"And you'd be absolutely right," I said. "But...while you're with them...do try to be careful. That's the only request I have for you."

He smiled. "Careful? I'm not sure I know how to be careful. Any tips?"

"I'm not sure I know how to be careful either," I said.

He was silent for a moment. "No," he said. "No, you were always ready to throw yourself at risks that terrified me. You were always the brave one..."

His phone *pinged*. He picked it up, looked at the message, and blew out a long breath.

"They're ready for me," he said. "They want me to come tomorrow."

"Oh," I said. "So soon?"

He tried to smile again, but it came out more as a wince of pain. "The sooner you go to jail, the sooner you get out, right? Might as well get it over with."

"Maybe," I said.

"But..." He looked down at the table. "I do have a request for you, Inna."

"What is it?"

He looked up at me. "I want...will you kiss me before I go? Just one kiss. I...I'm still all confused inside. But I keep thinking...maybe if I remembered what we had, I might...I might find some clarity. Some courage."

I got up from my chair and went over to him. For a moment I stood over him, looking down at him as he looked up at me. Then he caught me and pulled me down into his lap.

We sat like that for what seemed like a very long time, and yet no time at all. He moved several times as if to touch my face with the back of his knuckles, but could never quite bring himself to do it. His lips were parted, and his pupils were so dilated I could hardly see the gray iris around them.

I leaned forward and touched my lips to his. He froze, and then he was kissing me hungrily, desperately, his hands pulling me to him, his chest shuddering against mine.

We clutched at each other like that until I had to pull away.

"I need to breathe," I gasped.

He was breathing hard too. "Me too. And...I only asked for one kiss, didn't I?"

"I think that was more than one kiss," I said.

"Then I'll owe you." He grasped me by the elbows and lifted me up, then stood up himself. We were still so close we were almost touching. "It'll give me a reason to come back," he said. "I'll need to repay my debt to you." He bent forward and brushed his lips against the top of my ear. "But now I have to go," he said. "Or else I'll repay that debt early. But you'll be waiting for me, won't you?"

"I will," I said.

"And you'll be praying for me?"

"Day and night," I said.

"Then I'll have to come back," he said. And he left.

79

DIMA LEFT EARLY THE next morning. He knocked on my door before dawn. When I opened it, he stood there for a long time, looking at me.

"Come in," I said.

He shook his head. "If I come in, I'll never leave. I'd better go. I'll try to let you know I'm okay, but I don't know how often I'll be able to be in touch."

"Try to contact us whenever you can," I told him. "We worry. A lot."

He took a deep breath in and out. "Then I'll try." He smiled bleakly. "I must be getting old. This is the first time I don't want to go on an assignment. I used to thirst for this kind of thing like the water of life. But now I just want to stay here with you and mama. Some new stage of life, or something like that."

"I think Pushkin said something clever about that, but I can't remember it," I said.

"Yeah...blessed is he who...I can't remember the rest, either. Anyway." He shifted from foot to foot. "I'd better go."

"Come back soon," I said. "You owe me, remember?"

Something flared in his eyes. He was—deliberately, I thought—not smiling, but the dimple in his left cheek flexed into view for a second. I could tell, as surely as if his body were mine, that warmth was spreading through him at the memory of last night. "And you always collect on your debts, is that what you're telling me?"

"I intend to collect on this one," I said. "As God is my witness, I intend to collect on this one." I'd meant it to be a joke, but it came out as a solemn vow.

"Then pray for me, Inna. Pray for me, and I will return."

"I will," I promised.

He reached out. His hand hovered in front of my face for a moment, before one finger brushed my lips, soft as a butterfly. He inhaled sharply and pulled his hand away.

"Go with God, Inna," he said.

"You too," I told him.

He turned and left. I watched him walk down the stairs and into the pre-dawn semi-darkness. He held the hand that had touched my lips over his mouth the whole way, as if restraining a desperate cry of despair—or inhaling every last atom of a scent only he could sense. Then he was gone.

1

March

DIMA'S COMMUNICATIONS were few and far between. He spent a couple of weeks at the Security Solutions headquarters, before the Wolf Battalion was sent to Utah to train more survivalists and soldiers of fortune. Dima wrote to me and Galina Ivanovna in early February that he didn't think the Utah climate was doing his complexion any favors, but other than that, he was fine.

On Valentine's Day he sent me a private message congratulating me on the holiday and asking me if I was still intending to collect on the debt he owed me. I told him I was. He sent back a string of heart emojis. Then he went silent for the next two weeks.

Things were equally tense at work, with Mel and me both waiting to hear the results of our interviews. Would we be invited for the second round? Had the college really gotten so many qualified applications that they could afford to blow us off, and would they have the nerve to do so?

We didn't get our answer until March 1st. I was sitting with Galina Ivanovna as she got her weekly infusion, when I got a text from Mel.

Karen just told me they'll be using my first-year class for fucking teaching demos for the three weeks after spring break. Guess who's *NOT* going to be doing a teaching demo? That's right: ME! She didn't even address the fucking point, either. Just told me to prep my class to be used for teaching demos. No apologies, no explanation, no fucking NOTHING.

"Problem?" asked Galina Ivanovna. Although she was still basically in renal failure, she hadn't gotten worse, and she had, as promised, developed a tolerance for the treatment and no longer fell asleep during it.

"Mel wasn't invited for the next phase of interviews," I explained.

"Oh. And you? Any word?"

"I'll check." My heart was beating annoyingly hard. My face, which had hurt all week from muscle tension, spasmed, causing a bolt of pain to lance through my left eye. I hadn't been paying attention to my email notifications while I'd been sitting with Galina Ivanovna, but now I saw there was an email from Karen with the subject "Teaching Demos—Important!"

I opened the email.

Dear Rowena,

Please be advised that your 102 class will be used for our candidates' teaching demos the weeks of March 13, 20, and 27. I will be in contact shortly with the exact dates. Please prepare your classes accordingly. We want to be sure to shine for our candidates!!!

Karen

"Bad news?" asked Galina Ivanovna.

"I wasn't invited either." My voice sounded strange and felt like it was coming from a long way away. I moved to set my phone down on my lap and swayed alarmingly.

"Inna! You're hyperventilating and going into shock. Concentrate! I can't pick you up if you fall onto the floor."

I clutched at the arms of the chair, righting myself.

"Sorry," I said. "I don't know..."

"Shock," Galina Ivanovna said crisply. "Only to be expected when getting stabbed in the back by motherfucking assholes."

I laughed. She laughed too.

"Fuck 'em," she said. "Good riddance to bad rubbish. Now you can concentrate on finding a position commensurate with your worth."

"Sure," I said. "Of course."

2

GALINA IVANOVNA TALKED determinedly about other things for the rest of her treatment session, and on the drive home. Once we got back to the apartment, she insisted on listening to my lungs.

"Still a little wheezy, but about the same," she declared. "You had me worried there for a moment back in the hospital, but you don't have pneumonia...yet. Although you *have* been losing weight."

"It's stress," I said.

"Maybe," she said. "Try to eat more, Innochka. You mustn't waste away. Make double portions tonight."

It was only after supper (single portions for both of us, which was all we could manage) that she brought up the issue of my blighted job prospects again.

"I've been thinking, Innochka," she said. "About your career. We talked about you leaving America before, but we didn't really take it seriously. I think it's time to start taking it seriously. I know we said that you couldn't find work in Russia, and maybe that's true. Maybe that's true for Dima as well. Maybe you both need to start looking for work outside of Russia *and* America. Together."

She fixed me with a bright gaze.

"Um..." I said.

"It's time to think practically," she said. "And God knows Dima can't do it, so it's on you to do all the practical thinking for the both of you. You both need to find a new job and a new place to live. It will be easier to do it together. Maybe you can find something in your profession. Maybe he can find something in his. Or maybe he can apply to become a political refugee."

She made a face. "Tfoo! It's disgusting even to say the words. A war hero, and the son of a war hero, and he might have to run away from his own motherland! It makes me ashamed to be Russian, and I never thought I'd say that. But on the other hand, Dima would probably have to run away from whatever motherland he had. Probably if he had been born an American, he'd be taking refuge in Russia, like that...what's his name...Snowden? Dima would probably share his fate if he were American."

"Very likely," I said.

"But the problem is that *you* seem doomed to share his fate as well, Innochka, whatever it is."

"Um..." I said again.

She waved a hand at me dismissively. "I'm telling you all this for your own good, Innochka, since it seems no one else will. What does your mother say about your life? About your career? About your love?"

"She wishes it were different," I said. "But she's learned not to say that."

Galina Ivanovna nodded. "Of course. But, and I say this with the deepest respect for her maternal care and feelings, what does she really know about you? About you and Dima, that is. She's never met him. She's never even talked to him on Skype. Does she even know what he looks like?"

"She's seen a couple of photographs," I said.

Galina Ivanovna made another dismissive gesture with her hand. "But she's never seen the two of you together, has she?"

"One of the photographs..." I began, and stopped.

Galina Ivanovna fixed me with another bright gaze. "Yes, Innochka? One of the photographs?"

"One of the photographs...made an impression," I said. "On her, and on my brother. But...I don't think it was a good impression."

"Do you have the photograph? Show it to me."

I pulled out my phone and brought up the photo app. I still had the photo after two phone changes. In fact, it had its own special photo album, which I had labeled "Winter" because I was too embarrassed by...I wasn't sure what...to call it what it was, which was pictures of me and Dima together. Mostly taken in the winter, to be fair to myself.

I opened the photo and held it up silently.

"Oh," Galina Ivanovna said. "I see."

The picture been taken by a friend one snowy day in January when we had all gone walking around the Kremlin. Dima and I had just gotten engaged the day before, and a group of us had all gone out for a walking tour of the prettiest places in Moscow to celebrate. It was all the celebration we could afford, but I doubt any of the oligarchs bathing in gold bathtubs filled with French champagne had been half as happy as we were. It was so cold our breath was freezing onto our clothing, but we were so full of love and optimism that the freezing air felt warm on our flushed faces.

We had stopped in front of the Eternal Flame in the Alexander Garden. A couple was laying their wedding bouquet there.

"That'll be us soon," Dima said.

Our friends, who were sober but were acting as if they were drunk, started shouting the traditional wedding cry of "Bitter! Bitter!" to demand that the couple kiss in order to make the bitter wine sweet.

The newlyweds laughed and kissed. Dima and I turned and looked at each other. We looked at each other for a long moment, and then he caught my face in his hand and bent down and kissed me. The kiss went on for so long that everyone started whistling and cheering.

Afterwards, one of Dima's friends sent me the series of photos he'd gotten of the whole thing.

Frankly, Inna, I've got to get those photos off my phone, he told me. *I've taken some pretty intense photos*—he was a war correspondent who specialized in photographing combat—*but this might be the hottest stuff I've ever gotten. Afraid my phone might melt if I don't get rid of these pictures, and if my editor catches me with them, he might fire me for inappropriate behavior. So here you go.*

The photos were close-ups. We were wearing so much clothing you could only see a few square inches of our faces, but what you could see was, in the words of my friend Masha, "The very essence of love, distilled down to medicinal strength." Or as John had said when I'd shown him one of the pictures, "Jesus fucking Christ, just looking at that makes me want to scream at you to get a fucking room. I don't even want to know what happened afterwards."

"It was a freezing cold day in the middle of Moscow," I said. "Nothing happened."

"Yeah, well...I still didn't want to see it."

My mother had just said, "Oh, *my*. He looks so...Russian. And so do you." It had not endeared her to Dima the way I'd thought it would. Instead, it had made me look like a stranger to her.

I explained all this to Galina Ivanovna.

"Of course," she said. "I understand. She doesn't want you running off and marrying some foreigner. Frankly, Innochka, when Dima first brought you home, I wasn't too thrilled about the idea of him running off and marrying some foreigner either. But then I realized that, for once, Dima's heart was smarter than mine."

She snorted. "Too bad it didn't last. But you can't fight fate, so I understand that we need to face facts and be practical. So let's face facts and be practical, Innochka. You and Dimochka are destined to be together, that's clear. So let's make a plan for how you can both live with that."

"Um..." I said. "Shouldn't he be part of this conversation?"

The gaze she fixed me with this time was stern. "Would he bring any sense or a clear understanding of what must be done to it?"

"Well..." I said. "It's, um, just that, well, it's his fate too we're deciding."

She snorted again. "Dima has always been a fool when it comes to fate. He keeps trying to fight it, and when he can't win, he runs away from it. Neither is a good strategy for the long term. So tell me true, Inna: Are you intending to marry him?"

She fixed me with an even sterner gaze, like a strict teacher waiting for the right answer from her star pupil.

"Um..." I said. "Well..."

"Do you not know your own mind, Innochka? Is that the problem?"

"No." My voice was suddenly strong and sharp. "I know my own mind. And you're right. We're meant to be together. It's fate. But he doesn't know his own mind. I'm not going to marry a man who isn't sure whether or not he wants me. I'm not going to marry a man who's doing it because he's being told to. If he wants it, let him ask me himself, of his own free will."

Galina Ivanovna froze for a moment. Then she laughed. "Akh, Innochka. Of course you're right. And this is why you two are destined to be together. But still, we must make plans. What are the practical ramifications if you get married? What will that mean for your citizenship? Where can or can't you live? What kinds of jobs can or can't you get? Would it help or hurt his chances of getting asylum as a political refugee?"

"I don't know," I said.

"Then we should find out," she said. "Because I think you're going to need to know. Oh! Is that him?"

My phone had just *pinged*. I looked at it.

"No," I said. "It's my brother."

John's message was short and to the point.

Ro! Call me. Mom and Dad are going off the deep end.

3

GALINA IVANOVNA EXCUSED herself, saying she'd let me talk to John in peace, but that I needed to start looking into the marriage and work situation right away. I promised I would and then, wondering how much more excitement I could take tonight, called John.

"Ro!" He picked up on the first ring. "Thank fuck you're there! We need to have a major powwow. I think Mom and Dad have finally cracked. And right when I'm having problems with Camila, too..."

"Oh no!" I said. "What's happening?"

"With Camila? Or Mom and Dad?"

"Start with Camila," I said. "Mom and Dad have been taking care of themselves their whole lives. They can do it for a few more minutes. I'm more concerned about you and Camila."

"You won't be once you hear what they're up to...and it's...with Camila...I don't know...the usual fucked-up shit, I guess." He sighed heavily into the phone. "Don't know if this is just normal, or I'm being paranoid...or maybe it's just normal for me? Maybe the problem is me? After all, I've fucked up every other relationship I've ever been in. Why should this one be any different?"

"It should be different because I like Camila and I want to keep her around for myself," I said. "Therefore, I insist that you take every possible action to preserve the relationship."

"Yeah...you remember I told you about the guy who was kind of stalking me?"

"Uh-huh."

"Well, now he's *really* stalking me. I've seen him a couple of times lurking outside my apartment. The last time he sent me a picture of myself he'd taken with his phone, and told me he knew where I lived and I'd better watch out."

"Um..." I said. "That's bold. Does he know who you are? What you do?"

"I think he tailed me back and forth to work a couple of times, so unless he's a fucking idiot, which is highly likely, now that I think about it, he should have some idea."

"Have you informed the police?" I asked.

"What am I gonna tell them? Some guy's sending me vaguely threatening messages?"

"Some guy with a history of stalking your girlfriend? You sure are," I said.

"He's not actually doing anything illegal," John pointed out. "There's nothing they can do. Their hands are tied until they find my dismembered corpse in a dumpster somewhere."

"At which point the report you filed will come in real handy," I said. "But seriously, you should tell them, and maybe security at work as well."

He groaned. "That'll do my reputation a lot of good. I'll look like a real pussy."

"You know what I always say about pussies..." I said.

"Yeah, yeah, they take a pounding a lot better than balls. I know. And you're right, too, but..."

"Tell them there's a dickhead stalking your girlfriend and you want to catch him doing something criminal," I said. "They'll probably be more sympathetic to that."

"I'm not looking for sympathy!"

"Well, it'll make you look more manly, then," I said.

"I think you're dicking with me and my masculine pride a little, Ro, but I appreciate the advice, and you're probably right. Camila's been after me to do it for a while now. I'll have to tell her she's right, too."

"It'll do you good," I said.

"Yeah, whatever. Now that we've fucked over my self-esteem, can we get to the real reason I wanted to talk to you?"

"Sure," I said. "What's up with Mom and Dad?"

4

WHAT WAS UP WITH MOM and Dad, it turned out, was that they'd gone back up to Virginia. To go house shopping.

"What?" I said. "Wait, *what*? What about the property down here in Georgia they just got? What about the tiny home hand built from reclaimed materials they're working on? What about the family practice Mom is supposed to be starting?"

These were all recent developments. My parents had spent a year with Doctors Without Borders, and when they'd gotten back, they'd decided to overhaul their lives. They'd quit their jobs in Atlanta, bought a plot of land in the country near Macon, and were planning to start a family medical practice.

"I *knew* it was too normal to last," I said.

"Only you would think building a tiny house with your bare hands is too normal, Ro."

"Well, by their standards, it's positively mainstream," I said.

"Too fuckin' true. So I guess we shouldn't be too fuckin' surprised they've decided to join a cult instead."

"Are they definitely going ahead with it, then?" All my worry, anguish, and rage for the day had already been taken up by the job news, so the only thing I had room for was a kind of numb despair.

"They haven't come out and fuckin' said so, but it doesn't look good, does it?"

"Why *are* they saying they want to move up there?" I asked.

"They want to be closer to Dennis and Alexandra. They're going through tough times, they need family, blahdeefuckin'blah. So Mom and Dad are saying they need to go take care of them."

"They've just met them!" I burst out. I paused. "Well, obviously that's not true. In fact, that's completely insane. But you get what I'm saying. They've been perfectly content to be out of Dennis and Alexandra's lives for decades now. And Dennis and Alexandra have been perfectly content to be out of their lives. So why the sudden need for closeness?" My voice was rising higher and higher, threatening to get out of control. Anger that had been searching for an outlet all afternoon gathered inside of me.

"They say that Dennis and Alexandra aren't getting any younger..."

"Neither are Grandma and Grandpa! What about them?!?" I paused again. "Um...you know what I mean."

"I do, and I'm right there with you, Ro. Grandma and Grandpa have always been there for all of us, even when Mom and Dad were fuckin' around with stuff they thought was bullshit. They're the ones we should be standing by in their old age, not people who can't even bear to look me in the face."

"What?"

"Yeah...the whole fuckin' time I was there, they couldn't ever fuckin' bring themselves to look me in the fuckin' face." John stopped, sighed, and laughed painfully. "Sorry, Ro. I guess I got a lot of fucks built up inside me again. I'll try to tone it down."

"It's fine," I said. "Perfectly understandable. I don't mind at all. In fact, I feel like you're saying them for me."

He laughed. Painfully. "Thank fuck, 'cause I don't know if I can talk about this without blowing my fuckin' top off. Anyway. Mom and Dad are saying that yeah, of course Grandma and Grandpa might need family nearby to help 'em out, but they've got you, since you'll be working in Georgia for the foreseeable future—"

"Actually," I said, "I probably won't be."

"Wait. *What?*"

I outlined the non-interview situation.

"Are you fuckin' *kidding* me, Ro? Those motherfuckers won't even ask you for an interview for your *own fuckin' job?!?!*"

"Yep," I said. "So I probably won't be in Georgia for more than a couple more months."

"So where the fuck're you supposed to go after that?"

"I don't know," I said. "Options are being considered."

"Such as?"

"Um, well..."

"Wait...you're not...*Ro, are you thinking of moving back to Russia? With HIM?!?!*"

"Probably not back to Russia," I said. "But maybe somewhere outside of the US. If I can get a job. And maybe with him."

"Fuck, Ro! Now is not the time for you to go fucking off overseas! We need you to stay the fuck in Georgia!"

"I know," I said. "Unfortunately, my employer does not. And I am unlikely to get any other employment in Georgia, at least not in this job cycle. So unless you want me to take up panhandling, I'm probably going to have to move. Out of state, if not out of the country."

John did some deep breathing on the other end of the line. "I know it's not your fault," he said eventually. "I know it's not what you wanted. But fuck, Ro, couldn't you have found some better line of work to get in-to?"

"Apparently not," I said. "So what are we going to do about Mom and Dad?"

John did some more deep breathing. "I guess...maybe you should talk to them? Maybe ask them what's going on, you know, all innocent-like? Maybe if they hear themselves explaining it to you, they'll start to hear how batshit-crazy they sound."

"We might as well try," I said.

"Don't sound so fuckin' optimistic about it," said John. "Although you might fuckin' well be right about our chances for success. But we gotta do *something*."

"We do," I agreed.

"And maybe we'll have some allies. I told you that Dennis and Alexandra want to marry us off to church members, right?"

"Uh-huh," I said.

"Well, they've got some girl called Jennifer picked out for me. I told them about Camila, but they don't want to listen. Keep going on about how isn't she Mexican, shit like that, while this Jennifer is a nice Virginia girl...thought I was gonna punch 'em in the fuckin' face...anyway. The guy they've got picked out for you is actual church royalty. Isaiah Jones, the pastor's son."

"I feel the need to break out into 'Son of a Preacher Man,'" I said.

"Yeah…I talked to him a couple of times. He doesn't seem that bad, actually, although he's got a bad boy reputation in the church…might be right up your alley, Ro. And he certainly seems interested in you…He did keep asking about *him*, which was pretty fuckin' weird, but whatever."

"Uh-huh," I said. "Sounds like a match made in heaven for sure."

"Yeah, whatevs. Anyways, it's looking more and more like a fucked-up freak show all around, and I'm getting nowhere."

"I'll call Mom and Dad tonight," I promised.

"Thanks, Ro," said John. "For the advice, and for helping out, and for kicking me up the ass when I need it."

"No problem," I said.

5

I CALLED MOM'S CELL phone. No answer. I called Dad's cell phone. Also no answer. On the off chance that they hadn't left yet for Christiansburg, I called the house phone. No answer there, either. I texted my lack of results to John, but heard nothing back.

I tried calling twice more, but got nothing. I finally left a message asking them to call me ASAP, since I had important news. I tried to make it sound like it wasn't good news. Since it was, in fact, true that I had important but unpleasant news, I hoped it came across as authentic.

There was still no reply when I got up the following morning. Nothing as I got ready for work, or as I headed out to campus. I was starting to worry. This was unlike my parents. Sure, they were a little...unusual. But they were also basically responsive and responsible people. Not answering a message from me was not their usual MO. So either something bad had happened to their phones, something bad had happened to them, or they were giving me the silent treatment. They'd never done anything like that before, but maybe they were deeper in the cult than we'd thought.

I drove over to campus on my own, but ran into Mel and Chloe at the faculty parking lot beyond the football stadium. Mel was explaining that she had a doctor's appointment this afternoon that required her to head out straight after class, so we weren't carpooling today.

"Makes sense," said Chloe. "And...maybe I need to get the name of your doctor from you. There's still something just not right with me, and no one can figure out what it is. I feel like I've been to every doctor in Atlanta, and all of them say I'm perfectly healthy. But I don't *feel* perfectly healthy. What do you think: could your doctor help me?"

"You might as well try," Mel told her. "You've gotta fill out an application form for the clinic, and they decide whether to accept you. So they'll decide upfront if they think they can help you or not."

"Or if they can get money from me," said Chloe.

"There's probably some of that, too, but the doctor I'm seeing does seem like she genuinely wants to help—and she has," said Mel. "So I'd say yeah, you might as well try. I'll send you the link to the application."

"Thanks. Maybe I'll work on it this weekend." Chloe made a face. "I was hoping to have, well, a *date* or something this weekend, but no. I told you I decided to start dating again, didn't I?"

"Uh-huh," I said. "I take it that it's not going well."

Her shoulders slumped. "I carefully went through several dozen profiles and messaged my top ten choices based on our match rating, mutual interests, geographic proximity, how well I fit the description of their ideal date, and how much I liked their photos. Half of them never got back to me."

"And the other half?" asked Mel.

"The other half also never got back to me, but they blocked me first. Not sure if that's more or less hurtful. I mean, at least I know they got my messages, but their response was to cut off all possibility of contact."

"I thought men keep saying they want women to make the first move," said Mel.

"Yeah...they do, don't they? Either they don't know what they really want, or I'm so hideous that they turn to stone as soon as they see a photo of me."

"Fuck 'em," Mel said crisply. "You're not a Gorgon, and if that's how they're going to play it, then don't bother messaging them first. Sit back and let them come to you."

"I've tried that too...I did get some messages, it's true. Most of them were scammers who ghosted me as soon as I suggested a video date. I've learned to ask right away to weed out the fakers who just want to steal my money."

"Uh-huh," Mel and I said together.

"I did get a few real guys, though. One jumped right in on our first text exchange to telling me that I needed to submit to his big black dick, and when I said no thanks, he had a meltdown and then ghosted me. One asked me if I wanted to have kids, and when I said yes, he said he did too—sons. He went on and on about how important having a son was to him and how the male life was more difficult than the female life but also more meaningful. I asked him how, exactly, it was more meaningful. He blocked me instead of answering me. The last one said he admired strong, independent women with their own careers, which sounded promising. But then he started ranting about how higher ed was a scam and I should leave it. When I said I didn't want to leave it, because I'd worked really hard to get here and also because I needed a job, he told me I was a de-luded tool of the Machine and ghosted me. So no, it's not going well."

"Ugh," I said. "I'm sorry."

"I don't get it," said Chloe. "My dad isn't like that. My uncle isn't like that. My brother isn't like that. But every man I meet in the dating world is like that. Or...maybe my dad and my uncle and my brother *are* like that, and I've just never seen that side of them. Maybe they're monsters on the inside, just like all those guys, and I've only ever seen their smiling ro-bot façades, but the vampire is lurking there underneath, waiting to break free whenever they're around women who aren't their blood kin. Any-way. I was hoping to have *something* to look forward to for spring break, but now I just want to curl up in bed—or maybe under the bed—and cry."

"How about helping me catch my scammer instead?" proposed Mel.

"You're still working on that?" Mel had told Chloe about Evil Mel and her attempts to unmask her. Chloe had been dubious about the ad-visability of the undertaking from the get-go. Mel had said she needed to take a few risks in order to bring Evil Mel down. Chloe had argued that the person Mel was most likely to bring down was herself.

"Whatever," Mel had said. "It's not like anyone fuckin' cares, anyway."

This had led to a heated exchange between them in which Chloe had insisted that lots of people cared, including her. Instead of winning Mel over, though, this had only made her angrier. She had been thin-lipped and short with Chloe all week.

Now, maybe softened by Chloe's tale of dating woe, she appeared to be extending the olive branch. Unfortunately, Chloe had responded in a rather judgmental tone. Mel's face suggested that she hadn't appreciated it.

"You know, when you first told me about it, I thought it was silly," said Chloe. She must have recognized the danger signals Mel was giving off as clearly as I did. "But after my latest foray into the world of online dating, I'm ready to drain that damn swamp." She paused. "That was probably a bad metaphor," she said. "I must have listened to too much political news recently. But you get what I mean. Online dating feels like a disgusting...well, swamp, I guess."

"Or cesspool," put in Mel.

"I didn't want to go there...but yeah. Most of the profiles you find there are scammers, and the real people are if anything even worse. So you know what? I *do* want to help you catch your scammer. I'm feeling all...vigilante. I want to do *something* to clean things up, at least a little."

"Fuckin' A," said Mel. "Welcome to the team." She checked her phone. "Oh shit. We'd probably better get to class. But how about we get together tonight? We could even go out on the town, have a little Friday-evening fun while we do our scammer-takedown-planning session."

"What town?" Chloe said dourly. "There's no town here to go out on. If there was, we wouldn't be putting ourselves in the sights of the scammers on CheapHookup.Com." She put her hand over her mouth. "Oh, shoot! That was crude, wasn't it?"

"Maybe even crass," Mel said solemnly. "But Ro and I will forgive you, won't we, Ro? Especially if you help us paint the town red tonight."

"I think I'm more up for painting the town a light pink at best," I said. "But yeah. Going out tonight would be fun. And if we can take down a ne'er-do-well while we're at it, that would be even better."

6

I STARTED TO THINK better of Mel's proposal to go out and paint the town red when I got home from campus and checked in on Galina Ivanovna. It would mean leaving her on her own all evening, and would it even be any fun? Probably not.

"I don't have to do it," I told Galina Ivanovna. "I'd be very happy—more than happy—to stay home with you."

"Nonsense, Innochka! You should go out and enjoy yourself. Here you've been sitting at home for the past two months, taking care of an old lady—you need a break. I'm perfectly capable of taking care of myself for an evening. I feel just fine after the last infusion. Actually, I feel better than fine. I think the treatment might be working."

"Really?! That's great!!!"

"Yes, I've been feeling better this week than I have in months, so I'm taking that as a good sign. And in any case, you should get out, spend time with your friends, enjoy yourself. I know you're a homebody and an introvert by nature, Innochka, but even a sit-at-home like you will benefit from occasional informal social interaction—what today's youth call 'partying.'"

"I don't think we're actually going to party," I said. "Not in that sense. And I don't like leaving you here by yourself..."

"I'm ordering you as a doctor, Innochka," she interrupted me. "I'm prescribing you social interaction. You've had a mentally challenging week, and all you've been doing is work and take care of me. Go out, have fun, forget about your troubles for the evening."

"Well...if you're sure..."

"I'm very sure, Innochka. Now go! Go get ready to have fun!"

274

I went back to my apartment. Maybe Galina Ivanovna was right. Maybe I should do something wild like take the rest of the afternoon off, and then go out and...well, not *party*, but I might have a glass of wine. I might have *two* glasses of wine.

My thoughts of letting my hair down were interrupted by the discovery of a pool of cat vomit on the kitchen floor. I searched around, hunting for Fevronia, and found her under the bed. She looked fine. But this was the third time she'd thrown up this week.

I went back into the kitchen and performed a careful examination of the evidence. No obvious signs of worms. Maybe it was just hairballs?

What if it's something more serious? I asked myself. *She's never thrown up this much before.*

I went back and looked at Fevronia again. Was she crouched under the bed in an especially sickly, painful way? Or was this just her usual surliness?

*What if her usual surliness is a sign of a chronic condition? What if I'm a terrible, self-absorbed, neglectful pet parent? What if...*I cut off those thoughts by pouring some more food into her bowl and resolving to monitor her over the weekend and, if she didn't get better, call the vet Monday morning.

Okay. That's taken care of. Now I can focus on relaxing for the rest of the afternoon.

I was just contemplating how, precisely, I might do that, when the phone rang. Hoping/fearing that it might be Dima, I checked the caller ID.

It wasn't Dima. It was my mother.

7

"ROWENA? YOU CALLED us a bunch of times yesterday. What's going on? Are you okay?" Her voice sharpened with anxiety. "Is John okay?"

"We're both fine," I said.

"Oh, thank goodness." Her voice went breathy with relief. "You hardly ever call, so I knew it had to be something important...and of course, my first thought was John...So if it's not him, what is it? Is it...*him?*" She injected almost as much venom into that pronoun as John would have.

"No," I said. "If by 'him' you mean Dima, he's fine too." That might or might not actually be true, but I didn't want to get sidetracked by a discussion about what Dima was up to. "And so's Galina Ivanovna," I added. "She thinks the treatment might be helping."

"That's his mother, right?" Now my mother sounded muddled and uncertain. Which was not her style at all. She might be an oddball who marched to the beat of her own drummer, but she was also a sharp cookie. She'd always expressed confusion at everything about Dima and his family, though. I didn't even think it was feigned. I suspected that she found the very idea of Dima so painful that she had a mental block on everything that had anything to do with him.

"That's right."

"Well, I'm glad to hear that."

Awkward pause. My mother's words had been so obviously insincere that we both had to take a beat to let it pass.

"I'm actually calling about you," I said eventually.

"About me? Whatever for?" Her voice sharpened again. With, I thought, guilt.

"John said you were thinking of moving up to Virginia? I guess I wanted to find out more about why you were thinking of doing that. Are you planning on selling the place down here in Georgia?"

"Well, we don't know, sweetie." Her voice still held a faint tang of guilty sharpness. "We're just looking at all our options. It was so good to connect with Bobby's parents and repair that relationship after all these years. And it couldn't have come at a better time, since they really need family right now. You know about Dennis's cancer diagnosis, of course."

"Yeah," I said. "How's that going?"

"The first round of treatment has gone better than expected." Now she sounded like a doctor again, brisk and competent. "But the overall prognosis is still poor. We may have bought him a little more time, but the one thing we know for sure is that he's not a young man and he already had a lot of issues going into this. He could have five months, he could have five years...he could have fifteen years, but that's not likely. So every week is precious, and he wants to spend those precious weeks with family."

"Uh-huh." I had no doubt that this was all true. I still didn't like Dennis or my parents' newfound infatuation with him and Alexandra. "What about Roseanna?" I asked. "Have you talked to her?" I'd told my parents that I'd gotten in contact with Roseanna. So far they'd responded by ignoring everything I said about her. This time was no diffcrent.

"So we thought we'd look into the feasibility of moving up here to spend however much time he and Alexandra have with them," my mother was saying, not acknowledging my question. "We'd be sorry to give up the new property, but, really, honey, there are some *lovely* houses up here, and I might be able to get a good position as a GP here as well—probably better than anything I could get for myself in Macon. So it might be the practical choice as well."

"Uh-huh." Alarm bells were going off louder and louder in my head. When had my mother ever argued in favor of something by saying it was the practical choice? When it had been a bad idea, that's when. My mother only couched things in terms of practicality when she was trying to rationalize a terrible decision.

"You know what, sweetie? You should come up here and see it for yourself. While we're here. You could come see the town, meet Dennis and Alexandra—I mean, I know you've met them before, but you've never spent much time with them, have you? You should get to know them while you have the chance."

"Yes," I said. "How long are you up there?"

"For the next four days. Can you come up this weekend?"

"I sure can," I said. "That's a great idea. Thanks for suggesting it."

"Oh, *wonderful*, darling! I can't wait."

"Neither can I," I said.

8

I REGRETTED MY OFFER as soon as I hung up the phone. What would Galina Ivanovna do without me? What if Dima suddenly reappeared while I was gone? His time in Utah was supposed to end any day, although he hadn't been able to tell us which day, exactly, it was going to end. Because he didn't know? Or because he didn't care enough about us to give us this basic and essential information?

He cares, I told myself. *He's just not very good at showing it sometimes.* But that was cold comfort. People who weren't very good at showing they cared tended to do a lot of the same selfish shit as people who didn't actually care.

It's only a few hours away, I told myself. *If you need to, you can be home the same day you get a call asking you to come. It's no big deal.*

That was all very true, but I'd also been looking forward to getting in a few days' rest and relaxation, or at least catch-up. Especially since I needed to start looking for jobs ASAP. I'd spent about a nanosecond contemplating legal action against Crimson, claiming that they were essentially firing me in retaliation for the part I'd played in revealing Anthony Wainwright, III's criminal activities. Then I'd decided I'd be better off keeping a low profile and getting another job. But that meant I really needed to spend the weekend going through the recent job postings, not chasing after errant relatives who were older and should be wiser. Plus, it was pretty much guaranteed to be full of super-awkward encounters and opportunities to have full-on blow-out fights with my closest family members.

All in all, I was in a black mood when I drove over to the tiny downtown. I was supposed to meet Mel and Chloe at Smokey Joe's, which was a kind of bar-cum-barbecue joint. None of us had ever been there, but Mel had been assured by other faculty members that it was the best place to go for a good time on Friday nights.

"Apparently they have karaoke," she said, as we walked over from the tiny public parking lot to the neon-emblazoned bar front. It had a giant, bright pink pig smiling and waving happily with a glowing front leg, its jolly expression a million miles away from the trembling, terrified, shit-stained reality of the pigs you saw being trucked to slaughter. "And if they hate you, they shower you with barbecue."

"Really?" asked Chloe, her voice somewhere between skeptical and alarmed. "You're not planning to sing, are you?"

"Depends on how liquored up I get," said Mel. "Whaddya say, Ro: should we hit 'em with a duet? We could do..." She paused, thinking. "What's a good duet song?"

"Paradise by the Dashboard Light?" I suggested.

"Niiiiiiice," said Mel. "That'd be a hell of a song for two women to cover."

"Two women who can sing, maybe," I said. "I can't carry a tune in a bucket, so I will definitely not be getting up on that stage."

"I can't carry a tune in a fuckin' bucket either, but that's never stopped me," said Mel. "That's how I met Jewell, by embarrassing myself at a karaoke bar..." She trailed off. Jewell was the ex back in LA who had kicked her out and replaced her with someone who was just like her only six inches shorter and much less well educated. That had been three years ago, but Mel was still all hung up on her, even though, from my perspective, Jewell sounded like a shallow, selfish, manipulative, bitchy...I made myself stop before I thought thoughts that were unworthy of me and my feminist vow of sisterly solidarity.

"I'll get up and sing with you, if you want," Chloe offered.

Mel and I both stared at her in surprise.

"I mean, I'm no Aretha Franklin, but I sang in a gospel choir all through elementary and high school," she said, looking embarrassed.

"Daaaaamn, girl, you're just full of surprises," said Mel. "You're on!" Humming an off-key rendition of "Paradise by the Dashboard Light," she opened the door and ushered us into the bar.

It looked about the way you'd expect a small-town dive bar/barbecue joint in the South to look, except that it also looked kind of like the movie set version. There was a sign above the bar that said "proudly serving the Greenfields community since 2010," which maybe explained the movie set appearance. At 7:00pm on a Friday, it was half full. Because things wouldn't get started for another couple of hours, or because Greenfields was a dead zone at any hour of the day or night?

"Right." Mel looked around with the air of a commander surveying her terrain. "Let's go get that corner table before anyone else does. Then we can order."

We hustled over to the corner table and staked our claim. No clamoring hordes attempted to contest our conquest. In fact, no one of the half-dozen little groups there appeared to notice us at all. Oh, no, wait, was that a group from Math looking our way...?

"Are they *checking us out?*" Chloe hissed out of the corner of her mouth. "I never can be sure."

"I think they might be," I hissed back.

"Hot *dang!*" she whispered. "We're getting attention from the Math faculty. I don't know how to feel about that. Am I supposed to be flattered or embarrassed? I never know in these situations. Or am I supposed to be creeped out? Are they creepy?"

I gave them a covert glance. "They seem extremely uncreepy so far," I whispered. "I doubt they pose us any physical danger. The main concern would be if 1) they're married, especially to someone else on campus, or 2) they take a dislike to you and decide to scupper your chances at tenure."

"True." Chloe sat down with her back to the three presumed members of the Math department, her shoulders slumping. "Everything's so high stress. You can't even go out on a Friday night without worrying about accidentally committing adultery or ruining your chances for tenure."

"I think you can only commit adultery if you're actually married," I said. "Technically, you'd just be fornicating. *He'd* be the one committing adultery."

"Yeah…it'd probably fornicate my chance for tenure either way, though."

"Drinks," said Mel in a loud voice. "And food. Whaddya ladies want?"

We had a brief skirmish over who would pay, which Mel won. A few minutes later she was back with a beer (for her) and two glasses of Moscato (for me and Chloe), plus a basket of fries.

"They also have actual food, of a sort," she announced, setting down a couple of menus next to the fries. "If you call barbecue, slaw, and hush puppies real food."

"Cole slaw can be a very healthy dish," I said.

"I'm guessing not the way they make it," said Mel, taking a long pull from her beer. "Oh my fuckin' *God*." She closed her eyes. "No alcohol for two solid months while I was on the antibiotics. I even did a couple of weeks of this shit that will literally make you puke yourself to death if you mix it with booze. I thought the doc was pulling my leg when she told me that, but I got nauseous just from taking it with juice, so I became a believer."

"But you're off all that now, right?" Chloe asked. "You're all cured now, right?"

Mel shrugged. "Maybe. I *feel* a lot better, except for my stomach. And my face looks normal, and my joints don't hurt, and I don't feel like I have the flu all the time, and I haven't had any weird twitch-y, seizure-y episodes for a couple of weeks, so we're cautiously declaring me cured. For now."

She looked down at her beer and then at the fries. "I'm sure my doc would tell me not to do any of this. She's a big believer in clean living—no booze, no sugar, no carbs, no coffee—but you can only live like that for so long. At least I can. And it's an open question how good that lifestyle is for you anyway. People in the Mediterranean are chowing down on pasta and coffee and red wine all the time, and they're supposed to be super healthy. Anyway." She took another slug of beer. "I'm going to act like I'm back to normal, and see what happens. And that includes trying to take down Evil Mel. Which is where you two ladies come in."

Chloe was perusing the menu. "I think I'm going to have some real food," she announced. "Or at least something to soak up the alcohol. Will you mind if I eat?"

Mel popped a fry in her mouth. "Fuck, no. I'll be chowing down right alongside you."

"Great. Rowena, what about you? And let me get it. It'll be my treat." She looked faintly embarrassed. "You know, I don't think I've ever treated anyone to dinner at a restaurant before. But, now that I think about it, that's silly. I mean, it's a fun thing to do, and I can totally afford it, at least at these prices."

I surveyed the menu. Unsurprisingly, vegetarian options were few and far between. I chose fried mushrooms with a side of slaw, on the theory that somewhere under the breading and the mayonnaise they would have protein and phytonutrients. Chloe took our orders with an expression as serious as if she were a doctor listening to the description of a critical patient, and set off, somewhat nervously, to the bar.

"At least I'm doing some good in the world," Mel said when she was gone. "Getting her out of the house and introducing her to life. I may not have accomplished much when I get kicked out of here in a couple of months, but I can take pride in teaching Chloe how to go to a bar and even make an order. We might even work up to ordering drinks by the end of the evening."

"I think she might be ordering drinks even as we speak," I said. "Look: the bartender is making cocktails."

"Hot *damn*. What's come over the girl?"

What had come over her, it turned out, was an offer of free drinks. Chloe had been confused by it, but hadn't been able to refuse in time to stop it. She set down the three Cosmopolitans on our table with an apologetic air.

"No worries," Mel told her. "I don't normally go for Cosmos, but free drinks are free drinks. And it's no mystery why he gave them to us: we're the only girls-only table in the joint. They're probably hoping we stay here the rest of the night."

"Oh." Chloe looked around nervously. "There's a woman over there," she pointed out.

"With her date," Mel pointed out in reply. "We're the only ones here for the single guys to hit on."

"Oh. That...that sounds nice in theory, but in practice, it doesn't sound so great. Especially when you look at the guys who are actually here."

"A couple of them are cute," said Mel. "As much as I can tell. Who knows? This could be your lucky night."

Chloe took a hasty sip of her Cosmopolitan and choked on it.

"Or not," said Mel. "Anyway, wanna hear about my cunning plan to take down Evil Mel?"

9

"FIRE AWAY," I SAID. Chloe took another hasty sip of her Cosmopolitan and choked again.

"Gosh," she said, still coughing slightly. "I know I'm not making it look like it, but these are pretty good."

"Have mine." Mel pushed hers over to Chloe.

"Are you sure?"

"Damn sure. I have my dad's tastes for liquor: beer and whisky. Anything fruity and pink turns my stomach."

"Well...I guess...if I finish this one and feel like some more...although I still have more than half a glass of wine..." She surveyed the alcohol before her. "This is all a sign of terrible taste, right? I mean, it's all sweet. Isn't that supposed to be bad? Isn't it wrong to like sweet drinks?"

"It's wrong because women on average have more sensitive taste buds and therefore prefer milder, sweeter drinks," I said. "Liking dry wine and peaty whiskey generally means you have a weak sense of taste and smell, which is more common for men."

"Oh...well...I guess I should just own who I am, anyway, right?"

"Right," I said. "So what's the plan to bring down Evil Mel?"

Mel took another long swallow of beer. "So," she said, "I think I've finally convinced her to meet me in person."

"Whoa!" I said. "Really?"

"That sounds dangerous," Chloe said.

"Yes to both," Mel told us. "I really do have a real, in-person date with her, and yes, it might be dangerous. Maybe. I guess she could pull a gun on me or something. Although I get the feeling she's not really the gun-pulling kind. Whereas I"—Mel took another long pull from her beer—"intend to show up ready to rumble. Which is where you two come in."

Chloe had taken a big gulp of her Cosmopolitan at the word "rumble" and was now choking so hard I slapped her on the back.

"Thanks," she coughed. "I don't see what I could add to this...madness," she added once she could breathe again. "I always thought this was a bad idea, and the fact that you're planning to show up ready to *fight* just goes to prove..."

"What, exactly, is your plan?" I cut her off before she could piss off Mel again. "Maybe if we knew the details we could figure out how we might best help."

"My plan." Mel tossed back the rest of her beer. She contemplated the bottom of her glass, then set it down with a decisive motion.

"Here." Chloe pushed the extra Cosmopolitan towards her. "You take it. It's yours anyway."

"Nah. I'll get something when they bring us our orders. You take it."

"Are you sure?" Chloe eyed the glass full of pink liquid doubtfully. She turned to her own glass. There was only one small swallow left in it. She picked it up and tossed it back. This time she hardly choked at all. She pulled the full glass over, contemplated it for a moment, and then took a dainty sip.

"I think this one's even better than the other," she said. "More orange-y."

"That's Cointreau," Mel told her.

"Really? What's that?"

"A kind of orange liquor they put in Cosmos."

"Oh. Okay." Chloe took another dainty sip. No coughing or choking at all. "So," she said. "Ready to rumble. Do we need to be packing heat?"

"Only if you want to," Mel told her.

Chloe looked at me.

"I'll bring my phone," I said. "Maybe I can call 911 if things get desperate."

"I think I have some pepper spray," said Chloe. "I could bring that. If it still works. I got it when I lived in Manhattan." Chloe had gotten her PhD from Columbia. She frowned. "And if I can figure out how to use it. I took a self-defense class when I first moved to New York, but I never had to use it. It turns out New York isn't actually as dangerous as they tell you, even Harlem, as long as you're smart about it." She frowned again. "Or lucky. Maybe I was just always really lucky. Maybe my luck is about to run out! Maybe..."

"Take a drink," Mel advised her. "And maybe you were little bit lucky, but I'll bet you were smart, too."

Chloe took another dainty sip. "Yeah," she said. "I was pretty smart about not getting hurt, I guess."

"Great. That's the kind of person I want on my side when this goes down. So: the plan." Mel wrinkled her nose. "It's not actually as exciting or as clever as I'm making out. It's basically just for me to meet with Evil Mel, get her talking about her scheme, and record her telling me all about her evil criminal intent. She's been sharing little bits and pieces of it with me for the past few weeks, and I've been sending her pictures of my 'art,' trying to convince her I'd make a good partner. I think she might be about ready to cut me in on it."

"Oh." Chloe took another dainty sip. Despite the apparent daintiness of her drinking style, the second Cosmo was now almost half gone. "So what do you need us for?"

"For backup," Mel told her. "I need you to have my back in case Evil Mel does something evil. Then Rowena can call 911 while you pepper-spray the fuck out of her."

"Oh. That doesn't sound so bad, actually." Chloe took another dainty sip. "When and where is this operation supposed to take place?"

"Next Saturday," Mel told her. "A week from tomorrow. I wanted to make it this weekend, but she said she had plans. So we're doing it next weekend. In Augusta. Y'all up for a day trip to Augusta?"

Chloe was smiling faintly, a light sheen of sweat on her neck and temples, making the scars from excessive hair straighteners stand out sharply in the artificial light. "Sure," she said. "A day trip to Augusta sounds fun. Especially if it involves taking down a genuine evildoer." She giggled. "Chloe Taylor, crime fighter extraordinaire!"

"Damn straight," said Mel. "And look, here comes our food. This evening is going great already."

10

OVER FOOD WE IRONED out the details of our plan, such as it was. Mel had originally suggested a coffee shop for the date with Evil Mel, but Evil Mel had said she wasn't really a coffee shop kind of girl, and suggested a bar instead. So now they were set to meet at a sports bar near the riverfront.

"Not ideal," Mel admitted. "It'll probably be real loud, so hard to get a good recording. But it'll probably be busy, so she won't be able to try anything too evil."

"Unless she spikes your drink and lures you away to a quieter location where she kills you, cuts you up, and dumps your body parts in the Savannah River," said Chloe.

"Daaaaamn, girl, I didn't know you had that kind of imagination," said Mel. "And that's what you two'll be there to prevent."

"Yeaaaaaaah." Chloe took another sip of her drink, which turned into a slurp. When she set the glass down, it was empty.

"Why do I feel so warm?" she asked, fanning herself. "Is it really hot in here all of a sudden?"

"Nah, you're just drunk," Mel told her.

"You're sure? What if I'm coming down with something?"

"You just knocked back a glass of wine and two cocktails on an empty stomach. You're drunk off your ass."

Chloe picked up her pulled pork sandwich and waved it in front of Mel. "I'm eating! It's not on an empty stomach!"

"It was for the first glass and a half, and you're a little thing and you hardly ever drink, am I right?"

"I'm not little!" Chloe insisted. She looked down, surveying her body. "I wish I were. I've always wanted to be one of those waif-like fairy girls. But instead I've always been what Carolyn Keene would call 'pleasantly plump.'"

Mel squinted at her. "Is that a Nancy Drew reference?"

"Uh-huh."

"Well, cool, but you're not 'pleasantly plump' anymore. You're downright skinny."

"Yay! I think. If I'd been working out and dieting, I'd be thrilled, but since it's just happening, I'm...I'm scared." The last words came out as a whisper.

"You've been tested by all the best doctors in Atlanta, right?" Mel said.

"Right."

"So they're probably right when they tell you you don't have leukemia or some shit like that."

"Even good doctors can be wrong," Chloe whispered.

"Yeah, but I'm still thinking they're probably right about you not having leukemia or lupus or type 1 diabetes or any of that shit. They kept telling me I was fine, and it turned out I was—except for the fuckin' Lyme disease. I'm betting for you it's that mold crap that Diane and Julie are researching. Plus all the stress you're under."

"Stress can certainly make you lose weight," I put in. "I've lost, like, at least ten pounds this semester, and I'm pretty sure it's all from stress." I pulled at the waistband of my pants to make my point. The unwanted weight I'd put on last year from my enforced lack of exercise had been melting off for the past couple of months without me even trying. I was chalking it up to stress and not having the time to eat on Thursdays. I hoped that was all it was. At any rate, my clothes were now pleasantly loose.

"Chronic stress can cause all kinds of scary things," Chloe said, still in a whisper.

"Yeah, but so far it probably hasn't for you," said Mel. "So far it's probably just tied your guts all up in knots, and that's why you're losing weight. I'm not saying it's good. But it's probably not immediately fatal."

"Yeah...I guess..."

"You gonna drink this?" Mel lifted up the third Cosmo, the one sitting in front of me.

I shook my head. I was still nursing my glass of wine. I was less of a lightweight when it came to drinking than Chloe, but I wasn't a heavyweight, either. And I just didn't feel like drinking. None of this felt like much fun to me. Part of me was sitting there smiling and pretending to have a good time, and another part of me felt like it was floating somewhere above my left shoulder, looking down on the scene with detached eyes, and a third part of me was fretting about Dima, and my parents, and Dima, and Galina Ivanovna, and Dima, and John, and Dima...

"Here." Mel pushed the Cosmo over to Chloe. "Drink up. It'll make you feel better."

"But I'm already drunk!"

"Not drunk enough, apparently," said Mel. "Especially since it looks like they're warming up the karaoke machine."

"What?! No!!!"

"You were the one who sang in a gospel choir," Mel said. "I think we need to hear you. I think you'll be depriving the good people of this bar of the biggest talent in here if you don't stand up and show them what you've got."

"I wasn't much of a talent," Chloe said, mumbling into her glass. "Not like my cousins or my brother. There's a reason I gave it up when I started college."

"Sure," said Mel. "You only sang in an Atlanta gospel choir for—how many years was it?"

"Twelve," mumbled Chloe.

"For twelve years. I'm sure you have a *terrible* voice."

People had been arriving in a steady stream for the past quarter of an hour, and the place was now almost full. Apparently karaoke night was a bigger deal here than I'd thought. Well, it wasn't like there was a lot else to do.

There was an increasing bustle around the karaoke machine. It resolved into the bartender being ushered/pushed, in what I sensed was a regular ritual, onto the little stage. The opening bars of "Don't Stop Believin'" filled the room.

"Oh God," Mel muttered. "Please let him be good. Please let him be good..."

He was respectable. The bar broke out into enthusiastic applause when he was done, and he retired behind the counter, looking both embarrassed and pleased. Mel grinned at Chloe, but Chloe shook her head, saying there was no way she could top that.

This was followed by an off-key rendition of "Born in the U.S.A." The singer, a cracker-y-looking guy who had been pushed up onto the stage by his buddies, sang the lyrics in a flat, slightly behind-the-beat monotone that suggested he was finding them a surprise. He stumbled badly over the words "Khe Sanh," "Viet Cong," and "Saigon," but rallied, and his entire table screamed out the chorus.

"Gosh," said Chloe. "That...that..."

Before she could say what that was, a heavily made up woman wearing a tube top two sizes too small was pushed up onto the stage by her friends. All of them were stumbling drunk, even though it was barely eight o'clock in the evening.

The woman wove back and forth on the stage for a moment while her friends made their selection. "Fantasy" by Mariah Carey started to play.

Chloe perked up. "I *love* Mariah Carey!" she exclaimed. "I used to sing along with her all the time! She got me through some really dark moments in high school. She was kind of the reason I stayed in choir, actually."

The woman on the stage started to sing. Chloe winced. She winced even more when the other two women in the group joined in the chorus. By the time the song was over, she was hunched up in physical pain.

"Let me guess," Mel said. "You could do better than that."

"Well...I mean, yeah..."

"You're up, then. Whaddya wanna sing? Let's check out the Mariah Carey selection."

"No, no, no...And that would be so mean..."

While they argued, someone else got up and performed Whitney Houston's "How Will I Know." It was better than "Fantasy," but that was a low bar. By the time it was done, I was seriously considering stabbing my own ears out.

"First they blaspheme Mariah, then they desecrate Whitney," Chloe muttered.

"So get your ass up on stage and show 'em how it's done," Mel said.

"I don't know..."

"Well, I fuckin' do." Mel, who was on her second whiskey, grabbed Chloe by the wrist and marched her up onto the stage. "What's it gonna be?" she asked her, loud enough for the whole bar to hear. "Mariah? Whitney? Or something else?"

The bar was now packed. I was sweating too, even though I wasn't drunk. People started cheering and calling out suggestions.

"Uuuhhhhh..." said Chloe, her eyes deer-in-the-headlights wide. "Mariah Carey. 'Dreamlover.'"

Raucous applause. Chloe looked like she might faint. The music started.

For an instant, I thought she wasn't going to sing. Then she opened her mouth. The bar went silent.

Her voice was barely above a whisper at first. It was still pure and clear and perfectly on key. By the second verse, she was singing. She didn't have Mariah's five-octave range, but she did have a sweet, rich voice that hit all the notes and was infused with emotion.

There was a long moment of silence when she was done. Then the bar broke out in wild applause.

She tried to leave the stage, but there was a vociferous outcry.

"Um...okay..." she said. "Um..." She looked over at me and Mel. "What should I do next? Um...maybe something from 90s R&B? I, um...know a lot of it by heart..."

"*What's the 411!*" shouted the Math table. "Do something from *What's the 411!*"

"Um...yeah...it's not my strongest suit, but I could probably do that...I had a bootleg tape of that album from my cousin and I listened to it so many times the tape snapped...Um...how about 'Real Love'?"

More wild cheering. Chloe launched into a very respectable version of "Real Love." This was followed by an even more respectable rendition of Toni Braxton's "Unbreak My Heart." The entire bar was in paroxysms of joy. Calls for another Mariah Carey song got louder and louder.

"Heartbreaker!" someone screamed from the back. This was taken up as a chant by the entire bar.

"Um...okay...but I need someone to do Jay-Z's part..."

Pause. All the men looked at each other.

"Oh fuck," Mel muttered to me. "Do I need to get up and do Jay-Z's part?"

"Can you rap?" I muttered back.

"Fuck no, but that'll just make Chloe look better."

"Wait...is that...I think she's found her Jay-Z."

The most junior member of the Math table was being pushed forward by his colleagues. He was a skinny guy, about 5'6", with a distinct air of "East Coast Jewish intellectual" about him. I guessed that he felt no more at home in Greenfields than Chloe did.

He came shyly up to the stage. "I...I'm not great, but I can probably do the Jay-Z part...it's only one verse, right? I mean, I won't do it like him, but I can kind of mumble along...my older sister played the album so many times when I was little I think I know every word by heart..."

"Come on up," Chloe told him. They launched into a spirited rendition of "Heartbreaker." The Math guy wasn't as good as Chloe, but he gamely did his best, showing a surprising ability to rap. The bar filled with more rapturous cheering.

"I think...I think I'd better sit down for a minute...woo...I feel a little lightheaded..." Chloe announced when they were done. She made her way a little unsteadily, accompanied by thunderous applause, back to our table. Math guy shadowed her solicitously.

"I think I've seen you around at faculty meetings," he told her. "And at new faculty orientation. Aaron Shapiro. Math."

"I remember you," Chloe told him. She sat down and began to fan herself.

"Yeah...I remember you too..."

Aaron looked like he wanted to say more, but wasn't sure what it was. His two colleagues came over, full of congratulations.

"We were hoping to get him up on the stage," they told us. "But we weren't counting on such a spectacular partner for him...you have to come back next week! You guys have to work up a duet routine!"

"'Paradise by the Dashboard Light,'" Mel muttered to herself.

"Aaron can do it!" the taller of the other two Math guys said, while the shorter one nodded enthusiastically.

"I don't like that one so much," Chloe said. "I guess I could try it, though..."

"There's lots of other duets we could try," Aaron said eagerly. "Doesn't Mariah have some more?"

"Yeah...like with Boyz II Men..." said Chloe, still fanning herself. "Jeez! I'm still feeling kind of woozy...but it could be fun when I'm feeling better. Here." She stopped fanning herself long enough to fish a business card out of her purse and hand it to Aaron. "Maybe...send me an email or something...we could maybe practice together some-time...gosh...I haven't done any singing in years...I'd forgotten how fun it is...might be a fun thing to do to take my mind off things...oh jeez. I think I need to go lie down, but I don't know that I should be driving right now..."

"Mel and I can drive you and your car home," I offered. We said goodnight to the Math guys and helped the slightly stumbling Chloe through the throngs of her newfound fans and out the door.

11

IT WASN'T EVEN TEN o'clock when I got home from dropping Chloe and her car off at her house. This was good, because I had to set off early the next morning.

What was less good was the pool of vomit that greeted me at the door. I tracked down Fevronia, who was under the bed. That was normal for her. She looked at me suspiciously when I peered in at her. That was also normal for her. When I retreated to the kitchen, she came out and sniffed hopefully at her food dish. That was also normal for her. I reached down and felt her ribs. She swiped at me halfheartedly. Also normal. Less normal was the distinct feeling of rib bone that I got under her fur. Oh God. Where was I going to find the money for a vet visit? I poured out some more cat crunchies in case her problem was simple underfeeding. Maybe she'd taken to working out in my absence and had higher caloric demands than she'd had in the past. That was more likely than a terrible disease, right? She was only five years old. Cats didn't develop terrible diseases at that age, did they?

Some do, I told myself.

The sight of Fevronia chowing down on the cat crunchies was reassuring, though, and I went to bed in a reasonably calm frame of mind. This was broken at two in the morning when she barfed all over the bed, including in my hair. By the time I had cleaned up after that, including washing out my hair, I was wide awake. I only dropped off to sleep again sometime after four. This was unfortunate, since I had to get up at six in order to set off for Christiansburg at seven so that I could meet my parents by three in the afternoon.

I woke up, feeling groggy and out of it, at 6:15. When I saw the time, I cursed myself for not setting my alarm. I normally didn't need to, but an early-morning departure after a night out was an exception. Okay, it hadn't been that late a night out, and it wasn't that early a departure, but still...

Fevronia was unusually affectionate, rubbing her head against my calf as I stumbled around the kitchen making coffee and trying to pull together snacks for the road. Rather than reassuring me, this made me more worried. Was she acting like this because she could sense her end was near? Was she trying to tell me not to leave her at this critical juncture? It was moments like these when I felt my lack of experience with animals.

There had been goats and chickens on the commune, but I hadn't interacted with them much. My mother had gotten a cat when we'd moved into the "real house," as we called it, but I'd never been the primary caretaker. Galina Ivanovna had had a cat when I'd first started seeing Dima, but the cat had passed away shortly afterwards and they'd never gotten another one. Fevronia was my first ever pet who was all my own. I cared about animals in the abstract, but one of the main things I'd learned by acquiring Fevronia was that I lacked a lot of basic know-how when it came to interacting with other species.

A knock at the door made me spill my coffee. When I went to answer it, I found Galina Ivanovna standing on the welcome mat.

"Why are you here so early?" I said. It came out much more accusingly than I meant it. "You didn't have to get up..."

"Nonsense," she said briskly. "Someone has to see you off, Innochka. And I wake up early these days. Especially this past week...I think I'm gaining energy. It's pleasant, but it's making me wake up at four in the morning. So I came over to see you off and to say hello to my charge." She bent down to look at Fevronia, who was skulking behind my legs. "Such a pretty kitty. And so fluffy! But do you think she's a bit thin? I think she's lost weight."

I explained my fears for Fevronia's health while ushering Galina Ivanovna inside, cleaning up the coffee I'd spilled on the counter, pouring myself more coffee, and starting tea.

"It could be anything," Galina Ivanovna told me. "The first thing you need to do is a full physical examination, blood work, probably a stool sample to check for worms...it probably is just worms. Or maybe allergies. I'll monitor her over the weekend, Innochka, and let you know what I observe."

Galina Ivanovna's voice was brisk and efficient, with forty years of medical experience behind it. I felt myself relax. At least Fevronia would have the care of a medical professional while I was gone. Okay, a human doctor with no access to medical equipment, but still, medicine was medicine, and Galina Ivanovna was also an experienced cat caretaker.

"Thank you," I said. "Take care of her. And yourself. And you can call or text me at any time, day or night, and I'll come right back down..."

"Innochka." Galina Ivanovna patted my hand. "Don't worry. Ronechka and I will both be fine. Go to your family. And take care of yourself. *You* call *me* at any time, day or night, if you think you're in trouble. And call Dima too."

Something in my face must have given away my doubts on that score. "Dima is a blockhead," she said. "At least when it comes to regular communication. But if you really need him, he'll come in, guns blazing, no question."

"Yeah." I imagined various scenarios that would involve Dima coming in, guns blazing, in order to rescue me from my own family. I privately resolved to avoid that if at all humanly possible. "I know," I said out loud. "Well, I'd better get going."

"Go with God, Innochka," Galina Ivanovna told me.

She'd never said that to me before. It was always something we said to Dima before he set off on some risky venture where blazing guns were pretty much a certainty.

"I'll be back by Monday at the latest," I promised, and, gathering up my disorganized pile of overnight gear, left.

12

THE GROGGINESS SLOWLY dissipated as I headed north. By the time I was in Augusta, I felt fairly awake. This gave me time to do lots of pondering between Augusta and Columbia. This led to even more pondering between Columbia and my old stomping grounds of Charlotte, where I'd spent an extremely impoverished semester adjuncting at UNC-Matthews. Mostly it had been a bad experience, but there had been good moments, too. John and I had reconnected after his last deployment, and Alex...I shied away from that thought. We'd connected pretty closely then, to put it delicately, and I'd thought that maybe we were on our way to climbing out of the hole we'd both found ourselves in and creating something good. In the end, though, the magnetic pull of our past lives and past loves had been too strong.

I spent most of the drive north from Charlotte contemplating the magnetic pull of past loves and whether I was doomed to stay fixated on a man I'd met in my 20s. Was that moment of connection I'd felt when my eyes had met Dima's across a crowded airport been real, or just some kind of gosling-like imprinting on someone I'd been thrown together with during a turbulent and transformational time in my life? And what did "real" even mean in that context? Imprinting was a real feeling, just like any other. Just because an emotion or sensation was caused by hormones and neurons didn't make it not real; in fact, that made it much more real than something untethered to physical reality. It was real, just like any other natural phenomenon, and now I could observe it and make a conscious choice about how I wanted to react to it.

By the time I hit the Virginia state line I'd concluded that my love for Dima when I'd first met him had been real, and my feelings for him now were also real, even if different than they'd been more than a decade ago. It felt like my old love for him had died back to the roots, but now I was regrowing a whole new love for him, for the new person he was becoming.

As I turned from 77 to 81, I also concluded that this new love was going to have to be different, with different rules. When we'd first met, Dima had been my guide, teaching me about Moscow, about Russia, about the dark and dangerous underworld he'd dived into when he'd taken up opposition to the ruling powers. But now, more than a decade later, he was still trapped down there. For both our sakes, I was going to have to lead him out, Orpheus-like, into the land of the living.

That's a terrible metaphor, I thought as I turned off of 81 at the Christiansburg exit. *Orpheus failed.*

I drove through an attractive town square and turned into a neighborhood of gracious older homes. All of them looked to be at least twice the size of anywhere I'd ever lived. I experienced a rare moment of class envy and insecurity. Normally I assumed I was cultured enough to fit in anywhere. Faced with the half-million-dollar home of the grandparents who'd never wanted me, though, I felt poor, graceless, and uncouth.

Bullshit, I told myself as I pulled up to the curb. *Who's got the PhD in literature here? You, that's who! You've got way more culture than everyone else here combined.*

I got out of the car and walked up to the front door. When I went to ring the doorbell, a moment of cowardice swept through me, and I almost turned tail and ran.

But I didn't. I didn't even look back.

The door opened.

"Oh," said Alexandra. "It's you."

13

ALEXANDRA LOOKED LIKE my father. I'd never thought about it much before, but now, standing face-to-face with her, everything my grandmother—my *other* grandmother—had told me about her at the forefront of my mind, the similarities between them clobbered me in the face. She was also slender and slight, with wispy hair that desperately wanted to stick out everywhere. While my father indulged his hair in its natural tendencies, though, Alexandra had hers combed severely back into a tight bun at the nape of her neck. She emphasized the natural colorlessness of her complexion by what I could only describe as an aggressive commitment to no makeup. I never wore makeup, and neither did many of my friends and colleagues, and I generally took it for granted. Somehow on her it was clear that she Wasn't Wearing Makeup, rather than that she was just not bothering to wear makeup. She was wearing a long dress that also, somehow, made it clear that she was Wearing a Modest Dress. My grandmother—my *other* grandmother—normally wore modest dresses and skirts, as did Chloe, but again, on Alexandra, it was a Statement, not just a comfortable way to wear clothes.

"We were expecting you an hour ago," she said. Her fine mouth, slender and shaped just like my father's, remained turned resolutely downwards at the corners. If she was filled with tenderness at the sight of her only granddaughter, she was hiding it well.

"Traffic," I said. In fact, traffic had been minimal, and I was only a few minutes later than I'd said I'd arrive, but it seemed like the thing to say.

"Well," she said. "I guess you'd better come in. Wipe your feet on the mat, and leave your shoes by the door—there, on the rack. We don't wear shoes indoors here."

"No problem." I also didn't wear shoes indoors. It was a filthy habit and I couldn't understand how so many Americans did it. But the suspicious way that Alexandra was watching me slip my shoes off, and then fussily indicating exactly where I should place them on the rack, made me want to go tromping all over her house in muddy boots.

"This way." Still no smile on that downturned mouth, let alone a hug. My grandmother—my *other* grandmother—would have already showered me with so many hugs, kisses, sweet words, and offers of food and drink, that I'd be staggering under their physical and metaphysical weight by now.

Maybe she's feeling awkward and embarrassed, I told myself. *Maybe she's just not a touchy-feely person. Or maybe her ability to experience real emotions was burned out of her decades ago with electroshock therapy and forced sterilization.*

Or maybe she's just a jerk, I answered myself as I followed her deeper into the house.

I contemplated the question of what were "real" emotions and what it meant to have "real" feelings after having your brain and sex glands brutally assaulted and destroyed. If you could no longer produce the hormones and electrical impulses that led to feelings, what were you? What was your experience of life like? And if you somehow managed to produce an outward facsimile of feeling, was it "real"?

I got no answer to those questions from Alexandra's stiff, narrow back as we made our way through cave-like rooms and corridors paneled with dark, heavy wood to a large room in the rear of the house. This room was also depressingly cave-like from all the dark, ornate paneling, but it had a couple of table lamps that provided pools of warm yellow light in amongst the gloom. One illuminated my parents, sitting side-by-side on a loveseat upholstered in dark leather. Another lit one side of the face of the man who I in no way felt was my grandfather.

There was a long moment for me to contemplate what "real" feelings meant here, given that Dennis Halley was indubitably my grandfather, whatever I might feel about him. He and my parents sat in a frozen tableau for much too long, allowing me to examine his face and body and see that, yep, he looked pretty much just like a much older version of John, and an awful lot like me too. Also a lot like Roseanna. The rangy build and Black Irish features had skipped a generation in my father, but come out strongly in me and John. I'd always thought we looked like our grandfather—our *other* grandfather—but there was no doubt now that the person we *really* took after was Dennis.

Dennis was staring at me. Was he thinking the same thing? If he was, it wasn't bringing him any joy.

"You took your time getting here," he said. "Alexandra was all in a fuss, sure something had happened to you."

I glanced back involuntarily at Alexandra. She didn't look like someone who had been all in a fuss. She didn't look like someone who could ever be all in a fuss. She didn't look like she had any feelings at all.

Maybe still waters run deep, I chided myself. *Maybe she's full of grandmotherly anxiety and joy on the inside. Some people are like that: all cold on the outside and full of feeling on the inside.* **Dima's** *like that, and you'd never say he's unfeeling.* But such people normally gave themselves away with the brightness of their eyes, a sudden look, a sudden gesture, not to mention their dedication to various movements and causes...Dima's apparent coldness was a very thin shell indeed, that could be melted by pretty much any form of internal or external warmth, revealing the volcanic passions underneath.

Maybe Alexandra's passion is the cult, I thought. *Maybe that's what she's poured all her passion, all her feeling that can't be given to anything else, into.*

"Let me show you to your room," she was saying. "Then you can freshen up and join us for some hors d'oeuvres." The words were exactly what you'd expect from a gracious Southern hostess. But they were delivered in a chillingly robotic tone, and she didn't meet my eyes as she said them.

"That would be lovely." My own voice came out much too loud and warm and enthusiastic for the heavy gloom of the room. I thought that everyone else actually winced, as if at a ray of light suddenly piercing the darkness.

This is going to be a very long visit, I thought, and followed Alexandra to my room.

14

MY ROOM WAS THE SAME one John had stayed in, Alexandra told me in her flat, slightly reedy voice as she led me down another dark corridor to yet another back room. She still didn't look at me as she spoke.

She kept her eyes cast firmly down as she brought me into the room, which was a small study/den fitted out with a foldout cot, and as she showed me where the bathroom was, and told me that I could rejoin them when I was ready.

"Great!" I said, much too perkily. I thought she winced a little again. I was going to have to rethink my entire communicative strategy. Normally being upbeat and perky worked for me. But here it was like whistling a jolly tune in a churchyard. I just didn't know what would work any better. Cold silence seemed rude, and I certainly wasn't going to chatter on about my work and my personal life. Probably every aspect of everything I did would enrage them, so I'd have to find other topics of conversation. I just didn't know what those might be.

Besides, warmth and caring were some of the main features of my personality. And they tended to work pretty well. Deep down, everyone—well, almost everyone—liked to be treated with warm interest. Only extremely damaged people couldn't handle it.

I watched Alexandra's stiff, slender back in its Long, Modest Dress go out of the room and down the hallway. Maybe she was one of those people who were too damaged to receive any kind of warmth and affection. Maybe my charm offensive would come to a crashing disaster with my own family.

Just like it has with the people you most want it to work on. Karen, Dima...face it, the charm offensive never works when you really want or need it to. Too many people see warmth and caring as a sign of weakness, or distrust it as self-serving manipulation.

You don't know that, I argued back with myself. *Dima might be finally able to receive it. And maybe it was never supposed to work on Karen. Maybe there's some other, better person out there it's actually supposed to work on. And in this situation, it's all you've got, so you might as well deploy it. Besides, when it doubt, always do the kind thing. When it doubt, always say the nice thing you think the other person needs to hear.*

With that encouraging pep talk, I rejoined the others.

15

"SO, ROWENA—IS THAT what you go by? Or have you changed your name?—tell us about yourself."

Dennis's face was strangely stiff as he spoke. Excessive Botox? That didn't seem in character. I tried to examine him from my position in the unpleasantly deep armchair I'd been put in without being obvious about it. Was one side of his face slightly droopy? Did he have Bell's palsy? Or maybe Parkinson's? Was that why he seemed so stiff? Or was he just terminally uncomfortable around me?

"Rowena is fine," I said.

"So you haven't changed your name?" His voice suddenly rose, angry and challenging.

"No," I said.

"Because so many people are doing it these days." He turned his head towards me, bringing both sides of his face into the gloom that filled the room. His voice dropped, coming out of the darkness in a strangled hiss. "Seems like everyone's changing their name these days. Except when they get married—then they *don't* change their name, isn't that right? I'd ask you if you'll change your name when you get married, but it sounds like there's precious little chance of you ever getting married, is there?"

"Well..." I tried to give him a warm, caring smile. The trick was to smile more with your eyes than your mouth. Hard to do when tears were threatening to burst out of every outlet in my face. I blinked them back furiously to stop them coming out of my eyes, and they ran into my nose, down the back of my throat into my mouth, and even, it felt, into my ears.

I swallowed, choking slightly on salt. Had that been the most hurtful thing anyone had ever said to me? Dennis *must* be family, then, because only family could hurt you that badly. I cleared my throat and smiled widely. Just with my lips. My eyes, I could tell, were cold and mocking, and there didn't seem to be anything I could do about it.

"You never know what life is going to throw your way," I said. "For example, it was a surprise to hear that Mom and Dad were thinking of moving up to Christiansburg." I looked over at them. "Are you thinking of moving into this neighborhood?"

"Well..." My mother made an indecisive fluttering motion with her hand. "We're not sure yet..."

"This neighborhood is probably a bit out of our price range." My father's words were firm and decisive. Unusual for him. I peeked out of the corner of my eye at him, trying to make out his expression through the gloom. Was he about to come to his senses and declare this whole thing a folly and a farce, stand up, and tell me and Mom we were leaving right now? It would be extremely out of character for him, but as a sign of returning sanity, I would have welcomed it.

Dennis waved his hand in a copy of my mother's motion, but angry rather than fluttery. "And I told you, Bobby, we'll give you money for the down payment...heck, this house here will be yours soon enough."

"I believe you said it would be John's." My father's voice was quiet but still firm. The corner of my eye was unable to focus on his face well enough to see what he was thinking.

Dennis made another angry hand wave. "What's John's is yours."

The corner of my eye thought my father made a small, dry smile. "John never was very good at sharing, was he, Rowena?" he said, turning to me.

"Well...not when he was little, no," I said. "But I think he might have grown up some since then. It might be nice to have your own place, though. Especially if he and Camila..." I made myself stop, appalled that I was tacitly encouraging this madness. It was just *so* easy to fall into social pleasantries and go along with the others, even when the others were driving straight towards a cliff.

"Yes." Alexandra's lips seemed to go even thinner and drier. "He didn't talk much about this Camila, but it sounds like they might be serious. Is that so?"

"Well...I hope so..."

"Is it true that she's Mexican?" Alexandra's voice was even thinner and drier than her lips.

"Well...I guess her parents were...I think she's spent her whole life here, though..." I hated how wishy-washy my voice sounded. I wanted to stand up for Camila. I also wanted Alexandra to like her, which maybe meant not standing up for her right now. It was so hard to know how these total strangers who happened to be close blood kin would react to anything.

You're here to get intel, I reminded myself. *Focus on the mission!*

"You both do seem to have a thing for foreigners." Venom was seeping into Alexandra's thin, dry voice. "John's taken up with this Mexican girl, and Bobby says you're with some *Russian*." She made Russian sound even worse than Mexican. I filed away that piece of information on American xenophobia for future contemplation.

"Well..."

"In fact, he's here with you right now, isn't he?" Alexandra looked around as if expecting Dima to come leaping out of a dark corner. I fought off an incongruous desire to laugh

"Actually, right now he's in Utah. But his mother's with me in Georgia."

"What it is with you and John and foreigners?" Dennis's voice was rising into an angry shout again. "Can't you find any decent Americans? Or there aren't any who would take you?"

"I believe Camila *is* an American," I said, and then regretted it. *The mission! Focus on the mission!*

Alexandra sniffed. Then she gave me a sickly-sweet smile. A nasty crawling sensation ran up the back of my scalp.

"Well, there are plenty of nice Americans in the church," she said. "We should introduce you to some of them. I believe John is already quite taken with Jennifer, isn't he, Dennis? I'm sure he'll forget all about this Camila person before long. And...let me see...Dennis, what do you think about Isaiah for Rowena? Don't you think they'd do nicely togeth-er?"

Dennis gave me a cold up-and-down. "Maybe," he said. "If she learns how to keep a civil tongue in her head, that is."

"We'll be sure to introduce you tomorrow after service," Alexandra told me.

My lips smiled. My eyes, despite all my efforts, were, I could tell, cold and hard as stone in January.

"That sounds lovely," I said.

16

DINNER WAS AN AWKWARD affair. No, that's not right. Awkwardness requires a certain amount of liveliness. Dinner was too cold to be awkward. Alexandra spoke only to ask people to pass the dishes. Dennis spoke to me only to demand if I really was going to refuse the pork chops.

"I'll just have bread," I said.

"Rowena has always had the courage of her convictions," said my father. He looked down at the pork chop on his plate. When he looked up, he couldn't quite meet my eyes, and he ate only the tiniest sliver of it before pushing it aside.

"I've been thinking," my mother said brightly, turning to Alexandra. "What if we went out for a drive tomorrow afternoon? After church? We could show Rowena around the town, look at some potential neighborhoods, see what kind of houses are for sale?"

Alexandra grimaced but said nothing. "That's not really appropriate for the Sabbath," Dennis told us.

My mother looked like she wanted to say something, but didn't know what. "Rowena will only be here for a day," said my father, still in that same firm, even tone he'd been using earlier. "If we want to show her the town, we'll need to do it tomorrow afternoon. You're planning on leaving Monday morning, isn't that right, Rowena?"

I nodded, although at this rate, I wasn't sure how I was going to make it to Monday morning. The three hours since I'd arrived felt like the longest one hundred and eighty minutes of my life. I almost wanted to be off doing an interview, just in order to not be here.

"And Bev and I will need to head out on Monday too," my father continued. "So tomorrow afternoon is the only time we can go out. I'm sure the Lord will understand."

"Maybe," said Dennis. We all lapsed into silence. I tried to figure out what my parents were up to. As far as I could tell, my mother was falling for this whole cult thing hook, line, and sinker. Or maybe she was just being super nice? Maybe this was her way of trying to get out of here all in one piece? I couldn't tell.

I was even less sure what my father was doing. The only time I'd ever heard him use that voice before had been when John had done something really, really beyond the pale. But then we'd all known where my father stood on, for example, driving while stoned (John had had an extremely brief flirtation with weed between the ages of sixteen and a half and seventeen, before giving all that up to focus on military glory).

Now, though, I couldn't tell. My father was speaking to Dennis as if he strongly disapproved of everything Dennis said or did—but he was going along with this church thing and this moving to Virginia thing. He was even actively going against Dennis in order to go house hunting here. So what gave? Was he playing some kind of very deep game? Or was he stumbling along blindly like the rest of us?

We finished dinner in frosty silence. The rest of the evening yawned cavernously ahead of us. I was about to plead extreme exhaustion and retire for the night when my mother suggested, her voice bright and perky, that we all watch *Antiques Roadshow*. Apparently Dennis and Alexandra were big fans. So we all trooped back into the den, arranged ourselves in even deeper gloom, literal and figurative, and watched *Antiques Roadshow* until Dennis dozed off.

I was just getting up to flee to my makeshift bedroom when my phone *pinged*. Ignoring the disapproving glare from Alexandra—the first time she'd noticed me in over an hour—I pulled it out and checked my notifications. I was expecting it to be from John and fearing it would be from Galina Ivanovna.

Instead, it was from Dima.

Inna! Can you talk?

17

I'M FREE, I wrote back. It had been thoroughly drilled into me never to call Dima unless he specifically told me that I should call him at exactly this moment. What if he was in the middle of a delicate interview or a silent stakeout and my call messed things up? That was a perfectly rational and reasonable concern. But now I wondered about his need to be in a profession where that was a perfectly rational and reasonable concern. Was his choice of vocation a way of keeping people like his mother—and *me!*—at arm's length? Was this a way of never having to settle down into a normal life and develop normal connections? As it was, he was hyperconnected with the whole world, but his bonds with those closest to him were always on the verge of snapping. Because he was always on the verge of snapping them.

My phone rang. Too late, it occurred to me that I should have silenced it. Now Alexandra was probably listening at the door. Well, I hoped her Russian was damn good, then.

"Inna? Where are you? Mama said you were in Virginia."

I gave him a quick run-down of the latest developments in the Virginia situation.

"Why are you are whispering? Is someone eavesdropping?"

"Maybe," I whispered. "They don't approve of cell phones here. Or the internet."

He snorted. "Sometimes I don't approve of them either. But seriously, Inna, no fooling: are you in danger?"

"I don't *think* so."

"You don't *think* so?"

"These are my nearest and dearest. If I'm not safe with them, where am I safe?"

"Your nearest and dearest are often the most dangerous people in your life."

We both took a beat to think about how admirably Dima himself fit that description.

"Anyway," I said. "What's up with you?"

"Why did I call, you mean?"

"Well...yes."

"I'd like to say it was out of sheer concern for you, Inna, but I'd be lying. I *am* concerned for you, and if you need help, call me, okay?"

"I will," I promised.

"But I'm also calling to tell you that we're about to leave for Germany."

"Germany!" I said. "We!"

"Yeah...The Wolf Battalion, that is."

"Oh. Okay. I thought maybe Galina Ivanovna..."

"No, she's planning to stay in Georgia. But the Wolf Battalion is going to go do joint maneuvers with the Americans in Germany, and they want me to go cover it."

"Which 'they' wants it?" I asked.

He laughed, not very humorously. "All the theys. The Wolf Battalion wants it, and my masters back in Moscow want it too. So that works out nicely for everyone. Of course, if all the theys find out about each other, none of them will want it, so..." He paused, as if looking around. I bit my lip to keep from asking if he was on a secure line. I had to assume he was in as secure a situation as he could be, or we wouldn't be having this conversation.

"But I've asked for a couple of days off before we leave," he said. "I told them I wanted to see mama, which is true, and they said I could go back to Georgia for a couple of days. Will you be back home by Tuesday?"

"Yes," I said.

"You're sure? You won't need to stay longer to help your parents?"

"I'm sure," I said. "If I can't help them by Monday, I can't help them at all. And I'm coming back for your sake."

"Well...thank you, Inna."

"I'm coming back for your sake," I repeated. "And my own. I'm coming back for us."

"For us," he said. His voice was full of doubt and wonder. "I wish I had your courage, Inna. I wish I *deserved* your courage."

I got that out-of-body sensation that kept overtaking me at bad moments, along with a wave of crippling doubt. What was I doing? Was I making a horrible mistake that would ruin both our lives? Maybe I should just give up on him, on us, and go in search of someone else, or resign myself to living and dying miserable and alone.

"I'm coming back for both our sakes," I said.

He laughed shakily. "Is that a promise or a threat? Never mind. Go with God, Inna, and I'll see you on Tuesday."

"Till Tuesday," I said.

I hoped it was a promise. In this gloomy house, it sounded more like a threat.

18

IF ALEXANDRA EAVESDROPPED by my door, she didn't mention it the next morning at breakfast, which was another frostily silent affair.

Just another 24 hours, I told myself. *Just another 24 hours, and you'll be out of here.*

First, though, I had to make it through the church service. I was anticipating it with a mixture of curiosity and dread. My innate desire to find things out was looking forward to attending an attempted indoctrination into a cult. My dislike of emotional disharmony was dreading the inevitable disagreements it was sure to bring.

The first disagreement started up as soon as breakfast was over. I had brought my interview suit to wear to the service, as it was less obviously falling apart at the seams than my other two outfits. At least the stress-induced—I hoped—weight loss of the past couple of months meant those seams were no longer under dangerous strain.

Alexandra, however, roused herself from her apathy to tell me that all women had to wear skirts to service. She herself was already wearing another Modest Dress that somehow managed to look both unattractively loose around the waist and hips and uncomfortably tight around the bust and arms. That was a particularly impressive feat since she didn't have much bust.

"Oh," I said. "I don't have a skirt, though."

"Didn't your mother tell you to bring one?"

"It wouldn't have done any good," I said. "I genuinely don't have any skirts. At all. My wardrobe is not extensive."

Alexandra sniffed. "Is this some kind of hippy statement about materialism?"

"No," I said. "It's a statement about not being able to afford new clothes. I can barely afford to cover groceries and rent. I haven't bought any new clothes in five years at least. This is my interview suit, and it's the only thing I own that is fit to wear to church."

Alexandra's stiff face worked, ghosts of expressions trying to make their way onto it. She seemed to be struggling to speak. When she finally did, there was something almost grandmotherly in her tone.

"It's too bad we're not the same size," she said. "I've got lots of clothes that would look good on you. But you take after Dennis more than me. And Rose..." She trailed off, then rallied. "Bev, do you have a spare skirt? You're closer to Rowena's size than I am."

"I do...Rowena, honey, let's go try it on."

Half an hour later I was squeezed into my mother's spare skirt, which was a loose kind of peasant-y affair with an elastic waistband. Said waistband dug into my midriff, and the floor-length hem only came halfway down my calves, but it was the best we were going to do. I wore my blazer over it. I had tried on my mother's shirts, but all of them had threatened to split at the shoulders when I pulled them on.

"I always think of you as the little one," my mother said after I had struggled out of the third shirt. "But you're only little compared to John, aren't you? I don't know where you get it from...of course, Grandpa is pretty tall—my father, I mean—and so is Dennis, and, well, Rose..." She stopped abruptly, her face going scarlet.

"I know about Roseanna," I said. "We've been in contact."

"Have you? Oh...honey..." My mother took a deep breath, scrunching her eyes shut. When she opened them, she looked me up and down critically. "You...it's funny...you look *so much* like her now...I used to tell myself you didn't, I was just imagining things, but my God, Rowena, you could be the spitting image of her when I first met her...she must have been a bit older than you are now, but she looked young for her age then, just like you do now...how is she?" The last words came out in a half-whisper.

"Still young for her age," I said. "She wants to get to know me. And she desperately wants to be in John's life, too. I think she'll be disappointed if I don't go see her while I'm in town."

"Oh...Rowena..."

"Maybe I'll go see her on the way home," I said.

"Oh...Rowena..."

"Are you ready?" Alexandra called through the door. "We need to leave now or we'll be late."

"Oh!" My mother jumped guiltily. "Come on, Rowena, we'd better hurry."

Who are you and what have you done with my mother? My mother had never had a particularly strong sense of punctuality, and she had always considered church services to be an immoral waste of a good morning. And yet here she was, chivvying me out of the door to make sure I made it to church on time.

Sucking in my stomach to keep the elastic waistband from eating into my skin, I followed her out the door and into the car.

19

THE CHURCH WAS IN A different, less nice part of Christiansburg. Not that it was bad. It was just not the kind of upscale place I would have expected Dennis and Alexandra to go to. Maybe that was part of the charm. Maybe they hadn't found what they'd been looking for at their old, elegant church, and thought this new church offered something raw and real.

On the outside, though, it just looked like a brick box with a plain white and not very imposing steeple. On the inside it looked about the same. The pews somehow managed to look cheap and unattractive, even though they seemed exactly the same as every other pews I'd ever seen. Because the church genuinely couldn't afford decent-quality pews, or because they were deliberately going for a look of poverty in order to squeeze more money out of their parishioners?

Despite Alexandra's fears of being late, we were able to get good seats only three rows back from the pulpit, right behind the choir. Alexandra and my mother started making cold, awkward small talk, sort of including me but not really. Dennis and my father were completely silent, each apparently lost in his own thoughts. I fixed my lips into a semblance of a smile and scanned the crowd, which was growing and growing. By the time Alexandra and my mother had run out of cold platitudes, the temperature had risen at least ten degrees, and every pew was full.

There was an expectant pause. Everyone was fidgeting and whispering to each other, like concertgoers waiting for the star to burst onto stage. Sweat began trickling down my sides.

The doors suddenly swung open. A collective "Oh!" made my ears pop.

"There he is!" Alexandra hissed to me. "That's Isaiah!"

Everyone else was staring at the man coming up the aisle, so I did too. Medium height, medium build, a little younger than me, dark curly hair, a faint five o'clock shadow at ten in the morning...bright blue eyes that swept over the crowd and then stopped, fixed, on me.

Electricity went up the back of my neck and over my scalp. Isaiah Jones was the most attractive man I had ever laid eyes on. And it wasn't a matter of looks. I mean, yes, he had even features, good cheekbones, a strong jaw, and that five o'clock shadow that spoke of a virility trying to burst through his civilized skin, but it was more than that. I could feel the warmth, the emotional openness, the strong desire to connect, radiating out from him and enveloping everyone in the church. Especially, when his eyes met mine, me.

I held his gaze. He was *definitely* staring at me, staring into my eyes. Trying to get me to look away first? Was this the game we were playing? I could feel the corners of my mouth rising into a not very nice smile. Did he honestly think he could fuck with me? For Christ's sake...

The doors opened again, eliciting an even louder "Oh!" and breaking his concentration. He shook his head, gave me one last megawatt smile, and turned to look at the man coming up the aisle.

People were spontaneously leaping to their feet as he came level with them. He was nodding right and left, occasionally stopping to shake hands or share a few words. As he drew nearer to our pew, I saw that he was an older version of the man who'd gotten into a staring contest with me.

"Is that Jeremiah Jones?" I whispered to Alexandra.

She gave me a distracted nod, her whole being focused on the man now walking towards us. As he passed our pew, he turned and nodded at Dennis. He caught sight of me and did a barely perceptible doubletake. One quick measuring glance, and then he was moving on again, jumping up onto the pulpit with athletic agility.

Everyone was on their feet by now, clapping like the main act had just taken the stage. Jeremiah Jones made damping-down motions with his hands. Reluctantly, people took their seats, but the church was still buzzing with the sheer excitement of being in the same building with him.

"Good morning, folks!" he said.

"Good morning, Jeremiah!" everyone called back.

"What a beautiful Sunday to come together to worship the Lord!"

"Praise Jesus!" rose from various corners of the church. Including from Alexandra. I glanced over at her. Her cheeks had flushed pink, and she was gazing up at Jeremiah Jones with the adulation of a teenager watching a boy band.

I snuck a quick look at Dennis. Did he mind his wife's obvious infatuation with their pastor? But he was gazing at Jeremiah with what he would no doubt call firm, manly admiration, but looked an awful lot like adoration.

Jeremiah made a few more remarks as the crowd settled back into their seats. Isaiah slipped quietly away from his place by the pulpit and headed down the side wall towards the back of the church. This brought him right by me. As he passed, he stopped, caught my eye, and held out his hand.

I instinctively held my own hand out to him. He reached over and clasped it. His palm was warm and strong and surprisingly callused. Something crinkly cut into my own palm. Before I could respond, he let go and continued down the wall towards the back of the church.

I looked down into my palm. A small piece of paper nestled in it, crumpled up by our shared handclasp.

Alexandra had her back to me, her whole attention focused on Jeremiah up on the pulpit. I uncrumpled the paper. A short note, in square bold pencil.

Meet me outside afterwards. I.

20

I WENT TO STUFF THE note into my pocket, realized my ill-fitting skirt didn't have pockets, dithered, bent down to get my purse, got a glare from Alexandra for causing a disturbance, froze, then went ahead and shoved the note into the first pocket I could find in my purse. Then I settled down to listen to the sermon.

It was enlightening. Maybe not in the way that Alexandra and Dennis had wanted it to be for me, but certainly enlightening. Jeremiah Jones was undeniably, irresistibly, wildly charismatic. I spent a while trying to analyze why. Yes, he was good looking, but that was only a small part of his charm. It was more the way he poured out his passion on everyone around him. Just being in the same church with him was like taking a warm bath after a long day out in the cold.

He also sounded reasonable, even persuasive. As long as you didn't listen too closely to what he was saying, that is. At first even I found myself nodding along occasionally. Yes, yes, people didn't care enough about each other anymore, we were all lonely and disconnected, we needed to stop being so selfish and self-absorbed and start helping each other out again, and soon society would be revived into a warm and caring place where everyone felt loved and accepted, just like in the good old days...

Wait, wait, WAIT! I jerked myself out of the pleasant reverie I had been swimming in. Had I really just been fantasizing about joining the church, even—Jesus *CHRIST*—marrying Isaiah Jones like Dennis and Alexandra wanted and becoming a part of the church royalty? I mean, not seriously, but those thoughts had been idly running through my head...it was so nice to feel part of a warm and caring community, and what if Isaiah really had fallen in love with me at first sight, and was now going to do all the work of wooing, winning, and wedding me, while all I had to do was sit back and be adored? Wouldn't that be *wonderful*...I was so tired of fighting, fighting, fighting to get even a scrap of anything I wanted and needed, including the love of the man I was fated to be with...fate shouldn't be this hard to find...I just wanted to dissolve into oneness with everyone around me, float away into the clouds of fantasy...

The good old days were TERRIBLE, my rational mind told me. *You've read the deepest outpourings of the hearts of those who lived through them, and they were MISERABLE. And these were the richest, healthiest, most privileged people to walk the earth in their respective eras. The rest were too poor, oppressed, sick, and illiterate to leave anything for you to read. Now may not be great, but then wasn't any better, and in many ways was a lot worse. Besides, the only way out is always only forward.*

I focused my attention on Alexandra, who was still gazing raptly at Jeremiah Jones, her lips slightly parted. Dennis, rather than being jealous, was wearing the same expression as he listened to the sermon, which was now explaining how we would all return to a simpler life by giving ourselves over to a higher power.

This is how scammers, grifters, and populist dictators get you. They tell you what you want to hear and play on your deepest fears and desires. I wonder what deepest fears and desires Isaiah Jones is planning to play on with me?

"And now," announced Jeremiah Jones, "let's finish off the good work we have done here today by bathing ourselves in the Good Lord's love. Ladies and gentlemen, the choir has something special prepared just for you!"

The people in the first two rows of pews got up and moved in front of the pulpit. The rest of us rose, ready to join in the singing. The service must be wrapping up.

If Isaiah has something bad planned for me, I guess I'm about to find out.

21

THE CHOIR BROKE INTO a spirited rendition of "Every Heart-beat." Whoa. I was promptly transported back to my early-adolescent self, sitting with my friends and listening to bootleg copies of *Heart in Motion*. Their parents had disapproved of Amy Grant's turn to main-stream pop and my parents had disapproved of her still overtly Christian messaging, making her irresistibly rebellious to all of us.

I glanced over at my parents. They were singing along. Was there even a flicker of awareness of the irony that they were now singing songs they had forbidden me to listen to when I was eleven? And now I was thinking I needed to forbid them to listen to this dangerous music they had tried to keep me away from twenty-five years ago.

Alexandra and Dennis were also singing along. My mother looked over at me and motioned for me to join in the singing. Conveniently, I still remembered all the lyrics. The fruits of a misspent youth.

The choir switched to "Baby, Baby." If I remembered rightly, Amy Grant had written it about it her newborn daughter. I tried not to look over at Alexandra, but my traitorous eyes turned to her anyway. She was singing along, oblivious both to my gaze and, as far as I could tell, the tragic irony of what she was singing. Her cheeks had flushed even pinker, and she looked genuinely, intensely happy.

Don't cry! My eyes prickled anyway. I jerked them away from Alexandra's face and focused on singing along with the rest of the church. Every-one was singing, swaying, tapping their feet and clapping their hands in time with the music and each other. It was the closest thing I'd ever seen to an orgy...no, that wasn't right. I didn't like what was going on, but it wasn't an orgy. It was...well, it was an ecstatic religious experience.

The choir moved on to "You've Got the Love." Spontaneous cheers broke out. Jeremiah Jones, who had moved into the background when the choir had started singing, stepped forward, nodding and waving his hands in the air.

"You've got the love, brothers and sisters!" he shouted. "You've got the love of the Lord! Follow me on out the church!"

He started down the aisle, singing along, half-dancing, waving his hands and bobbing his whole body in time with the music. The choir followed, half-dancing as well. It should have looked silly, but once again, it didn't. Instead, it was a pure experience of primal joy. I couldn't quite share in it, but I could feel it all around me.

People in the pews started filing out into the aisle after them, also singing and dancing. My parents joined in with the others, then Dennis and Alexandra, and then—oh God—it was my turn. Dennis, I saw with relief, was only singing, not dancing and waving his hands. I took this as permission to keep my hands at my side, but I tried to shimmy with the music as I made my way down the aisle. At least I knew all the words to this song, too.

The choir formed up again once they got out the doors. They gave one final rousing chorus of "You've Got the Love" and then transitioned into a soft, gentle version of "Amazing Grace." Everyone broke into clumps, talking animatedly about the service. Dennis and Alexandra, trailed by my parents, joined a clump of two other couples about their age. I stood slightly back, hoping to avoid notice.

"Nice dancing. Maybe not quite appropriate for church, but nice dancing."

Jumping out of my skin and whirling around like a dervish would be wrong. I made myself turn slowly towards the speaker.

"Thanks." In truth, it hadn't been great dancing, but probably it had been a lot sexier than anything that church had seen for a while, maybe ever. I was not a fabulous dancer, but it was generally agreed that I had natural rhythm and a sinuous, whole-body style that drew the eye. Oops. Should have toned that down. I'd just been so thrown by the situation I'd reverted to my basic instincts.

Isaiah Jones looked me up and down. Despite what he'd just said, the examination seemed more scientific than sexual. Up close and head on, he was even more attractive and charismatic than before. But his eyes were contemplative, even uncertain.

"You're Alexandra and Dennis's granddaughter," he said. "Rowena, right?"

"That's right."

"Your grandparents are some of our strongest members," he said. "And your parents are looking to become just as strong. What about you?"

"I'm just visiting," I said.

He looked me up and down again. Another flash of uncertainty in his eyes. It must be tough to be Jeremiah Jones's son, and to be that good-looking and sexy on top of that. I laughed at myself as I thought that, but I was also pretty sure I was right.

Decision replaced uncertainty in his eyes. "We should talk," he said. "Come on." He turned and started walking away, expecting me to follow.

I went after him. Out of the corner of my eye, I saw Alexandra watching us and smiling. Her plan to get rid of Dima and marry me off to church royalty must seem like it was working.

Isaiah and I went around the corner of the church, to the overflow parking lot. It was gravel rather than pavement, and empty except for a late-model Cadillac and a Kawasaki Ninja motorcycle.

Isaiah went over to the Kawasaki and walked around it, looking it over, before settling into a half-sitting, half-leaning position against the seat.

"Nice bike," I said.

"Thanks." He ran his hand over the seat. "My dad hates it, of course." He looked up and grinned. "But I tell him I'm in the Lord's hands whenever I'm riding it."

"Sure," I said.

"I talked to your brother when he was up here a few weeks ago," he said. "He's quite a guy."

"No kidding," I said.

"He told me a lot about you."

"Uh-huh?" I said.

"He made me think..." He looked down at the gravel at his feet, which was getting white dust on our shoes. He studied the white marks for a moment, then rubbed his shoes clean on his pant legs.

"Do you need something?" I asked. "Help, for instance?"

He looked back up. "Yeah," he said, not quite meeting my eyes. "Maybe I do. And from what your brother said, maybe you're the one who can give it to me."

"I'd be happy to," I said.

22

"GREAT. HAVE DINNER with me tonight."

Isaiah straightened up and gave me the full benefit of his megawatt smile as he said it. I resisted the urge to roll my eyes. Yes, I could feel the sex appeal rolling off of him in waves. Yes, part of me could feel the pull of the fantasy of a happy ending with him. But another, more cynical part of me suspected that any ending with him wouldn't be very happy. I had a good nose for fucked-up men—after all, they seemed drawn to me like moths to a flame—and Isaiah Jones practically reeked of fucked-up-ness. Under other circumstances I might have found it intoxicating, but my fucked-upness receptors had already been occupied by Dima. Isaiah's fucked-upness was sliding off me like I was coated in Teflon.

"Sure," I said. "Sounds good." It didn't actually sound good, but it sounded better than spending another evening with Dennis and Alexandra. Possibly more productive, and definitely more entertaining.

"Great! I'll come by and pick you up at six. Don't worry: I won't bring the bike. Unless you want me to." He gave me another megawatt smile and let a little more bad-boy-preacher's-son sex appeal ooze into the air between us.

"Whatever you want is fine." I didn't actually like riding motorcycles, but maybe it would help him let his guard down.

"Maybe for our second date." Another grin. "Six o'clock, then?"

"I can't wait."

23

I WAS PRETTY SURE I got a lot of covert glances as I came back around the corner of the church and rejoined the knots of people talking. No doubt I would be a major topic of conversation at a lot of Sunday dinner tables this afternoon.

"Oh, you're back." Alexandra broke off from her conversation and gave me a quick, satisfied smile. "Were you talking to Isaiah?"

"Uh-huh." I felt weirdly like a teenager, with everyone around me speculating about whether I'd just been off necking with a boy. I suppressed a smirk. If only they knew...not that there was much to know, but what there was probably wasn't what they were thinking it was...

"He's such a *nice* boy, isn't he?"

"Uh-huh," I said.

"What did you talk about?" Alexandra's eyes were bright and curious. I didn't like this church, but I had to admit that at least it brought Alexandra out of her usual semi-catatonic state.

"Um..." I said. "Not much." Everyone else in the little clump around Alexandra had stopped talking and was now listening avidly. Should I announce my dinner date to all of them? Isaiah hadn't said whether he wanted it kept secret or not. Dammit! This is one of the many problems of getting into a conspiracy with someone you hardly know. You can't guess what they want you to do.

"He's turned out *so well* after...well, young men!" said one of the women in the clump around us. She laughed. Everyone else chuckled along with her. I smiled as if I were in on the joke.

A few more platitudes, and everyone had wound down enough from their post-service high to head home.

24

I HAD BEEN HOPING WE would go out to eat after church, just for something to do, but instead we repaired back to Dennis and Alexandra's house, where we had a meal of cold cuts and stale bread. It wasn't actually that bad, but the pre-sliced bread was your standard pre-sliced bread, and the cold cuts were your standard cold cuts. Everyone else acted like taking this pre-packaged food and turning it into sandwiches was a big treat. Maybe it was. Maybe this was the culinary highlight of Dennis and Alexandra's week. Maybe it felt like exciting junk food to them. It certainly would to my parents.

After that we went for the promised post-prandial drive. I had been hoping that Dennis and Alexandra would stay home for a Sunday afternoon nap, but no such luck. All five of us crammed into Dennis's car, and we set off on a tour of prospective properties.

I gathered that my mother had come up with a list of places she wanted to visit, but hadn't been able to print it off since, of course, Dennis and Alexandra didn't have a printer. She was also obeying their injunction against using cell phones. I sympathized in theory with their anti-technology stance. I considered a lot of modern technology to be figuratively and literally toxic—I'd read some very alarming things about the giant toxic waste dumps where old smartphones go to die. In practice, though, not using modern technology was highly inconvenient. I ended up whipping out my own smartphone and looking up houses for sale so we could do drive-bys of them. Dennis and Alexandra looked askance at me, but they agreed to go check out the properties.

The neighborhoods we went to were less fancy than Dennis and Alexandra's, but still cozy and pleasant. I would have moved into any of those houses in a heartbeat. My mother made encouraging remarks. If she was thinking in her heart of hearts that they were boring, mainstream, petit bourgeois materialist trash heaps that weren't a patch on the handbuilt tiny home she'd been dreaming of, she hid it well.

Dennis, though, snorted and made disparaging remarks about all of them. One was too small, one was falling apart, one had no decent yard, one had no garage, one was on the edge of a bad neighborhood.

"You can't possibly be thinking of buying anything like *that*," he said, after we'd made three slow passes past the last house on the list.

"It's what's in our price range," my father answered evenly.

"If you'd gone into a decent line of work, you could afford to buy a decent house," Dennis told him.

"I went into the line of work I was called to," my father said, still with that same calm, even tone he'd been using with Dennis all along, the one I'd only ever heard him use with someone he was very disappointed in. "Should I refuse to answer the calling I was given?"

Dennis snorted again, but headed home without answering.

We got back a little before five. My mother and Alexandra both insisted I go straight to the shower, in order to prepare for my dinner with Isaiah. They'd both turned bright pink and gushed like schoolgirls when I'd told them about it. Dennis had said "Hmph," but on balance had seemed pleased. My father had given me a searching look but said nothing.

I dutifully took a shower, although I didn't feel particularly dirty. At least not physically. Spiritually might be another matter. At Alexandra's insistence, I put my mother's skirt back on. I had shed it gratefully after the service, noting the bright red line where the waistband had dug into my skin. It felt even less comfortable when I put it back on, and to my eyes, made me look dumpy and oversized. My recent weight loss sometimes made me a little nervous, but I certainly liked how I looked in the mirror. This skirt, though, gave me a muffin top and hit my calves at their widest point, making my legs, which were in fact long and lean, look short and fat.

Who cares? I pointed out to myself. *It's not like you want to seduce anyone here. Maybe an unflattering outfit is your best defense against what-*

ever Isaiah is planning. He hadn't come across as someone planning on turning dinner into a night of steamy sex, but just in case he was, this skirt would probably cool his ardor.

"You look beautiful!" Alexandra told me when I stepped out of the bedroom. "Here...let me get you something...we're not supposed to wear vain adornments, but a little necklace won't hurt anything..." She rushed off to her bedroom.

I expected her to come back with a cross on a chain, but instead she handed me a pearl necklace. Even I, who knew nothing about jewelry, could sense the elegance—and the expense. When I went to undo the clasp, I noticed a little tag that read, in elegant script, *Tiffany & Co.*

"Um..." I had to be holding the equivalent of a semester's rent in my hand.

"Oh, take it, take it! I've always wanted to see you in this...here, let me help you."

"Okay." Alexandra was acting more and more like a grandmother, as if the service had freed up something in her, allowing her better nature to come through. I hated to quash it now. I was afraid I was going to disappoint her, though. Tomorrow I was going to head home—after stopping by to see her arch-nemesis Roseanna—leaving behind the church and returning to people she desperately disapproved of. The chances of me ending up married to Isaiah, as she hoped, were almost nil, while the chances of me ending up with Dima, whose very existence she despised, were high. Also, I was afraid of breaking the necklace. But I didn't know how to stop her without hurting her, so I let her put the necklace on me.

"You look *beautiful.*" She was positively misty-eyed. "You're such a pretty girl, Rowena, if only you'd take the trouble..." She stopped herself, remembering the injunction against vain adornment.

A car pulled up in front of the house and stopped.

"Oh, that must be Isaiah! He's here!" She fluttered around me for a moment, adjusting the necklace, straightening my clothes, and flicking my hair into place, as nervous as a high schooler before her first prom. Or so I assumed. I'd never been to prom myself.

There was a knock at the door.

"Dennis!" she called. "Dennis, get the door!"

"I'll get it myself," I said. The thought of Dennis inviting Isaiah in and all of us engaging in awkward small talk was unbearable. Also, it might break our cover. I wasn't exactly sure what our cover was or what it was covering up, but I was sure we were up to something illicit.

"Oh, but..."

I brushed past her, neatly cut off Dennis in the hall, and got to the door first, pulling it open with a wrench that caused my too-small skirt to cut painfully into my midriff.

"Hi," I said to Isaiah. "Ready to go?"

25

I WAS OUT THE DOOR before he could answer, closing it firmly on whatever Dennis was about to say. "Nice to see you," I said briskly. "Shall we go?"

"Sure." He followed me down the steps, bemused but also amused. "Gosh, you sure are in a hurry."

"They were going to invite you in and make small talk. I figured neither of us wanted that."

"Okay. Sure." He tried to cut around me. Why was he...oh, right, he was probably trying to open the car door for me. Nothing nefarious, I assured myself.

He did indeed open the car door with a gentlemanly flourish. I responded with a stiff smile. I'd always been horribly embarrassed by the rituals of American dating, on the extremely rare occasions when I'd been directly exposed to them. Going through the motions for a fake date was both more and less awkward. And I didn't want to give Isaiah any false ideas, just in case I'd completely misread the whole thing, or he decided to try to get some sexual satisfaction along with the other help he was looking for.

"Okay," I said as soon as we were both in the car. "What do you need my help with?"

"Jeez." He laughed. His voice was strained. "Don't you at least want me to take you out to dinner first?"

"I have a feeling this might be a long conversation," I said. "And maybe one best not held in public."

"Okay...yeah, you're right. So...I don't know where to start..."

We were driving slowly down the tree-lined street. Isaiah almost clipped a parked car, overcorrected, and almost plowed into the one car coming the other way.

"Maybe we should go park somewhere," I suggested. "So we don't get in a wreck."

He laughed shakily. "Yeah...um...I hate to be a jerk, but how do you feel about takeout pizza? We could eat it in the car. It's not classy, I know, but..."

"Takeout pizza sounds great," I said. "And maybe, if you can focus enough, you can tell me on the way there why you think I, specifically, can help you."

He blew out a breath and almost ran the stop sign at the end of Dennis and Alexandra's street. Once he'd screeched to a halt, he laughed shakily again and said, "Wow, I'm even more worked up about this than I thought. Haven't been this nervous about taking a girl out since sophomore year in high school."

"I doubt it's the taking me out part that's making you nervous," I said.

"Yeah." We were still stopped at the intersection. He looked both ways and then pulled through with exaggerated caution. "Yeah...it's even harder than I thought, you know? Ratting on your father?"

"I imagine," I said.

"And in answer to your question, it's not you I think might help me. Not exactly. Your brother mentioned something...he suggested you know, um, well...a journalist. An investigative reporter. A real pitbull, from what your brother said."

"That is true," I agreed.

He glanced over at me. He was still driving with exaggerated caution, swinging wide around all the parked cars looming out of the gathering dark. "Sounds like your brother doesn't like him much."

"He doesn't know him," I said. "I'm sure if he knew him...well, he'd probably still hate him. Both of them have a powerful need to be the biggest man in the room."

Isaiah glanced over at me again. "I know all about that." He navigated carefully around another parked car. His fingers were tight on the steering wheel. "My dad...he might seem all love and light, but...he's..." He shrugged convulsively.

"I'm sure," I said.

"Yeah, so...I don't know...I thought...I thought..." Isaiah swallowed hard, his Adam's apple bobbing in a throat that was, I had to admit, extremely sexy. What, I wondered, was it like to be a minor sex god stuck in an evangelical church? The physicality and pheromones radiating off of him said that he liked sex, *needed* sex, the way a lot of men think they do but only some really, really do. Tough to try to corral that into what the church wanted from him. Tough, but also a potent weapon his father could use.

"You thought maybe you could give your story to my boyfriend"—I felt weird calling Dima my boyfriend, but I didn't want to make things any more complicated than they already were—"and you were hoping I could help you," I said.

He give me an intense look of relief. "Yeah...yeah, exactly. I was thinking"—he swallowed again—"that maybe I could tell you, and you could tell him, and he could look into it, and my name would never even have to come up."

"Why don't you tell me what you know," I said.

26

THERE WAS QUITE A LOT he wanted to tell me, as it turned out.

It took the better part of an hour for him to start on the story, though. We did in fact get takeout pizza—"Everyone's going to be talking about this tomorrow," he said, his lip curled in a mixture of amusement and disgust. "It's a good thing you're leaving tomorrow morning, 'cause by tomorrow noon they're going to be calling you a painted Jezebel and the Whore of Babylon"—and then we headed over to the local city park. We parked in the parking lot overlooking the playground and dug into the pizza.

"I used to come here on real dates when I was a teenager," Isaiah said, gazing wistfully out over at the swings. "We'd come out here and eat pizza and swing and slide and make out. We thought we were so grownup, but we were still more than half kids—must've been why we wanted to come to a playground." He grinned, but to himself. "We thought we were so bad, but it sounds pretty innocent now." He glanced over at me, looking up almost shyly through his lashes. They were, I noted idly, thick and lustrous. "Probably sounds pretty pathetic to you, I bet."

"My friends did about the same thing," I said. "I don't know what you think I'm like or who you think I am, but I'll bet we've got a lot more in common than you're thinking."

"Yeah...I was imagining you'd be this badass, big-city...I don't know what. That you'd look down on little old us."

I bit back a laugh. "I think you're grossly overestimating my sophistication and worldliness. But I *do* know an investigative reporter who might know someone who might be interested in your story, so fire away. I'm listening."

"He wouldn't do it himself?"

"He doesn't speak much English," I said.

Isaiah looked startled, like that had never occurred to him. "Oh...yeah, I guess I can see that...but you think he'll know someone who can help?"

"He'll probably have some good ideas," I said. "So what do you want to tell the world?"

27

WHAT ISAIAH WANTED to tell the world without the world knowing he was the one telling it was one of those tales as old as time that you still keep running into in this relentlessly modern world.

His mother had died when he was ten. "Cancer," he said briefly, his face closing. His father had been distraught. The church, which back then had been the local Presbyterian church that Dennis and Alexandra and Roseanna had all gone to as well, had been his only solace.

"It was like he couldn't even bear to look at me," Isaiah said, staring straight ahead at the swingset sticking up angularly out of the darkness, like a mechanical giraffe. "Everyone says I look a lot like him, and I do, but once my mom was gone, everyone said I reminded them a lot of her, and I guess that's true. Dad couldn't even bear to be in the same room with me, for months and months afterwards he'd turn his face away and leave the room whenever I came in."

He swallowed hard and busied himself with the pizza for a while before continuing.

"And then more and more people started gathering around him. Bereaved people, mostly, like him. They all had something in common, something to bond over—and they thought they didn't have anything other than each other."

He shook his head angrily. "Most of 'em had families—husbands, wives, brothers, sisters, aunts, uncles, even kids, just like Dad—but their living families didn't mean anything to 'em. It was like all they cared about was their grief. They hated the living because we kept trying to pull 'em back into life when all they wanted was to sink into death so they could be with the people they'd lost forever."

"Uh-huh," I said.

"So then"—he sighed—"they started holding their own special meetings, you know, just for bereaved people. The meetings got bigger and bigger, till they turned into their own services. And then"—he sighed again—"they turned into the church."

"How old were you when this happened?" I asked.

"When the church started? Fifteen. Mom had been gone for five years, and I wanted to move on. But Dad didn't, even though I'm pretty sure that's what she would have told us to do. Not until he started the church. Then it was like he got a new lease on life. He finally had something to care about. Not me, but the church."

"Uh-huh," I said again.

"It started off real small. Dad still had his day job, and then he'd hold these small services on Sunday, for just a couple dozen people. It all seemed pretty normal."

"Uh-huh," I said for a third time.

"But then I went away to college."

"Mmmm," I said.

"I thought Dad didn't even really notice I was alive, but he must've, 'cause he really went off the deep end when I left. I was only an hour and a half away, in Lynchburg, and I came home most weekends at first. But then I started getting involved in stuff there, stopped coming home so much. I guess I didn't come home the whole fall semester of my sophomore year. I went on a mission trip over fall break and spent Thanksgiving with a friend. When I came back for Christmas, I could tell something was wrong."

"Mmm-hmmm," I said.

"He said he'd had a vision that he needed to grow the church. It was already more than twice as big as when he'd started it. He said he was being called to grow it into the biggest church in Christiansburg, that he needed to take it on full time. He was planning to quit his job and devote himself to his vocation."

"Mmmmm," I said.

"I just accepted it. I assumed he knew what he was doing. And I guess he did, 'cause he quit his job, but we only got richer. I mean, we weren't rich before. We weren't poor, but we weren't rich either. And we weren't rich when he first quit his job, but we weren't doing much worse. And then the church really took off."

"Uh-huh," I said.

He swallowed some more. "I still wasn't questioning it. Actually, I was thrilled. I totally bought what Dad was saying about taking his grief and turning it into service to the ministry. I was proud of him, and for the first time in years, he seemed proud of me. Until I screwed up, that is."

"Mmmm," I said.

"Senior year in college, I started questioning stuff. Something really bad happened to a friend of mine, she got attacked while walking home one night, and campus security and the powers that be just hushed it up, insisted she was lying. I was like: Is this how Godly folk behave? And then she started drinking to deal with the pain, and I started keeping her company."

"Mmm-hmm," I said.

"We weren't dating or anything, but she was probably the closest friend I had in college, and I was so angry about what had happened to her, I couldn't believe that something like that could happen to someone I knew was a good person. When she tried to report it, they accused her of making it up, and then they accused her of bringing it on herself, of being the kind of girl that sort of thing happened to. I knew none of those things were true. I tried to tell them that, but they literally ran me out of the room. I was so mad"—he swallowed again and clenched his fists convulsively—"and I couldn't get anyone to listen to me, and I started questioning everything I'd been taught. When I tried to tell Dad about it, he told me the same things campus security and all those deans and stuff were saying, that she was a bad girl who was either lying or asking for it. So I...I broke off contact with him. I didn't talk to him, didn't invite him to graduation, I refused the job he'd gotten me with someone in the church, said I'd make my own way, got the first job I could get in Roanoke, and started living my own life."

"Uh-huh," I said.

"Only turns out I wasn't very good at it. I was drinking every night, hanging out with people who said they were my friends but weren't…I found that out real quick when I got behind the wheel with one too many whiskeys in my system, crashed into a guardrail, and ended up with my good arm handcuffed to a gurney in the ER while they put a cast on the arm I'd broken."

He passed his hand over his face. "Thank God I didn't hurt anyone other than myself," he said. "My arm healed up just fine, but my faith in myself took a pretty big beating. I lost my license, lost my job 'cause I'd lost my license and couldn't get to work anymore, lost all my fair-weather friends…the only thing I had left, it turned out, was my dad."

"Mmmm-hmmm," I said.

"He came and got me when no one else was even speaking to me, said the Lord had called him and told him to go to me. The funny thing was that I hadn't told him what had happened. We hadn't spoken in over a year. But he woke up in the middle of the night one night—we later figured out it was the night of the crash—sure there was something wrong with me and he had to get to me. It took him a while to find me, but he did, and he came and took me home."

"Wow," I said.

"Yeah. So, you see, I kinda owe him everything."

"Uh-huh," I said.

"He sat and prayed with me every night, refused to let me go out drinking, helped me get sober, helped me get my license back, helped me turn my life around…gave me a job in his ministry, which was growing by leaps and bounds."

"Mmmm," I said.

"He said it was a sign that we were doing the will of the Lord. And I figured he was right. After all, going against him hadn't worked out very well for me, but working for him was going great for both of us. He seemed happier than I ever remembered him, happier even than before Mom died. My life was turning around too. And the church was getting new members every week. People were coming up to us after every service and telling us this was what they'd been searching for, this was what they'd been needing and couldn't get anywhere else. And the money was coming in."

"Ah," I said.

"I'm pretty sure most of it was legit." He fidgeted uncomfortably in his seat for a moment, scratched at his jaw, swallowed again convulsively. His voice cracked on his next words. "But some of it wasn't."

"Uh-huh," I said.

"Maybe it was just a misunderstanding," he said. "At least at first. The IRS has a lot of rules, and I sure as heck don't know all of them. But from what I understand, churches don't have to pay taxes, but pastors do. But some of the money we were getting for the church was going straight to us, tax-free. I didn't know that at first, and then I didn't know that we probably should have been paying taxes on it. Maybe Dad didn't either."

"Maybe not," I said.

"I don't think it was intentional fraud." He finally looked over at me. The yellowish glow from the sodium-vapor streetlights around the parking lot lit his face just enough for me to make out the pleading in his eyes. "I know it wasn't for me, for sure. But then it got worse."

"Mmmm," I said.

"We wanted to upgrade the church. The old church building, that is. It just wasn't big enough for us anymore. Originally we had modest plans to expand the parking, put in an annex—simple stuff. But then Dad started talking about doing something on a much grander scale."

"Oh," I said.

"You're surprised, right? The church doesn't look like it's had 2.5 million dollars spent on it, does it?"

"Wow," I said. "Uh, well...no."

"That's cause it hasn't. We spent maybe a quarter million, tops. We re-did the basement to turn it into a rec room, upgraded the HVAC system, got new pews and a new steeple, and expanded and repaved the parking lot. I know 'cause I oversaw most of the work. Most of the bills passed through my hands. It was a lot of work, yeah, but nothing like what Dad was talking about doing—or what he said we'd done. I saw some emails he sent out after it was done. He was saying we'd spent 2.5 million bucks on it, blown through all our money. But we *hadn't*."

"Oh," I said.

"Yeah...at first I thought maybe it was just, you know, the kind of thing you say in fundraising emails. It didn't sit well with me, but fundraising never does, you know what I mean?"

"I sure do," I said.

"But then I got to thinking...I got to wondering where that other 2.25 million went to."

"I can see why," I said.

"I had access to some of the church's bank records 'cause I'd been paying for the work being done. And I had access to some of Dad's bank accounts too. I was basically our business manager by then and was in charge of paying both our salaries. So...I'm not proud of this...I went in and looked at the accounts, gave 'em both some pretty close scrutiny."

"Uh-huh?" I said.

"And what I saw was...well, it didn't look good. There was a lot of money coming into the church, I'm not sure from where—like most churches, we get a lot of cash, you know? As well as people signing over their houses to us...their whole estates...sometimes their families would come and complain, but they'd done it of their own free will...So there was all this money coming in, over two million dollars, best as I could reckon, and all this money going out—again, over two million dollars—and most of it was going out into Dad's personal account."

"Oh," I said.

"But the weird thing is it wasn't staying there. And not 'cause he was spending it on stuff. I mean, he was, a bit. He got that fancy car and stuff like that. He had to show the world how good the Lord could be if you were good to the Lord, he said. But most of it was just being transferred to other bank accounts."

"Hmmm," I said. "Do you know who those bank accounts belonged to, by any chance?"

He shook his head. "Sure wish I did. I tried a couple of times to ask Dad about it—just asking general questions, you know, about what kind of charities we were supporting. 'Cause that's what he said most of our money was going to. He'd changed his tune from saying the money was going into renovations for the church to saying it was going to charities abroad. I figured they were both kinda true, too. I mean, we did renovate the church and spend a good bit of money on it, even if it wasn't what he was saying it was. I figured we were sending the rest of that money to *someone* abroad, and I was hoping it was charities, just like he was saying. I was hoping he'd come out with a list of names, send me pictures of food baskets being distributed and wells being dug, tell me what good work we were doing for the Lord. But he just brushed me off, told me it was too complicated to go into."

"Oh," I said.

"And maybe that's true," said Isaiah. "But I'm afraid—I've been getting more and more afraid—that the money's being used for something much worse."

"Like what?" I asked.

"I'm afraid," he said, looking down into his hands, one side of his face in deep shadow, the other distorted by the sodium-vapor orange glow, "I'm afraid it's being used to buy guns."

28

"OH," I SAID. "GOSH. What, uh, makes you think that?"

He was still looking down at his hands. "At first I didn't think anything of it. I figured it was just folks talking the talk. You know, fighting for the Lord, fighting the good fight, that kind of thing."

"Uh-huh," I said.

"But then I overheard Dad talking to some other guys after the service one day, and they were saying stuff about how our dollars were being put to good use in CAR. At first I thought they meant cars, which was weird enough, but then my dad said something in the next service about CAR, and I figured out he meant the Central African Republic."

"Oh," I said.

"And I thought, oh, well, that's just fine. I'm sure they need our help. And I'm sure they do. But I think the thing we're helping them with is buying guns for their fight against the Muslims. I guess there's a lot of Christian-Muslim conflict going on there right now."

"I guess so," I said. "I don't really know much about the region."

"Yeah, me neither, but I started looking into it, and I guess there's kind of a low-key religious war going on. We've been supporting a network of churches over there, but from what I can gather, they've been using our money to buy arms, not build churches and schools."

"Do you think people over here know?" I asked. "Do you think your dad knows this?"

"I'm sure of it," he said. "'Cause he was the one talking about how our money's buying weapons for the Lord. Not out in the open, not to everyone—not even to me. But I overheard him talking to some of the deacons—I'm not a deacon, you understand; the congregation isn't quite ready for that"—he flashed me a small grin before turning back to look at his hands—"and it sure seemed to me like they thought the money was going to guns, and they approved."

"Wow," I said. "Although, I have to say I don't know enough about this kind of thing, but I'm not sure that's actually illegal. It seems like it should be, but I don't know it actually is."

"Yeah...I don't know either, but it doesn't sit right with me, you know what I mean? I thought and thought about it, tried to look at it from all the angles—I mean, these are guns going to protect my brothers and sisters in the Lord—but eventually I decided it just wasn't right. At the very least, all those grieving parents and little old ladies who put their money in the collection plate every Sunday should know where their dollars are going."

"Yeah," I said.

"So will you help me?" he asked.

"I'll see what I can do," I said.

Isaiah turned to look at me again. "Thanks," he said. "After my experience after college, I kind of gave up on people outside of the church. But you're showing me that there are still a few good folks out there."

"There are good folks everywhere," I said. "Bad folks, too."

"For sure," he said.

29

ISAIAH OFFERED TO TAKE me out to a movie or something, but I said I was fine. In fact, I was tempted to go to a movie just to avoid going back to the house, but I thought that might be A) disingenuous, and B) cowardly. Plus, I should probably get in touch with Dima about Isaiah's problem.

Isaiah brightened up noticeably when I declined his offer and asked to be taken home so I could talk to Dima. This was a little hurtful, but I couldn't really blame him. It was clear that neither of us was even a tiny bit interested in the other romantically (although I could still feel his sex appeal humming around me like a high-energy magnetic field), and appearing together at the local movie theater would be sure to generate lots of gossip. We'd both be better served by me calling up Dima.

I got Isaiah's number and email address before getting out of the car. Apparently the church's aversion to modern technology didn't extend to the point of completely eschewing phones and email. He watched me with open envy as I entered the information in my smartphone.

"I've wanted one of those for a while now," he said with a sigh. "I keep trying to convince Dad that it would be good for business for at least one of us to have one, but he won't budge. And if business is running guns to Africa, I guess maybe that's not a very good argument."

"Smartphones have a lot of downsides," I said. "But they also have a lot of upsides. And—it's probably wrong of me to suggest this—you could always get one for yourself on the sly and only use it when he's not around. Although they're pretty addictive. You'd have a hard time stopping yourself from using it in front of him."

"Yeah...if this all goes down the way I'm afraid it will, I might have to get my own secret phone anyway." Another long sigh. "I hope I'm doing the right thing."

"You're doing the right thing," I said.

"Yeah. Yeah, I think you're right. Okay, Rowena, thanks again, and let me know what your boyfriend says."

"Will do," I said, and got out of the car. Isaiah, to my relief, made no move to open my door or walk me to the house, although he did watch until I got inside before driving away.

"You're home awfully early." Alexandra let me in at my first knock. She sounded disappointed.

"We both had big days planned for tomorrow," I said.

"Oh...well...well, how did it go?"

"Fine," I said. "We had a lot to talk about, as it happens."

"That's wonderful! Did you talk about the church?"

"Yes," I said. "Yes, that's the main thing we talked about."

"That's wonderful!" she repeated. "Do you think you'll talk to him again?"

"It's very possible," I said.

Her whole face lit up. Ugh. Now I was giving her false hope, if not deliberately deceiving her. I didn't like her, but I didn't want to hurt her.

"You never know how these things might go," I said. "But now I'd better get to bed, if you don't mind. I've got an early start planned tomorrow."

30

I GOT UP BRIGHT AND early the next morning. Unfortunately, it turned out Alexandra was also an early riser.

"Are you sure you have to leave right away?" she asked me over tea and toast. Coffee was not drunk in this house, it turned out, but tea was okay. "Isn't this your spring break? Aren't you off all week? It seems a shame for you to leave so early, especially now that you're just starting to get to know people in the church, make connections..."

"I'd love to stay, but I've got people waiting for me back in Georgia," I said, only semi-mendaciously. "But I might be back soon." I wanted to kick myself as soon as I said that. I had zero desire to come back here. Alexandra, it was true, had warmed up to me, but most of that warmth was predicated on me playing a role I didn't think I could sustain for long.

On the other hand, it might be true that I'd be back soon. If my parents did actually decide to move up here, then I'd probably come visit them regularly. If I was still living on the East Coast of the United States, that is. If I got a job abroad, the whole mess was John's problem.

"Please do!" Alexandra was saying. "We'd all love to see you, sweetheart." *Sweetheart* sounded stiff and false coming from her lips, but I thought she meant it as much as someone like her could mean anything. Even with this new warmth she was showing me, she still gave the impression of someone who'd read about emotions and human interactions and was trying to do her best to imitate them, but didn't actually understand what she was doing. It was like she'd been beamed in from Alpha Centauri and put on a skin suit and was now trying to pass as human, with only partial success. I felt sorry for her, and wished I could help her, and wanted to spend as little time around her as possible.

"I'd like to see you again, too," I said. I felt rather like I was manipulating a cold, rubbery skin suit myself as I was saying that, but it seemed better than not saying it.

"Well...come up as soon as you can, darling."

"I will," I promised. I told myself that "as soon as I can" was a vague term that had no particular time attached to it.

"And maybe you can see Isaiah again too while you're at it!" she added. "I didn't want to pry, but..." She lowered her voice. "Did he seem *interested* last night? You know..."

"He said he wanted to talk to me again," I said, honestly.

"Oh! That's wonderful...did you make any definite plans to keep in touch?"

"We don't have another date planned, but we did exchange contact information," I said, once again with complete honesty.

"Oh! And correspondence can be so...*romantic*, don't you think?"

I caught myself staring at her in surprise, and forced myself to stop. Even in the pale early-morning light, her cheeks were visibly pink, and she looked positively girlish. My stomach clenched from the pain of seeing how she must have once been, back before everything that had happened to her—had been done to her. Once upon a time she had been a young woman full of romantic hopes and happy dreams of love and marriage and family, dreams so strong they could make her giddy just remembering them. But now she was a hollow shell of that old self, only capable of experiencing the faint traces of once-strong sensations.

Stop being so judgmental! I told myself. *We never really know what's going on inside someone else's soul. Lots of people think you're always pretty, pleasant, polite, and happy, after all. Maybe Alexandra is full of deep feelings that others can't even fathom as well.*

But I doubted it. I thought the church was the only thing capable of bringing out any warmth, any emotion at all, in her. Which made me all the angrier at the thought that it might be misusing funds and running guns. I wasn't thrilled at the idea of any of my family members getting sucked into this semi-cultish organization, but if that was what it took to give Alexandra any semblance of peace and joy, then so be it. It just needed to deserve the faith and devotion she was pouring into it.

"Correspondence can indeed be very romantic," was what I said, though.

"Dennis and I had to wait a year before getting married so he could finish school," she said. "We wrote to each other every other day the whole time." She sighed wistfully. "I wrote Mondays, Wednesdays, and Fridays, and he wrote Tuesdays, Thursdays, and Saturdays. Going to the mailbox was the most exciting part of my day...sometimes there wouldn't be a letter from him, and I'd be cast down all day, but then, as fate would have it, there'd be two letters from him the next day, and I'd be in the seventh heaven..." She looked up at me. "I don't know if you young folk can understand that. I guess you don't get real mail anymore? Seems like a shame. Waiting and waiting to hear from someone...and then finally getting a letter that the man you love has written with his own hand..." She sighed again.

"Getting something handwritten does sound nice," I said. "But even if it's electronic, we know all too well what it's like to wait and wait to hear from someone." I suppressed the gag reflex engendered by the idea of Dennis inspiring romantic longing and sexual desire.

I also suppressed my own sigh. I'd texted Dima last night, asking if we could talk. No response. I'd sent another text outlining the situation with Isaiah and the church. As of—I checked my phone—7:15 this morning, there was still no response to either text, although the little blue checkmarks at the bottom of the message were telling me that he'd gotten them.

I told myself he had an excellent reason for not answering my texts. I also told myself that the excellent reason was not because he was tied up somewhere in a basement having his fingernails ripped off because he'd fallen afoul of Dahmer and Bundy. Everything was just fine, he was not in danger, he still loved me, and he wasn't answering my texts because...because he was out of service range or something.

Maybe you need to stop making excuses for him. Whenever Dima went incommunicado, which was often, I tried to come up with reasons that put both of us in a flattering light. But I could never shake the niggling doubt that he felt very differently about our relationship than I did. Well, there was no question about that. I was constitutionally incapable of ignoring a message from him (or pretty much anyone else, for that matter). If he asked me to talk, I would have neither peace nor rest until we'd spoken. Whereas he obviously got my messages and made a conscious decision to get back to me later, like maybe next month.

*What is he feeling when he does that? Irritation? Fear? Something he can't even put a name to but is clearly aversive? Does he even think for a moment about what **you're** feeling when he does that to you? Does he ever think about what you're feeling at all? Maybe all that stuff you said about collecting on your debt when he got back was stupid delusion about the possibility of you ever being together. Maybe you should give up on him and search for someone else instead. Maybe Isaiah is worth giving a second look to. Maybe this church isn't so bad after all...*

I stood up, breaking my death spiral of despair and delusion before it made me do something insane. "Thanks so much for breakfast," I said. "Can I help clear up? And then I'd better get on the road."

"Oh...of course..." For an instant I was sure Alexandra was going to ask if I was going to drop in on Roseanna on my way out of town. I could sense the question forming, trying to force its way out from between her teeth...she snapped her mouth shut. All her earlier giddiness and warmth was gone. The cold, rubbery skinsuit was back.

"I'll clean up," she said, not looking at me. "You go pack up your things. I'll take care of things here and make sure Dennis and your parents are up and ready to say goodbye before you set off."

"Thanks. I really appreciate it." My mouth felt cold and rubbery as I said that.

31

DENNIS MERELY NODDED coldly at me when it was time to go. My mother hugged me and said she hoped I'd had a good time and I'd be back soon. My father hugged me and told me to take care of myself. He still seemed off, a little distant and hard, but I had no better idea of why or what he was thinking. I told everyone it was great to see them, promised I'd be back just as soon as I could, and set off.

I drove to the closest gas station, pulled over, and called Roseanna. She picked up on the first ring.

"Rowena? Is that you?"

"It is," I confirmed.

"Oh good...I was worried something would happen, or they'd convince you to stay away somehow..."

"I didn't tell Dennis and Alexandra anything about coming here," I said.

"And your parents?"

"I've told them that we're in touch, and mentioned that maybe they should get in touch with you too. So far, no luck, but maybe I've sown some seeds. In the meantime, can I come by? Or we can meet at a coffeeshop or something if that would be easier."

"Oh...a coffeeshop would be fun, but if anyone recognized us and told Dennis and Alexandra about it...well, they've already cut me off, but they might make things unpleasant for you. Let's meet at my house. If you'll forgive the mess. I don't get a lot of company these days."

"Of course," I said.

And when I showed up, there was no mess to be seen anyway. Roseanna's house was a brick cottage tucked away in a corner lot of a pleasant older neighborhood. It was less ostentatious than Dennis and Alexandra's place, but much more welcoming, even if you could hardly see the house from the street. I parked at the curb, wended my way through the wooded lot that she had instead of a front yard, and rang the doorbell.

"There you are!" A tall woman with steel-gray hair threw open the door before I could take my finger from the buzzer. Despite the decisive lines bracketing her nose and mouth and the spots on the back of the hand that held open the door, she looked younger than mid-80s. She also looked a lot like me. We even had our wavy hair in similar shoulder-length cuts. Hers framed slightly tilted blue eyes just like mine and curved around a fine jaw that still maintained its lines despite decades of gravity pulling it downwards.

"Goodness," she said. "You really do look just like me. Or like I did fifty years ago." She squinted at me, looking at me first with one eye, then the other. "I can make out a bit of Bev in your cheekbones...and in the curl of your hair; it's got a tendency to ringlets mine never did...and you have her fuller figure...you must be fighting off the men with a stick."

"Not really." I smiled politely and told myself that that comment about my fuller figure was meant as a compliment. Apparently my weight loss hadn't gotten to the point of making me look waif-like and sickly. That, I told myself, was a good thing.

"Too competent, are you? That was always my problem. Well, that and my stick thinness." She shrugged what were undeniably very slender shoulders. John and I had both inherited our grandfather's—our *other* grandfather's—broad shoulders. They were more noticeable on John, but standing next to Roseanna, I could see how I had them, too.

"Men always thought I looked elegant at their side," Roseanna was telling me. "They thought I was a lot less elegant when I was explaining to them how to streamline their production processes. I was an efficiency expert back when women didn't normally go into business, especially in-to a business like that."

"Wow," I said. "I thought you must be good at something like that, so I'm not surprised, though."

"No? I'm glad to hear it. And it gave me a way to support myself when all those men who asked me out chose someone less elegant and more compliant to actually marry—someone who didn't have a nephew depending on her. Every penny that went into this place"—she waved a hand at the house and lot—"was mine and no one else's."

"Wow," I said again. "That's impressive."

"Maybe it doesn't seem like such a big deal now, but it was when I was doing it," she said.

"It's still pretty impressive," I said. "I'd certainly love to be able to do that."

"Yes...your current job is a bit of a dead end, isn't it? Well, maybe it's time to move on. Come on in and let's talk."

She stepped back and motioned me into the house. It was dark, but rather than being gloomy and cold like Dennis and Alexandra's, it seemed cozy and cool.

"It must be nice here in the summer," I said as I stepped in.

"It is. Half the time, I hardly have to run the AC at all. I may be old, but I keep up with the news. I know all about climate change, and I think all the time about what my actions today will mean for you and John tomorrow."

"That's great," I said.

"Is it? I think it's sad. I'd rather be able to do whatever I want, whenever I want." She stopped in the dark hallway and considered. "Well, that's what I *think*. I've never lived that way before, so I probably wouldn't like it as much as I think I would. I've always been frugal and future-oriented, and nothing's changed now that I'm in my 80s and I don't know how much future I have left."

I opened my mouth to say something comforting, but before I could come up with anything, she went on, "Now, don't go feeling sorry for me. I've had a good long life, even if it wasn't the one I planned, and now that I'm getting to the point where I don't have to worry as much about my own future, I can think about other people's futures instead. Frankly, that was what I always preferred anyway. I always was a fixer. That's how I became an efficiency expert: I liked fixing other people's problems. Is that something you got from me as well?"

"Well..." I said. "Um...maybe."

She led me through the house, which was mostly shrouded in cool darkness, out to a screened-in back porch.

"Have a seat." She pointed at a chair, one of those patio chairs made of springy wire that acts as a rocking chair. Its cushions were covered in a fabric with huge white peonies against a light green background. I sat down.

"Coffee?" she asked. "Tea?"

"Oh...I actually just had some. I'd better not have any more—it's a long drive back to Georgia."

"True." She surveyed me in silence for a moment, then said abruptly, "So. How are Dennis and Alexandra?"

"Well...I don't know. I don't know them well enough to know if they're doing better or worse than normal."

She nodded. "Did Dennis tell you anything about how his treatment's going?"

I shook my head. "He hardly talked to me at all."

The corners of her lips turned up in a non-smile. "That's Dennis. Not the most sociable person, especially when it comes to women and children. A granddaughter must be his worst nightmare to interact with."

I bit back a laugh just in time. Roseanna saw it anyway. We shared a brief smile.

"He was so proud when John was born," she said. "For all that he and Bobby never got along, and he was furious with your mother, when he heard he had a grandson, he was just about busting out of his britches with pride. He was sure he'd do something wonderful, finally be the heir he'd always wanted. And actually, John has done that, hasn't he? Maybe not exactly how Dennis imagined it, but John did the whole Citadel thing, and then the military—Dennis's been bragging about him for years, telling anyone who'd listen about his grandson the officer."

"I wonder what he thought when he actually spent a little time with John," I said, and then regretted it. But Roseanna only laughed.

"That boy! I always knew he'd be a pistol. I can't wait to meet him—do you think he'll stop by and see me the next time he comes up here?"

"I'll tell him he has to," I promised.

"I'd love to see him...he was the prettiest boy, although I'm sure he'd hate to hear me say that. But you know what I mean. I dare say he isn't what Dennis would want him to be, if what you've said about him is true, but Dennis has always been good at shutting his eyes to things he doesn't want to see. Like his granddaughter, for example."

She gave me a sharp look. I shrugged.

"I never did see what he and Alexandra saw in each other," she said after a moment. "He was always so stern and cold and by the book. You might not think it to look at her now, but when she was young, not only was she a real looker, she was as dreamy and romantic as a young woman could be."

"Opposites attract, maybe," I said.

"Yes...it sounds so good in books and movies, doesn't it? Whether it works as well in real life is another question."

"True," I said.

"Well, anyway, after...everything that happened to her, she lost all that dreaminess and romance and became a dried-up old stick. That was almost as hard for me as, well, the other stuff. I'd never really gotten along with Dennis, even though we're blood kin, but Alexandra and I hit it off right away. Opposites attract there too, I guess. She was everything I'd never been able to be, and I guess I was living all my dreams of being pretty and girly and in love through her.

"But then...well, it doesn't bear speaking of. I lost the sister I thought I'd gained, along with everything else that happened. And then...well, there's been so much water under the bridge between us over the years, but losing her to this 'church'"—her voice took on a venomous inflection that made the skin on the back of my neck prickle—"was a particularly hard blow. Just when I thought we'd finally gotten all that bad stuff behind us and were on the path to becoming friends again, she threw all those decades of friendship—of sisterhood—of everything I did for her, I sacrificed for her—she threw all that in my face for the sake of some pastor with a silver tongue and a pretty face."

She stopped. I couldn't tell if she was fighting back tears of sorrow or howls of rage. Maybe both.

"I knew Jeremiah Jones back when he was just another member of our church," she said, once she'd brought herself back under control. "He always was too good-looking for his own good, not to mention too charming. He could always get his way in anything and everything, and that's not good for a person, is it? Well, almost anything and everything. He couldn't get his way with his wife's illness. I do believe he sincerely loved her, as much as a man like that is capable of loving anyone other than himself. Probably he loved her as much for the flattering picture of himself he saw in her eyes as for who she was on her own, but he certainly was devastated when she died. I don't think he believed it would happen until it did. He was so sure that Jesus would save her if he just sweet-talked him enough.

"Some of us tried to explain to him that Jesus doesn't work that way, at least not very often, but he was so sure he was special, that he had a special relationship with Jesus and what was true for the rest of us wasn't true for him—and then she died anyway. It must have been a terrible shock to him, worse than it would be for the rest of us. If it'd been me, I would have had a terrible crisis of faith after something like that, and maybe he did. He stayed in that house for three months, not coming out even to go to church, and with that little boy locked up in there with him—did you meet Isaiah?"

"I did," I said.

"Is he as good-looking a man as he was a boy? Because he was beautiful as an angel when he was little. Even better than his father, because he cared about other people, not just himself."

"He's still very good-looking," I confirmed.

She gave me a look. "Oh, really? Made quite the impression on you, did he?"

"He did," I said. "But not because of his looks. He gave me some information that might be the key to breaking up the church, prying Dennis and Alexandra away from it, and saving John's inheritance."

32

I GAVE ROSEANNA A QUICK outline of what Isaiah had told me.

"I'm not surprised," she said when I was done. "There was something not right about it from the start, I remember thinking that then. And not just because he was stealing away our members—my friends. Sometimes people need more than what one particular church can give them, and I can understand why those early parishioners felt that way. Ours is a big church with a big social life, full of newlyweds and young families."

She reflected. "Well, maybe not so much now as we used to be, but still, we're doing pretty well these days, all things considered. We're definitely a younger, livelier, happier crowd than a lot of other churches. I like it—it keeps me young, too. But I can see how someone who'd just lost someone dear to them would find it difficult. I know we—Alexandra, Dennis, and I—found it pretty hard sometimes after...well, all of Alexandra's problems. But we stuck it out and we had the support of our community through all of that. Or I thought we did."

She reflected some more. "No, we did," she concluded. "It just wasn't enough for Alexandra. Not after she got out of the hospital that last time. There was something missing in her after that, and nothing any of us did could replace what had been taken from her. She spent the next thirty years as a ghost of her former self. It was...it hurt to see. But it hurt even worse"—she clenched her fist—"to see that *snake* Jeremiah Jones pretend to be able to give her what those of us who actually cared about her couldn't!"

"Do you think he's just faking it?" I asked. "Do you think he's intentionally trying to defraud people?"

"I don't know that 'faking it' has much meaning with someone like him," she said. Her voice had taken on an acerbic edge that matched the sharp lines of distaste forming up all across her cheeks and around her eyes. "I think Jeremiah Jones is a charmer and a people-pleaser through and through, and there's nothing more to him. If you were to dig down into him, right to the very core of his soul, all you'd get is what he thinks you want to hear. There's nothing else there."

I nodded.

"But I also don't know that he could intentionally defraud anyone," she continued after a moment. "That would entail having a plan and a sense of self separate from everyone around him, and I'm not sure he's capable of that. If you want my best guess, I'd say he's just fallen into this situation because he didn't have the sense not too. He just went around telling people what he thought they wanted to hear, and the next thing he knows—*if* he knows; he might not actually know what he's doing—he's cheating on his taxes and getting parishioners to sign their houses and bank accounts over to him and using the money to run guns to Africa."

"What do you think?" I asked. "Would Dennis and Alexandra leave the church if they found out about this?"

She stared out through the screen into a patch of woodlands beyond. "Squirrel!" she said. "Oh, and chipmunk!"

I turned and looked. A chipmunk whisked out of sight into the undergrowth just as a squirrel disappeared up a tree.

"I love watching them," she said. "Especially chipmunks. I sit out here and watch them for hours, sometimes." She smiled in reflexive self-deprecation. "That probably sounds foolish to you."

"No," I said. "I think it sounds lovely."

"Yes. Well...Dennis and Alexandra...in answer to your question, I honestly don't know. I think if they genuinely thought he'd done something wrong, then yes, they'd leave. But if we told them, or if they read about it in the paper, my guess is that they'd insist it was all lies. Or if they could be persuaded that it's actually happening, they'll say it's for the greater good. After all, no one's *forcing* all these people to sign their property over to the church. And they'd probably say that the tax fraud was just a mistake—and it may very well have been—and the guns are going to protect fellow Christians being unjustly persecuted by infidels and godless heathens."

"Yeah," I said. "That's kind of what I thought, too."

"What about John or Bobby?" she asked. "Do you think they'd believe you if you told them about this, or if it got into the news?"

"I don't know about my dad," I said. "I can't tell what he's thinking about all this. John would for sure. It's just the kind of thing he's waiting to hear."

She smiled faintly. "Why am I not surprised. From everything I know of him, that's always been the kind of man he is."

"Um, yeah, I guess," I said. "In any case, I'm sure he'd be on our side in this, with or without revelations of tax fraud."

"Hmmm." She put her finger to her lips in thought. We both sat there for what felt like a long time but probably wasn't. Another chipmunk—or maybe the same one—zipped across the yard and back into the shelter of the woodland. A crow came to investigate something on the ground near the house, saw us, *cawed* in disgust, and flew off. A squirrel hung head-downwards from the nearest tree and peered through the screen at us for a moment before shooting back up into the bare branches, out of sight.

"Do I have it right that you have a friend who's a journalist?" Roseanna suddenly said. "And Isaiah wants you to tell him about this so he can write up something about it?"

"Um, basically," I said.

"But that will most likely take a while, won't it? Your friend will have to investigate it, interview sources, follow leads, all that kind of thing, and then actually write the piece—and get an editor to accept it. I take it he's freelance?"

"He has a home paper," I said. "But I don't think they'd be interested in something like this."

She nodded. "So we've got time. Let him look into it if he wants to. Maybe it will do some good. Meanwhile, you and I can work on John and Bobby and prepare Dennis and Alexandra. Maybe if they hear it from them, they'll be more likely to listen."

"Maybe so," I said.

33

I LEFT SHORTLY AFTERWARDS. Roseanna and I agreed that, while it would be fun to have lunch together, I needed to hit the road in order to make it back to Georgia by a reasonable time.

Besides, I wasn't so sure it actually would be fun to have lunch together. Meeting Roseanna in the flesh had been unsettling. Every time I looked at her, or listened to her, or even thought about her, I had the feeling that I could be looking at myself forty-five years down the road, and I wasn't sure how I felt about that.

Since Roseanna was a good person, even an admirable person, it should have been comforting, and to a certain extent, it was. But it was also odd. And there were aspects of her biography that represented some of my deepest fears. She was a successful career woman who'd never had a family of her own. Instead, she'd thrown herself into her work and caring for her nephew and sister-in-law. I was profoundly grateful for that, since I probably owed my very existence to her generous behavior. But I was also profoundly depressed at the thought of following in her footsteps.

On the other hand, I reminded myself as I headed back towards the interstate, the chances of me following in her footsteps were slim. My career was circling the drain, and John seemed unlikely to provide me with nieces and nephews. So I had little reason to fear ending up like Roseanna.

I spent a good deal of the drive home making plans for how to avoid that fate. Most of the plans were vague or based on wildly optimistic scenarios. The only conclusion I came to was that I needed to be proactive. Setting concrete goals never seemed to work for me, so after a couple of hours of trying to come up with actionable targets such as having such-

and-such a job by such-and-such a date, and having a stable and committed relationship by thus-and-such a time, I gave up and simply recommitted to the one thing that came through for me more than anything else. I would act according to my convictions, and keep my eyes open for opportunities. Of course, it could be argued that that approach didn't work for me very well, but I couldn't think of anything better to do.

For the final hour of the drive I weighed the man I wanted to marry and the man my family wanted me to marry in the balance, and tried to see which way the scale tipped. I eventually gave that up as a fruitless exercise. I knew Dima so well, and Isaiah so poorly, that any comparison between them was impossible. My current frustration with Dima made dumping him and taking up with someone new tempting, but I suspected that closer acquaintance with Isaiah would reveal many, many shortcomings, and possibly a fundamental incompatibility. At least I knew that, for all our flaws, Dima and I fit together in a way that no one else was likely to be able to match. We were like...proteins that had specific lock and key formations that only allowed them to bind with their matching counterpart. Substituting some other protein/partner would be pointless because the reaction would never happen at all.

It was getting on towards dusk as I pulled into the apartment parking lot. I stopped at the mailbox and went through the routine of jiggling the key this way and that until I made the magic motion that caused the door to pop open. I pulled out the fistful of junk mail that was all fate had sent me in my absence and got back into the car, where I was greeted with half a dozen notifications on my phone screen, now that my phone was connected to its regular network. All of them were from Galina Ivanovna.

My heart clenched. Not waiting to read them, I called her.

"Allo? Inna, is that you?"

"Galina Ivanovna? I just got back. What's happening? Are you all right?"

"What? Me? Oh, yes, I'm fine."

"Thank God." I literally patted my chest with my free hand. "What's going on, then?"

"Two things. First of all, your cat."

Another heart palpitation. "What about her?"

"She was fine until this afternoon. Then she ate a big lunch, threw it up, and hid in the bathroom. When I checked on her, I noticed her hair was coming out, and I think there was a faint rash on her skin."

"Oh my God!"

"I think she has allergies, Innochka. Probably to her food."

"What?" I couldn't make sense of the words. "Allergies...is it serious?"

"If I'm right, and I'm a doctor, not a veterinarian, so I may very well be wrong, it's serious if you continue to feed her the same food, but if you can find something she's not allergic to, she'll be completely fine. Of course, if she's allergic to something in your apartment, that's a different matter, and more difficult to resolve. But either way, there are treatments. If I'm right, that is."

My brain was catching up with her words. She'd said "allergies" and "treatment options," not "cancer" and "terminal outcome." She'd said it could be as simple as switching Fevronia's food.

"You know," I said, "I think this may have begun when I started feeding her a new, cheaper food."

"There you go. If I were you, I'd switch to a better food and see what happens."

"I will." Now, here was a concrete, easily actionable goal that I could actually realize. "I'll go get some this evening."

"Good idea. I bet she'll start feeling better by tomorrow."

"That would be great!" The relief that Fevronia's problems could potentially be solved by something as simple as switching foods was so great that I could feel tears welling up behind my eyes. Of course, the reason I'd switched foods in the first place was because I was having a hard time paying my grocery bills, and I was about to be unemployed, so this wasn't going to be as easy as I'd like, but still, it was something that could be done.

"Excellent. So, we have solved that problem. Now, about the second thing."

"What? Oh, right." She'd said there were two things. Probably the second wouldn't be so easily resolved as the first one. With a certain amount of trepidation, I asked, "What's the second thing?"

"The second thing," she said, "is that Dima is here."

34

"WHERE ARE YOU?" I ASKED. "In my apartment, or yours?"

"In yours, Innochka, in order to sit with Ronechka. She seemed to pine for you, so I've been sitting with her. We're both in your apartment."

"I'll be right up," I said.

But instead of getting out of the car, I sat there frozen for a long moment. The last parting between me and Dima flashed before my eyes, and I involuntarily did a quick run-through of all the thoughts I'd had about him and us and whether I should give up on our relationship and go off in search of greener pastures. Ouch. It seemed wrong to have our next meeting in front of witnesses. But there wasn't any way around it that wouldn't be even more weird and awkward than just going through with it. I got out of the car.

It was a very long walk up the two flights of stairs to my apartment. Then the door opened very quickly, before I could even get my key out.

"Inna."

Dima was standing in front of me, holding the door just open enough so that we could see each other, but Galina Ivanovna couldn't see me. "You came back. I did too."

Oh God, what did I say in reply to that? Every word I could come up with in both English and Russian seemed trite and silly and entirely inappropriate. All that stuff I'd been thinking about breaking things off with him and searching for someone else was revealed to be the purest bullshit. Whether we liked it or not, our lock and key structures had already fitted together, and now our structures had folded into each other to create some new, bigger and better, protein...*was that how that even worked?* My knowledge of molecular biology was limited at best.

"I'm glad," was what I finally managed to say, wrenching my thoughts away from the BIO 101 class I'd taken almost two decades ago.

"Me too." His eyes did a slow survey of my face. "I know you have something to tell me," he said. "I have something to tell you, too. I..."

"Is that Innochka? For the love of Christ, Dimochka, let her in, let her in! Don't make the poor girl stand on the stoop until she dies of cold."

One side of Dima's mouth twitched. He stepped back and said, "Come in. Wait—this is your house. I guess I shouldn't be inviting you in."

"Too late," I said, stepping in. "You already did."

Fevronia came streaking over from the bedroom. Just before she barreled into my leg, she stopped, leaping backwards as if in surprise at my sudden appearance. She advanced the last foot between us with slow caution, sniffed at my pant cuff, gave my shin a sudden headbutt, and then streaked back into the bedroom.

"See? She's been pining for you, Innochka." Galina Ivanovna came over and gave me a hug. "You look tired," she said. "Of course, that's no surprise—after such a long drive! Are you hungry? We can make you something. Or would you prefer to order something. Maybe we should order something—or even go out to a restaurant! We could celebrate all being together again! What do you think, kids?"

Dima and I exchanged glances. Galina Ivanovna was in a state of nervous excitement that was most unlike her.

"How do you feel?" I asked. Maybe this was a side effect of the treatment. Maybe she was about to go into some horrible downward slide! Maybe...

"I feel fine," she said. "Better than I have in a while. I think the treatment is really starting to have an effect. You know how I would always feel so sleepy and tired for a couple of days after each infusion? Well, this week I just felt normal after the infusion—and then yesterday I started to feel better, better than I have in a long time. You remember: they told us this could happen after a few weeks of treatment. Then it didn't, and we all assumed the treatments weren't working very well, even though according to my most recent labs my kidney values were trending positively, as they say. But now I feel so much energy, I don't know what to do with myself!"

"That's great, mama," said Dima. I could read, plain as plain, his thoughts, which were the same as mine: desperate hope that this was the miracle cure we'd been praying for, which would stop or even reverse the damage to Galina Ivanovna's kidneys, obviate the need for a transplant, and give her many more years of healthy, active life; mixed with fear that this was only a false hope, maybe even a sign of decline. Galina Ivanovna was certainly acting manic, almost febrile, compared with her usual self, and I didn't like it.

"Let's go out," said Dima. "We have a lot to celebrate, and we need to go get new food for Ronechka anyway, don't we? Let's go out and enjoy ourselves."

"That sounds great," I said.

I told myself that I was being paranoid in thinking that one reason Dima wanted to go out was to put off talking to me one-on-one for as long as possible. I also told myself that just because you're paranoid, though, doesn't mean they're not out to get you.

35

AFTER SOME MORE DISCUSSION, it was agreed that we would do takeout rather than go to a restaurant, so that Galina Ivanovna could stay on her special diet. She acquiesced, but not very happily.

"You just said yourself, mama, that you've finally started to feel better," Dima said. "I wouldn't jeopardize that for anything, and certainly not a quick dinner at one of the crappy restaurants—sorry, Inna—in this tiny town."

Galina Ivanovna complained a bit, but was quickly talked around. "As a physician," she said, "I have to concede your point, although as a human being I don't like it."

"If you don't think like a physician right now, mama, you may never get to act like a human being in the future," Dima said. "And I'd never forgive either of us if I let you do something that messed up your recovery."

"Is this my son? I don't believe it. Could my son be making arguments in favor of prudence and caution? It can't be! It must be some imposter, perhaps an alien from another galaxy, pretending to be him for unknown nefarious purposes!"

Dima and Galina Ivanovna glared at each other. Then they both burst out laughing.

"It's a nice evening out—I can't believe it's only the beginning of March—and there's a table out under the trees on the edge of the compound," said Galina Ivanovna. "Let's have a picnic. That's my final condition."

Dima and I agreed that was acceptable. We also agreed that we would all go together to pick up the food, both human and feline, so we would have some kind of outing together.

"Pizza," said Galina Ivanovna, when Dima asked me what kind of food we should get.

"You can't even eat any of it, mama. Why do you care?"

"I get to watch you eat it, don't I? I can live vicariously through you. Besides, Dimulya, I know you have a weakness for Western pizza."

Dima looked at me.

"Sure," I said. "Pizza sounds great." Actually, two back-to-back pizza picnics seemed a little excessive to me, but if it would make Dima and Galina Ivanovna happy, I was game.

I called ahead to order the pizza. Dima tried to pay for it, but I hissed at him that he should keep his money, especially since I had a big favor to ask him.

"Ooooh," he said, raising his eyebrows. "A big favor. Should I be scared?"

"It depends on what you think about corrupt churches and gunrunning," I said.

"Now I'm intrigued. Clearly your trip to Virginia was more interesting than anticipated. I can't wait to hear all about it."

"You're in luck," I said. "Because I've specifically been asked to tell you all about it."

"Curioser and curioser...are you ready, mama?"

Galina Ivanovna came back from the bedroom, where she claimed she'd been settling Fevronia in for a rest.

"She's like a baby," she said. "She needs to be rocked and put down for a nap like a tiny infant."

A bolt of guilt went through me. I'd always accepted Fevronia's moodiness and standoffishness as just part of who she was, and never tried to break through it. I thought I'd been honoring her wishes and her basic underlying nature. But what if I'd been doing the absolute worst thing possible? What if a lot of her peculiarities were the result of physical and emotional pain, and what she really needed was medical attention and enforced cuddling and snuggling? What if, in my quest to suppress my natural tendency to be officious and controlling, and to give everyone around me the autonomy and respect I craved for myself, I was giving them what they neither wanted nor needed, and they were suffering as a result? What if *I* neither wanted nor needed autonomy and respect...

Don't be silly! Of course you want and need autonomy and respect. And you've always wanted to give fate a free hand, hoping it would give you equal freedom, but maybe you need to reach out sometimes and grab it by the throat.

"Is she sleeping now?" Dima was asking Galina Ivanovna with all seriousness.

*Maybe **Dima** is the one who most needs me to reach out and grab him,* I thought. *Maybe as I was rushing towards the fate I was so certain we shared, I should have looked back from time to time to make sure he was following. And made him keep up when he fell behind. Maybe by giving him the thing I myself wanted in a relationship—autonomy and respect—I wrecked things for both of us.*

"Like an angel," Galina Ivanovna told Dima with equal seriousness. "Shall we go?"

Dima ushered us to the door and held it open with a ceremonious flourish. Galina Ivanovna went through. When I went to follow her, Dima caught my hand in his. Just for a second, he ran his fingers through mine. When he released them, he took my elbow and held it all the way down the stairs.

Maybe I haven't wrecked things entirely.

36

GREENFIELDS DIDN'T have a pet store, but the cat food selection at the main grocery store was extensive enough that Galina Ivanovna and I spent over a quarter of an hour perusing my options. She recommended avoiding as many of the ingredients of the current food as possible, although, she said, the main problem was probably not the ingredients themselves but their cheapness.

We eventually settled on the most expensive bag of cat food in the store. It promised ethically sourced, humanely harvested wild-caught salmon as its main ingredient. I assumed this was mainly humane- and greenwashing, and that it was almost as much an ethical and environmental disaster as other seafood products, but its hefty price tag gave me hope that it wouldn't make Fevronia sick, at least.

After that we picked up the pizza and headed home. It was already full dark by then, but the night was mild, more like May than March.

"This is lovely," said Galina Ivanovna when we settled ourselves, our pizza, and her tray of special food at the picnic table. Just like my picnic last night, it was lit with the orange glow of sodium vapor lights, which I always found vaguely eerie and unsettling, but Dima and Galina Ivanovna didn't appear to mind.

"Really lovely," Dima seconded. "You know, I could get used to living in a place like this."

There was a pause. "Like Georgia?" Galina Ivanovna clarified. "You want to live here in Georgia?"

"Well, it wouldn't have to be Georgia, although it's been nicer than I'd been expecting. But Utah was really nice too, in its own dry, desert-y way. I didn't enjoy most of what I did there, but I did enjoy Utah itself.

I even took some time off and visited some of the parks there. Have you ever been to Canyonlands, Inna? It's amazing."

"No," I said. "I've never been to Utah at all."

"You should go! We should go together! All three of us. You'd love it too, mama, I'm sure of it. It's a landscape like I'd never seen before. Kind of like Central Asia, but also unique. I could feel the history and the geology of the region as I walked around there, I could sense millions of years of the earth's formation, and thousands of years of human habitation, and it was all completely alien to me, and yet also so familiar..." He trailed off and took a bite of pizza.

"It's funny," he continued. "The main inspiration for my writing has always been uncovering the evil deeds of the corrupt and powerful. But while I was there, I experienced an immense power that wasn't corrupt. It was neither good nor bad; it just *was*. And I wanted to write about it. Not to share my rage with others, but to share my wonder. I guess that sounds silly." He took another bite of pizza, ducking his head and not looking at either me or Galina Ivanovna.

"It doesn't sound silly at all," she said. "It sounds good. Maybe this is the next phase in your career, Dimulya. Maybe it's time for you to transition from sharing rage to sharing wonder. Just like with Innochka, what might seem right now like a detour or a setback is actually the path that will take you to where you need to go."

Dima brought his head up. "What detour or setback is Inna facing?"

I did a rapid-fire review of my vocabulary to find the words I needed to explain my current job situation in Russian. I knew more or less how to do it, but it wasn't something that translated well into another cultural context, and it had been a long day, and...

"They're firing her," Galina Ivanovna said.

"WHAT!?!"

"They're not *firing* me." Words started forming in my mouth. "They're just not interviewing me for the tenure-track job."

"So you'll get to stay here, then?" Dima demanded. "They'll just be hiring a second person?"

"No," I said. "Once my contract ends in May, I'll have to leave."

"So they're firing you," he stated.

"Well...not exactly, but the end result is the same."

"Motherfuckers!"

"Exactly," said Galina Ivanovna, nodding in approval. "That's just what I said."

"Well, fuck them," said Dima. "You don't need them anyway, Innochka. You're better off without them."

"I wish that were true," I said. "But I don't have any other job right now, so in a couple of months I'm going to be unemployed, and maybe unemployable. Besides..." I'd wanted to add that not being chosen for a campus interview for what was, to all intents and purposes, my own job, made me feel like a failure, or worse, like I was *bad*.

Frank had told me last year that deep down, I was *bad*, just like him, and that's why I hung out with him and people like him. The sting of those words had faded a little in the intervening nine months, but now, faced with this clear example of how people I had put so much effort into pleasing considered me to be not even worth talking to, it came back. I wanted to share the pain and the crushing self-doubt that this revelation was causing me with Dima and Galina Ivanovna, so that they could tell me I was wrong, but I ended up just gulping and choking before finally saying, "I'm tired of being on the job market."

Dima was watching me closely, as if he could tell I was about to burst into tears. When he spoke, his voice was unusually gentle, with none of the anger that was usually waiting to explode through the thin walls he tried to contain it in.

"Maybe something better is just around the corner, Innochka," he said. "Maybe you won't have to be on the job market much longer." He paused, apparently in deep thought, then said, "Maybe we should..."

Our phones both *pinged*.

"God DAMN it!" he said. He pulled out his phone, looked at it, and grimaced. "I've got to take this." He pushed himself up from the picnic table and stalked off, frustration and worry in every line of his body.

I checked my own phone. It was a message from Mel.

I looked out my window and saw the three of you having a picnic—fun! Did you just get back? Are you free sometime tonight to work on the takedown of Evil Mel?

I looked over at Galina Ivanovna.

"It's something important, isn't it?" she said. "No worries. I'll clean up here and go check on Ronechka. You go take care of your business."

"Are you sure? There's a lot to carry..."

She waved a hand. "I think I can handle half a pizza, Innochka. I'll take it back to your apartment and you and Dima can finish it off when you're done with your phone calls. And I'll give Ronechka some of her new food. Normally for cats you're supposed to change their food slowly, but in this case I think we'll be better off doing it all at once."

"Okay," I said. "Thanks."

"Of course. Now go take care of your call, Innochka. I can tell by your face that it's something important. And urgent. That conversation you were having earlier was also important, maybe more important, but I don't think it was urgent. I think you can have it tomorrow, or next week, or next month, and it will still be just the same."

"Thank you," I said, and went off to answer Mel.

37

DIMA HAD GONE OFF TO the edge of the parking lot and was standing under the line of pines, one more tall dark silhouette against the starry sky and the waxing gibbous moon that hung over all of us. He was talking intensely into his phone, his back to me. As I walked past, I heard him say in Russian, "...No, I don't think *you* understand. Even if I could, I wouldn't, but I can't, so it's a moot point."

I picked up my pace in order not to hear any more. Whatever he was discussing, I didn't want to know about it.

I stopped by the entrance to Mel's building and texted *I'm free right now for a bit if you are.*

I got an immediate reply. *Come on up!*

She was waiting for me at the top of the stairs. "Thank fuck you're here," she said. "It's only Monday and I'm going stir crazy. I thought for a moment there I was even going to do something totally fucked up like go visit my parents."

"Gosh," I said. "Glad I'm able to help prevent that."

"Yeah...I was all looking forward to spring break, but now I'm going out of my mind. No interview to prepare for, just a lot of injustice to rage over, and no real outlet for it."

"Yeah," I said.

"I mean, I guess I could work on grading. Or, fuck it all, an article. But it all seems so fuckin' pointless. Like, why the fuck would I do any of that if I'm about to leave this fuckin' profession?"

A woman with a small child holding each hand gave us a sharp look as she walked past us. Both the kids gave us curious glances, the younger one frightened, the older one gleeful.

"Maybe we should go inside," I suggested.

"Before we get run off the apartment complex on a rail, you mean? Come on."

She ushered me inside, indicated the frail loveseat, and plopped down on the floor, legs crossed. Her knees popped, and she winced.

"Dammit! My doctor wants me to do another round of antibiotics," she told me. "I got a lot better during the first couple of rounds, but now that I've been off them for over a month, my joints have started hurting again, and the twitching and the tasing sensation has come back. Not as bad as it was before, but pretty fuckin' annoying, and she said it's a bad sign. She said a lot of people have to do months or years of antibiotics."

"Oh," I said.

"Yeah, so I've got that to look forward to on top of everything else."

"Maybe you'll feel lots better afterwards, though," I said.

She wrinkled up her nose. "Maybe. But I'll definitely feel worse while I'm doing it. Oh well. Fuck it. You gotta do what you gotta do. I know you've probably got stuff to do this evening, so let's make this quick. Evil Mel and I have been in touch some more, and I've been thinking, and I've got a concrete plan for what we'll do on Saturday."

"That's great," I said.

"Yeah. You know, this has been the only fuckin' thing I've enjoyed this whole fuckin' semester. I'm *definitely* more cut out for this shit than for academia. Kinda sucks I got a PhD before I figured that out, but whatever, right?"

"Or maybe this is just a fun distraction from your real job," I said.

"Maybe. Or maybe all that was just a fuckin' awful distraction from what I was really meant to do, which was intel work. Broadly defined. I've started reaching out to PIs, asking if they'll take me on as an apprentice or whatever the fuck you call it."

"Oh," I said. "Here?"

"Fuck no—how many PIs do you think there are in Greenfields? A couple in Atlanta and Augusta, just to be near my folks, but mostly in LA."

"Oh," I said.

"Yeah. I guess I'm a sucker and a fool, 'cause I can't stop thinking about going back to LA."

"There's a lot of opportunity there," I said.

"Yeah...a lot of opportunity to be broke and get carjacked, but whatever. I've always liked things that are bad for me. Anyways. Saturday. I'll run through my plan, and you can tell me what you think, give me suggestions for improvement."

"Sounds great," I said.

38

MEL'S PLAN WAS STILL basically the same as it had been last week. She'd meet up with Evil Mel at the sports bar near the waterfront. Chloe and I would shadow her and try to record the conversation. Mel had driven out to Augusta over the weekend, scouted the bar and its environs, and sketched maps of the interior of the bar and the neighborhood around it.

"Wow," I said. "Maybe you really are cut out for this line of work. And these maps are great."

She shrugged. "I always liked finding stuff out. Why I thought academia was the place for me, but like I said, maybe I was wrong about that. And I always liked drawing things, too. I've always had a talent for making maps and stuff from memory. So anyway. Like I said, I think you should sit *here*"—she indicated a table by the door—"and Chloe should sit *here*"—she indicated one end of the bar. "We might have to mix it up a little if it gets busy, which it probably will, but you get the general idea. I want one person on me and one person on the door."

"Got it," I said.

"And then we're gonna *nail* Evil Mel, and I can chalk one up for truth and justice."

"That would be great," I said.

"Yeah. Might help my karma. I've been thinking a lot about it, recently, you know? Karma, I mean. How all these shitty and frankly fuckin' bizarre things keep happening to me, and why that is. Karma is the best explanation I can come up with. I never used to believe in that shit, but now...I mean, maybe the universe is just random and we're all fucked in the end, but that's not how it *feels*, is it? Whenever I think about how it *feels*, it feels like karma to me. Besides, it's a comforting thought. Like everything I've been going through has a meaning and a purpose, and if I do something right now, I can help myself out in the future."

"That's probably true even if the more esoteric aspects of karma and reincarnation aren't," I said. "Actions do have consequences, after all."

"Yeah. I've been reading some stuff by this Buddhist monk who keeps talking about how the only thing we really own are our actions and we can't escape their consequences. It's kinda scary and kinda hopeful, you know? Like, we have the power to affect our lives and the world, and the effects of our actions will live on long after we're gone, but on the other hand, what you do matters and you can't run away from that."

"Yeah," I said. "Scary."

My phone *pinged*. It was Dima.

Inna, are you free now? We need to talk.

39

I MET DIMA AT THE PICNIC bench. He was sitting there waiting for me as I came up, but he jumped up as soon as I made to sit down.

"Let's walk," he said. "I can't sit still. I need to move around, clear my head."

"Let's," I said.

He took my arm and set off towards the pines. We paced under them, stumbling occasionally on tussocks of dead grass. This area of the complex was allowed to go wild, with little mowing or maintenance. In general, I liked having a wildlife- and pollinator-friendly space outside my building. Right now, I was hoping that the dead grass meant that ticks were still in hibernation and we weren't dooming ourselves to an ordeal like Mel's.

"Let's go over to the play area," I said after I tripped over a tussock for the third time. "It's too difficult to walk here, and I'm afraid of ticks."

"What...oh yeah, right." Dima stared down at the grass around his ankles with distaste. "A friend of mine got borreliosis last year and is still sick. I forgot that you can get it here, too."

"Hopefully not this time of year," I said. "But it's a warm night, so just to be on the safe side, let's get out of the grass."

We went over to the play area, which had a slide, a swingset, a sandbox, and another picnic table. I thought Dima would head for the table, but instead he plopped down on one of the swings.

I sat down on the other swing. He pushed off and began a slow swinging motion, moving only a couple of feet.

"I used to love swings when I was a kid," he said. "I'd swing as high as I could get and then jump out at the top of the arc. For a moment, it felt like flying."

"I used to do the same thing," I said. "It worked even better if you were wearing a skirt."

"Really? I never tried that, obviously"—he grinned at me, his dimple showing darkly for an instant—"but it makes sense. I had kind of the same experience with big winter coats. Like a sail." He swung a little higher. "Probably if we tried that now, we'd break the swings. And/or ourselves."

"Probably." I started to swing slowly too. I was trying to match Dima's swing, but the differences in our relative size and weight meant that we soon got out of synch and were passing each other only in the middle of our arcs.

"So," he said on our third pass. "That phone call."

"Uh-huh?" I said as we passed each other again.

"My, ah, 'handlers', you might say, back in Moscow."

"Uh-huh?" I said as we passed each other.

"Yeah. They really want to get rid of this Anthony Wainwright."

"I can't say I blame them," I said.

"Yeah, me neither. Sounds like he's making progress with convincing your American Congress to buy the drugs and give them to their own soldiers."

"What could possibly go wrong," I said.

He laughed at that, smiling and giving me a thumbs-up as we passed in the middle of our arcs. By the time he was at the apex of his swing, he was sober again.

"The whole world might be about to find out," he said. "The Russian government is still very interested in these drugs too, and I've heard rumors that the Chinese government is as well. Three of the world's biggest militaries could be about to be hopped up on new, untested drugs. We've been talking a lot about it."

"We?" I asked as we passed each other. "What 'we'?"

"The Wolf Battalion." Another arc of his swing. He was going higher and higher. The swing frame was starting to creak from the strain.

"That's weird, right?" he said as he passed me. "Or it's Stockholm syndrome or something like that, right? I'm starting to identify with people I don't like, who don't like me, and who might want to kill me?"

"Watch out," I said.

"Yeah, no kidding. These guys scare the shit out of me, Inna."

"I'm sure, but I meant watch out that the swing doesn't fall down."

"What? Oh, yeah." He slowed his swing, gradually coming to a stop. I brought my swing to a stop too. We twisted slightly so that we were facing each other.

"I'm supposed to leave for Germany tomorrow evening," he told me. "I'll meet back up with the guys—the Wolf Battalion—there. We—they, dammit, *they*—are supposed to do joint exercises with NATO troops. But that's not all."

"No?" I said.

"No. The rumor is"—he looked up at the treetops, at the gibbous moon shining down on us, then brought his gaze back down to the ground, carefully avoiding me—"the rumor is that they're going to test the drugs out on us."

40

"BUT NOT ON YOU, RIGHT?" I said. "After all, you're not a member of the battalion. You're a journalist. They can't give you orders, and they shouldn't be testing anything out on you. It doesn't make sense. It would mess up their data."

"I may not be in their official chain of command, but they can certainly make me do anything they want." He was still looking down at the ground, his voice low. His recent talk about longing to be coerced into doing what he really wanted notwithstanding, Dima *hated* to be controlled. Our shared desire for autonomy and respect was one of the things that had brought us together. I'd often thought that his relentless opposition to the Russian government was as much about proving his independence from the power structures around him as it was from any particular political or ideological commitment. But here he was, saying that others could force him to do things against his will. I wasn't sure if that was a sign of personal growth, or the saddest thing I'd ever heard.

"Do you *want* to take the drugs?" I asked. Dima was also the kind of person who would do something reckless out of sheer curiosity, or just to prove that he wasn't afraid.

He shuddered. "No. Well...no! I have to confess I'm curious, of course, but what I've seen of them already was the most terrifying sight of my life. Well, top three, at least. Those thugs holding a gun to your head and mama getting sick were top two. But the drugged-out crazies who came after me like zombie hyenas were definitely right behind that. The only thing scarier than being chased by them would be to become them."

"Good," I said.

"Good?"

"At least you still have *some* sense left."

He laughed in surprise. "That suggests that you think I once had sense, Inna. I'm not sure I deserve that, but I thank you for it anyway."

"You're welcome," I said. "So how are we going to keep you from becoming a drugged-out zombie?"

He shrugged. "I don't think force of arms or strength of will are going to do me much good here. I think we're going to have to rely on my weakest skill, but one I'm striving hard to improve."

"Which is?" I asked.

"Cunning."

"And how are you going to use your wits and your cunning to outsmart these people?" I asked.

"That I'm still working on."

A figure came out of my stairwell. It stopped and waved at us.

"Mama!" said Dima. "I'd probably better go walk her home." He stood up from the swing. She made sit-down gestures at him. When he took a step in her direction, the gestures increased in vehemence. Dima stopped. Galina Ivanovna nodded encouragingly. He sat back down on the swing. She gave him a double thumbs-up and set off across the parking lot towards their apartment.

"She looks like she's walking better, doesn't she?" he asked me, once she had disappeared into the stairwell to their apartment. "Like she's stronger?"

"She does," I confirmed.

"Maybe it's just a temporary thing," he said. "You know, this disease has ups and downs, like any other. Maybe it doesn't mean anything. I'm still grateful that she's getting a few days of feeling better."

"Yes," I said. "And maybe the treatments are working and she really is getting better and she'll have many more healthy years."

"Maybe...I can't hardly bear to think of it." He was looking down again, his voice hoarse, like he was being strangled by unshed tears. "I thought there could be nothing scarier than watching her get sicker and sicker, but the hope that she might get better is almost unbearable."

"I know," I said. "I'm scared, too."

Now he looked up. "You are? You always seem so calm and brave, In-nochka. I confess that I envy you. I keep wishing I could be like you."

Now it was my turn to laugh in surprise. "What? Really? I'm not calm and brave at all. Certainly not in comparison to you. *I'm* not the one embedding with a hostile battalion, risking torture and death if they find out why I'm really there."

"Thanks for pointing out my situation to me, Inna. I hadn't fretted about it for at least, oh, two or three minutes."

"No problem," I said.

"But to your point, I'm not afraid of that. At least, not as afraid as I probably should be. But doing what *you're* doing—sitting at sickbeds, reconciling families that have fallen apart—*that* scares the shit out of me. I wish I could borrow a little of your courage."

"If it would be helpful to you, I'd give you all of it if I could," I said.

"I know you would, which is why it's good you can't. You need to keep it for yourself and not let selfish bastards like me suck it all away."

"You're not selfish," I said.

"Yes, I am."

"No, you're not."

"Yes, I am...goddammit, are we fighting? Fuck! I swore to myself I wouldn't pick fights with you, no matter how severe the provocation. But here I am, arguing with you because you keep trying to tell me I'm not selfish. You have to admit that is a *very* severe trial, though."

"I admit no such thing," I said.

We both glanced at each other out of the corners of our eyes. Our gazes jerked apart, then met again. This time they held.

"Innochka," he said slowly.

"Uh-huh?"

"You remember how I asked you before to wash over me like a wave?"

"Uh-huh," I said.

"Well, I'm asking again. If the offer's still open. And this time I mean it."

I stood up. "Give me your hand."

I held out my own hand. After a moment, Dima took it.

41

LATER, DIMA AND I SPECULATED how he could sneak back into his apartment without waking up Galina Ivanovna and/or alerting her to what he'd been doing.

"Brings me back to my wild youth," he said. "Especially the parts I spent with you."

"I'm pretty sure she had a pretty good idea of what we were doing, no matter how sneaky we were about it," I said.

"Yeah, but appearances must be maintained. We all have to go through the pretense that we passed the evening in the purest innocence. That's how we prove we're civilized people."

"*I* think we passed the evening in the purest innocence," I said. "There's nothing we did that I feel guilty about."

"Of course not, Magdalene. The rest of us are not so lucky, though. And mama's an old Soviet at heart. She prefers to remain silent about the more romantic side of life, or at least its physical manifestations. It's a wonder she survived as a doctor all these decades, really."

"She's tougher than you think," I said.

He took a deep breath. "Maybe. In some ways. In others, she's much more fragile than I ever imagined. Especially in her more physical manifestations."

"I know," I said.

He took another deep breath, or tried to. The tightness in his chest and throat was so strong I could feel it coming through my skin and entering my own body, his pain threatening to crush my breath as well as his.

"Promise me something, Innochka." There was a slight wheeze to his words, and he choked and coughed at the end of the sentence.

"Of course."

"Take care of mama."

"You don't even have to ask," I said.

"I know. But I'm asking anyway. Because...well, just in case it's for the long term. I was so worried I was about to lose her. I still am worried. But what if she loses me? It's always been possible, our whole lives it's been the more likely outcome, and I always dismissed it as not my problem, but now...now I keep thinking about what will happen to her if I'm not around. Not just for a few months here and there, but for good. At first I kept thinking that she'd be better off without me, without all the heartache I cause her, not to mention the political problems I bring raining down on her head, but these past few months I've been thinking more and more about how she needs me. Or at least, she needs someone to take care of her. I'm probably the worst person for the job. You'd be much better suited for it. Frankly speaking, you've already taken over it. I should cede the field to you—but for how long? How long could you continue to take care of her? She's not even family to you—"

"She is," I interrupted.

"Not legally," he said. "What will happen to her if something happens to me while I'm in Germany?"

"She's of sound mind," I said. "She can make decisions for herself."

"But what if something happens to her? What if she needs next of kin to make important decisions for her, and I'm not there?"

"Well," I said, "maybe we should do something about that." I paused, trying to come up with the phrase "power of attorney" in Russian.

Another deep breath from Dima. "Yeah..." A coughing fit. "Goddammit, I'm not even smoking! Although I'd really like to light up right now."

"You could go outside," I suggested. "Smoking is permitted out there."

"No. I don't want to leave you right now. And I think this conversation should be held without mind-altering substances, even nicotine." A deep breath, this time without a coughing fit. "You're right, Innochka.

Of course. We should put mama's situation vis-à-vis you as next of kin on a proper legal footing. What do you say?"

"Of course," I said automatically. "What do you want to do?"

He held up his phone and started searching something. "What's the procedure here in the US? Do you have to declare banns like you do in England?"

"Banns?" I repeated, confused. I'd never heard that Russian word before. "What are banns?"

"Maybe that's not the right word? Something like that, though. In some places, like England, you can't just go to the marriage bureau and get married. You have to publish these 'banns' first. Do you have to do that here?"

"Oh, marriage banns! No. But you do have to get a license. I'm not sure what the exact requirements are here in Georgia."

"Great! Do you think foreigners can get a marriage license here in Georgia?"

"Um...probably?" My mouth, brain, and body all seemed to have disconnected from each other. "I'm sure that information can be found out..."

"Great!" He put down his phone, kissed my cheek, and jumped out of bed. "You find that out. Probably we won't be able to get one tomorrow, right?"

"Um...I don't know...that's why people go to Vegas..."

"Where are my pants...how the fuck did they end up over there...and my shirt's on the complete opposite side of the room...Vegas is far away, right? We wouldn't have time to go there and back tomorrow before my flight to Germany?"

"Um...no..."

"Yeah, I didn't think so. Okay, well, I guess we'll be walking under God until I get back...there's my wallet; how did it end up in this corner over here...but get everything ready for getting married as soon as I get back, and in the meantime, take care of mama, okay?"

"Of course." I wanted to demand if what I thought was happening was in fact happening, but I was frozen by astonishment and also the fear that if I said it out loud, Dima would deny everything and I'd ruin it.

Don't look back, I told myself.

"Great!" he said. "Where's my jacket...by the door, I guess...you know, Innochka, I'm really glad you proposed. Some of my comrades complain about women taking initiative in things like that, and I always thought I'd hate it too, but actually, it took an enormous weight off my shoulders. I've been thinking and thinking about it, desiring and fearing it in equal measure like St. Augustine before his conversion...and then you did it for me! My own personal garden in Milan! So thanks. I won't say you won't regret it, but I'll try to make you regret it as little as possible."

"Great." Was I hallucinating? What was even happening?

"No, no, don't get up—you look so cozy there under the covers. Stay there and sleep. It's been a very long day for both of us. I'll just slip out and lock up after myself. And I'll think of something to tell mama—well, whatever, I'll tell her our plans and she won't care about anything else, will she?"

"Probably not." My voice sounded muffled and hollow in my ears.

Dima patted himself down, checking that everything was zipped and buttoned in place and he was ready to go out onto the street. The remnants of pre-combat gear checks, he'd told me, a habit that he just couldn't kick. "I thought I'd feel scared, but actually, I feel great!" he said. "You can't believe what a huge burden you've lifted from me, Innochka...well, I guess I'd better go."

"Yes." My need to suppress a cough made my word come out more tersely than I'd have liked, but Dima only grinned, kissed my hand, and left.

42

GALINA IVANOVNA TEXTED me first thing the next morning, her message overflowing with exclamation points and congratulations. This at least was proof that I hadn't dreamed the whole thing, which had been my first thought on waking up.

She followed up by an in-person visit, sans Dima, whom she'd ordered to remain behind so the two of us could have a girls-only chat, to reiterate all her delight at our engagement and her sorrow that we couldn't get married right away.

"Because you should seal the deal as soon as you can, Inna," she advised me. "Remember what happened the last time you waited! I know that wasn't your fault, but we both should have put all our feet down on Dima and forced him to the registry office the moment he proposed. None of this waiting around until circumstances are just right. Circumstances will never be just right, so go for it as soon as you can, that's what I say."

"Yes," I said.

"You're not rethinking this, are you, Innochka?"

"No," I said honestly. I had been carefully examining myself for cold feet ever since it had happened, but so far my toes remained warm and toasty. Yes, it was sudden, inasmuch as getting re-engaged to someone I'd known for more than a decade, had lived with, and had planned to marry, could possibly be called sudden. Yes, we both had a lot of uncertainty in our futures, such that some might say getting married right now was reckless. Yes, I hadn't actually meant to propose at all and Dima had completely misread what I'd said.

Or had he? More like he'd read what you'd wanted to say with complete accuracy, because it was what he wanted to say, too. You were both synched up perfectly last night, and things worked out exactly as they should have.

That was a comforting thought. This wasn't the result of impulsivity and a farcical failure of communication. This was the result of years of events leading us to exactly this point. One could even say it was fate.

"You probably won't even have time to go get a ring," Galina Ivanovna was lamenting. "I know that's important for you Americans."

"Well..." I said. "I still have the old one."

She stopped. Then she said, her voice warm with approval, "Of course you do, Innochka. Go get it."

"Um..." I said. "Maybe I should ask Dima first?"

"Why? Do you want him to give you a proper proposal? Don't you Americans expect the man to get down on one knee and hold out the ring? A bit medieval, but charming in its own way. Dima might agree to do it if that's the proper custom for your people. He's so grateful to you for proposing that he'd probably agree to anything right now. He told me he thought you'd both reached such an impasse of old feelings and new problems that he didn't see how he'd ever break through it, and then—babakh!—you up and proposed. He said he was surprised, but he should have known you'd be the one to take action, break the chains, all that. We both knew we could always count on you, Innochka."

"That's great," I said. "But I don't expect a fancy proposal from him. What I meant was we should ask him about security. Wearing an engagement ring is a big deal here in America, and people are going to notice. I'll need to tell them something. Do we want the world to know that he and I are officially planning to get married?"

My scalp prickled as I said those words, and I found myself putting one hand on the kitchen counter to steady myself. Like most wonderful things, in the here and now this was mainly a lot of stress. I let my mind wander for a moment over to possible plans for the future. Our prospects were so bleak that I promptly snapped my thoughts back to the present.

"Good question, Innochka," Galina Ivanovna was saying. "I suppose we should ask him. But don't let him say you shouldn't just because he's scared to publicly acknowledge your connection!"

"Of course," I said.

43

DIMA SHOWED NO HESITATION in wanting me to wear my old ring. In theory. In practice, he said it seemed like bad luck and I should have a new ring. Also, I was probably right in thinking that flaunting our engagement might be putting a target on my back.

"She could always say it's a secret," Galina Ivanovna mused. "Or say she's engaged to someone else."

Dima leveled a death glare at her. "I'm not having my fiancée going around saying she's engaged to another man!"

"A secret engagement, then," Galina Ivanovna said.

"People who know us will guess," I pointed out. "People who don't know us will speculate wildly. There will be talk, and someone unfriendly could put two and two together."

"True," said Galina Ivanovna. "Maybe, for safety's sake, you shouldn't wear the ring, Innochka."

"I don't want my fiancée to be ringless!" Dima said. "If that is the custom amongst her people, then she should damn well wear a ring! Besides, I want other men to know to stay away from her. She's *mine* and I don't want a bunch of worthless lowlifes sniffing around where they shouldn't."

"I could wear the ring on a chain under my shirt," I suggested. "That way I'll still be wearing it in some fashion, at least. And I don't normally have a lot of problems with worthless lowlifes sniffing around where they shouldn't. I don't encounter a lot of lowlifes, and the ones I do, I can normally send packing."

Dima argued against this a little more, but Galina Ivanovna and I eventually talked him around, and he agreed that I could wear the old ring hidden under my shirt, but that he was getting a new, better ring while he was in Germany, which I would absolutely wear on my left ring finger as soon as it was safe to do so. I argued back that there was no need to spend a bunch of money on *another* ring, especially since we would need to get wedding rings as well. I suggested we get cheap steel bands. Dima said we were certainly worth gold and we would just have to find the money. I countered that steel was a lot stronger than gold. Dima conceded this point, and also the point that steel might be more appropriate to our relationship.

"Meanwhile, do you have a chain to put the current ring on?" he asked.

"No," I admitted.

"I'd say we should go out right now and get you one, but this is Wainwright territory, after all. If someone saw us shopping for jewelry together, they might guess things we don't want them to know. Best to keep a low profile."

"For sure," I said.

"Are you upset, Innochka? If you really want to wear the ring, you should do it. We'll find a way."

"I'm not upset," I said. "You're right. Safety first. Your word means more to me than all the rings in the world."

This was true. It was also true that not wearing a ring in some form or fashion felt a little bit...risky. Not wearing a ring was my idea, and I thought it was a good one. It was founded on a rational assessment of the risks I faced.

But not wearing a ring also felt like it was tempting the gods. Until I had a wedding band, preferably of strong steel, sitting snugly on my ring finger, along with a marriage certificate locked up in a safe, I wasn't going to feel secure. Not because I thought Dima was going to back out, but because I thought fate might have it in for us.

I didn't say any of that, though.

44

BY EARLY AFTERNOON Dima and Galina Ivanovna had calmed enough down from the engagement thing to focus on other issues. I turned to Isaiah Jones's request with relief. It wasn't that I wasn't excited about the prospect of finally, at long last, marrying Dima. I was. It was more that it was so overwhelming that I couldn't really be happy about it, or even believe in it. I'd be able to do both those things about six months after the honeymoon was over, I guessed.

Oh God! The honeymoon! Something else to plan! And we were very likely to have no money to do it with! Maybe I could talk Dima out of that, too. He just seemed extremely set right now on giving me everything he thought American traditions called for. It was a sweet gesture. Unfortunately, American wedding traditions called for a lot more free time and spare cash than we could expect to have this year, or maybe ever. And what about kids...

Stop, stop, stop!!!! I couldn't even let myself think about the possibility of us having kids, or I'd spend all afternoon crying and being sick from anticipated joy and heartbreak.

"Isaiah Jones," I said firmly. Dima and I were having lunch at my dining room table. Galina Ivanovna had delicately retreated to her own apartment, claiming she preferred to eat her special meal in peaceful solitude and then rest. I suspected she was giving me and Dima some time alone so that we could get to work on providing her with grandchildren, should we be so inspired...what if we already had...I found myself making mental timekeeping calculations and cursing myself out for not keeping better records of my own cycles...there were apps for that these days; why hadn't I invested in one?

"Isaiah Jones," Dima repeated, breaking me out of my hopes and fears of an unintended pregnancy. "Why do Americans have such difficult names, Innochka? Is that really easy to say? It feels like a real jawbreaker in my mouth."

"Isaiah is a somewhat unusual name from the Old Testament, but it's not hard to pronounce," I answered, my mouth on teaching autopilot while my brain returned from its journeys through the distant fields of family planning. "Jones is extremely common and very easy to pronounce."

"Really? A voiced affricate plus a diphthong and a voiced dental at the end is easy for Americans to pronounce?" Dima laughed at my look of surprise. "See? I was paying attention when you talked about phonetics. Even when you were explaining why English words were hard to pronounce, because Russian words have none of those things I just mentioned."

"I see," I said. "Too bad my actual students never seem to listen."

"They don't have my motivation. So tell me about this Isaiah Jones and what he wants from me."

I outlined Isaiah's story and his concerns as concisely as I could. Partway through, Dima stopped smiling. When I got to the end, he was frowning.

"That certainly sounds like a story," he said. "It even sounds like it could be a story for me. But I'm about to leave for Germany, maybe for weeks, maybe for months."

"I know," I said. "This is probably something more suited for an American journalist, anyway. I just thought you might know someone."

Dima pulled out his phone and started scrolling through his contacts. "I might...no, no, FUCK NO, probably not..." He stopped scrolling and looked up. "I'll need to think about it a little. I'm sure there's someone out there who'd love to do this story. I just need to find them. I'll keep thinking about it. I'll have some time on the flight over to Germany. Searching for rings can't take more than a couple of hours."

"I suspect you'll get tired of it long before that," I said. "Have you ever had the slightest interest in jewelry?"

"No, but this is different. This isn't some cheap—metaphorically speaking—piece of trash to show off our ill-gotten gains. These are our *wedding rings*."

"Very true."

Dima checked his phone. "I should probably get going. I need to leave early to drop off the rental car, and getting through Security at Atlanta can be really slow."

"Oh." I checked my phone. "Yes, of course. Of course it's time for you to go." *So much for another attempt at conception. That's probably a good thing. Don't need to add another layer of complexity to an already complex situation.*

Dima stood up. "Wow," he said. "This is a lot harder than I thought it was going to be."

I stood up too. "Uh-huh." Oh shit! Was I about to cry?

"I should probably say something heart-stirring and romantic, but I'm afraid I'm about to cry," he said. He smiled as he said it, but his eyes looked like they were on the verge of filling up with tears.

"Same here." I swallowed and sniffed. "Crying is so unattractive! It always makes my nose run. Come on. Let's go to Galina Ivanovna. She'll keep us from crying."

"Yeah," said Dima. "Let's...oh, hey, kitty."

Fevronia came running out of the bedroom. She went right up to Dima, butted his leg with her head, and then stood on her hind legs and clawed gently at his trousers, mewing at him. He scratched her behind the ears.

"Someone's feeling better," he said.

"And she really likes you," I said. "She must know you're about to leave."

He bent down and picked her up. Fevronia, against everything I'd ever seen of her before, not only allowed it, but snuggled against his chest and purred.

I threw up my hands. "I guess she's been your cat all along. I'll just try to keep her alive and healthy until you return."

"Please do." Dima looked at me over the top of Fevronia's head, which was now rubbing ecstatically against his chin. His eyes were half-hooded and dark, the way they got when he was saying something very, very serious. "Keep both of you alive and healthy until I return."

"Only if you promise the same," I said.

A pause. Then he said, speaking slowly, "Like Pushkin says, I swear by even and odd. I swear by my sword and righteous battle." Another pause. "Of course, I don't have a sword, but if I did, I'd swear by it. If you'll do the same."

"I swear," I said.

45

I WENT WITH DIMA OVER to Galina Ivanovna's apartment, and stood there while he packed up his things—that didn't take long—and walked out to the car with him, and smiled cheerfully and told him we would be fine until he got back. We didn't even hug, just in case we were being watched. Just because you're paranoid doesn't mean they're not out to get you.

Galina Ivanovna and I watched until his car had gone through the complex gates and turned onto the road and disappeared.

"I remember saying goodbye to him the first time he went away to war," she said. "He looked so little then. He wasn't even his full height yet—he grew another two centimeters on the front—and so skinny. I didn't see how he could carry all his kit, let alone something like a gun. At least his father had been a full-grown man when he went off to his death. Our son was just a little boy. All the other wives and mothers at the station were crying, but I just smiled and smiled and smiled. I quoted Blok to him, and he quoted Blok back to me, and I knew I'd done at least one thing right in raising him. That made letting him go into the meat-grinder even harder."

"Uh-huh," I said.

"I almost didn't let him. I thought about hiding him away, smuggling him out of the country, bribing officials...I didn't have a lot of money, but I still had enough of my looks that I was pretty sure I could get some ugly bureaucrat to sleep with me. I even looked into it. I checked out all the men who could potentially keep Dima out of the military, or, once he was in, away from the front, and I made a list in my head of all the ones who looked particularly desperate, and made a plan to approach them and offer myself to them...it all came to nothing, of course. Dima forbade me to do anything to keep him out of the military when his draft notice came up, even though we probably could have gotten an exemption for him, as the only son of a widow, and he went and volunteered for the front once he was in. I tried to talk him out of it, I screamed, I begged, I pleaded, I told him what I was prepared to do to keep him safe, but that only made him more determined. He told me he was going with or without my approval, and if I tried to stop him, he'd run away and never speak to me again. Faced with the choice of definitely never seeing him again versus maybe never seeing him again, I chose maybe."

She sighed deeply. "We've never talked about it. About whether he regretted his choice, about whether he wished he'd listened to me. I think that day, on the platform, he did, and other times too, but now, almost twenty years later, I don't know. Maybe it's not something anyone can regret. Maybe it was his fate and he was right to listen to it."

"And now?" I asked.

"And now maybe this is his fate too," she said, staring at the road that had taken him away from us. "Or his...what's that Indian word? Kamra...no, karma. Maybe this is his karma, so that he can expiate everything fate has made him do."

"Maybe," I said. "As long as it's also his karma to come back."

"Yes," said Galina Ivanovna. "Well." She blew out a long breath. "Let's go check on Ronechka, shall we?"

46

FEVRONIA RAN OVER TO Galina Ivanovna as soon as we came into the apartment. My relief at seeing her happy and apparently in good health fought with my jealousy and my feelings of total failure and inadequacy. Apparently I couldn't even take care of a cat properly.

"I should check my email," I said. I had only checked it once in the past twenty-four hours, and it was making me antsy. Withdrawal, or legitimate concern? It was hard having to use an addictive substance—broadly defined—for my professional life.

"Check it, check it, Innochka. Ronechka and I will sit here and snuggle."

I opened up my laptop. Now that I was able to feed my email addiction, I didn't want to. I wanted to turn it off and go snuggle with Fevronia too.

She'd probably run away from you if you tried that. The thought did not make me feel better, but it did spur me to open my email.

You at least need to keep your job for the next couple of months. And find a new job. You may not be good for much, but maybe you can do that. **Maybe.** In fact, I was highly skeptical of my ability to find another job, and for good reason. Getting the kind of job I was qualified for was time-consuming and difficult. My attempt at leaving academia and working for the government had, as far as I could tell, failed. Marrying Dima was only going to make getting any kind of job that required a security clearance more difficult, if not absolutely impossible.

That was unfortunate, because marrying Dima was also going to make steady employment even more important. He had a job, but it was not very remunerative at the best of times, and these were not the best of times. I'd always expected to be the breadwinner in our relationship. My willingness to hold down a steady job had been the main asset I was bringing to the table. But willingness wasn't enough. You actually had to get a steady job, and that was harder than it looked.

Maybe I could be a cashier at a grocery store. How bad would that be? I was sure it would be dull as dishwater, but I could stick it out for a while, right?

But would it pay enough? Ah, there was the problem. Even if I were willing to do a steady job, and they were willing to hire me, they weren't willing to pay me enough to support me, Dima, and any children we might have...I broke out into a sweat of mingled excitement and anxiety at the thought.

Enough of this. I started skimming through my personal inbox. Maybe there would be a job announcement...wait, what was this?

It was an email from Masha, my best friend from grad school. *Inna, have you seen this? Just in case your current tenure-track thing doesn't work out. They're looking for researchers on Tsvetaeva for next year's fellowship!*

I scrolled down. Below her message was a forwarded email about a fellowship at an institute in Helsinki. As in Helsinki, Finland. They were indeed putting together a working group on female poets, and were specifically looking for a Tsvetaeva specialist.

"Inna! What is it!"

I put my hand over my mouth, choking back the shriek that was trying to leak out.

"A job announcement," I said. "One in my area of specialization."

"You see!" said Galina Ivanovna. "It's fate."

"Yeah," I said. "If fate means moving to the far north, then I guess so." I was already calculating my chances of getting the fellowship. Surely everyone would be applying for this, right? My chances were maybe one in a hundred, if that.

But it felt like fate, even so.

47

I SPENT THE NEXT COUPLE of days determinedly not thinking about Dima. At least, not mooning or pining over him. I told myself at least I didn't have to worry anymore about whether or not he loved me. He'd demonstrated that very clearly, right? Okay, it was a little—or a lot—hurtful that he'd obviously been full of doubt and fear about it, but he'd *done* it, hadn't he? Now I just had to worry about him coming back safely to me.

That was a scary thought, though, and not one I could do a lot about, so I forced myself to focus on something I could control, i.e., applying for more jobs. The thought of being unemployed while also being the chief breadwinner for the family was very scary too, but it was something I had some agency over, so I decided to work on that.

Having other people rely on me might be frightening, but it also gave getting a job a purpose it had never had when I'd just been doing it for myself. I felt unexpectedly calm as I went through the job announcements, making a list of everything I could have even an outside chance of getting.

Along with the Finnish fellowship, which looked promising because it was specifically in my area of research but less promising because was it only for one year and was open to anyone in the world, I found two one-year visiting positions in small colleges on the East Coast, a couple of positions at various military bases (I wasn't sure if my connection to Dima would rule me out of those, but I decided to apply in any case), and a program director job in Kyrgyzstan for next fall.

The upside of having submitted so many job applications was that I already had most of the materials I needed. The two visiting positions were the easiest, with just a couple of tweaks of my cover letter required, so I sent those off first. The military positions took a little more work since the US government had very specific information and formatting requirements for job applications, but I was able to get those done in a couple of hours as well.

The Finnish fellowship was more challenging since I had to write a cover letter and research proposal explaining how my current project fit in with the institute and working group's theme, and how I would benefit from access to the institute and working group's resources. I spent most of Thursday's session in the hospital looking up information about the institute and reworking my basic research proposal to fit the guidelines. Galina Ivanovna, who was very interested in all of this, particularly the Finnish fellowship, gave me a lot of advice, some of which was actually useful. She continued to be alert and lucid throughout her infusion, and walked out to the car afterwards with no difficulty.

"I'm getting stronger, Innochka," she told me. "Stronger by the hour. I can feel it."

"That's great!" I said. "The treatment's really working!"

"Yes," she said. "Although I think your good news is a big part of it, too."

That was another layer of stress added to the stress lasagna piling up all around me—what if I became a source of bad news and drove her to a relapse?—but I kept myself from telling her that and talked cheerfully about future plans instead.

I spent Friday writing up the Finnish fellowship application. Chloe, who was back from visiting her family, proofread it for me, and then I proofread it again out loud, finding a mortifying double "the" from my original research statement that had already been sent out in dozens of applications. That almost sent me into a tailspin of crippling self-criticism and despair, but I managed to pull myself out of it in time and send off the application. Then, for a cool down, I threw together the application for the job in Kyrgyzstan and sent that off too.

By Friday evening my eyes were burning and I had a splitting headache from grinding my teeth while staring at the computer, but I'd submitted six job applications. Six was a totally inadequate number if I actually wanted a job, but it was a start. Besides, sometimes when you rolled the dice, you came up sixes on the first throw. Now all I could do was wait and worry. Fortunately, I had the entrapment of Evil Mel that weekend to distract me from too much fretting.

48

THE MEETING BETWEEN Mel (call sign "Nickie") and Evil Mel was scheduled for 3:00pm on Saturday. We set off for Augusta in a two-car caravan at noon, Chloe and I in my car, Mel in her Jeep. We rendezvoused at a parking lot on Broad Street. Chloe and I waited in my car until Mel had finished sweeping the area and declared it clear of Evil Mel.

"How do you know what she looks like?" I asked when Mel came over and told us it was safe to get out. "Maybe she's watching us right now."

"First of all, no one's watching us, period. Second of all, I talked her into a video call last night."

"Whoa! How did she explain the fact that she's not you? And how did you explain the fact that you *are* you?"

"She said the pictures are real old, which is true. She might not even recognize me from them. And she does actually look kind of like me, to be honest. Maybe we're distant cousins." Mel shuddered. "Fuck! That makes it even creepier. And I said I'm Nickie, and Nickie and I really are first cousins and really do look a lot alike."

"Okay," I said. "So now what?"

"Now we split up again and sweep the block around the bar, looking for her or for any suspicious-looking confederates. Here. I took some screen shots from our video call last night. I'll send 'em to you so you can recognize her."

Mel texted me and Chloe a couple of low-quality screenshots of a woman who did, in fact, look kind of like Mel. I'd never confuse the two of them, but I could see how Evil Mel could think she might get away with claiming Mel's old photos were actually of her. She had the same firm bone structure and wide, mobile mouth, both accentuated in her case by an unhealthy thinness that was only partially obscured by long, straggly dirty blonde hair.

"She looks like she's on drugs," said Chloe. She clapped her hand to her mouth. "Oh, shoot! That's the kind of insensitive thing I'm probably not supposed to say."

"'Cept in this case she probably is on drugs," said Mel. "She hasn't said anything about using at the present, but she mentioned a couple of stints of rehab in her past, and hinted that she needed money for stuff to 'keep her healthy,' and also that she knows some drug-dealer-y type people. She sure seems like a real mess."

"A real mess who's hurting people!" said Chloe.

"Yeah..." Mel shook her head, as if shaking off an unpleasant thought. "Okay. Let's go do this thing. Rowena, you go down Broad Street that way and circle back on the riverwalk. I'll go the other way. Chloe, you go take up a seat in the bar and start surveillance inside. We'll all text each other if we see anything."

"I have to go into the bar by *myself*?" exclaimed Chloe in horror.

Mel gave her a measuring look. "Yeah, good point. You don't really look like a bar-y type of person. Ro, you go take up a position in the bar. Preferably by the door. Let us know if Evil Mel is already there, or if you see her come. Once we've seen the lay of the land around the target and you've given us the picture inside, Chloe and I'll enter separately and take up our own positions."

"What if she *is* already there?" Chloe asked. She looked like she was starting to regret being part of this. Conducting a slightly over-the-top illicit operation to confront a scammer had sounded all fun and games when we'd been planning it back in Greenfields. Now, though, the opportunities for embarrassment and appearing ridiculous were multiplying exponentially.

"Then Ro'll tell us where she is, you'll go in first, just like we planned, and I'll go in and greet her, just like I'm supposed to. We'll just know ahead of time exactly where she is."

"What if I find her while I'm 'sweeping' the area?" Chloe asked, not looking reassured.

"Then you text me that you've seen her and you follow her, real quiet-like, so you see where she goes and who she talks to."

"And if she spots me 'tailing' her?" Chloe was now looking like she was on the verge of a panic attack.

"You're a tourist. Tour. Look around, take a couple pictures, generally act like you don't know what you're doing."

"I can do that." Chloe was starting to calm down at the idea of a task well within her scope.

"I know you can. And I don't mean that in a bad way. But no one's gonna think you're a badass investigator on the tail of a criminal, which is why you're perfect for this assignment."

"Oh. Okay." Chloe looked dubious, but she set off in the direction Mel indicated.

"Godspeed," Mel said to her retreating back, sounding less confident in Chloe's abilities now that she was out of earshot. "You good, Ro?"

"Yep," I said. "Shouldn't be any problem at all."

49

I MENTALLY KICKED MYSELF all the way down Broad Street to the bar. What a stupid thing to say! But I'd wanted to look strong in front of Mel, so I'd said the first thing that came to mind. Now I'd probably jinxed us.

I was so busy berating myself that I almost walked right past the sports bar that was the designated meeting point. It had an understated white brick façade, a small sign that read "Sports Bar," and a bigger but still not very large sign advertising Budweiser. When I ducked inside I was greeted with cave-like unfinished brick walls, a couple of battered booths, a few tables covered in checked tablecloths, and the smell of fried food. The impression was of a place devoted entirely to watching sports, with food and alcohol as a secondary concern.

If there had been a lunch rush, it was over now. Two men were sitting in one of the booths, watching basketball with the sound off. Every other table was empty. I was glad we hadn't sent Chloe. She would have stood out like a sore thumb. Unfortunately, I stood out almost as much.

The bartender was sitting propped against the back wall, reading a battered paperback copy of *Master and Margarita*. Well, what do you know. I did a lightning-fast calculation and decided to take a chance.

"Sorry to disturb your reading," I said when she reluctantly slid off her bar stool and came over to take my order. "That's one of my favorite books."

She gave me a double take. I guessed her to be in her mid-thirties, although a heavy smoking habit—I could smell the smoke from hundreds of old cigarettes coming off her shirt—and a bad bleach job and haircut had added ten years to her appearance.

"It's 'cause of a bet." She had a heavy local drawl. "A friend bet me I couldn't read nothin' serious 'cause all I read are magazines. I wanna go to college someday and my friend said that in college you gotta read all kindsa hard stuff. She did one semester afore she dropped out and she said she had to read this book for some kinda, I dunno, literature or culture class or somethin', but it totally kicked her ass and she flunked the class and dropped out of college for good. She's been tellin' me I'll never make it either, so I bet I could finish the book that destroyed her. I'm real motivated 'cause I *really* wanna go to college. I wanna run my own business, and they say a business degree really helps for that. And I wanna make something of myself, you know what I mean?"

"That's cool," I said.

She shrugged. "Only problem is, this book is kickin' my ass too. I'm havin' a real hard time followin' what's happenin' here. Some parts are cool, I guess, but the names are all weird an' there's, like, stuff that happens in, like, Russia, I guess, an' stuff that happens in...I don't know, Rome, I guess? Although I keep thinking it's Jerusalem, but my friend says no. We got a side bet on that, too."

"It is Jerusalem," I said.

Her overly mascaraed eyes lit up. "I knew it! So why do they keep talkin' about Rome if they're in Jerusalem, then? That's what we keep arguin' about."

"Jerusalem was ruled by Rome then," I said.

"Really? Huh. And there's all kinds of weird stuff about them plannin' to crucify some guy...kinda like in the Bible or somethin', I guess. Is it, like, the Bible story?"

"Yes," I said. "It's a retelling of the Gospels."

She shrugged and grinned. "I never paid much attention in church, so I'm not good at this kind of stuff. Anyway, it's weird, but I'm kinda into it, an' when I finish it, my friend can't say I couldn't make it in college, especially when I tell her I won our side bet. So what'll you have? The kitchen's closed; all I got is what's on tap."

"Oh...when will the kitchen reopen? I've been walking around all day and I just need to sit and take a break for a while."

"We're showing a replay of the Boston-Denver game at 3:00. It'll re-open in time for that. If you wanna sit, why don't you get a drink and I'll tell the cook to open up a little early." She gave me a semi-friendly smile.

"That'd be great," I said. "Thanks so much!" I ordered Sprite, talking at length about how I really wanted a beer but should probably wait until I had some solid food in my stomach before getting one, but I'd definitely order one when the kitchen reopened...Since I was going to stand out here no matter what, I figured the best strategy was to have a good cover story. That way the attention would be focused on me rather than Mel and Chloe. I doubted it mattered in the slightest, but if we were going to run this like a security operation, we might as well go all out. At the very least, it added entertainment value to what was otherwise a fairly boring day.

I took my Sprite to the table closest to the door, as planned, got out my phone and texted Mel and Chloe that I was in position and the only woman in the place.

Halfway through the sweep. No sign of Evil Mel yet, Mel texted back. *Be there in half an hour.*

I sipped at my drink, wishing I'd brought a book. Half an hour was a long time to sit and wait. I had my phone, but I didn't want to look up anything important in case I got distracted or blew my cover. I wasn't sure why that would matter or what cover I had to blow, but as I kept reminding myself, just because you're paranoid doesn't mean they're not out to get you.

With some maneuvering I was able to sit so that I could keep one eye on the door and the other on the game. I didn't follow basketball and didn't even recognize the teams, but judging by the reactions of the two men in the booth every time one of the guys in red scored, it was a big deal. The bartender came back out of the kitchen, give me an encouraging nod, and settled back down with *Master and Margarita*.

After about ten minutes of this, two more men came in and took up another booth. They were followed by a small knot of college students, and another pair of men. I was still the only woman in the joint. I took another sip of my Sprite. I was genuinely starting to feel hungry. I paced myself, not wanting to chug down the soda and end up with a sugar rush and a full bladder just as things started to get exciting. If they ever did.

The door swung open, letting a little afternoon Georgia sunshine into our dark cave.

Another man, I thought, already bored. *No...no, wait! That's not a man, that's a tall woman. Is that...*I squinted into the light, trying not to be obvious about it. *It is! That's Evil Mel!*

50

DESPITE THE LONGER hair, which she'd curled and teased into an 80s big hair style, she really did look a lot like Mel. Disconcertingly so. I kept my eyes fixed on my phone as she walked past me and took a seat at the bar.

She's here! I texted once she'd sat down. The bartender came over and started talking to her. I couldn't make out all the words, but I got enough to guess that they knew each other...wait, were they talking about *Master and Margarita*?

"*She* says it's Jerusalem," the bartender was saying, nodding towards me.

Oh shit! I really should have kept my mouth shut.

Evil Mel turned and looked at me. I gave her a small smile in return and went back to my phone.

She and the bartender are friends, I texted. *Also, the bartender has specifically pointed me out to her (long story). We're the only women in the place right now.*

Don't worry about it, Mel texted back. *We'll deal.*

The bar was filling up more and more. The basketball game finished. The two men who'd been watching it high-fived each other and ordered another round. The bartender got out a remote control, turned on more TVs, and switched on the sound. The bar went from semi-asleep to a blaring wall of noise in an instant.

Chloe came in, looked around, clocked Evil Mel, took an involuntary step back, then, looking awkward and uncomfortable, took one of the few empty seats left at the bar, far back in the corner. She wouldn't be able to hear anything Evil Mel said from there. Of course, with the sound this loud, I doubted Mel would be able to hear anything from the bar stool Evil Mel was guarding zealously to her right.

Chloe was trying to watch Evil Mel while pretending to watch the pre-game commentary. Another group of college students, all black, came in and, by unspoken agreement, crowded around her. I caught glimpses of her fidgeting uncertainly in the middle of the knot of Celtics jerseys, and then she went still, apparently resigning herself to being stuck.

The door opened. Mel stood limned against the light, peering into the dark bar. Evil Mel turned to look over her shoulder. Her face split into a grin of genuine joy. An unpleasant prickle ran up my neck. The joy of seeing her prey come into sight, or joy at finally meeting the woman she considered her soul mate? Either way, if things went the way I hoped they would, that joy would turn to sorrow by evening.

Mel came over and said something to her. Another knot of people in Celtics jerseys came in and swarmed around the bar, blocking my view. When they collected their drinks and moved over to the last two open tables, Mel was sitting at Evil Mel's side. They were taking turns shouting into each other's ears.

The bartender kept trying to catch my eye, probably to tell me that the kitchen was open and I could order food now, or maybe to tell me to get out of there if I wasn't going to watch the game. It was now standing room only at the bar. A couple of women came over to my table.

"Hi!" one shouted. "Are you expecting someone? Because we were wondering..." She nodded towards the empty side of the table.

"No, no, please have a seat," I said, not seeing any way out of it.

The two women sat down and promptly turned their chairs to face the nearest screen, their backs to me. The game started, eliciting a cheer that made the room shake. A man from a neighboring table leaned over and shouted something at me. After a couple of tries, he managed to convey that he wanted the remaining chair at my table, if I didn't need it. I pantomimed that he should take it. He did. When I turned my attention back to Mel and Evil Mel, they were getting up from the bar.

Chloe slid off her bar stool and promptly got stuck in the middle of the group of die-hard Celtics fans surrounding her. She struggled through them, pushing and shoving, but everyone was so intent on the game that no one noticed her.

I kept my eyes fixed on the screen as Mel and Evil Mel walked past. Mel paid no attention to me, but Evil Mel stopped and said something in Mel's ear, pointing at me.

Mel shrugged, looking bored, and shouted something in Evil Mel's ear, pointing at the door and ignoring me. After a moment, Evil Mel turned away from me and followed Mel out the bar.

Chloe was still fighting her way through the thronging hordes of basketball fans, only halfway across the floor. I stood up and moved slowly towards the door.

"Hey! Hey, you!" The bartender had come out from behind the bar and was waving at me. I smiled and mimed going out the door. She pushed her way past the women who'd taken over my table and grabbed me by the arm.

"Don't you want your food?!?" she screamed into my ear.

"That's okay," I screamed back. I tried to free myself from her grip and slide out the door, but she only gripped harder.

"Come into the back!" she shouted, pulling at my sleeve. "We'll make sure you get something before you go! I owe you—you helped me win my bet!"

Chloe had fought her way free of the main crush and was hurrying to the door. As she passed, our eyes met for an instant. I made a split-second decision.

"Sure!" I screamed into the bartender's ear. "Thanks!"

Chloe dived out the door, after Mel. I, praying I wasn't making a terrible error, turned and went the other way, following the bartender into the back.

51

"THE BACK" TURNED OUT to be a sort of storehouse-y room off the side of the kitchen. The bartender, who introduced herself as Desi ("Short for Désirée" she said with a shrug), explained that I couldn't go into anywhere that food was being prepared, but they had a kind of a break room back here where I could sit, catch my breath, and have something to eat.

"Thanks." I tried to think of a subtle and artful way to ask how Desi knew Evil Mel, and what Evil Mel's real name was, and whether Desi knew about Evil Mel's scams, but before I could come up with anything sufficiently clever, Desi turned and went back to her customers, who were presumably clamoring for her attention.

The cook came into the storeroom/breakroom, introduced himself as Jose, and asked me what I'd like to eat. I requested fries. He asked if I wanted a burger to go with that.

"Or I do a mean fried PB&J," he said before I had to get into why I didn't want a burger. "House special."

"That would be great." I shifted a little, feeling how the waistband of my pants slid loosely over my skin. Fries and a fried PB&J on top of a soda wouldn't do too much damage, right? Besides, I didn't actually have to eat all of it. This was more a ruse to gather information, right?

Jose gave me a warm smile and said he'd be right back with my food. My conscience twinged. So far Desi and Jose had both been nothing but nice to me, including doing things they probably weren't supposed to like invite me back here into an employee area. And I was using their niceness to try to get them and/or their friend in trouble.

Well, since I was here, I might as well snoop. I walked around the store room/breakroom, examining the metal wire shelves. Big cartons of paper napkins, ketchup and mustard, all the things you'd expect in the back of a bar and grill. Wait...what was that...

Jose came back with a plate piled high with steaming fries and a golden-brown sandwich that promised about three thousand calories of high-fat goodness.

"Careful, it's still hot," he warned me. "You can sit over there." He indicated a vinyl-covered barrel-back chair with sloping sides that looked to be older than I was. It was pulled up to a coffee table of similar vintage that wobbled on its single central leg. Remnants from a previous incarnation of the bar, I guessed.

"Thanks. This is really nice of you."

He grinned at me. "Desi said you helped her out, so it's the least I can do. Desi and me, we help each other out. Me and Desi and Tiff, we're a trio. We stand by each other. And anyone who helps out one of us, gets help from all of us in return."

"Tiff?" I asked.

"Yeah...you probably saw her...she came in earlier for a bit. Kinda tall? She's going through a tough patch right now, but we've been helping her out." He shook his head. "She was working back home for a while, but her shithead manager—oh, sorry!"

"No worries," I said.

"She'd had a lot of problems, went back home...we told her not to, we told her to stay here in Augusta with us and we'd help her get back on her feet, but she wanted to leave the city—too much temptation, you know what I mean? She had a little drug problem...sorry if that's TMI."

"No worries," I said again. "Happens to lots of people."

"Yeah, that's what we told her. She'd had a tough childhood, but don't we all." He grinned again, but with pain rather than warmth. "My family came up here in the 80s to work the fields...ended up working in broiler barns and hog farms...most people have no idea...hell on earth exists right here in Georgia...I made friends with Desi and Tiff in school...they didn't have it too good either...we came to Augusta together but Tiff got into trouble, like I said, went back home, got into even more trouble there...we're helping her get back on her feet, though."

"That's great," I said.

"Yeah, she's doing better now. She's even gone into business for herself."

"Wow," I said. "That's *great*. She must have a real entrepreneurial spirit."

"She sure does! She was always the one with the ideas. Desi and me, we just wanted a steady job that wasn't in broiler barns. We got jobs here and we've been working here ever since. We're part-owners now." He grinned some more, this time with pride.

"Good for you," I said.

"Yeah, we wanted to bring Tiff into it, but she was always restless, you know what I mean? Couldn't handle being stuck behind a bar or in a kitchen all day, couldn't stand working for someone else. She always wanted to go into business for herself, ever since she was a kid. And it looks like now she's finally managing it."

"That's great," I said. "What kind of business has she gone into, do you know?"

Jose held up one finger in a "wait" motion. "I've got her card here somewhere." He dug through his pockets, pulled out a battered wallet, went through it, and fished out a slightly dog-eared business card.

"Here. She gave me a couple so I could give them to potential customers. If you don't need it yourself, maybe you'll know someone who will."

"Thanks." I looked at the card. It was embossed with a silver urn and an amethyst necklace. In florid silver script it said:

Tiffany Wilson
Precious Memories
Custom Jewelry

"SHE TAKES ASHES FROM, like, pets and stuff, and turns them into jewelry and decorations. Real nice stuff," said Jose. "She always was artistic."

"Wow," I said. "That's amazing. Is it okay if I keep this?"

"Sure. Like I said, maybe you'll know someone who needs it."

Desi came bursting into the room. "Jose! I've got orders up the wazoo…sorry."

"No problem at all," I said. "Jose was just helping me. You both have been so nice and helpful, you can't possibly imagine."

"Like I said, we help our people out," said Jose, and with one final smile, retreated into the kitchen.

52

WHERE ARE YOU? I texted Mel. I picked at the food while I waited for a reply. I was starving but unwilling to get bogged down with actually eating.

Three minutes. Five minutes. Seven minutes. When ten minutes had passed and there was still no answer, I abandoned the half-eaten food and went back out to the front.

The game was in full swing. The noise was still at permanent-hearing-damage levels, but there was a lull in orders at the bar as everyone's attention was fixed on the screens.

I sidled over to where Desi was leaning against the bar, watching the game along with everyone else.

"Your friend!" I shouted into her ear. "Tiff! Do you know where she went?"

Desi turned slowly to look at me, her eyes still half-focused on the nearest screen. "What?" she shouted.

"Your friend Tiff!" I shouted. "She was here earlier. Do you know where she went?"

Her focus slowly switched more towards me. "Why?"

"I need to talk to her," I said.

Desi's attention was now fully focused on me, and turning into suspicion. "Why?" she repeated.

"Okay, so here's the deal," I said. "I'm here with a friend of mine who was supposed to meet someone—she wanted me here as her wing-woman—and I think the person she was supposed to meet was your friend Tiff. But my friend has some medical problems and I think she might have forgotten her meds. I can't get her on the phone. I thought maybe if I could find Tiff, I could find her and make sure she has her meds." I wasn't sure whether I felt worse about the truth or the lies in that statement, but it was the best thing I'd come up with when I'd been sitting in the back trying to figure out what to do.

"Oh...right...Tiff *was* meeting someone on a date...makes sense the date would bring a wingwoman...after all, that's why Tiff wanted to meet her date here: so I could be there. I think they probably went to the Riverwalk."

"Anywhere in particular?" I asked.

Desi shrugged. "Just the Riverwalk. They're probably walking up and down it, talking. You know how first dates are."

"Yes," I said. "Thanks. I'll just go look for them."

There was a huge cheer. The Celtics must have scored. Desi's eyes slid back to the screen.

"Thanks," I repeated, and left.

53

I LOOKED UP AND DOWN Broad Street. No sign of Mel or Tiff or Chloe. I turned up Sixth Street and walked briskly towards the river, looking right and left, scanning passing pedestrians. Nothing, nothing, nothing...I got shouted at for stepping out into traffic while crossing Reynolds Street. I waved apologetically and sprinted the rest of the way across the street, slowing to a jog when I hit the sidewalk and jogging to the start of the Riverwalk.

I did another quick scan. Nothing to the right. I jogged along the red sidewalk and turned left.

Why didn't I wear running clothes? Other joggers were out and about, enjoying the March coolness. In running clothes, I would have blended in perfectly. But in jeans and carrying a purse, I was obviously running because of an emergency, not for exercise.

Nothing, nothing, nothing...my left knee was twinging, and I was starting to get winded. I wished I'd kept in better shape. But to keep in better shape I'd have had to have had a functional set of knees, and I hadn't, so...wait, was that Chloe?

Yes, that was definitely Chloe. She was standing in the middle of the path, in front of the entrance to an amphitheatre, wringing her hands and looking up and down anxiously.

"Rowena! Rowena! Thank God you're here! I didn't know what to do!"

"What's going on? Where are they?" I resisted the urge to fold over with my hands on my knees and pant.

Chloe pointed towards the amphitheatre. "They went that way, into the trees...Rowena, I think she's got a *weapon*! Evil Mel, I mean. Should

424

we call 911?" Chloe's voice was high and the whites were showing all the way around her eyes.

"Have it up and ready on your phone." There was a nasty stitch in my side. This was humiliating. And dangerous. What would Dima say? But it wasn't like I was out of shape because I *wanted* to be...I wrenched my mind back to the actual emergency at hand. "We don't want to get the police involved unless we're sure we need them," I said. "They might make things worse. Cue up 911 and let's go."

We skirted around the amphitheatre. No sign of Mel or Tiff.

"Where do you think they've gone?" Chloe whispered.

"The trees?" I whispered back. There were thick clumps of trees on the very edge of the river. They hadn't fully leafed out yet, but they still provided enough cover to half-hide someone from the riverwalk.

Moving slowly, we stepped into a clump of trees. Nothing. I heard Chloe exhale in relief behind me. We started to retreat from the clump of trees in order to go around to the Japanese garden next door.

"*Wait!*" Chloe hissed.

We froze. I could hear the sound of people going down the River-walk, and, more faintly but resonating deep in my bones, the sound of the river, and...

"For Chrissake, what the fuck d'you think you're doing with that thing?"

Chloe's eyes met mine. She pointed wordlessly towards the far side of the trees, where they ended in a rocky bank that tumbled down into the river.

"I *told* you, I'm not here to hurt you!" Mel's voice was more angry than frightened. I started to creep in its direction. Chloe checked her phone and started creeping after me.

Two figures appeared through the trees. One was Mel. She was backed up against the fence that ran along the very edge of the bank to stop people from tumbling onto the rocks and the river below, her hands in the air. The other woman had her back to us. She was holding up something at Mel's chest.

"I'm not here to hurt you," Mel said again. Her eyes flickered as Chloe and I stepped out from behind the trees, and then focused back on Tiff. "I really did just want to meet you, like I said."

Tiff hissed out something, her voice too distorted by stress and anger for me to make out the words. I nodded *left* at Chloe, and started circling right. After a moment, Chloe moved hesitantly to the left.

Mel was talking to Tiff, her words low and soothing. As I came around their side, I saw what Tiff was holding.

Not a gun. Thank God! Wait...what is that? Is that a taser? Oh jeez...

"Tiff! TIFF!"

Chloe and I whirled around.

"Oh shit!" Chloe yelled. She didn't even cover her mouth in embarrassment afterwards. I couldn't blame her. Our problems had just gotten a lot bigger.

Jose came bursting through the trees.

54

"TIFF!" HE SHOUTED. "They're..." He saw me and skidded to a stop. "Don't move!" he ordered. "Don't move or I'll..." He pulled something bright and shiny out from the front of his chef's jacket.

"*Eep!*" Chloe shrieked.

Fuck!

The bright and shiny thing was a chef's knife, as long as my forearm. Not a gun. Okay. That was good. We could handle a knife.

"I think there's been a misunderstanding," I said.

"Damn right there's been a misunderstanding!" Jose shouted. "The fucking misunderstanding was that you came in and tricked us!"

"We never wanted to trick you." I hoped I looked more honest than I felt as I said that. "We just wanted to get to know you. Well, Tiff." I nodded towards Tiff, who was still holding a taser up to Mel's chest. "We just wanted to make sure our friend was safe." That, at least, was true.

"So you came as a trio, you *spied* on us, you tried to get us to talk...you *did* get us to talk!" Jose brandished his knife in my direction. "You *used* me!"

I put my hands in the air.

"I'm sorry," I said. "I wasn't intending to hurt anyone. I just wanted to make sure my friend was okay. Just like you're doing for Tiff. I feel about Mel"—I nodded towards Mel—"the way you do about Tiff."

Jose lowered his knife about a quarter of an inch.

"We don't want to cause any trouble," I said. "I swear. We don't want to hurt anyone. We just want to make sure everyone's okay. Mel's had some problems in her past, and it sounds like Tiff has too, and we just wanted to make sure that everyone was okay. That was it. I swear."

I kept my eyes fixed on Jose's, willing every ounce of warmth and sincerity I possessed into my gaze, my tone, every line of my body.

He lowered his knife another inch.

"Well..." he said. "You coulda been more upfront about it! You didn't have to run this like a sting operation!"

"I know," I said. "I'm sorry. We should have been more honest with you from the beginning. But we didn't know what we were getting ourselves into."

Jose's posture relaxed a tiny bit more. We were going to get out of this. If everyone could just stay calm, we were going to get out of this...

"They're tryna trap me!" Tiff shrieked. "They wanna send me to prison!"

Jose stiffened. Tiff jabbed the taser at Mel. Faster than anyone thought possible, Mel brought her hands down, grabbed the taser, gave it a hard twist, jerked it out of Tiff's hands, spun Tiff around, and ended up standing behind Tiff with the taser pressed against her neck.

Everyone froze in shock. Then Jose reached over, grabbed Chloe, and held his knife to her neck.

Fuck! And things were going so well...

"We don't want any trouble." I stepped slowly so that I was in between Jose and Mel, who were staring each other down. I turned to face Jose, my hands still in the air. "We really don't," I said. "We just want everyone to get out of here safely."

"So why are you holding a taser to Tiff's neck!" he shouted. His hand jerked from agitation, the tip of the knife nicking Chloe's skin. She bit back a whimper and closed her eyes.

"Let's not let things get out of hand." My voice wanted to crack. I pitched it as low and calm as I could. "I get why you're upset. I'd be upset if I were you, too. Let's just all walk away before anyone gets hurt."

"Let go of Tiff or I'll stab her!" Jose shouted, jerking his knife against Chloe again. A tiny trickle of blood started to ooze down her neck.

"Why don't we have Mel and Tiff walk out of here together," I said. "Then, once they're out, Mel can let Tiff go, and you can let Chloe go, and we'll all walk out of here and nothing bad will happen to anyone."

"They're gonna call the cops on me!" Tiff yelled. "You know what that means!" Her face was twisted up in a feral snarl that, discomfitingly, made her resemble Mel even more.

"We're not going to call the cops on anyone," I said. "We have just as much to lose from calling the cops as you do. We just want to walk out of here unharmed. No one's been hurt yet"—Chloe's eyes opened and she gave me an *Are you kidding?!?* look, but I plowed on—"so we can all just walk away from here and nothing bad will happen to anyone."

"We're gettin' out of here," Mel declared. "We're gonna walk out of here nice and slow, just like she"—she nodded at me—"said, and then I'll let your friend go, and you'll let my friend go, and nothing'll happen to anyone."

"Until you call the *cops*!" Tiff shrieked.

"I'm not gonna call the cops," Mel said. "Like she said, we've got just as much to lose as you do." She started shuffling towards the path back to the main riverwalk, pushing Tiff in front of her.

Jose tensed. Chloe shut her eyes again.

"Here," I said. "I'll come over to you. You can hold me hostage too. You can hold us both until Tiff comes back."

Jose gave me a suspicious look. "You're tryna trick me," he said.

I shook my head. "I just want to help out my friend. Wouldn't you do the same for Tiff?"

He hesitated. Mel pushed Tiff faster towards the riverwalk. Jose fidgeted in indecision, accidentally driving the point of his knife into Chloe's neck again. She yelped. Mel stopped. There was a brief but extremely tense moment of staring. Mel started moving towards the riverwalk again. I let out a breath I hadn't realized I'd been holding.

When she got to the edge of the trees, Mel stopped and turned.

"Let Chloe go," she said. "Once I see her start walking towards me, I'll let her"—she shook Tiff by the shoulder—"go."

There was another brief but extremely tense stare-down between her and Jose. After a moment, he lowered the knife from Chloe's neck.

The shock made her stumble and almost go down, but he gave her a shove in my direction and she half-ran, half-fell towards me.

"I got her!" I shouted, grabbing her by the arms to keep her from faceplanting onto the ground.

Mel jumped back, pushing Tiff away from her. Tiff, unbalanced by the sudden shove, came stumbling and weaving past us and straight at Jose. He instinctively reached out and caught her.

"Come on!" I hissed at Chloe, and, still holding her arms, dragged her after me at the fastest run we could manage back to the boardwalk.

55

MEL CAUGHT ME BY THE hand and we ran like some kind of drunken game of crack the whip, with Mel as the head and Chloe flying along in the rear, getting jerked this way and that as Mel dodged oncoming pedestrians.

"Stop...stop...STOP!" Chloe shouted. "I'm bleeding!"

Oncoming pedestrians were starting to point and stare.

"Here." Mel pulled us over to the side of the path and stopped. "Let's have a look. Yep, a little nick...nothing to worry about. Here's a tissue. Apply pressure to the wound until the bleeding stops. Yeah, like that. Now let's get out of here before the cops or the criminals come after us."

She shoved the taser into her pants pocket and set off down the path at a brisk walk. Pressing the tissue to her neck, Chloe followed her. I took up the rear, glancing back to see if Jose and Tiff were coming after us.

"Excuse me." A woman with a concerned face stopped us. "Are you hurt? Do you need help?"

Chloe opened her mouth, probably to say *yes*.

"Just a little scratch," Mel said briskly. "We were admiring the Japanese maples and leaned in a little too close. Freak accident, but nothing to worry about. We're heading back to the car and we'll clean it up there. I've got a first aid kit."

"Oh..." said the woman. "If you're sure..."

"Thanks for asking," Mel said. "Really appreciate it, but we've got this."

"Well...okay..."

The woman took a step back. Mel continued her brisk march down the path, one hand firmly on Chloe's elbow. I hurried after them.

There was still no sign of Jose and Tiff when we turned off the boardwalk onto 10th Street. We crossed Reynolds unmolested. Still no tail that I could see when we turned onto Broad, or when we made it to our cars at the parking lot.

"Let me have a look at that," Mel said, pulling Chloe's hand away from her neck. "Yep, just a tiny scratch. Bleeding's already stopped. If you like, I can clean it with alcohol wipes and put a bandaid on it. I really do have a first aid kit."

Chloe looked like she wanted to yell something angry at Mel, but she swallowed it down and said in a small voice, "Okay."

There was still no sign of Jose, Tiff, or Desi when Mel was done cleaning the cut. I still wanted to get out of there. Augusta now felt malevolent to me, as if unfriendly eyes were watching me from all around. Some of those unfriendly eyes were from my own conscience, reminding me of all the lies I'd told here.

"Well," said Mel. "That was a little more exciting than I was expecting, but no one got hurt—"

Chloe made an angry sound.

"*Seriously* hurt," Mel corrected herself, "and at least we got a visual of the target and her associate. Wish we coulda gotten more intel, though. I recorded as much as I could, but I don't think I got anything actionable. And what kept you, Ro?"

She said it casually. I couldn't tell if she was angry with me or not.

"I had an opportunity to gather more, um, intel," I said.

"No shit! Whaddya get?"

I held out the card Jose had given me.

"I got our target's true name."

56

"I LOVE YOU," MEL SAID. She snatched the card out of my hand. "God *damn*, she really does have my last name. Maybe we're cousins or some shit like that."

"You do look a lot alike," I said.

"I know." Mel made a face. "Makes the idea of us hooking up pretty disgusting, doesn't it? I mean, there's no danger of inbreeding, obviously, but...yeah." She shuddered. "Now I'm getting sick just thinking about all the talking we did about the special connection between us. And even sicker thinking I really felt something."

"Maybe the thing you felt wasn't the opposites attract of erotic connection, but the like calls to like of family ties," I said.

Mel shuddered again. "Hate the thought of having a family tie with a scammer like...what's her name? Tiff? Tiffany, I suppose." She stopped, her face going introspective. "Wait...was there a story about some distant cousin named Tiffany? Or am I imagining that, trying to make a coherent narrative out of a bunch of fuckin' random facts..."

"We should go," Chloe broke in. "I don't like standing out here. What if they come for us? What if they send the cops after us? Wait...are we *criminals*? Oh my God! We're criminals! I could have a criminal record!"

"They're not gonna call the cops on us," Mel said. "So we're not gonna get charged with anything, even if we did anything wrong, which we didn't."

"I didn't mean wrong," Chloe said primly. "I meant illegal. There's a difference. And I don't want to do either."

"Good point," said Mel. "Don't think you've got anything to worry about here, but let's get out of here just to be safe. Everyone good to head out?"

I nodded. After a fraction of a second, Chloe nodded too.

"Great. And great work, Ro." Mel slapped me on the shoulder. "That was quick thinking, changing plans like that and getting that intel."

"It was mainly luck," I said.

"Still, good thinking. And good work from you, too, Chloe. You stuck with me the whole way, and kept your cool when things got tense. Bet you thought you didn't have it in you, did you?"

Mel grinned at Chloe. Chloe stared down at her shoes and mumbled something about still thinking she didn't have it in her.

"We'll make a kickass operative out of you yet," Mel told her. "All right, let's move out. See you back at Greenfields in two hours."

She hopped jauntily into her Jeep. Chloe and I got much less jauntily into my Civic.

Chloe sat in tense silence all the way out of Augusta. She only started to relax once we were in the country.

"Do you think they know who we are?" she asked. "I mean, you and me?"

"I never gave them my name," I told her. "Did you?"

She shook her head. "I never said a single word to them. But what if Mel told them?"

"I doubt she'd do that," I said. "And if she did, I doubt they'll do anything about it. They don't seem like the Mob. More like three people who've come up through the school of hard knocks and are just trying to survive, even if that means doing some things that aren't 100% honest."

Chloe stared out the window for a while.

"I wish you'd been there," she said suddenly. "I wish you hadn't left us."

"Yeah," I said. "That wasn't great. I wish I hadn't had to do that, too. But I couldn't see a good way out of it, and I did get key info. I got Tiff's name and business card, and I also saw some of her stuff. I snooped around in the back room while I was there, and I saw what looked like boxes of ashes, and little knickknacks and stuff that she's turning them into. I think she really did have a legitimate business, if you can call it that, turning pet ashes into keepsakes. Maybe she still does. But then she decided it would be more lucrative to scam people rather than to deliver the actual service she'd promised to provide."

"She's keeping *ashes* in the back of a restaurant?" Chloe had turned away from the window and was now looking at me, her face screwed up in disgust.

"That's what it looked like to me. And yeah, it's probably not code. But I don't think that in and of itself is doing any harm. They're just sitting there in the breakroom/storeroom."

"Still..." said Chloe. She shook herself. "I knew this was a bad idea from the moment Mel proposed it. Then I let her talk me into it, and I talked myself into thinking it would be a fun adventure—you know, something to get me out of my regular routine, shake up my life. I've felt like I'm stuck in a rut for a while now, just teaching and writing and teaching and writing and getting nowhere, and nothing I do seems to break me out of it. I thought letting Mel push me out of my comfort zone might also push me out of my rut. And maybe some of it did." She straightened up, smiling a little. "I have a...gosh, maybe it's even a *date*, to meet with Aaron to practice for karaoke night. I know it's not much, but it's a big deal for me, and I have a good feeling about this."

"That's great," I said.

"Yeah, although if it does go well, I'm not looking forward to bringing him home to meet my family. He's not really the kind of boy they've wanted for me...lots of cultural stuff there..."

"He seems like a nice man," I said. "If it goes well, they'll be happy for you to have found someone like that."

"Maybe." Chloe didn't sound very confident in that. "But anyway, that was okay. Good, even. But this..." She reached up and fingered the bandaid on her neck. "I didn't realize how awful it was going to be. First of all, it never occurred to me that I could be, well, *held hostage* like that. And second of all, I didn't realize how scary it would be. Has anything like that ever happened to you?"

"Yes," I said.

"Really? When? I mean, if you don't mind sharing, that is."

"I don't mind." That was not, strictly speaking, true, but maybe it would do Chloe good to hear about it. "Some not very nice people didn't like what Dima was doing, and basically kidnapped me and held a gun to my head to get him to stop."

"Oh my God! What did he do?"

"He shot them."

"Oh my God!"

"Not fatally," I added hastily.

"Still! I don't know how I'd feel about a boyfriend who *shot* people. Sorry! That was insensitive. I didn't mean it like that. I just meant...I guess I just meant I don't think I'm cut out for that type of thing. For *this* type of thing." She fingered the bandaid on her neck again.

"That's probably a good thing," I said. "Because you'd probably be wasted if you decided to pursue it. The world doesn't need you to do this kind of thing. But it does need you to do what you're good at. Weren't you saying you had come up with a really ambitious, far-reaching, inter-disciplinary research project for your next book? One that might turn the whole field on its head?"

"Yeah, but...I mean, I probably won't succeed in any of that."

"You're more likely to succeed at that than either Mel or I are," I told her. "Everyone knows you're the scholarly superstar, Chloe."

"Oh God! That's so much pressure!"

"Pressure you can handle," I said. "You held up pretty well when someone was holding a knife to your neck. But you're right: there are lots of other people who could have handled that just as well or better. But when it comes to putting out some truly groundbreaking research, my money's on you."

"You don't even know my research." Chloe clapped her hand over her mouth. "Oh shit! I mean...sorry, I don't know what's gotten into me...What I meant was that you're my friend and of course you're going to support my work and I appreciate that, but the people actually judging it are *not* my friends and *won't* be supportive."

"The people actually judging it have been pretty supportive so far," I said. "Didn't you win some kind of big fellowship in grad school, and get published before you even defended—*in the PMLA*—and get a tenure-track job straight out of grad school, and get a book deal your first year out of grad school, and isn't your book nominated for a big prize now?"

"Several prizes, actually," Chloe said in a small voice. "But it's not going to get any of them. They probably nominate everyone for them."

"Still. You see where I'm going with this."

"Yeah...I guess..."

"You have talents," I said. "Talents you've honed through years of dedication and hard work. Talents that have nothing to do with dealing with knife-wielding thugs, and everything to do with re-envisioning how we see the world. So focus on what you're good at, that's what I'm saying."

"Yeah..." said Chloe. "I guess...I just wish I knew how it would all turn out, that's what *I'm* saying."

"Don't we all," I said.

57

WE MET BACK AT CHLOE'S house, where I gave Mel a thorough rundown of everything I could remember from my conversations with Desi and Jose.

"Damn," she said when I was done. "I thought I was the one with the skills here, but you got the real intel, Ro. Good job."

"Yeah," I said. "So, um, what are you going to do about it?" I didn't say what I was really thinking, which was that the more I thought about what I'd done, the less good I felt about it. I'd just been going with the flow, doing what seemed best at the time, concerned mainly with getting me, Mel, and Chloe out of there safely and, hopefully, successfully. But in doing that, I'd lied. I'd knowingly deceived people who were already having a hard time, with the specific intent of extracting information from them that would hurt them.

People who hurt other people! I reminded myself. *People who would have hurt you!* That was true. It still didn't make me feel good about what I'd done.

Mel was turning Tiff's card over and over in her hands. "I think I'm going to find out more about Tiffany Wilson," she said slowly. "I don't want to go to the cops with this, partly 'cause I think we might get ourselves in trouble if I do that."

I nodded. Chloe made a face and rubbed at the bandaid on her neck. She pulled her hand away and wrapped her arms around her body. I thought she was shaking slightly.

"I want to fuckin' stop them," Mel said. "Don't get me wrong there. But I don't want to send them to prison—or get in trouble with the law myself. So I think...I think I'm gonna ask around, see if I can find out more about this Tiff and if she really is family, and maybe find some way of stopping her that doesn't hurt her. I feel responsible for her in a way, isn't that fuckin' weird?" She shuddered. "I guess this means I've gotta go talk to my family, doesn't it?"

"It seems like the most obvious first step," I said.

She shuddered again. "Ugh! Well, no one to blame but myself, I guess. I'll call my dad tomorrow and ask for a deep dive into Wilson family fuckups." Her wide, mobile mouth twisted into a grimace of distaste. "That'll be a fuckin' long conversation. Better start early. Leastways I know my dad won't be at church tomorrow morning, so we'll have all day."

"Sounds like a good start," I said.

58

MEL AND I LEFT SHORTLY after that. Chloe invited us halfhearted-ly to stay for supper, but looked relieved when we declined. She was still hugging herself and shaking as she walked us to the door.

"Are you sure you're going to be okay by yourself?" I asked.

"I'll be fine." Unspoken were the words *Better by myself than with the people who got me into this*, but I could hear them nonetheless. How long before she recovered from this, and how long before she forgave me and Mel? She hadn't uttered a word of reproach to either of us, but I was pretty sure she was thinking hard thoughts inside, at Mel for getting her into this mess, and at me for not coming after them like we'd original-ly planned. Yes, I'd broken the plan for good reasons, and my decision had ultimately turned out well for the mission, as it were, but Chloe had been the one who'd paid the biggest price, in terms of nerves and risk, for things not going according to plan. Physically she was going to be fine, but mentally it might take a while for her to bounce back.

"Call me if you need anything, or if you just want to vent," I told her. "Like I said, I know exactly how you feel."

"What...oh, right. Um, okay. Thanks. Will do." Not looking very re-assured, she ushered us out the door.

Mel said she was going to get home and get to work, and jumped into her Jeep and drove off. I followed more slowly in my own car, losing her at a light and arriving back at the apartment complex by myself.

The first person to greet me when I stepped into my apartment was Fevronia, who came running up, headbutted me, and rubbed her cheek against my calf.

"I think she's doing much better, don't you, Innochka?" Galina Ivanovna said. She'd been sitting with Fevronia all day to keep them both company.

"Yes," I said, reaching down to scratch Fevronia behind the ears. Instead of swatting at me, she purred and turned her head so I could get the other ear. "I almost don't recognize her." Since we had switched from the cheapest to the most expensive cat food in the grocery store, the rash on her stomach had gone away, there had been no more vomiting, and her mood had undergone a sea change. I felt terrible for making her feel bad for so long with bad food. I had to hope that she, like Chloe, would forgive me in time.

"How did it go?" Galina Ivanovna asked. I'd told her in very broad strokes what we'd been planning to do. Now I told her, also in very broad strokes, what had actually happened.

"So you think this person who was using Mel's identity actually is a relative?" she asked when I was done.

"It seems possible," I said. "They have the same last name—although it's a very common one—and they do look alike. Mel's going to look into it."

Galina Ivanovna nodded approvingly. "Maybe then she can help her. Helping family is the most important thing."

"Yes," I said.

"Speaking of such things," said Galina Ivanovna, "Dima called while you were gone. He thinks he might have found someone who can look into your church problem."

"Oh?" I kept my face carefully blank. Every time Galina Ivanovna mentioned speaking to Dima without me, a twinge of very unwelcome, very unworthy jealousy went through me. I hated to miss any crumb of communication from him.

"Yes. He asked you to call him tomorrow, when you'll both be awake."

"Great," I said. "Thanks. Will do."

59

I TOLD MYSELF I WAS going to wait until a decent hour to call Dima on Sunday. The decent hour I waited until was 7:00am my time. He answered immediately.

"How did it go?" he asked. "Your operation yesterday?"

I gave a short description of the highs and lows of Operation Catch a Scammer and Mel's planned course of action. Dima responded with mingled delight at my quick thinking, and horror at the danger I'd been in.

"Yeah," I said. "It made me think."

"Think about what, Innochka?"

"That maybe I don't want a career where that kind of thing happens all the time."

"Were you planning to have such a career?"

"No, but Mel is talking about taking up something in that sphere, and she's suggested I join her. She thinks I would be good at it."

"I'm sure you would be good at it, Innochka, but would you enjoy it? Do you need the adrenaline?"

"No...I don't think so...No," I finished strongly. "That's not how I get my highs."

"How *do* you get your highs, then, Innochka?" He sounded amused, and also genuinely curious.

"Love," I said.

He laughed.

"Also finding things out," I added. "But I'd rather not have to deal with physical violence."

It took him a while to stop laughing. When he did, he said, "I'm very glad to hear that, Innochka, and I swear, I'll do all I can to supply you

442

with the kind of highs you prefer. I'll also try to reduce the amount of physical violence in your life as much as possible, even if it means not having as many of my own highs."

"I don't know if you'll ever be able to get clean from physical violence," I said.

"I don't either." His voice was sober now. "But the highs are getting less and less high, and the lows are getting lower and lower. Isn't that how it is for junkies? You need a higher and higher dose to get less and less satisfaction? Until the only thing left is desperation and self-loathing?"

"More or less," I said.

"I wish there was rehab for violence addiction," he said. "Especially because I'm going to need it after this assignment. I guess you'll have to be my rehab for me."

"Is there really so much violence in what you're doing right now?" I asked. "You're not even on the front—are you?"

He blew out a breath. "No. Not on the front. Thank God. I guess. But it's constant training, day in and day out, and it's feeding my addiction—our addiction. I can see it in everyone's eyes. Every time they take us out and make us shoot at targets, the craving grows to shoot at people."

"You're shooting too?" I asked.

He blew out another breath. "Yes. I'm shooting too. They have me doing all the same training as the actual battalion." He laughed, this time bitterly. "It should cure me of my combat addiction once and for all. It's pretty clear that all these boys half my age are stronger, fitter, and crazier than me. I should leave the field of battle to them. But..."

"But," I prompted.

"But there's so much I know that they don't, and, God help me, I can't help but share what I know with them. It's terrifying, Innochka. These are kids who've fantasized their entire lives about killing Russians. Or maybe they've been brainwashed into it the past couple of years, but it's certainly the main focus of their lives now. All they want to do is kill, and kill my people. *Our* people, because half of them have Russian names and speak Russian as their native language and spent their childhoods with their grandmothers back in Tver or Perm or Vladimir. But now they want to burn that part of themselves out with fire and blood. And I'm helping train them. And...and I *care* about them, Innochka. They're my friends...no, they're like my sons, almost. Some of them are young enough to be my sons, and...and that's how I feel about them. And they call me 'Uncle' and 'Papa' and 'Dmitry Vladimirovich' and come to me for advice about girls."

"What do you tell them?" I asked.

He laughed, even more bitterly. "I *should* tell them to get the fuck out of this crazy cult they've fallen into and go home and hook up with their high school sweethearts, or maybe go to college and meet some smart college girls, but if I said that, they'd cut me off in a heartbeat, so I tell them to take a shower, act friendly, and show respect."

"Well, that's not bad advice either," I said.

"I know, but...I care about these boys like they're my own, Innochka, and they like and admire me...and I'm helping train them to kill our own people. And...and part of me is enjoying it. My violence addiction is over-powering everything else."

"If you didn't have it, you wouldn't be able to reach them," I pointed out. "And maybe you're doing something good. Maybe when it comes time to start the actual killing, they'll remember you and they'll rethink what they're doing."

"Maybe." Dima didn't sound very convinced. "At least the only ad-diction I have to worry about is violence. So far. They haven't started us on the drugs yet, and they haven't said anything about doing it right away."

"Maybe they won't do it at all," I said.

"Or maybe they're just biding their time," said Dima. "Waiting for just the right moment so they can get us hooked and show us to the high-est bidder."

"Maybe you can get out of there before that," I said. "How much longer are you supposed to be there?"

"We're supposed to be in Germany for at least another month, maybe more. And I'm supposed to stay with them as long as I can. I might be here until May."

"Until May!" The words burst out before I could stop them.

"I know, Innochka. I don't like to think of it—I *can't* think of it—either. But maybe it won't be that long."

"Let's hope not," I said.

"And that's not why I wanted to talk to you, anyway. I had a thought. About your church problem."

"Uh-huh?" I said.

"I'm probably not the man for the job—plus I'm stuck in Germany—but what about that journalist you told me about? The one in California?"

"Heather Ramirez?" I said.

"Yes, her. I know a little about her work. She loves corruption. Maybe she'd be the one to take this on."

"California is an awfully long way away," I said.

"Journalists," Dima said dryly, "travel, in case you hadn't noticed. Do you still have her contact information?"

"I should."

"Give her a call. If she can't do it, she'll probably know someone who can."

"Okay," I said. "Thanks. That's a good idea."

"I know." He laughed. This time it was intimate and low. "I had it yesterday, was sure it was such a good idea that you'd already had it, was about to text it to you anyway just to initiate contact, then I thought, no, I'll tell mama to tell you to call me so I can hear your voice."

"Well," I said, "I'm glad. Although you don't need a special occasion to hear my voice."

"That's right! We're about to get married. We can call each other up whenever we want, just to talk." His voice was full of wonderment and delight at the thought. "Although maybe not right now," he added. "I can't take calls for a lot of the day. They even take away our phones sometimes."

"Oh."

"I know. Bad sign, right? The first time, I thought I was about to be slaughtered like a steer. But nothing's happened. So far."

"It will be fine," I said. I didn't believe it, but saying something ominous and foreboding didn't seem helpful.

"Sure," said Dima. "So will you call this Heather?"

"I will," I said. "Will you call me whenever you want to hear my voice, just because?"

"If I did that, Innochka, I'd never do anything other than call you, but I will call you when I can, just to hear your voice. I promise."

"Good," I said.

"And we'll see each other again in the flesh"—his voice dropped again—"very soon. By May at the latest."

"I don't think I can wait until May," I said.

1

May

MAY 1st. Dima was still in Germany. I was still surviving the separation, although I wasn't sure how.

The good news was that Fevronia continued to thrive on her new, expensive food. I just wasn't sure how I was going to continue to provide it to her after my contract here at Crimson was up. I'd applied to twelve jobs and fellowships, which was everything I'd seen that looked remotely relevant to my skill set. So far I'd had one telephone interview, only to hear through the job wiki that an offer had been made to someone else. My last Crimson paycheck had hit my bank account this morning, and I didn't have another one lined up for June 1st or any other month after that.

Galina Ivanovna, on the other hand, had made substantial progress. While she wasn't the vibrant, vigorous woman I remembered from our first meeting, she was noticeably stronger and more alert, and had taken to going on long walks every day. Even better, according to her, her BUN and creatinine levels—I had only the haziest conception of what that was, but it seemed meaningful to her—had improved markedly. She was the first patient, the doctors and nurses were saying, to reverse kidney damage so significantly from such a late stage. There was much rejoicing over at the hospital, and much discussion over whether to continue the infusions or take her off them and proceed with the special diet alone.

"I am just happy to serve science," Galina Ivanovna would say whenever it came up. "Simply tell me what you think is best, and I will follow your orders."

It was agreed that there would be an extensive workup of her labs at her visit this week, and then decisions would be made. I didn't know what I hoped. I hoped they would make the decision that would best help her health, of course. I just didn't know what I hoped that decision would be for my own sake. My lease ran until the end of July, so I could stay here until then—if I could come up with the money. If Galina Ivanovna was released from the weekly treatments and decided to use her plane ticket to go back to Russia at the end of May, I wouldn't be able to go with her. And what would Dima do? She probably shouldn't be left on her own. But, now that I was so, *so* close to finally having Dima for myself, in the legal sense of the word, I didn't want another lengthy separation.

When we discussed this, Galina Ivanovna said philosophically that we'd stick together no matter what. If it seemed best for us to stay in the US, because either Dima or I got a job here, then that's what we'd do. If neither of us got steady employment here, we'd go back to Russia, where Dima ostensibly still had a job.

"And maybe this work he's doing for the government will turn into something," Galina Ivanovna said. "Maybe he can settle down in some state job and start bringing home a steady paycheck."

I looked at her. She looked at me. We both laughed ruefully.

"Okay, maybe not," she said. "I think for that to happen, both Dima and our government would have to be very different. They've been trying their damnedest to change each other for more than a decade, with absolutely zip to show for it. Isn't there something in physics about an unstoppable force meeting an immovable object? That's what we seem to be seeing here, with expected results. But maybe you can get a job there, Innochka."

"Doing what?" I asked.

"Teaching English? There's still a demand for people who can teach real American English."

"Okay," I said. "That's something I could do. Would it pay enough to support us all?"

"Hmmm...depends on how many clients you got...if you labored like a draft horse around the clock, you could probably make it work. But that's only until you have a baby." She gave me a sharp look. "No hope on that front?"

I shook my head. To my intense disappointment and rather superficial relief, I had received incontrovertible proof that I had not gotten pregnant. I consoled myself with the thought that the only thing that would have made our current situation more fraught would be the news that a baby was on the way, and that we hadn't done the deed on the right day to have any chance of conception, so my lack of pregnancy was simply from poor timing and not a sign that I was sterile, barren, hopelessly infertile...

I had unwisely spent a while browsing the internet about conception and fertility, and discovered that my best years were probably a good decade behind me—*when I had tried so hard to convince Dima that we should have a child, and he'd said no*, I thought furiously, and then quashed that thought as hard as I could—that it was entirely possible that I could no longer conceive, or at least not without tens of thousands of dollars of medical intervention, that even if I conceived, the child had an alarmingly high chance of having birth defects, one that grew by the month, that my body might already be too frail to support a pregnancy, and that, in general, I was old, decrepit, and doomed.

The funny—in the sense of ironic—thing was that I didn't *feel* old, decrepit, or doomed. Yes, I was incredibly stressed out by our uncertain economic situation, not to mention what might happen to Dima in Germany. But ever since we'd gotten re-engaged, I'd felt, underneath all the worry and fear and doubt, a rejuvenating flush of vitality spreading throughout my body and soul, telling me that things weren't hopeless, that, on the contrary, there was a future ahead of us, one full of possibilities. I might not have conceived an actual child, but I felt pregnant with a simmering hope and joy that kept wanting to bubble up and spill over everything. It was wonderful. I just hoped it wasn't a complete delusion.

Meanwhile, I had final exams to deal with. Classes had ended on Friday. It was now Monday. Unusually, I did not have my first final during the first exam slot on Monday morning. Instead, it was Monday afternoon. I had a second final first thing Tuesday morning, and then—naturally—during the last exam slot on Friday afternoon.

The Monday exam was for RUS 202. I had offered to hold a review session over the weekend, but no one had wanted to come in for that—including me—so we'd agreed to hold a review session immediately before the exam. I'd never tried that before, but I was moderately optimistic that the review material might stick long enough for it to have an actual effect during the exam.

The exam was scheduled for 1:00 to 4:00. As agreed, I showed up at 12:00. The only person there was Miranda.

"Oh, hi," she said. She was fidgeting and scratching at her face and winding her hair around her fingers, obviously agitated.

"I don't think you need to be that worried," I said. I sidled past her to the front of the room, surreptitiously hitching up my pants so that I didn't trip over the hems. I'd continued to lose weight, and now my clothes were falling off me. I yo-yoed between joy at the return of the slender figure I'd always considered to be my birthright, and worry that there was something sinister behind my mysterious weight loss. Then I remembered how much I was worrying this semester, and how little time I had to eat, and decided there was probably nothing mysterious about it.

"What?" said Miranda.

"You look nervous. I don't think you need to be nervous. You've pulled a solid A on every quiz and test of the semester so far. Chances are excellent you'll do fine on the final."

"Oh...yeah, right. The final. That's not what I'm worried about."

"What's the problem, then?" I asked.

Miranda looked over her shoulder. We were still the only people in the cramped, water-stained classroom.

"It's Jamal," she said, turning back to face me. "He's being kicked off the team, just like we feared. And maybe expelled."

2

"WAIT," I SAID. "*What*?! Have they given an official reason?"

"They said 'conduct charges.'" Miranda tried to make a brave face, but it crumpled into a sob instead.

"Sorry." She sniffled, wiped her nose, and straightened her shoulders. "It's just so...*unfair*! Because those conduct charges weren't about anything he actually did that was...bad. It was because he was trying to make things *better*! He gave some interviews and participated in some seminars and stuff about reducing sexual assault in sports and frat culture. He said a bunch of stuff about how he was brought up as right as his mother could bring him up, but when he ended up in college he was surrounded by a lot of peer pressure and it was hard to remember what he knew was right, but then he remembered, but he didn't want others to end up in the same situation and do stupid shit—sorry—that would wreck their own and other people's lives, and sports teams and fraternities needed better leadership on this issue, and he wanted to help provide that leadership...and now the college is saying he's a bad representative of them and has committed honor violations, and..."

"Couldn't Irene help?" I asked.

"She tried. She *tried*. But I guess the Wainwrights decided they had to take Jamal down, and even Irene couldn't save him. So he's been kicked off the team and they've yanked his scholarship, so he won't be able to afford to stay here, and they're talking about expelling him on conduct charges as well, and...what's he going to *do*? No one's going to want him after getting expelled on conduct charges! This was his big chance! He'd kind of given up on turning pro—like, who's going to recruit someone from Crimson for the NFL?—but we were talking about how he could get a decent degree from here, a *real* degree; like, actually earn a good degree that people would respect, and get a decent career for himself after he graduates, and take care of his mom...he's been studying really hard, even with all the games and practice and all the other stuff he's been working really hard on his classes all year, and he's gotten all As and Bs in all his classes, and he was thinking about getting a business degree—in fact, he's been really enjoying his classes, even talking about going on and getting an MBA—and just really doing well, and then *this.*"

She rubbed her eyes angrily. "Sorry. It makes me *so mad!* And I can't even write about it. I pitched a piece to the *Champion*, but it was turned down flat. I want to *scream* at the world about it, and I can't even write an article for my own paper!" She swiped furiously at her eyes again.

"I'm sorry," I said. "Does he have any plans for what he'll do if he does have to leave?"

"We've talked and talked about it...the only thing he can think of is to join the military."

"Oh," I said.

"Yeah, I know, right? But he said it's a job and pay and they'd maybe teach him something and then he'd have that GI money to go back to college when he got out. It's better than anything else he can think of. And his mom's having some health problems and just lost her job. So he's pretty desperate."

"Gosh," I said. "I'm sorry. That's tough."

"Yeah. Hey—didn't you say your brother was in the Marines?"

"He still is," I said. "So I have a lot of thoughts about the pros and cons of joining the military."

"Oh. I was hoping you'd say it's great."

"Sorry," I said. "There are upsides, but there are also major downsides. I'll ask Irene if there's anything else we can do. And I'll also ask someone I know about maybe helping you write that article and getting it published."

"Really? Wow! Who?"

"Let me put you in touch with Heather Ramirez," I said.

3

MORE STUDENTS SHOWED up then, so we had to start working on review. Several of the students expressed what sounded like genuine gratitude for all the work I'd done for them (although we skipped any mention of the shooting in first year), and disappointment that I wouldn't be coming back next year. I had told them after the campus interviews—which I had been kept resolutely segregated from—that I was leaving for other opportunities, but someone else would be coming in on a long-term appointment, and there might be a chance to get a minor or even a major in Russian. Most of them had said they didn't have time before graduation, and also they didn't want to take Russian from someone else, and couldn't I stay?

I told my students I was sure that whoever the new hire was (the hiring committee was being resolutely silent on the subject), she would be highly qualified and do an excellent job, and if they felt so moved and it became an option, all the current sophomores and juniors could probably squeeze in a minor, and it would make me very happy if they did so. Jackson and Isobel both said they would consider it. Jessica narrowed her eyes and said that she had a very full schedule and probably the new person wouldn't be any good compared to me.

Since I'd always assumed Jessica considered me to be an incompetent screwup, I was touched, but told her that the new person was likely to be at least as good if not better than me. She narrowed her eyes some more and said she'd consider it, but no promises. Isobel said she'd try to take at least one class from the new person just to offer support, and Jackson said he'd take a class in order to suss them out and make their lives hell if they turned out to be unworthy.

"No accidentally-on-purpose accidents!" I told him sternly.

This reminded everyone of how Jackson had engineered a messy prank on Karen involving a cup of iced coffee last semester, and they all laughed heartily for much longer than was decent.

Once they'd gotten their chortling under control, we held the actual final. I felt reasonably good about the chances of everyone other than Miranda. By this time most of the no-hopers and chronic underperformers had been weeded out—not that we got a lot of those in Russian classes in general—and the remaining students were a highly honed and polished cohort. Sort of. In any case, I had a high degree of confidence in their ability to get a good grade on the final.

But Miranda kept fidgeting and twisting her hair and chewing on her pencil throughout the exam. At one point it got so bad that I went over to her and whispered, "Concentrate!"

"What?" She looked up, confused.

"You won't help anyone by flunking the final. Concentrate on the exam, and we'll work together to help Jamal afterwards." I thought about adding something about Lenin graduating from high school with a gold medal for top grades the same semester that his brother was executed, but decided that Americans probably weren't ready to hear that story.

Even without the Leninist peptalk, Miranda settled down enough to finish the exam. While I was waiting, I emailed Heather Ramirez, outlining the situation and asking if she had any advice on how Miranda could get the story out there.

Heather and I had been in touch on and off ever since I had contacted her about Isaiah Jones and the Church of the Holy Light. She'd leapt on the story with joy, saying there was hardly anything she liked better than taking down a corrupt church.

I was pleased about that, but also worried. What if she succeeded? Then what would happen to Dennis and Alexandra? Not to mention my own parents? Alexandra would have the one thing that gave her comfort pulled out from under her, and my parents would look and feel foolish. What if they found out it was my fault? Okay, it wasn't entirely my fault, but I'd been the one to bring Isaiah and Heather together. If the church underwent a massive public implosion, I would be the catalyst.

I wasn't expecting an immediate response—Heather, like Dima, tended to be an inconsistent and dilatory correspondent, making me wonder if there was something about journalists that made it impossible for them to stay on top of their inboxes—but Heather's reply popped up on my phone screen just as Miranda was starting the last page of the final.

Whoa, sounds like an even bigger story than the church one! Hook me up with her and we'll talk. I'm just wrapping up Holy Light so I'm looking for the next thing.

I desperately wanted to know what the outcome of the Holy Light story would be, but Heather had made it clear she wasn't going to utter a peep about it until it was out. I told myself for the hundredth time that it was going to be okay and I definitely hadn't betrayed my family or ruined their lives, and sent an email introducing her and Miranda to each other.

Miranda, unusually for her, was the last student to finish the exam, almost two hours into the time. She brought it over to me, proffering it in one shaking hand while twisting her hair around the fingers of the other so fiercely that I was afraid she was going to yank it right out at the roots.

"I set you up with Heather Ramirez," I said. "She's an investigative reporter who, well, investigates this kind of thing. She sounded very interested. She might want to cover the story herself rather than letting you do it, but at least it would get out there, and probably to a much bigger audience than you could manage yourself."

"Yeah. Thanks. I don't care about the byline, to be honest, as long as it helps. Although it might be cool to see someone like that in action."

"Maybe she'll take you on as her assistant," I said.

"Yeah." A ghost of a smile flitted across Miranda's face, to be replaced once again by worry. "Is it wrong of me not to care? I mean, I care some, but the main thing I care about right now is helping Jamal. Is that wrong? Is it stupid? Am I one of those stupid girls who only cares about her boyfriend and nothing else?"

"You cared enough about your studies to come and take this final," I pointed out.

"Yeah...I guess when you put it that way, I've been studying for all my finals and I'm planning to take them. And I got that internship at that paper in Brighton Beach, and I'm planning to go do it. But the whole time, the main thing I'm thinking about is Jamal and how I can help him. Is that wrong?"

"I don't think it's wrong at all," I said. "It's not wrong to want to help someone you care about. As long as you're not throwing everything and everyone else in your life away."

"No...I guess I'm not doing that...I just worry about it, you know what I mean? Like I'm losing myself in him and being stupid when I think I'm doing the right thing...but maybe I *am* doing the right thing and *not* caring so much about him would be stupid and selfish...I just can't tell where being a good person stops and being a gullible idiot starts."

"That," I said, "is a very difficult boundary to establish sometimes. But I think so far you're doing pretty well. I hope Heather's able to help you, and I'll reach out to Irene and see if she has any ideas for next steps."

"Thanks. Oh, and I'll probably see you again before you go, but, uh, I just wanted to say thanks. For, like, everything. Including, like, saving my life." Miranda gave me another ghost of a smile, and, twining her fingers through her hair in a way that looked deliberately painful, trudged out of the classroom.

4

I GATHERED UP THE PILE of exams, put them in a folder, and headed out of the classroom after her. I saw no sign of anyone I knew all the way out to the parking lot. Exam week was weird that way. Our regular schedules were all flipped around, and you often found yourself on campus at strange, unpopulated times like early in the morning or late in the evening.

3:30pm on a Monday was a pretty normal time to be out and about, but campus was still half-empty. Except...

"Oh, hello, Rowena!"

Theresa Mayfield, former chair of the Modern Languages department and current Dean, was unlocking the car next to mine.

"Gosh, um, hello," I said. "I didn't know you parked out here."

"Normally I *don't*—the Dean has a special parking spot in front of Lee—but they're currently doing work there, so I'm back to my old haunting grounds of the faculty parking lot. I'd forgotten what a hike it is over to central campus, and how hard it is to get a decent spot." She eyed the football stadium thoughtfully. "And what a shabby old eyesore this is. I wonder if it could be converted into something useful."

"Like classrooms?" I asked.

"I was thinking of a multi-level parking deck, actually. If we go ahead with this expansion everyone's talking about, we're going to need a lot more parking. Now, of course, we'd all like everyone to bike into work or take public transport, but we know that's not actually feasible, don't we? There's no off-campus public transport in Greenfields, and no safe places to bike, either. Plus, half the faculty lives in Macon."

She gave the stadium another sweeping once-over. "It would still be a schlepp, but at least we'd have ample parking space, and we could put in charging stations for electric vehicles. That's more aspirational than anything right now, but we might as well plan for the future."

"Yeah, of course," I said.

"But I hear you'll be leaving us anyway," she said. "That's such a shame. Where are you going next? I hope you got an offer you absolutely couldn't refuse, to take you away from us. The person they're bringing in to replace you is ABD—she doesn't even have her degree yet. I'm sure she's great, but she doesn't have your experience, and it'll be a real loss to the college to lose that."

"Um..." I said.

"Theresa! Theresa! There you are! How's the remediation going?"

We both turned. Diane from Biology was coming over to us.

"Oh..." said Theresa. "I'm not enjoying it right now, but I'm looking forward to it being over." She coughed, then smiled ruefully. "You see? I've had this nagging cough for the past *year*, my doctor can't figure anything out, and then Diane here suggested it might be *mold* in the building. It'd never occurred to me, but I said, 'Let's get my office tested,' and you know what? It *is* full of mold! Diane here assures me it's a particularly nasty variety, too. You've got an article coming out about it, don't you, Diane?"

"I do," said Diane. "To my surprise, it was accepted right away. And a lot of our buildings have concerning amounts of several nasty varieties of mold, including *Stachybotrys* and *Aspergillus fumigatus*. Plus high levels of PFAS chemicals and PCBs."

"Oh," I said. "Gosh. That's, uh, scary."

"Very scary," said Theresa. "Makes me wonder about all the people in the office with their autoimmune diseases and fibromyalgia and chronic migraines. And the woman who's out with kidney cancer right now."

"Whoa," I said. "That sounds serious."

"Very serious," said Diane, while Theresa said, "Yes, but you didn't hear any of this from me. The Provost and the Chancellor and the Board are all determined not to hear about any of it. But I managed to arrange to have my own office remediated, as a sort of test case."

She shrugged. "Maybe we'll be able to work on the other buildings over the next few years. I know that's not ideal, but it's better than nothing, and Diane and I are going to keep pushing things forward with the upper administration. There are some alarming court cases happening right now over stuff like toxic mold and PCBs in university buildings. We're trying to convince the powers that be that it's better to lay out a little money now rather than be the center of an ugly court case later."

"For sure," I said. "And, uh, good luck. That sounds like a worthy project."

"Yes...we might as well put some of that Security Solutions money to good use, don't you think?"

"Um, yeah," I said.

"That's just what I say. Now, Diane, about that email you sent me..." Theresa and Diane walked off a few paces, talking intently to each other. When it became apparent they weren't paying any attention to me anymore, I left.

5

I STOPPED AT THE MAILBOX on my way home. The lock had gotten even stickier as the weather had warmed, and it took me four tries to open it. I went through the small pile of envelopes, checking for rejection letters from the various jobs and fellowships I'd applied to, but all I found was junk mail. I told myself maybe that meant fate would still be kind and send some employment my way.

When I got into my apartment, I pulled out my file of finals and looked at them. Then I called Irene Collins.

"Rowena, honey! So good to hear from you! Although...is it true that Crimson *fired* you?"

"They didn't fire me," I said. "They chose to hire someone else for the tenure-track position that is replacing mine."

"Couldn't they have given the tenure-track position to you?"

"They could have," I said. "But they didn't."

"Those *rats*! Well, hun, you're better off without them. Do you have anything in the pipeline yet?"

"I've applied for a number of jobs," I said. "I'm still waiting to hear back about them." I didn't say anything about Dima. I still hadn't told anyone about our engagement. He had sent me a silver chain and I'd put my old ring on it and started wearing it under my shirt, where no one could see it. It was getting too warm to wear anything high-necked, though, so I was going to have to stop wearing it or come clean to the world. I seesawed back and forth on how I felt about that. Mostly I wanted the wedding to happen as soon as possible. I thought, rightly or wrongly, that as soon as we made it official, a huge weight would roll off my shoulders. Whatever else happened, at least we'd be legally married.

On the other hand, I dreaded telling my family about it. My grandparents—my Macon grandparents—would be nice about it, and would maybe even be genuinely happy for me. My parents would be sad and disappointed, I was sure, even if they tried to put a brave face on it. John would tell me I was an idiot. Dennis would disapprove. Alexandra would disapprove, and also be disappointed that I wasn't marrying Isaiah. Although maybe the romance of it all would win her over. Under all the terrible trauma and scarring, she was a romantic at heart.

Like you, I thought, and then shook my head in surprise. It had never occurred to me that Alexandra and I had anything in common, but in our devotion to love and romance, maybe we did. I just had to hope that my love would turn out less tragically than hers.

Maybe she doesn't think it's tragic. After all, by some measures, she's been very fortunate. She married the love of her life and has been with him for over sixty years. She has a son and two grandchildren. She's got a church she finds fulfilling and a community that supports her.

Okay, but a lot of that was based on lies. Still. I couldn't deny that there was a little bit of Alexandra in me. Maybe there would be enough for her to forgive me for marrying Dima.

"Well, hun, I'm sure you'll get something soon—something better than Crimson," Irene was saying.

"Yeah," I said. "No doubt. That's not why I'm calling, though. I'm actually calling about Jamal Warner."

"Oh hun, isn't it just *awful* what they're doing to him? Not that I'm surprised, of course. In fact, I warned him that just this sort of thing might happen if he decided to go around talking about what happened. But of course, he did anyway. That boy's got more courage than sense, Rowena honey, if I do say so myself."

"Well," I said. "That's not surprising. He is an athlete, after all."

"True, hun, true, and I admire him as a player and as a person, but he went and courted disaster. Not that I can blame him. *Someone* needed to say what he's been saying, and he decided to be the one to say it. All power to him—except that if he gets kicked out of Crimson and ends up on the street, he won't be doing anyone any good."

"Apparently he's thinking about joining the military," I said.

"Well, maybe that will turn out well for him." Irene sounded doubtful. I couldn't blame her. I was doubtful too.

"Maybe," I said. "Meanwhile, is there anything more we can do. I know you've probably done everything you can, but..."

"Honey, I have screamed, I have cried, I have threatened to go to the governor, but when it comes to a showdown between me and Anthony Wainwright, we all know who's going to win. Especially him. I may have some pull, but the Wainwrights have a lot more. And not just in Georgia. Word is that they've made some friends in *very* high places a couple states north of here." She dropped her voice. "If I told you the rumors I've heard...I'm friends with the wife of the lieutenant governor, and she's whispered some things that...well, you wouldn't believe them, that's all I'll say."

"They wouldn't happen to be about drugs?" I said. "A new super-drug to create super-soldiers?"

Irene actually gasped, the sound so loud over the phone it was like a movie effect. "Sugar, how did you *know?!?*"

"I have my sources," I said.

"They must be incredible sources, if they're better than mine. I didn't know you had friends in the government."

"I have a few," I said. "And not just in the US government."

"Yes...wait, *what?*"

"Um," I said. "This is just between us, okay?"

"Okay...but what if it's something that really needs to be shared? Like with the government?"

"I think the government already knows about it," I said.

"Okay...my lips are sealed, hun. What's this about other governments?"

"Well," I said. "If the drug is the one I think it is, then it was developed in Russia. But by a joint enterprise including Security Solutions and a Russian company. They've been testing it out in the various hot spots in the former Soviet Union. Now they're trying to sell it to both the US and Russian governments."

"Isn't that treason?" Irene said.

"They're private companies selling their own goods to the highest bidders. The Russian company might have an agreement with the Russian government and might be engaging in some questionable behavior there, but Security Solutions doesn't. They can sell to whomever they please."

"Yes, but...is the drug any good?" Irene asked.

"From what I've heard, it's pretty terrifying," I said. "And not very reliable."

"We're not really going to drug our own soldiers, are we?" Irene said. "With some Russian drug that we haven't even tested properly?"

"Maybe we're going to start by drugging our allies and our private contractors," I said. "They can be the test subjects. And maybe this is all completely wrong. But everything I've heard suggests that Security Solutions has friends in very high places in Washington as well as Atlanta, just like you said."

"Yes...and poor Jamal has been going around telling everyone about how the Wainwright heir is a sex predator." She laughed dryly. "Isn't it ironic that Wainwright Junior used drugs on his victims, and now his father's planning to use drugs on our whole country, basically."

"Maybe not ironic," I said. "Maybe it's how they operate."

"Yes, they're just a bunch of drug pushers when you get right down to it, aren't they?"

"Of a sort," I said.

"And now they're pushing Jamal out of college, and maybe right into the military, where he might be given their drugs anyway, with no way to say no."

"Yeah," I said. "Ironic, isn't it."

"Or evil," said Irene.

"That too," I agreed.

"You know, I've known Anthony Wainwright pretty much his whole life. Not well, but we've run in many of the same circles ever since he started college. I never liked him much, but I never thought he was *evil*." She paused. "Okay, well, those for-profit prisons are pretty evil, but somehow this takes it to the next level for me. And I still can't shake the feeling that it's treasonous, somehow."

"Funnily enough, I know some Russians who feel the same way," I said. "It's also ironic—and tragic—that the most substantive US-Russian cooperation we seem to be able to manage right now is a joint enterprise to sell dangerous drugs to use on our own soldiers."

"Yes...you know, I hadn't even thought about this from the Russian perspective, but I suppose it looks even worse to them, doesn't it? I mean, if it was developed in their country, using their money and their people. And now some American company is trying to sell it to the US military."

"I believe they consider it to be in very poor taste," I said.

"Maybe they'll send someone from the KGB to take Anthony Wainwright out!" she said.

"Um," I said. "I, uh, don't know if they'd consider that effective."

"Isn't that what they do, though? Assassinate people they don't like?"

"Um," I said. "Sometimes. But not normally prominent US citizens currently inside the US."

"Well, I wish they'd make an exception!" She laughed dryly again. "Goodness! Just look what I've turned into! Wishing that someone I don't like would get assassinated by a foreign spy! What my pastor would say if he could hear me...well, I don't like to think. I'd better stop talking about it before I get all het up and do something I regret. I've done everything I could to help Jamal, and none of it's worked, and now I guess I'd better just go slinking off with my tail between my legs and lick my wounds."

"Well, thanks for trying," I said. "And if it makes you feel any better, there might be a big exposé about it splashed across all the papers soon."

"You promise, hun?"

"I can't promise," I said. "But it might happen. So I don't want to mess that up."

"Fair enough, hun, fair enough...I'll just keep my mouth shut for the moment—and hope that exposé comes out soon enough to save Jamal."

"Me too," I said.

After I hung up, I looked at my file of finals some more. Then I picked up my phone again. After a moment's hesitation, I dialed Frank.

6

HE PICKED UP ON THE second ring. "Ro!" he said. "What's up?"

"I think I might need some help," I said.

"Always glad to help you out, Ro, you know that. Whatcha need? Backup? A big fist and a bigger gun? Or something more personal?"

"No," I said.

"Damn. And here I was getting my hopes up."

"What I actually need from you," I said, "is advice."

He emitted a bark of laughter. "I bet the only person more surprised than me to hear that coming from your mouth, is you. But I'm flattered. And seriously, Ro, if I can help, I will, even with advice. So fire away. Whatcha need advice on?"

"If I tell you something kind of crazy, will you listen all the way through and not tell me that I'm, well, crazy?" I asked.

Another bark of laughter. "Now this I gotta hear. Sure, Ro, I'm game. In fact, I can't wait. Hit me with your crazy story."

"You know how you, um, expressed your concerns about Dima?"

"You mean Kuznetsov?"

"Yes."

"What's he done now?"

"Well...I don't know exactly, and that's not exactly why I'm calling either, but, um, I am concerned about certain aspects of the situation around him."

"No shit," said Frank.

"Yeah...anyway, I'm actually really calling about Security Solutions."

"Why? You got more intel on what your boyfriend's planning to do to them?"

"Um..." *Tell, or don't tell?* If I told Frank what Dima was actually supposed to be doing with Security Solutions and Anthony Wainwright, would that reassure him, or only fan the flames of his suspicions? And he could just say that this was merely what Dima was telling me, not the actual truth. And that was true. Maybe Dima *was* just spinning me a likely-sounding story, when really he was here to assassinate Anthony Wainwright's body, not just his character.

Think! There's no one in the world who knows Dima better than you, maybe not even his mother, and probably not even himself. How likely is that?

*Not likely. Except...*Except when I remembered the look on his face when he'd taken out the men holding the gun to my head back in Moscow. That had been the face of a man who would kill. And who had immediately turned around and killed our relationship, our love.

Except he didn't. You're still together. Now you have to save the both of you.

I realized I was fingering the engagement ring through my shirt. I made myself drop my hand.

"Dima really is working as a journalist," I said. "He's embedded with the Wolf Battalion, who've been doing joint training exercises with Security Solutions and various Western militaries. It's all open and aboveboard, more or less. But it seems that Security Solutions may be trying to sell a Russian-developed drug—which the Russians believe should be their exclusive property—to the US military."

Silence at the other end of the line.

"But that's not what I'm calling about," I added quickly. "I'm actually calling about what Security Solutions might be doing to take down a student of mine—well, sort of a student of mine—and how I might stop that."

Frank cleared his throat. "Whoa, Ro, that's a lot to throw on a man all at once. I don't even know where to start."

"Maybe with the small stuff," I said. "The big drug stuff is probably above our paygrade."

"Yeah, but I can't exactly fuckin' ignore it. Especially if your boyfriend is involved in it. Is he still your boyfriend, by the way?"

"Um," I said. "Yes..."

"You don't sound too sure, Ro. Things not going great between you?"

"Actually," I said. "We got engaged." Crap! Now why did I do that? Why did I tell Frank before telling my friends, my brother, my own parents?

Maybe because Frank needs to know.

"Well shit, Ro, that's some heavy stuff. Congratulations. Although it only confirms my opinion of you. Not only are you *bad* deep down, but you're crazy as a fuckin' bedbug."

"Jeez," I said. "Thanks."

"It takes one to know one, Ro, it takes one to know one. Okay. So you're now engaged to a crazy Russian who may or may not be working for some very unsavory folks in Moscow, who may or may not have ordered him to assassinate a prominent American businessman—"

"I think what they want from him is a character assassination, not an actual murder," I blurted out.

"That what he told you?" asked Frank, sounding just as skeptical as I'd expected.

"Yes. But it would certainly fit his skill set better than, um, contract killing."

"If you say so." Frank continued to sound deeply skeptical. "So what was this about drugs?"

I outlined everything I knew about the development of the supposed super-soldier drugs in the former Soviet Union, and Security Solution's subsequent plan to sell them to the US military.

"Well, shit," said Frank. "I'd say that sounds totally batshit insane, but I've been working for the government long enough to know that batshit insane can sometimes pick up a surprising amount of traction. And if the drug does what you say it does..."

"From what Dima said, I got the impression that it doesn't actually work very well," I said.

"Half the gear I got didn't work very well, and I don't want to get into the fuckin' drugs and vaccines they gave me. I've got this weird fuckin' numb patch on my left shoulder from all the shit they shot into me, and they won't tell me what half of it was...you ever hear of Gulf War Syndrome?"

"Uh-huh," I said.

"So that was a little before my time, but a bunch of us in Iraq ended up with some pretty similar problems...anyway, you don't want to hear about all that, but my point is that we expose our soldiers to all kinds of toxic shit all the time. And if this drug is so great, well...we might be willing to take a pretty big risk on it."

"Or have a bunch of Ukrainians take a big risk on it for us," I said.

"Yeah. God*damn*, Ro, I don't want to be this cynical, and I really don't want you to be this cynical, but there are a lot of bad folks out there, and there are even more folks who are greedy and thoughtless and easily convinced by pie-in-the-fuckin'-sky schemes. Tell people what they want to hear, and they'll pretty much always believe you."

"Uh-huh," I said. "Which gets me, sort of, to my reason for calling, which is what to do about this student."

"So how'd one of your students get involved in all this?"

I gave as concise a précis of Jamal's situation as possible.

"Sweet Jesus, Ro, you sure do know how to pick 'em, don't you? Is there anyone in your life who isn't a desperate fuckup?"

"I don't think Jamal is a desperate fuckup," I said. "I think he's a kid who's ended up in a bad situation..."

"Yeah, whatever. He's still a guy with poor judgment skills that you're currently trying to save, whether he deserves it or not."

"So, what?" I asked. "I should just let him get kicked out of college?"

Frank sighed. "When you put it like that, I guess not. But I think you might be overestimating your influence here."

"I have a low estimation of my ability to succeed," I said. "But I have to try."

"And you think I can help," Frank stated.

"I don't know. I just couldn't think of anyone else."

"Glad I'm your call of last resort, Ro. No, really, I'm honored. Okay. Here's what we're gonna do. I am, for better or for worse, gonna look into Security Solutions and Anthony Wainwright and maybe also this drug thing, although that last is *way* above my paygrade. But I'll do some general digging, see what I come up with. Maybe I'll find something that'll get Wainwright and his company to back off your student."

"Thanks," I said. "I...I really don't know how to thank you."

Another short laugh. "I coulda told you how, but if you're engaged to this Kuznetsov fellow, I guess that's off limits now. But I'll take your gratitude. You know, Ro, I turned fifty this year. It really made me start to think. The G-man could come to collect my debt to him any day now."

"I don't think..." I began.

"Yeah, I know, I know, I could live another fifty years, easy. Or not. Frankly, I haven't lived my first fifty in a way that makes it likely I'll have another fifty. I've burned through my body faster than I should have, and I've burned through my soul even faster. At this point I don't know who has the biggest claim to either, but whoever he is, Jesus or Satan, I feel like he's waiting in the wings, ready to make me pay up whenever I put a toe out of line. So doing something like this—I don't know, it makes me feel like it might earn me a little more time—if not more time on this earth, then less time in Purgatory. You believe in Purgatory, Ro? You believe in Hell?"

"I don't know about the afterlife," I said. "But I'm pretty sure they both exist right here on earth."

"Yeah. Yeah, they do, and I've seen 'em. I've been down in 'em pretty much my whole adult life, and I'm fuckin' tired of it. So I'm looking for a way to climb out. Maybe that means stopping this Wainwright guy and his money and his mercenaries from doing something that'll fuck up your student's life, and maybe get a bunch of Americans killed in the bargain. Shit." He laughed mirthlessly. "I used to think I was such a hero. Then I thought I was a sucker. But now I'm thinking maybe my chance to be a hero has finally come around."

"Oh," I said. "Well, uh..."

"And I don't know if I'll be thanking you for it or damning you to fuckin' hell for it, but you're the one bringing it to me, so...yeah. I guess that makes you my guardian angel, or some shit like that."

"I don't think guardian angels do that..." I began.

"No, you're right. Maybe you're the snake in the Garden of Eden."

"Well, jeez," I said.

"That didn't come out right, but what I'm trying to say is that you've set this task before me, and now it's up to me to carry it out." He took a deep breath. "Man, that got heavy real fuckin' quick, didn't it? Didn't mean to lay all that on you, Ro, but you brought it out in me."

"Yeah," I said. "I do that a lot."

"Yeah? Well, there you go, then. I knew you were special the minute I laid eyes on you, Ro. I just figured we'd have a different kind of special relationship than the one we've got. But maybe the old man upstairs knows what he's doing better than we do. Maybe this is just the kind of special relationship I've always needed, and you're the one finally giving it to me."

"Um," I said. "Maybe."

He laughed. Shakily. "Whoa. I haven't felt like this since...well, maybe we don't need to go there. Let's just say I'm feeling real naked right now, and it's kinda exciting and kinda scary."

"You don't have to be scared of me," I said. "Anthony Wainwright, yes, but not me."

"You say that, Ro, but I've been dealing with guys like Anthony Wainwright a long time. Yes, he's a big snake, but he's still just another snake. While you..." He stopped, cleared his throat, and then went on, "Well, you know what I mean. Or if you don't, just take it from me that it's good. Scary, but good. So yeah, Ro. I'll help you out. I'll start digging into it tomorrow."

"Wow," I said. "Thanks so much. I mean, really, I wasn't expecting..."

"But you called me anyway," he interrupted.

"Maybe I was hoping that you had it in you to help me," I said. "You have before, after all."

"Yeah. Yeah, I have. That's one mark on the 'good' column in St. Peter's ledger. Now I need to put another one in. So I'll look into this, but meanwhile, Ro?"

"Yes?" I said.

"You take care, okay? And I mean that. You watch out for yourself. 'Cause I really don't like what you've gotten yourself mixed up in."

"I don't either," I said. "But I think most of it is far away."

"Anthony fuckin' Wainwright could be right down the street from you, Ro. And I know you can take care of yourself and all that, but he's got guys at his beck and call who could mess anyone up real bad. They're just down the road from you, and I'm over here in California and Kuznetsov's in Germany. And you're taking care of his mother, right? Who's sick, right?"

"Um...yeah, right," I said. "Although she seems to be doing better now."

"Even so. I was Anthony Wainwright, I'd come after both of you."

"Yeah," I said. "I would too."

"So you watch yourself real good, okay? Swear to me, Ro, swear on your mother's life you'll watch yourself real good."

"I swear," I said.

7

AFTER THAT I TOLD MYSELF I really, really should settle down and do a little grading. I had barely opened the folder, though, when my phone *pinged*.

Okay, I got a little dilemma, Mel texted. *About what to do about Tiff.*

What's the dilemma? I texted back.

Too long to explain over text. Wanna come over for supper and talk it out? 6:30?

Sounds good, I wrote.

Sadly, 6:30 was just far enough way to give me no good excuse to avoid grading. In fact, it was far enough away to mean that I might as well just grind through all the exams instead of knocking off a little early and calling it a night.

When I showed up at Mel's door at 6:29, my shoulders ached, my right hand was cramping, my vision was weird and shimmery, and I was getting stabbing pains at various points across my scalp and around my eyes whenever I turned my head. So about normal after a concentrated grading session. Well, it meant I could just relax and read during tomorrow's final.

"Great!" Mel said when she saw me. "I've got homemade falafel ready. Anything to avoid grading."

"Sounds great." I followed her into the apartment. It seemed even barer than usual.

"Oh, sorry about the lack of furniture. Looks like I am gonna be heading back to LA, so I've started getting rid of stuff."

"Oh wow," I said. "So it's decided, then?"

"Yeah. I asked around, got in touch with an old buddy who was an MP, and guess what? She's currently working as a PI in LA. Said she'd take me on as her apprentice."

"Wow," I said. "That's great. If, um, that's what you want to do."

Mel shrugged. "I can't think of anything better to do. Might go back to school—fuck!—and get some training in criminal justice, but frankly I don't have the strength of will or, let's be honest, the fuckin' money to spend a lot more time in school. And I was never gonna be able to hold down an office job. But I'm damn good at asking questions, digging up answers, and coming to conclusions, if I say so myself."

"Yeah," I said. "It's kind of the definition of what we've been trained to do."

"Yeah. And I got all those people skills from all that teaching, too. So why the fuck not? What else am I gonna do with my life?"

"That is the question," I agreed. "Well, if that's what you want, I'm glad you've got this opportunity. When are you leaving?"

"Supposed to show up June 1st. Figured that'd give me time to wrap up the semester, get all my shit packed up here—and deal with the Tiff issue. Which is where you come in."

"Sure," I said.

Mel dished up the homemade falafel, pita bread, hummus, lettuce, tomato, and tzatziki sauce on two plates, and we went over to the table. As usual, I lowered myself gingerly onto the loveseat, while she plopped down on the floor.

"And look at that," she said. "I didn't even scream. My knees are feeling a lot better. Doctor says I'm lucky: there doesn't seem to be permanent damage to them. She said I was damn lucky to make so much progress after just a few months of antibiotics. I just have to hope everything keeps getting better."

"Did she have any recommendations for someone to see in LA?" I asked.

"Yeah, I asked the last time I was there, and she gave me the name of a clinic. I'm just hoping I don't have to use it. It's all expensive as fuck and

I'm gonna be making next to nothing for a while—and paying LA rent on top of that."

"Ouch," I said.

"Yeah." She took a bite of falafel. "On the other hand, maybe I can get a side hustle cooking Middle Eastern food, whaddya think?"

I took a bite of falafel too. It was crunchy on the outside, moist on the inside, and delicately flavored with herbs and spices. It was possibly the best falafel I'd ever had.

"This could be your true calling," I said.

"Yeah. Sure." She took another bite, chewed, and swallowed. "Damn, that's good! I think I better keep it for myself and a small circle of the chosen few, though. You don't wanna go giving away your best treasures to just anyone, right? I think I got a lecture about that in Sunday school."

"Probably," I said.

"Anyways, we'd probably better face up to the Tiff situation. So, like I said, I've got a little dilemma there, and I could use a sounding board."

"Shoot," I said.

"So I've been asking around, and damned if we're not cousins." She put down her plate and made a face. "Really makes you think about what kinda stock you come from, you know what I mean? Like, do you come from bad blood, that kind of thing. 'Course, my whole family is bad blood, so I don't even know why I'm wondering."

"I don't know that I believe in bad blood," I said.

"You believe in DNA, don't you? And it's a fact that some DNA is better than others."

"Yes, but...we can't always know which DNA that is. And DNA that's better in one context might be worse in others. Like..." I struggled to come up with an example.

"I know what you mean," Mel said. "And sure, under some circumstances, being trashy and dishonest *is* probably the winningest strategy. But a lot of times it's not, and I don't know that I want to be associated with it anyway."

"If it makes you feel better, I've got cult members in my family tree," I said.

"Yeah, you told me. And I gotta say, I'm not surprised at all. No offense."

"None taken," I said. "What turns out well in one generation might be a disaster in another. Anyway. Let's not beat up on your family. They're doing the best they can."

"Yeah, it's just not very fuckin' good," said Mel. "So Tiff. She's a fourth cousin or something. Born outa wedlock, of course, to the black sheep of my dad's family, which, considering my dad's family, is saying something. We probably actually met a couple of times when we were kids, at family reunions and stuff, but then her mom went off the deep end with drugs, ODed, died in a back alley in Augusta...you get the picture."

"Uh-huh," I said. "Poor Tiff."

"Yeah. I guess she was an innocent little child at some point, huh? Probably when we were running around blowing bubbles she was okay—although if she's the little girl I'm thinking of, she stole my wand and blamed Nickie and Nickie got whipped with a belt for it, so I don't know that she was ever that sweet and innocent. Nickie is still sore about that, by the way, and says she hopes I send her to prison for a good long while."

"Even worse," I said.

"Yeah, I guess so. I'm not gonna cry too hard about it, though. So then Tiff was doing what she could to make her way in the world on her own—though it sounds like she had Desi and Jose as backup, which I gotta say, is more than a lot of folks have—and she got into drugs just like her mom."

"Uh-huh," I said.

"And then, between all the drugs, she got a job at the local grocery store, just like she told me, but she had to fight off her piece of shit manager, and she got fired and then she was really desperate."

"Uh-huh," I said.

"Desi and Jose offered to give her a job at the bar, but she'd have to go clean to do that. I talked to Jose about it—yeah, I know, but what can I say? I think I've got a talent for this. I went back to him and got him to talk to me. He was pretty forthcoming, too. I think he's hoping I'll help Tiff get clean and go straight, 'cause he can't do it."

"Oh," I said. "Do you think you can?"

She shrugged. "I don't know that anyone can help Tiff get clean and go straight. But I do want to stop her from scamming, and she is family, of a sort, so maybe I can nudge her in the right direction."

"You might as well try," I said.

"Yeah. I guess. So anyways, Desi wanted to give her a job at the bar, and Jose said sure, but she had to go through rehab first and start attending NA meetings and do regular drug tests. I gotta say, respect to Jose."

"For sure," I said.

"So Tiff said no, of course. Instead, she started doing these memorial pieces where she incorporates the ashes of a loved one, normally a pet, into a piece of art—'art'—so people can have, like, long-lasting physical mementos that contain the actual, you know, physical remains."

"Okay," I said. "A little weird for my taste, but okay."

"Yeah. Apparently a lot of people say it helps them, so who are we to judge? And Tiff was good at it." Mel wrinkled up her nose. "She's actually not a half-bad artist. Another thing we've got in common."

"Okay," I said again. "But then, I'm guessing, she turned to a life of crime?"

"Yeah...I think she mighta been living a life of crime for a while, doing some low-level dealing and shit like that. But, from what I gather, she didn't like it, which is one thing in her favor, I guess. She wanted to go legit, or at least not make her living meeting lowlifes in the kind of back alleys where her mom died. And she liked doing the art thing, and she had an Etsy shop and was making a little money, but it wasn't enough, especially since she was still using. Then she had a brainwave."

"Uh-huh," I said.

"She heard about some scams other people were pulling, with getting people to send them the ashes of their loved ones and then claiming they were stuck in customs, they needed a couple extra thousand dollars to get them out, shit like that. That gave her the idea to start padding her expenses, asking for more money after the fact, when she already had the ashes. Someone'd send her the ashes of their favorite dog, something like that, ask her to make them into a sculpture. She'd say sure, but then she'd write again and say that oops, there was an unexpected problem, she couldn't get the special clay she needed, or the glazes were on back order and she had to get them special-ordered from Germany, or there was a delay at the kiln and she'd have to go get the piece fired at a more expensive studio at the next town over. And she'd add a couple hundred onto the price tag each time something like this came up, so that people who thought they'd agreed to pay a grand were finding themselves on the hook for two or three grand."

"Okay," I said. "Not exactly major fraud, but not exactly honest, either."

"Yeah. And if they said they didn't want to do it or they couldn't afford it and could she send the ashes back, she'd say, oops, so sorry, the ashes have already been incorporated into the piece and the only choices are to finish it or discard it—and the ashes."

"I see," I said.

"Yeah. And most people who've gone to the trouble of arranging for something like this aren't going to agree to just throw the ashes away, so they'd normally pony up the extra money. And she would in fact do what they'd hired her to do, and they'd get their piece and it would be nice—just for two or three times the price they thought they'd be paying for it."

"Hmmm," I said.

"Yeah. Things that make you go 'hmmm' for sure. But then word started getting around, both that she was good at making this shit, and that she was padding the expenses and raising the prices. So on the one hand she was getting a big influx of orders, more than she could handle, and on the other hand she was getting a lot of angry customers, who started leaving angry reviews on her Etsy site, shit like that. So then she decided she needed to change her name and address. And she picked mine."

"Did she do that on purpose?" I asked.

Mel shrugged. "She says—'cause I've talked to her about this on the phone—that she wasn't consciously thinking about me and the name just popped into her head, but then she remembered that she had a cousin with that name, and she looked me up and got my parents' address and started having stuff sent there. She was taking way more orders than she could fill and she thought she'd just leave the ashes there until she could get to them. She swears she meant to do what she'd been paid for eventually. And then when she found out I'd been in the military, that's when she decided to use my identity, start impersonating me on dating sites so she could do sweetheart scams, and then she got the bright idea of filing for unemployment and disability under my name. Which is how she finally blew it, so I guess she wasn't as smart as she thought she was."

"Criminals rarely are," I said.

"Yeah...she swears she didn't remember who Nickie was and that she and Nickie were related when our profiles connected." Mel twisted up her face in an expression of extreme disgust. "And I fuckin' well hope that's fuckin' true, 'cause otherwise, we went to a real fuckin' weird place."

"Given that you were both catphishing each other, I wouldn't worry about it too much," I said.

"Yeah, I guess. Makes you think, though, doesn't it? I mean, what kinda family do I have?"

"The usual kind," I said. "Extremely fucked up."

"Yeah, I guess so. Anyway, when she met Fake Me online and found out I could do art too, she started to think that maybe she could bring me into the business and go legit again. She says she hated scamming people who were already hurting, but she didn't have a choice 'cause she was desperate."

"She had a choice," I said. "She had people offering to help her, and she turned her back on them and consciously chose to go into scamming instead."

"Yeah, but...fair enough," said Mel. "And here's where we get to the dilemma that I need advice on."

"Hit me," I said.

"Sooooo...I mean it's obvious, right? What my problem is? What do I do about Tiff? I can't stand the thought of letting her get away with everything she's done, or not stopping her if I could. I mean, she hasn't killed anyone—that I know of—and the money she's scammed is pretty small potatoes, but she's *hurt* people. I mean, when I think about it...scamming bereaved people is about as low as it goes. And don't say it was mostly just dogs. I'm pretty sure my dad loves Bluey way more than he loves any of his blood kin."

"I know," I said. "And in a way it's worse, because she's taking advantage of people who've been through a devastating loss but don't have any socially acceptable way of marking it. The kind of thing she's offering is pretty much all they've got, and she's using that heartbreak and desperation to squeeze money out of them."

"Yeah. And the sweetheart scam thing—when I think about how much what Jewel did to me hurt, and then I think about going through all of that for something that was never even real in the first place, was something someone faked in order to get money out of me—well, prison seems too good for someone like that."

"I think those kind of scammers rarely end up in prison anyway," I said. "A lot of the time what they're doing isn't even technically illegal."

"Yeah. Fuck! I can't let her get away with it. But whenever I think of turning her over to the authorities...well, I can't imagine looking myself in the face each morning and liking what I see after doing that, either."

"Is there a way you can stop her from doing it anymore without turning her in to the authorities?" I asked. "Especially since, as you said, a lot of what she's done isn't technically illegal, anyway."

"What she needs is treatment," said Mel. "But even if she could afford it, and we could get her to check into it, I'm not sure she'd be allowed to bypass the criminal justice system and go straight to rehab."

"I don't know either," I said. "But I know some people who would. Let me ask my parents. If we could pressure her into going to rehab, that might be the best all around."

"Rehab's expensive," Mel said. "Since she never actually got my unemployment insurance, all the money she has is whatever she was able to bilk out of the pet scheme and sweetheart scams. Probably more than I've been making, but since she's been blowing most of it on drugs, I doubt she has enough for a stint in a clinic."

"What about NA?" I asked.

"You gotta actually go to the meetings," said Mel.

"Let me talk to my parents," I repeated. "Maybe they'll have some good ideas. They'll definitely know what the treatment options are. And then we can come up with a plan."

"Look at us," said Mel. "Saving the world, one druggie scammer at a time."

8

I WAITED UNTIL AFTER the RUS 102 exam to call my parents. I told myself it was because I didn't want to disturb them late in the evening—it was after eight when I left Mel's—or early in the morning. Really, though, it was probably because I didn't want to talk to them.

The 8:00am exam went about as well as 8:00am exams generally do. Three of the students were late, one by more than an hour, and one burst into tears when she got to the essay section. All of them expressed sorrow and regret that I would be leaving, and then skipped blithely off—even the one who'd cried—as soon as the exam was over.

When I got back home, I played with Fevronia for a while—in her new, cheerful persona, she had developed a fondness for string—and then looked at the folder full of exams. Then, telling myself I should get it over with, I called my dad's cell phone.

I was hoping he wouldn't pick up. He was still working at the addiction clinic in Atlanta. It was entirely possible that he was with a client and couldn't take my call. That was what I was hoping for. That way I could leave him a brief message, and he could call back and leave *me* a message, and maybe we could solve this problem without ever actually interacting.

I'd never felt this way about my parents before. But I was more than half convinced they were going off the deep end and there was nothing I could do to save them, and I just didn't want to deal with that. Plus, my secret engagement with Dima was weighing on my conscience. I might not need my parents' consent to marry, but I didn't like keeping secrets from them, and this was an awfully big secret to keep. They would be hurt if they found out how long I hadn't told them, and I didn't want to deal with that, either.

"Rowena? What is it? Is everything okay? Is it John?" My father had picked up on the second ring. Dammit.

"John's fine," I said. "I'm fine. I'm actually calling about, well, a friend of a friend, I guess you'd say, who's, um, having some problems with drugs, and, um, I thought maybe you'd have some suggestions for what we could do for her."

"Oh." That single syllable held a wealth of meaning: mostly relief that his ever-present worries about John had not been realized, but also pleasure at being able to help me. I'd never asked him for help in a professional capacity before, and while I was sure he was glad I'd never had to ask for myself, he was, I realized, delighted to be able to do the one thing he was really good at for me.

"I'd love to help you, honey, and I will. But first, I need to tell you that Dennis isn't doing too well."

"Oh. I'm sorry to hear that," I said, my mouth moving on autopilot.

"Yes, we were all so hopeful after the previous round of treatment, but this current one isn't going so well. He wants all of us to come up this weekend. Are you free? I know it's short notice, but...well, this isn't the kind of thing you wait too long on. I'd actually just left a message with John about it, which is why I thought when I saw your number that maybe it was you calling to tell me something about him...I know that isn't likely, but I'm so used to worrying about him, and, well...never mind. What will happen, will happen, but if you're available to come up to Virginia this weekend, Dennis would love to see you."

"Of course," I said. "I'd be happy to."

9

AFTER THAT, MY DAD talked over various options for Tiff, and sent me some information about treatment programs and counseling services.

"It will only work if she voluntarily enters treatment—and means it," he warned me.

"I know," I said.

"And if she ends up facing criminal charges, that will change the situation."

"I know," I said again. "But at least we have somewhere to start."

"You do. And that's good. But hun? Don't get your hopes up too high."

"I won't," I promised. "They were never very high to begin with. We just feel like we have to give her the best chance we can."

"You do," he said seriously. "But the best chance she has still might not be very good. You have to learn to detach yourself from outcomes in this business."

"There's probably a lesson in that somewhere." If my father, who was probably the most idealistic person I knew, was telling me to keep my expectations managed and detach myself from outcomes, I was going to listen.

"No doubt. And hun? Maybe detach yourself from any outcomes involving Dennis, too. Or Alexandra. *Especially* Alexandra."

"I don't think I'm attached to any particular outcomes with them, but thanks," I said.

"I would do almost anything to give you and John a good relationship with them," he said. "But I don't know that that's an outcome that's going to happen. They're...well, they're them. They've never been capable of finding good outcomes, even when they're being handed to them on a platter."

I thought about remarking dryly that this was the least forgiving speech I had ever heard come out of his mouth, but I ended up just saying, "Oh."

"But now they're trying to reach out, mend bridges that they've burnt, and with my father maybe...not having a lot of time left, and with the chance that they might do something for you and John...well, I'm willing to overlook a lot. You know, I never really wanted money, but now when I think about how, if I'd lived my life differently, maybe I could be putting John through law school if that's what he wants to do, helping you out while you look for your next job—I guess what I'm trying to say is that I can't do that, but Dennis can, and, well...I'm trying as hard as I can to make my peace with him."

"I appreciate that," I said. "But I think Uncle Sam can and should put John through law school, and I'll be okay, so don't worry about it. If you'd lived your life differently, maybe you'd be trying to mend bridges you'd burnt between me and John, and what good would your money do you then?"

He laughed. Shakily. "Good point. I've always managed to stay in John's life, even when he made it as hard as possible, so I guess I can't judge myself too harshly. But now I need to do the same with my father, and that's proving to be a lot harder. I thought nothing would be tougher to swallow than John joining the Marines, but now..." He cut himself off abruptly. "Well, never mind. So you'll come up this weekend? That's great. And in the meantime, let me know if you have any more questions for this friend of a friend."

"Will do," I said. "Thanks again."

10

MY DAD EMAILED ME INFORMATION about various treatment programs in Georgia. I forwarded them to Mel. She thanked me and said she'd look into them.

I spent Wednesday morning grading finals and entering my final grades for the two classes that had already held their finals. Final grades weren't due until the following Wednesday, but I was looking at a busy weekend, and I didn't like to leave things to the last minute. The online grading portal had a nasty tendency to crash on the due date.

Wednesday afternoon I got a text from Mel.

Going to go talk to Tiff, Jose, and Desi this evening. Wanna come be my backup?

Where is this meeting? I wrote back. The thought of driving the two hours each way to Augusta tonight, when I had the 90-minute drive to Atlanta early the next morning, followed by the 7-hour drive to Virginia over the weekend, did not appeal. The cost of gas alone was likely to be prohibitive. On the other hand, the thought of letting Mel go meet with knife-wielding criminals on her own did not appeal either.

Macon, Mel wrote.

How'd you get them to agree to come out to Macon? I asked.

I told them I had enough on Tiff to get her arrested, but maybe we could do a deal, and we should get together in Macon. I didn't feel like driving all the way out to Augusta again. Let them come to us :)

What's the plan? I asked.

I told them God's honest truth. I *do* have enough on Tiff to get her arrested, but I don't want to do that. I looked at those treatment options your dad sent you. A couple of them allow you to work at the center in lieu of pay-

ment. I want Tiff to get into one of those and get clean. Then she can grad-uate to NA. I want Desi and Jose to be her guarantors. I'll be checking up on her regularly, and if she stays on the straight and narrow, I'll keep my mouth shut. The only thing she's done that's really illegal is that fraudulent unemployment claim, but she failed at that and I don't think anyone other than us knows that she's the one who did it.

You're just going to talk? I wrote.

That's the plan. Jose and I came up with it. This is basically an interven-tion. I think he's already got a spot for her at one of the work-for-pay treat-ment centers. If she agrees, he'll drive her straight there after the meeting and check her in. I don't think it'll be dangerous, but backup is always good, and you witnessed their criminal behavior too. Remember: Jose threatened someone with a deadly weapon, so we've got him too.

Okay, I texted. *When and where do we meet?*

11

THE MEETING WAS SET for 6:00pm at Carolyn Crayton Park, on the Ocmulgee River. Mel and I drove over in separate cars, parked, and walked together to the bridge over the pond. I wasn't sure if it was whimsy or some deeper spiritual sense, but Mel and Jose had agreed to meet on the bridge, over water.

We showed up at 5:55. At 6:03 Jose, Desi, and Tiff came over from the opposite direction. Jose was walking in front, with Tiff walking reluctantly in the middle and Desi holding up the rear and, I thought, pushing Tiff along.

They stopped at the edge of the bridge and looked us over.

"We're here," Jose said, holding up his hands to show he was unarmed. "Ready to talk. No funny business, okay?"

"No funny business," Mel promised, holding up her hands too. "Thanks for coming. You can come closer. I don't mean you any harm, I swear, and I don't think we should be shouting at each other so the whole park can hear. If we stand in the middle of the bridge, no one can sneak up on us."

Jose eyed the bridge dubiously. "Or you could just tip us into the water."

"It's not very deep water," Mel told him. "If I were going to do something to hurt you, I'd throw you into the river. You're safe, I swear it."

Jose continued to look dubious, but after a moment he stepped onto the bridge. Tiff and Desi followed even more dubiously. After a little cautious jockeying for position, Mel and Jose ended up side by side in the middle of the bridge, leaning on the railing and looking out over the water. I stood a pace back from Mel. Tiff and Desi stood a couple of paces away. Tiff was glowering and fidgeting. Desi was also glowering, but she was holding Tiff firmly by the elbow.

"So here's how it's gonna go down," Mel said. "Jose, you got that place booked for Tiff at the rehab center?"

"I don't need to fuckin' rehab!" Tiff yelled.

"Ssssh!" Desi hissed.

"I got a place reserved," Jose said. "I looked into those places you sent me, the ones where you can pay your way by working, but they're all part of churches. Tiff, she's not much of a churchgoer."

"Neither am I, but if it gets her off drugs, we might all change our tune," said Mel.

"So I got her a place at one of the others, one of the private clinics."

"Those are expensive," Mel said.

"Yeah, but Tiff's actually got health insurance—I made sure of it when she lost her job, and she's kept up the payments—and that'll cover some of it, and I've got a little money set aside. What am I gonna spend it on if not on Tiff? She's like family to me."

"Okay," said Mel. "Sounds good. So you get Tiff checked into this place, and she cleans up her act and she stops taking drugs and she stops with the fuckin' scamming, and—I can't fuckin' emphasize this enough—she makes what restitution she can for what she's done, and I won't say a word about the unemployment fraud or anything else that might land her in prison. And Rowena won't either, right, Ro?"

"Right," I said.

"And I can't make any promises 'cause I don't know what my financial situation's gonna be for the next few months, but if she needs a little more time in rehab and you need help paying for it, I might be able to kick in a little money. She might be like family to you, but she *is* family to me. I got a vested interest in keeping her out of trouble. So I'll be checking up on her from time to time, making sure she doesn't step out of line. Our cousin Nickie might too. Nickie has got some old issues with Tiff, but she's willing to overlook 'em for my sake."

"Fair enough," said Jose. "Whaddya say, Tiff?"

"Fuck you!" said Tiff. "You ain't trying to send me to rehab—you're trying to send me to JAIL!" She was struggling harder against Desi's grip.

Desi was determined, but Tiff had a good six inches and forty pounds on her.

"Come on, Tiff," Jose said. "This is the right call, you know it is. We talked about this. We already decided this is the right thing to do. We just wanted to meet with Mel here so she could lay all her cards out on the table—and so you could hear how serious she is. 'Cause I think she's serious about sending you to prison if you don't do this, aren't you, Mel?"

"Serious as a fuckin' heart attack," said Mel. "I'll be honest, Tiff: Everything I know about you tells me you hurt people. Not 'cause you mean to, but 'cause the only person you care about is yourself. But you're not alone, Tiff. You've got people who care about you, even if you don't care about them. So I want you to take this chance that's being handed to you by people who care about you, show 'em you deserve all the care they're giving you. And if you don't, so help me God, I will make your life a living hell—GET HER!"

Tiff wrested her arm out of Desi's grip. For a moment she froze. Mel and Jose both dove towards her. Instead of turning tail and running back towards the parking lot, Tiff bolted forward, knocking hard into Jose and sending him reeling into Mel. Both of them stumbled backwards in a tangle of limbs towards the bridge railing.

I leapt forward, trying to trip Tiff in a soccer tackle. My left foot connected solidly with her right ankle. My left knee shrieked in protest as we both went down, Tiff on top.

This is embarrassing. Mel and I are better than this. The thought flashed through my head and then Tiff was crawling over me, attempting to get free. Her knee dug into my stomach—*thank God I'm not pregnant!*—knocking the wind out of me, and then she was shoving me aside so that my head ended up under the railing, half-hanging off the edge of the bridge.

This could go really, REALLY badly. I lashed out with my right foot, catching Tiff by the ankle again and dropping her to her knees. I slithered on my back out from under the railing and tried to grab Tiff, but she was shrieking like a banshee and writhing like a snake.

"Tiff! TIFF!" Desi, Jose, and Mel all descended on her. There was a moment of flailing chaos, and then they had her on her feet, with Mel and Jose gripping her firmly each by an arm twisted behind her back.

"TIFF!" Desi shouted. "Listen, Tiff, listen! We're trying to help you!"

"FUCK YOU!" Tiff screamed.

I rolled over onto my front and pushed myself up onto my hands and knees. My left knee twinged ominously.

"Come on, Tiff!" Desi was saying. "It's me, Desi! We're like sisters, Tiff! We even took a blood oath back in eighth grade. Do you remember, Tiff? We pricked our fingers and held hands and swore we'd always be there for each other. Do you remember, Tiff?"

Using both hands on the railing, I pulled myself to my knees. I was struggling to breathe normally and not vomit.

"YOU'RE NOT MY SISTER!" Tiff screamed. "I AIN'T GOT NO ONE!"

I carefully got my right foot under me and pulled myself to standing. As long as I didn't put any weight on my left leg, I was fine. Oops, no, I was going to barf...nope, nope, false alarm. I concentrated on breathing slowly through my nose.

"You've got me, Tiff, you've got me! And Jose. And even Mel here. And Mel's friend Rowena. We all showed up for you, Tiff, we all came to help you, even after you pushed us away, even after you hurt us. That's why Jose and I wanted you to come meet Mel again. 'Cause we wanted you to see that even the people you've hurt are trying to help you. We're here for you, Tiff, 'cause we know that you'd do the same for us. If Jose or me was in trouble, you'd do anything to help us, wouldn't you? And we're doing the same for you. And you heard Mel. She said you're family. Family, Tiff! You're always saying you ain't got no one, but that's not true, Tiff! You got lots of people. You got me, and Jose, and Mel, and Mel's cousin Nickie, and even Rowena here—we're all here because we love you and we want to help you."

I continued to grip the railing and breathe slowly, trying to calm down the violent rebellion in my solar plexus. I couldn't say I felt a lot of love for Tiff at that moment, but luckily I couldn't say anything, so maintaining a benevolent silence was easy.

Tiff's struggles were growing less violent.

"You really won't send me to prison?" she asked. "You're really sending me to rehab, not to jail?"

"As God is my witness," Mel and Jose both said.

"If I let go of you to show you the reservation, will you not run away?" Jose asked.

"I got her anyway," Mel told him. "Go ahead and get your phone out and show her."

There was a brief rearrangement, and then Mel was holding Tiff while Jose got out his phone. He scrolled through it for a moment, then held it up for Tiff to see the screen.

"See?" he said. "Confirmation for a place for you at Whispering Pines Treatment Center, if I bring you there tonight. It's real nice, Tiff. I went over there and checked it out this morning. It's the nicest place you've ever stayed, I promise you. It's worth it just to spend a few weeks in a spa like that. Here. I'll show you the website."

"It does look nice," Tiff said after a moment.

"Don't it? And the staff are all super nice there too. I went and talked to 'em. They'll treat you better than you've ever been treated by anyone, Tiff. This is the best day of your life, Tiff; I know it might not seem like it right now, but it is. You're surrounded by people who care about you, who came here just to help you, and all you have to do is say yes and we'll take you to the nicest, fanciest hotel you've ever seen, and they'll help you get clean so you can go live your best life. And we'll all be here for you every step of the way."

"It does look nice," Tiff said again. "I guess...I guess I could try it out."

"Just try it out, Tiff, just try it out! What's the harm? You can spend a month in a nice spa, getting pampered and taken care of, and if you don't like it, well, at the end of the month you can always leave."

Out of the corner of my eye I saw Mel open her mouth to argue, then shut it.

"I guess...that doesn't sound so bad...I guess...I guess I can try it."

"That's great, Tiff! Let's go right now."

"I gotta pee," said Tiff.

"We'll stop at the restroom on the way to the car."

"And I'm hungry."

"We'll stop at a drive through on the way there."

"Um...I guess...okay. Let's go."

"I'll walk with you to the car," Mel said.

"I said I gotta pee!" insisted Tiff.

"I'll take you to the restroom on the way. You coming, Ro?"

"I'll just wait here," I said.

"You sure you're okay?"

"I'm fine," I said. "I'll just rest here for a bit." My words came out as a hoarse croak.

"If you're sure." Mel gave me a worried glance, but then, deciding I wasn't in immediate danger, started walking Tiff towards the bathrooms and Jose's car.

I leaned against the railing and concentrated on my breathing and told myself I should appreciate the beauty of the bridge and the pond and the trees on this fine May evening. By the time Mel came back alone, I was more or less able to breathe and talk normally.

"We packed Tiff in the car and they're on the road," Mel said. "Hopefully she doesn't try to dive out of the car while they're going down the highway."

"Hopefully." I flexed my left knee experimentally. Ouch.

"You sure you're okay?"

"It's just my bad knee," I said.

"Yeah. Shit! That went a little crazier than I thought it would. I guess I should've been ready for something like that, what with Tiff being who she is and all."

I took a cautious step. My knee twinged but held.

"I think I'm going to be able to make it back to the car," I said. "But going forward maybe we should have better plans for our clandestine ops."

12

MEL SUGGESTED WE GO to urgent care to have a doctor look at my knee.

"I have a doctor back at the apartment," I pointed out. "And I'll be seeing another one over the weekend."

"If you're sure," Mel said. "I know you don't want to pay those urgent care prices if you can avoid it."

I took a few more cautious steps. "I'm sure," I said. "Let's go."

"Okay. You need a hand?"

"I think I'll be good if we walk slowly."

We set off at a restrained amble towards our cars. "You're right," Mel said after a few steps. "Both times we faced off with Tiff it went a lot worse than we'd planned for, and that's on me. I should've known better. Hell, I *did* know better. I was trained better than that. But somehow I fuckin' figured that the rules were different in the civilian world. I knew Tiff was a lying piece of shit, but somehow I didn't think she'd be dangerous, even though you warned me she might be."

"It all turned out okay in the end."

"You're limping, so no, it fuckin' didn't. And that's on me. I should've actually used my training and my instincts instead of suppressing 'em 'cause I didn't want to make things too heavy or think ill of people or...I don't know. I kept telling myself things were going to go okay because I didn't want things to be as bad as I knew they could be, and you got hurt because of it."

"I helped with the planning, and came along of my own free will," I said. "And Tiff was the one who knocked me down."

"Yeah, but I should've taken the danger she posed a lot more fuckin' seriously. I just didn't want to think...hell, maybe I'm too soft. Maybe this PI thing is a bad idea."

"You got a better one?" I asked.

"No, goddammit, which is one reason why this is fuckin' killing me."

"I doubt you're too soft," I said. "Or that this is a bad idea. You just have to relearn how to treat everyone as a scumbag lowlife, instead of giving them the benefit of the doubt, like you would a student."

"Yeah. You're right. I'm sure it'll all come back to me. Lord knows I got plenty of experience dealing with scumbag lowlifes. You gonna be okay driving home?"

"I'll be fine," I said.

We stopped at my car door. "You sure?" Mel asked. "Because I don't mind driving you. Hell, it'd make me feel better. Especially since I might not have many more chances to drive you around."

Our eyes met. Something passed between us. Not lust, and not even love, not exactly, but something deep and powerful, that spoke of what-ifs and futures we were never going to see, but that might turn out better for us than what we were actually going to have. For a heartbeat, I could imagine the two of us together, and I could sense, as clearly as if she'd spoken it out loud, that Mel was imagining the same thing.

I looked away. It was never going to happen, because I'd already chosen Dima. And that was the choice I wanted to make, even if it meant giving up all kinds of other things. Even things like the special closeness I felt sometimes with Mel, which I knew right now I was never going to feel again, not like this. This was our moment, and it was the last one we were ever going to have as anything other than casual friends.

"I'll be fine," I repeated. "It's not that bad."

"Sure." Mel smiled. "Not that bad at all. Let me know if you need help tomorrow, okay?"

"Sure thing," I said, and got into the car.

Operating the clutch turned out to be less easy than I'd been hoping, but I still made it home without so much as an embarrassing stall-out. Bypassing the mailbox and the daily struggle with the mail key and my own foolish hopes and dreams for what fate might send my way, I drove straight into the closest parking spot to my entrance that I could get. The stairs took me twice as long as normal, and I had to rest on the landing before I could manage to open the door. Galina Ivanovna was waiting for me when I limped into the apartment.

"Innochka! What happened to you?!?!"

"I got knocked down," I said.

As I'd predicted, Galina Ivanovna insisted on performing a thorough exam of my knee. When she'd finished, she pronounced it to be mildly strained.

"The concern is not so much the current injury as the cumulative damage of all the previous traumas," she said. "It needs to be immobilized—Innochka! You can't drive me to Atlanta tomorrow."

"I can and I will," I said.

"No, no, maybe we can skip tomorrow's session..."

"We're not skipping a session," I said. "Especially since they're supposed to do a lot of important tests."

Galina Ivanovna made another attempt to dissuade me, but succeeded only in extracting a promise that, if my knee was dramatically worse tomorrow morning, I'd see if I could get someone else to drive her. It was a big ask, but I was hoping that I could play on Mel's sense of guilt if necessary.

After she'd supervised the fitting of one of the several knee braces I still had, and brought me supper, and lectured me on the importance of keeping the joint immobilized and elevated, and ordered Fevronia, who was hanging around purring and walking back and forth under my elevated leg, to watch over me, Galina Ivanovna set off for her own apartment.

I considered going straight to bed. It would be an early morning tomorrow, and I didn't feel like dealing with email. But I was pretty sure I'd lie awake worrying about the contents of my inboxes if I didn't check them. So I turned on my laptop and started going through my various email accounts.

A notification on my Crimsonmail that my account would expire at the end of the month. Well, at least I wouldn't have to worry about checking it anymore after that. I went over to my personal email account and started scrolling through it. Junk, junk, junk...wait, what was that? From the foreign email address that I didn't recognize, but that looked oddly familiar...?

I hesitated a moment, afraid it might be some kind of phishing account, but then clicked on it.

The contents didn't *look* like a phishing account, but I couldn't make sense of them at first. Why were they...Oh my God! It was an email from the fellowship I'd applied to in Finland. And it wasn't a form letter rejection. No. After reading it three times to make sure I wasn't hallucinating, I had to conclude that they were, in fact, inviting me for an interview.

13

THAT WAS THE GOOD NEWS. More good news was that the interview was supposed to be a short, informal affair held over Skype. The mixed news was that they wanted to hold it on Friday.

Some calculations of relative time zones told me that the interview times they were suggesting were in my morning, so I should be able to do the interview and then make it to campus on time to administer my last final. That didn't sound like my idea of a pleasant day, but at least the pain would be concentrated. It also gave me almost no time to prepare, since I'd be driving Galina Ivanovna to Atlanta and back tomorrow.

I thought for a nanosecond about requesting an extension on the interview, but 1) I was afraid that would look bad, and 2) that would push it back to after I went to Virginia, thus merely stretching out the problem of stress and lack of preparation. So after hemming and hawing for a few minutes, I wrote back saying, with more truth than usual, that I would be delighted to talk to them on Friday, and requesting the earliest interview slot they could give me.

That done, I limped stiff-legged off to bed. I considered texting Dima to tell him about the interview, but I didn't want to wake him in what was the very early morning in Germany, and I also didn't want to get into a lengthy conversation when I really should be going to bed.

I slept better than I had been expecting, and the knee looked less bad the next morning than I'd been fearing. I still forgot to suppress a wince when I shifted the car into reverse as Galina Ivanovna and I were setting off from the parking lot, causing her to suggest that we stay home.

"I'm fine," I insisted, and carefully not showing any sign of pain, shifted the car into first.

Once we got on the highway and I was able to turn on cruise control things were fine. I told Galina Ivanovna about the upcoming interview.

"You see, Innochka! Everything is working out wonderfully."

"I still don't have the fellowship yet," I warned her. "It's just a simple Skype interview."

"Yes, but it's a good omen. Have you told Dima?"

"Not yet."

"You must," she told me sternly. "And you must tell him about your knee, too. You are about to get married. Spouses should have no secrets from each other."

It was on the tip of my tongue to ask how well she thought Dima was going to live up to that maxim, but fortunately, I was able to suppress that. I promised I would tell Dima about both things as soon as I got her settled in at the hospital.

This time, instead of sending us up to the infusion room, we were first sent to a phlebotomy booth, where Galina Ivanovna had what looked like at least a pint of blood drawn. This was followed up by a urine sample, and then we were told to go to her regular room for the infusion.

Kathy bustled in and hooked her up, talking all the while about how good she was looking, what a success she was, and maybe this would be the last time they'd see her. Then she bustled out, and Galina Ivanovna told me I *must* tell Dima my news.

I obediently texted him with both pieces of information and a picture of my knee in a brace. Although I needed to prep for the interview, not get in a long discussion of either issue, I was half-hoping he'd text back with an acknowledgement and maybe some sympathy for the knee thing and congratulations for the interview thing, but my phone remained resolutely silent. I resigned myself to an hour of uninterrupted interview prep, got out my notepad, and opened up the institute's webpage on my phone.

I was wrapping up the list of potential questions to ask the interviewers when my phone *pinged*. It was Dima.

Finland, huh? Could be fun. Good news: I'm almost done here. I'll be coming home next week.

14

I TEXTED BACK FOR MORE details, but Dima only said that he was still working on getting his tickets, and he had to go.

"Good news," I told Galina Ivanovna. "Dima is planning to come home next week."

"At last! Did he give you any instructions about the wedding?"

"No," I said.

"No, of course not, what was I thinking. I'm afraid it's on you to organize everything, Innochka. Can you go get the license now?" I had researched requirements for getting married in Georgia and tried to explain them to Galina Ivanovna, but she still had a shaky grasp of the details. The fact that requirements for a legal marriage varied on a state-by-state basis flummoxed her, and she kept asking me if a marriage certificate from Georgia would be valid in the rest of the country, or if we'd have to get remarried if we moved across state lines.

"Both of us have to be present in order to get the license," I said. "We'll do it when he gets here."

"When is he supposed to arrive?"

"He doesn't know yet."

"You'll go get the license the next day. If he arrives in the morning, you'll go get the license on the way home from the airport."

"Yes," I agreed.

"What's the place called where you can get a license?"

"A probate court," I told her.

"That doesn't sound very romantic to my ears, but maybe it sounds better in English."

"It doesn't," I told her.

"Well, never mind. Look up the closest 'probate court' to the airport, Innochka, and the closest one to the apartment, so you can be prepared when he arrives."

I duly looked up the addresses for all the probate courts in this whole half of Georgia, noting down their hours and whether they also performed wedding ceremonies. It was not, as Galina Ivanovna said, a very romantic experience. But my stomach tingled with butterflies of excitement even so. Maybe by this time next week Dima and I would have a marriage license, or even be married. Galina Ivanovna was saying something about rings and dresses, but to me, the marriage certificate was the only thing that really mattered.

"I don't have a dress," I told her. "And I don't want one. They're expensive, and what would I do with it? I just want to get married."

"I approve, Innochka, but what will your parents say? Will they be disappointed? I know how you Americans value huge white dresses and enormous cakes—they don't look very good to me, but what do I know—and flowers and all kinds of expensive things. You all get married like princesses."

"My parents will be fine." In fact, I thought they probably would be disappointed, although because the groom was Dima, not from my lack of a fancy white dress. But I certainly wasn't going to say that to Galina Ivanovna. Instead, I told her that my parents hadn't gotten married until after my brother was born. She took it in stride and confided to me that she'd already been expecting Dima on her wedding day.

"But as the great Dostoevsky says, the crown covers everything. Once you get married, all your past transgressions are wiped clean."

I wasn't too sure about that. I was pretty sure that karma didn't stop dogging your heels just because you put on a piece of jewelry and got a fancy piece of paper. But I still really, really wanted that piece of paper, and I also wanted Galina Ivanovna to be calm and happy, so I smiled and nodded and made agreeable small talk as Kathy came and unhooked her from the IV, and told her they'd be in touch once the labs came back.

"We'll probably call you on Monday or Tuesday with the results," she said. "Dr. Azarian will talk to you then about whether you need to come back in or not."

"Please accept my most heartfelt thanks for all your care—and my most heartfelt wishes that I don't have to come back," Galina Ivanovna told her.

Kathy laughed and said she was a sweet thing, and then we left the hospital and drove off into the early evening gathering darkness.

15

I GOT A TEXT FROM MEL when I got home saying that Jose had confirmed that Tiff had successfully checked into the rehab center and was starting detox.

So I say we call it a win, Mel wrote. *How's the knee?*

Not too bad, I texted back. In fact, it was noticeably stiff and sore, but it wasn't too swollen and I could still put weight on it, so I was declaring that a positive sign.

You need a ride to campus tomorrow?

I'd better drive myself, I wrote. *I've got an interview tomorrow morning.*

Mel texted me congratulations and the instructions to knock 'em dead. I promised I would.

The interview was scheduled for 9:00am. I arose in good time, calmly made myself coffee and breakfast, checked that I was prepared for the exam in the afternoon, and then sat down to calmly go over my notes. At least, I told myself, I was an old hand at this. Admittedly, I'd never been interviewed for a research fellowship before. Oh God. Now I was starting to get nervous. I was used to being asked about my teaching and service work. I had answers on those topics that I could reel off in my sleep. But what was I going to say about my research? I had a topic. I even had a book contract. In my fellowship application I'd said I'd finish preparing my manuscript for publication over the summer and start a new project, one that was also on Tsvetaeva, when I started the fellowship. I had some vague thoughts on the potential new project, but what little bandwidth I'd had to give to my research this semester had been consumed by my sloth-like attempts to revise my current book. I was closing in on the end

of the process, but I wasn't going to be able to send the revised manuscript to my publisher until after finals. Oh God! I was a complete failure. I was wasting everyone's time...

With a jolt, I saw that it was 8:55. I opened Skype, praying it
wouldn't try to update.

My luck held. Skype opened smoothly. A few minutes later, the call
from the interview committee *blooped* onto the screen.

There were three of them, a tall, slender blonde woman, a tall, slender, dark-haired man, and an older woman who was clearly Russian.
The Nordic-looking woman introduced herself as Helmi. The man introduced himself as Aksel, and explained that he was originally Norwegian
but had been at the institute for the past ten years. The Russian woman
introduced herself as Natalya Andreyevna. All of them spoke English,
Helmi and Aksel with light Nordic accents and Natalya Andreyevna
with a thick Russian accent. She, unsurprisingly, was running the show.

There was a couple minutes of small talk, where I described my upcoming final and the literature course I'd been teaching this semester.
Everyone was interested in it and asked me several questions about the
texts I'd chosen and how American students had responded to them.

"Well," said Natalya Andreyevna when we'd exhausted that topic
of conversation, switching to Russian. "You're not against me speaking
Russian, are you? You said you are preparing a book for publication.
How is that going?"

I switched to Russian too and gave the most upbeat and optimistic
assessment of my progress that I legitimately could without overt lying.

"I see," said Natalya Andreyevna when I was done. "That is all very
interesting, but of course what we really care about is the project you
would do while you're here with us. As you know, our theme this year
is 'Female Poets Reimagining the 20th Century.' We are particularly interested in including the Silver Age in our reimagination, and especially
Tsvetaeva. Explain to us, please, how your proposed topic fits in with our
theme."

I launched into an explanation of how I intended to continue my examination of identity and gender in Tsvetaeva's work in a way that would

reimagine our conception of her and her place in the 20th-century Russian literary canon.

"I see," said Natalya Andreyevna. "I have two questions for you. Firstly: It seems that you might have some trouble because you're talking about 'literary transvestism.' Is that not an issue in the West right now?"

"I'm working closely with my editors to find the correct approach to the issue," I said.

The corners of Natalya Andreyevna's lips twitched, as if she knew and appreciated a bullshit answer when she heard one. "Secondly," she said. "Can you explain in more detail how your second project will differ substantially from your first book? Why, frankly speaking, should you receive a fellowship for something that's the same as what you've already done?"

The muscles around my right eye and temple were starting to cramp and spasm, and my head seemed to be floating about six inches off to the side of my body. When I opened my mouth to start talking, my lips and tongue felt strange and foreign, and my voice sounded like it was coming from far away.

Somehow I strung together a bunch of words and trotted them out, though, and Helmi and Aksel nodded along as if I were making sense, especially when I said something about using my time at the institute to refine and develop my ideas through interactions with other scholars working on similar topics. Natalya Andreyevna listened with her eyes narrowed and her lips pursed. I couldn't tell if that was because she was listening attentively, or because she despised everything I said.

Eventually I wrapped up what felt like a wordy and yet vague and substanceless answer. Helmi and Aksel smiled and nodded and, switching back to English, told me about the institute's resources and what the fellowship would entail.

"We might be offering some classes at Helsinki University," Helmi told me. "That was why we were so interested in the literature class you are teaching now. We might need someone who wants to teach a class on literature and is able to do it."

"I'd *love* to teach a class on literature!" I said, with probably too much enthusiasm. But it was also the first really sincere thing I'd been able to say for the whole interview, so I let that sincerity and warmth come out.

"Do you have any questions?" Natalya Andreyevna interjected in Russian.

I asked a question about the visa and housing situation. Aksel launched into an encouraging description of the ease of acquiring a visa and the high-quality housing available near the institute.

"Will you be coming alone?" Natalya Andreyevna demanded. "Or do you have a family?"

Helmi and Aksel both looked embarrassed and faintly apprehensive.

"Don't worry, this is 'off the record,'" Natalya Andreyevna told us. "I know I am not supposed to ask that kind of question. But I care about you as a person, so I'm asking it anyway. Will you be bringing a husband? Children?"

"No children," I said. "But, um, my, um, husband will probably need to join me."

Natalya Andreyevna nodded briskly. "It's not good for spouses to be separate for so long. How long have you been married?"

"We're, um...planning to get married soon," I confessed.

"I see. So this would be something in the way of a honeymoon for you."

"Um," I said. "I guess you could say, um..."

"Don't be shy, Rowena. I know you Westerners are not used to talking about these things, but we must be frank with each other. I care about you as a person, as I told you, so I must know the full details of your situation in order to help you. What is your future husband's profession?"

"He's a journalist," I said.

"Ah, a journalist, that's good. Does he work for a major American news source?"

"He's actually Russian," I said. "He works for, um, *Nezavisimaya Pravda.*"

All three of them jerked upright as if electrified. They exchanged glances.

"We understand if you do not want to talk about this more..." Helmi began.

"Does he need to get out of Russia?" Natalya Andreyevna demanded.

"Um..." I said. "Maybe...I mean...you understand what the situation is like right now..."

"We all read *Nezavisimaya Pravda* regularly," Natalya Andreyevna told me. "Would we recognize his name?"

"Um," I said. "Maybe?"

She clicked her tongue a few times as if in thought, then snapped her fingers and said, "Wasn't Kuznetsov involved with some American woman?"

"Um..." I said.

"Are you telling us," said Natalya Andreyevna, "that you're about to get married to *Dmitry Kuznetsov*?"

"Well..." I said. "Um...yes?"

"God watch over and preserve you, child," she said.

16

I ENDED THE CALL WITH the sense that it had either gone really well, or really terribly. I tried to recall what it was I'd said in response to their questions about my actual research, but all I could remember was some word salad and inane babble. The natural fracturing of a traumatized memory, or an accurate picture of what I'd actually said? In any event, I was pretty sure none of us was thinking about anything other than my revelation that I was about to marry the infamous Dmitry Kuznetsov. My candidacy for the fellowship was, I guessed, going to be evaluated mainly on that. And, to be fair, it was the thing I cared about most right now, and maybe ever, so I'd probably be better off being judged on my commitment to that than to my research.

I tried to work up some feminist outrage at decisions about my career being made on the basis of who my husband was, but I was too emotionally wrung out to muster up anything other than a hope that the effect would be positive and they'd give me the fellowship out of pity. I had zero sense that I deserved it for my own merits, but I was desperate enough for a job to accept charity.

After splashing my face with cold water to try to bring some feeling back into it, I went to check through my messages and make sure I had everything for the final. It wasn't even 10:00am yet, so I didn't need to leave for another couple of hours, but I didn't want to go talk to Galina Ivanovna until I'd calmed down a little.

My inboxes were full of nothing but junk. I deleted it and started composing a thank-you note to the interview committee.

I was staring at my laptop, trying to decide whether to mention the one thing that I was sure they were all thinking, when a notification popped up on my phone. It was a message from Dima, asking how the interview had gone.

I don't know, I wrote back. *I think they have doubts about my research, about my fundamental approach. It seemed like a good idea when I picked it more than five years ago, but now everyone worries that it will come across as "anti-trans."*

Fuck them, was Dima's response. *The world is literally on fire, and the top priority of the West's best and brightest is to browbeat everyone, Petruchio-style, into saying that real women have penises. When they're not explaining how the real rapists and predators are women. And they take pride in it! Meanwhile, no one wants to be a sister of mercy, which is what the world really needs right now. I don't know if I can fucking stand the West, Inna.*

Well, we may have to leave it anyway, if I can't get a job, I wrote.

Something will work out, Dima told me.

Where's my fiancé and what did you do with him?!?!

He's right here, making plans to turn pro and start making real money if necessary.

No! Don't do it!

I obey, Comrade General)))))) *But I do have faith that something will work out. Someone will recognize your undeniable talent and offer you the situation you deserve.*

They'd better do it fast, I wrote.

Yes. Meanwhile, I'm supposed to fly in Tuesday evening. Can you meet me at the airport?

Of course, I wrote. *I can't wait.*

17

THE LITERATURE FINAL Friday afternoon suffered from a certain amount of chaos. Several students came trailing in late, saying they'd been detained by room inspections, since they were leaving campus as soon as the exam was over. Dorm checkout had to be completed by Saturday morning, and all the students were more focused on that than on the exam. I chivvied them through it as best I could, and gathered up the exams afterwards with a sense that grading them was likely to be a very disappointing experience.

I spent the evening with Galina Ivanovna and Fevronia, both of whom were in good spirits. After her weekly check of my lungs, which made her frown and say I wasn't getting worse, but I wasn't getting better either, Galina Ivanovna talked a lot about all of us, including Fevronia, going back to Moscow in a few weeks. We researched the requirements for bringing pets into Russia, and discussed whether Fevronia would tolerate being in a carrier for an entire day.

"I'm sure she'd be an angel," Galina Ivanovna said. "But just in case, we can sedate her. What are the rules for bringing pets into Finland, Innochka?"

We researched that as well. Galina Ivanovna made a list of the necessary vaccinations for both countries, and advised me to make an appointment with a vet, "Just in case, you know. Because we can't leave Ronechka behind."

I said I would, which Galina Ivanovna took as a pleasing demonstration of my faith in our future rather than a cowardly avoidance of gloomy topics. She wished us both a good night, promised to check in tomorrow morning before I set off, and left.

"You are clearly no longer my cat," I said to Fevronia.

She walked under my leg a couple of times, brushing it with her tail, and followed me into the bedroom, jumping up onto the pillow rather than hiding under the bed when I turned in for the night.

18

FEVRONIA SLEPT ON THE pillow next to me all night and didn't vomit on it once. I hoped this was an auspicious omen for my upcoming ordeal. I also wondered what Dima would think about having a cat on his side of the bed. Their previous cat had normally slept in her own cat basket, but Fevronia preferred to be in the bed or at least bed-adjacent. So far Dima had been charmed by Fevronia, so I had to hope they would work it out peaceably between them.

After a hasty breakfast and a brief farewell with Galina Ivanovna, who promised to spend all her time pampering Fevronia and to send me regular updates on her, I set off in the dawn light, heading north.

The drive was uneventful, giving me plenty of time to think about what I would do when I got there. Last I'd heard from Heather Ramirez, she'd said the story was scheduled to go live by early next week. I'd shared a couple of texts and phone calls with John over the past few weeks, strategizing how we'd break the news to our parents and Dennis and Alexandra. We'd ended up deciding to take the cowardly path and wait for the story to come out. Meanwhile, I was planning to be as pleasant and polite as possible. It was a good strategy that rarely let me down.

My plan was tested as soon as I pulled up to Dennis and Alexandra's house. Dennis was waiting out on the front porch. When he saw me, instead of coming over, he disappeared into the house. A few seconds later, he and Alexandra came out together.

"Rowena!" Alexandra looked almost animated. "We weren't expecting you so soon!"

"You're the first one to arrive," Dennis said. Coming across loud and clear was his dismay at having to deal with me without the buffer of my parents or John. They wanted or at least needed my parents and John, but Dennis would have strongly preferred me not to be there. Dennis, I guessed, would have strongly preferred me not to exist at all.

"We're so happy to see you!" Alexandra said. She was smiling in a way that looked painful, like her face wasn't used to it and the muscles in her cheeks had never built up the necessary strength, nor the skin the necessary flexibility. I resisted the urge to rub my own cheeks in sympathy. At least her grandmotherly instincts hadn't been completely destroyed by whatever terrible things had been done to her. Somewhere, deep down, my real grandmother, the grandmother I should have had, was still there.

"I'm delighted to be here," I said, with my best interview face. "Any news on when the others are supposed to get here?"

"Your parents are running late," Dennis announced. "Something to do with Beverly's practice...she's never been much for punctuality, has she?"

"Well," I said. "Um...she normally manages to get by." In fact, my mother's lack of punctuality had caused me much anguish in my childhood, but medical school, residency, and practice had trained her to be a punctual-enough person, and I would be damned if I'd say a word against her in front of Dennis. And, in all seriousness, sometimes doctors did get held up by emergencies. It was sort of a feature of the profession.

"And John should be here by now." Something almost like tenderness warmed Dennis's face for an instant, and was then replaced by an equally out-of-character expression of worry.

"There was a wreck on the interstate," I said. "He's probably caught in that."

Dennis and Alexandra instinctively stepped closer together, their faces registering identical alarm.

"I'm sure he's fine," I said. "If something happened to him, I'm sure he'd text me."

Dennis and Alexandra continued to look alarmed, and also annoyed at the reminder of the existence of cell phones. After a moment, Dennis visibly pulled himself together and said, "Let's go in, shall we?"

The house was just as dark and gloomy as I remembered. They offered me water, which I accepted, and then we repaired to the den in the back, where we sat in the semi-darkness.

I sipped at my glass of water and went through possible topics of conversation. *So, I hear you're not doing so good*, didn't seem like a great place to start. *Did you know your beloved pastor might be a crook?* didn't seem any better. They didn't have any pets we could talk about, and I didn't know about any hobbies. Talking about myself seemed equally fraught: any sort of honest account of my current situation would start with my lack of a job, and end with my engagement to a man they didn't approve of.

"Your flowers are looking nice," I finally managed. There was a narrow bed along the driveway that was lined with what I thought were petunias, plus some other flowers I couldn't identify.

"That's Alexandra's doing," Dennis said. "I couldn't even tell you what was there." Like many husbands commenting on their wives' interests, his ostensibly humble words were filled with a seething undercurrent of resentment and contempt.

"Oh, do you like to garden?" Alexandra asked.

"I don't have much of a chance," I said, truthfully. "But I like flowers." That seemed safe enough.

Alexandra talked about flowers for a while. We narrowly avoided catastrophe when she quizzed me on my experience gardening, and I almost brought up working in my grandmother's—my *other* grandmother's—garden, but I caught myself just in time and said something about my mother growing vegetables in my childhood. This was no better, though, and launched Dennis on a tirade about the commune and how it was all my mother's fault that we'd lived there. I sat and smiled and said nothing, while Alexandra tried to soothe him.

Just when I thought I couldn't take any more, the doorbell rang. Alexandra launched out of her seat as if on springs and rushed off to answer it. Dennis got up and followed her more slowly, and I kept far enough back that I didn't have to interact with him.

"John!" Alexandra was exclaiming when we got to the door. "John's here!"

"About time," said Dennis, but he was smiling a small, not very friendly but still genuine, smile as he said it.

Alexandra pulled open the front door with a wrench. "John! We've been so worried! Rowena said there was a wreck on the interstate..."

"Yeah, that was mostly cleared up by the time I came through," John said. "Sorry I'm late. I was held up a little setting off. But I'm here now, no problem."

"I hope it was nothing serious!" said Alexandra.

"Nothing serious at all," said John. He looked over Alexandra's head at me and mouthed *Camila's ex-boyfriend.*

I raised my eyes quizzically.

Tell you later, he mouthed, and let Alexandra usher him deeper into the house.

19

JOHN'S ARRIVAL TOOK some of the pressure off me, and our parents' arrival half an hour later allowed me to disappear into the background. At least until Alexandra asked me, as I was helping her set out dinner, if I was planning to see Isaiah while I was here.

John, who was carrying a pitcher of water (no wine for us!) to the table, stopped to listen.

"I might see him tomorrow," I said, trying to pitch my voice low. "I'm not sure yet."

"But of course you'll see him in church tomorrow morning, won't you?" Alexandra said, with what felt like deliberate loudness. "And what about afterwards?"

John was listening avidly. Everyone else, I noted, was inching closer.

"We might meet tomorrow evening," I said guardedly.

"For dinner, you mean?" Alexandra asked.

"Possibly," I said. "If you don't mind."

"Normally I'd say family dinner on Sunday is sacrosanct, but for this...of course you should go out to dinner with him! Do you think you'll do anything afterwards?"

John looked like he was choking back an expression of mingled outrage and amusement.

"We haven't decided yet," I said.

"Of course, of course...best to see where the evening takes you...but please, Rowena, don't worry about coming back early for our sake."

"Thanks," I said, while John continued making a face of mingled outrage and amusement.

In fact, Isaiah and I had been in touch over the past couple of days, and had discussed the feasibility of holding another non-date while I was here in order to share info, but so far no concrete plans had been made. He'd been too strung up over the impending release of Heather's article to make any commitments, and I'd been worried that it would cause us problems. But now I was worried that not doing it would cause even more problems. Of course, I was going to have to tell everyone about Dima at some point, but in the meantime, I wanted to stay in everyone's good graces.

Conversation over supper was as benign as a conversation with that crew could be. Dennis was mostly silent, Alexandra was trying to be as warm and charming as she could, and John was on his best behavior.

It was only when Alexandra brought out a dessert of blueberry pie that things took a turn for the worse.

"Why are you always feeding me blueberries?" Dennis demanded. "Seems like every meal you're stuffing blueberries into me. You know I don't like blueberries. Can't we have banana cream pie for once instead of these danged blueberries?"

"Blueberries are full of, what are they called, phytonutrients," Alexandra said.

"So?" Dennis demanded.

"So you know you should be eating as healthily as you can..." said Alexandra, faltering.

"Why? Only the Good Lord can save me, not these danged blueberries. If I eat any more, I'm going to turn blue all over! You'd be better off praying for me, not pushing this crap on me!"

Dennis's cheeks, gaunt and lined from age and illness, were flushed a bright, veiny red, and he made angry jabbing motions at Alexandra with his dessert spoon.

"If you want to eat blueberries yourself, you just go right ahead!" he said, his voice rising. "Maybe if you'd eaten more blueberries when you'd been expecting *him*"—he jabbed his spoon at my father—"you'd have been a better mother to him. You certainly could have prayed more for salvation, but no! All you did was complain! But *now* you're trying to save me with blueberry pie, and I won't hear of it, you hear me! Tomorrow night there'd better be banana cream pie, or..."

He started to cough, and coughed and coughed, his thin frame spasming, until he was breathless, his face an alarming shade of purple.

"Why don't you take a sip of water, Dad," my father said. He'd been sitting perfectly still throughout all of this, his expression carefully blank. His tone was now cool and measured, as if these people had nothing to do with him.

Dennis waved him off, glaring daggers at him between spasmodic coughs.

"*Best just to leave him be, Bobby,*" Alexandra whispered. "*Once he gets in these states, there's no pleasing him. It's the **drugs**, you know—they mess with his mind.*" More loudly, she added, "Pie, dear?"

"Please," said my father, his voice still cool and measured. "Bev, what about you?"

"Yes, please," said my mother, while Alexandra said, her voice full of false brightness, "You know, I don't think I've ever told you, Bev, dear, how much I've always liked your name. So elegant and classic and yet also modern, don't you think? *Beverly*. It sounds like something out of an English novel, don't you think? And of course it starts with a B, just like Bobby. You know, when I first heard it, I thought it was a sign that you two were meant to be together."

"That's...lovely," said my mother, looking extremely startled. "Um...thank you."

"B...b...I wonder what it is about that sound?" Alexandra mused, while Dennis's coughing continued in the background. "And of course, you hear it twice in 'Bobby,' don't you? *Bev, Beverly, Bobby*...that sounds very similar, doesn't it? I wonder why that is?"

"Rowena would be the one to know," my mother said.

"Really?" Alexandra turned to me. "Why's that, dear?"

"Um...I'm not a phonetician, but I have to know some basic phonetics in order to teach language," I said.

"Oh, I see. Of *course*. So why do they sound so similar?"

"Well..." I said, seeing icebergs ahead. I glanced over at Dennis. His coughing had gone from whole-body convulsions to minor shudders, but he was still glaring daggers at everyone. I plunged ahead, hoping to provide a distraction.

"*B* and *V* are both voiced labials," I said. "*B* is a bilabial, and *V* is a labiodental, but they're very similar."

"Bilabial..." Alexandra said musingly. "What an odd word. It sounds Latin. I wonder why they call it that?"

My traitorous eyes flicked in John's direction. He had his napkin to his mouth and appeared to be breathing into it deeply, trying to stifle a laugh.

"Um..." I said. "Because you, uh, say it with your labia."

John choked into his napkin. My parents sat there stonefaced. Alexandra looked mildly curious.

I glanced over at Dennis again. He was still glaring daggers at everyone. I pressed on.

"Your lips," I explained. "*B* is a bilabial because you pronounce it by pressing your labia, that is to say, your lips, together."

"Beh...beh..." Alexandra said experimentally. "John, dear, are you all right?"

"Allergies," John said hoarsely, coughing into his napkin, his shoulders shaking.

"And *V*?" Alexandra asked. "What did you call it?"

"A labiodental," I said, carefully not looking at anyone else in the room. "You, um, pronounce it by pressing your teeth against your labia, that is, your lips."

John convulsed, choking.

"Water," he gasped, and fled to the kitchen, tears streaming down his face, his whole body shaking.

"Should we do something for him?" Alexandra asked, looking alarmed.

"He's fine," said my mother, poker-faced. "He just...found what Rowena said to be a bit...amusing."

"Oh. Why? What am I missing?" asked Alexandra, looking bewildered and a little hurt.

"It's, um, some medical terminology," said my mother delicately. "I, um, could explain it to you later. It's, um...well, like I said, it might be considered funny if you know medical terminology."

"Oh. And of course Rowena and John grew up learning medical terminology," said Alexandra. "Well, I'm glad you have your inside family jokes. Pie, everyone?" She stopped and repeated the word "pie." "Is that also a, what do you call it, a bilabial?"

"It is," I confirmed. John, who had been coming back from the kitchen, whirled around and fled, his shoulders shaking.

"It's voiceless," I said, trying to steer the conversation into less rocky waters.

"Which means?"

By the time I had finished explaining the difference between voiced and voiceless consonants, Alexandra had dished up pie for everyone, and John had returned from the kitchen, wiping his face and determinedly not laughing. Dennis accepted his piece with reasonable grace, and asked for seconds when he'd finished, saying he guessed it wasn't so bad after all, and if it was good for him, he might as well try it.

When we were done, Alexandra told us that they'd taken to holding evening prayers after supper, to support Dennis's treatment, and would we join them. None of us could say no, so we went and sat in the den and held a very awkward half hour of joint prayers. John was openly struggling not to yawn by the end of them, so we both pleaded exhaustion and fled for the night.

20

I'D BEEN PUT ON THE fold-out cot again. John had been put in what turned out was an actual guest room next door.

"Well shit," he said, when we both went into it. "Why the fuck didn't they put us up in it before?"

"I think it had to be cleaned out," I said. "Look...is that Dad's stuff?"

We poked through a pile of toys that looked like they'd been swept off the bed and dumped into the corner. There were stuffed animals, blocks, toy trucks from fifty years ago...everything you'd expect from a little boy's room.

"Damn," said John, stirring through the pile. "I guess this was his old room, huh? Do you think they've been keeping it as a shrine to him all this time?"

"Looks like it," I said, going over to the desk across from the twin bed. "Look: is this an old yearbook?"

We opened up what was indeed a yearbook from our father's high school graduation. We flipped through it until we found him, looking the picture of a nerd with sticking-out hair and big glasses.

"Jesus Christ," said John. "I don't know that I can handle seeing this kind of shit. It's gonna give me nightmares."

I shut the yearbook. "I think it's sad," I said. "I wish we could have seen this when we were younger. I wish we could have known more about where we came from."

"Yeah, whatever," said John, surveying the room. "Turns out where we came from was a pretty fucked-up place, so we were probably better off not knowing until we were old enough to handle it. Although I don't know if I'll ever be old enough to handle it. I keep hoping someone will jump out and tell me I'm adopted."

"Little chance of that," I said. "And that would just mean coming from an even more fucked-up situation. So what's the deal with Camila's ex-boyfriend?"

"Oh, yeah. Speaking of fucked-up situations..." John threw himself down onto the bed, which creaked alarmingly.

"Shit," he said. "You might be better off on the cot, Ro. I think this damn thing's about to fall apart. And the mattress must be, like, fifty fuckin' years old."

"Probably," I said. "So what's the story with Camila and her ex?"

John groaned and threw an arm over his face. "Motherfucker had to try to break into my place at four o'clock this morning. He musta followed Camila when she came over and sat outside all night waiting. I gotta admire his commitment, at least. Wish I could get that kinda performance outta my own guys sometimes."

He yawned, his arm still thrown over his eyes. "Anyway, the stupid fuck tried to come in through the bedroom window at 04:00. Guess he was gonna set us on fire."

"What?!?!"

"Obviously he didn't," John told me.

"Well...okay. So what happened?"

"I woke up 'cause I was thirsty and heard something at the window. Thought it was a tree—there's a big-ass tree right next to that window—so I didn't pay any attention to it at first, but when I came back from getting a glass of water, something didn't seem right. Camila'd woken up and she said she'd been having a nightmare about monsters trying to come in through the window. She was pretty freaked. That's not like her, so we went over to the window to prove to ourselves there weren't any monsters there—and found Mr. Ex prying it open."

"What'd you do about it?" I asked.

"Camila screamed bloody murder and opened the window all the way and punched him in the face so hard he fell off his ladder and crashed onto the concrete sidewalk two stories below," John said.

"Jeez. Well, understandable under the circumstances."

"Yeah. He looked like he'd been winded pretty good, but I wanted to make sure he didn't get away, so I jumped out the window after him." John paused, grimaced, and rubbed his knee. "Seemed like a good idea at the time. Twenty years ago it wouldn't have been a problem, but my fuckin' knees let me know it was a dumbass move. But I crawled over and put him in a chokehold until the cops came."

"So he's been arrested?" I asked. "He's not threatening you anymore?"

"Oh, he threatened me plenty," John said. "But he's currently nursing multiple broken bones in custody, so I don't think he's gonna be hurting anyone anytime soon. The cops found a can of gasoline and a book of matches on him, so it looks like he was planning on setting fire to the apartment."

"My God," I said.

"Yeah, good thing Camila punched him in the face in time, huh?"

"I'm sure you would have punched him at least as well if she hadn't been able to," I said encouragingly.

"No fuckin' shit, but I like the fact that she got to get her justice in like that, don't you? I'm hoping it makes her feel better about herself. She was pretty down about it afterwards. Freaked out about almost getting flambéed in her own bed, of course, but also guilty about having such horrible taste in men, and putting me in danger, and causing me to jump out the window and fight with her ex while buck-ass naked."

"Wait...you were naked for all of this?" I asked.

"As a motherfuckin' jaybird," John said cheerfully. "Certainly gave the cops quite an eyeful when they showed up. Camila brought some clothes out for me while we were waiting, but I didn't want to let go of her ex until he was cuffed and loaded up into a cop car. So I got to give everything a good airing and break the hearts of every cop who showed up. And all the neighbors who came out to see what the ruckus was, of course."

"Well," I said. "It's, um, good that you're not, um, easily embarrassed by that kind of thing."

"Yeah, so many people have seen my junk at this point that what's another dozen more? As long as they don't bite it off...speaking of which,

Ro, thanks a bunch for that whole thing about, what the fuck'd you call them, labiodentals."

"I couldn't think of anything else," I said. "So I told the truth."

"Yeah, well, not that I don't like a good laugh, but I think I strained a couple of ribs this morning, and holding it in tonight may have broken 'em."

"Do you need to see a doctor?" I asked.

"If I wake up in the middle of the night and start to worry that they've punctured a lung, I'll go get Mom," he said. "But I'm fine." He yawned. "Just tired. And worried about Camila. She seemed to be taking the whole thing a lot harder than she needed to be."

"Well," I said, "anyone would be pretty shaken up after something like that."

"Yeah, whatever, but it's not her fault, and I'm not blaming her for it, which is what she seemed to be the most afraid of, even though she wouldn't come right out and say it. She's way too tough to admit to something like that, you know? But...you know, it's weird: I've heard other people talk about just *knowing* what someone else is thinking, being in synch with 'em somehow, but I gotta be frank: I've never had that with a woman. Not even when we were fucking. Just guys I was under fire with. But at that moment...I don't know, it was really fuckin' weird, but I *knew* she was scared I was blaming her and I was going to leave her, so I just...fuck, you're gonna laugh, but I just dropped down on one knee and proposed to her on the spot."

"Wait...*what?!?* You *proposed* to her? What did she *say?!?!*"

"Shh, Ro, keep it down. Don't wanna interrupt the prayer session down the hall, and I'm too much of a coward to tell everyone out there about this yet. She burst into tears."

"And!?!"

"And then she said yes."

"So—John Ivanhoe Elladan Halley, are you *engaged?!?* To be *married?!?*"

"You don't need to sound so shocked about it," he said, but he was grinning. "Yeah, I'm engaged. Although I won't feel good about it till I get her a ring. I felt real bad about not having one, but it was just kinda...I just got swept up in the moment, you know? But as soon as I asked her, I knew it was the right thing to do, and she was gonna say yes, and...to be honest, Ro, I know it makes me sound like a sap, but this is maybe the happiest day of my life. I just worry a little about the ring. I mean, what kinda girl says 'Yes' when there's not even a ring? How's she gonna know I'm serious about it if I don't put out? It were me, I'd expect a guy to be on the hook for at least a grand before I even thought about it."

"You're not a sap," I said. "And you'd just jumped—naked—out a second-story window to defend her. I think she could feel a reasonable amount of confidence in your seriousness."

"Yeah...anyway, timing kinda sucked, 'cause I had to come up here right afterwards. I offered to stay, but she said no, this was important, so I came...but I'm heading home tomorrow afternoon, come hell or high water. I don't care what Dennis wants to talk to us about, I'm outta here by 15:00 tomorrow. I got a fiancée to get back to, a ring to buy...oh fuck, I guess we'd probably better start planning the wedding, huh?"

"I don't see any reason to put it off," I said. "It's not like you're getting any younger."

"Ouch, Ro, but fair point. Okay. I'm gonna look at potential rings tonight on my phone, narrow it down to the top few choices, and ask your opinion tomorrow morning."

"I think you should ask Camila's opinion," I said.

"She said she wanted something I'd like. But I just want something she'd like."

"Okay, well, I'll help you narrow it down, but you should definitely ask her once you get to the top three," I said. "I've never even met her in person, remember? Although now we need to set up a meeting ASAP."

"Okay. Will do." He yawned again. "Damn, I'm getting soft in my old age! I only missed a couple of hours of sleep and I'm about to pass out here. I'd better let you go, Ro, so I can start ring shopping before I fall into a coma."

"Sounds good," I said, getting up and turning to go.

"Oh, and Ro?" he said as I reached for the door. "What about you? Seems wrong for a fuck-up like me to get married before a goody-two-shoes like you. When am I gonna be blinded by a ginormous rock on your left ring finger?"

"I don't know," I said, and slipped away before he could ask anything further.

21

JOHN CAME INTO MY ROOM at 6:30 the next morning with a list of potential ring options and a request not to tell anyone about it until he'd made it official.

"Once she says yes, I think it's official," I said.

"Yeah, but I'm not gonna feel good about it till I see that ring on her finger. It's like putting down earnest money, isn't it? You can talk all you want about how you want to buy a house, but until you put that earnest money down, it's all just hot air." He paused. "At least, that's what I think. I've never bought a house. *Or* gotten engaged. Oh fuck! Camila's probably gonna want to buy a house, won't she? She's just renting an apartment right now, same as me, but she's probably already house shopping as we speak."

"Quite possibly," I said.

"This is fuckin' terrifying," John said, but he was grinning as he said it.

Breakfast was as pleasant and polite as it could be, given who was around the table. We finished in good time and got ready for church. This time my mother had intentionally brought a skirt for me, so dressing was less fraught than last time, and we were all sufficiently dowdily attired when we set off.

The service was very similar to last time. So much so, in fact, that I found it a little tedious, but everyone else appeared to be swept away by it. Everyone other than John, of course, who had installed himself at the very end of the pew and was struggling to contain his boredom and scorn.

Things livened up for him towards the end of the service when, just like last time, Isaiah made his way down the outside of the pews towards the front doors. He slowed down as he passed our pew, reached across John, and passed me a folded piece of paper. Then he continued on his way out the church.

"*What the fuck?!?*" John whispered in my ear.

I glanced around. Alexandra, who was on my right, was watching Jeremiah Jones with rapt attention. I unfolded the piece of paper.

Meet me in the parking lot. **_Need to talk_**.

John read the note over my shoulder and raised his brows at me.

"*I'll tell you later,*" I mouthed at him.

This gave us something to think about for the rest of the service, and what felt like only a few minutes later we were all singing and dancing our way down the aisle. I tried to keep it restrained and not accidentally sway and shimmy too much.

When we got out and everyone gathered in knots and clumps to chat and gossip, I slipped off into the overflow parking lot. Isaiah was waiting there, leaning against his motorcycle.

"Nice dancing," he said. "I caught the last few seconds of the performance. You got any training?"

"No," I said. "And, um, I was trying to keep it down."

He grinned. "I don't think you could keep it down if St. Peter himself was telling you that was the only way to get into heaven." His grin faded. "I always liked music," he said. "Whenever I hear it, I want to dance so bad it hurts. When I was a little kid, I'd dance and dance for hours. But after Mom died, Dad took away all my music, said dancing was wrong. All through high school I was never allowed to go to any dances. I went a few times in college, but I always felt so weird, like there was all this dancing inside of me trying to get out, but I was trapped in a steel suit and couldn't move like I knew I should. When Dad started doing the music and dancing to end the services, I worked with him to pick the songs, 'cause I could just *feel* 'em move through me. But the first time he saw me dance to 'em, he got this weird look on his face, said I shouldn't be part of it. That's why I always leave early. We say it's to deal with stuff after the service, but it's really to keep me away from the music and the dancing."

"Oh," I said. *What a waste*, I thought. With his good looks and charisma, Isaiah probably could have had a real career as a dancer. I knew a lot of people who desperately wanted to be dancers but didn't actually have the bodies, the rhythm, or, let's be frank, the looks to make it in the big time. But Isaiah certainly did have the body and the face, and he exuded the air of someone with more feel for music than he knew what to do with.

"Maybe you could take ballroom lessons or something," I said. "I think there are a clubs that do ballroom, salsa, swing, that kind of thing."

"Maybe." He shook his shoulders (rhythmically, I thought), and pushed himself away from his bike. "But that's not what I asked you here for. I wanted to tell you that I think the police are gonna raid soon."

"What? Why?"

"'Cause we're criminals, that's why."

"*You're* not," I said.

"I am a little bit," he said. "I knew or guessed about a lot of stuff that I should have spoken up about, but didn't. I signed off on checks I probably shouldn't have signed off on. I definitely cashed checks I shouldn't have cashed. I'm part of this, Rowena, and when they take my dad down, they're gonna take me down as well."

"Why now?" I asked. "Is it because of Heather?"

He shook his head. "I don't think so. In fact, I told her about it yesterday and she said she didn't know anything about it. No, we got a notification that we're gonna get audited. I checked and the IRS can only audit churches if a 'high-level Treasury official' has a 'reasonable belief' based on written documents that the church is cheating on their taxes. Heather's article hasn't come out, and I don't think she'd turn us in before she finished it. I think someone else must have turned us in."

"Do you know who?" I asked.

He shook his head. "I wish I could say it was me, but it's not. The only person I've talked to about this other than you is Heather." He squinted at me. "It wasn't you, was it?"

Now I shook my head. "No, I wanted to leave the field clear for Heather to do her thing, too. I told my brother a little bit about it. Oh, and Roseanna—my aunt. But they haven't said anything about going to the IRS."

"Well, we've got auditors coming on Monday, so someone did something." He shrugged. "I can't say I'm thrilled about it, but I'm kinda looking forward to having this off my back, you know? Like, even if I end up going to prison—"

"Surely they won't send you to prison over this!" I exclaimed. "This isn't your fault!"

"Yeah, but I've still been part of it, like I said. But whatever happens, it'll be a relief to get it over with. At least, that's how I'm feeling right now. But I wanted to let you know. Maybe you can warn Dennis and Alexandra about it. I know you want to get them out of the church; maybe this will help you do it."

"Maybe," I said. "Thanks. And good luck. I hope they don't come after you, too. You've been trying to make this right all along."

He shrugged again. "Sort of. Anyway, I really do have to go prepare for this audit, so I guess we won't be going out tonight." He smiled with one side of his face, but his eyes were bleak. "Too bad. I could have used even a fake date to give me something to look back on when I'm in prison."

"You don't know that you're going to prison," I said. "At the very least, surely you can do a plea deal to provide evidence in exchange for a lighter sentence. Do you know any good lawyers?"

"We got some of the top lawyers in Christiansburg right here," he said, nodding towards the front of the church. "I'm sure some of them will step up if we need them."

"Okay, good. And, um, keep in touch, okay? Let me know how it goes. Or if you need any help."

"Will do," he said. "And thanks. Most real girlfriends would have already dumped me, but here you are offering to stand by me through thick and thin." He suddenly stepped closer, put his arms around me, and kissed my cheek.

"Sorry if that was too much," he said, releasing me and stepping back. "I just needed...I guess I needed at least the illusion of having someone in my life who cares about me."

"I'm sure you have lots of people who care about you," I said auto-matically.

"Yeah, but you and Heather are the only ones who've actually helped me." Now he smiled with both sides of his mouth. "Maybe I should try that with her, whaddya think?"

I reflected. "I think she might actually like it," I said. "But only if you do it right. Otherwise, I think you might get smacked in the face."

"Isn't that always the way," said Isaiah.

22

"WELL?" ALEXANDRA ASKED when I rejoined the group. They were just saying their goodbyes to the two older couples they'd been chatting with. She gave me a conspiratorial look. "Are you on for tonight?"

John took a step closer, not at all subtly eavesdropping.

"Isaiah has something going on tomorrow morning he has to prep for," I said. "He won't have time to go out tonight."

"Oh. Well...it's nice that he wanted to tell you that in person, though, isn't it?"

"Yes," I said. "And he really does have something very important going on, that he wanted to tell me about in private." I tried to give John a meaningful look, but only ended up giving it to Alexandra instead. She smiled encouragingly in response, looking very pleased. I resisted the urge to groan. The more she thought there was something going on between me and Isaiah, the more she was going to be disappointed when the truth—about the church, about me and Dima—came out.

We drove home and had what I believed would have been called back in the day a cold collation. It included traditional delicacies such as jello salad with canned fruit. As a child I hadn't been allowed to eat that kind of thing, which my mother considered to be disgusting and unhealthy. John and I had both told ourselves we were going to eat all the jello salads and cream pies we could manage when we went off to college. Both of us had separately discovered that our mother was right and they were, in fact, disgusting. And now scientific research was showing they were unhealthy as well. Score two for Mom. But Alexandra apparently still believed that it wasn't proper entertaining without a quivering pile of sugar and artificial coloring in the middle of the table.

"Well," said Dennis when we were done. The cold collation had been finished off with a banana cream pie, which my father had run out and gotten first thing in the morning. When she'd found out, Alexandra had told him he didn't have to do it, but when she brought out the pie, she told Dennis that Bobby had gotten it specially for him. Dennis had made a face, but had devoured two pieces.

"It's his favorite dish, and one of the few things he can eat much of," Alexandra had whispered to me, as I'd tried to gag down a few spoonfuls of the overly sweet, sticky pie. "The chemo kills his appetite, you know, and causes his mouth to burn. I know it's not good for him, but starvation's even worse."

I'd nodded in agreement and concentrated on forcing down another spoonful of what had to be one of my least favorite dishes of all time.

But now the banana cream pie was safely down—I hoped—and Alexandra was clearing the table, and Dennis was obviously about to start the conversation that he'd brought us all here for.

"Well," he repeated. "I'm glad you all are able to be here with us. I know Alexandra and I both appreciate the effort you've made to come here, and to reconnect with us after all these years. I know Alexandra wishes things had been different and she'd been able to be in your life more. She hasn't been the mother and grandmother she wishes she could have been, but she's trying to make up for that now."

My father, who was sitting next to me, stiffened. I couldn't tell if he was upset by the reference to the admittedly terrible things that Alexandra had done in the past, or the fact that Dennis was putting all the blame on her and not acknowledging his part in it.

Alexandra, who had been in the kitchen and (I hoped) out of earshot, came back into the dining room and stood behind Dennis, one hand on his shoulder, like a wife in a nineteenth-century portrait. "Have you started yet, Dennis?" she asked.

"I'm getting to it." Irritation flashed across his face, making the veins on his sunken cheeks stand out redly, but he swallowed it down and continued.

"As you know, the Good Lord has seen fit to send me a trial. He's sent me plenty in the past, but apparently he decided I needed another one, because he gave me cancer. We thought I might beat it, but the latest round of treatments haven't been as effective as we'd hoped. We're going to continue fighting, because the Good Lord helps those who help themselves, but the doctors say I should put my affairs in order, just in case."

We all nodded solemnly. The more Dennis talked, the less I liked him, but there was something about being addressed by my dying grandfather that was making me feel extra-serious, and possibly...oh dammit, was I tearing up?

"We've got a good bit saved up, and of course, the house," Dennis said, waving his frail hand to indicate the house. "Alexandra and I have discussed this, and we've agreed that once one of us goes, the other one will move into assisted living."

Alexandra made a slight face. I guessed that she was expecting to be the one to move into assisted living, and wasn't thrilled by the idea.

"We've set aside money for that, but we should still have some left over to take care of our grandchildren. And, of course, the house. John." Dennis turned to him. "As we discussed before, we want to leave you the house. But on the condition that you join the church, tithe to it regularly, and get married to someone in it. It's long past time that you settled down and started acting like the head of the family that you are."

My father made a face and shifted in his seat, but then, with an obvious effort of will, sat still again. My mother appeared to be attempting to disappear into her chair. I tried to imitate her. Yes, it was sexist and unfair for John to get everything, but frankly, I didn't want to have to deal with any gifts from Dennis and Alexandra, so let him reap the rewards of being the firstborn and the eldest male, whether he wanted them or not. It was a little harsh to pass right over my father, but he'd explicitly stated he was putting up with this solely to benefit me and John.

"Uh, well, thank you," John said. Even he was looking serious. "I appreciate it, I really do. But I still have to live where the Marines tell me to."

"But your term of service will be up soon?" Dennis pressed.

"Well, yes, but..."

"And you still don't have any plans for what to do with yourself afterwards?"

"I'm looking into going to law school," said John.

"There are several excellent law schools right here in Virginia," Dennis said. "You can live here, in your own home, while you work on getting your JD."

"Uh, I suppose so," said John.

"So you'll agree?" said Dennis.

"I appreciate the offer of the house, I really do," said John. "And the church has been very, uh, welcoming to me. I don't mind attending services while I'm here, as long as it's running." He gave me a brief glance, and then continued. "But I can't agree to marry someone from it. You see, I already asked someone to marry me, and she said yes."

"Camila?!?" my mother cried. "Are you engaged to Camila?!?"

"Yes," John said firmly. "And I'm not breaking my word to her, not for anything."

My father jumped up from his chair and hugged John, giving him his heartiest congratulations. My mother joined him, although she was too choked up with what I hoped was joy to actually say anything.

"Well," said Dennis, when my parents' effusions of delight had calmed down enough for him to get a word in edgewise, "I see you've already decided to settle down. I wish it had been with a woman from the church, but I hope this 'Camila' is a worthy helpmeet for you. From what you've told us about her so far, I have a hard time seeing her as a good wife and mother, but the Lord moves in mysterious ways."

"She's about the only one who'll put up with me, so she's got that going for her," said John, but he was grinning now. "Seriously, she's hardworking and responsible, and smart as a whip. But she's licensed to practice law in North Carolina, not Virginia. I'll have to discuss any plans with her before I agree to anything."

"Of course," said Dennis. "Bring her up here so we can meet her, and we can discuss the appropriate steps to take regarding the house and your share of the money then. We're planning on leaving the bulk of our estate to the church, of course, but we want to make sure you're provided for."

"Sure thing," said John.

My parents sat back down. The mood in the room was distinctly lighter. I was hoping the talk was over, and we could all get on with congratulating John, and…I wasn't sure what else we could do to kill time this afternoon—plan the wedding! That should furnish enough conversation for three weekends…

"Rowena," said Dennis sharply. He curled his thin upper lip as he said it. It was almost imperceptible, but not quite. "You know, I never asked: Do you really *like* your name? We told your parents not to give it to you, but they insisted anyway."

"I do," I said. Okay, there had been times that "Rowena Arwen" had caused me some minor embarrassment, but on the other hand, I'd never been one of six Catelyns or Jennifers or Elizabeths or Jessicas in a room, so my name had that going for it. No one ever forgot me or mixed me up with anyone else.

"Very well. Now, we wanted to make sure to provide for you as well. We want to set up a trust fund in your name. It will have a starting value of $250,000. We will of course add to it if we can, and it should grow with the market."

"Two hundred and fifty…that's, um, very generous…" I said. My lips felt numb, and shadows flickered in my peripheral vision.

"As with John, we have stipulations, of course. We want to ensure that you, too, settle down and find yourself in a stable situation, especially given your, as I understand it, precarious career." His upper lip curled slightly again. "We hope this will enable you to give up your job, such as it is, and settle down to start a family—if it isn't too late, that is."

"Um," I said faintly. "That's, ah, very kind of you…"

"So as with John, access to the trust fund is contingent upon you joining the church, tithing to it regularly, and marrying someone from the congregation. As I understand it, there is reason to be optimistic on that score: Alexandra tells me you have developed a connection with Isaiah Jones?"

"Well…" I said. "Um…"

He waved a hand dismissively. "I know better than to ask a woman to tell the truth about her relationship with a man, but I saw you slip off to talk to him after service this morning. If you're going to be slipping off to talk to men, I suppose Isaiah Jones isn't the worst choice you could make, although he does have a bit of a reputation."

"But he's straightened up *beautifully* since he's rejoined the church!" Alexandra added anxiously. "Rowena, my dear, you have to see that we *care* about you and we want you to have the same happiness and good fortune we've had"—I felt my father stiffen beside me again, but he managed to stay silent—"and, well, if you *could* end up marrying Isaiah—or any other decent man from the church—we'd be ever so happy for you, and, well, I've really enjoyed getting to know you, and, well, it's not a happy thing to talk of or even think about, but if I do, well, end up alone and in an assisted living place, well, having you settled down nearby would make it so much easier for me to face..." She trailed off, clearly having a lot more to say about her lack of desire to go into assisted living, but unwilling to say it in front of Dennis, who was looking more and more irritated.

"I understand," I said. "And I'd like to be able to help you out in whatever way I could. And Isaiah is a very nice man, in his own way. But I can't make any promises."

"Of course not, of course, but you'll *think* about it, won't you? You'll at least try?"

"Um..." I said.

"I mean, it's not like you're likely to find anyone better than Isaiah," Alexandra pressed. "He's so handsome and charming, don't you agree? And if, well, if you don't *quite* feel in love with him at first, well, that kind of thing can grow with time. So please, *please,* Rowena, tell me you'll give it a try. Haven't you enjoyed spending time with him so far?"

To lie, or not to lie? Give them false hope now in order to ease Dennis's last days, or tell them the truth?

"Isaiah is very nice, but I really don't think we are likely to get married," I said. "We, um, had a nice evening together, but I don't think we'll ever be more than friends."

"Oh, but...*why*?" demanded Alexandra. "Is there some *other* man who's caught your eye? Someone else from the church?" she asked hopefully.

"No," I said. "But you see, I'm actually, um, in a relationship with someone else. A very serious relationship."

My father stiffened again. A grimace of pain crossed my mother's face. John, to my surprise, smiled slightly.

"Oh, but then...it can't have been that serious if you've been going out with Isaiah...Rowena, *what* have you been up to?" Alexandra demanded. "Have you been leading that poor boy on? I thought you were better than that!"

"Well..." I said. *Oh God. Better just come out with the truth. It'll less painful in the long run.* "Isaiah and I were never dating," I said. "He just wanted to talk to me about some stuff. But we both knew it was nothing more than that. You see"—I looked down at the table—"I'm actually engaged to someone else."

Audible gasps rose from everyone else in the room. They all opened their mouths to speak.

"So why were you running around with Isaiah, then?" Dennis asked, beating everyone else's exclamations to the punch. There was something sharp in his eyes, something that made me see that, no matter how much I might not like it, I'd gotten some of my brains from him.

"Well..." I said. "You see..."

Rat-tat-tat!

We all jumped. Someone was knocking at the door.

Rat-tat-tat!

It wasn't hard enough to be the police, but it was sharp and full of determination. After a moment's pause, Alexandra rose and went to answer it.

We heard her heave the door open with a creak. Another short pause. Then she shrieked, "What on EARTH are *you* doing here?!?!"

23

THERE WAS A GENERAL scramble for the door, which John won handily. I came in second, my knee letting me know it didn't appreciate this kind of mistreatment after yesterday's long drive.

I didn't know who I was expecting to find at the door, but it hadn't been Roseanna. That, though, was who was standing there. Alexandra was leaning against the door knob as if that was the only thing keeping her upright, her mouth open in slackjawed horror.

"Aren't you going to invite me in, Alexandra?" Roseanna asked. She nodded at the rest of us as we arrived, panting, at the door. "John. So good to finally see you in person after all these years. Rowena. Bobby and Bev. Dennis. Aren't you going to invite your own sister inside?"

"You're no sister of mine." Dennis was too out of breath from the dash to the door to snarl, but there was something feral and angry in his gasping.

"That's where you're wrong, Dennis. We are definitely brother and sister. Alexandra, stop gaping and let me in."

Alexandra moved obediently aside, still speechless with shock. Roseanna stepped briskly inside. I wouldn't exactly say she strode like a young lion, but she moved pretty spryly for a woman in her 80s as she went past all of us and straight for the dining room.

"Still the same," she said when she came to a stop by the dining room table. "Alexandra, I know you've had a lot on your mind, but couldn't you refresh your décor once a decade? I swear I recognize every inch of everything in this room, and time has not been kind to it."

I involuntarily looked around. Indeed, the paint was fading, the curtains were shabby, and the furniture had been in style back when I'd been a child. I just didn't tend to notice or care about that kind of thing. Not so Roseanna, apparently.

"You know you're not welcome here." Dennis had drawn himself upright and was fixing Roseanna with a glare that was supposed to look imposing but was only irritated.

"I know, and I've stayed away for all this time, respecting your blamefool wishes even though they didn't deserve it, but I've had enough. The time has come, Dennis, for you to face the truth. I know it's never been your strong suit, but you're past eighty and could be coming to the end of your time here on this earth, so you'd better do this now. And I can't let you ruin their lives"—she nodded at me and John—"over a lie."

"I don't know what you're talking about!" I'd heard the phrase "sputtered his words" before, but this was the first time I'd ever seen it in action. Dennis was undeniably sputtering. Outrage, I thought, and maybe also a little bit of guilt. He knew on some level that what Roseanna was saying was true. He just didn't want to face it.

"Jeremiah Jones and the Church of the Holy Light," Roseanna told him. "Jeremiah never was one of the righteous, not even when he was acting right on the surface. Always too smooth and eager to please. And now he's committing tax fraud and running guns to Africa."

"What?!?!" cried Alexandra. My mother looked shocked too. My father only looked resigned. And Dennis looked guilty.

"You're talking through your hat, Roseanna, like always," he said.

"I wish I were, Dennis. I wish the church that has brought you and Alexandra a little comfort at long last deserved the faith you've given it. But it's nothing but a shiny surface on top and a lot of greed underneath, just like the man who made it."

"You're making this up," Dennis said. "You're just saying this because you want to stop us from leaving our money to the church. *You're* the one who's greedy." He spoke firmly, but I could hear the doubt and desperation underneath.

"Yes, I *am* saying this to stop you from leaving your money to the church, Dennis, but the reason I don't want you to leave your money to the church is because it doesn't deserve it. If you're going to leave your money to anyone, leave it to *them*." She nodded again at me and John.

"We were just discussing the legacies we plan to leave them!" Dennis said defensively. "We're planning to take care of them, don't you worry! And what would you know about taking care of family anyway. *You've* never had one. *You've* never bothered to take a husband or have children. Why should anyone listen to *you* about family responsibility? All you've ever cared about is yourself and your career!"

"And Bobby," said Roseanna. "I cared about Bobby. When Alexandra...was too sick to take care of him, and you were talking about putting him in foster care"—my parents both gasped in shock—"yes, foster care!" Roseanna continued resolutely. "I never told anyone, but I'm telling everyone now so they know what it was like for us all back then! You were desperate and at the end of your rope, you couldn't bring yourself to care for your own son, you were talking of putting him in foster care or giving him up for adoption"—"WHAT!!" screamed Alexandra.

"She's making it up!" insisted Dennis, but his face said she wasn't.

"You couldn't bring yourself to take care of him and you wanted to give him up," Roseanna went on firmly. "So I stepped up and took him in. You said I never bothered with a family, but *Bobby* is my family. I raised him when you couldn't. You know, I was on the verge of getting married then. Do you remember Bill Perkins? We'd been going steady for a while then, and were talking of getting married. It was almost settled. But then you and Alexandra...had your troubles, and someone needed to take care of Bobby, so I did. Bill got resentful of all the time I was spending on him, said he wasn't going to be the father to some other man's child, and broke things off. And after that there weren't a lot of other suitors. No one wanted a woman whose every spare minute was taken up with caring for her brother's child."

"My God!" my father exclaimed. "I'm...I'm so sorry..."

"Don't be," Roseanna told him crisply. "You saved me a lot of trouble and heartbreak, Bobby. Imagine if I'd married one of them and only discovered afterwards what a selfish bastard he was. What if Bill and I had already gotten married by the time you came along, and he tried to stop me from taking you in? I'd have had to divorce him, and I don't generally believe in divorce. No, Bobby, taking care of you was the best thing I ever did. The fact that it drove away all the shallow, selfish men who were sniffing around me like hound dogs was merely a bonus."

"Oh," said my father. "Well..."

"So don't you dare tell me I don't know anything about taking care of family, Dennis Halley. I'd say of all of us here in this room, I'm the one who knows the most about it. I'm the one who's stepped in when someone needed to step in, and stepped out when someone needed to step out, no matter how much it cost me. I stepped in and took Bobby when it needed to be done, and I stepped out and left him and Bev to raise him"—she nodded at John—"on their own, even when I thought they were making a hash of it. I'm glad to say I was wrong about that, or maybe you just can't ruin good material.

"And then I stepped out again when you and Alexandra left our church to follow Jeremiah Jones. I knew he was a snake-oil salesman, but I hoped he wasn't a snake, and you'd tried everything else and it hadn't brought you any peace, so I thought you might as well try his special brand of snake oil, no matter how much it pained me to lose you to him. But I was wrong there too. Now I'm stepping in again to tell you we were all wrong, Dennis. You were wrong to believe anything that Jeremiah told you, and I was wrong to let you go. But I'm here to right that wrong now. And I'm starting by telling you that Jeremiah is a liar, a fraud, and a criminal. Auditors are going to show up tomorrow to start an investigation into tax fraud. It wouldn't surprise me if the FBI followed closely on their heels to look into this gunrunning he's supposedly doing with church money."

"Where are you getting these crazy stories?" Dennis demanded. "This is nonsense! Jeremiah isn't getting audited!"

"Tell him, Rowena," Roseanna said.

"Actually, um, that's what Isaiah wanted to tell me today," I said. "That's what he'll be busy with tonight. Preparing for the arrival of auditors tomorrow morning."

"And no doubt by 'preparing' he means 'trying to cover up as much as possible,'" said Roseanna. "But from what I hear, the IRS has already dug up a lot of damning evidence on them. This audit will just be the icing on the fraudulent cake."

"So you're getting this nonsense from Rowena!?" Dennis cried. "She's the one feeding you this, this *bullshit*!?"

"No," said Roseanna calmly. "It was Bobby."

24

AUDIBLE GASPS ALL AROUND.

"Actually," Roseanna continued, "I initially got it from a journalist who's investigating the church. She approached me because she heard I might have an axe to grind with it. I said I did, but unfortunately, I didn't have a lot of information on it. But we kept in touch, and I pointed her Bobby's way, since I knew he'd been going to services regularly these past few months. Bobby got in touch with me afterwards, and we've been communicating ever since. He told me about the progress she's made in her investigation, and the potential audit tomorrow—and that he and everyone else was going to be here this weekend, and could I help stage an intervention."

"An intervention!" Dennis exclaimed. "We're not...how dare you talk to us like we're lowlife addicts!"

"You might not be lowlifes, but you are addicts, Dennis," Roseanna told him. "You're so addicted to the false good feelings the church gives you that you're ignoring all the real blessings you have. Yes, I know you're ill, maybe dying, and it's a terrible thing, but look at all the good things you have! You've had a heavy burden laid upon you, it's true, but you've also been given grace beyond all your deserts. You have a wife who's standing by your side, a son and daughter-in-law who've come to stand by you despite everything, and two grandchildren who've come back into your life even though you've done nothing but push them away. Only the Lord Above knows how much time you have left, Dennis, but however much it is, don't waste it! You've been given something precious to spend your last days on; don't throw them away on a con man and his false church."

"Seems like you're the deceivers here," Dennis said. His initial rage had passed, and an ugly expression of resentment was filling his face. "You're the ones who've been going behind my back—you, and Bobby, and Rowena—I never did trust her, I always knew she was a snake in the grass..."

"Dennis!"

It was Alexandra. She had been listening, white-faced and silent, for all of this, but now she burst out.

"You and Roseanna can say whatever you like to each other, call each other whatever names you like, but you will not slander my only granddaughter in front of me!"

She stopped. Everyone looked astonished at her outburst, her most of all.

"I'm sorry about letting you think there was something romantic between me and Isaiah," I said. "He asked for my help, and this was the easiest way we could think of to do it. But, um, I didn't feel good about deceiving you, and, um, I'm really glad to have gotten to know you." And I meant it. If I'd been asked ahead of time, I would have said I didn't want someone like Alexandra for my grandmother. But I had her, and she was turning, against all odds, into a halfway-decent representative of the species.

"Well..." she said. "I suppose...if what Roseanna says is true...I can't believe it, but..." She turned to me. "Never mind the church," she said. "We have more important things to think about. Is it true you're getting married? You and John both?"

"It is," I confirmed.

She clasped her hands together. "A double wedding!"

John opened his mouth to object. I shot him a death glare. He shut it.

"Maybe we can introduce you to Dima and Camila soon," I said.

"Yeah, and you can introduce the rest of us to Dima as well," John said, deflecting the second death glare I sent his way.

"What? Well...I see we have a lot to discuss...Dennis! Dennis, are you okay?"

Dennis was clutching the table with one hand and his chest with the other.

"I...I think I got a little too riled up..." he gasped.

My mother jumped forward and felt his pulse. "Do you feel dizzy?" she asked. "Stick your tongue out."

Dennis gave her an outraged look.

"I want to see if your facial muscles are responding symmetrically," she told him.

He only glared at her more.

"State your name and date of birth," she told him. "Can you smile?"

More glaring.

My mother peered into one eye and then the other. "Bobby," she said, "go get the car. John, help me walk him to the door."

Dennis moved his mouth, but no sound came out.

"We're going to take you to the ER," my mother said calmly. "Alexandra, the closest hospital is Presbyterian, isn't that right?"

"Yes...the ER?" Alexandra had gone white again.

My mother pulled out her phone while John came over and put his arms around Dennis. She checked the map app and said, "Less than ten minutes away. Good. John, as gently as you can. Dennis, you try to stay calm and we'll get you to help. Rowena, you stay here with Alexandra and look after her."

A minute later John had half-carried Dennis out the door, put him in the car, and they were gone.

25

AS SOON AS THE OTHERS were gone, Alexandra sank down onto a chair, gripping the table as if she were about to faint, too.

"I don't feel so good," she said weakly.

"And no wonder," Roseanna told her. "You've had a shocking day and isn't even midafternoon yet. Pull yourself together and let me get you a glass of water."

I reached into my purse and palmed my car keys just in case this half of the party also needed to make a quick trip to the ER, but after resting a bit and drinking a glass of water, Alexandra revived enough to make it to the den under her own power.

My mother texted me then to say that they'd checked in at the hospital and were going through triage, and a few minutes later to say that Dennis was alert and answering questions but they were concerned he might have had a minor stroke and were sending him to get a rapid CT scan.

"Dennis is alert and answering questions," I told Alexandra and Roseanna. "They're sending him to get a CT scan just in case."

"Why a CT scan?" Alexandra asked.

"Um, in case...just to rule out a minor stroke," I said.

She burst into tears.

"Pull yourself together, Alexandra," Roseanna told her crisply. "You heard Rowena: he's alert and talking. This is just a precaution."

"I'm sorry." Alexandra sniffed and dabbed at her nose, but the tears kept trickling out. "It's just...I know I can't keep him forever, but...and...and I'm so selfish!" she burst out. "Every time I think about losing him, I think about how I agreed to go into assisted living so we could give the house to John, and...and...and I don't want to!" she finished fiercely. "I hate the thought of leaving this house, and I hate the thought of living in some kind of center, among strangers, even more! I think...sometimes I even pray that God will take me soon, just so I don't have to go through that!"

"I'm sure John would be happy for you to continue living in the house," I said.

"Oh, but...he's getting married...surely his wife won't want some strange old woman in her house...and...and...and to be honest...I'm so selfish...I don't know that I could stand to go live in the guest room and see some other woman as mistress of my home of the last fifty years!"

"First of all, even if they do decide to move up to Virginia, it will take John and Camila a while to sort themselves out," I said. "John still has to finish up his time in the Marines, so he won't be leaving Camp Lejeune until next year at the earliest. If he does decide to go to law school, he'll have to apply this fall to get in next fall. And Camila is licensed to practice law in North Carolina. If she wants to move her practice to Virginia, she'll have to pass the Virginia bar exam first. They won't be able to move here for another twelve to eighteen months at the least. And I'm sure if they knew how you felt about moving out of this place, they'd insist that you stay."

"Yes, but the whole point of this was to make sure John and his wife could be settled somewhere stable and safe, somewhere that has ties to his family!"

"And I'm sure John appreciates that, but I'm also sure he'd hate for you to be miserable," I said. "That would make him miserable too. He's not happy unless he's being a hero, after all. You can still leave him the house in your will, and stay here as long as you like."

"Well...it's not what Dennis and I agreed...Dennis is dead set on John moving into this house...sometimes I think it's the only thing that makes him happy, the only thing that keeps him going..."

"What Dennis doesn't know won't hurt him," Roseanna said sharply. "You can leave John the house and work something out with him on the side. And if you're determined to get him into this house anyway, well, then, don't go live in a nursing home"—she and Alexandra both made involuntary faces of disgust as she said the words—"if you don't want to. You know you'll always have a place with me, Alexandra."

"Oh. But..." Alexandra began, faltering. "But...you're older than me, Roseanna."

"We'll hire home health care if and when we need it," Roseanna told her. "I know I'm not the easiest person to live with, and we've had our differences in the past, but you'll still be better off with me than with whatever roommate they stick you with at whatever nursing home you end up in."

"Roommate!" exclaimed Alexandra in horror.

"Yes," Roseanna said firmly. "You often have to share a room, you know. So you might as well share a house with me instead."

"Yes...well...why are you doing this?" Alexandra demanded.

Roseanna gave her a steely look. "Is there anything you know about me that makes this out of character, Alexandra?"

"Well...no..."

"I'm making this offer for lots of reasons, including the fact that you're Bobby's mother and there's nothing I wouldn't do for him. But maybe the main one is that, deep down, I like you, Alexandra."

Alexandra stared at her in surprise.

"I know you're not a very likeable person at this point, Alexandra." Alexandra bridled at that, but Roseanna continued inexorably, "You have your reasons for that, and I know them and forgive them. But I liked the romantic young woman you were when you married Dennis, and now, God help me, I like the romantic old woman you are now, who's thrilled at the thought of a double wedding of your grandchildren and genuinely believes all that rose-tinted snake oil Jeremiah Jones is selling. Jeremiah is a sleazebag, but *you're* not, Alexandra. Deep down, you've got the pure heart that actually deserves the truth behind the cheap crap he's peddling. He's a fake, but deep down you're the real deal, Alexandra."

Alexandra opened her mouth, but no sound came out.

Roseanna waved her hand at her. "Don't worry about answering just yet if you can't find the words. You just sit there and listen while Rowena tells us about this man she's marrying. I'm sure we're all dying to know everything about him."

They both turned to look at me expectantly.

I cleared my throat. "Well," I said. "Um...he's a little hard to describe..."

26

THE OTHERS CAME BACK that evening with the news that the CT scan had shown no sign of a stroke.

"Probably just a dizzy spell from the chemo," my mother said calmly. "It's a common side effect. They recommend a follow-up soon, and so do I, but for the moment, Dennis appears to be fine and can go about his business as usual."

Alexandra burst into tears again at this news. Dennis was cranky, probably to hide his embarrassment and fear. Roseanna said she was glad to hear it, and shouldn't we think about supper?

Alexandra said despairingly that she hadn't even started on supper and she didn't know what to do. Roseanna said we could get takeout. This occasioned some back-and-forthing over what kind of takeout was acceptably elegant and healthful, but by 7:00pm we had been furnished with takeout from a local restaurant. By 8:00pm we were finished, and Dennis and Alexandra were both visibly drooping. Roseanna insisted they go to bed early, and said she would take her leave as well.

"But I'll be back tomorrow morning to see you all before you head out," she told me and John. Our parents were planning to stay for a few extra days to help out, but John had already put his departure back from this afternoon and was determined to leave at the crack of dawn the next morning, and I didn't want to leave Galina Ivanovna alone any longer than I had to. Besides, I had to pick Dima up at the airport on Tuesday.

Roseanna did show up at 7:00am the next morning, bearing bagels. She congratulated John again on his engagement and told him he had to bring Camila up to meet her as soon as possible. John promised he'd do what he could, but said in an aside to me that he wasn't showing Camila off to anyone until he got her a ring he could be proud of.

"*I'm sure she doesn't care about that,*" I whispered to him.

"*Yeah, but I do,*" he whispered back.

He was on the road by 8:00am. I'd wanted to leave then too, but my parents had convinced me to wait for a couple of hours in case Dennis wasn't feeling well again.

Dennis, however, seemed no worse than usual. My parents, I realized as we sat around the table, were determined to interrogate me about Dima, and were trying to lead the conversation in that direction.

I thought about stopping them, but that seemed wrong. They had a very natural and legitimate curiosity about him. I tried to say things that would make him look good in their eyes, but I could tell with every answer I gave that everyone else was more and more horrified by what I was saying. To them, I realized, he sounded like a semi-psychotic fanatic with no good economic prospects and the very real possibility of bringing death and destruction down on my head. Plus, he'd abandoned me as soon as things got hard, only to get back together with me once he needed my help, but had run off again, leaving me to care for his ailing mother.

Well, okay. There was a grain of truth in some of that. But...but...I remembered how our eyes had met when I'd met him at the airport in January. That was a much bigger truth, even if it was harder to explain. I remembered Roseanna's story of her almost-engagement that had gotten broken off when she'd taken in my father. Dima, I was sure, would never break things off between us if for some reason I had to take in a niece or nephew. Dima, I was sure, would insist on taking them in. Dima had a lot of problems, but he wasn't the kind of man who put his own selfish desires before the needs of a baby. And for me, that trumped money and titles and pretty much anything else.

I tried to explain this without saying it directly, since I didn't want to upset Dennis and Alexandra, but I could see by everyone's faces that I had failed utterly.

"Are you planning on a long engagement?" Alexandra asked, making it clear she hoped the answer was "Yes."

"No," I told them. "We'll probably do it this week."

"This week!" Alexandra and my mother both exclaimed in protest. "You can't possibly put together a wedding in a week!"

"We don't want a wedding," I said. "We want to get married."

"Well...well...but you'll let us know when it is, won't you?" Alexandra pressed. "So we can all be there?"

"Um..." I had zero desire to have Dennis and Alexandra come to whatever we ended up doing, which would necessitate inviting my grandparents—my *other* grandparents—as well, along with my parents, and John, and—I looked over at her and confirmed my guess—Roseanna also. That was a lot of organizing and hassle.

On the other hand, I didn't want to create some kind of scene around my wedding that would cause decades of enmity and estrangement and bad blood, as had happened with my parents.

"We'll figure something out," I said. "Maybe a reception that we can take a little more time to organize..."

"Is there a *reason* you're in such a blamed hurry?" Dennis demanded, an unpleasant expression on his face.

"Dennis!" Alexandra chastised him.

"There are bureaucratic reasons why having it official is desirable," I said. "Plus, it's my birthday this week. Might as well make it one to remember." I spoke flippantly, trying to lighten the mood, but the mention of my birthday only made my parents and Alexandra wince guiltily.

"Hmmph," said Dennis, still looking suspicious. My natural desire to tell the truth wanted to assure them all that I wasn't pregnant, but as the words started to rise up in my throat, so did a choking lump of tears.

Fortunately, my phone *pinged* just then.

"We told you to turn that thing off!" Dennis barked.

"Dennis..." Alexandra said soothingly. "It might be important..."

I looked at the screen. "It's from Isaiah," I said.

27

THE TEXT SAID, *The auditors have descended. It doesn't look good for Dad. And the article just came out. That looks even worse.*

Are you okay? I texted back.

I'm not being led away in handcuffs—for now, he wrote. *I'm sitting in a room by myself. They're keeping me and Dad apart. I've already said I'll tell them everything I know. I feel awful, but I'd feel even worse if I kept up the lie.*

I'm sorry, I wrote. *But I think you're doing the right thing.*

I hope so. Anyway, here's a link to the article. You can show it to Dennis and Alexandra if you think it will help. And you can tell them what's going on at the church right now.

Thanks, I wrote. *Let me know if there's anything I can do to help.*

Know any good bail bondsmen? JK :) I'm sure someone from the church will bail us out if we need it. I hate that, but I'll make use of it if I have to anyway.

Good luck! I texted.

I was about to tell everyone what Isaiah had told me, when another message came in, this time from Heather.

The article is live! She included a link too.

Congratulations! I wrote back.

Yeah, it's already getting a great response—and I hear the IRS is going through the church's books as we speak.

That is what I hear too, I wrote.

It's nice to know you've done something right :) :) And thanks for hooking me up with that Miranda kid and her boyfriend's problems—there might be another juicy story there. I should put you on retainer or something :) :)

No need, I wrote back. *I hope you can help Miranda and Jamal!*

"What does Isaiah have to say?" Alexandra was staring at me wide-eyed, aware that something bad had happened.

"IRS auditors are at the church right now," I said. Apologetically. I wasn't sorry the IRS was auditing the church, but I was sorry for the pain it was going to cause people like Alexandra and Isaiah.

"Oh my!" She clutched at her chest.

"And the article is out." I opened it and held up my phone.

Alexandra squinted at it. "I...I can't read it," she said tremulously. "Dennis, can you..."

Dennis turned his head away deliberately, refusing even to look at my phone.

"Read the article to us, Rowena," my father said. He spoke softly, but there was a steel in his voice that rarely appeared.

I started reading. In straightforward, hard-hitting prose, Heather laid out the formation of the Church of the Holy Light, its questionable tax practices and the ambiguities and loopholes around church income in the US in general, and then moved on to the gunrunning. She'd dug up a fair amount of information there, and concluded that Jeremiah Jones and several of the church deacons had knowingly supplied money for weapons being used in the current religious war in the Central African Republic. They'd then received a significant portion of the money back as "donations" from the warlords they were supporting, thus laundering the money and taking kickbacks simultaneously.

The Church of the Holy Light may have started off with noble intentions, she ended. *Many of its parishioners who spoke to me said it brought them support and comfort during the worst ordeals of their lives. But it used that support and comfort to line the pockets of its founder and senior members, and supply money and arms for a war that is currently devastating some of the poorest and most vulnerable people on the planet. The road to hell is paved with good intentions; we see that truth once again in the story of the Church of the Holy Light.*

"Nonsense!" Dennis snapped once I was done. "It's all a bunch of lies!"

"Oh, but Dennis...don't you remember...that collection for our sister church in Africa...there was talk then that the money might go for weapons for them to defend themselves...it was all just for self-defense!" Alexandra burst out. "We just wanted to help them defend themselves!"

"I know," I said.

"And the church *did* help us...so much...I'd felt torn apart, empty, destroyed, worthless, like life wasn't worth living, ever since...ever since my little girl..." She gave a great sob, then continued, her voice shaking, "More than half a century of sorrow, of wanting to die, and then Jeremiah came along...I don't care what else he's done, he saved *me!* He's done so much good in the world as well as..." She gestured at my phone.

"I know," I said.

Dennis pushed himself to his feet with both arms, and stood there, leaning against the table for support but glaring at me. "I think you should get out of here," he said.

"Dennis!" cried Alexandra.

"You've brought nothing but trouble since the day you arrived here—no, since the day you were born." His face was bright red, the veins purple and bulging, and he was visibly shaking.

"Maybe you'd better sit down," I said, as Alexandra cried out, "Dennis!" again.

"Don't 'Dennis' me!" he yelled, his face turning even redder.

"Sit down before you give yourself a stroke for real," I said.

He stared at me.

"I'm going to go now," I said. "I know it's been a lot to take in. But I didn't mean to hurt you, I promise. We all only wanted to help you. The church might have helped you at first, but it was going to drag you down in the end. I'm going to leave now so you can digest everything that's happened. I—"

My phone *pinged.* I checked it instinctively. Dima.

Inna, mama's test results have come in, but she's not confident enough of her English to understand them, and I don't speak doctor)))) Can you look at them and tell us what they mean? Here's the link.

That was followed by a second text.

And please hurry!! My nerves can't take much longer))))

28

I LOOKED AT MY MOTHER. "Care to explain some medical test results to me?" I asked.

"Are they yours? Is it anything serious?" Her forehead creased in concern.

"They're Galina Ivanovna's. They're to determine if she should continue the treatment or not."

"Oh. Oh!" My mother's face cleared with relief. "Renal disease isn't my area of specialization, but I can certainly take a look at them."

I brought up the results. My mother looked over them for a while in silence.

"These don't look too bad," she said eventually. "Stage One kidney failure, maybe Stage Two."

"She was Stage Four when she started the treatment," I said.

My mother stared at me. "Really?!?!"

"Really," I confirmed.

"Well, in that case, this is...this is *excellent*. So many of my patients could use this...of course, I'm sure it will be out of the reach of most of them, but still...the existence of something like this is a cause for hope for all of us...please tell her I'm thrilled for her."

"I will," I said.

"And I hope to meet her soon."

"I'll tell her," I said. My mother appeared to have gone from being dead set against Dima and everything to do with him, to having warm thoughts for his mother, at least. Galina Ivanovna had engaged her doctorly feelings, causing a paradigm shift in her emotions.

"I'd really better go now," I said. "Galina Ivanovna is waiting for me to come home."

Alexandra stood up. "Rowena—I don't care about what happens to the church—please let me know when the wedding will be. I understand that you might have to get married quickly—but at least let us give you a reception. I...I can't have found you just to lose you so quickly. And"—she gave me a ghost of a smile—"I may not be good for much, but everyone agrees I organize a good wedding reception."

"I will," I promised. "We'll...um, I don't know what's going to happen over the next few days, and we'll probably have a very quick civil ceremony as soon as we can, but as soon as we're able, I promise you, you can throw whatever kind of reception you want for us."

Alexandra's smile turned from a ghost into the real thing. "I've already got ideas for a slap-bang party running through my head."

"Great," I said. "Whatever you want."

She impulsively reached up and hugged me. "I'm so glad you came," she said. "No matter what else might have happened."

"Me too," I said.

She released me. I looked over at Dennis. He looked extremely uninclined to hug, but at least he didn't seem like he was about to have a stroke anymore. Maybe by the time the reception that Alexandra was cooking up happened, he'd be reconciled to my existence.

Roseanna came over and hugged me too. "Don't be a stranger," she said. "And even if you do have just a quick civil ceremony for the wedding, I insist on you having the reception of the summer."

"Of course," I promised.

My mother hugged me too, and repeated her desire to meet Galina Ivanovna. My father walked me out to the car.

"Well, that went less badly than I'd feared," he said. "Although I might have failed in my attempt to get you back into Dennis and Alexandra's will."

"I think I did that," I said. "I could have told Isaiah sorry, I didn't know anyone who could help him, let's just keep our suspicions to ourselves. But instead I hooked him up with a bulldog investigative reporter who brought the whole thing down around us." I thought for a moment. "I might be about to do the same to Crimson College," I added.

My father sighed. "I assume you think they deserve it?"

"Oh, I know they deserve it," I said. "It won't be anything but telling the world the truth. But if they go up in flames too, I'll feel a little bit like a...I don't know. Kali, goddess of destruction, I guess."

"Kali is also the slayer of demons and destroyer of ignorance," my father pointed out. "There could be worse things. Just don't let her destroy you along with the demons she goes after."

"Good advice," I said. "And, um...I'll let you know how everything goes. With, ah, with the wedding and everything."

"You do that," he said. "And same here. I don't know how things are going to shake out, but I'll keep you in the loop. Oh, and happy birthday in advance."

"Thanks," I said. "Well, I'd better get going."

"Stay safe," my father said.

29

I TEXTED DIMA AND GALINA Ivanovna from the car with the good news about the test results, and set off.

I had to stop half an hour later for a bathroom break—the downside of a dramatic exit—and then I got caught in traffic in Charlotte, which allowed me to spend a lot of time thinking about my semester there and how things were turning out so differently than I'd thought they would back then. For better or for worse? I couldn't tell yet.

Galina Ivanovna met me at the door when I arrived at my apartment. "Inna!" she cried as soon as she saw me. "Is it true? I've been looking and looking at the results all day, and I keep coming to the same conclusion, but I don't trust my eyes—or my pitiful knowledge of English. Of course, medical terminology is similar, and numbers are the same in any language. But is it true? I seem to have improved? A lot?"

"That's what it looked like to my mother," I confirmed.

"I must meet her," Galina Ivanovna said.

"That's what she wants too," I told her.

"Then it's settled. How was everything in Virginia?"

I gave her a brief update on all the drama in Virginia while petting Fevronia, who twined ecstatically around my ankles and didn't try to bite me once.

Galina Ivanovna said she was sorry for all the family upheaval, but overall, things had probably turned out as well as could be expected, it was wonderful about John, and Dennis would come around someday.

"Maybe," I said. "He's never been very quick to forgive before."

She held up her hands in a gesture of exasperation. "That's men. But he'll come around someday. Doesn't Ronechka look good?"

"She does," I said, scratching her behind the ears.

Galina Ivanovna left after supper. I wanted to take a shower and go straight to bed—I hadn't gotten a lot of sleep on the creaky cot—but I made myself check my email first.

Junk mail, junk mail, junk mail...wait, what was that?

It was an email from Natalya Andreyevna.

My heart sank. I didn't feel like dealing with a politely worded rejection right now. But I also wouldn't be able to sleep with it hanging over me unopened and uncertain, like a Schrödinger's Sword of Damocles.

I clicked on it.

Dear Rowena,

We are delighted to offer you the fellowship at our institute. You made a big impression at the interview with your warmth, your passion, and your commitment to following your own vision, and we think your research on Tsvetaeva would be a good fit for our theme of "Female Poets Reimagining the 20th Century." In fact, we believe your bold approach will revolutionize the field of Tsvetaeva studies. We would also welcome the opportunity to work with Dmitry Vladimirovich, if he will agree. It is possible that we may have a fellowship available for him as well. We are happy to discuss this with him if he is interested. Meanwhile, the details of your contract are below. Please connect with me if you have any questions, and we request your decision by 15 May, 2017.

With respect,
Natalya Andreyevna Simonova

30

I STARED AT THE EMAIL. Then I read it again. Then I read through the contract at the bottom. Then I screamed into my hand a little bit.

Once I was done screaming, I sat in paralysis for a while. Should I reply immediately? Tell Dima? What to do, what to do...

I ended up replying to say that I had received the offer, I was very interested, and I would look over the contract carefully and discuss the matter with Dmitry Vladimirovich. Natalya Andreyevna hadn't exactly said so, but it was clear from both the interview and the email that they were interested in us as a package deal. Well, so be it. Both of us had done pretty poorly on our own. If we were only interesting to prospective employers as a couple, then maybe that was a sign.

I texted Dima. It was the middle of the night in Germany, so I wasn't expecting an answer, but I wanted to make sure he got the news before he went to the airport, so he could think about it. Nothing like a trans-Atlantic flight to give you plenty of time to mull things over.

Two minutes later, I got a reply.

That's great! And they want us both?

That's what they said, I wrote. *They are only offering the fellowship to me, obviously, but they seem very interested in you, and they said that they might be able to find something for you as well.*

I wonder what they want in return.

I imagine they want to parade you around at talks and seminars. But is that any worse than what you're currently doing?

I don't know, he wrote. *I'll talk to them about it once I'm back with you.*

Okay. And shouldn't you be sleeping? When is your flight?

I have to leave for the airport in a couple of hours. But I haven't slept all night. Can't.

What's going on? Fear curled like poisonous smoke inside of me. Insomnia was Dima's default state, but something behind the words exhaled something sinister.

They gave us the drugs.

What drugs? The poisonous smoke inside of me thickened.

The ones they've been working on. They made us all take them as part of our last training session.

Why you too? You're not one of their mercenaries!

Hazing, he answered succinctly. *I had to prove I was one of them. It was that or get shot. So I took the drugs.*

Another text came in a few seconds later, while I was still trying to compose a coherent message.

It wasn't so bad. Nothing terrible happened to us. We just ran super-fast through our exercises. It was like magic, Inna! We knew exactly what each person was thinking, before he thought it. We worked together like a flock of birds, or a swarm of bees. It was the best thing I've ever experienced. And now, at long last, they trust me. But apparently severe insomnia is a side effect.

Extreme jealousy rendered me incapable of responding, or even reading the message to the end. Being told by your fiancé that a bonding exercise he'd done with a bunch of other people was the best thing he'd ever experienced was startlingly hurtful. It took several deep breaths and calming exercises before I was able to deal with what he'd said in a rational fashion.

How do you feel other than the insomnia? I asked.

Fine. I feel great, actually. Just sorry to leave them.

I did a few more deep breathing exercises.

How long are the side effects supposed to last? I asked.

Who knows? This is still a new drug, after all. We're just test subjects. What do rats know of the drugs being tested on them?)))))

Good point, I wrote back. I searched for the most conciliatory, least aggressive words I could find. *Just monitor yourself carefully. As you said, this is still a new drug.*

So is the drug they gave mama, and look how well that worked!))))))

True, I wrote. *And they've been monitoring her carefully all along.*

Very true. Well, I'll watch over myself, monitor all my vitals, as if I were in a clinical trial. And now I'll let you go, Inna: I know it's time for you to go to bed there.

Are you sure you'll be all right on your own? I asked.

I'll be fine. And I'm not on my own)))))) But I'm going to go ahead and head out to the airport soon. I'm sorry to be leaving the boys here, but I can't wait to see you!))))))

Okay, I wrote. *Have a good flight, and I'll see you tomorrow!*

Good night, Innochka! Sweet dreams!

Needless to say, Dima was not the only one to suffer from insomnia that night, and when I finally fell asleep, my dreams were anything but sweet.

31

I AWOKE TO A MESSAGE from Dima saying he'd boarded his flight from Munich to Charlotte. He had a layover in Charlotte and was scheduled to arrive in Atlanta at 5:36pm. He assured me he was feeling fine and his vitals were all perfectly normal.

I texted back to say I was glad to hear that, and that I'd meet him at the Atlanta airport. Then I tried to settle down to grade my literature finals. Grades were due by noon tomorrow and I had to leave for Atlanta by 4:00pm at the latest, so I really did need to buckle down and do them.

The phone interrupted me halfway through them. It was Dr. Azarian, calling to discuss Galina Ivanovna's test results and next steps. This took a while, since I had to go get Galina Ivanovna and call back. The end result, though, was that Galina Ivanovna was supposed to take this week off from the treatment and see how she felt.

"It's too soon in my judgment to discharge her from the trial," said Dr. Azarian. "But let's try pausing the treatment for a week or two and see what happens."

We agreed to that. I was thrilled that Galina Ivanovna was doing so much better, and also looking forward to not making a second trip to Atlanta in two days. If it weren't for the worry about Dima and the drugs, I'd be feeling good about the upcoming week. I shut down that line of thought as much as possible, and went back to grading.

By 3:00pm I'd finished all the finals. True, I can't say it had been my best work grading, but I was reasonably confident the grades more or less reflected what the students had earned. I hastily put everything into my spreadsheet, calculated the final grades, eyeballed them to make sure there were no egregious errors, and entered them into the online system.

The confirmation that they'd been received came at 3:55pm. I grabbed my purse and headed out the door. Galina Ivanovna had already declined to come, saying that she didn't want to take an extra trip to Atlanta if she didn't have to, and anyway, it would be more romantic if she weren't there. She'd just stay at home with Fevronia instead.

I was afraid that I'd left it too late and I'd get stuck in traffic, but I made it to the airport at 5:45pm. Dima texted while I was waiting in traffic at the airport exit that he'd already landed and I should pick him up at the curb. It took the better part of half an hour of negotiating traffic and waiting in line to get to the passenger pickup zone. I picked him out of the crowd as soon as I pulled up, but had to stick my head out of the car and yell to get his attention. Galina Ivanovna shouldn't have worried about making our meeting less romantic.

Dima came jogging over, his backpack slung over his shoulder. "Inna! You made it!"

"So did you."

The person waiting behind me honked his horn. Dima jumped into the car, and I pulled away as smartly as I could without rear-ending the car in front of me. The romance of the experience was increasing by the second.

"I'd kiss you, but I don't feel very fresh," Dima said. "But consider yourself kissed in spirit."

"Thanks." Chalk up another one for romance. It was true that Dima was giving off the usual airplane smell of old coffee and stale artificial fragrance. Underneath was another scent, one I had never smelled before but that I instinctively recognized as bad. It was both chemical-y and rank, like a combination of antiseptic and rotting meat, only stranger than that. It was very faint, but once I'd smelled it, I couldn't get it out of my nostrils.

I glanced over at Dima. He looked fine. I told myself he was perfectly fine, just a little tired from the long flight, and he'd probably gotten some kind of harsh disinfectant on him at some point during the trip. Didn't they spray planes down with pesticides in some places? I thought I'd read an article about that. That was probably what it was.

Dima rubbed his eyes. "I must be getting old," he said. "My eyes have been bothering me all day. The light hurts them."

We were stopped in traffic again. I leaned over and looked at him. His pupils were so dilated that his normally gray eyes looked almost entirely black. He was fidgeting as he sat there, rubbing his thumbs and index fingers together in odd, compulsive movements.

"What's your pulse?" I asked.

"Still measuring my vitals, Comrade Medic?"

"Yes. What's your pulse?"

He started the stopwatch on his phone and measured the pulse in his wrist. Then he frowned and measured the pulse in his neck. Then in his wrist again.

"Over a hundred every time," he announced.

"Was it like that last night?" I asked.

"Yes, but they told us that was expected and it would go back to normal in a few hours. It was close to normal this morning."

"How long since your last dose?" I asked.

He calculated, got confused by the time difference, tried again, and finally said, "About a day and a half. And it was only one dose."

"Okay. Do we need to go to the hospital?"

"And tell them what? That I was given an experimental drug for soldiers? They'll either dismiss me out of hand, or call the CIA. Besides, I feel fine."

We were moving again. If we were going to go to the hospital here in Atlanta, we needed to get off at the next exit. "Are you sure?" I asked.

"I've made it this far just fine, Inna. I'd rather deal with the side effects of this drug than get interrogated by the CIA."

"Well...good point. But if you start feeling worse, tell me, okay?"

"Sure thing, Comrade General Medic. So what do we have to do to get married?"

We spent the rest of the drive discussing the logistics of getting married, the reception that Alexandra wanted to hold for us, and the fellowship in Finland. By the time we got to Greenfields, Dima seemed less manic, although it was now obvious that he was exuding the unpleasant, chemical-y, rank smell from his pores. Even he noticed it.

"I must be sweating the drug out," he said. "Not very nice, huh? This is even worse than when I smoke—which I quit, by the way. They made us all quit, so they've done one good thing for me, even if I don't smell very good right now anyway. Good thing I was planning to wait to consummate our marriage until after the wedding, anyway."

"I think it might be a little late for that," I said.

"Yeah, but proprieties must be observed. Also, frankly, all I want to do is take a shower and go to bed. I mean, obviously I'd like to do other things, but all I think I'm actually capable of is taking a shower and going to bed."

"Good idea," I said. "Morning is wiser than evening anyway. You'll feel a lot better in the morning, and we can deal with everything then."

"Yes, ma'am," he said.

32

THE NEXT MORNING, SHOWERED and shaved, Dima said he felt much better. He felt so good, he said, that he wanted to get married. Today, if possible.

"I haven't actually gotten the rings yet," he said. "I looked and looked, but I couldn't find any that seemed just right. But we can get them later, right? Can we just go and get married today? And—wait—isn't today your birthday? The perfect day to get married!"

"It is," I said. "And I've researched the requirements thoroughly. Georgia doesn't require a waiting period. We can get the license and get married on the same day. Cobb County courthouse does daily wedding ceremonies at noon and six."

Dima checked the time. Not yet 8:00am. "How far away is Cobb County courthouse?"

"About two hours," I said.

"So plenty of time if we leave now. What documents do we need?"

Twenty minutes later, Dima, Galina Ivanovna, and I were all headed north to Marietta. Dima and I were in jeans and t-shirts. At least he was freshly showered. Galina Ivanovna was in the old dress she'd been wearing when we'd announced we were heading off to get married and did she want to come.

"You'll need a witness," she said.

"Not in Georgia," I said. "Oh, and it will be a group ceremony."

"Very early-Soviet," said Galina Ivanovna. "I'll come. Your parents won't mind, Inna?"

"They might, but let's do it anyway," I said. "I want to get married. They can have the reception they're planning afterwards."

Galina Ivanovna expressed doubts, but Dima said he wasn't going to wait another minute, and if Galina Ivanovna wanted to be there, she'd better get in the car ASAP.

We spent the drive up the all-too-familiar stretch of highway discussing the fellowship in Finland.

"Take it," Dima concluded. "And if they want to offer me something as well, I'll probably take it too. I'm pretty sure I'm going to get fired by *Nezavisimaya Pravda,* if I haven't been already."

"Okay," I said. "I guess we're moving to Finland, then." I'd passed briefly through the Helsinki-Vantaa airport once. It had seemed nice. That was enough to know about a place to decide to live there, right? And it was close to Russia. I'd sworn I'd go back there one day, to get Dima back and take blood vengeance on those who'd taken him away from me. Maybe I'd accomplish both those things without ever even setting foot on Russian soil.

"What do you say, mama?" Dima asked, twisting around in the car seat. "How do you feel about living in Finland? I guess we'll move there this summer? Maybe we can get our tickets back to Moscow transferred to Helsinki without losing too much money."

Galina Ivanovna twisted up her mouth. "I'll come visit with great pleasure, Dimulya, you know I will, but I think I'll just go back home to live. I've been talking to Uncle Sasha and we've agreed that I'm going to take my flight back to Moscow at the end of this month and then go live with him in Murmansk."

"What?! No! Mama, you can't do that!"

"I can and I will," Galina Ivanovna answered serenely. "I'm too old to start life again in another country, and I don't want to get underfoot during the first days of your marriage. It's been a real adventure to spend a few months in America, and I'll be forever grateful to it and to the doctors here and especially to you, Innochka, for helping out and giving me however much more time I have, but I want to go home. Living in a foreign country has made me realize the only place I really want to be is Russia. To misquote the great Akhmatova, I need to be with my people, where, unfortunately, my people are. So I'll be going back home as soon as I can. But Murmansk isn't that far away from Finland, so I'll visit often. After all, you will still be my people, too."

Dima shifted uneasily in his seat. "Now I feel like a coward for abandoning my people."

"Inna is your people now," Galina Ivanovna told him sternly. "Or she will be as soon as this wedding takes place."

Dima looked over at me. "What about you, Inna? Are you worried about leaving your people?"

"My people is you," I said. "You are no longer foreign blood to me."

"I thought foreign blood was the most desirable of all?" Dima was smiling as he said it, but there was also a tinge of worry in his words.

"Once the blood is joined in holy matrimony, it's no longer foreign," I said. "But the desire remains."

"There you go," said Galina Ivanovna. "Nothing to worry about. And I don't want to get in the way of the creation of this new nation...or new desire. Although if there are grandchildren, I'll be right over to help take care of them."

Dima grinned broadly, his dimple showing he was truly happy at the thought. But the grin quickly turned to alarm. "That makes it sound so...real," he said. "Like it could really happen!"

"Children happen very easily sometimes, especially for married couples," Galina Ivanovna said. "I'm telling you this as a medical doctor with decades of experience."

"But sometimes they don't," said Dima, sounding both worried and relieved at the thought.

"Sometimes they don't," Galina Ivanovna agreed. "But sometimes they do."

With that thought, we arrived at the Cobb County courthouse. It took a certain amount of wandering around and asking questions, but eventually we found the right office to get the marriage license. We presented the application I'd already filled out, our passports, and $56 in cash, and by 11:30 we were walking away with a marriage license.

We joined the growing crowd of couples on the third floor. Some of them were in street clothes like us, some were in what looked like their recycled prom outfits, and some were in full-on wedding attire. Expressions ranged from glowing excitement to near panic.

At noon the magistrate showed up. All the couples organized themselves into ranks while friends and families ranged around us. Dima and I were at the back of the group, which didn't stop several people from leaning over and telling Dima to smile. He had put on the serious face that Russians normally wore for solemn events. After the third person told him to smile, he attempted it, but the result was so ghastly that I told him he was better off not doing it.

We all repeated after the magistrate as she led us through the ceremony. Ten minutes later, we were married. Dima and I, I noted with relief, were not the only ones who didn't even have rings, although several of the couples had elaborate and obviously expensive wedding ring sets. Whatever. We were all equally married in the eyes of the law.

Afterwards, we turned in our license to the magistrate to be signed and submitted to the court. The certificate would be mailed to us within 30 days, we were told. And that was that.

"I thought I would cry," Galina Ivanovna said as we left. "But I didn't. Inna, did you cry?"

"Not even a little," I said.

"Disappointing. How do you feel now? Any different?"

I did a full scan of body and mind. "Psychologically, exactly the same, only somewhat relieved," I said. "Physically, I feel like I can breathe easy for the first time in forever. It's good to have it done. Although I think I'll only really feel good about it when we have the certificate."

"And rings," said Dima. "Shall we go shopping for rings this afternoon?"

"Let's!" said Galina Ivanovna. "Although maybe you'd prefer I didn't come along?"

"We're not going to leave you in the car, mama," Dima said. "You can come."

"Well then, let's do it. But let's get lunch first. All of a sudden I'm ravenous."

"Me too," I said.

"I'm not," said Dima. He fanned himself. "Is anyone else really hot?"

"It's a little warm, but not terrible," said Galina Ivanovna. "But you probably have jet lag. Here. Let's go sit down on that bench over there."

Dima continued to fan himself after we sat down. "I must not be used to this American heat," he said. "I got unaccustomed to it while in cold and gloomy Germany."

"You do look flushed," Galina Ivanovna observed. She reached over and felt his skin. She frowned. She put her hand on his wrist and felt his pulse.

"Maybe you're coming down with something," she said. "Maybe you picked up a cold or something on the plane."

Dima suddenly started like a wild animal catching sight of a predator. "What's that?!" he demanded.

Galina Ivanovna and I looked around. Nothing. "What's what?" I asked.

"That man...there's something wrong with that man..."

I followed his pointing finger. A medium-sized, very fit black man with a shaved head looked up and caught my gaze.

"That's Carl," I said.

"Who's Carl?" Dima cried.

"He works for Security Solutions," I said.

As soon as the words were out of my mouth, I knew something was wrong. Carl must have been sent to spy on us. But why? And how had he found us? And surely it wasn't with any ill intent, right? I might hate Security Solutions, but I trusted Carl. I'd always had the sense that he liked me, or at least found me amusing. Surely *Carl* wouldn't hurt me, right?

"He's coming this way," said Galina Ivanovna.

33

AS CARL DREW CLOSER, I could see that there was something wrong with him, too. He was sweating in the mild May day. While I could believe that Dima wasn't used to the heat, Carl was. The thermometer had barely cracked 80. No Georgia native was going to be sweating through their shirt for a piddling little temperature like that.

He was also wearing sunglasses even though the sky was cloudy. I glanced over at Dima. His pupils were huge, filling up his eyes and turning them into lightless black pits.

"What is it?" I demanded as Carl came up to us. "What are you here for?"

"Sure is good to see you, Miz Rowena," he said. "Or is that Doctor Halley? Or is it Missus now? I saw the two of you coming out of the courthouse together."

"It's always Doctor," I said. "What is it, Carl? Are you here about the drugs?"

He took off his sunglasses, winced, and put them back on. "What makes you say that, Doctor Rowena?"

His voice was the same as it had always been, but he was talking in jocular, drawling sentences rather than the clipped phrases I'd always heard him use before.

"You're sweating and your pupils are dilated, just like Dima's," I said. "Either you both came down with the same disease at the same time, or you both took the same drug. I'm betting on the latter."

"And you'd be right, Miz Doctor Rowena. I were you, I'd go get a lottery ticket or put a bunch of money on the ponies today."

As he was speaking to me, Carl was eyeing Dima. Dima was doing the same to him. I had the bizarre sensation that they were communicating in some unspoken fashion, like animals. The hairs rose on the back of my neck.

"Most of what we perceive is filtered out by specific processes in the brain designed to do just that," Galina Ivanovna said in a low voice, speaking just to me. She must have been sensing whatever was going on with Dima and Carl too. "But extreme stress, or certain hypnotic or meditative states, or certain pharmaceuticals or hormones, can shut off those brain circuits, allowing us to receive our perceptions more completely. We can become hyper-aware of our surroundings and everyone in them. Dima often told me about the sense of clairvoyance and omniscience he experienced in combat. It is useful in certain survival situations. But the human brain is not designed to deal with that much unfiltered information over the long term. To make matters worse, the experience can become addictive."

She and I looked at each other, at Dima and Carl, who were still sizing each other up and engaging in what appeared to be nonverbal, even telepathic, communication, and looked back at each other.

"When did you last take the drug?" I asked Carl.

"Two days ago," he answered, still looking at Dima.

I stepped closer to them and sniffed. Both of them emitted that same rank, half-rotten, half-chemical-y odor that had been coming off of Dima yesterday.

"The drug used to get flushed out of your system in a couple of hours," Carl said, still watching Dima. "They've been working on extending its halflife. But now there are recurring side effects for several days afterwards."

"Are they dangerous?" I spoke softly, as if to a wounded animal, trying not to spook them.

"Sometimes," said Carl, still not looking at me. "Especially when you mix them with other drugs, including alcohol or nicotine. They made everyone stop drinking and smoking when they found that out. But even so, sometimes they cause strokes...seizures...psychotic episodes...That's what I came to tell you. I knew your man Dima here was set to be given the drug. I didn't want anything bad to happen to you, Miz Doctor Rowena. So I slipped a tracker in Dima's wallet"—Dima yelped in outrage, yanked his wallet out of his pocket, and began going through it feverishly—"and I followed you here to warn you. But the side effects are getting to me too. Recurring, like I said. I felt fine this morning, but they're getting me again now."

"Is there a cure?" I asked. "An antidote?"

"They got stuff they can give you to help you ride it out more safely," said Carl.

"Stuff you can get at the ER?" I pressed.

He shook his head, his eyes still on Dima, who was tearing apart his wallet. "I don't know what it's called, and I doubt they have it at your average hospital. No, the only way we can get it is to go straight to the source. Security Solutions."

Dima cried out in triumph, pulled a small round plastic object out of one corner of his wallet, held it up, and then dropped it on the sidewalk and smashed it with his heel.

Carl winced. "That's a damn expensive piece of equipment to treat that way," he said.

Dima glared at him.

"Where would Security Solutions have this antidote?" I asked.

"At headquarters," Carl said, still looking down at the smashed-up tracker in dismay.

"Okay...Dima! Dima!"

Dima was ripping up his wallet, dumping out cash, credit cards, ID, everything most important in his life, onto the pavement.

"There's another one in here! I know it!" he shouted.

"Paranoia's a bad sign," said Carl. "Normally the next step's psychosis. And if you don't get hurt real bad doing something you'll regret, that's often followed by seizures and stroke."

"How far is headquarters from here?" I asked.

"About an hour."

I put a hand on Dima's arm. He pushed me back, shoving me away from him so hard I almost stumbled into Galina Ivanovna.

"Dima!" she cried.

"Do we have an hour?" I asked Carl. His eyes, I noted, were starting to go strange, as if a demon were peering out from somewhere deep inside his skull. "Do *you* have an hour?"

"I don't know," he said. His voice had become an eerie, rasping whisper. "But we sure as hell don't have much more than an hour if we just sit here."

34

GALINA IVANOVNA AND I got Dima and Carl loaded into my car. Carl was cooperative about it. Dima kept asking where we were going. At first he sounded reasonable, and accepted what we told him. By the time we got to the car, though, he was demanding angrily that we tell him the truth, his voice loud enough that people were turning to look at the tall man shouting in Russian.

"Just get in the car, sweetie," Galina Ivanovna kept saying. "Get in the car for mamochka."

Dima got into the car, but then started demanding again where we were going.

"Where *are* we going?" I asked Carl. "And why is it affecting him so much worse than you?"

Carl shrugged. "It affects different people differently. And we took our doses at different times, and maybe they gave him more, or gave him a different version. They're still testing them out. As for where we're going, head for the Security Solutions headquarters."

"Which is where, exactly?" I asked.

"Give me your phone so I can put it in your GPS app. I'll try to give you directions, but I don't know how much longer I'll be lucid."

I gave Carl my phone, and tried to examine him without being too obvious about it while he entered the address into my GPS app. He was sweating and his pupils were dilated, but nothing like Dima's.

He handed the phone back to me. Something demonic peered out from his eyes for a moment. He blinked. It retreated. But it was still back there, I was sure.

"Thanks," I said. "Good thinking. I'll try to get there as quick as I can."

I put the car in gear and started making my way slowly away from the courthouse and through Marietta. According to the GPS app, it was a 47-minute drive to the Security Solutions headquarters.

"Dimochka, Dimochka, sit still, please," Galina Ivanovna was saying in the back seat. "It's like he's two all over again," she said to me. "But a lot bigger."

I tried to glance at him in the rearview mirror, but a black SUV pulled out suddenly in front of me, forcing me to brake hard.

"Oh shit," Carl muttered.

"How so?" I asked.

"Don't look back," he said quietly, "but those are SS cars in front of and behind us."

I snuck a quick peek in the rearview mirror. An identical black SUV was behind me.

"What are they doing?" I asked. "Are they going to stop us?"

"Let me ask. Maybe they'll tell me." He pulled out his phone, called someone in his contacts, and spoke softly to them.

"They say they're going to escort us to HQ," he said. "They would like to speak to Mr. Kuznetsov. And you." Carl did a passable job of pronouncing Dima's name.

"Why?" I asked.

"I guess they're not done with him," Carl said. "As for you, I couldn't say."

That didn't sound good at all, but I didn't think I could escape from the black SUVs, and I wanted to go to headquarters anyway, so I kept following the route on my phone.

Dima and Galina Ivanovna were arguing in the back seat. Even without looking at him, I could tell that Dima was growing more and more restive, twisting and fidgeting in his seat, talking to himself and then bursting out at Galina Ivanovna when she tried to soothe him.

"We're trying to help you, Dimochka," she told him, speaking in sugary tones as if to a sick child. "We're taking you to nice people who can help you." In a more normal voice, she asked, "Do you have a plan, In-nochka?"

"Um..." I looked over at Carl. "Any suggestions for a good plan?"

"They want to talk to you. Both of you. I suggest you agree on the condition that they give Mr. Kuznetsov the necessary meds first."

"And you," I said. Carl was still looking better than Dima, but he was starting to shift in his seat and rub his hands together nervously. When our eyes met, the demon looked straight at me for an instant.

"Thanks for thinking of me." The demon disappeared, and I was talking once again to Carl, who probably wasn't a very nice person in the grand scheme of things, but had always been nice to me.

"Of course," I said. "And I have a plan. Can you bring up my contacts for me? I have some people I need to call."

At my direction, Carl dialed Mel.

"Ro!" she said. "I thought you were eloping."

"There's been a slight hiccup," I said. "How do you feel about maybe taking on your first case?"

"That doesn't sound good."

"The good folks at Security Solutions want to talk to us. We're heading there right now. And they gave Dima a weird super-soldier drug a couple of days ago, and he's currently freaking out from the side effects."

"That sounds even worse."

"They say they have an antidote. I'm hoping to get it for him. But if you don't hear from me by this evening, come looking for us, okay? Tell...I guess tell everyone you think should know, but especially my brother John and Frank McAvoy at the FBI, and come looking for us. If you can't find us, find out everything you can about Security Solutions, and see if you can nail them to the motherfucking wall. The journalist Heather Ramirez might be able to help you."

"Got it." Mel's voice was calm and businesslike. "When should I start?"

I glanced at the time. Barely 1:00pm.

"Give us until five," I said. "If I don't call you by then, start raising hell."

"Will do," said Mel.

"Thanks," I said.

"No problem. Good luck."

After Mel, I called Heather. She didn't pick up, so I left a message detailing the situation. I didn't have Camila's number, so I called John and left a message with him, telling him to set Camila on Security Solutions if he didn't hear from me again by this evening. Then I called Frank McAvoy and left a message with him.

"I don't know how much good it will do, but at least a bunch of people will know where we went if we disappear forever," I said when I was done.

"Good thinking," said Carl. "And this probably wasn't how you expected your wedding to go, huh?" He tried to smile, got into a wrestling match with the demon, and eventually won, but only by squashing down the smile as well.

I tried to look back at Dima, but was distracted by the black SUVs both speeding up and signaling to turn off at the next exit.

"It wasn't how I'd always dreamed of my big day, but knowing Dima, it seems about par for the course," I said.

"One thing's for certain," said Carl. He and his demon got into a wrestling match again.

"What's that?" I asked, once he had gotten the demon back under control. Each time they fought, I could feel, with some visceral sixth sense that spoke of ghosts and dragons and terrifying things that rose out from the muck of the underworld and the unconscious, how he pushed it back down into those dark waters—but also how each time it stayed a little closer to the surface.

I glanced quickly down at my phone. 20 minutes to ETA. My hands, I noted with detached calm, were gripping the steering wheel so hard the knuckles had gone white. When I tried to loosen my grip, I discovered they had stuck to the wheel with sweat.

Carl turned to look into the backseat. I tried to look too, and this time actually managed a quick peek of Dima in the rearview mirror. Galina Ivanovna was holding his hands in hers, speaking to him in a low continuous voice.

"Let GO of me!" Dima shouted, jerking his hands free. For a moment our eyes met. I wished they hadn't. The demon that was flirting with me coyly out of Carl's eyes was staring out of Dima's at full strength, hungry for blood.

"You're having a real destination wedding," said Carl. "One you ain't ever gonna forget."

35

"HEY!" DIMA WAS SHOUTING from the backseat. "Hey, hey, HEY! This is Security Solutions!" He was slurring his words slightly, as if he'd had a couple hundred grams of vodka and was contemplating whether another hundred grams was a good idea.

"It is," I said, not taking my eyes off the road. We had exited off the highway, driven on a two-lane road through some rolling trees and pastures, and had now turned onto a paved one-lane road that was closed off by a very serious-looking gate, with a chain link fence topped with barbed wire disappearing into the trees in either direction.

The black SUV in front entered a code into the pinpad by the gate. It swung open. A hand in the SUV waved me forward as the vehicle pulled through the gate. I followed. The SUV behind us held up the rear. The gate swung closed behind us.

"Why are we at Security Solutions?" Dima demanded.

"To talk to them," I said, still not taking my eyes off the road and the SUV in front. We were driving down the one-lane blacktop through a lightly wooded area that opened up into a compound surrounded by a much higher fence, made of chain link with rolls of razor wire angled inwards at the top. The gate was eight feet tall and had a sentry booth next to it.

"Jesus," I said. "What is this, a maximum security prison?"

"Sometimes they do bring prisoners here," Carl said.

"Whatever for?!?"

"They say work release, but it's mainly to use them in training exercises, or maybe to train them if they're close to getting out and have signed a contract with SS to work here after release."

"That sounds like something I really don't want to know the details of," I said as the driver of the SUV in front leaned out of his door to talk to the sentry by the gate.

"You're right about that," said Carl, while Dima burst out furiously, "You don't want to be here! Inna, you don't want to be here!"

I looked back at him. It was the first time we'd had direct eye-to-eye contact since we'd gotten in the car.

For a moment it was Dima looking at me. I recognized his humor and his anger, his intense belief in making a better world and his fury that that better world didn't exist yet...his love for me and the fear that love engendered. The things I would call his good side, and the things I would call his bad side, and how they were opposites, pulling him in opposing directions, keeping him upright and functional when they were in balance, and tearing him down and destroying him when they got out of control.

"Inna," he said softly, "this is a bad place. This is the last place I would ever want you to be. Why did you come here?"

"To save you," I said.

He shook his head in a convulsive spasm. "I'm not worth it," he said.

"You are to me," I said. "And you can't convince me otherwise."

He opened his mouth to say something. Instead of words, though, what rose up inside of him was the demon. I could almost see it like a physical stain as it tightened his neck, tensed his jaw, turned his mouth into a snarl. It engulfed his eyes last, sucking away the tenderness, the love, the care for others that was such a big part of who he was, even if he had a hard time facing it. What was left were two dilated pupils that had become lightless pits leading to a place of selfishness, rage, and pain.

"Don't look at me, Inna," he said. He had started trembling all over, like a dog quivering to attack.

"I..." I began.

"DON'T LOOK AT ME!" he screamed. "*HE'LL* GET LOOSE IF YOU LOOK AT ME!"

I turned to face forward. The skin on my scalp and the nape of my neck was crawling and burning with the sense of something huge and dangerous just behind me.

Don't look back, I ordered myself. Gripping the steering wheel so hard my whole hands went white, I pulled through the gate.

"Lord Jesus Christ, son of God, have mercy on me, a sinner," Galina Ivanovna whispered. "Have mercy on all of us."

The gate clanged shut.

36

OUR THREE-CAR PARADE drove up to a beige metal building and parked in front of it. There were other beige metal buildings dotted around the complex, but this one was clearly the one in charge.

Two men in black Security Solutions uniforms got out of each black SUV. The one who'd been driving the SUV in front motioned at me to get out as well.

"Inna, what do we do?" Galina Ivanovna asked. Her voice sounded thin and frightened. She'd been stalwart in the face of illness, and gone into the hospital with a calm smile that had shamed the rest of us, but now her voice shook like a scared child's.

"Get out and follow them," I said.

A growl emanated from the back seat. It took a moment for me to realize it was coming from Dima. I started to turn to look back at him. The growl rose to a snarl. I snapped my head around to face front again.

"I'm getting out," I announced, in Russian and then in English. "You can follow me when you're ready."

I got out of the car. Carl got out the other side. He nodded at the other Security Solutions employees. One of them nodded at him and stepped forward, his hand outstretched as if to shake Carl's hand or take his arm.

Carl snarled and launched himself at him. It was so fast and unexpected, he had the other man down on the ground before anyone knew what was happening.

"Shit, shit, shit!" the man's partner shouted, diving down after them, while the other pair called for backup.

Carl was rolling around on the ground with the first two men. They were just as fit and trained as he was, and with odds of two to one they should have been able to restrain him, but he was writhing out of their grip, punching, biting, willing to do anything to hurt them, while they were trying to restrain him without damaging him. It took all four men to immobilize him so that the two more men who came running out could inject him with something and restrain him with flex cuffs.

"Is that the antidote?" I asked when they were done. Carl was still thrashing and screaming in their arms, his eyes bugging out of his head.

"Sedative," one said briefly. "We'll give him the antidote when..." He stopped talking when the driver of the first SUV glared at him and shook his head in a "shut up" motion.

Oh great. My peripheral senses were aware that Dima and Galina Ivanovna had gotten out of the car, but I didn't dare look in their direction. Dima was standing there fairly calmly, but I was afraid that one look from me would set him off.

"Rowena Halley?" said the driver of the first SUV.

I nodded.

He held out his hand towards the front door of the beige metal building. "This way, please. Mr. Wainwright wants to see you."

I nodded again and, not trusting myself to speak, followed him inside.

37

THE INTERIOR OF THE building looked like any cheap institutional structure. I could have been in a new but not very nice high school. But I wasn't.

I followed the SUV driver down the linoleumed hallway. I could hear Dima and Galina Ivanovna walking behind me, and a little farther back, the others dragging the still-struggling Carl after us.

We came to a junction. The corridor ran right and left. Straight ahead, stairs led down to the basement level. Instead of going down them, we turned left. When we came to a door at the end of the long, echoing hallway, the SUV driver stopped and knocked.

"Come in!" a man's voice called.

We stepped in. It could have been the principal's office in the cheap high school. But the man sitting behind the desk was wearing a suit that no high school principal could afford. He was tall and slender and was accessorizing the suit with an expensive hair cut and a tan that spoke of vacations most of us mere mortals could never manage.

"Rowena Halley?" he asked as soon as I came in.

I nodded.

"My son said you were pretty." He gave me a once-over as he spoke. He tried to make his voice and his face dismissive. But I could tell from both that he, just like his son, thought I was, in fact, pretty.

I gave him a faint smile.

"And they tell me they think you got married today." He gave me another once-over. "But you're in old jeans my wife wouldn't wear to muck stalls in, and I see no sign of a ring on your finger."

I shrugged.

"Give me your phone," he ordered.

I hesitated.

"Give me your phone or he'll take it from you," he said, nodding at the SUV driver.

I held out my phone. After a moment, Anthony Wainwright II stood up from his desk and took it. Our fingers brushed. His were cold and dry. Up close, I could feel the agitation he was hiding under his smooth surface. He was trying to play it cool, but something was churning inside of him, threatening to tear him apart as it broke loose.

"Search her," he ordered the SUV driver. "Search all of them."

I stood there with my arms out, not resisting as the SUV driver searched me. I had briefly contemplated trying to record the meeting, but I'd guessed they might search me. I'd been right. I was glad I hadn't wasted my time and gotten myself into more trouble by attempting to sneak a recording device past them, but I felt extremely naked without my phone.

Galina Ivanovna didn't protest when they searched her and took her phone. Dima started to struggle as soon as they approached him, jerking out of Galina Ivanovna's grip and running for the door.

"Stop him!" shouted Anthony.

There was a scuffle at the door as at least six Security Solutions employees tried to restrain Dima while also keeping Carl under control. They only succeeded when another man came in. Even watching out of the corner of my eye so as not to upset Dima, I could see there was something...odd about the man. He moved with a strangely animal grace, rolling slightly from side to side as if his limbs were both incredibly strong and not quite where he expected them to be. As soon as he came into the room, his eyes met Dima's. Dima stiffened. Then, I swear, they *sniffed* at each other, inhaling until their nostrils flared.

The other man put his hand on Dima's shoulder, leaned close, and said something in Dima's ear. Dima nodded and, meek as a lamb, followed him out the door.

"Where's he taking him!" Galina Ivanovna cried.

"Where are they going?" I asked Anthony, I hoped more calmly.

"Just for a chat," Anthony told me. "We dosed Mykhailo there as soon as we knew you were on your way. The drug allows them to communicate with each other in ways the rest of us can't."

He smiled a faint, unhumorous smile. "Oh, it's not magic. It's just a hit of hormones—oxytocin, testosterone, cortisol, that sort of thing—and other substances our bodies produce naturally. Give people the right amount extra, amp it up with some uppers like methamphetamines or cocaine derivatives, and you have superfighters who can read each other's body language so well it seems like they're telepathic. They also produce pheromones and other things that they can literally smell on each other, so as long as they're under the influence, they can pick each other out of a crowd. They always know who else has had the drug, and are instantly drawn to him."

"Too bad about the side effects," I said.

Anthony shrugged. "Yes. We thought we'd finally hit on the perfect formula. We gave it to some of our own men here, including your friend Carl, and then the Wolf Battalion, including your boyfriend—husband??—a few days ago."

A thin smile. "The results were truly astounding. The best training exercises any of us had ever seen. A fighting group using this drug would be unstoppable. A true breakthrough in the technology of warfare."

"But then the side effects hit," I said.

He nodded. "Two members of the Wolf Battalion have already stroked out this morning during a regular training run, and three more are having psychotic episodes in padded cells. The rest are experiencing various arrhythmias, blood pressure events, and hallucinations."

"But you have an antidote," I said. "A treatment."

Another shrug. "We've got drugs that have successfully stabilized subjects experiencing side effects from previous versions of the drug and helped them metabolize it more quickly. We don't know how well they'll work on this variant. But we wanted to bring in your Kuznetsov before he drew attention to himself or you took him to a local hospital and caused the wrong people to ask the wrong questions. And maybe we can get some answers, figure out how to tweak the formula to reduce side effects."

"Yeah," I said. "I don't see the US government being happy about giving something like this to their soldiers."

"You might be surprised," he said. "But it could cause some unpleasant backlash. As long as it's confined to Security Solutions and the Wolf Battalion, no one's going to care, but if it hits the general military population, we might have a PR problem on our hands."

"That's one way of putting it," I said.

Anthony's phone, which was sitting on the desk in front of him, buzzed. He looked at it.

"They have Kuznetsov in a safe place for observation," he said.

"And the treatment?" I asked. "When are you going to start the treatment?"

"I told you," he said. "It might or might not work."

"But it has in the past," I said.

He nodded. "It has in the past, and we're reasonably confident it will this time too, but we want to observe him a little while longer before we give it to him." He reached into a drawer in his desk. I tensed.

"No need to worry." He put something from the drawer onto the top of the desk. When he withdrew his hand, I saw the thing he'd taken out was a small syringe.

"The 'antidote,' as you called it," he said. "They've got plenty down in the medical bay, of course, but I kept some up here just in case we needed it. It's fast-acting."

"That's nice," I said. "So what do I have to do to get you to give it to him?"

Anthony smiled, a cold, thin-lipped smile. "You know," he said, "I've thought a lot about meeting you, Rowena. I heard a lot about you from my son. He admired you, you know. Thought you were pretty *and* smart. Even after you ruined his life, he kept insisting you were a good teacher and a good person."

"That's nice," I said. "And I think your son ruined his life himself. Along with the lives of several others."

Anthony shook his head. "That's what he says, too. You know, he keeps saying he's really sorry for what he's done? He keeps wanting to apologize to...I can't remember their names, but various girls..."

"Brittany?" I suggested. "Aishat? Alicia?"

Anthony shrugged. "Maybe? And that football player, Jamal...my son feels bad about what happened to him, too. He wants to apologize to him, and to the whole Crimson community...I don't know what's gotten into him. We keep trying to talk sense into him, but he won't listen. It's like he's a different person now."

"Sometimes a major life tragedy can do that," I said. "Sometimes it makes you re-evaluate your past and decide to be a better person in the future."

Anthony stared at me as if I'd suddenly started speaking in Martian. Then he said, "So I decided I had to meet you. The woman who wrecked my son's life, who turned him against me and everything I've raised him to be."

"I don't think I can take all the credit," I said. "I think your son always had that in him."

Anthony gave me another half-angry, half-perplexed look. "And I asked myself: what was I going to do to you, once I got you here? What price should you pay for destroying my son's life?"

He reached into the desk drawer again.

"I thought of all kinds of things, each grislier than the last," he said. "But then I thought: You're a businessman, Tony. Be sensible. This is a chance to do business."

He withdrew his hand from the drawer and held it open. Another small syringe balanced on his palm.

"I assume you had some kind of plan when you showed up," he said. "I assume you were planning to offer me some kind of a deal."

"I was," I said. "I was going to appeal to your better nature."

Another thin-lipped, humorless smile. "I'm touched that you think I have one."

"Apparently your son does. He must have gotten it from somewhere. And it looks like he's seeking a path to redemption. I was going to offer you one, too."

"And if I turned you down?" he asked.

"I was going to offer to take myself, and more importantly, Dima, away from here. I was going to offer to take us both out of the country and leave you alone. If you left me, and Dima, and Jamal Warner alone, I'd offer to do the same for you."

He eyed me distrustfully. "And you'd do that? More importantly, you'd convince Kuznetsov of that?"

"There are a lot of bad guys out there," I said. "He'd find other targets to go after. And you said yourself there are problems with the drugs. I was going to let you take your chances with Congress. Poisoning a bunch of American soldiers is just the kind of thing to start a bipartisan witch hunt. Or better yet, the Duma and the FSB. Security Solutions is fooling around with the kind of thing that could get a whole bunch of you terminated with extreme prejudice. Or all this stuff you're doing with the Wolf Battalion and other Ukrainian nationalists. Everything I've seen of those guys makes me think they're total loose cannons. You said that two of them have died just this morning because of your drugs? The US government isn't going to care about a couple of dead Ukrainians, but I'll bet they have friends back home who are going to care very, very much, and who have the will and the means to take you out in a very violent fashion."

"You have an odd way of appealing to my better nature," said Anthony.

"I'm not asking you to turn into my idea of a good person," I said. "I'm laying out the situation so you'll understand it. From what I can see, you've already made some very ugly enemies in Moscow, in Grozny, in Donetsk, in Kiev, and who knows where else. And you're playing a dangerous game with Atlanta and Washington. Unless you change something, one of these days one of these groups is going to take you out. Dima and I won't have to do anything. But we could not make things worse for you. We could even help you, if you'd let us."

"And if I refuse?" Anthony asked. "If I refuse to let you 'help' me, and if I refuse to give you the antidote?" He nodded at the small syringe on his desk.

"Have you heard of Camila Rodriguez?" I asked. "What about Heather Ramirez? One's a lawyer, and the other's an investigative journalist. Both of them would *love* to take you down. Maybe you noticed Camila's campaign to get rid of for-profit prisons in North Carolina? Or maybe you caught Heather's piece on the Church of the Holy Light that just came out? Or her piece last year on US involvement in torture and corruption in Iraq? I called both of them on the way here and told them where I was going and why. They're supposed to start digging if they don't hear from me in the next couple of hours." That was a slight distortion of the truth, but it was true enough that I was able to say it convincingly.

Anthony made a dismissive face. "Camila Rodriguez is a gnat. Not even worth swatting. And Heather Ramirez is a mosquito. Annoying, but all she does is whine until you squash her. No one cares what journalists write."

"Tell that to the Church of the Holy Light," I said. "And they aren't the only people I called. I also have a PI and an FBI agent waiting for my call this evening." That was also a tiny bit of an exaggeration, but it was close enough to the truth that I sounded convincing, even to myself.

Anthony shrugged. "PIs have no power. And the FBI is on our side. But since you're willing to do a deal, I do have a deal for you." He held up the syringe in his hand.

"You see," he said, "we've been getting requests for a version of the drug made for women. The US, and Russia, and Ukraine, all have enough female soldiers that they want to be able to use this on them as well. But there's concern that the effects won't be the same. Something about the way that women process hormones differently. We haven't had a chance to test it on many female subjects yet."

He smiled a smile that got all its pleasure from other people's pain. "It occurred to me that you, Rowena, would be the perfect first subject for our newly reformulated version for females. What do you say?"

"What do I get out of it?" I asked.

"Other than scientific glory? Isn't that what you academics care about more than anything? Don't you routinely test your ideas on yourselves?" His smile had taken on a mocking tinge.

"This isn't my idea," I said. "I want to get something other than glory out of it."

"So you do have a mercenary soul when it comes down to it," he said, his smile still mocking. "Very well. As one mercenary to another, here's the deal I'm offering you: Sign an NDA and take this dose, and once we're done observing you, we'll give you and Kuznetsov both the antidote and let you walk away free. If you survive, that is."

I looked at the syringe in his hand. It was so tiny, no more than a couple of milliliters of liquid. To think that something so little could change my life. To think something so little could kill.

"Inna," Galina Ivanovna suddenly spoke up, "what is happening? What is this man offering?"

I explained the deal Anthony had offered me.

"Tell him you might be pregnant, and as everyone knows, you can't perform first-round tests on pregnant subjects. Not only is it unethical, but the hormones can invalidate the results."

I opened my mouth to say I certainly wasn't pregnant, saw the look on her face, and shut it.

"Tell him," she continued, "that if he wants to test it on a female subject, he should test it on me."

"No!" I cried out instinctively.

"Inna! Think! I've already lived a long life, much longer than yours. I lost my husband a long time ago, and my son, at long last, has finally gotten married and has someone to look after him. I'm ill. I may not have much time left, and what time I do have left might be full of sickness and suffering. If by doing this, I can save you and Dima, I will do it gladly."

"No!" I repeated.

"Do you have a better plan?" she demanded.

"Is she offering to take the dose instead of you?" Anthony asked. "I understand a little Russian. Not every word, but enough to get the gist. You're arguing over who's going to take it, aren't you? How touching. But futile. I'm not going to waste it on her. Not a lot of call to use combat-enhancing drugs on postmenopausal women."

I translated what he'd said for Galina Ivanovna, stumbling a little because I realized partway through that I didn't know the Russian word for "postmenopausal" and ended up just saying "old" instead.

"I see," said Galina Ivanovna when I was done. "Yes, I understand. There is no value in testing it on me. Ask him how we can trust him to keep his word and let us all go after he tests it on you."

I asked.

"Camila may be a gnat, and Heather a mosquito, but I'd still rather not deal with gnats and mosquitoes if I don't have to," Anthony said. "I'll let you all go if you agree not to bring them down on my head." Another thin-lipped smile. "At some point, though, we all have to start trusting each other's word."

I translated that to Galina Ivanovna.

She nodded. "I understand. In that case, I have one final request. As you know, I am a trained medical doctor with many decades of experience. Let me be the one who injects Inna with the drug."

"It's a simple intramuscular injection," Anthony said. "Anyone can do it, even me. And we have trained medical doctors here, too."

"Even so," she said. "Intramuscular injections can go wrong if you hit the wrong spot. And I have many years' experience specifically in women's medicine. Plus, I am a diabetic and have been injecting myself daily for many, many years, and am extremely familiar with how to inject into lots of different places in a woman's body. A woman's upper arm, for example, is smaller and has a different fat-muscle ratio than a man's. Someone who is used to injecting men could miss the muscle entirely and go straight into the joint."

Anthony was staring at her, bemused. Apparently his Russian knowledge didn't extend to medical vocabulary.

"She wants to do the injection herself," I said. "She says that she is specially trained in women's medicine and knows how to avoid errors that doctors without experience in women's medicine are likely to commit."

Anthony looked back and forth between me and Galina Ivanovna for a while. Then he said, "That sounds like bullshit to me, but just in case it's true, and to shut you up, sure, go ahead."

"Right now?" asked Galina Ivanovna.

"Yeah, right now. I want to see you two put your money where your mouth is. We could administer it by force, but like I said, at some point we're going to have to start trusting each other. Consider this the first test. Go ahead and give it to her, and once I'm satisfied you're going to uphold your half of the bargain, I'll take you down to Kuznetsov."

"Very good." Galina Ivanovna walked over to Anthony and held out her hand. "Give it to me."

He gave her the syringe. She held it up and examined it, observing the amount of liquid in it and checking it for air bubbles.

"Now, Innochka," she said, turning to me. "This will only take a second."

She uncapped the syringe and raised it. I rolled up my left sleeve.

Galina Ivanovna examined the syringe one more time. Then, in one swift motion that spoke of decades of practice, she plunged the needle into her own stomach.

38

FOR A MOMENT, ANTHONY and I froze in blank astonishment. Galina Ivanovna snatched up the other syringe from the desk and pressed it into my hand.

"Run, Inna," she said. "Run and give this to Dima. Just take the cap off, stick the needle into his shoulder and press down on the plunger." When I continued to stand there in shock, she slapped my arm. "*RUN!*"

It's amazing how fast the brain can work under stress. One part of my mind was wondering if she'd just ruined everything by proving to Anthony that he could not, in fact, trust us to keep our word. Another part was visualizing everything I'd seen of the building to figure out where Dima was and how I could get to him, and how I'd get past the guards that must be around him. A third part was wondering if the syringe she'd just thrust into my hand actually contained the antidote, or if this was all part of some crazy double- or triple-fake and I was being tricked into administering a fatal poison to my own husband.

Anthony was starting to rise, his face distorted with rage.

"*RUN!!!*" screamed Galina Ivanovna.

I ran. One hand clutched the precious syringe, which I told myself contained the antidote and not poison. The other jerked open the door and slammed it shut behind me. I wasted half a second checking to see if I could lock the office door from the outside. Not, alas, without keys. Then I took off down the hallway.

It was empty. There were closed doors on either side of it. I sprinted past them, my footsteps loud on the linoleum. They'd spoken of observation rooms and padded cells. Those wouldn't be next to this building's equivalent of the C suite. No, they'd be down the stairs we'd passed when we first came in. They'd be underground.

No one came bursting out of any of the doors, including the one behind me. Faint shouting came from that direction. It sounded like Anthony and Galina Ivanovna were fighting. I kept running.

No one stopped me as I came to a skidding stop at the top of the stairs and started down them. No one other than myself, that is. I had to use one hand to hold the precious syringe. The other wanted to hold onto the banister, but ended up having to hold up my pants to keep me from dripping over the hems and tumbling head over heels to the bottom. My descent slowed to a fast walk.

It was too fast for my left knee. The faint twinges it had been giving me all day morphed into lancing pain every time I put weight onto it. I must have wrenched something in my mad dash down the hallway. And now I had another hallway to run down, and maybe a lock to pick, and a bunch of armed, highly trained mercenaries to fight...

Stop! THINK! You're never going to fight your way past them. You have to use the weapons you actually know how to wield.

When I got to the bottom of the stairs, I kept walking, rather than breaking into a run again. I couldn't hear anyone coming behind me. Galina Ivanovna must still be occupying Anthony. I just had to hope she was able to keep him from calling the others and warning them about me.

By walking, I could hear what was going on around me. At first, all I heard was the muffled *whooshing* of the HVAC system in the walls and the high-pitched *innnnnnnnnnggggggggg* of the fluorescent lights above me. Then, as I proceeded down the corridor, I could hear voices.

The voices were muffled too. Because, I realized as I came to the end of the passageway, they were behind the door that the corridor dead-ended into.

The door was made of heavy metal, with a small grilled window and a lever-type handle. I walked up and turned the handle like I belonged there. Before I could think better of it, I heaved the door open—it was very heavy—and walked in.

Two men in black uniforms leapt to their feet in surprise, their hands reaching for the sidearms on their belts.

"Mr. Wainwright sent me down here," I said. "For observation. He gave me the new formula, the one for females. Now I'm supposed to be observed. Along with Kuznetsov. We're supposed to be observed together. Where is he?"

The guards hesitated. The story sounded crazy. But it also was based on things they knew to be true, and I sounded confident, and they were used to obeying commands.

"You need to bring me to him immediately," I said. "Part of the observation process is to see how we interact when the drug takes effect. They've tweaked the oxytocin levels for female subjects, but they don't know what that will do for group interactions. You need to bring me to him immediately."

I could see the question forming, like a cartoon bubble, over the guards' heads, of why I was there by myself. Shouldn't I be under escort? Who *was* I, anyway?

I shuddered. "It's kicking in!" I cried. "I can feel it! You need to bring me to him immediately!"

The question in the cartoon bubbles over the guards' heads was replaced by the certainty that they didn't want to have anything to do with anyone who was under the influence of this drug. It was astonishing how extreme stress had made me clairvoyant. If this was what the drug did to anyone at any time, I could see why so many governments would want it.

"This way, ma'am," said one of the guards. By his looks and his accent, he was South American. Cheaper to hire mercenaries from war zones in the developing world rather than Americans. Ex-Rangers and former Navy SEALs don't come cheap, but Africans, South Americans, and East Europeans can be recruited at half the price with twice the combat experience.

He walked me briskly to another metal door with a small grilled window at the far side of the foyer. Faint words were coming from it, too low to make out, but that sounded like repetitive muttering, not a conversation.

The guard knocked briskly. The faint muttering stopped.

"Who is it?" someone called through the door. Male. American. No noticeable regional accent.

"A female test subject is here," the guard said, in careful English.

"Already?" the American voice called back. "Well, bring her in. Davidson, watch over the subjects. Keep them back by the wall."

The door swung open. A man in a white lab coat looked me over, frowned, and ushered me in. The door swung closed behind me with a resounding *clang*, followed by the *click* of an automatic lock.

"You're the female test subject?" the man in the white lab coat said. "They sent you down on your own?"

I took a quick look around. We were in a room of about 20' by 20', with, indeed, padded walls and a floor that was faintly springy underneath, like firm rubber. Other than the man who had let me in, there was another man in a white lab coat, two more guards, and, backed into the far corner, Dima and Carl. The other lab-coated man was recording them on a handheld video camera. The guards were both standing back from them, but watching them alertly, their hands on what I guessed were electric cattle prods.

"Why'd they send you down on your own?" the first man asked. "And you look a mess. Are you limping? Are you having trouble breathing? We only want healthy subjects."

"I'm fine," I said. "And I'm the subject you have. Mr. Wainwright was detained, but he wanted to send me down as quickly as possible. He already administered the drug and wanted observation to begin as soon as it could."

White lab coat frowned, sighed, and rolled his eyes. "He had some bee in his bonnet about administering the dose himself. I tried to convince him it would invalidate the results, but non-scientists never understand proper lab procedures." He looked down at a large watch on his left wrist. "Can you say at what time the dose was administered?"

"Um…" I said. "Less than five minutes ago, I guess. I came straight here afterwards."

White lab coat sighed and rolled his eyes again. "Okay, let's say at 1:30, then. Jesus! This is going to really fuck up my results. Davidson, did you get that on the recording? She got the dose at approximately 13:30. We'll write it up later."

"I'm supposed to go over to them," I said, indicating Dima and Carl. They had both started muttering and pacing in their corner. "Mr. Wainwright wants to see how the female-specific formula affects group interactions."

Another sigh and eye roll. "He does, does he? And now I have test subjects telling *me* what donors want? Jesus Christ! I should have stayed at Auburn, I really should have...fine. Get over there. Hey! You!" He snapped his fingers at the guards. "Stay alert, okay? We don't know how they're going to react when she goes over there. Be ready to stop them if they attack."

I set off at a slow walk over to the corner where Dima and Carl had stopped muttering and pacing, and were now watching me with interest. Not the interest of someone seeing a friend approach. The interest of predators watching prey.

I passed the guards. They both stepped aside instinctively, as if afraid of me with a visceral fear that their body armor and cattle prods couldn't entirely shield them from.

I angled my walk to take me up to Dima. When I was three paces away, he suddenly flung up his hand in a "Stop" motion.

I stopped.

"Inna," he said. His voice was hoarse, as if he hadn't spoken in a week, or had been screaming for hours. "Inna, is that you?"

"Yes," I said.

He turned his head, deliberately averting his eyes.

"Inna," he whispered, his words barely carrying to me. "Inna, *don't look at me.*"

I dropped my gaze to the floor.

"Can I come stand next to you?" I asked quietly.

"As long as you *don't look at me.*"

Keeping my eyes firmly fixed on the floor, I moved, slowly and gently, until I was standing by his side.

"*How do you feel?*" I whispered.

"What are you saying?" white lab coat called. "Don't whisper! We have to be able to get everything on the recording. Jesus Christ! Sometimes I miss the lab rats, I really do. At least they only bit you."

"*There's a demon inside of me,*" Dima whispered. "*I can kind of control him—as long as you* **don't look at me.**"

"Speak up!" shouted white lab coat. "Even if you're speaking Russian! It'll get translated when we go through the recording."

"I'm not looking at you," I said to Dima, speaking quietly but not whispering. "They don't speak Russian?"

"Not as far as I can tell," he said softly. He was fidgeting, turning half away from me and then turning towards me again, before jerking back as if burned by my very presence.

"I brought the antidote," I said quietly. "It's in a syringe in my left hand."

"Just one dose?" he asked.

"Yes."

"Give it to Carl."

"But..." I began.

"He needs it more. I can control myself—sort of—as long as you *don't look at me*. I think this wave of side effects is wearing off. My heart rate and blood pressure are going down, I can feel it. I think I'm getting out of the danger zone, at least for now. I've been faking some of my symptoms just to throw them off. But Carl is in bad shape."

I glanced over at Carl. He was sweating profusely, rocking back and forth and talking to himself, an insane, high-pitched gabble that held few recognizable words.

"I need to get you out of here," I said.

"Give the antidote to Carl. Then let him and me get us out of here. Wait—did *you* take the drug? Is that what you were telling them?" He sniffed my neck. "I don't smell it on you."

"It was a lie," I said, very softly.

Through my peripheral vision, I could sense Dima smile.

"Good," he said, very softly. Then, more loudly, "Carl! Carl! Come here!"

Carl shuddered all over and pressed himself into the corner, his high-pitched gabbling increasing in speed.

"Walk between me and the wall," Dima said quietly. "Let me shield you from their view...Carl...come here, Carl..."

With Dima moving between me and the others, I, still using those incredible stress-induced reflexes, transferred the syringe from my left hand to my right, uncapped it, and, before Carl could escape from me, shoved the needle right through his sleeve and into his shoulder and depressed the plunger with one quick squeeze.

39

THE LAB COATS YELLED. The guards both charged in my direction. They didn't make it.

I had seen Dima fight before. A little bit. Most of it had been training with me, which was basically play-sparring where his primary objective was not to hurt me. But I'd seen him go up against actual bad guys a couple of times, including that awful night in Moscow that I thought had ruined everything. He'd seemed preternaturally quick and strong then.

This was beyond anything I had imagined possible. Apparently it was beyond anything the guards had imagined possible, because he'd knocked them both to the ground, taken their cattle prods, cuffed them with their own flex cuffs, and taken their phones before any of the rest of us even knew what was going on. Then he went after the lab coats.

They were retreating, trying to huddle behind each other and make a dash for the door simultaneously. Their faces were masks of naked terror. I caught a glimpse of the side of Dima's face as he turned towards them and understood why.

"DIMA!" I shouted. "NO! DON'T KILL!"

He swiveled to face me. I immediately averted my eyes, but not before I got another glimpse of his face, this time full-on. It was going to haunt my nightmares for the rest of my life. If before I had seen him as Hel, with one half down in the underworld, now he was all three Furies at once, the personification of the earth itself as it rose up in vengeance.

The two lab coats were scrabbling in terror at the door handle, their fear rendering them clumsy and stupid.

"Dima," I said gently, still looking down, "help me. I need your help." I pointed to Carl, who was slumped against the wall, staring at the syringe sticking out of his shoulder in confusion. "I need your help with him. We need to get out of here, Dima. We need to get out of here and save your mother, and we can't do it without you."

Out of the corner of my eye, I saw him shudder. The lab coats finally got the door open and fled.

"Help..." Dima said hoarsely.

"That's right," I said. "I need your help, Dima."

"Help...me..."

"How can I help you, Dima?"

"DON'T LOOK AT ME! DON'T SAY MY NAME! IT SUMMONS **HIM**!"

"Okay. Sure. Sure."

"Help me calm down," he said, more normally.

"Sure. Of course. How?"

"Sing to me."

I repressed a wince. I had a terrible voice. If he'd asked me to dance, I would have felt on firmer footing, but singing was probably more soothing.

"Um...what do you want me to sing?"

"Something soft. For children."

My mind went blank.

"Do you know 'May there always be sunshine?'" Dima asked.

A classic Soviet song. I knew the chorus. Still keeping my eyes fixed on the floor, I sang, my voice shaking,

"May there always be sunshine,
May there always be blue sky,
May there always be mama,
May there always be me."

Dima laughed again.

Carefully not looking at either of them, I took Carl by the hand and started walking towards the door, still singing.

Carl followed along docilely. When I started the song for the third time, Dima joined in.

I was afraid the door was going to be locked, but it swung open when I turned the handle. I was afraid we were going to be met with a hail of gunfire when we stepped through, but there was no one in the vestibule outside of it. The guards who'd let me in had disappeared.

That door swung open into an empty corridor as well. Still singing softly, I led us down it. Carl followed along, his hand in mine. He couldn't understand the words, but he was humming along to the tune. Dima took up the rear, singing under his breath.

The long corridor through the basement was empty. We stopped when we got to the stairs.

"Where *is* everyone?" I asked quietly.

"I don't know," said Dima. "But I'd better go in front. No! Don't look at me. *He's* still trying to get out. And keep singing. It keeps him calm."

I kept singing and looked to the left as Dima passed by on my right. He scouted up the stairs, then came back down.

"Clear," he said. "Where *is* everyone? And where's mama?"

"She's in Anthony Wainwright's office," I said. "As for the others, I don't know."

"Phone," mumbled Carl.

I looked over at him.

"Phone," he said more clearly. "The guards' phones."

Dima pulled the guards' phones out of his pocket. "Lots of messages," he said. He handed the phones to me, careful not to look at me or touch me. As I took the phones, I felt how tremors were shuddering through his entire body, making him shake all over like a man in the throes of a raging fever or terrible fear or overwhelming desire.

The screens of both phones were full of notifications. I couldn't access the actual messages, but the notifications themselves told the story.

"I guess we know where everyone went," I said, showing the phones to Carl.

He twitched convulsively, then leaned in and read the screens.

"Office," he said. "Wainwright."

"What's going on?" asked Dima.

"It seems," I said, "that Galina Ivanovna is holding Anthony Wainwright hostage."

40

ALL THE GUARDS WE'D been expecting downstairs turned out to be clustered around the door to Anthony's office, along with a bunch more people in nice suits who obviously made decisions for the boots on the ground. There were also several white lab coats, including our two friends from the basement. They were the first to see us. They shrank back, emitting faint *eeps* of terror.

The rest of the scrum milling around the door turned too.

How to play this..."Galina Ivanovna!" I shouted. "We're here! I found Dima! We're all here!"

"Tell them to let us out!" she shouted back. "Me and this Anthony person! Tell them to let us all out, and no one gets hurt! But if they try to grab me, I have a syringe against his neck and I. WILL. USE. IT!"

I relayed the message to the roiling crowd. The uniforms reached automatically for their weapons. The suits and the lab coats looked back and forth at each other uncertainly.

"Anthony!" I shouted. "Anthony Wainwright! My deal still stands! Let us all out of here, and we won't hurt you! We'll even help you, if we can."

A pause. Then Anthony shouted back, "Why should I believe you? You already broke your word once."

"No," I said. "You got to give your new formula to a female test subject. Now I've got Dima and Carl. All we want to do is walk out of here. Let us do that, and we'll all get out of this just fine."

"Why shouldn't I just tell my men to shoot you all down where you stand?" he demanded.

"First of all, because Galina Ivanovna will inject you with whatever she's got in that syringe," I said. "You've already seen how quick she is with a needle. Second of all, because, like I told you, I told a lot of people on the drive over here where I was going, and told them to start hunting down everything they could about you and your companies if they didn't hear from me by this evening. Along with a hungry investigative journalist and a labor relations lawyer on a mission, if anything happens to me, you'll have a very pissed-off PI, an FBI agent who takes a special interest in my safety, and a US Marine looking for blood vengeance coming after you."

A long pause. "So how do you want this to go down?" Anthony eventually shouted.

"Tell all your people to put down their weapons and back off," I said. "They can go stand on the stairs. Then you and Galina Ivanovna can come out of the office. We'll all go together to my car. We'll all get in the car and drive out of here together. Once we're past the gates, we'll drop you off. They can come get you. But if anything happens to any of us, everything I said about a bunch of angry people with a nose for blood coming after you will happen. If anything happens to us, all hell will break loose in the media."

Another pause. Then Anthony said, half-dismissively, half-hopefully, "And you say you'll help me?"

"Dima was sent here to commit an assassination," I said. "A character assassination. Of you. And he could do it. He could tear you to shreds if he wanted. But if you help us, he can do the opposite. He can build you up rather than tear you down. A character resurrection, one might say, rather than an assassination."

I'd have to discuss that promise with Dima later, but it was the best way I could think of for getting us out of here. I had already decided I was okay with giving up on my pursuit of blood vengeance against anyone who'd wronged me or who'd had anything to do with the incident that had driven Dima away from me. If forgiving and forgetting could help me achieve my higher goals, then that's what I'd do.

Another pause. Then, grudgingly, Anthony Wainwright said, "Fine. We all walk out of here, and no one gets hurt. I don't go after you, and you don't go after me. And if I need help in the future—your kind of help—I'll come to you, and you'll give it to me. Deal?"

"Deal," I said.

41

ANTHONY ORDERED HIS people to lay down their weapons and retreat to the stairs. There was some hesitation and some looking back and forth, and then they did as they were told. A moment later, Anthony and Galina Ivanovna emerged from the office. She was standing behind him, holding a syringe to his neck. His posture was rigid and arched away from her as much as possible, as if it were a live asp she had in her hand, not a small syringe.

"Mama!" Dima cried. "How do you feel? The drug..."

"I've got the antidote in my pocket," she said calmly, nodding down to her left breast pocket. Four tiny syringes were sticking out of it. "Now let's get out of here."

We made our way slowly down the hallway. When we came to the top of the stairs, everyone standing there stared at us hungrily. When we turned to go out the doors, I could feel their glittering eyes boring into our backs. But no one made any move to stop us.

Out the doors. No one was waiting for us on the other side of them. The half a dozen steps to my car. No one stopped us. I felt in my pocket. Amazingly, I still had my keys. I unlocked the car. I had a moment of panic that maybe they'd boobie-trapped the car while we'd been inside the building.

"There's not a bomb or something in the car, is there?" I asked Anthony.

A rictus-like smile twisted his face. "Not by my orders," he said. "And it's not the kind of thing we normally do."

"Let's hope that continues to be the case," I said. I got into the driver's seat, and turned the key.

The ignition started up smoothly, with a complete absence of deadly fireballs. I relaxed my white-knuckled grip on the steering wheel a tiny amount. My fingers, I noted, were shaking. I hoped I could make it back to Greenfields without collapsing.

Galina Ivanovna was directing the others. Dima got in the back, on the passenger side. Then Carl got in the passenger's seat in the front. Then, last of all, Anthony and Galina Ivanovna got into the back, with Anthony in the middle, between Galina Ivanovna and Dima.

"Let's go, Inna," Galina Ivanovna commanded.

As carefully as if I were taking my driver's license test, I backed out of the parking lot, turned, and headed away from the building, towards the first gate. It swung open as we approached it. There were guards on both sides of the road as we drove through, but all they did was watch us, their eyes hidden behind sunglasses, their faces impassive and strangely inhuman as their heads tracked our progress out the gate and down the road.

No one came after us as we proceeded at a sedate thirty miles per hour down the one-lane road. The second gate swung open as we approached it, too.

"Stop on the other side of the gate, Inna," Galina Ivanovna ordered.

I drove through and stopped. Dima got out of the backseat. Anthony, after a last look at Galina Ivanovna, scrambled out after him.

"I'm getting out here too," Carl announced.

"What? Why? You should come with us!" I protested.

"And do what? No, I'm gonna get out here, walk Mr. Anthony back to the compound, and do a little damage control. For all of us. You helped me back there, Doctor Rowena, but Mister Anthony's helped me a lot too. He gave me a job when no one else would, and stood by me when another man would have thrown me out on the street. Time to return the favor."

"Um," I said. "Okay. If you're sure."

"I'm sure it's the right thing to do," said Carl, and got out of the car.

Dima got back into the backseat.

"Go, Inna, go!" Galina Ivanovna ordered.

This time I took off with a chirp of rubber, heading towards the main road as fast as I dared.

I took one last look in my rearview mirror when we reached it. Carl was walking Anthony through the gate and down the road towards the compound. Or maybe Anthony was walking Carl. They were walking side by side, supporting each other.

42

"SHOULD WE GO TO THE hospital?" I asked as soon as we were on the main road, heading back towards Marietta because that was the only way I knew how to go. "Galina Ivanovna? How do you feel? Is the drug taking effect yet?"

"I feel fine, all things considered," she said. "I didn't actually get much of the drug into me, you know. I shot a lot of it into the waistband of my skirt." She laughed shortly. "I have a *lot* of experience giving injections, both to patients, and to myself. The most common place to inject insulin is into the stomach, so I knew all the things that could go wrong, all the ways for an injection to not actually inject anything in that area. And it was a very small needle. I knew I could make it look like I was injecting myself without actually doing it. Most of it went into my waistband, and the rest went into my navel." She pulled down the top of her skirt and inspected her navel. "I don't even see a needlemark," she said. "I don't think I actually got even a drop of the drug into me."

"If you're sure..." I said.

She inspected her navel some more. "I'm sure," she said. "Besides, I have the antidote here." She patted the syringes in her left breast pocket. "Along with God knows what else." She pulled the syringes out and inspected them. "That's the antidote, see? It's kind of yellowish. And here's another dose of the drug—see how clear it is? And these three—this is what I used on Mr. Anthony." She held up the syringe she'd used on him, plus two more syringes from her pocket. All three were filled with a viscous, red and gold liquid.

"It looks like blood," she said, inspecting it thoughtfully. She laid down all five syringes on the seat between her and Dima. "Should I give you the antidote, Dimulya?" she asked. "Or are you feeling better now?"

"Better now," he said. "I think I'll skip getting injected with another unknown substance if I possibly can." He looked up, towards me. Our eyes met in the rearview mirror. I saw no trace of the demon in them.

"So how did you manage to take Mr. Anthony hostage, mama?" he asked. He was talking to her, but his eyes kept searching out mine in the rearview mirror.

Galina Ivanovna laughed again. "I swear, everyone thinks that if you're an old woman, you're stupid and incompetent to boot. Once you left, Inna, I started creating a scene, said my heart was failing, all kinds of stuff. I don't know how much he understood, but he got enough to open up that drawer again. I'd already gotten a glimpse of it and knew it was full of loaded syringes. He got the antidote out, told me what it was, and said he'd give it to me soon. I went crawling over there, begging for it, got a good eyeful of the drawer, saw how careful he was to avoid the red syringes, crawled right up to him, sobbing and making a fuss—and then grabbed one and threatened to use it on him."

She smiled. "That shut him up quick. I got these others, just for insurance, and demanded that he let you both go. It took him a little while to understand what I wanted, but by then you had shown up, so we got it figured out in the end."

"All's well that ends well, I guess," I said.

"Shakespeare, as usual, knows all," she said. "Let's go home, Inna."

My eyes met Dima's again in the rearview mirror. "Are you sure?" I asked him. "You're sure you're okay?"

His eyes held mine, calm and steady. "I am," he said. "Thanks to you, Inna. When I was down there, not sure who or even what I was, you appeared before me like a six-winged seraph and showed me the way. You saved me."

"Of course she did," said Galina Ivanovna. "Who else other than your wife should save you?"

"My wife...That's right! We got married! We're married!"

"Don't tell me it slipped your mind," said Galina Ivanovna. "It's been a long day, but honestly, Dimulya, a man should remember his own wedding."

Dima's eyes met mine in the rearview mirror again. This time, they were smiling.

"I didn't forget," he said. "Even in the depths of that basement, when there were all these hormones and chemicals churning through me, turning me into a monster, there was still something inside of me who remembered, who stayed *me*. I was able to cling to that and make a conscious choice, of my own free will, to be *me*, not the monster. And you were why, Inna. You reminded me that I had to stay *me* not just for me, but for mama and for you. For my wife. I'm just not used to saying it loud."

"We should celebrate," said Galina Ivanovna.

"I think we've already celebrated enough," said Dima. "Now I just want to go home. Take us home, Inna."

"Sure thing," I said. I could feel the adrenaline ebbing out of me like a great tide, leaving shakiness and tears in its wake. But every time my eyes met Dima's, I knew I would have the strength to get us all home.

43

I CALLED MEL, HEATHER, and John as soon as I got home to let them know that I had made it out of Security Solutions safely. Mel accepted the news with equanimity, saying only that it would have been a hell of a case to start her PI career with.

"Not that I wouldn't have thrown myself into it," she said. "But it's probably better to start small."

"Probably," I said. "But thanks for being willing to try."

"Of course. And if you ever need anything or anyone in LA, you know where to go."

"I do. And maybe I will."

"I'll hold you to that," she said.

Heather said she was glad I'd made it out of there safely. She mostly sounded disappointed, though, not to have a reason to go after Security Solutions."

"I can still investigate the hell out of this Jamal thing, though," she said.

"Sure," I said. "As long as you don't ask me to take down Security Solutions myself."

"Somebody has to," she said.

"And they will," I said. "But they let me walk out of there alive because I said it wouldn't be me."

"There has to be more to it than that," she grumbled. "You're holding back, I can sense it."

I hesitated. On the drive home Galina Ivanovna, Dima, and I had debated at length what to do about the syringes. We'd all liked the idea of turning them over to Heather to have them analyzed by an independent lab. But we'd eventually decided that would not be upholding our side of the deal.

"There's more," I told Heather. "They're pretty dirty. Um...once you're done with the Jamal thing, if you're kicking around for something to do, you could always look into a drug that the US military is talking about using on its soldiers."

"What kind of a drug?" Heather demanded.

"Um...a kind of super-soldier drug," I said. "Only they might be re-thinking that decision right now. But if they do decide to go ahead with it, you might want to look into it."

She blew out a breath on the other end of the line. "Fuck, Rowena, you can't tantalize me like that. Okay. I'll keep my eyes and ears open. And if I *do* find something, I'll be back, and this time you'll tell me every-thing you know. Okay?"

"Okay," I said.

The conversation with John was, predictably, the most exciting. He called me right after I got off the phone with Heather, demanding to know what the FUCK the message I'd left him was about.

When I gave him an abridged version of the day's events, he blew up. Of course.

"We're all fine," I assured him, once I could get a word in edgewise. "Everything was resolved amicably."

"Yeah, but I've heard things...those SS motherfuckers are NOT nice guys, Ro."

"I know," I said. "But we're fine, and I don't think they're going to come after us any time soon."

"If you say so...wait...you got *married?*"

I distracted John with a description of the courthouse wedding, which made him laugh.

"Not a half bad idea, though," he said grudgingly, when I was done. "Get it done nice and easy, no muss, no fuss. I wonder what Camila would say to that..." He hung up in good mood.

As soon as he hung up, my phone lit up again, this time with an in-coming call from Frank.

"Ro! What the fuck..."

I gave him a slightly less abridged version of the day's events.

"And now we don't know what to do with the syringes," I finished. "We've got them in the fridge for now. We don't want to just throw them away..."

"I'll call Atlanta, have someone come down and pick them up," he said. "You say they might be dangerous?"

"Anthony Wainwright certainly seemed scared of the red ones."

"Well, Jesus Christ, you be scared of them, too, then. Someone will be down tonight to get them."

"Thanks," I said.

"Any time, Ro. And the next time you're out in California, you let me know."

"Sure thing," I said.

I wasn't entirely thrilled about turning the syringes over to the FBI—what if they were used for nefarious purposes?—but it seemed less bad than the alternatives. Half an hour later, I got a call from Xavier Thornton, my contact in the Atlanta office, saying he and a biohazard expert would be there in two hours to collect the syringes.

That took up the rest of the evening. By the time they were gone, Dima had lain down "for a quick rest" and fallen so fast asleep that he only turned over and pulled the pillow over his head when I tried to wake him up for supper. I was worried it was a further side effect of the drugs, but Galina Ivanovna said sleep was probably the best thing for him and we should leave him.

By 9:00pm I was lying beside him. He continued to sleep like someone who was trying to catch up on a lifetime of insomnia. I was hoping to fall into the sleep of the exhausted myself, but instead I just lay there, my body buzzing with old adrenaline.

Not the most romantic wedding night, I thought. *But who the fuck cares!* I added. *You've done the most important bit. Everything else is just window dressing.*

Eventually, comforted by that thought, I fell asleep.

44

OVER THE NEXT FEW DAYS, Dima had a few minor recurrences of side effects, but each was milder than the previous one, and by the weekend they stopped entirely.

"Maybe someday we'll find out what was in that drug, and if there are any long-term problems," he said. "But for right now, I'm just happy to have it out of my system. Not being able to look at you or have you look at me was terrible. I don't know what it was, but there was something about your gaze that...well, from the first moment I met you, Inna, I felt like your eyes could peel back my skin, open up my heart, see what was really inside of me. Sometimes that was good. Sometimes it was scary. And when what was inside of me was the drug..."

We both shuddered. We both agreed that it was terrifying to know how easily everything that made us, "us," could be modified by the right cocktail of chemicals.

"But it didn't change me that much," Dima concluded. "Not really. I could feel the demon rising up inside of me, but I still didn't want to let him hurt you. So there was still something of 'me' in control."

"Yes," I said. I wondered how long that would last after multiple doses. I changed the subject instead of speculating.

There were plenty of other things to talk about. I accepted the fellowship in Finland, and informed them that Dima would be coming along with me. They said they'd look for ways to provide a fellowship for him, too. We weren't too proud to accept their charity, especially once Dima got an email from his editor telling him he was no longer employed by *Nezavisimaya Pravda*.

"It's good to start off a new life with no old obligations," he said philosophically. "I'm not even angry about it. I actually feel free for the first time in years."

"Me too," I agreed. I'd decided to forgive and forget all kinds of offenses others had committed against me, starting with the Wainwrights and ending with Karen. Having good things come into my life to replace the bad ones certainly made it easier, but I also just felt lighter and freer without that anger and resentment hanging around my neck.

Negotiating things with Dima's handlers in the government took some more finessing. He didn't share the details, but I gathered that he appeased them for his failure to take down Anthony Wainwright, one way or another, by handing over lots of information about the Wolf Battalion.

"I feel a little bad about doing something that might hurt them," he said. "Some of the boys there are pretty decent. But Dahmer and Bundy...the sooner they get taken out, the better. And I never gave my word to protect *them*. I'll just stand back and let them go down while I work on the story about scammers that mama wants me to write. I can't do much for her, but I can do this."

We took Galina Ivanovna back to the hospital for follow-up testing after a week of no infusions. The results were positive, so it was agreed that she would go off the infusions for 3-6 months, depending on how she did, only following the diet.

"More astronaut food," she groaned. "But I guess it's better than the alternative. You know, I was all set to die, both when I came here to start the treatment, and when I was in that Mr. Anthony's office, trying to keep him from killing the two of you. But now...now I want to live again."

Dima had to leave abruptly after that. I found him a little bit later, surreptitiously wiping his eyes. He insisted he wasn't crying, then burst into tears and cried on my shoulder for a good five minutes.

In amongst all this, I informed the rest of my family that Dima and I had gotten married. This sent them into a variety of strong emotional states. The only thing that they could all agree on was that, since it was too late to stop me from sneaking off for a courthouse wedding, a proper reception was a must. Alexandra, Roseanna, and my grandmother—my *other* grandmother—actually established semi-cordial relations as they joined efforts to work on it.

They decided to hold a big do up in Christiansburg at the end of May. Meanwhile, Mel and Chloe threw a small party for me at Chloe's house, to celebrate the wedding and the new fellowship.

"I'm so *happy* for you!" Chloe said, gazing at me misty-eyed. "It gives hope for the rest of us."

"Yeah," said Mel. "How's Aaron, by the way?"

Chloe looked down into her glass. "Really good, actually. We're, um, planning to get together a few times this summer. So, um...that gives me hope as well. It's just sad that the two of you will be leaving. But with Aaron, and Diane, and Julie, and Sandra DeWitt, and Theresa Mayfield all on my side, it feels like I'm building connections here, you know? Like I'm making a place for myself here. And I have an appointment this summer with the same clinic that helped you get better, and my book's supposed to come out next month. I don't know how things are going to turn out in the long run, but I feel hopeful for the short term, at least."

"Yeah," said Mel. "Same here." We toasted that. Then Chloe said she'd better stop there—she'd learned her lesson about the dangers of overindulging in the demon water.

A week after Dima and I had gone to the courthouse, and then ended up down in that basement, and climbed back out, things were finally starting to settle down. I still felt like I could finally breathe easily, after years of holding my breath. Galina Ivanovna also said my lungs sounded better after I'd been away from Bedford Hall for a week. I told myself that I could expect lots of things, including my lungs, to keep getting better and better, and I actually believed it. Dima and I had a plan for the rest of the month, and a plan for where we'd be next year, and the start of a plan for getting to our new home and new life. We had a lot to look forward to.

"The only thing we *don't* have are wedding rings," Dima said. "I'll be honest, Inna: it's really starting to eat at me."

"Me too," I said.

"Every time I start to look, though, I'm overwhelmed. So many choices, and so many of them are so expensive. Two minutes later my head starts to spin, and I give up."

"There's a jeweler downtown," I said. "Surely they have something. Let's go right now. Keep it simple."

An hour later and we'd put down money on a set of rings. Steel. It seemed more appropriate than gold.

"It's a start," Dima said as we drove home. "It still doesn't feel real, though. I hardly even remember the wedding itself. I won't feel right until I have some external sign that we're officially bound together and no one can separate us."

"I know," I said. We were pulling into the apartment complex. "Oh look, it's the mail truck. It's late today. I'm just going to go check and see if we got anything."

I pulled up to the mailboxes. After an even longer fight than usual with the key, I managed to open my box. What had fate sent me today? A circular and a couple of envelopes that looked to be ads for cable TV services. And an envelope from Cobb County.

I almost put it with the junk mail. Then realization struck. I ran back to the car and jumped in.

"I think we just got what we wanted," I told Dima. I tore open the envelope, pulled out the piece of paper, my heart beating as if I were drawing lots from the urn of life and death, and held it up. "Look," I said.

He squinted at it, trying to read the English.

"Is that...?" he asked.

"It is," I told him. I read through everything just to make sure it was all there. "It is," I repeated. "Official proof. For the rest of my life, my people is you."

In my hand, at long last, was my marriage certificate.

The End

Want to find out more about Dima's backstory with Security Solutions? Scan the QR code below to get your FREE novella and sign up for my mailing list (but only if you want to).

From the Author

DEAR READER!

Thank you for joining Rowena on her heroic journey! *Terminal Degree* is the last planned book for this series, although who knows what might happen...In any case, this is the bittersweet ending to this arc of the story.

As in all the Doctor Rowena Halley books, *Terminal Degree* is fictional, but heavily inspired by reality. The drugs that Security Solutions are experimenting with are the product of my imagination, but based on (somewhat) real biochemistry and a long history of governments issuing performance-enhancing drugs to their soldiers. For example, you can read more about the US use of drugs for their soldiers during the Vietnam War in the *Atlantic* article "The Drugs That Built a Super Soldier."

Likewise, the prominence of private military companies in both the US and Russia is real, even if Security Solutions and Kavboyets are imaginary. Similarly, the Wolf Battalion is a figment of my imagination, but the use of serial killer names as call signs and the legends (I hope) of keeping wolves who are fed on the bones of Russian children are based on real battalions currently or recently operating out of Ukraine.

In keeping with the bent towards reality, the Russian-speaking characters use a number of sayings that I have translated directly from the original Russian, such as "We're all walking under God" (Мы все под Богом ходим), meaning something like "we're all in God's hands"; "Go with God" (Иди с Богом), which is roughly the equivalent of "God be with you" or "Fare thee well"; and the Hesychast prayer of "Lord Jesus Christ, son of God, have mercy on me, a sinner" that Galina Ivanovna utters as they enter Security Solutions.

The "sick building" issue is also common on modern American campuses, with multiple universities having problems with toxic mold, PCBs, and PFAS chemicals. The connection between "sick buildings" and health is only just beginning to be studied, but the health issues that the characters experience while on the Crimson campus are common for university workers.

More cheerfully, the literature, history, and mythology are all real. When Rowena thinks of Dima as an "unbelievably troublesome, meddlesome, and turbulent modern-day priest," she's referencing Thomas Becket, who provoked the ire of Henry II and ended up murdered by knights who took Henry's complaints that no one in his household will rid him of "this troublesome/meddlesome/turbulent priest" (the epithets are different in different versions of the story. Also, I guess that wasn't very cheerful).

Rowena herself is associated repeatedly with both Mary Magdalene, and specifically the "Magdalene" cycle of poems by Marina Tsvetaeva, and Orpheus, as well as passing references to Kali, the Hindu goddess of destruction. The poems Rowena reads to Galina Ivanovna are by the 19th-century poet Evgeny Abramovich Baratynsky, one of Russia's most important metaphysical poets; the frequent references to fate throughout the book are partly inspired by Baratynsky's own frequent references to fate in his poetry, including the poems "The Steamship" (Пироскаф) and "Of what use are dreams of freedom to a slave?.." (К чему невольнику мечтания свободы...), both of which are quoted directly. Dima, meanwhile, quotes Pushkin's "Imitations of the Koran" when he swears by even and odd, by his sword and righteous battle. He also mentions the poet Alexander Blok, whose poetry is often associated with him throughout the series.

Finally, the discussions of who are my people and being with my people no matter where they are is a reference to Anna Akhmatova's long poem *Requiem*, about her experience as the mother of a political prisoner in the Gulag system. Okay, also not very cheerful, but I hope that Dima and Rowena manage to transform the underlying material into a story of steadfast connection across borders and over barriers, staying true to each other against all odds.

Sid Stark

About the Author

SID STARK LIVES A LIFE very similar to her characters', only with more grading and fewer exciting chase scenes. She did once get held up in Heathrow on suspicion of being a Russian criminal traveling on an American passport, though, which was fun. She loves to hear from her readers, and can be reached by email at **sidstark@sidstarkauthor.com**, at her website at **https://sidstarkauthor.com/**, on Facebook at **https://www.facebook.com/SidStarkAuthor/**, and X at **@Sid-StarkAuthor**.

Don't miss out!

Visit the website below and you can sign up to receive emails whenever Sid Stark publishes a new book. There's no charge and no obligation.

https://books2read.com/r/B-A-NVEK-UVBHF

BOOKS 2 READ

Connecting independent readers to independent writers.

Also by Sid Stark

Doctor Rowena Halley

Campus Confidential: An Academic Thriller

Permanent Position: An Academic Thriller

Summer Session: An Academic Thriller

Trigger Warning: An Academic Thriller

Honor Court: An Academic Thriller

Total Immersion: An Academic Thriller

Under Review: An Academic Thriller

Terminal Degree: An Academic Thriller

Doctor Rowena Halley Boxed Sets

The Doctor Rowena Halley Series Books 1-4: Four Dark Comedy Mysteries

www.ingramcontent.com/pod-product-compliance
Lightning Source LLC
Chambersburg PA
CBHW031018030726
47497CB00004B/911